"*T*HIS is the Captain's cabin, Rosie," Darin said, opening a door. "Come in."

She entered the tight cabin, then suddenly lost her balance. "I feel peculiar."

"Ah, darling, maybe it's the motion of the ship."

He was at a complete loss when she burst into tears. He went down on his knees and embraced her impulsively.

Rosie's fears calmed beneath his touch, and suddenly she kissed him passionately, full on the lips, with a rare sort of wildness. Before he realized what was happening, Darin was responding, his emotions rushing forward with all the love he felt for her. His hands, which were around her waist, moved up slowly to caress her whole body.

"Darin," she whispered between kisses, "love me. I was made for our loving. Oh, darling, make love to me now!"

"Oh, God, Rosie..."

The Wild Harp

by

Jacqueline La Tourrette

FAWCETT GOLD MEDAL • NEW YORK

THE WILD HARP

Published by Fawcett Gold Medal Books, a unit of CBS Publications, the Consumer Publishing Division of CBS Inc.

ISBN: 0-449-14408-9

Printed in the United States of America

First Fawcett Gold Medal printing: June 1981

10 9 8 7 6 5 4 3 2 1

To my mother's Irish family

Quick to anger was Sweeny, the bard, and warrior King,
When Ronan, the saint, rang his bell in the morning
Quenching with its clamor the sweet, gentle stream
Of harp song he played for his white-throated Queen.

The King strode from his chamber in a blasphemous rage
And flew naked up the road to the steep hermitage,
His cloak torn away by the restraint of his wife,
Bearing javelin alone, and the harp he loved like life.

He drowned the saint's psalter in the monastery well,
And, in poetic frenzy, broke the rude-tongued bell.
With his javelin he pierced the sweet cleric's side.
"Die, like my murdered song!" the sinful Sweeny cried.

The dark monk raised his hand as though in benediction,
Pronouncing, not a prayer, but a woeful malediction:

'I banish you to branches, in restlessness to roam,
An outcast forever, in madness quite alone.
Fleeing before skylarks, naked to the rain,
Flesh rent by thickets, in everlasting pain.
You will graze upon cresses, and live in the yew,
With ashes on your head; on our tongue, bitter rue!

'And as for your fine harp that sang so fair,
It will spread discord and misery everywhere.
Clenched everlastingly in your profane hand,
It will bring despair throughout your green land.
The proud will be humbled, love will go awry,
From the wild harp's song beneath Erin's sky.'

—from *Buile Shuibni*, Gaelic, 12th C.

Part I

MARY

Chapter 1

ROSALEEN threw her dark head back and let the snowflakes melt on her small pink tongue. She had never seen so much snow. What had been called a "cruel winter" back home was nothing compared to this, and the flakes were still falling in wet clusters. From the creaking deck of the ship, Boston looked topsy-turvy, the houses tilted by the heavy drifts on the roofs. And icicles hung from the masts of the other ships in port like the mythic beards of druids. No fairyland she'd ever imagined was as beautiful as this. She wanted to show it all to Seamus, but they had thrown him into the sea. She felt a chill inside that did not come from the weather: she was five years old and grateful to be alive. Barefoot, her callused feet hardly feeling the cold, she and the other children on board, who had been cooped up in the hold during most of the trip, came gradually to life out on the deck.

The children improvised snowballs from the snow already heaping the rails; and Rosaleen's cousin, Darin, always wild and innovative, discovered they could slide halfway across the deck in the slush. Leaving the silent mass of people huddled at the railing, Rosaleen and her brother, Liam, followed Darin's example, skidding and slipping, ignored by their desperate parents. Others joined in, and an older boy with a petulant face watched, rolling a snowball around a chunk of ice. He soon found a target in the laughing little girl with the long dark braid and threw it into her face. Rosaleen was stunned at first; then her hand went to her burning face and tears welled up in her blue eyes. She called out for her cousin Darin.

The usual fight ensued. Though Darin denied it, he had been Rosaleen's protector since he had hauled her out of the River Bride when she was three; and, as though the life he saved belonged to him, he had been looking after her ever since. He deeply resented the little girl's following him around, but he jumped to her defense whenever she was in trouble, and Rosaleen had a peculiar knack for getting into trouble. If she did not find it herself, it usually came to her, as swiftly as the well-aimed snowball.

As the two boys rolled on the deck, punching each other, Rosaleen watched Darin with admiration. She stood in the circle of wide-eyed children, which had formed around the combatants, unnoticed by the adults. A weathered seaman in a striped shirt finally separated the brawling boys and, holding the still-thrashing, black-haired Darin at arm's length, grinned at the unholy blue anger in his eyes. The dispute was settled as far as the sailor was concerned when he knocked the boys' heads together and dropped them on the deck; but it erupted a few minutes later in a snowball fight, with the Noonans lining up against the other boy and his relatives. Her face still stinging from the first snowball, Rosaleen clung to the torn tail of Darin's homespun shirt, hampering his movements, until he pushed her away forcefully.

"Git away with ya! You're like a flea on a dog. This is no place for girls. Go back to your ma!"

Crestfallen, the instigator of the fight rejoined the tightly packed group of adults at the rail, who were staring at the pier, waiting for the captain to get clearance from the authorities for them to disembark. They had been standing in the cold for nearly an hour, but not one had returned to the relative warmth of the stinking hold, where they had been crowded together, dirty, seasick and dying, during the rough winter crossing. Rosaleen grabbed the safe folds of her mother's ragged skirt and insinuated her body between her and Aunt Doirin, enjoying their warmth after the romp in the snow. Mary's hand found her little daughter's head and rested on it protectively. Mary's husband, Tomas, who stood beside her, exclaimed suddenly, "Civilization! There *are* human beings movin' around in all that muck, aren't there?"

There were a few thin smiles, a couple of laughs ending in coughs, but the woman at his side did not respond to the

10

humor. Mary stood stiffly, clutching her black shawl across her breast with tight white fingers, her face showing no emotion. Though she was painfully thin, her bone structure retained its beauty, much remarked upon in both herself and Doirin, in the days when the sisters were admired for their spirit and dark, flashing eyes. They had been the pride of Rathcormac. When they married the handsome Noonan brothers, the whole village expressed satisfaction, innocent of the tangled emotions between the two couples.

Doirin, the older, whose looks had suffered more from the troubles, tugged at Mary's shawl and whispered maliciously, "He's a great one with the jokes. Sure, Tomas is a terrible heartless man. It'll be a pub he's after seeking when we set foot on this cold land."

Mary did not defend her husband. Though Doirin was known for a wicked tongue, what she said was true enough, so much a fact that it did not need voicing. Mary was grateful that Brian held the money for all of them, though she had not been able to ascertain how much it was. There was a slight mystery about their salvation from starving, though no one but herself seemed interested. She could not understand how Brian, fine and winsome as he was, had managed to talk the estate agent out of the landlord's emigration fund. Mr. McGee was a hard man and avaricious: he had not even told them about the fund until confronted by Brian. After he got the money, Brian insisted on the long trek to the West country, though they were faint with hunger from the famine, instead of boarding a ship in nearby Cork City. They had followed Brian like pitiful sheep, not daring to ask any questions. He had spoken little then and all during the voyage. Mary lowered her lids and glanced out of the corner of her eyes at him, a device she had employed to study him since she was a girl, even before Brian had married her sister. He was leaning over with his hands clutching the rail, but it was not a position of relaxation. After all the years of loving him, Mary knew him better than she knew herself, and trouble moved in her heart.

She had heard that a mandrake plant shrieks when it is pulled from the earth, with a cry that freezes the blood, and the silent cry in Brian's blue eyes made Mary feel cold inside. Torn from the land he loved, he did not seem the same man. His face was pale and blank with a hint of weakness about the fine lips, an expression of fear upon him as he looked at their new home from the deck. He had gotten them this far, but he was at the end of his rope. He was always too sensitive. The voyage had been more a nightmare for him than the others, bearing, as he did, the extra sorrow of leaving his own piece of land. Though he was the only one who still had tears left in him when her Seamus died, he seemed to have dried up completely now. There was gray in his black hair she had never noticed before: he looked ten years older than the last time she had seen him in daylight. She moved her gaze away stealthily, with a sigh in her throat that did not escape her lips.

She knew she must, for Brian's sake, take control again, and she wondered if she had the strength. She was just a woman . . . what did God expect of her? During the past year, it was she and she alone who had kept the two families together and alive while the men looked for work in the city, bringing home a few shillings or a small bag of grain at irregular intervals. She had been the one who had persuaded Brian to ask for the emigration fund. She had often pondered, in the last hard months, why she seemed to have all the strength in the family, a burden she would gladly have discarded. She was intelligent enough to recognize that there was not much grit in the Noonan men. Her husband, Tomas, would probably drink himself into an early grave. And Brian, God love him, was not practical. On his own land, where he knew every groove and clod, he was a passable farmer, though his head was in the clouds. And Doirin, her sister, was so turned in upon herself she was no help at all when needed. Only her young sister-in-law, Veronica, could be depended on: she was a plucky girl, but she was far from well.

As though somehow sensing the problems Mary was to face, a small hand reached up and found hers, the little fingers warm and strong. Mary looked down into her daughter's beautiful Noonan eyes, which were grave and merry at the same time. She did not smile at Rosaleen: her lips would not move. But the child seemed to understand. Things were bad, but they would be better: Mother would see to it. She always had. Mary took a deep breath and mustered all that was left in her to take up the burden again, for Brian and Rosaleen and the boys. Discarding the numbness that hung about her like a shroud, she willed herself to life, clearing her mind to solve their immediate problems.

The first was Immigration. Everyone on board lived in fear of the Public Health. The captain had warned them not to say anything about the fever deaths during the crossing, or the ship would be quarantined and anyone showing symptoms of illness would be thrown into a fever hospital to die. He was not concerened about their welfare: his only cargo was human. He wanted to outfit his ship and return for another load of passengers as soon as possible. Everyone thought they were going to New York or Montreal like the other immigrants. The captain had chosen Boston, quite frankly, "because it gets fewer ships and isn't aware yet how bad things are in Ireland."

Mary was worried about Veronica. Though the cough had begun before they left Rathcormac, she thought her sister-in-law had the fever. If it had run its normal course, she should be dead by now, but Mary was not sure of the fever's idiosyncrasies, though she had followed it through to the end with her young son. Veronica's cheeks were blazing hot, as Seamus's had been; her eyes were bright and the cough continued. Somehow she must be gotten past the Public Health and stay with the family. Unless a person was thrown into a hospital, there was a chance of recovery. When the passengers began to file down the gangplank, Mary had put her hand firmly under Veronica's elbow to keep her at her side. Then, in a low, even voice, speaking in Gaelic, she said to the whole family, "Mind you say nothing about the fever."

"But Seamus..." Rosaleen began, and Mary shook her head, cautioning her and the other children.

"Not a word about him. Not a word. You are to keep silent completely until we leave that building...that long shed."

Though she described the building in a word she knew, she had chosen the proper one. Not an official stone building such as she had seen in Cobh, this one was hastily constructed of wood to accommodate all the new immigrants. It was obvious Boston was ill-prepared to meet the situation, but, as the captain had implied, that was to their advantage. Mary's only thought at the moment was of Veronica: the rest should have no trouble.

"As soon as we touch the ground, start eating snow," she whispered, and Veronica's blue eyes widened.

"Mary, are you daft?"

"Do as I say. You're feverish. For God's sake and ours, keep eating snow until we get to that shed. It may cool you down a bit."

With no heroic thoughts about setting foot in a new world, Mary leaned forward and scooped up snow as soon as her feet

13

were on the ground. With imploring eyes, she thrust it into Veronica's hands, and, trying to cover her embarrassment, the girl began to suck on it. When the children observed what their aunt was doing, they imitated her, until all of them in the slow-moving queue were satisfying their thirst with snow.

"God bless them," Veronica said, her eyes smiling at the children.

"God help us," Mary replied shortly.

The comfort of the warmth from the grids of a potbelly stove just inside the door was the first any of them had known for a long time. Their impulse was to move toward it, but a man in uniform kept them in line, instructing families to stay together. A long wooden table occupied one side of the shed, and several officers and clerks were inspecting papers there. From ten feet away, Mary studied their faces, so she would know what to expect. None of the men looked very agreeable. One had a narrow, sour face with muttonchop whiskers. The other, younger man in uniform was a mite too efficient for her taste, reading every word on the sets of papers, asking questions before scribbling furiously and putting his stamp on them. The intonation of their voices was flat, though not really an English accent. The Noonans were next in line when a difficulty arose with the young couple ahead of them and loud voices were raised. The wife wore the red petticoat of Kerry, torn to her knees, and they did not speak English at all. When Mary heard what they were saying in Gaelic, her heart nearly stopped: they had not understood what the captain had said to all of them.

Before the frowning officer with the whiskers could call for an interpreter, Mary pushed Tomas aside and stood before the long table, clutching her shawl to steady her hands. A hush fell over the room at the sound of the loud Gaelic protestations.

"I can help," she volunteered quickly. The officer gave her a long look, placed his fingers together and leaned back in his chair.

"By all means," he said with faint sarcasm. "You'd think at least they could speak English."

In the long Gaelic harangue that followed, all of their worst fears were realized. Before even giving Mary his name, the young man was protesting conditions aboard the ship. They had paid seventy-five shillings each for passage, he said, and hard it was to come by. They had been promised bread and decent food. There was a loaf of bread on the counter of the ticket office, wasn't there? All they'd been given was beans, which made them sick because they'd never had them before. They'd nearly died in the filthy hold, crammed with over a hundred others, and the place was full of fever. Six people had died of it, one only a child, and they had been cast into the thrashing ocean without proper burial rites. The *Laura* was a hell-ship, for sure, and the captain should be hanged.

Mary mollified them with understanding and managed to extract their names and papers, which she gave to the official, who looked at her suspiciously with slate-gray eyes.

"Out of all that...that's all they said? Their names and county? Gaelic must be a strange language, indeed."

"A queer tongue, for sure, sir," she replied strongly while the other passengers in the line held their breath. "It's frightened they are, never having left their farm before. They seem to have some relatives in New York, but they were landed here. We'll look after them and get them to their folks."

His narrow eyes appraised her, but he shrugged and wrote down the information without noticing that the whole room exhaled as one. Mary told the Kerry couple she had registered their complaints, and they moved on to the forbidding door at the end of the shed, where the Public Health people would be waiting. With trembling hands, she rejoined her family, unable to meet Rosaleen's eyes. She had always been firm with the children about lying, and Rosaleen had received the most frequent scoldings for her imaginative whimsies about playing with fairies. With heat rising to her face, Mary observed the other children: her son, Liam, had a sly expression she did not like, and that young devil Darin showed open admiration for her clever lies. Doirin really should take that boy in hand. Her sister's older sons, Michael and Padraig, were more solemn, old enough to understand what had really happened and how close a thing it had been.

Unable to bear Rosaleen's steady stare any longer, Mary explained in Gaelic, "It isn't right to lie: it's a sin. But maybe once in your life you'll have to...if it's a matter of life and death."

A frown gathered on Rosaleen's brow, and Mary could almost tell what she was thinking. It would have to wait until later. The narrow-eyed officer was waiting for them. Mary glanced at Veronica. They would have to get through this quickly; in the warm room, the unhealthy heat would come back to Veronica's cheeks. Mary had assumed that

Brian would take over now, but it was Tomas who leaned over the table to address the officer.

"We're the Noonans from Cork, the whole lot of us," he was saying. "We speak English, and we don't have to sign our names with a mark. Cork had some of the best hedge schools in the country: we read and write, down to the smallest. Me brother and I married sisters, would you believe it? That makes all these children practically brothers and sisters...not wishing to confuse your records, sir."

Fury burst in Mary's breast. There was no snow for Veronica to eat in here, and that blatherskite Tomas would delay them further. She extended a shaking hand for the papers Brian was holding, and he relinquished them with an abashed expression she did not understand. What's the matter with the man? she wondered fretfully as she counted through the papers quickly. There was one too many: Seamus! The official was almost shouting at Tomas when Mary extricated her son's paper and balled it up in her hand, before pushing her husband aside.

"I'll give the information you need," she said, trying to forget her dead son's passage paper, which scalded her palm like hot tears.

Tomas's indignant look boded no good for later, but the procedure went quickly from there. When their papers were stamped, she felt giddy and sick and let the others push her forward with their momentum to the dark door at the end of the shed. They entered directly into another section of the shed to be faced by a man in a wrinkled white coat at a desk with a large slate on the wall behind him. Mary had never seen a doctor in her life, but only the village midwife, and she credited the medical man with almost supernatural insight. She must keep Veronica with her: it would be difficult for anyone to outwit such a knowledgeable man, and the girl certainly was not up to it. She saw the round red smudges of heat beginning to bloom on Veronica's cheeks again and felt a sinking sensation in her middle.

At that unfortunate moment, Doirin's tongue came to life again. "Quite taken with yourself, aren't you?" she addressed Mary. "Trying to get everyone's attention back there. Do you think you're the head of the whole Noonan household? You know that Brian—"

The dark flash of anger in Mary's eyes made Doirin take a step backward: her younger sister had been known to strike. Instead of physical force, Mary used Gaelic words. "Shut your mouth! It's Veronica I'm thinking of. Look at her! If we don't get past here, it's the fever hospital for sure, and quarantine for all of us."

When Doirin grasped the situation, she looked faint, and the small amount of color in her face faded to gray. The doctor was studying their papers, making inquiries of Tomas, who kept his answers to a minimum. Mary, looking around frantically, noticed the chalky slate on the wall and was quick-witted enough to maneuver as close to the slate as she could get. Slipping her hand from under her shawl, she ran her fingers along the bottom of the chalk-filled frame. Veronica started when her sister-in-law, standing between her and the desk, put something white and dry on her face, smoothing it out with trembling fingers to look like natural color.

"You're making me look like a painted woman!" Veronica said in Gaelic.

"What do you know about such things?" Mary said weakly, turning away, as a woman wearing a white apron emerged from the area behind the doctor to usher them into the adjoining corridor. The men and women were separated into the divided area, and the women were put into gray-curtained cubicles with the order to undress to the waist. Mary tried to hang onto Veronica, but the aproned woman put her into a space along the hall, allowing only Rosaleen to stay with her mother.

Shocked as much by the order to undress as by the loss of her young relative, Mary sat down on a bench with Rosaleen at her knee. Still fully clothed in ragged skirt and blouse, with only her shawl loose about her shoulders, Mary listened to a man's voice in the space next to them cajole someone into taking off her blouse. It was not decent. Only small children undressed before others. No woman ever displayed her naked body to a man, not even her husband. And, oh, God! . . . what about Veronica?

The man's voice was patient, as though he had been through the discussion many times. "You can hold your clothing over the front of you. I only want to listen to your chest."

Mary took off her shawl in a matter-of-fact way, anxious to get it over with as soon as possible and rejoin Veronica. She did not wish to expose herself before Rosaleen, but her mind was more with her sister-in-law than with her own modesty. She had hoped to distract the doctor with talking, so he would not notice too much. Alone, Veronica would remain silent, and all would be lost.

As though she had read her mother's thoughts, Rosaleen said suddenly, in careful Gaelic, "Can I go to Veronica, Ma? If I can make the doctor look at me, maybe he won't see that Veronica has the fever."

Startled, Mary took a deep breath and said, "Go!"

She had never felt closer to Rosaleen than at that moment, the daughter she had not wanted, but who had turned into her special child, the one to make her continue fighting in spite of everything. Shivering in the chilly room, Mary opened her hand and stared at the ball of paper, all that was left of her youngest son. Quietly and quickly, she secreted it in the waistband of her skirt, to be destroyed later.

Dr. John Townsend was extremely ambivalent about the Irish. He did not have to do this work, and he wondered why he volunteered in the first place. He put in several hours of work a week at the Lung Hospital, too, as well as teaching and carrying on his lucrative private practice. Now there was the threat of fever here, and he had to wear a surgical mask above his Harvard tie. When the ships had started arriving six months before, he was curious and had come down to have a look: he was touched by what he saw. He had not imagined such poverty existed, and today the immigrants were even quieter, thinner, more desperate than before. Why didn't he just leave? For the same reason he had become a physician thirty years before: humanity concerned him. Though born into a good family, he had chosen his profession, and he was needed here. Lately, humanity and human beings were separating into two distinct things, though: the one abstract, the other painfully real. And this was only the beginning. As the winter progressed, the ill and dying would start arriving. He knew the effects of the famine of 1847 had not begun to be seen in this country, and he wondered if he would have the courage to continue with his work then.

His wife and friends already objected. Where would small, well-ordered Boston put so many poor Irish? Who would employ them, dirty and illiterate as they were? And Roman Catholic, too. They had already brought down property values in the North End, where they had begun to congregate: tenements were springing up in the oldest area of town. There were not enough industries in the city to absorb them as a work force; they would be a burden on the taxpayers. Boston, after all, was for Bostonians.

All these arguments had a peculiar effect on Dr. Townsend.

He could not disagree with them, but when his friends spoke, he pictured the faces he saw here, and it made him stubborn. Compassion, paradoxically mixed with irritation, stirred in him. Basically, he was a kind man. Sandy-haired and nearly bald with a trace of red remaining in his whiskers, he looked younger than his age, because of the youthful, inquisitive light in his gray eyes. His poorly laundered Public Health coat hung on his long body, giving him the unkempt appearance suitable to the patients he examined. Once he had considered bringing in his starched white coats from Massachusetts General, but decided he was intimidating enough to these people as he was. When he first realized they were afraid of him, he tried to analyze their fear. His English name and Boston accent might have something to do with it, or just the fact that he was an authority figure. He knew they resented authority after being ruled by England for so long. Of course, most of them had never seen a doctor before, either. And they were such a straitlaced people they did not even want to take off their clothes for an examination. They were more puritanical than his own ancestors.

But there was a liveliness in them he admired, and they had an incredible use of words, from long hours of telling stories in the winter, or listening to someone else who told them well. Though, like any national group, they were not all beautiful, he had seen some remarkably handsome specimens among them. The woman he had just left remained in his mind, guarding her full breasts from sight with her hands, like a figure in a Renaissance painting. Her skin was like white cream stretched over her ribcage, and she had a certain dignity and pride. Remarkable face, marvelous dark eyes. Twenty-nine years old, in her fifth pregnancy, with only two children living. He had seen her sister, too...several years older, with a trace of the same good looks spoiled by tight lips and angry, suspicious eyes. She had stared at him as though he were going to defile her, at his age. What would they all do when they left here? Now, it appeared he was going to see yet another Noonan in cubicle four: yes, same last name, this time Veronica, age eighteen. He cleared his throat to give warning of his entrance through the curtains; then he heard the laughter within and forgot to replace his face mask. Laughter...in this place?

He could not understand what they were saying inside, because they spoke their own language, full of glottal stops and guttural slurs. He knew something of the history of

19

Gaelic, what an ancient language it was, that it had originated in the Danube Basin and spread over France to the British Isles before the arrival of the Romans. But suddenly, hearing it spoken, between laughs, with such ease and familiarity, he was struck by the downright stubbornness of these people. In all the centuries under the British, they had kept their old language, their own religion and national character. Though he could not say he was really fond of them, he admired their tenacity. Another burst of laughter from the cubicle interrupted his reflections, and he entered quickly to make up for the time he had lost.

The two girls looked up at him, and the smiles stopped on their lips. Dammit, he thought, why are they so afraid of me? He had a desire to communicate with these people, get to know them a little, but it was always stifled by their unreasonable fear. These two were so young, so pretty; they looked alike, but not as the other Noonan women had looked. Their hair was black, not dark brown like the others, and their dark-lashed eyes were as blue as cornflowers. They had been playing some kind of game: their fingers were still linked loosely. And, of course, they both had all their clothing on. Before he could repeat the old injunction to disrobe, the little girl moved shyly toward him and put her small hand in his, something that had never happened before and that left him speechless for a moment.

"Sure, it's the fine doctor himself," she said. "It's time for you to undress, Veronica."

The older girl straightened her narrow shoulders. "Don't be naughty, Rosaleen!"

"Ma says we have to get this over with as soon as we can," the child said, beginning to struggle out of her blouse. "I'll do it first." Then, glancing up at him, "Do you think I'm being naughty?"

"No," he reassured her, and lifted her up in his arms, disregarding his own advice to the staff about typhus and lice. "You're a sensible girl. In order to examine you, I must listen to your chest with this." He waved his cone-shaped stethoscope in front of her wondering eyes: it always worked with Boston children, and it seemed to be doing so now. What a little charmer! She was as friendly as a puppy, totally unlike all the others. For the first time, he felt he had made some kind of breakthrough. He smiled, and the little girl stared in fascination at his mouth.

"Veronica! He has a gold tooth...just like Ma's sovereign!"

"Does your mother have a gold sovereign?" he asked doubtfully, and Rosaleen's face became solemn.

"She had one hidden in the well. But it's gone now. She spent it for food when Da didn't get back from the city. Do the people here have gold teeth?"

"Only when they don't look after their own. Let me see yours."

She grinned with exaggeration as children do when showing their teeth. Every baby tooth was perfect, so white it was nearly translucent. Already he had noticed the difference between the teeth of city and country dwellers, and he knew this child came from the country, where there was very little caries and, for the most part, the teeth were clean.

"What do you brush them with?" he asked, expecting the formula for some homemade powder, but the child laughed as though it was the funniest thing she had ever heard.

"I brush"—she broke into laughter again—"my hair! How can anyone brush *teeth*?"

He put her down on the floor and knelt at her level. This was too good an opportunity to pass up: usually, these people were not so open. "What do you eat, Rosaleen?"

The child lost her merriment. "Beans, on the ship."

He felt embarrassed, realizing where his question had led them, but he was too interested to stop the inquiry. "I mean, what did you eat at home, before the trouble came?"

"Praties and milk. And sometimes pratie bread," she said wistfully.

"Does she mean potatoes?" he asked Veronica, who nodded solemnly.

"And nothing else?" he asked Rosaleen. "No green vegetables or meat?"

The child went silent, thinking about food, and Veronica answered, "On grand occasions—sometimes a chicken, or fish."

"What about wheat?"

"We grew it, sir, but it was sent to England. We don't know how to cook it."

"And green stuff makes us sick," Rosaleen volunteered. "Ma cooked a batch of grass and plants, and it made us sick."

"That was during the famine," Veronica said softly. "The Indian corn the Americans sent made people sick, too."

"Didn't you keep pigs? I thought all Irishmen kept pigs."

"Oh, yes. We raised a pig every year to meet the rent."

Potatoes and milk, their basic everyday diet. He wanted

to pursue the matter, but he had spent too much time with them already. He helped Rosaleen get out of her patched garment, dropping it to the floor.

"I know where my heart is," she said, regaining her high spirits. "I can feel it when I run fast."

He smiled. "I can hear it, too, and it's very sound, indeed. I'll let you listen, too." He looked at Veronica while the child played with the stethoscope, and the girl's eyes were cast down, knowing she would be next. He checked Rosaleen's torso for typhus lesions, listened to her lungs, and when he looked at Veronica again, the girl had turned her back and was slowly dropping the upper part of her dress. He stood up quickly, before she could throw her filthy shawl over her white shoulders.

Veronica's skin was clear and poreless like the others. She was pale, but almost everyone there was pale from lack of nourishment. When he put his hand on her forehead, it was cool enough, and there were no typhus lesions on her body.

"Have you had any headaches?" he asked.

"No, sir," she replied, holding her garment over her breasts.

When he put his stethoscope to her back, he did not like what he heard, and turned her carefully by the rigid shoulders to place the instrument on her chest. The moist rales were only too familiar. He resorted to percussion, hoping he had heard wrong.

"How do you feel? Do you cough much?"

"No," she said, lowering her eyelids. "I feel just fine, sir."

"Veronica can outrun me," Rosaleen said, tugging at his sleeve. "She's never been sick. I was once. My nose ran, but I didn't cough. No one in our family's ever coughed!"

"I'm sure they haven't," he said, touching the top of the desperate child's head. "Veronica, I'd like to speak to your sister."

"I have no sister, sir. Just two brothers."

"But I just examined two women named Noonan."

"My brothers' wives, Mary and Doirin."

"I see. I believe it's Mary I'd like to speak to."

Rosaleen released her grip on his sleeve. "That's my ma!"

"Is she, now?" he said with abstraction. "You run and bring her to me like a good girl." Then, he turned to Veronica. "You may dress, my dear. Go through the door at the end of the corridor. Your family should be waiting there."

*   *   *

Mary was breathless with alarm when she entered the cubicle where the doctor waited, with Rosaleen following close behind her. Dr. Townsend ignored the child and spoke to Mary.

"It isn't the fever, Mrs. Noonan. It's something slower, less contagious. Have you heard of consumption, Mary?"

Relief washed over her face. "They get well. The priest in our village had consumption, and he got over it."

"Yes, sometimes they do. With lots of rest and good food." He was not sure what to do. He knew what a pesthouse the Lung Hospital was, with whole families living there together. But, on the other hand, could these people provide for the girl well enough to save her? "How much money do you have?"

"Enough to settle in, I'm sure. And we can all work. We'll look after her, doctor—even the children. You don't know how much they love Veronica."

"We have to think of the children, too. She can't be near them, or they may get sick, too. Maybe it would be better if we put her into the hospital."

She folded her hands tightly in entreaty. "No! Please. We'll keep the children apart, I promise. We'll nurse her back to health. Doctor, please let our Veronica stay with us."

He rubbed his chin and stared over her head; then he glanced down at Rosaleen, who was almost the image of her aunt. The child's blue eyes were pleading with him. He reached into his vest pocket and thrust a card into Mary's hands.

"If you ever need me, send someone to this address."

"She can stay with us then?" Mary asked, a smile on her lips, the first he had seen there. He nodded. "Oh, thank you, doctor—" She looked at the card. "Dr. Townsend. I'll pray for you."

That one break in the darkness seemed to blow every cloud out of Mary's life. Joy rose in her heart, and she felt like singing as she started to leave the cubicle. Then, with one hand on the curtain, she turned back to look at the doctor.

"Do you suppose Veronica got the consumption from the old priest?" She smiled. "She's that pious!"

Chapter 2

THE SHOES were shabby and ill-fitting, and the threadbare coats, which had seen better days, smelled of cedar and naphtha. Rosaleen slogged through the snow in an old navy coat that nearly touched her ankles and boy's shoes that rubbed even her callused feet. At least they were all relatively warm as they straggled uncertainly through the streets. The clothing, tossed in large boxes just inside the exit of the immigration building, had been donated by the Charitable Society, a sign indicated, but no one was there to see to its distribution. Selection was made by rooting like so many pigs at a trough, with frequent outbursts between the new arrivals over a particular item. Veronica's coat had caused just such an altercation with another young woman. Though it was not the warmest, it was elegant: a rich blue velvet cut in the fashion of twenty years before. Doirin had shouted the other claimant down so her sister-in-law could have it. Mary held a man's tweed greatcoat around her like a cape, while Doirin put hers all the way over her head to protect herself from the falling snow. Tomas, at least, had fared better: his gray wool coat almost fit him, but Brian's was too small and had a ragged bit of fur hanging from the collar.

"We should look for the priest," Doirin argued, half-slipping on the cobbles. "If anyone can find us a place to stay, he would. I don't trust these people. Sure, they look like a bunch of cutthroats to me."

Mary, who was still in a light mood, laughed, the sound ringing clearly in the cold air. "You must have no notion of how *we* look."

"We should at least ask where the church is," Doirin persisted.

"Mary, we really should find the priest," Veronica concurred.

But Tomas had another idea, one that better suited his comfort. Across the street, which was tracked with ice and mud, a familiar painted window announced "Dugan's Pub," and even before the others saw it, Tomas began to head them in that direction.

"No one knows what's transpiring in a town like the pub-keeper," he said with authority, herding them over the ruts in the snow. "They know every bleeding thing that's happening. Ah, Brian, do we have enough for a bite to eat? There was no food on the boat this morning."

Once through Immigration, Brian had become more alert, as though some awful fear was removed from his shoulders. He surveyed his surroundings with interest, joking with his son, Darin, who was the most like him.

"Yes, we all need food," he responded. "But will a pub in this place provide it?"

Only whiskey fumes and stale smoke struck their nostrils when they entered the pub, but the room was warm from the stove and the human bodies huddled against the dark bar. Tomas was mystified by the reaction to their entrance: several patrons near the door picked up their drinks and moved away. The drinkers had a whispered conference with the big ginger-haired man behind the bar, who approached them wiping his beefy hands on a towel. Though the patrons kept their distance, they listened with interest. For a moment, Mary thought he was going to ask them to leave.

But, Tomas, in his own element, gave the man a broad smile. "Afternoon, Mr. Dugan. I'm Tomas Noonan, and this is my family. Your Boston's a cold place, for sure, man. We'd like a little something to warm our souls."

Mr. Dugan was hesitant; then, "Is it Cork I detect in your speech?" he asked. "I'm from Skibbereen, myself, but many years past."

The women involuntarily lowered their eyes at the mention of that village; even Tomas was silenced for a moment. But he recovered himself quickly.

"Skibbereen, is it? Sure, we have news of that place. But we're fair freezing and hungry, too."

Mr. Dugan put one large hand on Tomas's shoulder and ushered the whole family through a door beside the bar, into a room containing booths separated by colored glass. When the Noonans were suitably settled around a table, he winked and bent over them.

"Never mind that lot in there," he said, hitching his head in the direction of the bar. "There's been talk of fever, that's all. Sure, there's no truth in it, is there?"

"Fever?" Tomas asked blankly. "I've heard nothing. Have you?" He looked at the others.

Only Brian shook his head, but that was enough to convince the pub owner, for women counted very little with him. "You'll be cozy enough here," he assured them, "and I'll get you something to eat. This snug isn't used until later, so you'll have your privacy. Did you just arrive today?"

Not one of the children fidgeted while the men bantered: they had been promised food and they waited in silence, along with the women. None of them knew what to order in this grand place, and, uncertainly, Tomas ordered two jars of ale for himself and Brian. When Mr. Dugan disappeared into the bar to get them, they all put their heads together in conference.

"They must eat meat and Indian corn and things like that here," Tomas said. "Do you think we can afford it? But Mr. Dugan seemed like a fine fellow, and God knows I can tell him about his village."

"He may throw you out for that," Doirin said flatly. Mary watched Rosaleen put her little finger into the sugar bowl and lick it cautiously.

"Ma! It's sweet like honey!"

Brian exclaimed softly, "I believe to God it's sugar! Sitting right out on the table like this! I saw it once in a tea shop in Cobh when I went to market."

Mary picked up the cardboard propped between the sugar bowl and two glass containers filled with similar granules, one white and one black. She had never been in a restaurant before, but she was less inhibited than Veronica and Doirin.

"It tells what they have to eat, and the prices. Brian, how much is twenty-five C?" Mary asked.

He shook his head. "We must ask Mr. Dugan."

"And look like dull boys from the country?" Tomas said, appalled. "No. We'll eat what we like and then see if we can pay for it!"

"That way you won't look like dull lads from the country," Doirin said bitingly, "though that's what you are."

Mary looked up from the menu with an almost religious awe. "They have potatoes," she said in a half-whisper. "They have praties here."

"That settles it," Tomas said gleefully. "That's what we'll ask for. And a pot of tea, too!"

"Tea!" Veronica exclaimed.

"Tea, is it?" Doirin cut in. "It was so dear at home that in the good times we didn't have it often. Brian's handling our money, in case you've forgotten! He won't allow such extravagance."

Brian was silent for a moment; then he slipped quietly from his seat and reentered the bar. Mary felt a wave of pride and relief: he was taking over again. He returned shortly with the men's drinks on a small round tray and a smile in his deep-blue eyes.

Placing Tomas's ale in front of him, Brian took a swig himself and, wiping his mouth, said, "Mr. Dugan is aware that we're new here. He explained what he called the rate of exchange. We'll all have praties and tea—just this once to celebrate. But things are dreadful dear in Boston for sure."

"Did you get him to exchange our money?" Mary asked.

"No. I'll have to go to a bank for that. But he did change a pound note. This is what their money looks like."

When the big bowl of steaming potatoes arrived, with a pot of tea and a loaf of bread with butter, they were still poring over the coins and bills, trying to understand them. Only Rosaleen seemed to grasp the value of the new money quickly.

"It's easy," she said. "Four of these make a dollar, and there's near three dollars to a pound. These dark ones are pennies or cents and ten of them make a dime."

Mr. Dugan smiled broadly. "I believe to God you've a wee banker in your family," he said, putting heavy white plates on the soiled tablecloth and serving the potatoes from the bowl. "No eating from one pot here. You each have a plate and"—he lifted the cutlery—"a knife and fork! You eat your fill, now. I'll join you later, so you can tell me about home."

The unfamiliar forks were abandoned for spoons in the feast that followed. After a few minutes of diligent eating, however, Rosaleen began to choke and Mary dropped her spoon to help the child.

"Sure," she warned them, "it's too much, all at once. Our

stomachs are unaccustomed to it. We'll be sick. Remember that poor woman who came to the cottage when we still had some grain?"

They slowed down, and when they stopped eating the bowl was still half full. Carefully, Mary poured the precious tea into the big cups, and Brian pushed the sugar bowl forward.

"For the tea," he explained. "Just a small spoonful, now."

They tried it cautiously and decided the sweetness added to the tea. Tomas belched and rubbed his stomach. "Look at all those praties left. I used to eat that much at a sitting, when we were working the fields, but I'm fair full already."

"It's our stomachs," Mary said, savoring her tea. "They must shrink. By the time things got really bad, I had no hunger at all, just the weakness."

"It's true," Brian agreed. "But, since that's the case, why did the bellies of children in town swell up so much?"

She shook her head. "Let's not speak of it."

"I could stand another pint for the road," Tomas said cheerfully, but, much to Mary's relief, Brian shook his head.

"We don't have money to throw around—just enough to keep us until we get some work. And I still have to go to the bank."

Veronica, who had remained silent during the meal, eating lightly, almost with a reverence for the food, looked from Tomas to Mary, her eyes bright and feverish again.

"Do you suppose Mr. Dugan really had people at Skibbereen?" Veronica asked. "He's been so kind—it would be a disfavor to tell him about it. We shouldn't lie, of course, but maybe we shouldn't mention it at all?"

Tomas, who had become dejected and hostile from being refused his pint, gave her an angry look. "He's a man, isn't he? Well, then, he can take the truth. Didn't Brian and I see it for ourselves? A mass grave it was, with nearly every villager thrown in."

He looked at Brian to back him up, but his older brother's lips were pale and set. Brian ran one hand over his eyes to blank out what he had seen, and said softly, "Veronica's right, Tomas. No one should have to face that kind of truth. It'll please me if you don't tell our new friend, Dugan, about the mass burial in his village. A stigma attaches to the one who brings bad news."

* * *

They exchanged the news, some of it true, about the famine, with Mr. Dugan. Then he advised them to go to a house at the top of the hill, where a woman might put them up.

"Mrs. O'Toole's a hard one," he said, "but better than some. The streets up there are filling up, and they'll charge you all they can. It's one of the oldest parts of the city, and they've turned the houses into rooms. The Old North Church is right on top there."

"Is it Catholic?" Veronica inquired meekly, and he smiled at her ignorance.

"No, my dear. You'll learn all about it soon enough. The Catholic church isn't far away."

"I think we should ask the priest to help us find a place," Doirin said sharply, and Mr. Dugan laughed outright.

"You'll only see the priest when he's collecting, here," he said. "It isn't like home...too many people. If you get to know him at all, it'll be a blessed miracle. Now, it's getting on toward four and the light will be going soon. You'd better get yourselves settled in."

The snow had stopped, but a bitter wind tore through their clothes as they climbed the hill. The brick houses were dirty, fringed with icicles, furred with snow, and there was not a living soul on the street or looking out of the dingy windows. They reached the side street Mr. Dugan had instructed them to find and had to cling to the iron railings of the fences to keep from sliding head-first on the cobbles where garbage and debris were frozen firm into the ice. Mrs. O'Toole's house was no different from the others on the street, with shredded lace curtains and the paint peeling off the door. Brian thumped hard on the door, and they waited mutely for it to open. He had to knock again to be heard. Muffled footsteps in the dark hall preceded the opening of the door, and a strong smell of cabbage coming from within.

Mrs. O'Toole was a stringy woman with lank hair falling from the unkempt bun on top of her head. She held her hands beneath her apron and looked at them blankly until she heard Mr. Dugan's name. Then both hands came together and she wrung them in distress.

"I haven't any place to put you! The house is full. Praise be to God, you're really lousy, aren't you? Just off the boat? Well, come in...come in. The cold's harsh. You can warm yourselves by the fire before looking further."

She led them down the dim hallway, with the snow melting off their shoes onto the threadbare streamer of rug, to her own quarters: a small room with a cot in an adjoining alcove. There were not seats for all, so the men and children stood while they warmed their hands at a small grate under a mantle.

"I don't own this house," she made clear at once. "I only manage it for Dugan. Things are in a fearful state: the roof leaks, the pipes have burst, and there are already too many people here. It's the same all up and down the street. Even basements are going for a high price, dirt floors and all."

"Basements?" Brian asked.

"What we'd call cellars back home. There's some advantage to them. They're a bit warmer in the winter and cooler in the summer. Some people are getting two dollars a week for them. But, God help us, the one here isn't fit for human habitation. I don't go down to tend the furnace myself, if I can get someone else to do it. I don't even know what's stored down there, but I know there's rats and spiders."

Brian looked at Mary: their eyes held for a moment with perfect understanding. It had been so long since that had happened that she had to put her hand over her heart to still its frantic beating.

"We have money," he told Mrs. O'Toole, "and many hands to do the clearing. I'm sure we could make it livable in a week."

"You haven't seen it yet," the woman said, shaking her head. "It's so dark and dirty."

Mary stood up and faced her in front of the fireplace. "We've spent forty days in the hold of a ship. Anything would be luxury compared to that. And, as Mr. Noonan says, we could clean it."

"Do you have any of your things with you? Bedding, utensils?"

"Just what's on our backs, and that fairly crawling, as you remarked. Everything else was sold long since. But," Mary added quickly, "we can buy what we need tomorrow."

"You do have money, then?" Mrs. O'Toole considered, some of the blankness leaving her gray eyes. "You can pay two dollars a week?"

Mary looked at Brian, who nodded cautiously.

"We can pay," Mary said. "And we can work."

"The work may be hard to come by," the woman said; then she pursed her lips. "All right, for a while anyway. But I haven't even a pallet to lay down for a bed. And as for cooking, the others are doing it in the yard, out near the outhouse.

There's a stove in the kitchen, but it isn't enough for everyone. It's one whole family to a room here."

"They're that quiet," Veronica said, suppressing a cough with her fist. "Is no one at home, at all?"

"They're here," Mrs. O'Toole said grimly, lighting an oil lamp. "Where else would they be on a day like this? Come along, follow me."

"Aren't the men at work?" Brian inquired as she led them to the rear of the house.

"Not many," she said, using her key. "Work isn't easy to come by in this city. A few lucky ones get jobs on the docks."

They descended the narrow wooden stairs into an area of stifling blackness, with snow banked against the two windows in front of the house which might have provided some light. A skitter of rats made Rosaleen cling tightly to Mary's hand, her little body drawn up tightly in terror. There was nothing more fearful to her than the dusty darkness with rats where you could not see them.

"It's filthy!" Doirin exclaimed in disgust as the oil lamp played over the floor and stacked furniture. "Oh, we really can't..."

"It'll be fine," Mary said unevenly, touching her sister's shoulder. "If you could just give us the loan of your lamp, Mrs. O'Toole?"

"Indeed," the dour-faced woman said reluctantly, "but it'll be extra for the oil. Everything's dear these days."

Dust motes turned in the faint beam of light from the window. Mary closed her eyes again and snuggled warmly into the naphtha odor of the old coat around her. She drifted in half-sleep, content with the comfort of somewhere to lay her head. For a few minutes, she was back in Rathcormac on a summer day, and only a girl, barefoot, sitting on the stone wall near the path to the village, waiting as she always did for Brian to pass, experiencing the mingled exultation and trepidation she felt when he was near. Perhaps he wouldn't pass today, she thought despondently; but, soon, she heard his step, which could be mistaken for no other, on the lane beyond the dappled green hedge. Her heart took a turn as she braced herself for the greeting she had never been able to articulate, trying not to run away before he appeared. She loved him. She was fourteen and he was a man, but she loved him dearly. When he finally appeared, she stared raptly at his face, and it was like praying to a saint in church, but more uplifting. That beautiful face, the dark gentle blue eyes, bluer than the sky behind him, the hair, darker than the wing of a blackbird, falling over his fair brow. And he was tall—a head above any other man in the village, carrying himself with assurance. She watched him with a love that had no object but to worship, and when he saw her she turned her head away, as though the meeting were by chance and she had not been waiting over an hour. His smiling eyes met hers as he passed, and she nodded gravely, so he would not see that his glance melted her heart into her thighs, a sensation she did not understand, but which she sought in these meetings. He did not pause to pass the time of day with such a child, no matter how pretty, and she slid down from the gray stone wall to lie in the grass, staring up at the sky with a whispered prayer on her lips: "Oh, God, let him wait for me!"

A soft mewing sound beside her made her open her eyes to the light motes filtering the darkness again, and she was recalled to the present with a feeling of tragedy. It was morning and they were in Boston, a strange, cold, forbidding place. Moving in her sleep, Rosaleen repeated the little mewing sound. Mary shook her gently by the shoulder, with just enough force to wake the child, who, she knew, had to urinate and, if left to sleep, would do it where she was. Slipping the uncomfortable shoes on her feet, Mary lifted Rosaleen quietly, so she would not wake the others, and carried the child toward the stairs they had descended the night before.

She could see the basement more clearly now, without the aid of the lamp. It was big, extending back and away from them into impenetrable gloom, where a monstrous block of concrete and brick showed fire in its metal grill. The windows tried valiantly to let the sun shine through the accumulation of dust and snow on them. The earth floor was as even as that of her own cottage, but it was covered with a veil of black dust that puffed up as she walked. On the whole, it was not such a bad place, if it could ever be cleaned.

When she pushed the kitchen door open, the world seemed very bright again. A kettle was boiling on the wood stove, and Mrs. O'Toole and another woman, who was grim-faced and unclean, sat at the table with cups before them. Apparently it was too early for the others to rise and fill the kitchen until they boiled over into the back yard to cook. The woman with Mrs. O'Toole watched with narrow green eyes as Mary passed through.

Mrs. O'Toole, whose voice was rough, said, "It's that way—at the end of the yard. Come back and join us for a cup of tea."

"Thank you," Mary said and nodded. Though she did not see it, she felt their heads go together behind her, whispering. On either side of the broken path and clustered close to the house were buckets and basins and an old rusted stove, which still felt warm as she passed it. The adjoining houses had similar yards with high brick walls between them, and she could hear some activity there: sleep-fogged voices made occasional remarks as women stirred up the morning fire. A baby cried hungrily. The air was cold, but the sky was gray and clear. Mary did not much like the look of the woman with Mrs. O'Toole in the kitchen. She had the frantic, lean look of those who clawed at the cottage door toward the end, when there was nothing left to share, and who stole what they could if your back was turned.

After taking care of Rosaleen, Mary washed their faces with snow and dried them on her shawl. They were as grubby as the others, there was no denying that. In the clear, frosty air, she could smell her own body, and that was a sign one needed a good wash. It would be grand to wash again: she itched all over. When she reentered the warm, untidy kitchen, the woman with the green eyes got up and left, leaving her the empty chair. Mary sat down and then lifted Rosaleen onto her lap.

"Did you get any sleep at all?" the landlady asked gruffly, filling her cup. "Nothing bit you, did it?"

"It was fine," Mary said, leaving the cup on the table to cool. She did not want to seem greedy. Everyone, it appeared, drank tea regularly here. "The cellar isn't a bad place. With a little work, it will do fine."

Mrs. O'Toole moved a black kettle from one side of the stove to the other, holding it with her apron. "There are rats as big as cats down there."

Rosaleen stirred. "I dreamed of rats," she said. "I dreamed I was at Grandma's and..."

Mary shushed her softly, rocking her to soothe her. "You forget all that," she said, a flash of her own foolish dream flickering through her mind. "Dreams are only something that sneak up on you when you're asleep...things we daren't think about when we're awake. We'll get rid of any rats and they won't hurt you."

Mrs. O'Toole sat down heavily and poured herself another

cup of tea. "Last summer, all these rooms were empty. Some of the houses around here were boarded up. They could be bought for a song. Now, the place is teeming with people, and more to come if I'm not mistaken."

"I hope so," Mary said softly, sipping her tea and putting the cup to Rosaleen's lips. "I mean, I hope a lot of them can get out of Ireland."

"It's that bad?"

Mary nodded. She did not want to talk about it; she wanted to forget it all and start fresh. But something compelled her to say, "You wouldn't believe it, Mrs. O'Toole. Are you from the country?"

The woman grunted. "I should say not. I'm from Dublin. My husband brought me here ten years ago. Then he died and left me to starve. Thank God for Mr. Dugan and his wife. I was living in the same rooming house with them. He bought this place when he heard about the famine. He said lots of people would be coming...only I didn't expect so many."

"There are thousands waiting," Mary said, tempted to tell Mrs. O'Toole about conditions in Ireland, but she did not want to bring those troubles with her. "How long has Mr. Dugan been here? Is he long from Cork?"

"Twenty years or so. But he didn't come here with empty pockets. It takes money to make money. He's made something of himself, which is more than you people will be able to do. You're late-comers, and there are too many of you."

Mary took the last gulp of tea and let Rosaleen have the sugar at the bottom of the cup. "It depends on who you are, doesn't it? Back there, there were some who made it here and some who didn't...more who didn't. Just getting here makes us special, doesn't it?"

"You don't know what it's like," Mrs. O'Toole flashed, and for the first time Mary realized that her temper was quick because she had a heart and could not stand what she saw around her. "Half the men in this house aren't working. There's no work for them. There are too many of them, and they're ignorant...right at the bottom of the ladder, just like the niggers. And the people here don't like Catholics, either."

Mary experienced mild surprise. She was accustomed to the English not liking her religion, but she did not expect that prejudice in America. "Why not? I thought there was religious freedom here. We've done nothing to them."

"You'll see," Mrs. O'Toole said darkly. "They're afraid the Pope will take over the world. They consider our religious rites secret, because they're in Latin, and us dangerous. Being poor, dirty and stupid doesn't help us. How much money do you have?"

Mary remembered the green-eyed one, and soft alarm rang in her chest. Even if she had known, she would not advertise it, and she must tell Brian about the kind of people here. She simply shrugged, implying it was enough, and Mrs. O'Toole let the matter drop. She was studying Rosaleen.

"She'll be a pretty little thing when she gets some meat on her bones," she said. "Don't send her to the public school. The priest says it's the wrong thing to do. The Americans are Protestants, and they'll have all religion out of our children if they can. Father Donelly is against the state schools."

"What other kind are there?" Mary frowned. She wanted her children educated: it was the only way out of the trap of ignorance and manual labor.

"There'll be a parochial school here in a few years. The father's collecting for it, now. And they're going to build more churches. All of us must contribute what we can to fight the Protestants."

"Even if we haven't any work?" Mary asked, seeing some kind of unreason in that and disturbed about the schools.

"Every penny helps."

"What would the priest do if we sent our children to school?"

Mrs. O'Toole raised her eyebrows. "It's not him so much. It's what the others would do." She reached out and touched Rosaleen's cheek with her gnarled, dry hand. "Our own people would make it hard enough on your baby, to be sure, Mrs. Noonan."

Chapter 3

DOIRIN objected from the beginning and did less than her share of the work. It took nearly a week to get the basement into order, and most of it was dirty, filthy work, sweeping and scrubbing the hard earth floor. Their faces and hands were covered with coal dust, and they had to tie rags over their noses and mouths. They found a chair in the rejected furniture stored by the furnace, and Mary bundled Veronica up in heavy coats, to sit outside breathing the cold, clean air while they stirred up the dust inside.

"You take too much upon yourself!" Doirin declared. "This place is as bad as the hold of the ship. Only two small windows for light. And them rats dying in the traps you set—stinking up everything!"

Mary removed her shawl and wiped the accumulated dirt from the nearest window with several hard strokes. A long stream of light shone through, filtered only by the snow outside. She shook the dust and cobwebs from her shawl triumphantly.

"Was it a neat country cottage you were expecting?" she asked. "You're living in the city now, Doirin. When we get rid of the snow, there'll be enough light. This black dust beneath our feet is the biggest problem. Mrs. O'Toole says it's from the coal stacked there by the furnace. They burn it like peat."

A large chunk of shiny coal was carefully examined by all

of them. They could not understand how anything so hard could make so much dust, but they appreciated its long-burning qualities: a few shovelfuls in the furnace every day gave off continuous warmth. When they finished the floor on their hands and knees with water, it was not as clean as Mary's own cottage, but as clean as it would ever be. The men bought straw, warm and fresh to the smell, and made it into pallets for sleeping. They were pleasant to lie on, after making their beds on the floor at night, and Mary aired them every morning when the weather was clear to kill the lice.

Enough furniture was found in the storage by the furnace to answer their minimal needs: several chairs in assorted styles, most of which Brian had to repair, a couple of stools and an old door that served nicely as a table when set on wooden boxes. Their only expenditure was for cloth to divide the area into rooms, the way they had seen it done at the immigration shack. Partitioned into separate spaces for the two married couples, and for Veronica and the children at night, the basement became one large room again during the day, with the curtains pulled back on the ropes Brian strung across the ceiling. A few carefully doled-out coins bought a large secondhand bowl, a bent pot, and a bucket for cooking and scrubbing.

The greatest marvel had come first, before they started their domestic enterprise. Brian returned the first afternoon without a job, but with a fifty-pound sack of potatoes, which he placed carefully in one corner. The children cried out when they saw what the gunny sack contained: food, so much of it, for all of them. Their single daily meal was cooked outside on the stove and brought into the basement, where they ate from one large bowl. Milk was far beyond their means, but Mary insisted that Veronica have a pint a day: she had promised the doctor. And, with rest, time spent in the cold air and adequate food, Veronica had begun to look better already, though her cough still lingered.

Their needs, which had always been simple, were almost met, but after a month's unemployment the men began to come home in a state of dejection. Of the two, Tomas was the more cheerful, having cadged a few pints at Dugan's while Brian searched for jobs.

Finally, at the table one night, Brian told them, "We can't go on like this. Wherever we go, there are signs up saying 'No Irish Need Apply.' I don't understand it. Why do they dislike us so?"

"Our religion has something to do with it," Tomas said knowledgeably, from hanging around the pub. "They also think we're rowdies and thieves. I've never stolen anything in my life!"

Brian turned his face away, so the candlelight flickered on his neck and ear and graying hair: his expression could not be seen, but Mary knew he was going to start brooding again.

She spoke up. "We aren't trash, the way they think. We're poor and not so clean, though. Brian, if you'll give us a couple of dollars, I know where I can get you men some decent clothes. If I bargain right, perhaps I can completely outfit you. A friend of mine has a secondhand store not too far away."

She did not tell him that Mr. Rabinsky was a Jew: that would start another row. Both Tomas and Doirin hated Jews, though they had never met one. Mary, on the other hand, thought Mr. Rabinsky a very nice man, if overly sharp when it came to money, and difficult to talk with because of his accent. He, in turn, seemed to find her company unusual and not unpleasant.

"It's you women who need the clothes," Brian replied, not looking at them. "Sure you're in rags, without anything to wear even to Mass."

"Our coats cover that," she said quickly. "And we've no-where else to go. The important thing is that you get jobs, and you won't do that looking slovenly. I don't wonder there are signs! In the old days, I'd have turned you away for a tinker."

"You go out enough," Doirin said peevishly. "You're gone all afternoon . . . and your children, too."

Mary had asked Doirin to come with her, at first, but her sister preferred to sleep the whole afternoon. So, while Veronica rested, Mary and her two children had been exploring their new environment, taking in the city a section at a time. Up one hill and down another they had wandered, for blocks around, and all the way down to the dock, where they had seen men lined up looking for jobs, shabby and unwashed. As her physical strength improved, Mary went farther afield, until she reached the Common and Beacon Hill, where she observed servants with uniforms under their coats going about their outside chores, even riding in horse cars to do the daily shopping. At the foot of that hill, on the opposite side, she came to a shantytown as bad as their own, and both she and Rosaleen were unnerved at their first sight of a black man. The neighborhood was a small pocket, adjacent to a street of bars and saloons, and they hurried through it quickly, not knowing what to expect from people so different from themselves.

Mary knew the price of everything: butter, which she did not buy, yard goods, which she someday hoped to buy, and the impossibly expensive furniture in the better store windows, for which she had not the least desire, though she looked long and painfully at the frocks for little girls like Rosaleen. Mary had asked for jobs, herself, in some of the small neighborhood stores, and she had been turned away with disgust, so she knew something of what Brian was experiencing.

That she thought of Brian, and never Tomas, was not strange to her: it had always been so, though perhaps not to such an extreme. They had never lived under the same roof before, she had never been so conscious of his proximity. But her secret was so secure she did not feel guilty about it. It was part of her, as it had been for so many years. Sometimes she thought she loved Rosaleen so much because the girl looked more like Brian than Tomas. After all they had been through, her feeling for Brian was the one thing that did not change; indeed, under the present circumstances, it seemed to grow day by day, until Mary thought she could not contain her love . . . though she knew she would. There was no alternative.

Mr. Rabinsky traded like a tinker, but there was a softer light in his eyes, for trading was evidently something he enjoyed, apart from the money. There was a strange sympathy between them, the Irish woman rejected by the new society because of her religion, and the small Jew from Poland, who had never known anything but rejection. She wished his English were better so they could converse, without realizing that he wanted the same thing.

The pile of clothing she selected, with a few things thrown in for the children, came to more than her two dollars, and he could reduce the prices no more and make a profit, small as it was. It was then, through sign language and mixed Polish-Yiddish-English, that he indicated to her that she could have everything she wanted, if she would instruct him in English for one hour a day. Mary returned home jubilantly, laden with clothing, and Liam and Rosaleen followed, bumping a large half-barrel they had found down the basement stairs.

Doirin started up from the pallet, where she had been sleeping all afternoon. "What in the name of God?" she said foggily. "What's all the noise?"

"It's for washing," Mary explained. "Not just our faces and hands and feet...but all over, like in the tub Mrs. O'Toole showed me upstairs. You crawl into it and wash all of you."

"That's what you think," Doirin said, her hands hanging listlessly over her knees where she sat. Catching sight of the bundle of clothing in Mary's arms, she squinted her eyes. "And what might that be?"

"Trousers, shirts, jackets. In pretty fair condition, though the shirt collars will have to be turned. I even found a few things for the boys."

"Always the men, isn't it?" Doirin sighed. "We're nothing at all."

"They have to work," Mary said, laying the shirts out on the table, along with a spool of white thread and a packet of needles she had purchased. "They have some women's things at the shop, too, but nothing that would suit us. When we've a bit of money, we'll buy some cloth and make our own, as we always have. I thought maybe a nice gray gabardine, since I haven't seen much plaid about...but it'll wait."

Doirin still sat on her pallet, watching her sister thread a needle in the dim light. "Until the cows come home, I'll wager. Are you sure our old pattern will suit this fine town? Those shirts aren't the homespun the men are accustomed to wearing."

Mary's spirits, which had been high from the bargain she had struck and the invigoration of the walk home, began to sag slightly. "If they don't suit, we'll get another pattern," she said sharply. "Maybe it's a red Kerry petticoat you'd be wanting, Doirin? I swear to God, I don't know what's the matter with you."

Doirin lowered her head and rubbed her forehead with her fingers. "Neither do I," she half-whispered. "Neither do I...."

Mary reached into her parcels and produced a large brown bar of soap. "It was only a penny," she said. "You'll feel better when we've had a bath. Once we get rid of these wretched lice and fleas, we'll all feel grand!"

The luxury of the first full bath was reserved for the men that evening. With the curtains drawn around them, they screamed from the hot water and the sting of the soap. But they looked grand afterward, as though they had lost a layer of darkened skin. When they left next morning in search of jobs, even Brian's mood was sunnier, and Mary could not get over how well he looked in his new clothes.

As soon as they were gone, Mary washed the two younger boys, one at a time, in a single tub of water, because it took five trips down the stairs to fill it. Doirin's oldest boys, Michael and Padraig, insisted on taking their baths without her help, while Mary washed and dried their clothes close to the furnace, but she inspected their ears and hair to make sure they had done a good job of it. Then it was time to boil more water and carry it downstairs. She felt a surge of resentment against Doirin for not doing her share. More than ever before, she was finding it difficult to understand her sister. Doirin was not a lazy woman, but since they had arrived in Boston, she had not turned a hand with anything but cleaning the basement. And she slept too much: Mary had never known anyone to sleep during the day as Doirin did. The responsibility of the children and the meals was all on Mary, though Veronica was allowed to peel potatoes. It was not natural.

When the tub was full again, Mary bathed Rosaleen, who was torn between coos of enjoyment over the hot water and shrieks over the soap. Then to give an example to Doirin and Veronica, who did not want to take their clothes off, Mary stepped into the tub behind the curtain herself, making ecstatic noises and splashing loudly.

"Oh, it's fine! The soap makes a grand lather, and the itching's all gone!"

Actually, when the soap touched her skin, she realized why the others had screamed: it was strong enough to burn the skin off a pig. She decided it must really be for washing clothes. But since none of them was familiar with soap, except for one precious bar her mother had purchased from a peddler in a good year long ago, she neglected to voice her observation to the other two women.

If one word could be used to summarize Veronica's nature, it was obedient, especially since the diagnosis of her illness. Though she was more against disrobing than Doirin, and modesty was ingrained in her, she was the next to endure the scathing bath, while Mary, clad only in her overcoat, washed their scant, patched skirts and blouses and shawls and set them to dry as she had the boys' clothing. Maybe she was doing penance, but Veronica did not make a single outcry about the soap. After she dried herself, she emerged from behind the curtain buttoned up in her blue velvet coat, with her color high and amusement in her eyes.

"Ah, that was lovely, soothing," she said. "Doirin, it's your turn, now."

Mary, not yet familiar with the frenetic fluctuations of the girl's illness, stared at her dumbfounded. Veronica was so high-spirited, and actually trying to lure Doirin into the crucifixion of that soap. And her mood was contagious. When Doirin adamantly refused to bathe, Mary and Veronica actually undressed her, fighting her all the way, and shoved her into the now tepid tub. Before she could get out, Mary took all her clothes, including her coat, and began to wash the skirt and blouse vigorously while Veronica raised a lather on her sister-in-law.

"Sure it isn't that bad, is it? Get back in there, Doirin. Your clothes are gone! Now let's just clean the rats out of your hair, darlin'. It's been driving me daft for weeks. How often do you think we should do this bathing thing, Mary?"

Hanging Doirin's rags over boxes near the furnace, Mary answered, "I don't know. Once a month, do you think?"

The pennies the boys brought in from running errands was all there was for the next five weeks, enough only to keep them in potatoes, and to buy a pint of milk for Veronica every few days. The rent was paid, but that was the end of the purse Brian had brought with him. Even decent clothing did not secure work for him and Tomas in a city dead set against the Irish, with a growing flood of workers on the market. The men responded to the rejection in their own way: Brian, seething with uncharacteristic anger, withdrew from the others and ate very little; Tomas, whose temper was never even, became surly and spent more time away from home. Mary knew he had given up looking for work. His days and evenings were spent at Dugan's pub, cadging drinks from the clientele for his amusing and fanciful stories. The good humor he showed in his cups had never been extended to the family. In the morning, before the pub opened, he was short with the children and, out of some guilt in him for his behavior, his words to Mary were scathing, deliberately painful. When he returned at night he fell, fully clothed, onto the pallet beside her, attempting in his drunkenness to paw her before he fell into a heavy sleep.

"At least it's one less mouth to feed," Doirin said one evening at the table. "He's living off the spirits he drinks, and not off our praties."

But out of family loyalty, or perversity to his wife, Brian defended Tomas as he had never done before. "The man's near beaten," he said. "Being turned away so much does something to a man: he loses his pride...and hope. Every day when I go out it's the same. Hundreds looking for work, any work, and only a few jobs to fill. Unless a man wants to leave his family to starve, to work on the railroad or go to sea, there's nothing."

"I want to go to sea!" Darin piped up with an enthusiastic, glowing face. "If I go to sea, I can send money home."

"Never a bit of it!" Doirin said firmly, but Brian ruffled the boy's hair, which was so much like his own.

"You're a bit young yet, lad. They don't sign anyone on who's below twelve. And," he said quickly, looking at Michael and Padraig, "you're needed here. For the time being, you're the men of the family, for it's you who bring in the food."

Doirin was not to be put off the subject of Tomas with talk of her son's activities. "What," she asked maliciously, "was your fine brother's excuse at home? If he's drinking because he's depressed, now, he was gay enough in his cups then!"

Brian put down his spoon, having eaten less than usual, and said quietly, "You shouldn't speak so in front of his wife and children. Tomas is good enough at heart."

"I've failed to notice it. And Mary's put up with a lot from him, more than any woman's share."

"She married him, didn't she?" Brian asked vehemently with flashing eyes; then he brought himself under control. "Mary has more strength than the lot of us put together. If my brother's given her trouble, it's myself who's to blame. And I apologize for him."

For a fleeting moment, Mary thought Brian knew why she had married Tomas: it was a strange enough statement. But she quickly dispelled the thought, thinking there was no way anyone could know about her love for Brian. She remained silent during the conversation. She had only disgust for Tomas, and realized that her feelings had never been otherwise. It had been a grave mistake to marry a man just because of his physical resemblance to his brother, her real love. Unfair to Tomas as much as to herself. In a poor family, the girls married to relieve the burden, and she had waited longer than most, until she was twenty. Then she reasoned that if she must marry, she would have someone as closely resembling Brian as possible, in appearance if not character. So as they said back home, she had made her bed, but she was having an increasingly difficult time lying in it.

Brian's proximity was such that she could hear his quiet breathing beyond the curtain that divided their beds, and though the torment she felt was not physical, it was in her soul. Her behavior was probably, in part, responsible for Tomas's recent drinking, and she felt guilt over it. With Brian so close, she could not let her husband touch her, even in his rare moments of sobriety.

"It isn't decent," Mary had told Tomas one night, when they had retired earlier than the others. "I can't. Wait till we have a place of our own."

From that night on, her husband's surliness had increased. If she could have left his bed openly, with a scene, she would have done so, but they were too crowded in the basement for such an action to go unnoticed. Always before, the children had held things together: they were her only joy. But child-bearing, too, had suddenly turned into a monstrous trap. For many months, during the hunger and the stress of trying to find food for the children, she had not had her periods: other women confessed to the same physical upheaval during the troubles. But now she knew for sure that she was pregnant from the last time Tomas took her in their cottage back home, when she was so miserable and hungry she did not care what was happening. The flutter in her lower abdomen and the swelling of her belly told her the awful truth: she was nearly five months gone. She did not dare tell the others. Doirin would complain about another mouth to feed, and Brian...

She could not face Brian. Almost irrationally, she could not admit before him that Tomas had used her body, even in the depths of their misery. To avoid despair, she went about her chores, trying to ignore her condition, carrying the heavy pail up and down the stairs, scrubbing vigorously. If something in her mind suggested a fall from the kitchen to the basement, or prodded her on to carrying heavier loads, she turned it off before it became a thought. Every day, as she and Rosaleen walked to Mr. Rabinsky's on the icy walk, her thoughts turned to such things: one wrong step and you would slide down the hill; instead of stepping over that high curbing, you could jump. All repressed until she was almost unaware of them.

And poor Mr. Rabinsky, with enough prejudice against him already, knew no more than Mary that the "American" he was learning was with an Irish brogue. Though the debt for the clothes had been paid off in lessons, he had retained her for ten cents a day to continue teaching him. Unable to admit how she came by the money, Mary slipped it into the family "purse," a jar on the windowsill, muttering that she had done some ironing, or some other odd job, without realizing how much it shamed Tomas to have his wife bring in money, when he was not even looking for a job any longer.

Rosaleen liked Mr. Rabinsky and the visits to the back of his shop, where all his cluttered treasures from the old country were kept. He always offered them strong tea in little Polish bronze cups, and sometimes there was a bit of raisin cake.

Because Mary had warned her to say nothing about the English lessons or Mr. Rabinsky, Rosaleen knew there was something wrong about their association with the thin, bearded little man, but she accepted Mary's lies about the money with equanimity, because it concerned her, too. She enjoyed the visits. But the duplicity unwittingly revealed itself one night at the supper table and brought about the first family fracture.

Everyone was at the table. Even Tomas, uncharacteristically, was home for the meal, red-eyed and disheveled. As Mary carried the pail of hot cooked potatoes down the stairs, with the water only half drained from them, his angry voice shouting at Rosaleen, assailed her ears.

"That's Jew talk! I know Jew talk when I hear it! Where did you hear that, you little bitch?"

Mary hurried down the stairs. Tomas was shaking Rosaleen by the arm, nearly dislocating it. Tears streamed down the child's screwed-up face.

"Take your hands off that child!" Mary commanded, rushing forward and setting the steaming pail on the edge of the improvised table.

"You keep out of this!" he bellowed. "She's my child, too, isn't she? And she's talking like a Jew. She said it was a long *valk* to *vork,* and that it was nice and *varm* there! Are you ironing clothes for Jews, then? Have you no decency at all? The people who killed our Holy Savior!"

"Sure, what have you to do with our Savior at all? Take your hands off that baby, at once!"

"Are you working for a Jew, woman?"

"Yes! And a nice man he is, too, with a better temper and nicer manners than some I know!" Mary cried, rushing at him to get Rosaleen. Tomas backed off and, in his fury, twisted the child's arm, nearly lifting her entirely off the floor.

Angry and frightened, young Darin rushed around the table at his uncle. In an attempt to protect his little cousin, he began hammering the grown man's arm with his fists. With Tomas temporarily distracted, Mary moved in quickly, but her hip struck the makeshift table as she grabbed Rosaleen into her arms. Veronica rose with a gasp and stood against the wall with Doirin and the other children, watching Brian grab his brother's lapels with murder in his eyes. And, buffeted on all sides, the plank that made up the table, weighted by the pail of hot potatoes, suddenly flew into the air, striking Rosaleen and making Mary slip into the scalding mass on the floor. She lay there, dazed, for only a moment before she felt the burns on her arms.

Brian helped her to her feet, brushing the hot mash off with his bare hands, and young Darin picked up Rosaleen. A trickle of blood ran from the child's cheek, but Mary's neck and arms were scalded bright red.

"God in Heaven," Veronica said, guiding Mary to a chair, "there's nothing hotter than praties."

"Look after Rosaleen," Brian told his sister and knelt down beside Mary's chair to inspect the extent of her burns. When he looked around for Doirin to help him, he found her cringing against the wall, holding her hands before her face for her own protection.

"Wet some cloths," he told her and, when she made no move, he shouted, "For Christ's sake, woman, wet some cloths! Your sister's in pain."

As he put the cool cloths on her burning neck, tears welled up in Mary's eyes. She was unable to bear both the pain and his proximity. "Oh, Brian, Brian," she sobbed, holding his hand against her cheek. "I don't know what I'd do without you, sure."

"It'll be fine, Mary. I've seen a few burns before. Yours are painful, but they aren't too bad. There, there, don't cry, darlin'. We need something to protect you from the air. Michael," he said, turning to address his oldest son, "take some money from the jar and see if Mrs. O'Toole will give you some butter."

He held her to him until her sobs died out on his breast. She knew that now that she had been in his arms, the real pain could never leave her. Then, in a flash that almost hurt, she remembered Rosaleen and struggled to her feet. Veronica

46

was attending the child, who sat on a chair, while Darin held her hand, anger still smoldering in his eyes.

"Is it bad?" Mary asked, forgetting her own pain.

"It only bled a little," Veronica said. "To be sure, it's an odd thing. There's a dent in her cheek and it's bruising badly. The corner of the table must have hit her."

As Mary gathered her daughter in her arms and sat down with her on her lap, Darin carefully removed his hand and backed off to stand beside his father.

They heard someone retching in the vicinity of the furnace, and Brian picked up the lamp to investigate. Liam's white face, with a stream of vomit at the edge of his lips, was illuminated in the darkness.

"Are you ill, son?" Brian asked.

But the boy just stared at him, glassy-eyed and pale. Brian put an arm about Liam's shoulders and led him back to the living area, where he still would not speak, but sat trembling, with his gaze on his mother and Rosaleen.

No one even noticed Tomas leave: he was forgotten.

Liam was an odd, sulky child—he had been that way since he was a mere baby—so Mary did not concern herself too much with his ups and downs, which were, after all, part of the Irish nature, something everyone lived with. She knew her son was intelligent; he caught on to his lessons with the priest very quickly. She also knew he was something of a dreamer, the only Noonan characteristic he seemed to possess. His hair, instead of being black, was a nondescript, straight brown, and his eyes were as dark as hers. She fancied the boy at various times as a scholar, a poet...or a trouble-maker, though he had never really exhibited the latter in his behavior. Though he was inordinately fond of his father, he would do anything to get Mary's attention, from kissing her hand to being the victim of innumerable small accidents, from wetting his pants, when he was smaller, to skinning his knees too often, now, at eight.

She found it difficult to believe that Liam and his cousin Darin were the same age: her boy was a baby compared to Brian's aggressive son. And though the two boys got along well enough, Darin preferred the company of his older brothers, who were as bold and handsome as he. Liam had been very attentive to his own little brother, Seamus, happy, perhaps, to have a brother of his own to play with, though Seamus was two years younger than he. She remembered now that Liam had vomited after Seamus's burial at sea. Since the fight in the basement, with its ensuing accidental injuries, it occurred to her that Liam's vomiting was a way of releasing too much tension, and she tried to give him more attention, without ignoring Rosaleen. One of the curses of extreme poverty, she thought, was that one frequently forgot the emotional needs of children in trying to provide the physical ones.

Mary stayed in for two days after her burns, because the cold winter wind made them hurt so much, even when covered with a thin layer of butter. Liam went out with the other boys, working for whatever pennies they could pick up, and Rosaleen amused herself quietly for hours with a doll made out of a discarded sock. Mary had stuffed the sock with rags and Darin had fashioned a face out of charcoal, with two button eyes. In the morning, Veronica sat outside, where she could breathe the clean air, while she was bundled up in coats, and her sweetness made her many friends in the cooking area in the back yard, though she herself cautioned the children away from her, speaking to them only at a distance of several feet.

Left alone with Doirin while she nursed her burns, Mary's full concentration for the first time fell on her sister's unusual behavior and cutting attacks. It was bad enough that Doirin slept most of the time; it was worse when she was awake. Mary tried to remember back to when Doirin was a girl, though her sister was six years her elder. She recalled that Doirin went to church a lot, and though very beautiful—more so than Mary—her expression had never been happy. Not even on her wedding day. That day cut Mary like knives, because it ended any chance she might have had with Brian, but she deliberately thought about it now.

It was proper that the oldest daughter should marry first: it had never been otherwise, an established custom. And when Brian's parents both died the same winter of the grippe, it was necessary that he take a wife to look after the house for himself and Tomas. Veronica was no more than a child at the time. The courtship, closely observed by Mary, who kept out of the way for fear of betraying her own emotions, was not a particularly romantic one. Brian called and sat by the fire with the family—Doirin and her parents, since Mary was always absent, hovering in the wings. The talk was of the crops, of improving the cottage. Brian said he would make it fit for a wife to live in by spring. The parents approved of the young man: Doirin was passive. They had no moments of walking out together alone, because that was not proper. And, when the time came, Doirin faced the altar in the village chapel just as calmly, betraying nothing on her beautiful face. Mary, who was sixteen, found it almost impossible to attend the wedding: only her mother's prodding had gotten her to the church, and she disappeared for a while during the party that followed, to sit on the green bank of the river, under her favorite hawthorn tree, sobbing great tears.

Mary realized that she had never understood her sister, though they had lived together so closely in her mother's cottage. Doirin was not lazy then: she was a fine housekeeper. And though she spoke seldom, it was never with malice or sharpness. They had not been close, perhaps because of the difference in their ages, but Mary had thought of Doirin as sweet and kind. What, she wondered, had happened to her?

One afternoon, when the snow was falling and Rosaleen playing in her corner, Mary drew aside the curtain by her sister's bed. Doirin was lying there, hair uncombed, staring at the sooty ceiling: she was not yet asleep.

"May I come in, Doirin?" Mary asked, holding a cool cloth to her oily burns. "I was thinking perhaps we could visit a little."

Her sister turned her head and stared up blankly. "If you please," she said shortly, patting the pallet of straw she lay on.

Accepting the invitation, Mary sat down quietly, waiting for her sister to speak further, but no words came from her tight lips.

"I was thinking," Mary said, "it's daft, but it helps me forget the pain. I was thinking about home in the old days, when we were at mother's cottage... and you so beautiful and..."

Doirin grunted. "Don't fool yourself. Things weren't so wonderful then."

"No? I thought they were. At least, most of the time I was happy."

Doirin repeated the word. "What does it mean? Happy? I've never understood it."

"To me, it means content with the world," Mary said in a low voice. "When I was a child, I was content. Ma and Pa loved us dearly, would do anything for us. Sure, there were some bad times, when the praties went bad... famine wasn't a stranger, was it? But, even then, there was the warm fire, and the people you loved about you."

Doirin rolled her eyes to look up at Mary; they were so expressionless that they seemed not even to have color. Her face was lined beyond her years, her lips permanently tight, from some internal pain. "I've never known a moment of happiness," she confessed. "Not then or later. I've always felt a little miserable. And, now," she fanned her hand limply to indicate their abode with a sigh, "I find the only way to escape it is to sleep."

"Surely you were happy on your wedding day," Mary ventured, feeling a peculiar, poignant pity for this woman who was sleeping her life away. "There must have been times—maybe when your children were born?"

Doirin shook her head slowly where she lay. "I've never known joy or even understood it," she almost whispered. "It's as though, somehow, I'm afflicted. I've thought about it a lot. From the earliest time I can remember, I was miserable, like an apple with a worm tormenting its middle. I've suffered enough from being awake. Sometimes I wish the good Lord would end it."

Mary listened to the words with alarm: she had never realized any of this. Was it possible for a person to be born unhappy? At least it seemed so to Doirin. "Sure, that's no way to talk," Mary said sympathetically. "You have a fine family that depends on you. What would they do if you were taken from their midst? Michael, Padraig, Darin and . . . Brian? That's no way to think at all."

"Everyone thinks her own way," Doirin replied with some of the snap back in her voice, as though she regretted what she had revealed. "Veronica, ill as she is, is happy! And you, with that husband of yours—are you happy, Mary?"

"Sometimes," Mary said. "Yes, sometimes, even married to Tomas, I've been happy. The children have been such a comfort. I've known misery, too. Misery even you couldn't believe, because you've never lost a child. But life goes on and I suppose we make our own contentment. Maybe by ignoring and forgetting the things that make us sad. Yes, I think that every day, I feel some happiness; if it's only in combing Rosaleen's hair or trying to make things easier for Veronica."

"Good for you," Doirin said with that blank stare again. "Now, if you'll leave me be."

She closed her eyes to the world and turned away on her side with a deep expiration. Mary watched her for a while before rising from the pallet and closing the curtain slowly. Her sister was living a death-in-life which Mary could not comprehend. Turning away, her gaze rested on Rosaleen playing with her doll, and she approached her with a smile.

"Rosaleen, would you like to sleep with me tonight?"

The wide blue eyes looked up at her, and the bruise was still dark on the little cheek.

"What about Pa?"

"If he comes back, he can use your pallet," Mary said, and the little girl began to fidget with her toy.

Finally, Rosaleen agreed unwillingly, "Well, just for tonight, if you want me to."

"You don't want to sleep with your Ma?" Mary asked, feeling slightly hurt.

"Oh, I want to sleep with you," Rosaleen said. "But not all the time. When I'm sleeping between Darin and Liam, I'm not afraid of the rats. I really like to sleep with them."

"Most of the rats are gone," Mary comforted her. "And there are traps around for the others. Please don't be afraid. I would like you to sleep with me all the time."

A troubled expression crossed Rosaleen's face. "Do I have to? I love you, Ma, you know that. But I'd rather be with Darin."

The child's attachment to her cousin had not been overlooked by Mary; but since they were so young, it did not trouble her. She was glad that Rosaleen had such a champion, since her own brother did not seem to care about her. On the other hand, perhaps it was time to put some space between the two children. Darin was going on nine. Better that the rupture came now, instead of in a couple of years, when it would call undue attention to his puberty.

"Darlin', Mother wants you to sleep with her, now. You see enough of Darin during the day."

Rosaleen nodded her head, but Mary saw that her lower lip was trembling.

Chapter 4

ONCE a week, Doirin washed her face and combed her hair to go to Mass with Mary, Veronica and the children. Though she was extremely critical of the "worldly" priest and felt lost in a church so much larger than the stone chapel to which she was accustomed, on Sunday morning, Doirin shook out her shawl to cover her head and urged the others to hurry.

On the Sunday after the accident, Doirin and Veronica were shawled and had their coats on before they noticed that Mary was not coming with them. Mary's burns were still too sensitive to face the harsh winter wind, and she still felt weak in the knees from the shock of it, but Doirin did not want to go without her.

"Sure, your arms will be covered by your coat," she argued, "and you can put a cloth around your neck. How do you expect us to find our way? Mary, if anyone should be going to church, it's you! You haven't seen hide nor hair of your husband for these two days. You should be praying—"

"I won't find Tomas in church," Mary said with equanimity. "He'll come back when he's ready or not at all. Right now, it matters very little to me one way or the other. And I think Veronica can get you there and back. I'm not the only person with a sense of direction."

Doirin, who had drawn in her breath as Mary spoke, let it out through her teeth with a hiss. "A fine way to talk in

52

front of your children! What if he doesn't come back? You'll all be dependent on us, then—on what my boys can bring in."

Brian, who, like many young Irish men, did not go to church, intervened on Mary's behalf.

"There's no question of dependence here. We're one family, and God knows Mary's done plenty for us. Go on to Mass, Doirin, and pray for a little human charity. Here's a penny for you and one for Veronica, for the collection. It seems that all they do in church here is collect. Now, off with you. Mary needs a little time to recuperate. She'll be with you next week."

Doirin and her sons climbed the dark stairs with Veronica, who held Rosaleen's hand and looked back to smile at them. That girl, Mary thought, is goodness itself... and her health seemed much better, too. Veronica had regained some of her playfulness, and Rosaleen was very fond of her.

Mary sat down carefully at the infamous table, in place again and secured with a few nails, and folded her hands before her, feeling slightly awkward: it was the first time she had been completely alone with Brian since she had watched him from the wall as a girl. When the door finally closed above them, he pulled up a chair to join her, with an apologetic expression on his face.

"I didn't mention the money you've brought in from ironing. It would have thrown her into a worse fit," he said. "You have to understand Doirin—"

"Do *you?*" she asked seriously. "I confess that sometimes I'm ashamed to be her sister." There was a silent pause: there was nothing Brian could say without speaking ill of his wife. "I haven't been ironing," Mary said. "I'm giving English lessons to a very nice Jewish man from Poland."

He raised his dark eyebrows, his blue eyes twinkling. "Good. Oh, that makes me feel much better! The thought of you doing heavy work right now nearly drove me wild. If only I could get a job—any job!" He shook his head. "I've worked hard all my life, and I didn't dream there wouldn't be work for willing hands here."

"At least you keep trying...out every day in the snow from morning till night. You know, Brian, that those pennies for church could have found better use."

"I know. But without something for the collection, Doirin wouldn't go out at all. And"—he grinned—"they don't have farthings here. A penny's as low as we can go." He sobered as quickly as he had smiled. "We're about as low as we can go, Mary."

"We aren't living in hedges like some, and we've something to cover our nakedness. And one good meal a day," she reminded him. "We did right to come here. We'd be dead by now if we hadn't. Whatever you had to do to get our money from the landlord, it was worth it."

He looked at her with narrowed eyes. "Why do you say that? What do you think I did, Mary?"

She shrugged, but her heart had begun to beat hard, and what she was about to say was a lie. "I think you used your charm, pulled out the stopper on it." She smiled. "Whatever. You saved our lives, remember that. There's nothing you could do that wouldn't have my full approval, Brian. Even I did things that..."

She was alarmed at the length of his mild, penetrating blue gaze into her eyes, and at something she had never had with anyone else, the complete understanding of one person for another communicated in a look. After a few seconds, she broke the gaze, looking away quickly: the moment had been highly dangerous for her.

"It's a crazy life, for certain." He sighed. When she did not reply, he added, "If you think you have to apologize for your sister, what in God's name am I to do about my brother? Tomas was always a rowdy bastard and not good enough for you. You don't know how upset I was when you married him." He added quickly, "I knew the kind of life he'd give you. Mary, why did you choose him?"

She averted her eyes, struck almost silent by the irony of the question. "I was twenty years old," she said. "You know how it was. I couldn't be a burden on my family."

"Yes, but why *him?* Everyone knew him for a rascal."

"Ah, Brian, you don't know how women think they can change a man. He was the best-looking man around, and he had a certain charm in those days." She looked directly at him. "You were such a good man, I thought he could be the same."

He exhaled through his teeth. "I've been looking for him," he confessed. "If I find him, I may throttle him before I bring him back. What he's doing to you..." He leaned forward and put his hand over hers. "If he doesn't return, don't you ever worry about being dependent. Whatever we have is yours, and I hope we soon have more to offer. Doirin talks mad sometimes. I'll never forget that you kept my family from starving when Tomas and I were working in Cobh. I don't know how you managed that last time, when they detained us there. We thought we'd come home and find the whole lot of you dead. You're the strongest woman alive."

She swallowed hard, remembering. "It was my family, too."

"He'll come back before the baby comes. He has to. Not even Tomas could be that much of a—"

Her heart nearly stopped beating. Brian, the last person she wanted to know about the baby, somehow knew, and accepted it as something normal, not despicable.

"I didn't want anyone to know—not even Tomas," she said. "We don't need another mouth to feed."

"We'll manage," he said, squeezing her hand to give her confidence. "Together, we'll manage, Mary, dear. I know I behaved badly when we first arrived: I had something on my mind. But all that's behind me, now, and I'm better still for talking to you today." He cocked his head and gave her his sweetest smile. "The baby really gives me something to fight for! I couldn't understand why you were so quiet about it. You were always that delighted before. 'Another mouth to feed' is it? That's Doirin's language, not yours."

Hot tears stung her eyes, and she tried to brush them away with her free hand. "How did you know? Even she hasn't noticed."

"I notice everything about you, Mary. I always have. I remember you sitting on a stone fence by the path when you were just a girl...." His hand over hers lost its grip, went almost limp, and his lips drew tightly together. He did not finish the recollection, but his eyes met hers, penetrating and sad. "Life's so queer. Circumstances, tradition, expediency. It gets all mixed up, and we do things we wouldn't otherwise have done. Well"—he smiled suddenly—"we're a family, now, and that's what's important."

Her hand tingled when she put it over his with trembling fingers. "Thank God for—"

A scraping sound at the bottom of the stairs made them both look in that direction, disentangling their hands quickly. Liam stood there, pinched and pale, his dark eyes boring out of the semidarkness with an expression of open hatred. Though shaken by the interpretation he might put on what he had seen, Mary tried to behave as normally as possible.

Without rising from the table, she smiled and said, "Liam, why aren't you at church?"

He turned his face away and walked across the floor to the jar on the windowsill, dropping a few pennies into it with force. "Man needed some help with newspapers," he said tightly.

Then, without looking toward the table again, he ran up the stairs.

Brian rose to follow him, but Mary stopped him by putting her hand on his arm.

"I can explain to him," he said, but she shook her head.

"There's nothing to explain. Liam's an odd one, Brian. He'll believe what he wants to anyway, and he'll keep it to himself."

When he finally got work on the docks, Brian kept his word about new clothes for the women. As soon as he had paid the back rent and taken care of their necessities, he gave Mary three dollars for cloth. Knowing with what difficulty it had been earned, at first Mary refused it. Brian's callused hands, which had not worked for so long, were raw with blisters from loading and unloading ships in the cold for ten hours a day. But he pressed the money into her hand.

"Sure, it'll be good for all of you," he said. "Especially Doirin. It's hard to keep your spirit up when you're dressed in rags."

There was almost a guilt on him for Doirin's misery, Mary reflected. Though she felt sure he was not the cause of it, she did as he requested. One morning, she sat Doirin and Veronica at the table to consult with them about the fabric.

"Sure, cloth's dear enough here," she told them. "It'll be cheaper if we all choose the same. What color would you like, Doirin? Veronica?"

Doirin shrugged disinterestedly, but Veronica laughed and said, "Red?"

"Be serious, girl." Mary smiled, noting the hectic flush on her cheeks. "I can see you going to church in a red dress! I haven't seen any good plaid stuff around, but there's—"

"Why not black?" Doirin said flatly, with her hands hanging loosely in her lap.

Mary scrutinized her sister's face. "Black's for mourning, my dear," she said kindly. "We aren't in mourning at all."

"No?" Doirin asked. "It appears to me that someone's missing around here."

"Tomas isn't dead, I'm sure," Mary replied patiently. "I've not given that a single thought."

"He's been gone for five weeks. If he isn't dead, where is he?"

Veronica's gaiety over the new clothes left her, and tears hung just behind her eyelids. No one had thought Tomas dead, and Mary was angry with her sister for suggesting it, throwing a pall on their few light moments. She decided, however, for Brian's sake, to be patient with her sister.

"Let's stop all this nonsense of red and black." She smiled. "I saw some nice fawn-colored wool in one of the shops, and the gray gabardine I told you about in another. Our choice is rather limited by price, as it's always been. So, which is it, fawn or gray?"

"The gray would be nice," Veronica said, recovering herself because of Mary's practicality. "Don't you think that would be nice, Doirin?"

If Doirin had any fondness for anyone, it was for Veronica, so she said, "It doesn't matter."

"Would you like to come with me to get it?" Mary suggested, still trying to get Doirin out of the house in the afternoon, but her sister shook her head. Seeing the longing in Veronica's eyes, Mary smiled.

"I think you can come, dear," Mary said. "You've been outside for months, and the doctor didn't say anything about that. Do you feel strong enough?"

"Is it far?" Veronica asked, betraying for the first time that her strength was not what it once was.

"Not far. You and Rosaleen and I will go this afternoon. Are you sure you don't want to come, Doirin?"

"I'm sure. And I don't think Veronica should go, either. The girl's sick, you know that. It's daft to take her out in the cold."

Mary looked at her in disbelief. "But Doirin, it isn't that cold out at all. It hasn't been for the past three days. Look at the window: the sun's shining and all the snow's melted off the walks."

"I hadn't noticed."

"Sure, how can you notice anything if you only leave the house on Sunday for Mass? You're holed up in here like a rat! Please, just pull your shoes on like a good girl and come with us!"

But Doirin would not change her habits. All she had seen of Boston for over two months was on the walk from the ship to this house, and five blocks to church. It was almost as if she were building some kind of wall between herself and the world, Mary thought. She remembered old Mrs. Coughlan in the village, who kept completely to herself for six months and, at the end of that time, was taken away to the asylum in Cobh, completely out of touch with reality. But Mary felt sure that could not happen to her sister. Doirin was an intelligent woman who was just being slothful; for what reason, Mary could not understand. Even after their conversation about Doirin's feelings of misery, it was so far removed from Mary's own outlook that she could not comprehend it.

And, today, she was feeling really happy. She and Veronica and Rosaleen were going shopping! Liam no longer came with them, had not for some time. He lived in the basement like a little shadow, communicating with no one, unless directly spoken to; but that was not so unlike him, anyway, so Mary did not dwell on it. For her own peace of mind, she dismissed all their troubles from her mind for just one day.

Mary had wandered far enough to see the grand stores downtown, but she knew their limitations and they went to a fabric shop only a few blocks beyond Mr. Rabinsky's store. If the proprietor looked somewhat askance at their entry, he was soon drawn into their cheerful enthusiasm and completely charmed by Veronica's beauty, her color high and her eyes very blue in the velvet coat. Though they had just enough money to cover the purchase of the fabric they needed, he found himself throwing in the extra yard on the bolt "to make something for the little girl." Thanking him liltingly, they gathered together outside in conference.

"Thank God you were with us," Mary told Veronica. "If you hadn't been so pretty, Rosaleen wouldn't have such a fine dress. I was going to skimp on mine to make her one, but look what we have!" She hoisted the brown parcel in her arms.

Veronica, unaccustomed to the reactions of men, blushed scarlet. "Oh, Mary, I'm sure it had nothing to do with me," she said modestly. "And we've spent all our money. What on earth will we do for thread?"

"You'll see," Mary said archly. "I have credit with a good friend."

"We're going to see Mr. Rabinsky!" Rosaleen chirped, jumping up and down on the cobbled walk. "Oh, Veronica, he's such a nice man! And he'll give us tea and cakes."

Bewildered, Veronica stared at them. "Is that the... the... man you iron for?"

"Yes, only—"

"But he's... isn't he a Jew?" Veronica asked, torn between her own feelings of humanity and what she had been taught.

"He's Jewish," Mary said, "and there's nothing wrong with that. Sure we all believe in the same God. The only difference is that they're still waiting for the Savior."

"They don't know He's come?"

Mary smiled and shook her head. "They must not have been around when it happened," she said impishly, to which Veronica replied with a serious face, "Poor things."

They entered the dingy secondhand store, with its assortment of old clothes on tables and in bins, and various other household objects stacked against the walls: chipped china, pots and pans, old newspapers, books. A tiny bell on the door rang as they came in and Mr. Rabinsky appeared from the back of the shop, pulling on his dark jacket, and wearing the little black silk cap that always decorated his head. A smile broke over his small, pointed beard.

"Mrs. Noonan! Rosie! Come here to me, my little Rose of Sharon!"

Rosaleen rushed forward to be hoisted into the air, laughing, and Veronica hung back, near the door, until Mary introduced her.

With a bow, Mr. Rabinsky took her hand. "Such beauty... such beauty," he said wonderingly, sincerely, making Veronica draw away flustered. "And what can I do for you today, Mrs. Noonan? You haven't come with company for a lesson, eh?"

"No, for needles and thread and scissors," Mary said. "Which, if it's agreeable to you, we'll buy for lessons."

He flapped his arms like a blackbird. "Of course... of course! Sure, I can never thank you enough for what you've taught me, my dear," he said. "But, before the needles, may I please be offering you some tea?"

"That would be very nice," Mary said with dignity, beginning to follow him to the back room, but Veronica grabbed her coat.

"Is it all right?" she whispered. "He's so *different*, Mary. Are you sure it's safe?"

"For me, yes." Mary smiled. "For you, I'm not so sure. He may not be as old as I thought he was."

Hardly reassured, Veronica took Rosaleen's hand and followed like a child. When they went through the curtains dividing the man's living quarters from the shop, Veronica could not believe what she saw. To a young Irish country girl, it was all the luxury of the Orient: a faded Persian rug on the floor, shining tables, a cabinet full of china and bronze cups, and a large copper machine with a spigot such as she had never seen in her life. More curtains apparently separated this room from the sleeping area. Pushing chairs forward by one of the low tables, he encouraged them to sit down. Mary, who knew his tea ritual by heart, watched Veronica's amazed young face as he took the brass cups from the cabinet.

"And, little Rosie, would you like to draw the tea again today?" he asked. "This one," he said, shaking his head with one hand on Rosaleen's head. "Sure, she is my little ...uh...*servant?*" he asked Mary.

"Helper would be better, I think," she said. "A servant is someone who works for you. Rosaleen's only *helping* or *assisting*."

"Good. Two new words!" he said, passing around the cups Rosaleen had filled from the samovar. "And there is cake, too. Does my little helper want to cut the cake today?"

Holding her tongue between her teeth, Rosaleen carefully sliced off four slices from the pound cake. She put the pieces, one by one, on china dishes, trying to keep each piece intact. When she served them, she kept the one that had crumbled for herself, and settled demurely on a low stool to eat it.

"Vell," he said, and checked himself at once. *"Well,* here we are." He cleared his throat and smiled shyly at Veronica. "Your relative has told me about you, Miss Noonan. Are you feeling fine today?"

Veronica nodded and averted her eyes, sipping from the red-hot brass cup and taking it swiftly away from her lips. Mr. Rabinsky, she noted, drank it that hot, but Mary and Rosaleen, who had probably learned their lesson the way she just did, let the cups rest on the table awhile.

There was an awkward moment. Veronica felt she should say something, but the only thing that came to mind was the information Mary had given her about Jews still waiting for the Savior: she thought, perhaps, she should not bring that up. She wanted to ask him about his funny little hat, but thought that, too, might be impolite.

"Have you been in Boston long?" she finally brought out.

"Four, almost five years," he said. "There was bad trouble in my village, which is not unusual, you see. The Russians do not like Jews, and my country has been Russian for a long time. So many people hurt...cast out of town. I decided to leave there when my wife died."

Veronica was embarrassed to have blundered into memories that could only be painful for him. She felt she had to say something, though. "Why don't the Russians like the Jews?"

He shrugged, almost comically. "Why don't the English like the Irish?"

"They want our land. They...no, you're right, they don't like us. If they did, they'd have done more for us during the famine."

"Right now, during the famine," he said, "what they are doing is committing genocide. They want all of you dead. For years, in Central Europe, in Spain, in Russia, they have wanted us dead."

Veronica puzzled unhappily over this thought, found her tea was cool enough to sip and lapsed into silence.

"My dear young woman," he said and smiled, "I don't mean to make you sad. What I was trying to point out is that our religions have been blamed...just like here. Roman Catholics and Jews, sure they should stick together. Be friends." He raised his tiny brass cup, as though in a toast. "To my friends!"

"He's very nice," Veronica told Mary later. "He even talks like us. Should we mention our visit to Brian and Doirin? After that awful scene with Tomas..."

"No need to mention anything. Though I know Brian wouldn't object, I'm not sure about Doirin. It's strange, isn't it? What we don't understand, we distrust."

"But, at church, they taught us that the Jews—"

"You should listen more carefully there, Veronica. The Gospels say quite clearly that the Romans killed our Savior. Christ was a Jew, you know."

"I hadn't thought of that."

"You should do some thinking, then. No one should condemn other people because they're different. Not too long ago, Rosaleen and I went through a black district at the north end of Beacon Hill. We were terrified. But now I feel guilty about it. We'd just never seen anyone with black skin before. It's a fear I want to get over, but I haven't had the nerve to go back, because there were lots of saloons there and it seemed rather wild."

"Well, here we are," Veronica said, pausing in front of

their house. "Mary, I want to thank you. Not just for letting me come, but for taking me to see Mr. Rabinsky. I like him very much."

They had to wake Doirin to show her the fabric. But once they did, it lit some kind of spark in her. A good seamstress, she liked the feeling of the cloth beneath her hands. And when she saw the scissors, needles and thread, she went right to work without saying a word. Before supper, Doirin had all three skirts and blouses marked out, and a miniature of the others for Rosaleen. They had to persuade her to remove the project from the table so the potatoes could be served.

As Mary served the supper, the seed of an idea began to germinate in her mind. Doirin seemed to be all right when her hands were doing something she liked and did well. Maybe if they saved a little money every week, she could keep Doirin busy and out of bed.

The pattern was in their minds, and it was simple: a long skirt gathered at the waist, a blouse gathered at the wrists, both without bands, and only a simple neckline that tied in front. It had been the same for centuries, varying only according to county and color. Mary cut out the material next morning, deliberately leaving the sewing to Doirin, and to Veronica, whom her sister was instructing. Mary had set their chairs beneath the window for light, and when she finished her chores, she sat beside them to watch them sew. Doirin had always sewn a neater stitch than Mary, who was fascinated now to watch the needle skim through the material with ten small stitches to each pull, all equally even and neat. The blouses, which were the more complicated, were finished first; Doirin was still up, and it was past two in the afternoon. Mary felt happy.

"Sure, you sew like a machine—better," she complimented Doirin. "I've never seen anything like it. I wish I could do as well."

"You haven't the patience," her sister said, though she glowed slightly from the praise. "Ma tried to teach you. I tried to teach you. You were always wandering off somewhere, flitting about like a dragonfly. Veronica's far better than you'll ever be."

"Do you think it's too late, then?"

Doirin studied her for a moment, raising her eyes from her work. "Maybe not. You've calmed down some. Give us the length of that skirt, and let's see how it fits you."

Mary was prepared for this moment: it had to come some-time. But she found herself taking deep breaths out of nervousness when she walked from the table to the window.

"As a matter of fact," she said casually, "the skirt will have to be large at the waist for a while, just until the baby comes. After that, we can take it in again."

She did not look at Doirin but down at the cloth she held around her, pinching it in here and there to get a fit. There was silence from the two women who were sewing; then Veronica stood up and threw her arms around Mary.

"A baby! Mary, how wonderful! Why didn't you tell us? Doirin, a baby! When is it coming?"

"In about three months' time, I think," Mary answered, still listening for Doirin's reaction. She could no longer hear the movement of her hands on the cloth. Rosaleen, playing in the corner with her doll in the new skirt Mary had made for it, was so lost in her imagination she was not listening to them.

"Veronica," Doirin's weary voice said, "put on your coat and take the child outside with your friends."

"But, Doirin..."

"You heard what I said." The voice was more peevish. "Take Rosaleen outside with you."

With some intimation of Doirin's reaction, Mary nodded for the girl to go. Only when they were alone did she turn to look at her sister: she was shocked at the pale fury in her face.

"How could you let this happen?" Doirin demanded. "It's disgusting! And it's a terrible burden, too. Isn't it enough that we're taking care of you and your children? Do you have to bring another one into the world in times like these? What are you thinking of, Mary?"

"I'm thinking I'm pregnant by no will of my own," Mary replied. "I'm thinking when that happens there's nothing to do but bring the child into the world."

Her sister's bony hands twisted the cloth in her lap. She had already, Mary noticed, neatly stuck the needle in the shoulder of the blouse she was wearing, before Mary had turned to look at her, as though she needed her hands free for battle. Mary met Doirin's angry eyes calmly. Now that everything was known to Brian, it did not matter what her sister said.

"You ignorant creature!" Doirin declared. "Why didn't you tell me sooner? There are ways. How do you think I kept my

63

family down to three? All boys, too, thank God! I thought you knew more about the world, after the two miscarriages you had."

For once, Mary was absolutely amazed; her sister was right, she was ignorant indeed. She did not know what Doirin was talking about.

"Six . . . six and a half months," Doirin calculated. "Maybe it isn't too late."

Doirin rose, letting the new material fall on the floor, and hunted among the chairs. When she found the one she wanted, she steadied it and patted the wooden seat, indicating that Mary should come over. But Mary stayed where she was, watching Doirin's frantic movements.

"Too late for what?" Mary finally asked.

"To get rid of it, you fool! Stand on this chair and *jump*, just as hard as you can. Then do it again and again, until you break the waters. A six-month baby won't survive."

If her sister had threatened her with a gun, Mary would not have been more horrified: she could not believe what she heard. People did not do such things deliberately. She knew sometimes pregnant women fell, but accidentally . . . accidentally. Suddenly, she recognized the thoughts that had played at the edge of her mind a few months ago, when she had first realized her condition. Her stomach tightened, and the next moment she thought she would be sick. And, all the while, her sister stood there implacably, patting the seat of the chair.

"I swear to God, you've gone idiot," Doirin said. "You have no husband to support you! It's all on us. So, for God's sake, do as I tell you!"

Mary backed away slightly, clammy all over. "You . . . you've," she managed to articulate, "*done* this thing?"

"Not like this," Doirin replied. "Mrs. Desmond took care of us—sometimes with a drink of wheat rust and oil—sometimes other ways. You mean you didn't know?"

Mary shook her head slightly and stared with an open mouth. "Mrs. Desmond, the midwife? She did things like that?"

"And many's the client she had, too," Doirin snapped. "Now, I'm not sure this will work, but it's worth a try. Molly Blake did it, but she wasn't this far along."

"Doirin, you're after talking daft! I don't believe any of this."

"If you're so innocent, how did you lose your brats?"

The words hit Mary like a slap in the face. She could hardly answer. "It just happened. I didn't even fall, you know that. They both happened during the night." She held her hand up to silence Doirin. "No, don't say anything more! It's against nature, against God and the Church! You've said too much already."

"It's easy enough for the Church to make rules—a lot of celibate priests!" Doirin said, working herself up. "It's easy enough for men! They don't have to bear a child every year! Oh, God...oh, God!" she wailed, tears beginning to stream down her cheeks. "I hate women! I hate birthing and everything that goes with it! It's nasty, sickening, painful." Her expression shifted, her voice became more inviting. "I'm giving you a way out, don't you see? I've done it. Lots of women do it. If you can't keep men away from you with their filthy ways, it's the only chance we have. Why do you think I haven't had a child for eight years?"

"I've never thought of it," Mary said, though she had wondered about it. Speculated on whether Doirin let Brian make love. She knew they had not done so since they came here; her pallet was so close to their curtain, she would have heard. She thought perhaps they were just being decent, because they were so crowded. She really felt ill now, and her knees were shaking.

"I've been pregnant five times since Darin," the unrelenting voice confessed. "And each time I made a trip to Mrs. Desmond. The men don't even know," she said, shaking her head. "Men are so stupid about women! They don't know anything. And you've already miscarried twice, so this will just look like..."

Mary felt dizzy, detached. This woman had killed Brian's children...*Brian's!* Without realizing what she was doing, she turned and ran up the steps, out of the house, and down the street, still holding her hands to her head, forgetting she was not wearing a coat. Only after she ran up the steps of St. Mary's and fell on her knees in a pew in the cold, waxy-smelling dimness did she stop to think and to get her breath.

She did not want to hate her sister, who was obviously disturbed. No wonder she was depressed, with all those little lives on her soul. But hadn't she, Mary, had the same sort of thoughts, just a little, only a few months ago? True, she had not really considered doing anything, but, in her desperation, the thoughts had been there. Sobs began to shake her body, and she could not control them. She cried until she had no more tears left to shed: it felt good. It had been such a long time since she had cried, and not one tear after Seamus's death. Unsteadily, she rose and walked down the aisle to the statue of the Virgin, glowing from candles. Mary knelt, put her hands together and looked up into the untroubled Virgin's face and the infant crooked in the blue-clad arm.

"Hail Mary, full of grace..." she began, but it was too formal, not enough. "Oh, dear Mary," she cried in her heart, "help me to love and to go on loving. Please help me to get my family out of there! I can't live with her much longer! I know what I feel for Brian is a sin, but please forgive me. It's the only love I've ever known for a man. Dear, dear Mary, if you'll only help me through this, I promise you I'll...I'll give him..." Oh, God, she could not abandon him to such unhappiness, now that she knew everything. "Oh, dear Lady," she revised her promise, "I'll look after him always in purity. He's my sister's husband, and you must know that my sister's mad."

Chapter 5

THE INJURY to Rosaleen's cheek healed quickly; once the bruise was gone, it was forgotten, until Darin noticed something one night by lamplight. Brian had said something that made the little girl laugh, and her cousin put down his spoon, staring at her with fascination.

"Rosie didn't have that before," he said in a wondering voice. "Look, Aunt Mary, hitting the table gave her a dimple! There's a hole in her cheek."

Mary turned the child's face to the light, and Brian pushed the lamp closer: it was true. Just under her cheekbone, an indentation in the skin had appeared, which made a dimple when she smiled or laughed. Pulling her skin taut, Brian lightly rubbed his finger on it.

"Poor little thing," he said with laughing eyes. "That's the hardest way to get a dimple I ever heard of. But, it's there, sure enough. When the corner of the table hit her, it must have separated whatever's underneath." Brian kissed her quickly on the spot and smiled at Mary. "God help the boys when she grows up! She'll not only be a beauty, but one with a dimple. I've lost my heart already."

"All the Noonans are beautiful," Mary said and smiled. "You mustn't turn her head. I don't want her to grow up too taken with herself. I'd be happy if she were like Veronica."

Blushing, Veronica also looked at her niece and seemed content with what she found. "There's no harm in telling a girl she's pretty," she said softly. "It's the only way she really knows."

"For all the good it does her," Doirin put in, still eating.

Since that awful day two weeks before, Mary and Doirin had hardly spoken. She wanted to be forgiving, to feel something for her sister, but her tongue locked in her mouth when she attempted any pleasantry. Eventually, she knew they would have to start speaking again; for the time being, it was easier not to. She had said nothing to Brian about their confrontation: she could never tell him the things Doirin had said. And Doirin, conscious of having gone too far and of telling too much, let the matter of the baby drop after discussing it with Brian. Knowing that she brought in enough money for her own family's food gave Mary self-confidence, which somehow spread to the children and Veronica. And when it was carefully pointed out by Brian at the table one evening, all the children seemed to hold her in greater respect. Mary was not only a nurturer, she was a provider: Doirin's boys admired her, because she was so unlike their mother, without even realizing about her pregnancy, which was carefully concealed by her shawl.

"I'm afraid," Veronica said shyly, "that being more attractive isn't going to help her with that bunch outside. I haven't said anything, Mary, but those children—poor little things—are almost savage. Even when she's wearing her patched old clothes, they push her around. They've grown vicious from want, like some of the people back home...." But she let her voice trail off: almost silently they had agreed not to talk about the bad times. "Rosie's very brave and she keeps to herself. But only this morning, that Murphy girl threw her doll in the mud. And when Rosie went to get it, the girl tried to push her down, too."

"That isn't nice," Mary said, hugging Rosaleen, with a frown between her eyes. "Why do they pick on her?"

"Because she's different," Veronica said. "She's pretty. And she's loved. They see her go off with you every afternoon."

"All the more reason for taking her, then."

"Yes, but she should be able to play," Veronica said. "How will she learn to get along with people when she goes to school?"

Doirin raised her head. "What school?"

"Right now, there's only the public one," Veronica said. "Doirin, all the children should be sent to school."

"That isn't what the priest said," Doirin said flatly. "We're to wait until there's a Catholic school for them to attend. The Protestants will take their religion away from them."

"Not if we teach them at home," Veronica continued, growing timorous. "I mean, we could tell them stories just like at church, and there's always Mass on Sunday."

"There's Mass every morning of the week," Doirin said. "I just found out about it. I think we should take them to Mass every day and forget about school." ˙

The boys groaned, not at the loss of school, but at having to attend Mass so often; all but Liam, whose dark eyes looked interested.

"I'll go with you, Aunt Doirin," he volunteered quietly, and she nodded curtly.

"Ma, we have to earn some money," Michael said quickly. "First thing in the morning's when people want things delivered. Paddy and Darin and me should work." Three heads bobbed together in agreement.

"Sure, I have a regular job, almost—with the papers, Ma," Darin said. "And I'm working on something with the milkman, too. I'll go to church on Sunday, if I have to, but every morning's impossible."

Mary thought Doirin was going to fly into a fit and slap the boy: it happened too often. But, for once, her sister's practicality took over and she allowed her boys the freedom of the week mornings. Not, however, without looking at Brian reproachfully.

"It seems to me you could find some work that would keep us all," Doirin said. "With the rent two dollars a week, we've only a little left over."

"You should be glad he got a job at all," Mary muttered, in spite of herself. "Once we really get established, we won't have to worry so much."

"Do you know," Veronica said, "most of the men in this house have no work at all. The women tell me they're even behind in their rent. They get some odd jobs, sometimes, like the boys, but they haven't been as fortunate as we have. Both Brian and Mary working, and the boys bringing in what they can. Some of the people here still don't have enough to eat."

Doirin narrowed her eyes. "The bag of potatoes has been going down pretty fast. You haven't...?"

The girl averted her eyes, her face burning red.

"You have!" Doirin cried triumphantly. "Don't you know—"

"That will be enough," Brian cut across her voice with his

deep, soft baritone. He put out his hand to Veronica, with a smile at the edge of his lips. "None of us have suffered yet for anything Veronica might have done. Come on, darlin', look at me," he coaxed, and his sister's blue eyes met his innocently. "You'll use your head, won't you?" he asked her. "Once in a while, when it's really needed badly, but remember how many we are."

Veronica nodded with relief. "I've only done it twice," she confessed. "And it was really needed, Brian, it was! You know what the Gospel says about casting your bread upon the water."

He laughed aloud and squeezed her hand, but Doirin sniffed and said, "Nothing's ever found its way back to me. She should be thrashed."

He looked at her as though he had heard incorrectly. "Thrashed? Doirin, Veronica's a young woman! See here, now, I don't want to find you sitting on the potato sack, either. Veronica has good common sense." He shook his head wearily. "Women. It's my opinion that there's nothing wrong with a little charity."

"No one's ever given it to me," Doirin said with self-pity. "We were starving to death, and no one—"

"You have a short memory," he said patiently. "Don't you remember the broth and squirrel meat, just before Tomas and I got home? Mary didn't have to share it, but—"

Mary's face went white. "Don't," she said in a stifled voice, "please, don't. That's all in the past. We've agreed." She rose unsteadily from the table, clutching at her throat, and wavered slightly when she tried to pick up a dish. Brian was on his feet at once.

"Mary! You don't look at all well. What is it?"

She shook her head. Gaining control of herself, she began to stack the dishes without saying another word. Uncharacteristically, Darin rose to help her. They put the dishes in a bucket to take upstairs to wash, and he insisted on carrying the bucket for her.

A cloud-swept moon illuminated the littered back yard. They tried to avoid the mud, walking on pieces of boxes to the old black stove, which was still hot. The snow was almost gone, but the air was cold. Darin helped her lift their bucket off the stove to the ground, and they faced each other, bent over, each holding onto the handle. His eyes lit with merriment.

"Aunt Mary," he said, "that broth and meat you fed us

wasn't squirrel, was it? I saw your face just now. Of course it wasn't. I was so far gone, I didn't think about it until now. Everything was all kind of dreamy. There wasn't a squirrel or a rabbit for miles around, not even a bird. They had all been eaten. You can tell me, I don't care. It saved my life, for Christ's sake."

"Mind your language, Darin."

He twisted his face so he could look into hers, which was still averted. "Aunt Mary, what the hell did you cook up? We aren't cannibals or anything?"

Her lips trembled between weeping and smiling. He was such a little rascal, and the spitting image of his father. Too sharp for his own good.

"Aunt Mary, darlin'?"

"Get on with you!" she said, striking out at his backside. "Every woman has her secrets."

He jumped away, still smiling, quizzically, and paused on the top step with his hand on the kitchen door.

"We aren't cannibals," she said as he ran into the house.

She washed a dish in the hot bucket and put it on the steps; then her hands stopped moving. Pushing the hair back from her face, she sat down and let the tears flow.

Was there no forgetting all that?

She would have to talk to Darin, tell him the truth, before he had all the children speculating and they upset Rosaleen, who was every bit as bright as he was, and old enough to put things together in her mind. Her little girl must never know what she had done.

Rosaleen burrowed into her like a kitten at night, hiding her face in Mary's armpit, where her mother could feel her soft breathing. Mary found it difficult to change her position. If she gently put the child to one side, removing her arm from under her head, the little girl followed her in her sleep and protected her face against her mother's back. Mary had often found her that way when she slept with her brother and Darin, with her face always hidden beneath the coats they used as covers, usually pressed against her cousin's chest.

Rosaleen was an affectionate little thing, Mary reflected, lying on their pallet after the lamp had been extinguished. She was loving and intelligent, as well as pretty. Rosaleen deserved something more than she had had, but she could not think of any way to improve her daughter's position, unless she was allowed to go to school. More than Doirin's warning bothered her about that: she remembered Mrs. O'Toole's remark when they first moved in. Rosaleen was already having problems with the other children in the building, and they would most certainly bully her if she went to the public school. Liam worried her even more than Rosaleen, though she could not feel the same affection for him. She knew she was not imagining his avoidance of her since the night he saw her holding hands with Brian. The boy was more difficult to reach than before, and he had never been a sunny child.

From infancy, he had been beset by colds and illness much more than her other children. It was a wonder—and she felt guilt for the thought—that he had not expired on the ship instead of Seamus. Seamus had been blessed with the Noonan eyes, though his hair, somehow, had been blond, and there had been a kind of toughness in him; compared with Liam, Seamus had been the survivor. But it was he who died. She tried not to think about it, and realized she would be trying for the rest of her life. Every decision to forget the ordeal they had been through was thwarted each succeeding day. If it was not Seamus in her thoughts, it was her mother and father, shallowly buried in the floor of their cottage...or something like what had come up with Darin tonight. The whole nightmare was built into her blood and bones: she would carry it with her always, no matter how she appeared on the surface, smiling and joking with the children and Veronica, who had been too ill to remember most of it.

What she should really do was give some thought to the child that was coming, as she always had in the past. Poor little creature. Until now, she had only thought of it with guilt and misery: she must get past all that and think of it as a blessing. All her babies had been blessings: the only thing that brightened her life. She wondered vaguely if it would be a boy or girl, this time, and if she had any preference. A boy might replace Seamus, though not in her heart: each child had his special place. She thought, perhaps, she would like another girl, because girls were so much company.

Her daughter was breathing warmly right between her shoulder blades. Mary was warm and relaxed beneath the pile of coats, and her eyes began to close as her mind, which was so overburdened, drifted into sleep.

An unfamiliar noise made her open her eyes quickly in the darkness, squinting them as though it would make her hear better. The sound was on the stairs. There it was again.

Someone was coming downstairs into their flat. Mary remembered the hard, brutish face of the woman with the green eyes and the others like her; they seemed capable of anything, and she had seen a few of their men, who must be worse. Her first impulse was to confront whoever it was, but her heart grew weak inside of her: she was in no condition to confront an intruder, without any kind of weapon for defense. She remembered the kitchen knife, laid away clean for tomorrow, on a shelf behind the table. There was no way for her to reach it. Her heart thumped heavily as she sat up as quietly as she could, pushing Rosaleen away gently.

"Brian!" she whispered. He did not hear her, though she knew it was he who slept just beyond the hanging blanket, closest to her pallet. Pushing her arm through the bottom of the divider, she touched his shoulder and shook it insistently. "Brian!"

The lamp went on at the same time that Brian sat up, its dim light barely reaching them behind the curtains. He seemed to grasp the situation at once and rose in one long athletic motion, loosening his belt and drawing it out by the heavy buckle. Every man had been a rowdy little boy once, and knew how to defend himself. Mary got up too, rather clumsily because of the weight of her belly, and reached for her shawl. But before she could emerge, she heard Brian exclaim, "Tomas! What are you doing? For Christ's sake, where have you been?"

Tomas was seated at the table with the lamp before him, not absolutely sober. "It's me home, isn't it?" he asked. "I've come home to see me wife and kids."

Mary appeared behind Brian, her face a white blur in the darkness of her loosened hair, the contour of her body invisible under the black shawl. There was a moment of silence, during which she wished Brian would throw Tomas out, rid her of him forever.

"That's a point to be argued, my man," Brian said. "We've not seen a hair of you for over two months. Tomas, where have you been?"

Tomas rose unsteadily and held his arms out at his sides to display the fine clothes he was wearing, a tipsy grin on his face. "I've been at Dugan's. They gave me a wee room there with the family, over the pub. And I've been working." He explored the pockets of his striped suit clumsily, finally extracting something, and triumphantly threw a handful of coins in the middle of the table.

"That's fine, me boyo," Brian said ironically. "There must be all of a dollar and a half there! Either Mr. Dugan doesn't pay well, or you've put it all on your back."

"Ah, Brian," Tomas said in a conciliatory way, "sure, you can't hold that against me! I had to have clothes to work in such a fine place, didn't I? They'll be paid off in no time. Is that my Mary I see behind you?" he asked, squinting. "Indeed it is! You aren't after being inhospitable, too, love? I swear to God I didn't knock you down in those hot potatoes. You're all right, aren't you?"

She did not reply. He had the whole episode so mixed up in his mind he did not recall *what* had happened. She wanted to put her hand on Brian's arm to urge him to keep Tomas away from her, but she had made a vow not to touch Brian. Besides, Brian was angry, she could see it in the tilt of his head and his squared shoulders: perhaps it would be better to pacify him, before he throttled his brother as he had threatened.

"Mary's all right, no thanks to you. I'd be defaming our own mother if I called you what I'd like to. You bloody idiot! You've been away all this time not knowing if Mary or the children were alive or dead! Not knowing if there was enough to eat! Not even knowing if Mary was badly burned that night!"

Brian was working himself up, and though they were talking softly, if furiously, Mary heard one of the children turn in his sleep and looked down. She could not tell which of the boys had moved: they all appeared to be sleeping soundly.

"Brian," she whispered, "the children. Let's sit down at the table to discuss this, before one of you starts roaring with anger."

Tomas bowed to her deeply as they took their chairs. She wondered if it was sensible to try to discuss anything with him in his condition.

"So," she addressed him, "you've got yourself a job in the place you like best. Is Mr. Dugan paying you out of the taps?"

"Nooo...I swear to God this is the first time I've had a drop for a week. No, longer than that. Mrs. Dugan laid down the law right at the beginning. Said she might have a pub below her, but she'd have no drunks in her house."

"They booted you out, then?" Brian asked, dangerously pale, but Tomas chuckled slyly, shaking his head.

"When I have a snootful, I don't go up those stairs at all, man! She's a terror, that one. Tongue like a wasp and not above physical torment, either. Dugan's scared out of his head of her. She beats him, you see, with a broom! All six feet three of him, and she no bigger than a wasp."

"Do you still have a job?" Mary asked, and he vigorously nodded in the affirmative, reaching out to touch her shoulder.

"I am employed," he said rather grandly; then, softening his voice, "Oh, Mary, I've missed you so."

She shook his hand off and used her own to place it on his side of the table. "There'll be none of that," she muttered, averting her eyes.

"None of...but woman, I'm your husband! There's been none of that for far too long!"

Brian breathed out sharply in disgust. "So that's why you've paid us this visit," he said. "If you stay here, Tomas, you'll be sleeping there"—he hitched his head—"with the children. Goddammit, man, your wife's carrying your child! You didn't know that when you pranced away, did you?"

Tomas shook his head to remove the blur of the whiskey, and his eyes went blank. "Child? You mean a baby? But that can't be. No." His face tightened and went hard and stubborn. "What the hell's going on here? Mary, speak to me!"

"It's true," she said quietly. "I didn't know it, but I was carrying a child when I left home."

"If there's a child, it's not mine," he exploded. "Nor were you carrying it when we left Ireland! Ah, I think I understand!" He stared at her belligerently, with dark hatred in his blue eyes, the eyes that were like Brian's, and yet not like his at all. "That's how you kept the family alive when Brian and I were breaking our backs movin' rocks in Cobh for a road that didn't go anywhere! Why, you bloody bitch! Who was it, then? McGee? He was the only one who had grain or money."

"Shut up, Tomas!" Brian exclaimed, grabbing his arm to drag him from the table. "You're talking mad, saying things you won't be able to take back. Mary never did anything bad. She saved my whole family, and since we've been here she's brought more into this house than you have! You're talking to a saint! You'll not abuse her before me or I swear to God, I'll kill you with my bare hands!"

Whether it was the force of Brian's grip or the words, Tomas blinked and seemed to collapse in upon himself. "I'm sorry," he mumbled. "It's sleep I'm needing. Brian, help your drunken brother to bed, like in the old days, huh?"

Brian's angry glance met the dark torment in Mary's eyes; finally, she shrugged her shawled shoulders.

"Put him down with the boys," she murmured. "He'll forget all this in the morning."

Supporting Tomas's body, Brian helped Mary flatten Rosaleen's old pallet and dumped his brother onto it with more force than necessary. "Jesus," he said. "No wonder they call the drink 'the creature.' It makes a man inhuman."

"We mustn't mind what he says when he's like this," she said, brushing some wetness from the corner of her eyes. "He's mad."

Liam snuggled up to his father's inert body and put his thin little arm over Tomas's chest. His eyes were closed, and it was difficult to tell if he was awake or just restless in his sleep. Mary hoped desperately that her young son had not heard Tomas's drunken, irresponsible accusations: it was impossible to approach a child to explain such things. With a sensation of unease, she nodded goodnight to Brian and returned to her own bed, where she took Rosaleen in her arms and held onto her for warmth. The lamp was not extinguished for some time; apparently Brian could not sleep, either.

Doirin, who now rose as early as the rest of the family, to go to daily Mass, stood over Tomas's inert body thoughtfully for some time before she remarked, "The fatted calf has returned instead of the prodigal son. When did he drop in on us, then?"

"Last night," Mary replied, checking Liam's clothes and brushing the hair back from his white little face. "Don't tell me you didn't hear him? You must sleep like death."

Her sister adjusted her shawl over her head, carefully flicking away a wad of lint that had caught on the dark wool. "Did he bring any money with him? It looks as though he put everything on his own back."

"Indeed it does. He only had a dollar or two. He's employed, it appears, at Mr. Dugan's pub, and has been living above it all this time."

"If ever a job matched a man... Well, I suppose you'll have it out. Come on, Liam," Doirin said impatiently. "We don't want to be late."

Tomas slept on noisily until almost noon, when Mary woke him by shaking his shoulder and offering some cold potatoes from last night's supper. The innocence of his handsome face after causing so much pain amazed her all over again. Except for Rosaleen, they were alone. Veronica was outside in the sun, and on her return from church Doirin had gone to sleep again. If Tomas remembered the night before, he chose to forget it, without ignoring her pregnancy, which was evident enough to see.

"Is it a boy or a girl you want this time?" he asked conversationally, and her face flushed with his previous accusations.

"I'd like another girl," she replied, putting Rosaleen on a stool to brush and braid her hair. She knew that Tomas liked children, especially when they were too small to judge him. Indifferent to Liam's worship, he had already detached himself from his son, but he adored little Rosaleen. The girl's emotions seemed ambivalent. She accepted his kisses without returning them. And she kept away from him when she smelled alcohol: he had dropped her too often when bouncing her on his knee when he was drunk. As young as she was, Rosaleen was no one's fool, Mary realized. She greeted her father's return with more solemnity than happiness and had hung back, listening to him brag about his fine job, and observing his new clothes.

"So it's a pub you're working at?" the little girl asked gravely. "Uncle Brian's working on the docks, out in the cold...though the weather's getting better, now. Your face is all white."

"It's a good job," he reassured her, scraping the bowl. "My little darlin' isn't going to tell me where to work, is she? I probably make twice as much as Brian."

"You have a fine suit of clothes," Rosaleen observed. "And a new coat, too."

"A man must look his best in a job like mine."

"Uncle Brian bought us cloth. See? We have new clothes, too!"

Mary continued to brush Rosaleen's long, dark hair, without commenting, finding it difficult to speak to Tomas after last night. She had nothing to say to him until they were alone, anyway.

"I'll get you better ones than that." Tomas smiled. "And new shoes, too. You're still wearing those poor-fitting things from Immigration. Just give me a little time, sweetheart, and I'll fix my family up in style."

"I like my shoes," Rosaleen replied, dangling her feet from the stool. "They hurt at first, but now they feel fine." Then: "What time do you go to work, Pa? Uncle Brian's gone before we get up."

Tomas smiled. "That's one of the differences between Brian

and me, love. The work in the pub doesn't really get going until later...almost when Brian's coming home. Oh, there are a few things to do in the afternoon, but... If you're a good girl, I'll take you to Dugan's with me sometime. How would you like that?"

Rosaleen's silence beneath Mary's hands indicated that she would not like it at all. After a few seconds, she answered with composure, "Ma and I are usually busy in the afternoon. We have a job, too."

Cocking one eyebrow with displeasure, Tomas looked at Mary. "You aren't still working for that...?"

"Indeed I am. We were able to keep ourselves while you were away, without being beholden to your family." She paused, not wanting to say more in front of the child. Except in scenes with Doirin, she had never belittled him in front of the children.

Tomas's spoon clattered against the empty bowl, destroying the carefully kept peace, and Rosaleen started: like Liam, she was extremely sensitive to family outbursts. Before things could go any further, Mary spoke with deliberate obliquity to Rosaleen, so that only Tomas and not the child would understand,

"Your father understands the situation, I think. We're pleased he has some work, to relieve Uncle Brian of the burden, aren't we? If your father chooses to remain here, it will be like last night—with the children—since we're already settled cozily in our bed. It'll be a kind of trial period." Her dark eyes moved to his face and saw the trepidation there. "If your father wants to help the family like Uncle Brian does, he'll prove it to us, I'm sure. Is that agreeable to you, Tomas Noonan?"

His face was flushed, his blue eyes narrowed. "Yes. Yes, of course, Mary. You know my family means everything to me. But I don't like the thought of you going to work. No wife of mine is going out to work in your condition."

Mary's laugh was more ironical than warm. "If you can prove you can support us, I'll give all that up. I'll soon have to anyway. But, for the present, I need some security. Rosaleen, run up and tell Veronica it's time to leave."

"My sister's working there, too?" Tomas demanded as the child ran up the stairs.

"Not really. She just comes along to keep us company. Our employer is fond of her and likes to talk to her."

"What's his name?"

Mary shrugged and pushed the pins more firmly into her own hair. "Unpronounceable. Isn't it about time you were on your way to Mr. Dugan's? There must be cleaning up to do before the crowd arrives. Please give him my best regards. He was kind to us the day we arrived."

Tomas rose to his feet, smoothing his clothing. "Yes, I'll be on my way. And, Mary," he said with a husky voice, his innocent eyes entreating, "I'll prove myself to you, I swear I will. You'll never be ashamed to be the wife of Tomas Noonan. All I needed was a chance."

Chapter 6

FOR A WHILE, it seemed that the best thing that could have happened to them was the return of Mary's husband and the few dollars he brought home every week, because shortly after his arrival Brian was once again without work. Overloading himself with boxes, in order to meet an impossible quota under the surveillance of the dockmaster, Brian had a sudden pain in his groin and toppled the merchandise, breaking one of the wooden packing boxes and strewing its contents on the pier. When a workforce is unlimited, one mistake is all a man gets. Returning to work the next day, he found he had been replaced by a burly fellow from Mayo. He did not go home until late that night, and when he did it was obvious he had taken a few drinks on the way home.

Mary reflected that any man who had to face Doirin would have done the same; and, even now, Brian was not really drunk—just slightly anesthetized against both the pain and what he must listen to.

Doirin surprised them all by showing concern for him.

"Sure, you've ruptured yourself," she said. "You shouldn't have lifted such a load. You must rest for a few days before looking again. With our fine Tomas back, you can afford a few days' rest, God knows." Her eyes challenged Mary, who stood by helplessly. "People lived off us long enough. I'm sure they won't object."

"Of course not," Mary said quickly. "Rest is what he needs. Perhaps he should even see a doctor."

"I don't want a doctor," Brian said, moving toward his bed. "If I can just lie down for a little while..."

When she was sure he was sleeping, Mary invited the other two women to the table for a rare pot of tea. They watched as she poured the liquid carefully into their chipped cups, in silence, as though it were some sort of ritualistic act. There was no sugar, but it did not matter: they had only tasted it once. Gingerly, they lifted their hot cups and tasted the weak drink.

"I think that work's too hard for Brian," Mary said at last. "Not that he isn't a strong man...he is! But to see him slaving when Tomas has it so easy has bothered me a great deal."

"If only Tómas would bring home all he earns," Veronica whispered. "What is he doing with it? Last week there was little more than the rent."

Mary shook her head. "It isn't the drink," she said with conviction. "But with all his bragging and the suit of clothes on him, I'm sure he makes more than he brings home."

"Gambling?" Doirin suggested. When they looked shocked, she continued, "It wasn't unheard of for him to take a flutter on the horses at the fairs. With the weather getting fine, now, God knows what goes on here."

Darin moaned in his sleep, his face flushed in the lamplight, and they all looked down at him. Carefully, Mary turned the lamp lower so it would not disturb him.

"Sure, he's a grand beautiful boy," she said. "Never a complaint out of him. You should be proud, Doirin."

"Pride's a sin...like many other things," Doirin said shortly. "If he's beautiful, it will be his affliction. Don't tell him that, and don't fuss over him. You and Veronica are always teasing him. It's better for his soul if he's just a wee bit humble. Now, what are we to do? Our fine Tomas isn't being honest with us, and Mary won't be able to work much longer."

"I told Mr. Rabinsky today I wouldn't be back," Mary admitted, to their surprise. "Well, it wouldn't do to have the baby in the back of his shop, you know."

"Of course," Veronica said, smiling. "That wouldn't be suitable. I wish I could bring something in. I've been such a burden, with the milk and all. And I haven't contributed anything."

Both of the sisters objected: Veronica's temperament was

such that no one asked any greater contribution. Besides, the girl was still ill. None of them looked as well as they had in the old days, not even the children, but Veronica, in spite of her occasional high color, was as fragile as porcelain. Often, after she had walked the few blocks to Mr. Rabinsky's, she was short of breath, though in some respects the outing seemed to do her good: it was better, at least, than sitting in a chair in the back yard.

"We'll just have to confront himself," Doirin said, referring to Tomas. "Let him know that we realize he's holding out on us."

"I'll do that," Mary said quickly, wishing no quarrel between hot-tempered Tomas and her quick-tongued sister. "He made a promise. I'll keep him to it, even if it means..."

"What?"

"Never mind," she said, the color creeping into her cheeks. "I can handle Tomas better after the baby comes."

"I have an idea," Veronica said timidly. "I'm really ever so much better, you know. Why can't I take on Mr. Rabinsky's lessons? It's a dollar a week, and that's half the rent."

"Absolutely not!" Doirin declared. "It's not decent! Mary's a married woman with children, but you're just a girl."

Mary knew how much Veronica liked to go to Mr. Rabinsky's shop, as a break in her otherwise confined routine. Overcoming her own worries about the girl's health, Mary ventured, "Perhaps there wouldn't be any harm in it. As long as you don't wear yourself out, Veronica. If you promise to walk slowly. You can try it for a week, at least."

Outnumbered, Doirin scowled and bit her lip.

"It's really all right," Mary assured her. "He's a very nice man. Besides, Rosaleen will be there. He's helping her with her arithmetic."

Mary poured out the last few drops of tepid tea and lifted her cup in a mock toast. *"Slainte!"*

Delighted, Veronica clicked her cup against Mary's, and, when Doirin kept hers in both hands, they coaxed her into the toast, too.

"We'll get through this." Veronica smiled. "Things have been worse. The important thing is that we're still together—and that Brian has a little rest."

Though he was unable to do heavy work, Brian could not endure idleness and, after a few days at home, he began to make the job rounds again. His injury still made him limp a little, and Mary noticed that when he thought no one was looking, his hand went to his lower right side, pressing it for comfort. At first, Tomas was elated at being the breadwinner of the family; the position gave him the kind of boost to his conceit that he most enjoyed. On payday, he came in smiling, with only a hint of liquor on his breath, and distributed the funds for the week in little piles of coins, reserving the rest to pay the rent himself. The children began to look forward to those days, once a week, because it usually meant a penny to spend on themselves. Tomas beamed benignly on them as he played the generous uncle. The older boys secretly dropped their coins into the family jar on the windowsill, because they knew just how far a penny went toward keeping food in the house. Mary kept Rosaleen's for her, in case it might be needed before more money came in; for she lived with a deep anxiety, knowing from experience that, unless Tomas had reformed drastically, he could not be depended upon from week to week.

Mary had Veronica purchase some soft white cloth for her, and she spent her afternoons making a few baby clothes. She missed their trips, but Veronica brought her the news from Mr. Rabinsky's. The girl would come in smiling, dropping her money into the jar, and Mary realized that the color in her face was not from her illness any more. The weather had turned fine, early in May, and the walks seemed to be good for Veronica, because she was full of stories on her return and smiled often.

"Mr. Rabinsky's such an interesting man," Veronica said one afternoon, picking up a needle to help Mary with the sewing. "He's been everywhere—not just Poland, but France and Italy. And he has such a funny way of telling about the things he saw. He really loves Rosaleen, Mary. He says she has an incredible mind for figures. That's strange, isn't it? I mean for a child that's so imaginative and makes up such fantastic stories for her dolly. You'd think it would be the boys instead, who took to figures."

"They haven't had much of a chance, have they? Out there on the street, scrambling for pennies. At least one child's getting a little education," Mary said, straightening out a small garment, smoothing it on the table.

"That isn't for the baby?" Veronica asked, confused at the color of bright-red silk, and Mary smiled.

"No, it's for the doll. Darin saved his pennies for the material so Rosaleen's doll could be dressed as fine as Maebe," he said. I didn't even think she had a name."

Veronica laughed. "She doesn't ... or she has many names. I've listened when Rosie thought I was resting. Her dolly's all the fine characters out of the old stories Fiddler Murphy used to tell. If she isn't just an ordinary fairy, she's Maebe or Brian Boru or Conn himself. She hasn't forgotten one word that old man ever said, and she embroiders on it, too."

Mary shook her head and smiled. "She loved Fiddler Murphy and his stories. I think she looked forward to winter when he could stay awhile."

"She even named her dog after him!" Veronica laughed. "I wonder what happened to that old dog?"

Mary shrugged. "Who knows in times like that? We'd better clear the table, now. Tomas said he'd be sending Michael home with the potatoes so we can start dinner. What time is it? It feels like the boy's late."

The boys came clamoring down the steps in a few minutes, Darin taking the last five steps in one jump, and Liam walking over to put his pennies in the jar. Michael came last, his prepubescent face grim, his dark eyebrows drawn together over his short nose. But Padraig was the first to come out with the news.

"He only gave us enough for five pounds of potatoes," Padraig said with disgust. "He said that was all he had. And him sitting there playing cards with that lot at the pub."

Mary felt her heart fall; before she could say anything to the boys, Doirin was up and out of her blanketed cubicle.

"But it's payday!" she cried. "What about the rent? What about—"

Veronica quieted Doirin by putting her arms around her shoulders, while Mary went to the jar and dropped its contents, coin by coin, into her palm. One dollar and thirty cents: Veronica's money and the boys'. She had five cents in pennies tied into a handkerchief for Rosaleen. She looked into Michael's disappointed face.

"Is he still at it, then?" she asked. "Are they still gambling at Dugan's Pub?"

"They were half an hour ago," the boy said. "He said he was going to win, and wanted me and Padraig to wait around."

She knew if she followed her impulse to descend on him in the pub, he would lose his job altogether, so she swallowed hard and attempted a smile.

"You were good boys to come on home with the spuds. Who knows, maybe he will win. A man can't go on losing forever, can he?" She picked through the potatoes in the bag, selecting the best, and began to peel them, holding back furious tears. "We'll not say anything about this to your father. He has enough worries. Things will work out."

"Like hell they will!" Michael cried, with tears in his angry blue eyes. "It isn't just Uncle Tomas. It's everything! People treating Pa the way they do when he looks for work! The way those goddam yankees order us around! Do you know what it's like out there? Do you think we've been having fun all winter? Half the time we begged for pennies, when there weren't any errands. And most of the time we had to fight off the bloody bullies in this neighborhood to keep what we had! I'm fed up with it! I hate this goddam place. I'll be..."

Shocked, Mary stood, with the paring knife in her hand, staring at Michael. The quiet, self-sufficient boy had never even expressed himself before, and the sudden tirade with its revelations was completely unexpected.

Doirin finally recovered enough to say, "Michael! I won't have you talking that way! I didn't know you used such words! You just wait until your father comes home."

The boy looked at her with pity and revulsion fighting each other in his face. "For Christ's sake, Ma, don't you hear what I'm saying? I'll be twelve in a few weeks, and I'm going to sea! Maybe I can send money back that way. In any case, I'm not staying here."

Doirin responded as though he had slapped her; only Veronica's arms kept her from falling backward. Trembling all over, she tried to regain control of the situation.

"We won't mention that again, Michael. Sure, it's absolute fantasy! We've done all we can to make things bearable for you, and you have no gratitude at all!"

Michael, eyes blazing and lips trembling, gave Doirin a look of pure hatred and ran up the stairs. Padraig followed him, glancing back over his shoulder to reassure his mother. Doirin, at her wit's end, began to keen as though she were at a wake, holding her shawl over her face. Veronica gave Mary a frantic look.

"That'll be enough of that," Mary said firmly. "They'll be back for supper. There's no place else for them to go. Doirin, stop it! You're upsetting everyone, and Brian will be home soon."

Nothing would stop the wailing, though, so Mary set herself to peeling the potatoes, trying to keep her trembling fingers from slipping with the knife. Darin, still pale from the outburst, looked from his mother to Mary and back again; then he came up to Mary's side.

"I'll set the water to boiling upstairs, Aunt Mary," he said. "Where's Rosie?"

Mary had to think for a moment; she was so accustomed to the little girl playing in a corner that she forgot she was outside. "In the back yard," she said at last. "Tell her to come in, Darin. No, keep her there with you for a while, until your mother quiets down!"

"You made the dress for her doll," he observed.

"Yes," she said distractedly. "You can give it to her after supper."

He hesitated. "I'll come back for the spuds," he said. "It isn't right, you taking all those stairs."

For the first time since he had come in, she looked at Darin and saw the concern in his face. She also noticed something else, as though her senses were sharpened by everything that had just happened: the boy's pretty face was thin. The cold of winter had made the children look rosy, but now his complexion was almost gray. She turned to look at Liam and found him sitting in a corner with his arms around his drawn-up knees. He was even thinner. Her own arms looked like sticks. She had not observed that none of them were really thriving. Was it the basement or the food? The only thing lacking from their diet had been milk, and Veronica, who had been drinking it, looked better than any of them.

"Dear Jesus," Mary whispered. All winter, she had been fooling herself that they looked well, when they were scarecrows, pale images of what they used to be. Having no mirror, she saw her reflection only in others' eyes, and they were loving ones. When Rosaleen finally came downstairs with Darin, Mary had to work up the nerve to look at her.

Supper was silent. The two older boys had come back, and though Doirin's eyes were swollen from weeping, Brian did not seem to notice, any more than he noticed that there were fewer potatoes on the table that night. He tried to control the pain he felt after walking around all day, but occasionally there was a spasm in his face which Mary, with her new eyes, saw was very lean indeed. They looked no better than the other poor people upstairs, and she had a sudden conviction that they would all die if something was not done.

Darin touched her ankle with the toe of his shoe under the table, and she looked up at him, mildly surprised at first by his twinkling eyes. Then she remembered: the dress for the doll. As soon as the table was cleared, she nodded to Darin, but he shook his head. He would not give the present to Rosaleen.

"Rosie," Mary said, "we have a surprise for you."

The little girl's eyes widened. Mary went on, "Your cousin..." Darin shook his head more violently this time: he was to be left out of it altogether. Mary smiled. "A bit of material came my way, and I made this"—she put the small red dress on the table—"for your dolly."

Brian's face lost its intentness, and he smiled at the expression on his niece's face.

"Ah, that's a fine dress," he said. "She'll look just like a princess!"

"Let me help you dress her," Veronica offered, as the child's hands fumbled trying to put the garment on the sock doll, but Rosaleen shook her head.

"Please, let me!" Rosaleen cried in her excitement. Darin was the only one of the boys who laughed. The others either sat in moody silence or moved away from the distraction, too frivolous for their concern. Observing what a poor, dirty thing the treasured doll was, Mary felt tearful, but she put on a brave smile.

"Maybe we should wash dolly before we put on her pretty dress," Mary suggested, but Rosaleen held the doll close to her. "No! If you wash her, the face Darin put on her will come off!"

"I'm sure Darin will make her another."

There was a knock on the door upstairs, something they had never heard before. Mary's first thought was that it was Tomas, drunk and repentant, asking entrance, but the door did not open. They glanced at each other, and Brian finally rose to climb the stairs, taking the lamp with him to identify their company.

"Ah, come in, Mrs. O'Toole," Mary heard him say, warmly, but they did not return. The whole family sat in darkness while a whispering conversation went on over their heads; finally, the light disappeared as Brian stepped into the upstairs kitchen and closed the door behind him.

"Something fearful's happened," Veronica whispered in the darkness. "I've had a feeling that something was going to."

"Hush," Mary said, thinking of the children. They sat silently in the thick blackness of the basement, which suddenly seemed suffocating. Finally, after a few minutes that seemed much longer, the light returned and Brian came slowly down the stairs, his footfall hardly audible. When Mary saw his face in the lamplight, she involuntarily drew in her breath: his lips were set tightly, his eyebrows drawn together over his lowered eyes.

"What is it?" Veronica asked thinly, and when he did not reply, she raised her voice a little. "Brian, has something happened to Tomas?"

"I have to go out," he replied, reaching for his coat which hung from a nail on the wall. "Don't worry, Veronica, nothing's happened yet."

"For God's sake, Brian!" Mary cried, rising. "What's going on?"

The single glance he shot her was so full of anger that it made her take a step backward, as though it were directed at her. Observing her reaction, he put his hand around her arm and drew her to the foot of the stairs, out of hearing of the others.

"The bastard's really done it this time," he said. "He hasn't paid the rent for two weeks! Do you know where that puts us? I'm off to Dugan's to have a word with my fine brother."

"He'll lose his job!" Mary said. "I thought of it earlier. There's a card game going on. But if we burst in on him, he'll lose his job."

"Fat lot of difference that makes: it's doing the family no good! I may wipe up the floor of the pub with him."

"Wait!" Mary said. "I'm going with you. Maybe if Mr. Dugan sees how things are, he'll have a little mercy on us for murderin' my husband."

Mary remembered Brian going out that angry once before: when he went to get the money for their passage from the agent, Mr. McGee. What had transpired then she would never know, but it seemed safer to accompany him. They did not need any more trouble. They walked silently through the dark, cobbled streets, standing apart from one another, their hands not even touching, but she felt terribly close to Brian. She knew their minds held the same thoughts, their anger was the same. She knew they would both like nothing better at this moment than to physically lay hands on Tomas, to punish him for his irresponsibility.

When they came to the glass door of Dugan's, with its yellow light shining out into the street, Brian restrained her with his hand. "It isn't a place for you to be going into at night, Mary. You wait here for me."

The stubborn shake of her head made him surrender with a sigh and open the door for her. The light inside, full of tobacco smoke, seemed dimmer than what had filtered onto the street. Though there were many patrons, leaning over the bar and packed around the tables, the room was curiously quiet, the focus of all attention on a crowded table at the rear. Instinctively, Brian headed for that table, shouldering a path for Mary through the tightly packed, sweaty men.

Mary saw Mr. Dugan, briefly, standing behind the bar with his red head tilted, listening as intently as the others. The crowd of men did not seem to notice Brian, or that a pregnant woman had curiously appeared in their midst. They moved aside at Brian's bidding without taking their eyes off the attraction at the rear. The last row of broad backs directly around the table was difficult to penetrate, but Brian did so by directing attention to Mary with his eyes, and they moved away to make room for her.

Six men were sitting around the table with drinks in front of them. Tomas was one of them, his face red from the drink and the heat of the room, his eyes small and bright. He and another man were staring at each other in a bluff, but Brian did not pause to watch the play. He reached across the table and raised his brother by the shirtfront, to the astonishment of the other players and the amusement of Tomas, who threw his hand of cards down in triumph, calling, "Full house!"

At the same moment, Brian's fist connected with Tomas's jaw, sending him flying through the shattering glass of the window into the cobbled alley behind the building. After a moment of total silence, pandemonium broke loose, and the tension in the room snapped. There was a roar of raucous laughter. All attention focused on Brian, whose eyes were shooting blue fire, and Mr. Dugan elbowed his way to his side with a grin.

"What's this all about, man?" Dugan asked, his heavy paw slapping Brian's shoulder. "Your brother won, don't you see? He deserves another jug, not a crack on the jaw. What's the pot, now, lads?" Several voices answered at once. "See now! Twenty-five dollars! That's a small fortune."

Mary gasped and Mr. Dugan turned to her, to reassure her that what he said was true, but his smile faded at the expression on her face. Her dark eyes were wide and startled, and her face was pale. Grimacing with pain, she held both sides of her abdomen with her hands: it had come on so suddenly, without any preliminary back pain to signal contractions. She looked pleadingly at Mr. Dugan while Brian, still oblivious to what was happening, reached over and picked up five one-dollar bills.

"This belongs to the family," he said to the players. "He can blow the rest as he pleases, if I didn't crack his head in two. Dugan, how can you let this—"

But Dugan shook his head, indicating Mary with his eyes.

"Jesus!" Brian cried, putting his arms around her for support. "Oh, Jesus. Mary, darlin', do you think we can make it home?"

She shook her head firmly and muttered, "I don't want my baby to be born on the floor of a pub!"

"Upstairs!" Dugan said, clearing the way through his awed patrons. "The wife's there. She can help."

He led them to a staircase situated between the bar and the restaurant area where they had come on that first day of their arrival, and Brian lifted Mary in his arms. "It's all right, now, Mary," he said, as he ascended to the Dugans' living quarters. "Oh, God, if anything happened to you..."

She hardly heard him, conscious only of the strong, bearing-down impulse of imminent birth and of his cheek pressed tightly against her own.

Once they were inside the apartment, Mrs. Dugan took over, leading Brian into a small room, where he placed Mary on the bed. Vaguely, she noticed lace curtains and white linen before the next expulsive straining made her clasp the brass rails of the bed.

"Get out of here, both of you!" Mrs. Dugan said. "Start boiling some water and get some towels from the linen press! Don't stand there gaping! Help me! From what I see, there won't be time for boiling water, but do it anyway." She put her hand on Mary's forehead. "It's all right, now, don't be afraid, young woman. You were taken rather sudden, weren't you?"

"It's coming," Mary said steadily. "Please lift my skirt out of the way...."

One more expulsive effort and the birth was over. Mary's hands relaxed from the bed rails, and she hoisted herself up on one elbow. "It isn't crying," she said, straining to see over the piled gray drapery of her skirt. "Slap it again!"

Mrs. Dugan gave the tiny infant several strong slaps, but it made no sound and remained as blue as at birth.

"Put your finger in its mouth!" Mary directed. "There may be mucus there."

The woman's actions coincided with Mary's directions: she had attended births before.

"He's a poor wee thing," the woman said. "I think he's gone."

"Give him to me!"

Mary labored over the infant, while Mrs. Dugan tied the cord and cut it with a large pair of sewing shears. There were no pulses in the neck; the small body was slack and cold. After a few minutes, even Mary gave up, surrendering the child to the other woman, who held up an old petticoat to receive it.

"Surely it wasn't full term," Mrs. Dugan said. "It only weighs a few pounds."

"It was the hunger did it," Mary said bitterly. "Hardly eating all those months, when it was forming. I didn't feel any life until the fifth month, and it's been feeble since."

Putting the dead baby aside in a washbasin, Mrs. Dugan began to massage Mary's uterus to expel the afterbirth. Mary let her head fall back on the pillow, feeling an ache of loss for the baby that had not been wanted by anyone.

"What on earth were you doing on the street at this hour, with your time so close?" Mrs. Dugan demanded mildly. "You could have had it in the gutter, girl."

"In the pub," Mary said, closing her eyes. "I'm Tomas Noonan's wife. I'd heard about the card game."

The woman's thin little face brightened. "Tomas's wife? Sure he's mentioned you. Mary, isn't it? He's a one, isn't he? That man could charm a bird out of a tree. And so handsome! He's a bit of a rascal, but which one of them isn't?"

"His brother isn't. Is Brian still here?"

"In the kitchen. Those bumbling idjuts are slow enough with the towels." She gave a short laugh. "God bless them! I told them to boil water and the stove's banked for the night! Ah, there we are!" She extracted something from between Mary's legs, but Mary did not open her eyes.

"Did you get it all?" she asked indifferently.

There was a moment of silence while Mrs. Dugan examined it. "Yes. Now, I'll need cold water to clean up. Will you be all right for a bit?" When Mary nodded, Mrs. Dugan began to pull off Mary's bloody skirt and tidy the sheets. "I'll put this to soak right away. There's cold water in the pitcher."

Pouring the water over a corner of one of the sheets she had stripped off, she cleaned Mary's thighs and pulled the covers over her. "There. You're hardly bleeding at all. I'll be right back with clean linen."

"Mrs. Dugan?"

"Yes, dear?"

"Do you have any holy water in the house?"

"Yes. Oh, my God! I almost forgot!" She went over to the chest of drawers and returned with a small bottle. Then, with her back to Mary, she anointed the infant with the water, saying, "I baptize you in the name of the Father, the Son and the Holy Ghost."

Mary felt the tears running from the corners of her eyes as she stared at the cracked plaster ceiling, without knowing that at the same moment, in a much different chamber, another woman was looking at the elegant gold scroll on her canopied bed, and weeping too.

Mrs. Dugan would have had Mary stay on for a few days, even after she refused to see the bruised Tomas, but as soon as her clothes were dry and ironed, Mary insisted on going back to her children late the next morning. Brian, who remained helplessly in the parlor all night, staring at his hands, was the first person she saw when she woke. His face was haggard and he needed to shave, but his blue eyes were full of sympathy as he took her hand.

"I'm sorry," he said. "It's all my fault, Mary. If I hadn't let you come with me..."

Mary put her hand against his face. "No," she whispered definitely. "It would have happened anyway. The baby was like a little bird fallen from a tree, Brian. All those months of starvation in Ireland doomed him from the start, so don't go blaming anyone. Thank you for just being here."

"Mrs. Dugan says you want to go right home. Is that safe, darlin'? Shouldn't you rest here for a day, at least?"

She smiled without realizing how rueful her smile had become. "Sure, if we were at home in Ireland," she said brightly, "I'd be up tending the house and children today. I want to be with them." Then she frowned and her face grew dark. "What's to be done with the...infant?"

"I'll take care of that while you're getting dressed. Dugan's being most kind. He's even getting a horse cab for you to go home in. I think he must be feeling a bit guilty about all this." His hand covered hers on his cheek and tears stood in his eyes. "Mary, I feel as bad as if it were my own child. I..."

She could stand no more and turned her head on the pillow to gaze at the sun shining through the lace-curtained windows. "You'd better go, now, Brian. There's a lot to do."

She felt him lift her hand to his lips. Then he murmured, "Yes," and left the room.

The swell of love she felt for him nearly stifled her, and she moved quickly to control it, throwing the covers back and climbing out of the bed. For a moment, she felt woozy and had to sit back down; but when her head cleared, she looked carefully around the room. The marble basin had been removed, but she would never forget her baby's wizened little face and protruding ribs. When Mrs. Dugan entered, Mary was sitting on the edge of the bed with the sheets around her, crying softly, and the older woman sat beside her and put her arms around her.

"We've all had it happen, Mary. I only had one child and he died when he was three. There were never any more. At least you have the little ones at home." Mary nodded, gained control of herself and attempted to smile. Mrs. Dugan rose and held up her freshly washed and pressed skirt and blouse. "Do you want to get into these, now?"

Mary nodded. "They look fine. Thank you, Mrs. Dugan, for everything."

"You're welcome, I'm sure." The older woman turned her back so Mary could dress. "Only...what about Tomas? What are you going to do about him? I know he's a scamp, but..."

"Does he still have his job, then?"

"Of course! We're very fond of him. Tomas has brought a lot of new patrons in here with his stories and all."

"Why don't you keep him, then?" Mary said, smoothing her skirt, and Mrs. Dugan turned around, dumbfounded. "I mean it. He stayed here with you before, didn't he?"

"Yes, but he's your husband, Mary. Don't be hasty, please. All he needs is a chance. Look, we'll keep him for a while, make him pay his own board and room, and I'll keep an eye on him, to be sure. He'll straighten out!"

Mary eased her blouse into the band of her skirt, which felt loose, now, though her breasts were heavy and aching with milk. "You'll have your fill of Tomas soon enough," she said matter-of-factly.

"You didn't even ask if the poor man was hurt last night,"

Mrs. Dugan reproached her. There was a moment of strained silence between the two women who had been so close in a life-and-death struggle the night before; finally, Mrs. Dugan sighed and nodded her understanding. She came forward and embraced Mary, kissing her lightly on the cheek.

"I'll withhold some of his pay to send home," Mrs. Dugan said.

Chapter 7

AS THOUGH she had been wearing blinders for the past month, Mary suddenly noticed as the horse cab jogged along that it was a lovely day, and the tender green leaves were just coming out on the trees. Winter had seemed forever: she was almost surprised at the change of season and observed Boston with different eyes, because it was easier to look than let herself think. The North End was not a pretty place even when shrouded in ice and snow, but there was a park and a few trees grew from circles in the sidewalk, supplying a small amount of spring to the haggard neighborhood. She noticed how the old houses sagged and revealed their chipped masonry in the sunlight and that the garbage, frozen securely for so many months, was beginning to deteriorate and emit a stench now that it thawed. Conscious of Brian at her side, she did not remark on it, but gave a slight cry of delight at a tulip tree coming into bloom near the church. He took her hand and smiled down at her, though his eyes were serious.

"No matter what, you always manage to see the good part," he said. "It's a poor place to be sure, but we won't be here forever, Mary. Now that the weather's better, I'm sure I can get some work. Maybe tending yards. During the winter, we were all frozen into a chunk of ice: my mind would hardly work sometimes. I know that things will get better. They have to."

"We're still alive," she said, "and that's almost a miracle. If it weren't for you, we'd all have been under the sod these many months. You got us here: you saved our lives. We'll never forget that." She was answered by a tense silence, so she changed the subject. "Do they know what happened at home?"

"I sent a lad over as soon as we knew the baby was...well, yes, they know. I expect they won't be looking for you so soon, though. You should have laid up a day or so at Dugan's. They wanted you to stay."

"I couldn't do that. God knows, I was a great imposition on them as it was. You haven't been home yet, then?"

He shook his head. "I thought I should stay there last night, in case you needed me. It was silly of me, but..."

"It was not!" she said, then modified her tone of voice. "I did need you last night, very much. There was no one else to turn to. No one that was family, I mean." She paused as they passed the Catholic churchyard. "Brian, have you made any arrangements for the burying?"

"This afternoon. Doirin and Veronica can attend with me. I think you should get some rest."

"I don't want to come," she said in a hollow voice. "My feelings about this baby have been so mixed up. I believe to God, you're the only person who wanted it."

"And Rosaleen," he said. "You may not have been aware of it, Mary, but Rosaleen was looking forward to a real baby. She was even going to name it Seamus."

"I didn't think she even knew about it," Mary mused. "Poor little mite. How on earth did she know?"

"Liam told her, I think. After Tomas came back. He was awake that night, I'm sure. That's something that needs taking care of—you must talk to him. I watch him and try to think what's going on in his head. I suspect Darin could tell me. They're pretty close, but..."

"Liam's a queer one," she agreed. "I don't understand him at all, and he's my own son. There's something kind of sad ... and ... well, I can't think of any other word ... sneaky, about him. It makes me anxious when I'm around him, like I'm being watched all the time. He's that partial to Tomas."

"I think he's just shy," Brian defended her son, "and I'm sure he's attached to you. Every boy loves his mother. Surely you've noticed how Darin takes care of Doirin."

She smiled. "Darin takes care of everyone. He's been that

96

attentive to me these past few weeks. He's a strange one, now! You just label him a little devil, and then he does something kind and thoughtful you wouldn't expect.... Well, here we are."

Seen from the street, Mrs. O'Toole's lodging house revealed its squalor: paper blew from the railings they had clung to in the winter; the windows were bare of any curtains, except cardboard and newspaper used to keep the cold away; and the dark-gray paint seemed to be peeling more than ever. The cabdriver in his tall hat gave them a suspicious glance when they descended, until Brian paid the fare carefully, without knowing anything about tipping. The man switched his horse lightly and was gone before they reached the door. A host of shabby children poured out of the house before they could enter the hall. Mary turned to look at them; most of them she had not seen at all during the winter.

"They're like skeletons!" she exclaimed softly. "If I didn't know better, I'd think we were still in Ireland."

Brian put his hand on her shoulder and guided her through the open door into the same dark hallway, with its smell of cabbage and sweat. She was relieved that no one was in the kitchen when they passed through, and felt almost unreal as she descended the stairs to their own quarters, gray even at noon. Doirin and Veronica were sitting at the table, talking, but jumped up at once when they saw Mary. Veronica came forward to hug her tightly, whispering, "Mary, Mary, I'm so sorry!" She had tears in her eyes.

"There, now," Mary comforted her, at a loss for what to day. "Sure, the good Lord must have wanted it this way."

Her eyes met Doirin's eyes over Veronica's head, and she saw nothing but animosity there, which she could not understand. Doirin had been the first person to say the baby was unwanted. Disentangling herself from Veronica, but keeping her arm around the girl's waist, Mary asked her sister, "Where's Rosaleen?"

"I sent her out to play with the others in the back yard. I got tired of her sniffling around here," Doirin answered.

"But she doesn't get on with the other children!" Mary protested and turned to go up the stairs, but Veronica held onto her.

"You lie down," she said, "I'll get Rosie."

"You spoil that child to death!" Doirin exploded. "You're away from her for one night and she cries her eyes out. It isn't natural! Leave her alone, Veronica. Let her learn to take care of herself. She has to know how to get along with those children sometime."

"But they aren't our kind of children!" Mary said, not allowing Veronica to lead her to her bed. "They're mean and jealous. They're from towns!"

Brian stepped forward to assist Veronica. "Lie down, Mary. We'll get Rosie. You need your rest. How long has she been outside?" he asked, turning to Doirin.

"An hour or so. I can't understand all this concern for Rosaleen just because she's a girl. The boys have to go out, don't they? Do you think it's easy to see my boys going out on the streets every day?"

Veronica had gotten Mary to her pallet and was holding her down with both hands, her eyes entreating her not to get into the discussion.

"Did she take her dolly?" Mary asked in a whisper, and Veronica shook her head,

"No, it's all right. It's right over there in the corner where she plays, love. She knows the dolly makes the children angry."

The upstairs door slammed and the sound of small feet walking sideways down the stairs followed. Mary was the first to hear the sniffling sound and, pushing Veronica aside, rushed toward her little daughter, who had blood all over her face.

"Look at her!" Mary cried, almost hysterically, still off balance from her experience the night before. "Look at her!" she blazed, facing Doirin, with her hand below Rosaleen's chin. Then she fell to her knees to examine the child's face with wild eyes, only to realize that it was just a nosebleed. Veronica came forward with a wet cloth and Mary bathed the blood away carefully.

"She probably fell down," Doirin said relentlessly. "My God, it's just a nosebleed! You pamper her so."

But Brian put his hand on his wife's shoulder and, with one look, made her fall silent. "I think Rosie, herself, can tell us what happened," he said. "She's a big girl. See, she's stopped crying. Come on, Rosie, my love, what happened out there?"

Rosaleen looked up at her uncle with hurt and indignation in her eyes. She gave one more sniff before she answered, "They're savages, Uncle Brian! I was just standing there, watching them make mud pies. All of a sudden, they set upon me. Big, mean girls! They tried to scratch me, but I hid my face. Then one of them, that freckle-faced Sianid McCarthy, grabbed my hair and hit me in the nose! I think it scared them when they saw the blood, though."

"You stupid girl!" Doirin said. "Why didn't you fight back? We had hair-pulling matches in my day, too, but we could take care of ourselves. Mary, remember the Grogins? You either fought those girls or they kept you inside forever."

Mary continued to hold the damp cloth to Rosaleen's nostril. "The Grogins were a bad lot," she agreed, "but we were also older. Rosaleen's only five! And she's not a boy, Doirin. Please remember that. I don't want my daughter brawling in the streets like a hoodlum. Darin, where do you think you're going?"

The boy stopped dead at the foot of the stairs. "Outside," he said.

"You are not," Mary said severely. "It's one thing to beat up on boys, but don't let me ever catch you laying a hand on a girl. No matter what she's done."

"That's right, lad," Brian seconded her, and the boy returned reluctantly, with an angry frown on his face. Brian suppressed a smile. "Sure you weren't going to fight the girls?"

"I was going to wipe up the bloody lot of them," Darin declared.

"That isn't right, son. Though God knows they deserve it. You'll learn you have to suffer the abuse of females without hitting them. It isn't proper."

"If a man ever struck me, I'd leave him in a minute," Doirin said. "You're a bit too protective of your cousin, boy. It isn't natural."

Mary lifted Rosaleen in her arms. "I don't want her ever to go out there again, unless she's with Veronica or me. Now, I think Rosie and I will both take a little nap."

Mary drifted off into an uneasy sleep, conscious of the child's body in her arms. Though she was thoroughly weary, her mind would not shut off and kept going over the events of last night repeatedly, until finally they were woven into her half-waking dreams. Probably the most difficult part was talking to Rosaleen about it before the little girl nodded off. The child wanted to know what had happened to her "babby," using the Irish term, and her face was full of disappointment and tears.

"The little babby died," Rosaleen said, with reproach. "I wanted to take care of him so much. They told us about it this morning, and Veronica explained that God had wanted him, and Liam said it was just as well he had died, and that I'd understand when I was older. But he wouldn't say anything more. What was wrong with the babby?"

Puzzling over her son's statement, Mary replied gently, "He was very small, Rosaleen, too small to survive. And Veronica was right, dearest. God takes special care of tiny ones like that."

"Why couldn't I go to the funeral with Uncle Brian and the others?"

"I wanted you here," Mary said, brushing Rosaleen's hair back with her hand. "There's time enough for funerals, darlin'. I wanted you here with me."

When Mary finally heard the rapping on the upstairs door, it must have been going on for some time, because it had become very insistent. She opened her eyes with a start and, trying not to disturb Rosaleen, rose from the pallet. Calling softly, "I'm coming," she ascended the stairs. When she opened the door, the sight of the girl standing in the kitchen surprised her. She had never seen anyone in the house look so neat and clean. About twenty years old, and not particularly attractive, the girl wore a splendid uniform of black material with a small white collar. Mary gaped at her in amazement, not even asking her to come downstairs, but the girl smiled understandingly.

"I'm Bridie Tierney," she introduced herself. "My ma and pa and the kids live here, but I don't get home often. Are you Mrs. Noonan?"

Mary nodded. "I'm Mary Noonan."

Bridie looked slightly uneasy, though the smile remained on her freckled face. Mary noticed that her reddish hair was plaited carefully around her head and that her hands were clean, even the nails.

"Are you the lady who...had the baby last night?" the girl asked carefully, staring intently into her face. When Mary nodded again, she started talking as though she were unable to stop, out of sheer nervousness. "You see, Mrs. Noonan, I was home this morning on my day off. I don't always come here. I suppose I should, but it's so... Anyhow, Mrs. O'Toole told us about you. I'm awfully sorry about your baby, I really am! But, you see, my mistress, the lady I work for, had a baby last night, too." She stopped breathlessly, uncertain how to go on.

"That's nice." Mary smiled in encouragement, wondering what on earth the girl was about. "Was it a boy or a girl?"

"A boy. Yes, a boy, but it's not... Mrs. Noonan, my mistress can't nurse it. She's an older lady than you, and she can't nurse her baby. When I heard about you, I thought, well, maybe you'd like the job."

At first Mary was shocked, realizing why the girl had approached her so nervously; then she thought about the baby, somewhere in Boston, who might die if it did not have milk. Before she could reply, the girl was jabbering nervously again. "They tried to give it some warm milk on the end of a cloth, but it didn't work out because... I know it isn't done much in the old country, Mrs. Noonan, but wet-nursing is acceptable here, especially in the South, where they let the Negro slaves nurse their children."

"Is your mistress looking for someone, then?" Mary asked.

"I don't know, but it seems like a good idea. I wouldn't have thought of it at all unless I'd heard... I haven't offended you, have I, ma'am?"

"No. It's just a surprise," Mary said, trying to put all the information in order. "If the baby was born last night, it's been hours without any real food."

"They were trying a sugar tit when I left this morning," Bridie said. "But that won't do any good. In fact, cook said it would hurt the little fellow... make him loose, you know. Anyway, I'll be returning shortly and my friend—he's the coachman—will be picking me up, and I thought maybe you'd come along and..."

"Have I time to comb my hair?" Mary asked. "And clean up, like? I have to take my daughter with me, too."

A full smile wreathed Bridie's face, revealing her crooked teeth. "Oh, yes, it'll be at least half an hour yet! I'm so glad you'll do it, Mrs. Noonan. I'm not promising anything. Mrs. Maddigan might not hire you, though I don't know what else she can do. I'll tap on the door when Kevin comes."

Mary woke Rosaleen and began to clean her up. There was dried blood on her bodice from the nosebleed, which she tried to dab off with cold water, so only a little of the stain remained. She brushed the child's hair and then her own, to make it as neat as Bridie's, thanking God that at least her own clothes were freshly laundered. She wished she had a small white collar to put on her gray dress, but there was no time to make one out of the baby things.

Rosaleen groaned when she was told to get into her shoes: she had gone barefoot since the warmer weather set in, and the old boots were now too small for her. Mary helped her work her feet into them, exasperated that her daughter did not have something better to wear. Well, at least she would not be walking in them: they would be going in a buggy. It struck her as strange that she had never been in one before this morning, and now she was riding in a buggy twice in the same day.

When they were both presentable, as much as they could be, Mary sat down at the table and wrote a hasty note to Brian:

My dear Brian,

Opportunity for a job...don't know when we will be home. Please ask Mrs. O'Toole about it. She will explain.

Love,
Mary.

Bridie's tap on the door came sooner than Mary expected. She only had time to grab her shawl before she and Rosaleen went quickly up the stairs.

The vehicle awaiting them at the curb was not a buggy like the one that brought her home from the pub: it was an enclosed coach with two horses, perfectly matched, and when they got inside the cushions were of deep red velvet. Before Mary could say anything, Bridie giggled.

"This isn't allowed, you know," she said. "If Kevin and I weren't walking out together, we'd never ride in it. We'll have to get out before we reach the Square. Maids don't ride in fancy rigs like this."

"What Square?" Mary asked, helping Rosaleen to look out the window. The child was squirming with excitement, and she kept her hands firmly on her shoulders. "Behave, Rosaleen. I want you to be on your best behavior today, do you hear me?"

"Louisburg Square." Bridie twinkled. "The only place in Boston that's called the Square."

"On Beacon Hill, isn't it?" Mary said. "We've walked there. But those are very fine houses!"

"The Maddigans' is one of the finest," the girl said proudly. "They may not be accepted in Boston society, but their house is like a castle."

"What do you mean, not accepted? The rich are accepted anywhere," Mary said.

"Cook says that Boston society's very closed to outsiders. Mrs. Maddigan belonged to it before she married himself. But, like everywhere else in this town, the Irish are not in society. Sure he's been here for years. He came here rich, the way I hear it. But that doesn't make any difference to them. He's Irish and Irish is dirt," the girl finished a little bitterly.

"I understand it's the religion that bothers them," Mary said, keeping her eyes on the passing streets. "They think Catholics are trying to take over the world or something."

Bridie laughed. For such a plain girl, she had a bright spirit.

"They aren't Catholic," she said. "He came from the North, and she was Protestant enough when they married. In this case, it isn't the religion, it's the name of Maddigan."

"He's done well for himself, though, to get to the top of the hill," Mary remarked. "What business is he in, anyway?"

The girl shrugged and pulled a long face. "Banks...or shipping. I don't really know, maybe both. He's always that busy. But he's kind and he remembers my name. He may have lost the brogue, but he hires only Irish servants. Well, more and more are doing that, now, you know. Cheap labor. There are so many of us about, and more coming in all the time, I hear."

"You don't get a fair wage, then?"

"Fair enough, but it has to go too far. What with my family in Mrs. O'Toole's hardly making it, I don't keep a whole dollar for myself in a month. Still, it isn't bad at all."

"And Mrs. Maddigan?" Mary asked carefully. "What's she like?"

Something like reverence came into the girl's freckled face. "Sure, she's a lady, Mrs. Noonan—a lady born. She lets the housekeeper look after the place, and lives in her own world. You'd think we were bits of furniture where she's concerned. It isn't that she's unkind," she added quickly. "She's very nice, at Christmas and holidays, you know, but I'm sure she doesn't know the name of any living one of us! It's the way she was brought up, you see."

Mary pondered that, beginning to feel uneasy. The only comparison she could draw from experience was when the landlord came to stay in the big house in Ireland. His lordship visited his tenants, but the ladies remained inside or rode about the countryside, under chaperon. To them, in their fine clothes, the peasants were less than dirt: they hardly noticed them in passing.

"A housekeeper, is it?" she said in awe. "And who else in that house?"

Bridie made a face. "Mrs. Balfe's a witch! She notices everything we do and makes us go over things twice, and calls us lazy. You won't like her, to be sure. We don't see much of the governess, a French lady, who eats with the family. She teaches the three boys. And, of course, there's cook—a grand old lady—and, now, there's a nurse."

"To look after the baby?"

"To look after both Mrs. Maddigan and the baby right now. She's poorly, I understand. But we'll be there soon. Get ready to jump out so we can walk to the back door."

Even approached from the back entrance, the house was grand and imposing: a miniature of the great houses back home, built of fawn-colored stone, with a large garden in the rear and a metal plate to wipe your feet on before entering at the solid oak door. Though their feet were hardly dirty from walking a single block, Bridie dutifully scraped her shoes, and Mary and Rosaleen followed her example. The wonderful odor of fresh-baked bread emanated from the kitchen, and after walking down a paneled hall they stopped for a moment to meet the cook, a gray-haired woman with bright-blue eyes who looked as if she consumed what she prepared with relish: she was almost round from one side to the other. Bridie whispered a hasty introduction and explained why Mary and her daughter were there, and Mrs. Lynch surveyed them with a small frown.

"I guess they'll do," she said at last. "I heard himself say that if a wet nurse was to be found, it wouldn't be from the Irish section because of the disease there. But they look clean enough, I guess. You can give it a try. We'll have to have Mrs. Balfe ask her first, though."

Bridie looked as though she were about to burst into tears. "I can't. I'm too afraid of her!"

The older woman patted her shoulder reassuringly. "It's all right, love, I'll speak to her. The doctor's with Mrs. Maddigan now, and herself has gone to her room. Give Mrs. Noonan and the little girl some tea. I'll be right back."

The cups were so delicate that Mary was afraid that if she did not break one, Rosaleen would: she felt extremely uncomfortable, and did not really enjoy the tea and the slice of buttered bread that went with it, though it would have been a great treat at any other time. Rosaleen ate daintily, concealing her real hunger, and handling the cup with both hands, with great care, staring around the large kitchen, looking at all its hanging pots and pans and gleaming cupboards. By the time Mary heard footsteps coming down the hallway, she was nearly shaking with tension and wished she had not come at all.

The door opened and a thin woman in gray, whose watery eyes matched her clothing, entered. She could only be Mrs. Balfe, Mary decided from the way the woman carried herself and from the disapproving expression on her face. Mary rose from the table as she entered and held her own chin in the same proud way, staring at the woman, eye to eye. After a moment, Mrs. Balfe raised an eyeglass to one eye from a little brooch on her bodice, and walked around Mary, checking her on every side. Feeling like a horse at auction, Mary wondered briefly if the woman would inspect her teeth.

"Well," Mrs. Balfe said at last, "it's too bad you're Irish. The master said specifically no Irish. But you look clean enough to me, and we haven't much time for choice. Does the child have to come with you?"

Mary nodded. "Where I go, Rosaleen goes. She's a good girl."

Mrs. Balfe watched the child put her cup gently and carefully into the saucer, then gave a loud sigh of disapproval and defeat. "We've been searching all day," she admitted. "All right. Come along with me."

They entered a spacious hallway with shining wooden floors and flowered carpets, curtained from the sun by heavy gold-braided velvet curtains. All the tables bore crystal vases full of flowers, and the curving banister was painted white. Mary, who had never been in the big house on the estate back home, could not have imagined such luxury and found herself treading softly up the carpeted stairs behind the straight back of Mrs. Balfe, who did not choose to speak again. Only Rosaleen's ungainly footwear made a clopping sound as they ascended to a floor with more carpets. The little girl lingered for a moment to look back down the staircase, staring at a large chandelier with faceted crystals hanging in clusters around the candles. Mrs. Balfe told them to wait a moment, without turning to look at them, and Mary had a chance to retrieve her daughter. The housekeeper entered the first large double doors at the top of the staircase while Mary and Rosaleen stood gaping around them.

"Oh, Ma, it's a fairy castle for sure!" Rosaleen whispered. "Have you ever seen anything so beautiful?"

"No," Mary said, holding the child's hand so she would not disappear again. "The world's unevenly divided, that's for sure."

"What does that mean?" Rosaleen asked. But the doors opened again at that moment and Mrs. Balfe motioned them in, closing the door behind herself as she left. Mary found herself in a bedroom of cream satin and lace, with touches of gold on the furniture. After one quick look around, she fastened her attention on the woman propped up in bed and held Rosaleen's hand tighter so she would behave. Mrs. Maddigan had been crying: her eyes were red and swollen in her pale face with its delicate features. And her thick blond hair, graying slightly at the temples, fell over her satin-clad shoulders. Clutching a lace handkerchief in her hand, she stared at them with such a lost look that Mary, quite suddenly and inexplicably, felt sorry for her, and knew she did not have to lift her own chin quite so high. The lady in the gold and satin bed was far more miserable than she.

Laura Maddigan's smooth white fingers had been worrying the handkerchief, but they stilled and stopped twisting as she looked at the woman and child at the door. Poor they were, she could tell that from the clothes and the little girl's worn, unsightly boots...boy's shoes...but there was something appealing about the tall, slender, full-bosomed woman that she had not anticipated. She was beautiful, too, with her head held high, not lowering her fine dark eyes to anyone, her dark-auburn hair braided like a halo around her striking face. She had a strong face with a firm jaw and remarkable bone structure. And the child—a little girl, like she had wanted—was thin as a scarecrow, but her deep-blue eyes were singularly intense, intelligent. The thought nearly brought the tears again. Last night she had cried herself to sleep, and every waking moment since had been spent in tears. Why should this happen to her? It would have been better if the baby had been born dead: she had even said that to her husband, John, in hysteria this morning. But sound and stable as he was, he had embraced her tightly, assured her everything would be all right: these things always worked out somehow. No life can be perfect. "Into every life a little rain must fall," and equally consoling phrases, until he calmed her down. But not until this moment, staring at the woman and child before her, had she felt any consolation.

"Mrs. . . . ." she began, but realized she had been too preoccupied to even listen to the woman's name. "I beg your pardon, I . . ."

"Noonan. Mary Noonan. And this is my daughter, Rosaleen."

The soft lilt of the words, so unlike the harshness of American English. Laura did like to have John's Irish servants about, for that alone: it was a soothing sound. A gentle, humorous dialect. But she was forgetting what the woman had come about.

"Mrs. Noonan, please step over here, closer to the bed. I'm not well...not well at all." As the woman moved smoothly to her side, Laura realized that she, too, was just out of childbed. She felt like a weakling in the presence of the woman's stoicism.

"I'm sorry about your child," she said softly. Mary Noonan only inclined her head in an accepting nod. "Really, should you be up so soon?"

Mary smiled faintly. "Mrs. Maddigan, in Ireland we don't stay abed after birthing. There are usually other children to look after."

"I have other children," Laura said fondly, realizing she was trying to put off the discussion that faced her. Oh, God, why wasn't John home to take care of this? Why hadn't she just left it all to Mrs. Balfe? Her fingers began to twist her handkerchief again. How much had the servants told her?

"Mrs. Noonan," she said as clearly as she could, "you've probably been informed about our...situation. You have, haven't you?"

"I've been told your poor little baby hasn't had any milk."

Nothing was going to be spared her, then, Laura thought almost furiously, angry at fate and at herself.

"The child...a little boy," she said carefully, but the tears rushed out before she could finish. "The baby isn't right!" she cried out. "The doctor says he'll be an idiot!"

She closed her eyes and listened to the long silence. Then she felt a rough hand enfold her own on the smooth counterpane, holding it strongly.

"Such things happen, Mrs. Maddigan," the lilting voice consoled her. "When they do, we have to accept them and do the best we can. I think, perhaps, that if my baby had lived...he wouldn't have been right, either."

Laura opened her eyes and met the woman's steady, accepting gaze. She put her own smooth hand over the one that clasped her other one. "It doesn't repulse you?" she asked in a small, breathless voice. "I'm telling you the child doesn't *look* right. He's...odd."

Mary Noonan took a deep breath. "Sure, I've heard they can be the sweetest ones of all," she said softly. "But we won't have a baby for long, will we, if he doesn't get fed?"

"Thank you," Laura said, putting her head back on the pillow as the woman patted her hand. "You're right, of course. I'll see that you're well paid, Mrs. Noonan. And Mrs. Balfe will find a comfortable room for you near the nursery."

"We're to live here, then?" Mary asked, startled.

"Of course. Where else?" Laura asked, afraid she had lost her.

"I hadn't thought about it," Mary confessed. "Of course, I'll have to stay nearby to feed the wee fellow. Is it all right, ma'am...I mean, Rosaleen staying with me? I don't like to leave her down in that area...the children mistreat her."

"Anything you want," Laura said with weary relief; then she remembered her first impression of them. "Send Mrs. Balfe to me, please. I want her to get that child some decent shoes."

Mary was taken up another flight of stairs, where she heard the shrill wailing of an infant. "The nursery's on this floor," Mrs. Balfe said. "This is where you'll be staying. I'll take you to the baby first, so we can have some peace in this house. He's been squalling like that for hours."

There was not the least compassion in her voice, and she confirmed Mary's suspicion about the reason, when she stopped in front of the door the cries were coming from and did not go further.

"Nurse is inside. I don't want to see that baby unless I have to. Did Mrs. Maddigan tell you he was...?"

"Yes." Mary nodded. "I'll go to him now, if you please. The poor little mite is starving."

Mrs. Balfe stepped back and indicated the doorknob with her outstretched hand. Without a further glance at her, Mary opened the door and walked into the room, and Rosaleen followed close at her heels. An old woman with a white head covering was standing at the window, and she turned suddenly when she heard the door open. There were lines of grief etched into her face, and she looked as if she too had been crying.

"I'm Mary Noonan. I've been sent to feed the baby," Mary said, already loosening the string on her gray peasant blouse. If she had expected the old woman to be consoled, she was wrong. The worn hazel eyes met hers without feeling, but the nurse indicated the lace-trimmed bassinet.

"It would be better to let him die," the woman said, to Mary's shock. "It's amazing, isn't it? Three fine, bright boys...and then this. You can tell just to look at him he's not right. I've seen it before, a long time ago, but the baby died within a month. They're prone to lung disease, you know."

Mary was hardly listening. She had already lifted the small demanding bundle from the bassinet and was cradling it against her. Rosaleen pulled at her skirt, so she could see the baby, too, and Mary leaned down and moved the soft receiving blanket from his face. He was still crying lustily, and he looked like any other baby with his face all screwed up and red.

"Ah, the little darlin'," Rosaleen said, almost in a whisper. "Ma, we have a babby after all."

Mary went to the rocking chair by the window and put the infant to her breast, throwing her shawl across the front of her for modesty. At first he seemed to have difficulty sucking, but Mary adjusted his position until soon he was pulling away hungrily at her nipple, while she rocked the chair slowly. The absence of sound in the room was total, except for the creaking of the chair on the hardwood floor.

Mary forgot about the nurse, was conscious only of the baby at her breast and Rosaleen beside her, waiting to hold him when he had finished nursing. But then she heard the old woman's footstep on the floor behind her, saw her shadow fall across the wall.

"I've been here for thirteen years," the nurse said. "I've taken care of all of them, and I love them like my own. But I can't abide caring for this. It breaks my heart, but I have to go. The boys are old enough to do without me now: they'll soon be off to school. Are you willing to stay and look after it? If you are, there are some things I must tell you."

"I don't know if Mrs. Maddigan will want me, after the nursing's done," Mary replied. "If she did, I'd have to make arrangements. I've a family of my own. My sister would have to look after Liam and—"

"She'll want you," the nurse said acidly. "Who else would take such a job? But I must warn you that you'll probably be confined to this room, or the upstairs here, as long as the child lives. Mrs. Maddigan married beneath her, you see. I was her nurse, too. I love her like my own daughter, but her family won't have anything to do with her. They're proper folk—not as rich as Mr. Maddigan, but with an old name. And Laura's proud and stubborn. She won't want them to know about this idiot. Mrs. Noonan, you'll be confined here like a keeper. No one will ever visit, least of all Laura. If you feel you can accept that kind of existence..."

Beneath her shawl, Mary transferred the baby to her other breast. "It isn't as bad as you make out, ma'am," she said. "People change, and they're full of love. I don't know whether I'll be staying or not, but if I do, I'm sure his mother will grow to love him."

"They can't even be toilet-trained, you know."

Mary did not reply. She did not turn her head when she heard the old nurse leave the room. When the time came, there would be decisions to make, but not right now. She was here for only as long as it took to get the baby weaned. With the sun streaking warmly through the sheer lace panels on the window, she brought the quiet little boy out from under her shawl and looked at him, as Rosaleen strained over the arm of the chair to see, too.

He had a funny little face, a remarkable one. She had seen some like it in the old country. The eyes were wide-set, a little slanted, and his wide pink tongue protruded slightly from his mouth. There was nothing wrong with the shape of his head, from which soft blond hair grew. When she touched his little hand, she noticed that the thumb was short and pressed inward toward the palm. A gas pain made the corner of his mouth move, as though he were smiling.

Rosaleen laughed, voicing what Mary was thinking at that moment. "Ma, he's such a love! Did you see him smile? Why do they all say such bad things? He's beautiful."

"Yes, poor baby," Mary said, putting him to her shoulder and patting his tiny back. "He'll probably be kinder than some I've met today, even if he hasn't all his wits about him."

Chapter 8

THE MADDIGAN boys were about the same age as Doirin's, but they could not have been more different. Only rarely was romping or yelling heard, and they spent a good part of the day with the governess, whom Mary and Rosaleen had never seen. Though the classroom was on the same floor as the nursery, the boys must have been told to keep away, because they marched right down the steps after classes. They all favored Laura, Mary thought, fair and blond and delicately featured, though the two older boys had their father's dark eyes. Her first encounter with those eyes, hard and unyielding, had left her shaking. If Mrs. Balfe had not intervened, Mary felt she and Rosaleen would have been thrown immediately into the street.

Trays had been sent up to them the first evening they arrived, and they would have starved if Bridie had not crept up to take the food off the dumbwaiter and deliver it to their room. Because of the hollow cheerlessness of the huge nursery, Mary and Rosaleen had moved the bassinet into the room assigned to them by Mrs. Balfe. The room was small, but it had a double bed in it, along with a chest of drawers, a mirror and washbasin and pitcher. Compared to where they had come from, it was elegance itself. By seven o'clock, however, they were very hungry indeed, and Rosaleen had to use the privy and was afraid to go downstairs alone. If Bridie had not thought of them, the night would have been even more un-comfortable than it proved to be later.

Bridie rapped on their door, after not finding them in the nursery, and when Mary opened the door, the maid was standing there balancing their trays, one on each arm, in desperate danger of dropping one of them.

"Grab it!" she cried and Mary moved quickly to catch the teetering tray. "Sure, your food's as cold as ice. Didn't Mrs. Balfe tell you it'd be sent up on the dumbwaiter?"

"She may have," Mary admitted as the girl accompanied her into the room and laid the other tray on the chest of drawers. "If she did, I didn't know what it was."

Bridie giggled. "I'll show you where it is. The food's sent up from the kitchen, you see. A bell rings when it arrives."

Mary looked blank. "Oh." Then, she put her hand on Bridie's arm. "And what about the...conveniences? Is there a privy in the back yard? Rosaleen's had to..."

Bridie walked over to the bed, leaned over and pulled out a dark wooden box, opening it to reveal a chamberpot. "You use this," she said. Rosaleen immediately lifted her skirt and squatted down, making a hollow trickling sound into the pot.

"Does it stay here, then?" Mary asked suspiciously. "Right here in the room with us? Do we empty it somewhere?"

"No," Bridie said flatly. "I do that."

"You! But it isn't decent having someone else..."

"It's the way it's done," the girl said; then she became quite serious. "Look, Mrs. Noonan, if I was you, I'd eat up in a hurry. The master's home, and he's fit to be tied."

"Mr. Maddigan? He's the one who didn't want an Irish wet nurse."

"Yes. And, kind as he usually is to the mistress, he's raging in there...absolutely roarin'."

Mary crossed herself quickly. "You think he'll shove us out, then?"

"He can't, can he...unless he has someone else? But I think you might be expectin' him any time, now. I have to leave. Rosaleen, close the lid and put that back under the bed!"

They were left for, perhaps, half an hour in peace, nervously eating their dinner, which, though cold, was more food than they had ever seen at one time. Beef and potatoes and gravy and some little green things that tasted rather sweet. There was even a pudding, of sorts, rather mushy but good. Mary ate everything, because she knew she must make milk.

Rosaleen finished everything on her plate except for the suspicious-looking green peas.

They had expected a loud knock on the door to announce Mr. Maddigan's arrival; what they heard instead was a man's voice roaring, "Where are you, woman? Where is my child?"

Mary opened the door cautiously. "If you please, sir, we're in here."

The tall man standing in the hallway turned on his heel and was upon her at once, but he stopped short when he saw her face in the light.

"What's your name?" he demanded, his dark eyes hard. "I left strict orders..."

"Mary," she said, opening the door wide to let him enter and look into the bassinet. "You don't want Irish—like the rest of them. But you're Irish yourself, Mr. Maddigan, and so are all your servants."

"This is different! Times are different! I've seen the shantytown you've all made at Fort Hill and the North End. You're all half sick...I've seen it. I don't want typhus in my house!"

"Typhus? Oh, the fever. But, sir, we've been here for five months now and there's been no fever."

"Those shanties are pesthouses. How do I know what diseases you have?" She backed away from him and, reluctantly, he glanced toward the bassinet. "He's quiet now, at least."

"He is that." Mary smiled. "Would you like to hold him?"

Matthew Maddigan drew back sharply. "No!" He caught sight of Rosaleen, staring at him with disbelieving blue eyes. "Who is this child?"

"My daughter," Mary said nervously. "I brought her along because the children in the building set upon her like hounds every time she goes out."

"They're a nasty bunch of hoodlums. I've seen them myself. Dirty, snotty-nosed. Disgraceful—"

"Sir!"

His invective stopped in midsentence, he turned to stare at her, starting at the braid around her head and moving to her toes. "I beg your pardon," he said suddenly, wiping his forehead. "You seem clean enough, and your daughter, too. The fact is, Mary, I'm desperately ashamed of my countrymen right now. They're making a mess of this city. Boston wasn't ready for them. I'm not ready for them."

"No more are we ready for you," she said softly. "Have you tried to help them? Has anyone tried to help? Not even the Church, from my observation. We think Boston is hell."

The man's hard eyes widened, and something like amusement came into them. "You have the old spunk, haven't you? By God, I haven't seen it since I left home. All I've seen is sniveling and whining and laziness, even from my own servants. That's how I've tried to help. That and getting people out of Ireland before they starve, but to go to New York, mind you...not to come here! I have two ships running back and forth, constantly."

Mary did not take in anything else he said. She stood before him in silence, studying his heavy face and hard eyes, watching a stream of perspiration run from his temple to his jaw, where he wiped it away again. After a minute or so, he became aware of her scrutiny and noticed her silence, and asked, "What's the matter?"

"Your wife's name is Laura," she said.

"Yes, yes, so what? Are you daft, woman?"

"Is one of your ships named after her?"

"Why, yes. Wait! What are you doing?"

Mary was putting on her shawl. Looking him directly in the eyes, she said, "I'm leaving. I don't want to work for you."

He was dumbfounded. "Wait, I didn't say you had to go! In fact, I'm rather favorably impressed. I—"

"Mr. Maddigan, we came over on that hell-ship of yours. We spent eight weeks in its filthy hold, living on one small portion of beans a day. There were seven deaths on board, Mr. Maddigan—seven! And not all of them from fever, either. The old folks went first. Is that the way you're helping your countrymen? Sure it's a noble man you are, with your fine house and servants and food," she said, giving the tray a shove. "With two ships going 'back and forth' killing passengers, leaving the ones that live in their putrid holds, without any sanitation at all and not a cover to put over them in the cold. Your ship saved us from the famine, sure enough—for every shilling we could get together, which went into your pocket! You'll have to get someone else to care for the baby, God love him. I won't work for you at all!"

He had to restrain her physically, by taking her by the shoulders and spinning her around to face him. His eyes were like flints, his face looked haggard: he had ceased to sweat.

"Is what you're saying true?" he demanded. The expression in her dark eyes answered him. "I didn't know. I swear to God, I didn't know. Do you think I'd let a ship bearing my wife's name treat people like that?" His face became grim, businesslike. "This will be looked into. The *Laura* made port in Boston more often than New York last winter, and now I see why. I'm a banker, you see: I don't know anything about ships."

"For observing how the Irish are living everywhere in town, you don't bother to see to the arrival of your ships, it seems," Mary remarked, taking Rosaleen's hand and trying to pass him in the doorway.

A small cry came from the bassinet, and Mr. Maddigan said quickly, "You're not going, are you? I said I'd look into the matter. For God's sake, woman, I said I approved of you! Nurse has left and my wife's in a terrible state. Stay on and I'll pay you four dollars a month and keep. You won't beat that anywhere—it's more than my servants make."

"I didn't come here for the money, so I won't be staying on for that," Mary spat. "It's the baby I'm concerned about, since no one else seems to be. The poor little..."

"Then stay for him. You're right, there's no one else to do it. You can't just leave him, Mary. You aren't that kind of woman."

"Ma, we can't leave the babby," Rosaleen said, tugging at her hand. "The man's right, Ma."

Mary stood stock-still, considering the situation. Perhaps Mr. Maddigan did not know what went on aboard his ships: they were just an investment to him, after all. She had been dropped into a family in crisis, though she doubted very much if they really cared for anyone else. She thought of Brian, still out of work, and she thought of the basement apartment. Most of all, she thought of the baby, but she must not let that interfere with her judgment too much. Mr. Maddigan was a hard man; she would show him that she was hard, too.

"I'll stay," she said, "for five dollars a month."

That would almost cover the rent for the basement, and there would be two less mouths to feed. What the boys brought home and what Mrs. Dugan sent from Tomas's wages should make up the balance for living expenses until Brian was able to work. She did not take her gaze from Mr. Maddigan's face when she spoke. She had expected anger again, even refusal: what she saw was that glint of humor again, though he did not smile.

"By Jesus, I'd forgotten what a real Irish woman is like," he said. "The job's yours, for as long as you want it. There's only one thing: when my wife's physician comes, I want him to examine both of you."

* * *

Mary did not see Mr. Maddigan again for a while; but a week later, she was called to Laura Maddigan's room through Mrs. Balfe. Leaving Rosaleen to mind the baby, Mary followed the housekeeper down the stairs, though she knew where Laura's room was located. Mrs. Balfe knocked on the door, and when an airy voice said, 'Come in,' the housekeeper left Mary to enter alone. Mrs. Maddigan was fully dressed, sitting at her vanity table, adjusting the curls around her face. She still looked pale. There were dark smudges beneath her eyes, and deep lines from her nose to the corners of her lips. When she saw Mary's reflection in the mirror, she turned.

"You must have thought I'd forgotten you, Mrs. Noonan," Laura said. "I haven't, not for one moment. But I just got up yesterday. My doctor gave me so many sleeping drafts, I haven't been myself. I guess he thought I was losing my senses: maybe I was. But this morning I realized how inconsiderate I'd been. That's why I summoned you. Please, come closer and sit down."

Mary did as she was told, wondering what was coming next: perhaps Mrs. Maddigan would come to visit the baby after all. She could see the ghost of fragile beauty still in the lady's face, though she looked very sad. She did not ask after her baby at all.

"It occurred to me that you must have things to take care of: you will need some time off. And I want to give you an advance on your pay. The servants get a half day off every week, and one full day once a month. However, this would be inconvenient in your position. So I thought we should work something out together."

The woman was not going to mention the baby: she would not acknowledge he existed. Well, she was not going to be allowed to live in such a fantasy world. They would approach this problem like adult human beings or Mary would have none of it.

"As a matter of fact, yes, I do have things to attend to. My family must wonder what's become of me. I left a message, but that's the last they heard. I've been thinking about it, too. With the weather so fair, I was thinking, if you have a pram, I could take the baby along for the sun. Unless you object to his going to the North End."

Laura's face looked stricken; apparently she had hoped the subject would not be mentioned. Her hands twisted nervously in the lap of her light cotton dress. "Whatever you think is

117

best," she said at last. "I'll leave the whole thing to you. My husband and I have complete faith in your judgment." She smiled feebly, revealing even, white teeth.

Mary did not return the smile: she searched the woman's gray eyes instead. Sitting there, solid and strong, she could not accept the weakness in the pampered woman at the vanity: she would not accept it.

"Mrs. Maddigan," she said, "I'm just a woman like any other. I don't know if my judgment's always good, and I'm not prepared to take full responsibility for the child upstairs. What you're feeling is pride and self-pity, and there isn't a bit of compassion in it. When I lost my child, I felt guilt, pure and simple. Guilt for not wanting him in the first place, because we were so poor. Guilt for his little life being snuffed out because of the famine and my poor diet. You have nothing like that to face. The baby upstairs is nature gone wrong, Mrs. Maddigan. He isn't a judgment on you: he should not be an embarrassment. I love him. I love looking after him. But I want to speak about him in the open."

Color suffused Laura Maddigan's face: her hands stopped fidgeting. She looked away for a moment, but her eyes were drawn back to Mary's. Under ordinary circumstances, Mary felt that tears would have been her next defense, but she dared not cry in front of her.

"You can't just shuffle him off," Mary added. "For instance, don't you think it appropriate that he have a name? Or aren't you going to have him christened?"

From Laura's reaction, it was obvious that she had not given it a thought. The full horror of her rejection began to show on her face; for a moment, Mary thought she was going to collapse. But, almost imperceptibly, her body straightened, the narrow shoulders squared beneath the dainty fabric of her frock, and her gaze finally met Mary's directly.

"You're right," she said in a choked voice. "I've been dreadful. Only thinking of myself. Of what my family would say. You see...well, I can't explain all that, but when I was in such an hysteria a few days ago, my mother wouldn't even come."

"You're a grown woman, a mother yourself," Mary remarked. "It's too bad when families have fallings-out, but it isn't a tragedy, is it? Maybe your mother's just proud, too." Then, more brightly, "What shall we name him?"

Laura hesitated. "Is he very ugly?" she finally asked.

"Haven't you seen him, then?"

"No, they took him away at once. The doctor could tell that he was..." She groped for a word, and Mary offered her no help. "That he wasn't right. That wasn't fair, was it?"

"No, not at all," Mary agreed. "He isn't ugly—he's very sweet."

Laura's gaze was directed upward, as though she could see through the floor into the nursery. She clasped her hands tightly again and bit her lip. "No, not yet. But I will, soon. I swear I will! In the meantime, we'll find him a name. I had Ian in mind, but it would hardly suit, would it? Do you have any ideas, Mrs. Noonan?"

"The decision's yours, ma'am, just like the judgments." Mary smiled. "I'm sure you'll find him a good name." She rose from the chair with deliberation, feeling she had accomplished something with Laura Maddigan, and liking her much more than she had ten minutes before.

"If it's all right with you," she said, "I'll find the pram and we'll go for a walk to see my family."

Laura nodded, her face more peaceful than it had been when Mary entered the room. "I'll think of a name," she assured Mary. "A sweet name, Mrs. Noonan."

"You do that," Mary smiled at her. "Rosaleen can't go on just calling him 'babby,' can she? She's that fond of the little fellow."

Chapter 9

THOUGH THE large house seemed to run itself, it soon became apparent to Mary that this was not the case; and, as Bridie had told her, Laura Maddigan was not its real mistress. Fragile and kind, Laura lived in a world surrounded by the four walls of her bed-sitting room, seldom leaving her chamber, except to go shopping. A flighty, sheltered woman, she was wildly extravagant, and Mr. Maddigan gave her everything she wanted, whether it was for herself or someone else. The real power in the domestic sphere was Mrs. Balfe: the servants lived in terror of her. Thin and wiry, born in New England, neither her accent nor her sympathies were Irish, in spite of her name. Within the first few days at the house, Mary and Rosaleen had been introduced to the back stairs, which descended, rather narrowly and darkly, to the area of the kitchen and the back door: Mrs. Balfe made sure that everyone in the household kept her place. And though Mary's position was ambiguous and she was frequently summoned to Laura's room, she was nothing but a rather low-class servant to the housekeeper.

During the first weeks, when things were still so strange, Mary had no inclination to challenge the housekeeper's authority and probably would never have done so if it had not been for Rosaleen. It was almost impossible to keep a child her age in one room with herself and the baby all day long, even allowing for the long lessons and games they had together. Often when Mary and the baby took a nap in the afternoon Rosaleen slipped out to explore the forbidden territory of the rest of the house. Particularly fascinated with the large entry hall and the shimmering chandelier, Rosaleen did not keep the rules about the stairs, either, and several times she was returned by Mrs. Balfe to the room with a loud knock on the door which woke both Mary and the baby.

"If you can't control this child, she will have to go," the housekeeper said, though Mary recognized her words as a bluff, because she knew she had the protection of Laura. "If the room's too confined, move into the nursery, as you should. There's room enough for the child to play there without bothering anyone except Mrs. Maddigan, whose chamber is below."

"Can she play in the garden?" Mary asked, holding her temper.

Mrs. Balfe blinked her watery gray eyes. "I have no objection, provided she makes no noise and uses the back stairway. And, of course, avoids the Maddigan boys."

With a child as outgoing as Rosaleen, and so accustomed to the company of no one but boys, the latter condition was impossible to meet. Not only did she hover around their classroom, listening through the door, she frequently waylaid them on the stairs or in the garden. Finally, even the oldest boy, Matthew, who had made a face at her, first endured and then welcomed the little girl's lively presence. The middle brother, Harold, gentle-natured himself, followed Matthew's example, teasing the little girl affectionately, insisting she have tea with them. Only the youngest, John, kept to himself shyly, reading books and seldom communicating with her. Though outraged by the boys' invitation to Rosaleen to join them for tea, Mrs. Balfe found that she was powerless regarding the dark-haired little girl. When she protested, Matthew, who was ten and the apple of his mother's eye, stood up at the table and threatened to speak to his mother. Later, seeing how easily he had won that victory over the housekeeper, he reserved the same threat when anything concerning Rosaleen was questioned. He had never had a sister, and he and Harold were enchanted by the tiny, pretty child, who chattered on so readily and was so quick to smile at their jokes.

Mary was pleased with Rosaleen, not so much for befriending the Maddigan boys as for the way she seemed, without difficulty, to thrive in her present surroundings. Some of it, she realized, had to do with the nourishing food, which made the girl fill out and grow rosy; but much of it could be attributed to the light and air and fine living. One day Mary overheard Rosaleen, who approached the boys when they marched out of their classroom. She was appalled: her door was open because she had just collected their trays from the dumbwaiter, and she listened.

"I can talk like you do," the little girl said triumphantly. *"Je m'appelle Rosaleen. Qu'est-ce que vous dites? Honi soit qui mal y pense. Je vous aime beaucoup...."*

What on earth was the child doing? Mary wondered, her hand going to her throat. It was not Gaelic; perhaps it was the nonsense talk Rosaleen was fond of using with her dolly. The response of the boys alarmed her further, and she went to the door. They were standing like little men in their long-trousered summer suits staring at Rosaleen in amazement.

Suddenly, the oldest one began to laugh. "Her accent's better than yours, Harry! I doubt she knows what she's saying, but she's doing it well enough!"

"Where did you learn that?" Harold asked, indulgently for a nine-year-old. "Do you know what it is?"

"Français," Rosaleen replied, with a smile that showed her dimple. "I've been listening outside the door!"

All three of the boys laughed, then; even the quiet, mousy John smiled, holding his books to his chest. The governess appeared in the doorway behind them, dark-haired, in a gray dress with a lace collar, a puzzled expression on her sharp French face.

"Mamselle!" Harold cried. "You really must hear this! Rosaleen, talk to Mamselle Boucher."

Shyly, the little girl repeated by rote what she had heard; the governess's face took on a look of surprise, then softened somewhat when the boys explained how Rosaleen had learned it. "She has a good ear," she said in a thickly accented voice. "It's the little Irish girl, yes? How long have you been listening?"

"Every day," Rosaleen said, averting her eyes, the color rising in her face. "I sit on the floor when the door's open—with my back against the wall, so you can't see me. Do I have to stop?"

The woman's face became slightly sad. "No, *chérie.* I see no reason to stop, as long as Mrs. Balfe does not find you there. You'd make a good pupil."

At the mention of Mrs. Balfe's name, Mary appeared in

the hall, apologizing for her daughter's behavior. The governess stiffened, nodded her head and passed on down the stairs with the boys, who looked back over their shoulders, still smiling.

Mary thought that was the end of it, until there was a soft tapping on her door after dinner two weeks later. Worried that it was the housekeeper again, Mary smoothed her hair and nervously opened the door, taking a step backward when she saw Mr. Maddigan there. "Good evening, sir," she said, wondering what could have brought him upstairs. Then, thinking it must be the baby, she opened the door wide to let him enter her room. "He's sleeping. He sleeps a lot, the little lamb. Has Mrs. Maddigan decided on a name for him yet?"

He glanced only briefly at the baby in the crib. "She'll see you about it tomorrow. I believe she's decided on Philip. Rather pretentious, I think, but it doesn't belong to anyone else in the family. I didn't come about him, Mrs. Noonan—Mary, isn't it?" He cleared his throat. "I came about your daughter."

Oh, God! Mary thought. What's Rosaleen been up to now? She nodded, and was about to make an apology, when he continued.

"My sons fancy her quite a bit. She's a pretty, merry thing: I'm fond of her myself. She's even bringing John out of his shell a little. Well, I like to see my boys happy, Mary, and, though this is a little unconventional..."

"Un...con...what, sir?"

He looked embarrassed. "Unusual?" he asked, waiting a second to see if she understood that word. He was relieved that she did. "The boys—especially Harry—he's a good-hearted lad—would like your daughter to sit in on their lessons. Harry says she has a quick mind, and it's a shame to waste it. He says she picked up on French very rapidly."

"Sure what will Rosaleen ever need French for?" Mary asked frankly.

"God knows," he replied, equally honestly. "What will my own boys use it for? I don't know it myself. But, there you are. It's the way it's done here. And, when it comes right down to it, I guess everything you learn has some purpose. It's better than being ignorant."

"Rosaleen isn't ignorant, sir. She can read and write quite well. And she knows more about figures than I do."

"Well, there you have it. The child's smart." He appeared

to relax. "The boys are doing mathematics, too. No harm in her sitting in, is there?"

Mary started to bring up the matter of Mrs. Balfe; then she quickly realized she was speaking to the highest authority in the house. "No, sir, no harm. I'm concerned about her education. She'll be six next week and it's time she went to school, but no Catholic school's opened yet, and—"

"What's that got to do with it?" he asked rather harshly. "Jesus, you're all the same! Plunged into a sea of ignorance because the Church won't condone our good public schools. I—"

"I'd rather not discuss the Church, Mr. Maddigan, you being an Orangeman and all. Rosaleen can go to classes with your sons."

"An Orangeman, now, is it?" he exclaimed. His dark eyes began to twinkle; then, teasing, he said, "And why isn't my color green like yours? They've only given me the red, black and blue here."

"I thought it was white—the American flag, I mean."

"Not for any Irishman, it isn't. I was referring to being bruised, my dear. Why can't I have green?"

Mary began to feel nervous; if she did not know better, she would think he was flirting with her. But it could not be that: he was just having a bit of fun at her expense, trying to get her Irish up.

"You're a Protestant and you're from the North: nothing could be more Orange than that, Mr. Maddigan. I don't know why we say Orange, but we do."

"From the conquest of William of Orange, my dear, who freed us from the English oppressors, for a while. But I don't belong to the lodge, and never have. The goodness of the Orange hasn't been 'slammed, crammed and jammed into me so I wear it like a badge of pain.' I don't hate Catholics. I may despise them a little, but I'd never hurt them. As a matter of fact, goodness isn't really one of my strong points, but I'd like to help you, Mary."

"Goodness is sorry hard for everyone," Mary admitted, uncertain how to take the remarks of this large, sweating man. It must be all the stairs that do it, she thought. Both times she'd seen him, there had been perspiration on his heavy, florid face.

"Tell me about your husband."

She was so taken back that she knew it was revealed on

of course.

'I, but she's

'asses, I'll go

she quickly got her reaction under control.

...ike to know about him, sir?"

...living apart, and most men wouldn't

...go to a tenement in the North

...in the afternoon, when he

completely surprised

...ght, or cook. No:

...s the most

...'t live

at the flat, too, then."

He chuckled. "Yes, I know. I dropped into Dugan's Pub the other day and met him. And his brother, what's-his-name, too. Fine-looking lads they are. Now, under the circumstances, you aren't going to tell me there's any great attachment in your life, are you?"

She realized abruptly that they were alone on the third floor. Rosaleen had gone down to play with the boys in the garden before it got dark, and they often brought their games inside for a while before they went to bed. Mary had an unreal feeling, a sort of premonition, but she knew she was just putting two and two together. No employer paid that much attention to a servant, sought out her husband in a place like Dugan's, unless there was something else on his mind. And there was a teasing, warm expression in his dark eyes, which flicked hotly from her face to her full breasts and small waist. She had heard stories of landlords and their sons back home trying, and sometimes succeeding, in having their way with servants. Straightening her shoulders, she looked him right in the eyes as innocently as possible.

"I thank you for your concern, Mr. Maddigan. My feelings are my own, and you may not understand them. Yes, I am deeply attached. I've loved only one man all my life. Poverty and necessity sometimes bring temporary separations. Sure, whoever gave you so much information neglected to tell you that I visit Dugan's when I go home, too. In a household as large as ours, nearly everyone works—even living in if they have to."

She saw at once that her oblique confession, which she had never made to anyone before, and about which she felt excited and guilty, had the proper effect on her employer. He moved back almost at once to put his hand on the doorknob. "I admire you very much," he said hastily. "My wife wishes to keep you on to look after the baby as long as possible. We

want to make things more ... to the flat, when Rosaleen
Rosaleen may begin cla...

"Thank you, sir. ..ys had decided to give her daugh-
lively, and if she d...
after her."

Mary to ..... y and had invited her brother and cousin
was in ...et by the thought of the Noonan boys appearing
ter a ...
Da..

in their old street clothes and penniless because she had
turned her whole salary over to Veronica, Mary confided her
trepidations to Mrs. Lynch, the fat cook, over a cup of tea in
the kitchen the evening before, and the good woman was
quick to come to her aid.

After ascertaining the ages of the boys and their size, cook
said quietly, "Sure, there's a bundle of old clothes waiting to
be picked up for charity. Some of the young masters' things
must be in there. We'll just look and maybe take a few things
for charity ourselves."

"But wouldn't the boys recognize their old clothes?"

"Is anyone at home quick with a needle?" the woman said
and twinkled. Mary had mentioned that Veronica sewed well.
"The fabrics won't matter, if the styles are changed around
a bit, and a patch of velvet put on here and there."

"Thank you, Mrs. Lynch," Mary breathed out in relief.
"Darin and Liam are smaller than the older boys. Indeed,
they're smaller than even John, living the way they do. I
could take the clothes by in the morning."

Mary took the two winter suits to the flat, where she found
things going as badly as ever. There was food in the house,
and the rent was paid, but the battle of Michael was still
going on. Doirin insisted that Liam, to whom she had begun
to cling more than to her own sons, would not be interested
in coming to the Maddigans. "He's a religious boy, and not
full of high and mighty ideas," she said.

"He's my son," Mary told her, "and he's invited to a party
for his sister. He'll be there, do you understand? Do you think
you can do anything with the suits, Veronica?"

"It wouldn't be easy," Veronica confessed, stretching the
material, examining pockets and buttons. "I think the best
thing I can do is trade them to Mr. Rabinsky for different
ones. These are marvelous material. I'm sure we could work
something out."

126

"Fine. Anything," Mary said, close to distraction, wondering what Rosaleen herself would wear. "Just make certain they're clean and look decent and that their hair's combed and their nails aren't dirty. And make them polish their shoes. Veronica, I hate to ask, but have you half a dollar for some material for something for Rosaleen? I'd like to get a bit of ribbon, too."

Veronica went to the jar at the window, which was nearly half full of small coins. "You should keep something for yourself out of your own pay," she said, putting fifty cents into her palm. "You must have some needs. It's daft to give us the whole thing. Both the men are working at the pub now, and Mrs. Dugan's sending over part of Tomas's pay."

"Mary's more than looked after," Doirin said tartly. "I can't imagine what she'd need any money for."

Mary turned to Veronica. "You're right, Veronica. As long as things are going all right here, I'll keep a dollar a month for Rosaleen and me. The weather's getting warmer, and we'll need lighter things."

She would never have taken the money if Doirin had not interfered: it made her proud to help keep the family, though only her small son was living with them, now. She was still smarting from Doirin's meanness as she brought the pram in the back door of the Maddigan's house. A small package, containing the material for Rosaleen's dress and a yard of blue ribbon for her hair, was tucked into the carriage. The first person she encountered was an excited Mrs. Lynch.

"Thank God you're back," she said. "Mrs. Balfe's been down here twice! The mistress wants to see you. I told the housekeeper you'd taken the baby to the Common for some sun, since it isn't your day off. Hurry, now! I'll look after the little fellow. Were the suits all right?"

"Well..." Mary began, but the older woman bustled her off without an answer, in terror of Mrs. Balfe, who might appear again at any moment.

When Mary entered Laura's chamber, her eyes were dazzled by what she saw: bolts and bolts of the finest material, from batiste to satin and bombazine strewn almost carelessly on the tables and falling to the floor. Laura was standing on a chair in a full-skirted afternoon gown of sheer Indian cotton, turning gradually as the dressmaker, a dark woman with a tight black chignon, pinned the hem. Laura fussed with the neckline before a full-length mirror, her graying yellow curls falling down the sides of her face. When she saw Mary, Laura turned toward her quickly, much to the dressmaker's distress.

"I've been waiting for you!" she exclaimed pleasantly, waving aside Mary's explanation as though she did not want the baby discussed before the dressmaker. "I have the most exciting news. My husband told me this morning that the nursery is to be redecorated! We'll have such fun. You can keep your own room, too, of course, but you and Rosaleen will stay in the nursery. It's a nice big airy room, but he says it's too drab, and I must agree with him. We'll lighten it with white curtains and pretty coverlets. Oh, Madame Hurotte, this is Mrs. Noonan, the woman I was telling you about. Mary, madame is going to make some uniforms for you, too."

"Uniforms?" Mary replied dumbly, imagining herself dressed in black with a stiff white apron and cap like the maids. She preferred the loose peasant blouse covered by her shawl for nursing. Laura continued to pull at the crossed-over neckline of her dress.

"Are you sure this is right?" Laura asked the dressmaker. "It's uncomfortable. Can't something be done about it?"

"It's the fashion," Madame Hurotte replied through the pins in her mouth. "Please don't move about so much, Mrs. Maddigan."

Laura succumbed to the woman's authority with a sigh. "I wish fashion didn't change so much," she said a little petulantly. "My mother didn't have to go through all this. The narrow, princess gowns were in vogue then, without all these skirts! Of course, that went too far, too. At least in Europe, where so much bosom was shown. Mother absolutely wouldn't lower her neckline that far." She laughed, remembering. "None of the Americans would. They wore scarves across their shoulders to go to a ball. It isn't that I don't like the full skirts," she put in quickly, fluffing hers out at the sides. "It's just all the petticoats underneath them. Even in lawn, I'll swelter in the summer. What's the use of wearing a thin material and then putting it over cotton petticoats?"

There was a faint knock at the lower part of the door and, forgetting her talk about fashions, Laura smiled. "That will be your daughter, Mary. Come in, dear!" she called. "I asked her to come, too. She must have a birthday dress."

Rosaleen opened the door cautiously and stood transfixed by the abundance of fabrics and color she saw, not responding when Mary motioned her to her side. "Rosaleen," Mary finally said to attract the child's attention. Her hands were dirty, and Mary knew what a toucher the little girl was: it wouldn't do to get fingerprints all over the bolts of cloth.

When her daughter was safely by her side, Mary said to Laura, "It's very kind of you, ma'am, but she doesn't need one, really. I bought material to make her one myself."

Laura's face fell at the refusal; Mary was soon to learn that Laura did not like her bounty refused. Giving provided Laura with almost the only excitement she had, and she was like a child about it. "Oh, I'd hoped...madame and I had decided on a pattern, and...Rosaleen, dear, don't touch that. You've ink all over your hands. Go to the basin and wash them like a good little girl. Didn't the boys tell you about pen wipers?"

Mary thought quickly to extricate herself from the awkwardness of the situation. "I'll get the fabric, ma'am," she said hastily. "If you like, you can have it made to your pattern." Without asking further permission, she left the room and ran down the back stairs to retrieve the package from the pram. In the time she was gone, Rosaleen had washed her hands and moved out into the sewing area, fingering the silks and satins, drinking their luster in with her wide blue eyes, encouraged by Laura, who put Mary's objections aside.

"Every little girl likes pretty things," Laura said indulgently. "Now, Mary, show madame what you have."

Mary pulled the twine off the wrinkled package to reveal the printed batiste, and the blue ribbon fell to the floor. Rosaleen could not restrain her enthusiasm and rushed to pick it up.

"Is this for me?" Rosaleen asked, her eyes sparkling.

"Yes." Mary smiled. "It's for your birthday, but..."

The seamstress came over to inspect the fabric, hardly taking it between her fingers before throwing her hands out from her sides and muttering something in French. Apparently, the poor cloth did not meet her standards. Small wonder, Mary thought, with all this wealth of material at hand. As always, Laura tried to be kind.

"Mary, dear, madame thinks a birthday dress should be white. The ribbon would look lovely with that, don't you think? I'll tell you what, why don't you make up the print for an everyday dress? Rosaleen really needs several. And our gift to her will be a party dress...with your pretty ribbon, of course."

"That's very kind of you," Mary said, unable to thwart the

woman's generosity twice, even though it meant having no gift for her daughter from herself.

Aware that something was wrong, Laura changed the subject to Mary's uniforms. "I want you to select a pattern that suits you. And I don't think it should be in black, do you? A nice cotton. Something cool for summer. I suppose we must be conventional about the color. You're wearing gray—do you like that?"

There was that word again: conventional. Mary made a note in her mind to look it up. "Yes, I usually wear gray," she replied.

"Good. But we'll touch it up a bit, madame, with white lawn or organdy. You'll make several detachable collars and cuffs for the uniforms. Two of those should be enough."

"May I see the pattern, ma'am?" Mary asked.

"Of course—it's marked there in the book with a sheet of paper," Laura said, indicating the thin paper book the dressmaker had brought along with her. Mary opened it to the page marked, and her worst suspicions were confirmed. Full-skirted, though not as full as her mistress's dress, the uniform had a tight bodice which came to a V in front: the closing was in the back. Since she obviously was not to discuss the baby in front of the seamstress, she wracked her mind for a way of putting her objection.

Catching Laura's gaze and holding it, so she could express most of what she wanted to impart with her eyes, Mary suggested, "Under the present circumstances, don't you think it would be more fitting—more convenient—to have buttons in the front?"

From the flush on Laura's cheeks, she realized she had made her point. "Of course, how stupid of me. I really didn't think," Laura said, helping the seamstress undo the full-skirted dress. For a moment she stood on the chair dressed only in her tiered petticoats, camisole and corset, all trimmed with lace. Rosaleen stared at Laura as though she were a statue of the Virgin Mary herself, worshiping the undergarments with her eyes.

"She's wearing a dress underneath her dress," she whispered to her mother. "I like this one better."

Slipping on a light, cream-colored peignoir, Laura sat down at her vanity to touch up her hairdo. "Madame Hurotte, if it isn't too much bother, I'd like you to take Mrs. Noonan's measurements today, after you take Rosaleen's. And remember, we must have the child's dress by the day after tomorrow."

The seamstress, who did not seem happy about the whole thing, picked up her measuring tape reluctantly and faced Mary and the child. "Take off your dresses, please. I can't get accurate measurements over your clothing."

Perhaps it was the startled expression on their faces that indicated to her something was wrong, even before Mary stammered, "We can't do that, ma'am. It isn't decent."

Laura turned with a smile from her dressing table to reassure Mary, but the smile died when she, too, saw her expression. She looked at the seamstress; Madame Hurotte stared at her. Laura's voice sank slightly when she asked, as delicately as possible, "You do have something beneath your dress, haven't you?"

"No, ma'am," Mary said, without embarrassment. "I never have. We're lucky to have something over our skin."

"Oh, dear," Laura said, biting her lower lip, trying not to laugh. The French seamstress, however, drawn up to her full height, stared disapprovingly at Mary and her daughter. "Well," Laura said, turning back to her mirror, where she could observe them all without being seen clearly, "I guess you'll have to take their measurements over their clothing, madame. And, if it isn't too difficult, please, for goodness' sake, make them some lingerie." Wait until she told her husband about this *faux pas*, she was thinking. It was his idea, after all, that the "woman upstairs" have some uniforms, though Laura completely approved it. The thought of Matthew made her remember something else.

"Oh, Mary," she said turning again and suppressing a laugh at the expression of endurance on the Irish woman's face as she had her bust measured, "there's something else I was supposed to tell you. My husband doesn't object to your taking the ... to your going home during the day on your time off. But he expressly said he doesn't want you staying out overnight with your charge. You understand, don't you? He does worry."

Mary understood too well: more than her mistress did. She understood everything: the clothes, the redecoration of the nursery, and the insistence she keep her own room. If she had wanted to flee from the hands of the seamstress before, the feeling was now intensified, and all the kindness of her mistress crumbled into ashes. But she could not leave: she was too poor. The dreadful man was even trying to keep her from her husband at night, without knowing he had no need to give such instructions. The measuring and probing of the dressmaker was forgotten in the thoughts that dashed against her mind like the sea against a cliff. She had thought all that was settled the other night, or even that perhaps her mind had been playing tricks on her; but it was all too clear now. Well, she had tackled greater problems in the past few years: she could take care of Matthew Maddigan. She didn't really even like him. There was something unclean, almost bestial, about the portly, sweating man. You will have to look sharp and use your wits, she told herself as the dressmaker's tape pulled tight around her waist.

Out of the corner of her eye, Mary observed Laura's pale, gentle face in the mirror with pity—the woman who had given up everything for him, who filled her days, devoid of friends and family, with trivialities and spending money. Well, at least she had her children: they seemed to be good boys. And, sooner or later, Laura would come to see the baby upstairs: Mary was quite determined about that.

What she could not believe was that any woman, no matter how flighty, was unable to understand the man with whom she lived just as she saw through Tomas. A feeling of oppression settled over her chest: she needed Brian as she had never needed him before. Not to tell her troubles to him: dear God, if he knew the position she was in, he would go after Mr. Maddigan himself. She missed him sorely, though; and, if she could not be out after dark, she would never see him at the flat. That horrible man had seen to that, though he thought he was depriving her of Tomas's company.

Well, there were more ways than one to skin a cat, she decided. If she left little Philip with Veronica for an hour, she could go to Dugan's herself.

Her wish about Laura was fulfilled more quickly than she could have imagined. That very next evening, when she was sewing Rosaleen's print dress at the side of her bed, her mistress appeared, entering without even knocking, adorned with a smile and a tape measure.

"I thought we might make measurements of the windows in the nursery," she said, deliberately not looking in the direction of the crib. "I've been thinking of eyelet embroidery for the windows and the beds. Of course, we'll have the whole room painted first. What color do you fancy, Mary?"

Mary put aside her sewing and stared at her. If she were

not dressed, if her eyes were not open, the woman might have been sleepwalking, oblivious as she was to her duty. Rising from her chair, Mary lifted the sleeping infant from his crib and approached his mother directly to put him in her arms. Laura's arms remained at her sides, her gaze holding Mary's, dreading to look at the bundle she carried.

"It's your little Philip," Mary said, smiling. "Sure, he's missed his mother, ma'am. Hold out your arms." When Laura made no motion to do so, Mary resorted to a desperate measure. "Hold out your arms, ma'am, or he'll fall on the floor!"

She did not really release the baby until Laura's arms came up: it just appeared so. And once she was holding the warm, squirming bit of life, Laura could not help looking down at him. Mary moved the covers aside so she could see his face clearly.

"But," Laura said, sinking down on the edge of the creaking bed, "his head isn't misshapen. It's a nice little head. I thought...oh, I don't know what I thought. He's actually rather pretty—as pretty as any of the others were at his age."

"His eyes are different," Mary pointed out truthfully, "and his tongue protrudes a bit. Otherwise, he's just like any other baby."

Laura touched his fuzzy head, examined his hands, tight little fists that did not show the thumb anomaly, which was so slight that she probably would not have noticed it anyway. "Oh, Mary," she breathed, "I don't know what's been wrong with me! Not even to come up and see for myself. I just didn't have the courage. Matthew was so upset by the birth of a child that was different. It must have communicated itself to me." She looked up at Mary with tears in her eyes. "Thank you. You've helped me again. I may never be able to thank you." She brushed her eyes with the hand still clutching the tape measure and gave a little laugh. "I guess we won't be doing the nursery tonight. I'd just like to stay here with him for a while."

"Why don't you take him to your room?" Mary suggested, trying not to push too hard, settling down in her chair to resume her sewing. "It's so much easier to accept the things we can't change."

"Yes, I've been fighting hard. I'm all bound up inside," Laura admitted. "I'm not the total fool I appear, Mary. I can't take him down there, though. If I did, I'd lose my husband. Matthew wants the child kept out of sight."

Great loss, Mary thought ironically, wondering what

Laura would say if she told her that Mr. Maddigan had visited here himself—even if it had not been to see the baby. But Laura was probably right. She knew what was important to her, though someone else might not be able to see it.

"You love your husband dearly," Mary said. "You gave up a lot for him, didn't you?"

Laura shook her head, still rocking the baby. "It might appear so to some people, but that isn't true. Matthew's all that's ever really mattered to me. Oh, sometimes I miss the old life a little: I'd like to be reconciled with my family. But it really doesn't matter, as long as I have Matthew. He's my life. And I like to think I'm his." She smiled. "He's so good to me—the poor lamb feels guilty about 'depriving me of my way of life,' as he calls it, and I guess he always will. The truth is, I couldn't live without him. Have you ever felt that way, Mary?"

Though Mary nodded slightly, she maintained her silence: she was not going to confess, untruly, to this woman of a love that was not for her own husband. "Those who feel that way about their husbands are blessed, for sure," she said at last. "You're that fortunate, ma'am. You've fine sons and you love your husband as much as the day you married him."

"That's true!" Laura cried, as though the recognition of her good fortune were sudden; then she looked down at the baby again, and bent to kiss his sleeping face. "Maybe God does things like this just to test us...and if he sees we can accept it, it pleases him. Rather like Job."

"Little Philip's hardly a trial," Mary said and laughed. "He's joy itself. Have you seen Rosaleen? I want her to go to bed early tonight. She'll have a grand day tomorrow."

"She was in the parlor, playing a game on the floor with the boys, when I left the dining room. She's your joy, isn't she? I've never seen a mother and daughter so close. It wasn't like that in our family. My mother was rather cool and forbidding. I've wanted a daughter, though—mostly because Matthew wanted one so much. Rosaleen's a beautiful child."

"Don't tell her that. I don't want her putting on airs. Sure, she's being spoiled to death as it is."

"Spoiled?" Laura asked. "Oh, no, Mary! She should have an education so she can make a better life for herself. Do you understand that?"

"Indeed I do. It's what I want for her myself. Just because I don't wear drawers and a petticoat doesn't mean I'm stupid, ma'am. I don't want her getting used to fancy dresses, though, and the company of children like yours. They're way above her."

"One little party dress," Laura chided gently. "Please don't be too severe with her. She's completely open and charming. I wouldn't want her to change. As for the boys, the two eldest are simply delighted with her: she's such a bright little thing. Even poor old Johnny talks to her sometimes, and that's a real conquest. He's so painfully shy and unable to express himself. His whole little life is lived through books. Mary, your daughter is a blessing to this household, as you are, yourself."

Laura rose to put the baby down, leaning into the bassinet to kiss him. "Poor little Philip," she whispered. "Sleep well, my dear. You won't have any problems at all." Then she rose and straightened the taffeta flounces of her skirt, smoothed her hair. "I must go now. Matthew will be expecting me. I'd rather he didn't know I've been here yet. And Mary..." She bent down to embrace her, giving her a swift kiss on the cheek. "Thank you, once again."

Mary was touched, and felt she understood Laura better, but she did not reveal it. She was determined not to reveal her sentiments to either of her employers: a stubborn sort of pride made her want to keep to herself. "If you see my little 'joy' down there," she said, "please send her packing, ma'am. She's after being cranky when she doesn't get enough sleep."

Chapter 10

THE DAY of the party, Mary was more concerned with how the Noonan boys would look than Rosaleen and herself. She did not want them to be embarrassed by the others. Though there was some tension about Rosaleen's dress arriving on time, she put it to the back of her mind: if worse came to worse, Rosaleen could wear the print she had stitched up last night. She made sure the child was bathed and her hair brushed to a glossy black in a hairdo imitating Laura's, with side curls made by turning the half-curling hair over her fingers. Her daughter was so excited she could hardly keep her still.

When a knock finally sounded on their door, Rosaleen squealed, "Oh, Ma! It has to be my dress!"

The dressmaker's box, brought in by a bewildered maid, was tied with a white bow of better satin than the one Mary had purchased. When the striped box was opened, it revealed wonders in a billow of tissue paper. Gleefully, Rosaleen fought with the paper to get at the contents inside. On top of the sheer white dress with its wide skirt and single ruffle on the hem were petticoats and pantaloons trimmed with lace, which mother and daughter lifted carefully, uncertain about their use.

"Does it have long sleeves, Ma?" Rosaleen inquired, holding up the pantaloons. "Sure Mrs. Maddigan doesn't wear anything like this."

"It looks like trousers," Mary puzzled. "But, if it is, the dress is too short for them—they'll hang out at the bottom, and I don't think underpants are supposed to do that."

Mrs. Balfe, who had entered the room without knocking, stood staring at them, a look of disapproval on her face. "Mrs. Maddigan sent me up to help the child dress," she said, horrified by the exploded box and tissue on the bed. "What are those pantaloons doing on your arms?" she demanded of Rosaleen, who dropped them quickly to the floor, looking abashed.

"Sure, they're too long for the dress," Mary said, her eyes flashing dangerously at the woman. "All this lace shows at least half a foot below the hem."

"That's the style for children," Mrs. Balfe snapped. "Well, get into them, child. Take your dress off first."

The little girl's blue eyes sought her mother's. Not wishing to make trouble, Mary helped Rosaleen into the pantaloons before removing the gray dress as instructed, and took off her blouse only when she had the camisole ready in her hands to slip over the child's head. Mrs. Balfe handed Mary the two petticoats, one after the other, with a frozen face, and when both of them were in place she lifted the dress carefully by the shoulders.

"It's beautiful, isn't it?" Rosaleen asked, her enthusiasm returning. "Wait until Darin and Liam see me! They won't know who I am, I bet."

"Very nice indeed," Mrs. Balfe replied, shutting off speech by putting the dress over Rosaleen's head. "Mrs. Noonan, this isn't the child's fault, but I want a word with you later."

Mary did up the buttons in back without reply. She thought she knew what the woman would say, and there was some truth in it, but she did not want to spoil Rosaleen's party by discussing it now. A sash that matched the hair ribbon came with the dress, and Mary drew it around the little waist, tying it in a bow in the back. Mrs. Balfe made no objection, so she assumed she had done that right, at least. Taking the hairbrush in hand again, Mary brushed the child's long hair back from her face, tying it with the blue bow in back; then she patted her daughter and smiled. "You look very pretty, love. You can look in the mirror now."

As Rosaleen turned in front of the full-length mirror on the door, Mary used a discreet side glance to look at the housekeeper's face. Mrs. Balfe was standing rigid, with her hands folded in front of her, but, watching Rosaleen, a ghost of a smile touched the edge of her lips. Perhaps she was not altogether inhuman after all.

"It's time for you to go downstairs, Rosaleen," Mrs. Balfe said. "Please don't run on the stairs."

"Can I use the front ones, or do I have to go down the back?" the little girl asked.

"You may use the main staircase. But just today."

"Ma, are you coming?" Rosaleen asked, dragging at Mary's hand.

"You go along, darlin'. I'll be down later to help cook serve. I have to look after the baby first."

"I wonder if Darin's here yet," Rosaleen said, tearing by Mrs. Balfe and out the door. Mary cast her eyes to heaven, praying she would not break her neck on the stairs.

"Are you going down like that?" Mrs. Balfe asked.

"Sure, I've nothing else to wear," Mary replied. "My uniforms aren't ready yet. You had something to say to me, Mrs. Balfe?" she asked, carefully gathering up the tissue and folding it with the bow into the box.

"Yes, Mrs. Noonan. Please sit down."

Mary did so, still clasping the box over her knees.

"Mrs. Noonan, it seems to me that you're taking advantage of Mrs. Maddigan's good nature and generosity. What's happening here today isn't in good taste. It's deplorable! You have a pretty little daughter, but this isn't to her best advantage. I think you should exercise better judgment—"

"You're right," Mary replied, studying her face as she stopped in midsentence.

"I beg your pardon?"

"You're right, Mrs. Balfe. I don't approve of any of this at all. I told Mrs. Maddigan so last night. I don't want Rosaleen's head filled with frivolous things that have nothing to do with her. I don't want her raised up for a fall. But if anyone's being taken advantage of, it's my child: I don't approve of it, as I said. And I'll hope that it doesn't happen again. I do understand my position, you see."

Mrs. Balfe moved a step backward toward the door. "Well, if you understand, then there's nothing more I need say. When this party is over, I hope things will go back to normal in this house. The Maddigan boys—"

"—are lonely," Mary said. "I don't know why. I don't understand these things. If they've taken a fancy to Rosaleen, there isn't much I can do about that, since it seems to please their mother. But isn't it all just a tempest in a teacup, ma'am? The boys will be going away to school in a few months."

"They'll be leaving before that, if I understand the family plans," Mrs. Balfe said; then she seemed to consider the situation in a new light. "Yes, I think you're right, Mrs. Noonan. It will all blow over very quickly." The baby began to make noises in the crib, giving her an opportunity to interrupt the conversation. "Look after the baby, so you can come downstairs for a while. I think there's a long white apron in the linen room you can put over your dress."

"They're really something," Darin said with interest. "Sure, might I put them on for a moment? Jes... I mean, *goodness* ... I can't see through them at all!"

"I can't see well without them," John Maddigan said, warming to the Irish boy. "I'll have to wear them all my life."

"Well, they're fine to look at. With solid gold rims, I'll wager. They're splendid, really. You look like our land agent back home. Impressive, that is, not *like* Mr. McGee, who was a positive—"

"Darin!" Mary said from the table, where she had just put the cake with real candles. "I haven't seen you for a while, my dear. Come give us a hug."

She thought it particularly unfortunate that poor Johnny's spectacles should arrive on the day of the party, as promptly as Rosaleen's dress. Mrs. Lynch, the cook, had reported that Johnny had been sitting alone in a corner all afternoon; but when she entered the room, she overheard Darin's conversation and decided to put a quick stop to it: God alone knew what that boy would say about Mr. McGee, or what kind of language he would use. She had already made an overture to her son, Liam, who allowed her to kiss his cool cheek without responding in turn. That hurt. But, in truth, she did not know how to handle the difficult child. Though Darin would bear watching this afternoon, she was relieved about one thing: Veronica had done well by the boys' suits. Though they were slightly worn, and Darin's trousers a mite too short, there was little difference between them and those of the Maddigan boys. Though they came without hats and Liam's straight dark hair had a cowlick and Darin's black curls had been blown in the breeze, she blessed her sister-in-law for turning them out so well, probably with Mr. Rabinsky's advice.

When he heard Mary's voice, Darin rose quickly to respond

139

to her request, throwing his arms about her waist and pressing his head a little too tightly to her bosom.

"Aunt Mary, we've missed you," he said earnestly, while she was still trying to decide if he was too young to realize what he was doing. Carefully, with firm hands on his shoulders, she pulled him away and looked down into his face. If he had been up to something, it did not show: indeed, the boy's expression was quite serious, an unusual one for him. "There's trouble at home," he said confidentially. "Michael's gone. He left a note last night that he was traveling to Nantucket to get on a boat."

"Who's going to sea from Nantucket?" Matthew asked, overhearing. "Those are mostly whalers, you know. They go all over the world!"

"My brother," Darin answered politely, turning away from Mary to go back to the children. "He's only your age, Matthew, and we miss him already. My ma's fit to be tied."

Matthew's face was full of awe. "He must be a brave boy," he said. "Oh, what I wouldn't do to go with him! Just think of it—no more school. So many foreign places to see, and harpooning a whale! But, of course, he'll be gone for years."

"Years?" Mary asked, listening in on the conversation. "Did you say *years?*"

"Oh, yes, Mrs. Noonan! Those ships are out three years at a time at least. I guess he'll sign on as cabin boy, about all he could do now. But when he comes back, he'll be a real sailor."

"Maybe I'll do that, too, when I'm old enough," Darin said thoughtfully. "Ma will be used to it by then, I guess."

Before Mary could object, Rosaleen, who had been following her cousin around with pure joy in her eyes, suddenly stormed, "No! Don't you ever go away, Darin! There wouldn't be anyone to look after me, and you know how much trouble I get into." Tears rose in her eyes, and, with a deep sigh, Darin wiped them with a handkerchief that was not exactly clean.

"Not on your birthday, Rosie," he entreated. "That's a long time away. Four years, at least. Sure if you can't take care of yourself by then, you'd better pack it in. Besides, you have all these fine boys to look after you now. You'll do it, Matthew, won't you? She's a lot of trouble, but she's a good-hearted little thing."

"I may go with you," Matthew said, his imagination stirred, "but old Harry will do it, won't you?"

Kneeling on the carpet over a game, Harry chuckled. "Of course, I'll be her knight in shining armor. At least until I'm old enough to go to sea." He shrugged playfully. "And, when that happens, there's always good old John."

John went scarlet behind his gold-rimmed spectacles, mumbling in objection, "I don't like girls much."

All the boys laughed, and he grew redder than ever. "None of us do!" Darin said triumphantly. "Why do you think we want to go out with the whales? But Rosaleen isn't really a girl: she's too young for that." He put his hands about her waist and heaved her into the air, dodging her thrashing pantaloons and petticoats. "She's more like a toy or a little puppy. She's very loyal and she can get you into more trouble than you'd ever believe. Like a bloody idjut, I pulled her out of the river once, and I haven't been able to shake her since." He put her down on her feet with a grin. "I wouldn't want to, though, not as pretty as she looks today. And I can thank her for getting me into the best fights I've ever had."

"Fights?" Matthew asked, enthralled. "Have you really?"

Darin proceeded to tell them about some of the ordeals Rosaleen had put him through, including the one on board the ship, while the little girl stood by proudly, happy that the Maddigans liked Darin so much.

When it came time to blow out the birthday cake's candles, Laura appeared at the door, putting her finger to her lips, so Mary and Mrs. Balfe would not reveal her presence.

"You must make a wish," Harry told her. "Close your eyes and think of what you want most. Then you have to blow out all six candles at once. If one's left burning, you don't get your wish."

"And you mustn't tell it," Matthew instructed. "If you do, you don't get it, either!"

Rosaleen closed her eyes for only a moment; then she blew out all the candles, to the cheers of the boys. Mary, moving forward to cut the cake, told the children to take their places around the table before she served. Finally Laura came into the room and offered her congratulations. Joining the other two women on a velvet loveseat, she ate her portion of cake.

"She's adorable," she whispered to Mary. "And her brother's the image of her! How can you bear to leave him at home? He's such a handsome boy, and so clever."

Mary frowned. "Liam?" she asked, completely puzzled. Her closed-faced son had spoken fewer words than Johnny and was only playing with his cake instead of eating it.

"No, Darin. He's her brother, isn't he?"

Mary smiled. "No, ma'am, he's her cousin. That's my Liam, there beside your Harry." There was a short silence. "I guess he favors my side of the family," Mary said.

Laura nodded absently. "He's rather like Johnny, isn't he? They can be so difficult, those shy ones. I think I worry about Johnny ten times more than the others."

"Yes, ma'am," Mary said noncommittally, observing her dark-eyed son with a feeling of anxiety. Liam had been more open before he saw Brian consoling her that awful night Tomas returned home drunk, with his wild accusations. She was sure now that Liam had overheard them. She realized that the boy had changed so much since then. Why, he might think anything. Or he might just hate her for abandoning him to Doirin. She must get him aside and have a talk with him, but her head whirled at the thought of it. How does one come right out and ask a child if he has misinterpreted what he has seen or heard? Even while she watched him, he lifted his eyes, which seared her like a brand. The cake stuck in her throat, and she coughed.

"Excuse me," she said, rising, with her fist to her lips. "It went down the wrong way, I think."

"Let me help you," Mrs. Balfe said, joining her. "No wonder you're choking, I forgot to serve the punch!"

Of all the little gifts she got that day, Rosaleen treasured her new sock doll from Darin and her party dress most. Mary was not hurt when she discarded her blue hair ribbon on the floor of their room a few hours later: she was too happy for her daughter, who might never have such a wonderful day again—a thought that made her throat tight with emotion. The party had been generous: the Maddigans were good people. But they did not understand the child's position. Darin was right: Rosaleen was like a toy to all of them. As she helped Rosaleen off with the dress, which had not a single punch stain on it because the little girl had been so careful, Mary leaned forward and kissed her on the neck affectionately.

"Ooh! That tickles." Rosaleen laughed, squirming. "Do it again! It gave me a chill all the way down to my toes!"

"No, I won't do it again," Mary said, rising with a smile to hang the little dress in the mahogany armoire. "Give us the sash, now."

The little girl sat on the edge of the bed, playing with the blue satin sash, pulling it over her knees and holding it up to admire it. "This is the best day of my life," she said and sighed. "Almost."

Mary turned to look at her. "Almost? Sure I'd say it was the best one ever. What was better than this?"

The child's face was wistful, sad. She averted her eyes so her mother would not see the tears forming there. Mary moved to her side and put an arm around her, laughing in an attempt to make her happy again. She kissed her on the neck but got no reaction.

"What is it, love?" she asked. "Sure, you got such fine presents today—more things than you've ever wanted. The pretty dolly from the boys with the dress almost like yours, the dress from Mrs. Maddigan, and the sock dolly from Darin. Now you can throw the old one away."

"No! I'll never throw her away!" Rosaleen responded. "The new one's nice, but she can be a sister to my old one. And I got the holy pictures from Liam," she reminded her mother.

"Yes, I forgot: the lovely holy pictures of the Blessed Virgin and the Sacred Heart. If I save my money, I can buy you a missal to put them in for Christmas: they'll mark the pages when we go to Mass. Now, can you think of anything you didn't get? You mustn't be greedy, Rosaleen."

"I'm not," the little girl said, her lower lip starting to tremble.

"You're overtired, darlin'. It's been an exciting afternoon. Why don't you take a little nap?"

"The best day," Rosaleen blurted out, the tears running over, "was when Darin gave me my puppy, Murphy, when I was three!"

The shock was like an icicle being plunged into Mary's belly: for a moment, she was speechless with compassion, holding her own tears back. Gradually, with her arm still around her daughter, she gained control of herself: all that was in another time, best forgotten by everyone.

When she had confidence enough to speak without her voice breaking, she said, "Murphy was a good dog, Rosie, but that was long ago. We can't be happy all the time, so we must grab onto the things that make us happy and hold them tightly. Get into bed, now. Lie down and close your eyes, and think about this day, because you'll remember it the same way, sometime. It isn't likely to happen again, my darlin'." She bent to kiss the child's smooth forehead, wishing that she could take all the bad things that might happen to her child onto herself, so that Rosaleen would know only happiness, always.

Doirin would not speak, not even to Liam. She sat huddled in her shawl with her face forlorn, staring directly in front of her at the dark wall of the basement flat. Veronica reported that Doirin had been like that since Michael's departure, leaving only a note for his father and no word for Doirin.

"Dear God, it's frightening," the girl said, biting her lip. "I have to do everything for her, just like a baby, Mary—force some liquid food into her mouth, take her to the privy. I don't think she hears a word I say. Is it the madness that's on her? I just don't know. I've never seen anything like this before."

Mary handed the baby to Veronica and knelt down beside her sister, who appeared to have aged many years. There was not a flicker of life in her set eyes; she hardly seemed to be breathing. Taking her hand, Mary almost expected it to be pulled away: Doirin had never appreciated the affectionate gesture. But the hand remained in hers, limp and cold, as though it were not attached to her.

"What does Brian make of it?" Mary whispered.

"He's sorely tried," Veronica said. "You don't have to whisper. I'm sure she doesn't hear a thing. She's retreated inside herself like a garden snail when it's threatened. Oh, Mary, she was terribly hurt! I'll never forgive that boy! Never! The least he could have done was leave a message for his mother. I just don't understand."

"Sure, it was his mother he was trying to get away from," Mary replied, "as well as the streets. Maybe it's the best thing for him, after all. But this is worrisome." Mary was glad she had not brought Rosaleen with her today: the child had seen enough in one small lifetime. "You know, once a long time ago, when I was about ten, I remember something like this. Old Mr. Foley, after his wife died. He never came out of it, and they took him away to an asylum, because there was no one to care for him. But he was an old man and probably senile, not young like Doirin." Mary rose slowly, forgetting to brush the dust off the skirt of her new uniform. "And you, Veronica, how are you? Is there any cough now? Do you feel weak?" She put her hand on her sister-in-law's forehead: it was cool to the touch and there were no hectic smudges on her cheeks.

"I'm sure I'm quite recovered," Veronica said quickly.

"Really, Mary. I'm very well. As strong as in the old days, before..."

"Yes, but are you well enough for this? It must be hard on you, helping her around."

"I only have to do it in the afternoon and evening. Brian looks after her the rest of the time."

"And how is Brian?" Mary asked cautiously, afraid of what she might hear.

"Well enough, I think. Mary, you know he wanted the boy to get out of here. And he and Doirin haven't gotten on for years."

"Well, that's not for us to know. We only saw what was on the surface. Many couples squabble." Mary sighed. "Doirin's never been an easy person to get on with. Is Brian at the pub, now? I think I should talk to him."

"Yes, but Tomas is probably there, too. I mean...well, I didn't think you wanted to see him."

"I don't, but it doesn't matter. I can handle Tomas. Would you mind looking after little Philip for a while? He's been fed. You can just lay him down on one of the mats. I won't be long."

Walking down the hill in the late May sunshine, Mary felt that she was missing something; then it occurred to her how long it had been since she had been alone. She kept expecting the touch of a little hand in hers or the cry of a baby. She knew she should have felt free, but instead she was lonely, and slightly timid of the stares that followed her, as though people were asking, "What is that woman in the uniform doing, walking alone on her own two feet, without looking after someone?" Her trepidation increased as she reached the bottom of the hill and the cobbled street across from Dugan's Pub. It was only three in the afternoon, too early for many patrons; those who could afford to drink should be at work. Behind that door Brian and Tomas were working, and probably Mr. Dugan, too. She wondered how she could speak to the one without the others. She had not the time of day for Tomas, and she still resented Mr. Dugan for encouraging his gambling, though she would not mind speaking to his wife, who had been so kind to her. After several minutes, she took a deep breath and walked across the street, opening the pub door quickly, before her courage failed.

The dim interior, with which she had become somewhat familiar by now, was almost unearthly still, though she felt a presence somewhere within its confines. She opened the

145

door to the restaurant: it was quiet and warm, with only a fly buzzing against the windows. She did not want to call out; indeed, she was not certain that she could. Her mouth was quite dry at the prospect of seeing Tomas. She was upset enough, not in the proper emotional condition for a scene with him. With her hand on the polished bar, she took a few steps forward and nearly cried out when a figure loomed up beside her on the other side of the bar.

"May I help you with some—Mary!"

"Oh, Brian, you nearly frightened me to death! Sure where is everyone? It's like a church in here."

"Dugan and Tomas have gone after a supply of liquor. They didn't like the last we had from the dealer. Oh, Mary, it's so good to see you again." He stepped around the bar and moved forward with his hands extended, half smiling, his blue eyes very hurt; the next thing she knew, she was in his arms, instead of holding his hands, and they clung together, muttering each other's name, Mary crying.

"I can't stand to see things so," she said, pressing her cheek against his. "I can't bear to see you hurting so much."

When his lips met hers, it seemed the most natural thing in the world: she had kissed him so many times in her mind. And the reality of it was just as she had imagined, his lips gentle and firm, his breath clean as Tomas's had never been, for Brian made a habit of neither tobacco nor alcohol. As the pressure of his kisses increased, she responded without thinking, caressing his shoulders with her hands, clinging to the cloth of his shirt in back, then caressing again. There was no one else in the world at that moment. It was as inevitable as the passion that began to grow from the kisses, so overwhelming that it tore them apart suddenly, and they stood looking at each other in horror.

"Jesus, my brother's wife!" Brian exclaimed. "Mary, I can't."

"Nor can I," she said through the tears choking her and streaming down her face, remembering her oath in church. "Brian, I love you ... only you. I always have. But it's too late for us. I know that. I don't know what happened to me...."

"Or me," he said, almost in a whisper, the lilt in his voice so characteristic that Mary cried harder than ever. "Please don't, my darling. You must know it's the same with me. Oh, God! How did things get so twisted up ... so knotted! It should have been us and I always knew it. It should have been you, not Doirin."

At the mention of her sister's name, Mary turned her back, wiping her face with her handkerchief, trying to control the sobbing. "It's about her I came," she gasped. "I saw her just now. Brian, we have to do something...she's..."

"I know," she heard his voice say. "But I don't know what to do. It's too much for Veronica, and I don't want the boys to see. I've thought of everything. Mr. Dugan even suggested an asylum. Just until she's well again."

"An asylum!" Mary exclaimed, turning quickly, but her reaction became reasonable when she looked at him, saw the blue hell in his eyes. "Sure, they're awful places. At least they were at home. There must be another way." She tried to think, but his kisses flitted through her mind, confusing her. "I'll come home," she said at last. "If we partition the flat differently, keep her away from the children...I'm strong enough for all the work. I'll—"

"You'll do no such thing." His voice was firm, adamant. "For the first time in years, you've a small bit of comfort in your life. You'll not give it up for a woman who cares about no one...not even for the boys. That's my final word on it. You stay where you are. Besides..."

She waited and, when he did not continue, asked, "Besides, what?"

His gaze met hers, sank into it: she could feel it sink to her thighs, as it had when she was a girl. The sensation was not new to her when she was with Brian. She had never once felt it with Tomas, though. It was frightening.

"That's it," he said gently, as though he understood. "We couldn't live in the same house together, again. Surely you see where it might lead."

She averted her eyes. She had always considered herself strong, but she was no match for this. What he said was true. She could not live with him without touching him, wanting to kiss him. The power of his lips was wonderful, making her wish to submit completely: she would eventually welcome him with open arms. She could see it was the same with him, that he stood away from her now for no other reason.

"It's true," she said sadly, trying to will herself to be practical. "We can't leave her like that. But don't mention an asylum again, please! That would be hard on the children, too."

From his silence, she knew the answer was beyond him, and she thought of alternatives, none of which suited the situation. If they had been back home, they could have called

147

in the priest for a decision, but the clergy was too uninvolved here.

"Brian," she said tentatively, "do you remember the doctor who let us keep Veronica with us? Dr. Townsend, it was. I have his address still, at home in my room. He said to contact him at any time about Veronica."

"Doirin's not sick, Mary. It's her mind."

"I know. But I don't know where else to turn. He didn't favor putting Veronica into the lung hospital. And when Mrs. Maddigan was upset, her doctor gave her something to make her better...that was in her mind, too. If I write to him and ask him to come see her in the morning when you're there, would you agree to that?"

His face looked drawn, his eyes weary, from both passion and despair. "Whatever you say, my dear," he agreed. "Things can't go on like they are."

The next afternoon, Bridie came running upstairs to tell Mary that she had a gentleman caller waiting down in the parlor. "A real gentleman he is, too, Mary. Wherever did you meet him? He said his name is Dr. Townsend."

Without thanking the girl, Mary flew by her and ran down the main staircase, which was closest to the parlor, past the astonished Mrs. Balfe and into the first-floor room, where the doctor stood looking at the furnishings with interest. He turned as she approached, and a smile came to his face.

"Good afternoon, Mary Noonan," he said. "I must say, you've attached yourself to a curious household. I've never been here before myself."

"No, indeed, few people come," Mary said breathlessly, searching his face for what she wanted to know. "The mistress married an Irishman, and though he isn't even Catholic, they aren't accepted at all."

"That's a blunt assessment, if I ever heard one." He laughed. "There's more to it than that, though. But that isn't why I've come. I know you're anxious to hear about your sister."

"Please sit down, sir," she said, indicating the velvet settee and taking a place in the matching chair. "Can anything be done for Doirin? It was so kind of you to see her."

"Your sister's suffering from acute melancholia, my dear. Nothing in medical science can treat it, but I advised her husband against an asylum, for now, at least. Give it a little time. He explained to me the circumstances that led up to it.

I wish I could tell you something more hopeful, Mary, but..."
He shrugged. "We're at a complete loss about this sort of
thing. Some people seem to be melancholic by nature without
this ever occurring, but others... we just don't know why. All
of you have been through a lot... more than anyone should
have to bear. Since the Irish came, funds have been appro-
priated for two new asylums, but I don't recommend them.
When gentlefolk are mentally disturbed, they're kept at
home, unless they're absolute maniacs. Your sister isn't like
that, and the people in the asylums frequently are. We don't
want her there among them: she'd never recover."

"There's hope of recovery, then, sir?" She lowered her
voice. "My mistress was disturbed a few months past and her
doctor gave her something for it. Sleeping drafts, she called
them."

He smiled helplessly. "That wouldn't do for your sister,
dear. It might make her stay that way forever. Yes, there are
recoveries, and I think we can hope for one. In the meantime,
everyone seems to be caring for her as well as possible. Incidentally, I'm amazed at the condition of your young sister-
in-law. When I sent her away with you, I was sure she would
die, but whatever you did, you did it right. Her lungs are
clear, they sound completely healed. And she seems quite
willing to take on the nursing of Doirin." He cleared his
throat, coughed slightly into his hand, looking uneasy.
"There's one suggestion I might make, though I doubt if it
can be accomplished."

"Yes," Mary said, "anything!"

"If her living conditions could be improved, I think it would
be beneficial. That dreary basement isn't conducive to happy
thoughts. How much do you pay for it?"

"Two dollars a week, sir. It's very dear. But there's the
heat of the furnace in the winter, and no one else has been
affected by it. Of course, Doirin looks at everything a different
way. What was that word you used... melan..."

"Melancholic. Yes, that's the key, you see. What doesn't
affect others probably affects her, because of her nature. Two
dollars is dear, out of your incomes. I just don't know what
else to suggest."

"I know a nice, cheery place," Mary considered, "but it
would be a terrible imposition under the circumstances. The
men work for Mr. Dugan at the pub, and... well, Mrs. Dugan
has a fine, cheery flat above it." She shook her head slowly.
"She's a good woman, but it'd be asking too much."

"You never know until you ask," he said, rising, his hat in one hand and his stick in the other. "Maybe her husband can arrange something."

Mary walked with him to the front door, glancing around to see if Mrs. Balfe was still about, conscious now of her breach of the rules of the house. They were alone in the high white entry hall with the crystal chandelier casting colorful prisms on the walls. The doctor paused at the door, studying her reflectively.

"You're looking fine, Mary," he said, his eyes darting to the inside doorways, as though he, too, wanted to talk in privacy. "A word to you about that other matter—the social ban on the Maddigans," he said, lowering his voice. "It isn't just because he's Irish, my dear, though that's part of it. He isn't a decent sort of man, you see, in business or even in his personal life. Well, you might look shocked! I wouldn't say this, except that you're an unusually attractive woman. Keep your distance from him, Mary. He has a bad reputation. When Laura Parsons cast everything aside to marry him, she had no idea what a philanderer he'd turn out to be. For her sake, I hope she doesn't know it now. Just be careful, that's all."

Mary was left standing alone in the hall with her mouth hanging open. She did not understand everything he had said, especially the word he had used, though she caught some of its meaning in context.

She would have to look that word up.

Chapter 11

WHEN THE MADDIGANS took Rosaleen to the Cape with them, Mary felt as though the most important part of her was missing; but she could not refuse the child the trip to the seaside: it was difficult to refuse Rosaleen anything. Darin had gone, too, but Liam declined the invitation. Almost alone in the house, she made frequent trips across town to see Veronica and help to care for Doirin, always going at a time when she would miss Brian.

The embrace in the pub still bothered her. She thought about it every night before she went to sleep; and instead of pushing the pleasure of the moment away from her, she found herself submitting to its remembrance, knowing it was wrong. And it never seemed more wrong than when she was in the basement flat, in the presence of the pathetically disturbed Doirin.

"Would it be too much for you to watch Philip for half an hour?" Mary asked Veronica one Saturday. "I'd like to go to confession. Sure, I haven't been for a while with no Rosaleen to care for the child in church."

"He's no trouble at all," Veronica said, lifting him in her arms. "And there are some things you shouldn't neglect, Mary. God knows, you need a breather, if nothing else. Go along with you: we'll be just fine."

Mary wanted to discuss her feeling about Brian with someone with education and authority, in the hope it might help her control it: she could not do it on her own. And the only person Mary could think of with such credentials was a priest. She was unfortunate in her choice, though: young Father Donelly was fresh from Ireland, still wet behind the ears. Knowing nothing of human emotions, never having experienced the important ones, he filled in the deficit by pounding on the rules of the Church, verbally backing her into the corner of the confessional with the only thing he knew. Brian, he told her, being her sister's husband, was the same as a brother to her; she must think of him in no other way. Even if her sister, instead of being insane, were dead, and her husband dead too, there was no hope that Mary and Brian could marry: it would be against the laws of God.

"'Thou shalt not marry thy brother's wife' applies to sisters, too," he told her. "Sure, there are good reasons for such rules!"

He gave her no comfort, no direction to overcome her love, and she went away hurting as cruelly as before, her only determination never to go into his confessional again. He had told her nothing she did not already know, and his lack of understanding made love a mortal sin. Mary could not believe that any love, when properly contained, was a sin.

Mary thought she would be alone in the house with the two maids, one of whom was doing the cooking, but after only a month, Mr. Maddigan returned. He came up to the nursery one evening when Mary was changing Philip's diaper. She started and looked up from the table where the baby lay, unable to believe her eyes at the sight of him.

"Sir! I thought you were at the Cape with the family. Nothing's happened, has it? Is everyone all right? They said there was water there: Rosaleen can't swim."

"She can now." He smiled broadly. "No, everything's fine. The children are having a grand time. I took them to New Bedford to see the ships last week. But I never stay the whole summer, Mary. I've business here."

Mary finished pinning the diaper and raised the baby in her arms, her heart thumping heavily. She did not want to be in this house nearly alone with her employer; even before Dr. Townsend's warning, she had known what he was. "We'll have to see to some dinner for you—we weren't expecting you back at all."

"I've dined." He waved the suggestion aside, taking a few steps into the nursery and looking around at the white eyelet embroidery on the beds and windows, the striped and flowered blue paper on the walls. "Very nice...the room. It was my suggestion that it be redecorated, you know."

"Yes, sir, Mrs. Maddigan told me," Mary said, pushing her damp hair back from her forehead. "She decided on everything: she's very clever."

"Yes, when it comes to spending money, Laura's the best. Not that I begrudge her anything, of course. But don't I even get a thank-you?"

"For what, sir?"

"It was you I was thinking about. It's much more pleasant in here, now, isn't it?"

"It's pretty, sir. Were all of the boys in this room when they were babies?" she asked, wiping the perspiration off the baby's face and head, which were red with the heat.

"Yes," he said vaguely, "but that was a long time ago."

"Were they here in the summer, sir?"

"Of course not, they were down at the...I see what you mean: it is hot in here, isn't it? But I didn't want this baby down there: I don't really want him in the house. That's my wife's decision. But there was another reason I didn't want you to come to the Cape, Mary. I knew I'd only be staying a month or less, and I thought that we could keep each other company here."

Mary clasped little Philip closer, determined not to put him down while Maddigan was in the room. Feeling like a rabbit in a snare, she thought quickly. "There's no reason to be ashamed of him, for sure," she said. "These things happen. It's nature's fault alone, and it certainly isn't *his*. I think sometimes they happen to make better people of us, to remind us that none of us are excused from responsibility when it presents itself."

He took a large handkerchief out of his waistcoat pocket and mopped his face, which was getting as red as Philip's in the inferno of the nursery. "I didn't come here to discuss philosophy...or the child," he said impatiently. "I came here to see you. You aren't at all friendly, Mary."

"I try to keep my place."

"Your *place*." He laughed harshly. "Indeed. When I said I'd already dined, I didn't say where. I went to Dugan's Pub when I left the bank today. I saw some of your relatives there. When I introduced myself to your husband, Tomas, he asked me for a loan."

Mary's mouth fell open. It was like Tomas to be such a blithering idjut, but it put her in a bad position. "Tomas isn't always . . . conventional," she said, using the word for the first time. "He doesn't think before he speaks sometimes. I'm sorry he did it."

"I'm not. Dugan's put his pub up for sale, and the Noonan brothers want to buy it. Their only problem is that they have no ready capital. I only have to say the word and they're in business for themselves."

"Sure, why's Mr. Dugan selling out?" Mary stammered. "He has a good business there."

"Yes, and it isn't the only one, either: he has real estate, too. He's simply decided he doesn't want to work any more. Not there, at least. He's purchased a little farm in the country and wants to move to it with his wife. Leave it to an Irishman to go back to the land if he can."

Mary thought about it all for a moment, but her face revealed nothing. If the men bought the pub, they would have the apartment above it, too: the nice, light-filled upper floor which would be so good for Doirin. "Would it be a good investment for you?" she asked Mr. Maddigan evenly.

"I don't make one unless it's good," he said, wiping his face again. "To tell the truth, I don't think much of your fine Tomas, but his brother's another matter. He seems like a steady, intelligent, hard-working man."

"Brian is that," she said, but not too quickly. "He's always been most reliable. It was he who brought us all to this country."

"Oh?" Mr. Maddigan said, raising his eyebrows. "He's the real head of the family, then?"

"Yes, sir, being the oldest, I suppose he is."

"I understand that his wife is ill. He's married to your sister, isn't he? That's what Tomas said." He smiled. "I had your whole genealogy before I got away from him, and for only one drink."

"Tomas does run on," she said, exasperated by her husband's talkativeness. She could preserve very little privacy with him around.

"He's a blatherskite, all right. I know his type. I'm seldom wrong about men. Now, women," he said, laughing, "that's something else. I know when I want one, but seldom how she'll respond."

Mary turned away, wanting to put Philip down: her bodice was soaked from the warmth of him and he would be cooler in his crib. But, more than ever, she knew she must keep holding him. Mr. Maddigan's behavior was inconceivable to

154

her: she could hardly imagine such a blackguard. But he was an Orangeman, and there was no telling what he might do next.

"Please put that child down," he said. "You're wringing wet from holding him." When she did not follow his suggestion, he began to get angry. "Mary, I want to talk to you without that clod on your chest! Do you hear me?"

Suddenly she felt wetter than ever: her nerves had made her lose milk. She could not put the baby down now if she wanted to, because it had soaked right through her bodice.

"I'm sorry," she said, "he wants looking after, sir. I don't know whether you're considering the loan or not, but it has nothing to do with me. That's men's business."

"You haven't understood a word I've said. The loan depends entirely on you. Getting your sister out of that basement depends on you. I want you more than I've ever wanted any woman. I'll leave you now to think about that. I must be crazy with the heat to have come up here at all."

What to do? She could not turn to the priest and she dared not mention any of it to Brian. He would kill Mr. Maddigan, if he knew: no, she corrected herself quickly, Brian would never kill. He had got the money out of Mr. McGee just by talking to him. They had not left from Cork, but from a western port for some reason of his own.

After Maddigan's visit, Mary kept the baby in her own room at night with the window wide open for whatever breeze they might catch in the sweltering, humid Boston summer. She was unable to sleep, though her door was locked securely. But Mr. Maddigan did not bother her again: he left her in torment with her own confused mind.

Once, only once, after she had visited the basement flat in the North End during the day and found Doirin just the same, though the basement itself was cool, did she bring herself face to face with the thought of submitting to Maddigan for the good of them all. The very thought of him touching her made her recoil with disgust. The thought of any man but Brian kissing her made her feel that way. She loved Brian, though she tried not to think about him. She could not just put him out of her mind, or heart. As for Maddigan's suggestion, she could not do such a thing, even to get Doirin into better surroundings. She had sacrificed a lot, had done some unappetizing things to keep them alive in Ireland, but she had never done *that*, and she could not do it now. Damn

Tomas anyhow! Why couldn't he have gone to another banker looking for his loan? But the answer to that was simple: Mr. Maddigan was the only banker who was Irish, the only person who might consider lending money to penniless immigrants.

Maddigan spoke to her several times during the remainder of the summer; once he even summoned her downstairs to the parlor, where it was relatively cool. He must have realized that in the heat of the nursery, with his child at her breast, he had said things that would not further his desires. He chatted amiably enough, but sat sizing her up with his dark eyes, as if he expected an answer. Mary behaved as though she had never heard the proposition, let alone considered it. After half an hour, he dismissed her and went to the hall to put on his hat and pick up his walking stick. Bridie noted the next day that the master's bed had not been slept in all night: he must have stayed with friends.

Though Mary visited Veronica at least once a week—and a hot, weary journey it was, pushing the pram—she did not see Brian for the rest of the summer. He was not difficult to avoid, since he was at the pub when she went to the North End, and he made no effort to contact her, either, which made things easier on both of them. Doirin remained the same: Mary could hardly look at her, feeling that it was in her power to help her, if she could. Veronica kept her informed about what was happening in the family, while she helped Doirin take a cup of the tea or some of the cake Mary brought with her.

"Sure, Mr. Dugan's not leaving until the autumn," Veronica said one day. "He can't get anyone to take his pub. There are lots that would like to, but no one has any money. And Brian and Tomas haven't heard anything from the banker they asked for a loan." She shrugged. "Sure, who'd give it to them, anyway? They've nothing to match the money with."

"They'd have the pub," Mary said, relaxing in the coolness of the basement with her cup of tea.

"If that were the case, why doesn't someone else come up with a loan?" Veronica asked. "Any one of them would have the pub to put against a loan. Brian said the banker they asked sounded very hopeful at first, but they haven't heard from him again at all. Poor Brian. Was there ever a man who had so much against him, so much unhappiness...and he such a good man? My heart fairly breaks for him."

"Yes," Mary said. "And what about Mr. Rabinsky? Do you

see him any more at all? His English was coming along so well."

Veronica's cheeks colored. "I get there a few times a week, for an hour or so, when Liam's here to look after Doirin. Isn't it peculiar that your boy's the one most concerned about her? Of course, Michael's gone and never a word from him. And Darin's so young. But you'd think Padraig, who's older than Liam, would do something."

"Padraig lacks feeling," Mary observed. "Haven't you ever noticed? From the time he was a baby, no one could hold him or kiss him, without him turning away. No, Doirin can't expect much from that one: he's all for himself. Some children are born selfish, I think. The sad thing is that Doirin estranged all of her children, before this happened to her."

Veronica nodded, abandoning her attempt to get some tea between the close-set lips of her blank-eyed sister-in-law. "Sure, Mary, it may sound like treason, but would you put up with her if she weren't your sister? I mean, before this occurred. She has a tongue like a viper. And talk about selfish! God forgive me," she said, crossing herself. "One shouldn't speak evil of the . . . God forgive me again . . . I nearly said *dead*."

Mary looked at her sister: it was almost the same thing. She sat in one position, unless she was moved: she did not speak a word. "It isn't easy on you, is it, Veronica?"

Veronica smiled. "It wasn't at first. But then I remembered how you looked after me when I was ill, Mary: that wasn't easy on you, either. And, for the most part, I can ignore her when I'm here with her." Her blue eyes twinkled suddenly, mischievously. "It's like having a statue of the Virgin Mary in the room."

"Veronica!" Mary laughed. "May God forgive you for that, too! But I think I see what you mean. As long as you don't go daft and start praying to her."

In spite of themselves, they both dissolved into laughter. Covering her mouth with her hand, Veronica managed to say, "This is wicked, Mary. It's like laughing in church!"

And they both nearly went into hysterics again, for laughter was their only release: if they did not laugh, they might have cried.

Mary was the first to get herself under control. Wiping her eyes, she said, "That felt good. I don't know how long it's been since I really laughed. Remember in the old days, back home? Sure, Tomas was the wit, then. Either he's changed, too, or I have. He isn't funny anymore."

"The real wit was your father," Veronica said. "When Mr. O'Shea was around, no one kept solemn for long...even at a wake."

"Yes." Mary smiled; then she remembered the last time she had seen her parents and her mind veered away. "I've had another letter from Rosaleen. The children are having a wonderful time: picnics, swimming, boating. But her every other sentence, it's Darin this or Darin that...you'd think the Maddigan boys weren't along at all. Those two are so close."

"They are that," Veronica agreed. "You'd think they were brother and sister, instead of cousins. Darin pretends he hates to have Rosaleen following him around, and next thing you know he's making a doll for her or something."

"Mrs. Maddigan thought they were. Brother and sister, I mean. They're both certainly Noonans. Pretty, like you."

Her fair skin coloring again, Veronica rose from the table. "I think I'd better get Our Lady out to the privy before we've a catastrophe on our hands."

Mary put down her cup quickly. "Here, let me help you. I wish I could be here more often. I don't like it in that house in the summer, anyway, with so few people about."

"Is it haunted?" Veronica asked, taking one side of Doirin while Mary supported the other.

"I don't know. I think it is, in a way," she said, because she felt Mr. Maddigan's presence everywhere in it, even when he was not there. "It's big and empty without the children there."

"You can let go of her now," Veronica said. "After you once get her up, she'll let you lead her up the stairs."

The leaves were starting to color when Laura Maddigan, with her entourage of servants and children, returned. Rosaleen and Darin looked as though they had grown inches to Mary's eyes: their skins were brown and their eyes bright as they gabbled their adventures to her in the nursery. She noted, almost with dismay, how their bodies had filled out, too: all sign of skin-and-bone thinness was gone, and they were as hearty as the Maddigan children. Rosaleen brought her some seashells, which she presented proudly, throwing her arms around Mary's neck.

"Oh, I missed you so much, Mother!"

Mother? Mary looked into her face to make sure it was the same child: the eyes that looked back at her were full of love. "You used to call me Ma," she said, smoothing her daughter's curls.

"Aunty Laura said that isn't right," Rosaleen explained solemnly. "She says it isn't repect...respectable..."

"Respect*ful*," Darin corrected her. "I think that's true, Aunt Mary. You wouldn't be after saying 'Holy Ma, Mother of God,' now, would you? By the way, how's my mother?"

Mary averted her eyes. "She's the same, Darin. When Michael left the way he did, it broke her heart."

The boy's face was serious for a moment. "When a boy becomes a man, his mother should keep out of it, I think. Michael knew what he was doing and Pa agreed. By the way, we went to New Bedford with Kevin, and I found out what ship Michael's on."

"With Kevin?" she asked, surprised. Mr. Maddigan had said he took the children to New Bedford: he did not mention the young driver. "Sure, you didn't go alone with Kevin, did you? He's a nice young man, but didn't Mr. Maddigan go along, too?"

"Why would he do that?" Darin asked. "Kevin's loads of fun: we did everything with him. Why, we hardly saw Mr. Maddigan when he was there. He was off visiting friends of his own most of the time."

So, Mary thought, he lied about that: there was no telling where truth left off and lies began, then.

"I *like* Mr. Maddigan!" Rosaleen said with fervor. "He thinks I'm funny!"

"Sure do you want someone to think you're funny?" Mary said, bristling. "Do you want to be laughed at, Rosaleen?"

Darin broke in quickly and humorously, "She's a daft little thing, Aunt Mary. She is rather funny sometimes. Mr. Maddigan likes her. She amuses him. And Rosie laps up attention like a cat eats cream."

"Cream, is it?" Mary said, raising her eyebrows slightly. "Sure I guess milk's no longer good enough for you." Her mind was working hard beneath the children's conversation. Her first thought was to wonder if Mr. Maddigan had made any improper advances to her little girl, like that old man in the village made to the children years ago, feeling up their skirts and trying to put his tongue in their mouths. But Rosaleen was such an open, honest child that she would tell her about it without being asked; indeed, she would have told

Darin long before now. Rosaleen would not keep it to herself as Doirin had done, making Mary swear never to breathe a word to their parents. Strange: she had forgotten about that until this moment, and how upset her sister had been, calling the old man "filthy" and "nasty," wiping her hand across her lips and washing her mouth for days. Mary had been a very little girl, Doirin about eight. Mary shook her thoughts from the past when she realized Darin was getting ready to leave.

"Well, I guess it's time I got home," he said, almost reluctantly. "I'll be over when I can. Matthew and Harry are going off to boarding school next week, and Rosie and John will be starting classes again. I'm sure glad I don't have to do that! I hope that damn Catholic school never gets built!" Mary shook her head at his language, but his eyes were so merry that she did not reprimand him: he would continue to swear anyway, and as long as Rosaleen did not pick it up, it wasn't so bad.

"Come whenever you can, dear," she said with her arm around her daughter. "There'll always be cake for you. And don't forget to thank Mrs. Maddigan for the lovely summer you had."

He nodded, grinning. "She's a nice lady. A little..." He made a screw-like motion with his finger to his temple. "But nice. It's better to go that way than the way Ma . . . Mother did."

After he left, Mary gave Rosaleen a big hug. "My, don't we have pretty curls! Where did you get those?"

"Mrs. Lynch wrapped rags around them at night." Rosaleen smiled, shaking her head to make the long black curls dance. "Will you do that too? She can show you how."

"I don't think so, darlin'. I don't want you to get precious. No one likes a little girl who's too taken with herself. Besides, your own hair's as nice as it can be." Her daughter did not seem to care that much: she was into her wicker hamper, which had only been a box containing a few things when she left, pulling out one summer dress after another and holding one up to herself to show her mother as she did so, turning around to make the full skirts twirl. "And where did those come from?" Mary asked, trying to keep the concern she felt out of her voice.

"One day, Mr. Maddigan said I only had two dresses to my name," the child replied. "He told Aunt Laura to get me some, but"—she wrinkled her nose mischievously—"she did something even better! She made them herself!"

"Mrs. Maddigan made these?" Mary said with surprise, lifting one of the garments to study the stitches: they were beautifully sewn. "She did all this herself?"

"Yes. She said she had nothing else to do for the summer, and she ordered the material and patterns. Wasn't that nice of her? And it was nice of Mr. Maddigan, too."

Mary studied her daughter with mixed emotions, wondering where it all would end. Laura Maddigan had obviously taken a liking to Rosaleen; but Laura was flighty, as Darin had indicated: the attachment might terminate as quickly as it had begun. As for Mr. Maddigan, the very thought of him made Mary shudder.

"Rosie, is there anything you want to tell me?" she asked suddenly.

The wide blue eyes stared innocently into hers. "Yes, Mother. There are so many things I want to tell you! It was such a wonderful summer! I wish you could have been there with us."

With the child's arms around her neck, Mary thought she must be going as insane as her sister over her fear of Mr. Maddigan. She was making a child molester and a monster out of him. Still, from her own experience, she knew that he was a monster and a liar: it was probably natural to suspect the worst of him in any relationship. She was glad Rosaleen was home with her again, where she could watch over her, and she determined that if any improper advances were ever made to her child, she would go first to Laura and then to the police.

She would probably never find a job as good as this one again, but she felt she could always get some kind of work.

Chapter 12

THE NEW ENGLAND autumn, which Laura Maddigan
called Indian summer, came like a startling revelation to
Mary and Rosaleen, who did not know that leaves could turn
so many different colors. After Rosaleen's classes in the afternoon, they took a walk in the Common with the pram, just
to marvel at the splendor of the trees, spangled red and gold
and rust, some pure yellow like sunshine, others a deep, wild
red such as they had never seen in Ireland. They exclaimed
over each leaf Rosaleen retrieved from the ground, the cold
air making her cheeks red too.

"It's even nicer than spring," Mary said. "Sure I wish it
would be spring and autumn forever here...that there wasn't
any snow or heat. I wish we could keep the leaves just like
this."

"I saw a flower kept in a book," Rosaleen replied, bending
over to gather more leaves, holding them like a Chinese fan
in her hand. "It was dry, but it still had some color."

"What a grand idea," Mary said and smiled; then, suddenly
serious, "Where did you see that? Surely not in one of
Johnny's schoolbooks. Rosaleen, you haven't been taking
books off the shelf in the library when you should be studying
downstairs."

"But there are so many of them, Mother. Besides, that one
belonged to Auntie Laura, and she wouldn't mind."

"You mustn't touch things in that room, darlin'. You're

there to do your homework, because the light is better. Those books are the Maddigans' private property. You must ask first if you want to look at them."

Rosaleen skipped on the earthen walk, giving her new coat a swirl. "I did, Mother! Mr. Maddigan said I could read all of them if I wanted to. He said Johnny's the only one who's ever touched them."

"Does he come into the library when you're studying?" Mary asked quietly.

"He did once. He's so nice, Mother. He likes me."

"Indeed? Maybe you just miss having your father and Brian around. Come along, we must go home for dinner. The days are getting short, now."

"Why do they get short?"

"I'm sure I don't know. They get shorter before winter, that's all. They always have."

"What's that awful smell?" Rosaleen asked suddenly, wrinkling her nose. "It smells like something's burning."

"They're burning dead leaves," Mary replied, her mind contrasting the odor with the sweet fires behind hedgerows back home; for the first time, she felt a pang of homesickness for Ireland. The good times there had been good: all the greenness, the mist and meadow flowers. "Do you remember the hedge fires in Ireland?" she asked her daughter.

But Rosaleen shook her head. "I remember bad things...like when we took the broth to Grandma's."

"Then you must forget all of it," Mary said quickly. "There were things no one should see. Come along, now: help me push the pram up the hill. I wonder if you'll have your favorite pudding for dinner?"

In the evenings, everything was as soft and gray as the days were bright: a comfortable quietness pervaded the warm house, a kind of gathering in close together as they waited for winter. Often, after the children went to study, Laura retired to her room and summoned Mary. Both of them needed female companionship, and they found it in each other. Mary could hear the baby from the nursery above as they chatted, if there was a problem. Laura had been deeply pleased when Mary complimented her on her sewing, and when Mary admitted that she was very poor with a needle herself, Laura invited the Irish peasant woman for a few lessons. Mary's sewing improved immensely under Laura's patient eye and gentle admonitions, though she was in constant fear she would ruin the fine material she worked on. They were making squares for a quilt, but not with castoff remnants from the rag bag: that was not Laura's style. She had ordered several yards of every cotton in the store, patterned and plain in color, and she directed the mixture of them like an artist combining pigments.

"I used to embroider," she said. "It was considered proper for young ladies. But when you sew, you have something to show for your work. Something that can be used and enjoyed. Embroidery is rather tedious, and hard on the eyes, too. Do you know, I believe I'm getting short-sighted? I may end up with spectacles like poor old Johnny."

Mary was ashamed to ask her what embroidery was, but she would never learn if she did not ask questions. In her embarrassment, she asked another question that had been bothering her.

"Why do you always call him that, ma'am? The lad's only eight."

Laura laughed lightly. "Johnny's been old since the day he was born," she said. "A little wise old man. I'm sure he's dreadfully intelligent: the governess says so. But he's so solemn! He doesn't play like the other boys. His nose is always in a book. I must say, though, that Rosaleen and Darin were simply marvelous when he got his spectacles. They prevented his brothers from teasing him by pretending they were wonderful."

"I don't think they were pretending." Mary smiled. "They were very much impressed with them. Ma'am, begging your pardon, could you tell me what embroid—"

The door opened suddenly, without even a knock, and both women looked up from their work with opposite reactions to the dominating presence of Mr. Maddigan, who still had his waistcoat on, instead of his usual evening smoking jacket. While Mary's heart shriveled with dread at the sight of him, Laura smiled brightly.

"Hello, my darling! What a lovely surprise. I thought you were still working in the study."

"I am working," he said, without acknowledging her pleasant greeting. "Mary, I want you downstairs. This business of ours is to be settled tonight."

Her hands trembling so much she could hardly push the needle in the material, Mary said evenly, "What business, sir?"

"This nonsense about the loan for the pub. Your husband and his brother will be here shortly. I want you there, too.

It's a family business, so the whole family should be present."

Was he lying again? she wondered. Bluffing to get her downstairs alone with him? She studied his face: it was very businesslike. No, not even he would be so terrible, in front of his wife. Then another thought shook her: Brian was coming here this evening. She took a deep breath and, rising, put her patchwork square aside. And Tomas, too, she thought with a sinking sensation. She had not seen him for five months: she did not want to see him ever again.

As soon as he got her in the hall with the door closed behind her, Mr. Maddigan whispered fiercely, "If you think I'm doing this for you, you're daft, Mary! You've been decent enough not to say anything to my wife, but maybe it wasn't that, eh? More like survival, if I see it correctly. Christ! You have Laura eating out of your hand. You're a survivor, aren't you, my dear? Devil I should meet a woman like you! When Tomas approached me again at the bank yesterday, all I could think of was little Rosaleen. She needs some kind of security for the future."

He descended the staircase in silence, with Mary following a few steps behind him, loathing the sight of his neck bulging over his collar. By the time they reached the Turkish rug outside of his study, her temper flared suddenly.

"Mr. Maddigan, I'm not a schemer! Never a bit of it! I wouldn't hurt that lady for anything, just because I like her. Yes, I'm a survivor. God alone knows what I've survived. But not at anyone else's expense. You can only see others through your own eyes. You're not only ruthless, you're . . ."

Amused amazement crossed his face. "Oh, you're really trying to secure this loan, aren't you? Now, you don't give a damn about anything but your own self-righteousness. Mary's pure and blameless, and devil take the hindmost . . . in this case, the pub! You're absolutely extraordinary. And, Mary," he said, his voice softening, "if you knew me better, you'd find—"

The doors of the library exploded open, and Johnny came running out, laughing, with Rosaleen chasing him, her face screwed up and her hands extended like talons. When Johnny saw his father, he drew up quickly, and the little girl nearly bumped into him from behind.

"Rosaleen!" Mary exclaimed, and the child changed into her daughter again, staring at her with guilt.

"It wasn't her fault," Johnny intervened quickly, though quietly. "We were telling ghost stories, and—"

"Sure, you should be studying."

"We finished that a long time ago," the boy said. "When we help each other, we can finish in a hurry. Mrs. Noonan, it isn't true that there's a wailing banshee in Ireland, is it? I don't believe it, but she scared me half to death with her imitation."

"The banshee only wails for a death in special families," Mary explained with some embarrassment before the boy's father. "You've nothing to worry—"

"Like Maddigans," Rosaleen put in mischievously. "She wails only for the royal ones."

"Rosaleen!" Mary repeated, grabbing her by the arm. "Johnny, sure you've nothing to worry about. Rosaleen, I want you to go to the nursery. I won't have a repetition of this. You're acting like a hooligan! We'll talk about it later."

Mr. Maddigan was chuckling, and it infuriated Mary. She did not want the child encouraged when she was bad.

"Don't leave, Rosaleen," he said. "Some of your relatives are coming this evening. I think you should be here, too."

Rosaleen looked from him to her mother, wondering which one to obey. Mary shrugged her shoulders. "It's true. Your father and Brian will be here soon. You should see them, but you haven't heard the last of that other matter."

Together, they went into the study, one room that was always closed to them. It was Mr. Maddigan's private sanctum: he worked at night on his business in there. Mary turned around to see if Johnny had entered, too, but the boy had disappeared like an elf. The three of them were alone together. Mr. Maddigan indicated a low leather chair, and Mary sat down on the edge of it, keeping Rosaleen at her side. The study was sumptuous, but completely masculine: it even smelled of him. Perspiration and tobacco and brandy. He took his place behind the massive mahogany desk and filled his pipe from a rosewood canister engraved in silver with his initials. The silence was so heavy that Mary could feel it pressing down on her.

He must have felt it, too, because he finally said, "Well, Rosaleen, how are your lessons coming?"

"Just fine, Mr. Maddigan," the child said brightly. "Auntie Laura says if I do well with my French, I can take piano lessons after Christmas."

He nodded heavily. "I'm told your mathematics are as good as Johnny's. That's an odd thing for a little girl."

"I had lessons before I came here, from the nicest man in the world! He showed me how to do shortcuts. It's hard to explain."

"Well, you must show me, then. It sounds like something I could use. Who was this man who taught—"

The front door bell rang, mercifully, before Mr. Rabinsky was brought into the conversation. Mary wanted Mr. Maddigan to know as little about them as possible: their lives were no concern of his. But at the sound of the chimes, the sinking sensation returned: it would take every ounce of her strength to get through this meeting. It had been a long time since she had seen Brian: the last time, she had been in his arms.

"Ah, sure, it's a cool night," Tomas said as the Noonan men were ushered into the room. "Hello, Mary, darlin'. I was after hopin' you'd be here this evening for such a grand occasion. My, you're lookin' fine. And here's my little Rosaleen! Come to your old Pa, Rosie! Why, this one's the pride of the family, for sure. What's wrong, darlin'? Come to your Pa."

Rosaleen remained beside Mary's chair, eyeing her father suspiciously. It took a nudge on her mother's part to make her move toward Tomas, as though they were a happy family—an impression Mary thought it imperative to make in front of Mr. Maddigan. Shyly, the little girl let the effusive man, who was almost a stranger to her, lift her into the air and pat her bottom, which was so well covered by petticoat and skirt that she could hardly feel the familiarity. Her face remained grave, and when he put her down, it was with mutual relief.

While the paternal fiasco was taking place, Mary raised her gaze to Brian, to see how he looked, and if he was faring better than when she'd last seen him. This was one of the times that she should have given him her invisible, sidelong glance, but she did not realize it until their eyes met and held, with a force flowing between them stronger than ever before. With all of her determination, it was she who broke the glance first; and, the next moment, Rosaleen was pulling at Brian's coat, demanding his attention. With a quick change of mood, he flashed his white smile and crouched down to kiss the child, briefly, because he, too, was aware of impres-

167

sions, and it was obvious to everyone in the room that the little girl had snubbed her own father.

"Well," Tomas said, rubbing his hands together, looking younger, though stouter than he had ever been. "Good evening, Mr. Maddigan. You'll forgive my manners, please, but it's always such a joy to see my family. It's wanting to get down to business you are, though, I have no doubt."

"On the contrary, Tomas. I find your family most interesting. Little Rosaleen's a special pet of mine, too. As I explained to you in the bank yesterday, I'm doing this particularly for her."

Tomas smiled wickedly, arching an eyebrow, as though there were a secret between them. "Divil, you are! You're a businessman, sir, and so am I. Both of us are out to get all we can out of this transaction: I appreciate your good sense. By backing Dugan's Pub, which we're renaming the Noonan Pub, you're doing a sharp piece of business, to be sure."

"Tomas," Brian said, putting his hand on his brother's arm, embarrassed by the bluffing speech, "I think, perhaps, we should listen to Mr. Maddigan's terms. That is our reason for being here tonight."

He glanced at Mr. Maddigan, who was sizing him up beside his brother, and the banker nodded, extending his hand. "Please be seated. This transaction can be handled rather simply, and in a gentlemanly way, I believe. Mr. Dugan wants to sell out for nine hundred dollars, a loan I will carry for ten years. I think you can pay such a loan off in ten years with a business like that, don't you?"

Mary was appalled by the amount: they had never had so much money in their whole lives. Brian's face remained grave, and Tomas ran his finger under his collar.

"That's what the man said," Tomas agreed feebly, faced with the improbable amount in reality, instead of dreaming. "Begging your pardon, sir, you wouldn't have a little drop of something around to take the edge off?"

Mr. Maddigan's eyes glittered contemptuously. "Not until our transaction's finished, my friend. I believe in keeping a clear head with figures."

"Yes. Yes, indeed," Tomas said hastily, exceedingly parched from nerves. "I couldn't agree with you more. I was just saying to Brian on the way over here—"

"If we maintain the present profits," Brian interposed quietly, "we could certainly handle such a loan."

"Good . . . good!" Mr. Maddigan said, with the same glitter

168

in his eyes he had previously retained for Tomas. "Of course, there will be interest. You know what interest is, don't you?"

"Do we know what interest is!" Tomas exclaimed. "Indeed we do, sir. Didn't we have to pay it, and then some, to the *gombeen* man in our village, who sold meal most dearly during the hungry summer months until the spuds were in, and charged us interest into the bargain, when we couldn't pay in cash."

Mr. Maddigan cleared his throat and tapped his finger impatiently on the desk. "*Gombeen* men are usurers...little better than Jews," he said. "I'm a banker, and my rate of interest is fixed on a yearly basis. It is three percent."

There was a sudden silence: none of the Noonans could compute percentages, but no one wished to reveal it. Mary had a feeling that Mr. Maddigan's small dark eyes saw right through them.

"That's thirty-three fifty a year, as you know, in small payments in addition to your monthly payment. It isn't a high interest rate and should be agreeable to everyone."

"Twenty-seven dollars a year, sir," a small voice said, and everyone turned to Rosaleen, who was raising her hand as though in class. "Thirty-three fifty would be at three and a half percent on nine hundred dollars. I think you made an error in your multiplication."

Mr. Maddigan flushed deeply, appraising the little girl with his hard dark eyes. "Perhaps I did," he admitted lamely. "I should have done it on paper instead of in my head." And, noting that Rosaleen had not used paper, he quickly jotted down some figures: she was right, of course, but the exercise saved face, gave him time to think in order to cover the discrepancy. "Well, then, Rosaleen...you're right, indeed. One of your famous shortcuts, young lady? You really must show me how you do it." He cleared his throat again and addressed himself to the adults. "As I said, your payments will come to about a hundred dollars a year over ten years. Our little friend here has broken it down nicely for us, showing that the payments will be even easier than we thought. Would you like to sign the papers, now? I think, like Tomas, I'm ready for a drink."

Though she had no intention of joining the family above the pub yet, because she was sincerely attached to the baby and Laura, and because Rosaleen was getting an education there, Mary rejoiced with Veronica at the move and helped her furnish the sunny new flat. Mrs. Dugan was excited over her farmhouse and had decided to decorate it like her house in Ireland, where Mr. Dugan had been an overseer. So she left many basic and valuable items behind for the Noonans. They only had to purchase beds and some linens and stonewear: the dining-room furniture and most of that in the parlor was left intact. The thing that delighted Mary the most was that she also left the airy white lace curtains in place. The other furniture they could acquire as they could afford it: the flat was already like a castle to them all, after nearly a year in the basement.

Their decision to bring absolutely nothing with them but the clothes on their backs was mutual. They left the tenement with even less than they had had on arrival, discarding not only the pan and buckets, but the poor winter coats as well, not in an act of bravado, but to provide the furnishings for the next poor immigrant who appeared. And the Irish continued to arrive almost daily, some so weak and sick they had to be carried from the boat, or from the railway station. The North End and Fort Point were filled to capacity, but room was still made for more. The newspapers spoke out against conditions in those locations, saying they were like pestholes, breeding grounds for disease; but the fact remained that there was no place else for the refugees to go. Most of those who were here had already fled New York, which was overcrowded and sick with poverty from so many thousands pouring in without proper preparation for their arrival.

As conditions in the neighborhood declined, Mary was sick at heart. She went there, pushing the pram through slush and snow, during the early months of winter, usually alone, except for little Philip, while Rosaleen was getting an education with Johnny. And though it meant their livelihood, Mary was incensed by the number of patrons at the pub every afternoon—men spending the little money they had for ale, just as they had in Ireland. When she finally mentioned the fact at tea in the upstairs flat one day, she found that Tomas and Brian had different opinions of it.

"Every penny they spend is a penny more for us," Tomas said, lacing his tea with whiskey. "It's easy for you to talk, Mary, livin' as high on the hog as you do. But remember, we have to meet our payments and our livin', besides. And your poor sister needs caring for. What other people do with their

170

money is their own affair. We got what we have the hard way, God help us."

Brian leaned back in his chair, weary from working such long hours, though he seemed more content with their lot. Mary knew that he did most of the work, because Tomas was such a talker. But Brian had informed her, early on, that Tomas created the "goodwill" to bring people in. "Tomas knows we fell into an easy thing because of Mr. Maddigan's affection for you and Rosaleen," he said and smiled, and Mary's heart stopped for a moment, before she realized that he did not know what Mr. Maddigan's affection for her really was. Maddigan had been less persistent lately; he reminded her of a spider, biding his time. She spent a lot of time in Laura's company. "The truth is, Mary, we continue to give free meals to any poor souls who wander in here like we did, and we contribute to the Irish Benevolent Society. And I'm starting to put a bit aside each month to go into the parochial-school fund that's just getting started. Within two years, the boys will be able to go to school."

It still did not make up for the food snatched from the mouths of wives and children by drinking husbands, but Mary pretended to be pacified: she would say nothing that would hurt Brian.

"Sure, it's a dog-eat-dog world in this country," Tomas expanded, ignoring what his brother had said. "We can't educate every snot-nosed hoodlum in the slums. We'll be lucky to take care of our own."

As her thoughts always did when Tomas was talking, Mary's wandered, first to Veronica, who was looking slightly pale, then to her sister, Doirin. Though she sat at the table with the rest of them, clean and combed and putting on weight, she seldom spoke. The move had been good for her, as Dr. Townsend had predicted: within three months, she had shaken herself out of her stupor and begun to talk. But she was not the same as she had been before, which, according to one's way of thinking, was either a curse or a blessing. She still grieved for her lost son, Michael, and waited for letters from him that did not arrive. Mary would rather have seen her back in her old form, nagging all of them, slashing her wicked tongue, than sunk in such heavy passivity.

The "care" Tomas mentioned amounted to no more than her living there: all the work was on Veronica, and though it was not as heavy as when Doirin was totally catatonic, the girl was frail and the invalid still too confused in mind to give her much help. With winter now upon them, and the flat not quite as warm as the basement, they had to look after Veronica's health, so she would not be sick with consumption again.

"I'm thinking," Mary suggested, looking at Brian, instead of her husband, "with business so good, that you might hire a cook for the restaurant. Veronica wouldn't have to leave Doirin alone in the evening that way. Sure, there are hundreds of poor souls out there who'd take the job for a song and glad to have it, too."

"Veronica's only just learned the recipes from the cookbook we bought!" Tomas protested. "She's only beginning to turn out decent grub. She can even do a roasted meat now that isn't too bad."

"Any woman who can read," Mary said quietly, "could soon do the same. You might even find someone who was a cook somewhere back home. I know I'd have given my right arm for such an opportunity when we first arrived here."

"She'd steal food for her family," Tomas said quickly, when he saw Brian nod. "It'd cost us twice her pay."

"A good thing, too," Brian said, "if her children were starving. Sure, Tomas, all she'd want is leftovers and a sack of spuds every month to keep her honest. I think it's a fine idea. She wouldn't have to live here, and the spuds would be part of her pay."

"Well," Tomas considered, "when you put it that way...but Veronica would have to train her, from the book we bought: it cost two dollars. She'd have to cook at least as well as Veronica."

Veronica looked from Mary to Brian, a smile showing faintly at the edge of her lips, appreciation in her blue eyes.

"Sure," she said humbly, "any woman would be a better cook than I am. And I'd keep after her, never fear!"

The restaurant improved with Mrs. Flannery's cooking, and so did Veronica's health. By November, not only single working men were coming there to dine, but merchants and craftsmen from the surrounding area. Tomas was pleased with the decision and often commented on what a stroke of genius it was for him to have hired a cook.

Laura spent a short time each day with little Philip. Once she became accustomed to him, she began to enjoy him; his face was no longer strange to her. She came to the nursery every morning before lunch, and didn't glance at her lapel watch until it was about time to leave for the meal. His future clearly worried her, however; often Mary observed the pensive expression on her face when she held him quietly. Mary could not figure out whether Laura was worried that he would not survive to adulthood, or feared that he would. As a small baby, he was clean and sweet and delightful, grinning easily at any noise or responding to a smile. Mary thought that his mother must realize, as she did, that the baby days would soon come to an end and they would have a decision to make. Realizing that Laura was not much good at decisions, she approached the subject herself one morning.

"Something's troubling you, ma'am, and I think it concerns Philip. Would you be wanting to talk abou' it?"

The invitation brought Laura up straight, dispersing the clouds from her mind, scattering her vagueness. "Yes, Mary, I really would. After he starts walking, he's going to become more difficult, isn't he? I mean, the training and all...or inability to accomplish it? You've been so good with him, and he's simply blooming! But I've been wondering if I can ask so much more of you. You're such a young woman and have your own family. I keep thinking I should hire a nurse— someone trained to bear with such things. At the same time, I consider you more a friend than an employee, and I can't endure the thought of not having you here."

Mary smiled. "You're troubling yourself over nothing, ma'am. I'll be happy to look after your little boy. Sure, we don't want some vinegar-faced nurse caring for him, now, do we? He has a lot of affection to give, and he deserves some in return. You know I'm very fond of him."

Laura relaxed. "Oh, Mary, I was hoping—though I didn't really dare hope—that you'd say that! However," and her countenance saddened again, "I think it's only fair to point out that things won't be the same for Rosaleen after next fall. My husband has decided that Johnny really must go away to school, too. We've only kept him home this long because he was always ailing and he was so timid. You know how men are...'We must make a man of him,' that sort of talk. Anyway, the governess will be dismissed in the spring, and your daughter won't have any instruction here."

Mary's heart fell slightly: that was something she had not considered. She had thought of the governess as a household fixture like Mrs. Balfe. She did some rapid calculations in her head.

"The new parochial school will be built in two years, they say. It would mean that Rosaleen would only miss one year of instruction before then. Sure, she's ahead of the rest of the Catholic children, as it is. If perhaps she could have permission to use the books in the library until then?"

"Of course! But Mary, why can't she go to a regular public school like other children in her class? They say they are relatively good, and . . ."

"They won't allow it," Mary said with a sigh.

"For goodness' sake, *who* won't allow it?" Laura asked incredulously.

"The Church, ma'am. The priests are that much against a public-school education. They say if we can't educate our own—"

"That is the most outrageous thing I've ever heard!" Laura flared suddenly, with more emotion than Mary had ever imagined she possessed. "Are you telling me that all those ignorant children are being deprived an education—indeed, of any future in life at all—just because the priests say they can't go to our schools?"

Mary's embarrassment was caused by the fact that Laura had expressed her own hidden thoughts out loud. "Yes, ma'am. I think it's criminal, myself. God help me," she said, crossing herself. "But that's the way it is. The clergy's afraid the children will lose their religion and fall into wicked ways, which is the most important thing to them. I thought of going against it. I really did. But it wouldn't be the priests who'd be enforcing the rule. It'd be the other children, and a bad lot of hooligans they are, too. Rosaleen's had enough trouble from them."

Laura finally glanced at her watch. "Oh, dear, I'm late. Mary, my dear, Rosaleen can use the library all she wants next year. And there's one other thing: I want you to call me Laura, not 'ma'am.' It doesn't sound right, somehow, coming from you."

"Oh, I couldn't do that," Mary protested. "I'll call you Mrs. Maddigan, if you like."

"*Laura*," the small blond woman said emphatically, tapping her toe in mock displeasure.

Mary laughed. "I'm sorry. That isn't like you," she said, pointing to the tapping foot. "Very well, ma'am . . . I mean, *Miss* Laura. I think I'll call you that."

Laura bent down to kiss her cheek. "I think you're the only real woman I've ever known," she said. "You're the salt of the earth, Mary, and that's a very good thing to be."

Almost everything seemed to be going well for Mary: it was enough to cause some superstitious fear. She said a quick prayer of thanks to the Blessed Virgin, her namesake, who looks after women. She tried not to allow herself the euphoria that was sneaking through her controls. But her job was assured for Philip's lifetime, and she had money of her own to do with as she chose. The parochial school would be built just in time for Rosaleen and Liam and Darin to attend. Padraig could go, too, if he chose, but she thought he was probably too big to want to join the younger children: one never knew about Padraig. When Mary considered their situation a year ago this time... She crossed herself formally, slowly, to overcome the fear brought on by too much good fortune. In many ways, they were better off than they had ever been, and she could not help wondering if they really deserved it, especially herself. She almost had a precognition that something bad was in store for her. To free herself from the feeling, she started to make plans for Christmas: she and Rosaleen would have to start soon, if they were to make gifts for everyone. Pressing the happiness back inside of her, she began to make a list: as long as she was doing things for other people, she was all right.

She was safe. And, she thought hopefully, the rest of the family with her.

Thanksgiving, even when it was explained to them, seemed to embody the sin of gluttony to Mary. She and Rosaleen shared the meal in the kitchen alcove with the other servants, after the family above had been served. Never had she seen so much food in one place before: the rich browned turkey, piles of mashed potatoes, golden Indian squash, the inevitable peas, cranberry sauce and rolls with creamery butter. That feast for kings, partaken of by servants, too, was followed by two different pies. Mary was certain Rosaleen would be ill from all she was eating, and it did not take the thought of starving people to make her eat lightly. When the last piece of pie was consumed, young Kevin, the coachman, leaned back in his chair and undid his belt.

"Sure, I'll be good for nothing but sleeping the rest of this day," he said, belching. "There are some things in America of which I heartily approve."

"Tell me more about the Indians," Rosaleen coaxed the cook, Mrs. Lynch, who did not rise at once to clear the dishes. "Are there any still around? I'd love to see an Indian, wouldn't you, Mother? Johnny showed me a picture in a book. They helped the Puritans when they came here. They showed them how to grow corn and shoot turkeys, and kept them from starving to death."

"They did, that," Kevin groaned just as the bell rang, indicating service was required upstairs. "Sure," he said in disbelief, "it's from himself's study. I've never seen that bell ring before. Someone get up there quickly, he may be dying of acute indigestion!"

The first-floor maid, a quiet young woman named Peggy, rose and adjusted her white cap. She had hardly climbed the stairs, with Rosaleen still going on about Indians, when she returned again.

"It's Mrs. Noonan he's after asking for," the maid said to Mary's discomfiture. "Alone, he says: it's business. You're to leave Rosaleen here."

Mary rose stiffly and, without comment, left the room with the other servants staring after her. Well, it had not been such a grand day that he would spoil it for her. She was only thankful she had eaten little; if her stomach were full, she might take one look at the man and retch all over his Turkish rug. She considered the possibilities: something about the pub, perhaps, but she had thought all that was settled for Rosaleen's sake. Perhaps, contrary to Miss Laura's wishes, he had decided to dismiss her for being uncooperative in his clumsy advances: but would he do that on Thanksgiving Day? By the time she reached the study, she had exhausted all the reasons she could dream of for his wanting to see her so suddenly.

When she opened the door, she was relieved to see that at least he was sitting behind his desk in a businesslike way: it would be difficult to grope at her from there. His smile, though broad, was slightly sly, as if he had something up his sleeve.

"Ah, Mary, my dear," he greeted her, without rising. "And what do you think of our fine American custom of a Thanksgiving feast?"

She was immediately on the defensive, trying to guess his intentions. "Rather barbaric," she said shortly. "No one should eat himself into a stupor. Especially when people about are near starving."

He laughed, as though that was what he expected from her. "Oh," he said, "the charitable organizations will see that everyone gets a basket on a day like this. All the micks in the tenements will eat like high kings of Tara today...courtesy of this society or that. They were grand feasters and drinkers, our ancestors, you know: the Celtic appetites were strong. But then I suppose you have heard the old tales of green Ireland."

"I have, indeed. I can almost recite them by rote," she said, her pride rising beyond her discretion. "Fiddler Murphy in our village was a grand storyteller, and he took shelter with us every winter. I know about Conn and Brian Boru and the Cattle Raids, up north there in Coolie."

"Good! They were all heroes, weren't they? They'd never seen a cross, and they took whatever they wanted, whether it was another man's cattle or his wife. Rare men they were in a heroic time," he said, putting on his Irish brogue rather thickly. "Your village was Rathcormac, wasn't it?"

"Yes, sir," she answered innocently, but added nothing else to the conversation. If he had called her up here to chat about Ireland, he would soon enough find it boring and dismiss her to her own quarters.

"That's what I thought," he said, fixing her with his gaze. "You were one of the beautiful O'Shea sisters. The younger, too proud to marry until she was twenty years old." Mary's mouth nearly fell open, but she maintained a placid expression in spite of the throbbing in her temple. "I met a Cork man yesterday," he continued in a friendly tone. "Perhaps you know him. But that doesn't matter. Apparently, he arrived here after you did. By coincidence, he was from your village." He paused, waiting for her to speak.

"No great coincidence," she said mildly. "Everyone who could leave got out."

"Dreadful circumstances there," he said. "Though, apparently, Lord Leighton, your landlord, was a good sort and didn't evict anyone for nonpayment of rent. But it was a criminal thing that happened to his agent, Mr. McGee, who nobody liked very much."

In spite of herself, her attention was riveted on Maddigan, and her gaze rose to meet his. "He was a terrible man," she said.

He nodded. "Indeed. I've heard what these estate agents can be when they're hired to get the rent from tenants. Still," he said, scratching his chin, "to my way of thinking, no one's so terrible that he deserves to have his head bashed in so brutally. Oh, you didn't know? Mr. McGee met a fearful end and had money taken from him into the bargain. My acquaintance says he knows the Noonans well, both Tomas and Brian. And that there's a warrant for their arrest back in Cork. The older one, Brian, was seen going to Mr. McGee's house, and when the tragedy was discovered, all the Noonans had left. And not from Cork harbor, either. The British constabulary checked there at once."

Mary felt the floor coming up to meet her and had to grasp the arm of a chair. She was as cold as ice, and she could not speak or think, though she wanted to tell the man that Brian would never commit a brutal crime.

While her mind was still reeling, he shot out at her, "I don't wonder that you're white as a sheet! Don't you think I noticed the way you looked at him? You told me you were in love, making me think it was with your husband," he said sarcastically. "Then, right here in this room, you looked into Brian Noonan's eyes and I realized you'd made a fool of me! I don't like playing the fool," he rapped out. "I don't like it at all. Any more than I enjoy being held at arm's length by a woman I happen to want. Now, perhaps you'd better sit down."

She had no choice; her knees were buckling under her. She sank into the nearest chair, grasping the velvet arms with white-knuckled hands. It will pass, she told herself: it is all confusion right now, but it will pass. I will be able to think again. In the meantime, she had no choice but to listen.

"I summoned you here, Mary, to ask if I should pursue this story—through the proper authorities, of course. It would be the quickest and easiest way to get answers. However, knowing you as I think I do, I imagine you'll want to think about it for a while. There's no hurry, is there?" His voice was benign now. "I'm sure we can make an arrangement suitable to both of us. All that's needed is mutual cooperation. It's Thanksgiving, now, and the Christmas holidays are coming up. How about the first of the year? Yes, that's good: the beginning of a new life for both of us. I'm not a flaming romantic, Mary. I never have been, thank God. I have a businessman's brain, and I'm usually very direct. I haven't been direct enough with you in the past, but I'm going to be now. I've never wanted a woman as much as I do you: you're beautiful, earthy, warm. And I don't just want you for a night: I want you to be my mistress, my companion. I've actually been jealous of Laura, because she gets so much of your time. Eventually, I think you'll find that's what you want, too. Women don't consider me unattractive, and I can be very generous. However, tonight, I'm going to write a letter to the British authorities in Cork inquiring further into this matter. If the allegations are true—and from your reaction I'm sure they are—extradition could always be arranged. You don't know that word? It means, quite simply, that Brian Noonan would be sent back to Ireland to hang for his crime. We both know quite well that's the way it's handled. I'll date the letter January 1, 1848. That gives you a month to think it over. I'm sure you won't force me to post it at that time."

Mary did not know how long she sat in the chair, staring into space, after he left the study. During the next three days, she forgot everything but the substance of the conversation: she could think of nothing else. She found it very difficult to get out of bed in the morning at little Philip's first cry; she just did not want to face another day of pain and indecision. She went about her chores automatically, hardly speaking unless she was addressed directly. Her mind was in a numb fog. She found it impossible to get her wits about her, and wondered sometimes if she was going the same way as Doirin. That, at least, would be an answer to her problem. At one moment, she wanted to run to Brian, to find out the truth; but the action was blocked by the thought of his action: she did not want to probe his very soul and destroy him. She thought of going to the priest, but that was negated by the sure knowledge that a priest always made a man turn himself over to the authorities before absolving him. In a way, she felt she was a partner to whatever had occurred in Mr. McGee's house. She had sensed something wrong from the beginning and let it pass without question. The only thing she could not absolutely accept was the brutality of Mr. McGee's demise. That was not like Brian: he would never do that. Perhaps he gave the man a little shove, and he fell and hit his head; something like that was entirely possible. Or maybe someone came in after Brian left and finished the estate agent off...but no, that did not make sense, either. From the time he returned to their cottage, Brian was fleeing from something: walking them to the western port in their condition; frightened out of his wits when it came to going through Immigration, absolutely useless then, because he was afraid of something. And that amounted to only one thing: he feared the news had beaten him to port. He was afraid of being apprehended when they showed their papers.

Mary dwelt on all that for some time, because it kept her from facing the real problem, which she found it impossible to think about clearly. When Laura noticed how pale she was, she gave her a glass of port and sent her to her quarters, where Bridie looked in on her often, to make sure she was all right. Most of the time, Mary lay on her bed in her clothes, only stirring to take care of Philip's needs. She did not bounce him or kiss him, as was her custom; she attended to him and put him back in his crib to gurgle or sleep, forgetting him again at once. Rosaleen, who had never known her mother to be ill before, was almost mute in her presence. She carried the food trays from the dumbwaiter and watched during the few moments it took Mary to fiddle with her food; she took only a bite or two before pushing it away. Then Rosaleen crept off to her lessons or her play, leaving Mary to sleep, since that was what she appeared to be doing.

Mary wanted to be alone. At the same time, she wanted to be in the bosom of her family, where nothing could touch her until her strength returned. She was torn by opposing forces no matter which direction her thoughts took: she was limp from wrestling with everything that pulled at her from either side. After three days of struggling through quicksand in a haze, her faculties began to return. She was aware of it at breakfast when something told her she would grow weak from lack of food; and though she still felt no hunger, she forced herself to eat. She attempted to smile at Rosaleen and thanked her for looking after her so well. She was back among the living, but she did not know for how long. She had not even begun to tackle her real problem, which she saw clearly now.

The snow, which had been intermittent and late that year, began to fall in soft, clustered flakes, covering the street and disguising the dry bushes in the back garden until they looked like rolling hillocks or infinite sand on a white beach, which she had only seen once, before they sailed. The windows rattled with the first thrust of an oncoming blizzard, the wind sculpturing drifts as high as the iron fence. The house was a great, warm trap, from which there was no escape, its inhabitants caught equally together, though only she was struggling for her freedom—for her very life.

No matter how it came out, Mary decided as she and Rosaleen began making their Christmas presents, Brian must be protected, and he must never know that anyone in America knew about their past. Even if she could submit to Mr. Maddigan—and she knew she could not—Brian would be sorely hurt by her action. Somehow, if it were carefully thought out, she would beat the devil at his own game. But how? The question almost made her ill. Never in her life, except, perhaps, when they were all dying of hunger, had she felt so desperate.

If she were dead, Maddigan would not carry out his threat of exposing Brian: the letter would serve no purpose. To be sure, suicide was an unforgivable sin, but she spent one whole evening considering ways to go about it. She could hang herself, as crazy Mrs. Moore had done when they put her second husband to rest. But it would probably be Rosaleen who would find her, poor lamb, and that on her mind for the rest of her life. The only poison she knew about was every part of the potato plant, except the tubers: no chance of obtaining that here, especially in the dead of winter. If she slashed her wrists, the same argument of who would suffer came to mind: Rosaleen. If she could just wander out into the snow and never be seen again...

But no: she could not die. One person, at least, was completely dependent on her... her dear little daughter. The thought of escaping the situation by dying suddenly made anger burn in her face. She was not the one in the wrong: she had done nothing to encourage that terrible man's attentions. Maddigan was the one who should suffer for all the pain he was causing. Her tossing and turning in bed finally disturbed Rosaleen, who began to whimper in her sleep, so Mary lay as still as possible with her thoughts: deadly still.

To be sure, she could kill that man for his wickedness: for the threat he held over her. Not that she would ever think about it... but then... why not? Do away with him like the rodent he was, rid herself of him entirely, in one stroke. Still half-rejecting the idea, she found herself thinking of ways to carry it out. She could never take a weapon against another human: a kitchen knife or one of his guns, or even the poker, was out of the question. She could try to smother him with a pillow while he slept, perhaps, but he was a powerful man, and it would not do to be overpowered in his bedroom. Her heart beat rapidly and her mouth was dry. Something in his food: he was an enormous eater, and he would never notice it. But what? Her mind kept turning to poison and her complete ignorance of it.

Sure, there were all those books in the library, and hardly a soul about all day, until the children went there to study. With that many books, there must be something about poison.

Chapter 13

THE FIRST week in December, when the weather cleared, her Christmas shopping for bits and pieces of material to use in making gifts took Mary to Mr. Rabinsky's, for the first time since spring. Though his shop was swarming with poor Irish on the same mission, he dropped what he was doing the moment she opened the door and rushed to help her maneuver the pram through the entrance. She noticed briefly that he seemed an almost different man: much younger than she remembered him. His long hair was cut and clean, and he no longer wore the distinguishing black skullcap; moreover, with his face shaven, he was almost attractive.

"I have something I've been saving just for you," he said with excitement. "Come, push that carriage into the back room and we'll have a spot of tea."

"What about your customers?" Mary asked dully, but he waved them aside.

"They like to browse. Of all the good things I can say about the Irish, one of them is that they are not thieves. They'll be all right, Mary. Come along."

The small stove and the tea in his quarters only partly warmed Mary: she had felt cold for so long now. Every day that passed toward the new year seemed to take more warmth out of her body, until she was certain she would be a corpse before long. Her grave countenance and pallor were not lost on her old friend.

"What is it, my dear? Sure you've a terrible face on you. You aren't ill?"

"It's an illness of the soul." She smiled ruefully. "So far, the winter's been that hard. Where is this treasure you want to sell me?"

"Not *sell!*" he exclaimed, moving about more than she remembered: he could not seem to sit still and sip tea out of the little brass cups the way they once had done. "I have a gift for you. Two of them came my way, and I'm saving one of them for Veronica for Christmas." Her puzzled look interrupted his line of thought. "Mary, everyone else is celebrating Christmas, can't I do it, too? I know it means the birth of Christ. But even if I don't recognize him as the messiah, I've read the New Testament, and I think he was a good Jew."

A smile touched Mary's lips in spite of herself: he was a dear, good man, and she did not realize how much she had missed him. "Sure, you have my permission to do so," she said. "As long as it doesn't mean extravagant gifts. Because Veronica and I have no way to match them."

"*Gifts,*" he said disparagingly. "After all you and Veronica have done for me? It's nothing. And they aren't really extravagant anyway." He hurried to the wall cabinet, where he kept his treasures from Poland. "I couldn't help noticing, if you'll forgive me, that you and Veronica carry your money around in the corner of a handkerchief, tied so tightly that you have to struggle to loosen the knot. So, when I came by these, I thought of you at once."

He held out a small mesh bag, constructed of tiny metal links of dull gray. "I already have hers wrapped, you understand. But I want you to take yours now. I see you so seldom."

"What is it, then?" she asked, never having seen one before.

"It's called a reticule. You carry it with you to keep your things in. All ladies carry them."

"My lady doesn't," Mary said, examining it carefully in her hands. He had to show her how to work the clasp.

"*Your* lady, if I hear things correctly, doesn't carry money." He smiled, revealing a gold incisor she had not noticed before. "She charges everything and her husband pays the bills."

The thought of Mr. Maddigan cast a pall over her again. She thanked Mr. Rabinsky, as gratefully as possible, and prepared to leave. "I've a few things to get up front," she said. "Some cloth and thread. Then I have to go to the apothecary shop."

"Are you sure no one's ill? Rosaleen isn't with you?"

"She's in the classroom. I must get back before she finishes. No one's ill, Mr. Rabinsky. The problem is, we have rats. I have to pick up something to get rid of them."

"Oh!" He smiled. "Arsenic is the best thing. Though in my neighborhood back home people used lye. Yes," he said and laughed, "instead of killing them, they burned their feet so they would go away. Jews don't like to kill."

She took a deep breath. "Nobody does," she said, rather shortly, taking the handle of the pram to push it out of the room.

"I have some arsenic here," he volunteered. "It will save you a trip to the apothecary, and a few cents, too."

She stopped as though frozen into place. "Sure, what do you keep it for?"

"The same as your household. Rats. Living this near the dock, I had to overcome my squeamishness: the place is infested with them." He raised his hand. "Wait just one minute, my dear. I'll put some in a package for you."

Mary stood in place like a statue, with her hands still resting lightly on the handle of the pram. Her mind, which had not operated very well lately, tried to assess the pros and cons of the situation. Perhaps it was better to get the arsenic here than at the apothecary shop: no professional person would remember it. On the other hand, she did not want to implicate Mr. Rabinsky in any way. If somehow she was apprehended, she knew he would never speak up: he was her friend. And she simply would not disclose how she came by the poison. He was back sooner than she expected.

"Be careful with this, if you're the one who's using it," he instructed her. "A little bit on your hands, accidentally consumed, might make you slightly sick. However, even with all the ladies using it these days, there are few accidents like that."

"All the ladies?" she frowned slightly.

"Yes, didn't you know? It bleaches the complexion if it's used as a lotion. But you don't need anything like that. You and Veronica have the most beautiful skin I've ever seen."

"Thank you, Mr. Rabinsky," she said, for both the compliment and the small package he put into her hand. "I'll put it in my new reticule! I wouldn't want to keep it in the pram with the baby."

*   *   *

The only thing that kept Mary from wavering in her purpose, vague and uncertain as her plan was, was the conviction that she was saving Brian. Several times she put off using the package hidden in the mesh bag in her dresser: once, because of her sympathy with Laura, who loved the dreadful man who was her husband. Then, when she overcame that obstacle, by reasoning that Laura and her sons would be better off without such a corrupt influence and would want for nothing when he died, she postponed her action again, because Christmas was so close. God help them, she would let them have Christmas together, though it only left her one week from the deadline set by her employer.

Keeping to the upper floors as she did, she seldom saw Mr. Maddigan, and he did not press his case, convinced that when her verdict came in the outcome would be on his terms. Actually, from what little talk she heard, he was not spending much time at home. No one had seen him for more than a few minutes a day in several weeks' time. Laura fretted that he worked too hard.

"He's at that horrid bank all day," Laura said, putting the finishing touches on a bow on one of the many presents she was wrapping. "When he comes home, he goes out again right after dinner, and Lord knows when he comes in! I simply can't wait up. I get too sleepy. I only hope that he's getting all this work done, so he can have some time with his family at Christmas. The boys will be home next week, you know, on school holidays. He really should spend more time with the boys."

From the break in her otherwise bright voice, Mary knew that Laura wished he would give her more time, too. Though from the time Mary and Rosaleen had come to the house, she had observed that Laura saw very little of her husband. Their bedrooms adjoined, with a dressing room between them, but how often the door was opened at night was impossible to guess. The situation reinforced Mary's decision. Laura did not have him now, so she could not miss him much when he was gone.

"Miss Laura," she said, "I've been meaning to ask if it's all right for Rosaleen and me to spend Christmas Day with our family. We'll take Philip along, and he'll have a grand time."

Laura started to protest, but stopped herself at once. "How selfish of me not to suggest it!" she accused herself. "Of course, Mary, but we'll miss you very much. Especially old Johnnie, who's bought a very special gift for Rosaleen. I can't believe how much that boy has changed! She's the perfect little companion for him...someone he can instruct, and who likes books as much as he does.... Oh, dear ... I think I've given it away!" she said, putting her hand to her mouth with a smile. "I know what we'll do, so Johnnie won't be disappointed. The children can open their gifts to one another on Christmas Eve. And you shall have your gifts from us then, too."

Mary flushed, smoothed her apron to have something to do with her hands. "Our gifts are rather humble. Rosaleen's made pen wipers—stacks of them—for the boys. I hope they won't be disappointed."

"Anything she does they'll love. We really should teach that girl to sew, though, Mary. Perhaps next year, when she isn't in classes."

"Begging your pardon, Miss Laura, will himsel—will Mr. Maddigan be there Christmas Eve?"

"Oh, I had hoped so!" Laura said with scarcely controlled impatience. "But he told me specifically not to plan things around him: he's dining with a client. It's strange, isn't it?" she added, shrugging her shoulders helplessly. "I have hardly any friends at all, and he has too many. I can't remember the last social event I went to...even a dinner outside this house. But before I was married, this season was full of parties and dances. I needed five ball gowns, just so I wouldn't repeat myself too often, there were so many gay occasions."

And you gave all that up for nothing, Mary thought grimly: Laura was not very deep, but she was kind and tender.

"Sure, you'll be having two fine gowns for the holidays this year," Mary reminded her. "I'm especially fond of the cranberry taffeta with the lace around the shoulders and all those pretty petticoats! You should do your hair with lace and roses...the velvet kind: you'll be a vision, Miss Laura."

"I hope the boys like it," Laura said wistfully; then, cocking her head so that her gray-blond curls danced, "You like pretty things, don't you, Mary? I have a marvelous idea! Goodness, there are so many gowns in my dressing room, some of them hardly worn. Let's pick one out for you to wear on Christmas Eve! We'll have a real party!"

Mary drew back a step. "Oh, no, ma'am, I couldn't. I wouldn't know how to walk with all those skirts. Besides, it just isn't fitting."

"It is, indeed, in *my* house. Now, let's see, you're a few inches taller than I am, but otherwise...I do believe we'll have to take the waist in! And maybe let the bosom out...you know, you really do have a splendid figure. One would never know you were still nursing."

Any attentions from Laura were like rubbing salt into an open wound, and Mary instinctively recoiled from them. But, over her protestations, she was dragged into the dressing room to choose a gown. She was astounded at the rows of garments hanging there in every fabric and color imaginable, with neat lines of matching shoes beneath them. To placate her excited friend, Mary chose a shot-gray taffeta with a discreet neckline and narrow gray-and-white pleats that fanned out below the hemline. Laura threw her hands up and laughed.

"You've excellent taste, my dear. It's from Paris! But it's an afternoon dress, and it's terribly out of style. There's hardly any fullness to the skirt. Haven't you noticed how skirts are billowing out? If it continues, I don't know what we'll wear for petticoats! Are you positive that's the one you want to wear?"

Mary nodded. She really did not want to wear any of them, but she must accept gracefully to keep Laura's spirits up. God knows, they would be lowered soon enough. In spite of herself, Mary's eyes scanned the wardrobe for black, but she looked away quickly.

"I think I can alter it myself now," she said in a dead voice. "I've almost a week to do it, and I'll be that careful not to damage the fabric."

"You *are* a silly. The dress is yours, Mary. If you 'damage' anything it will be your own property."

Every evening, while the children were studying, Mary checked the package in the mesh bag, as she sat motionless on the edge of the bed contemplating how to use it. Time was going by too fast. Perhaps if she went in tears to Laura and spilled out the whole story, this drastic act could be avoided. But Laura was not strong enough to take that: the accusation about her husband would defeat her utterly, with no concern about Mary's attempt to save her relative. That would be a greater disaster than the other thing: death was shocking, but it was clean. In death, a man might remain loved, a perfect hero, and eventually the pain faded. If Laura knew her husband for the blackguard he was, she would never forget: she would be embittered. Every night, after similar dialogues with herself, Mary put the packet carefully away and hid it in her drawer, where Rosaleen would not come upon it accidentally.

She did not go to confession for Christmas: she could never do so again. But she did visit the family once during the preceeding week. The flat above the pub, though still not completely furnished, was warm and festive, and even Doirin seemed better. Veronica had adopted the custom of a tree with candles, which they had seen in Ireland only once, through the windows of the great house, when his lordship was in residence one year. The candles were not to be lit until Christmas Day, when they were all together; but already small brown-wrapped packages had begun to appear beneath the tree. Darin, always clever with his hands, was carving a nativity scene: the Holy Family and the Infant Jesus looked like people, but the only animals present were a pig, a chicken, a donkey and a horse.

"Sure, Darin, you must do a sheep," Mary suggested kindly. "You remember the sheep in the chapel, the one in the church here. Our Lord was a shepherd, you know."

"I've never seen a real sheep here, Aunt Mary. So how can I make him? As it is, the horse looks like a donkey, and the dog I made..."

"Yes? What about the dog you made, love?"

"He looked like Murphy," he said, with an effort. "I'm going to give him to Rosaleen."

Mary suppressed a shudder: would that dog follow her around forever? And, if a dog could do it...what about a man? She rose and left suddenly, feeling sick and frightened.

Veronica followed her downstairs, "Mary, I've something to tell you."

"I must get back, dear. Won't it keep until another time? I'll be here on Christmas."

The girl lowered her eyes. "Yes, it'll keep. But I'm going to need all your support. Even Brian will be furious."

"Brian? It has something to do with Brian?" Mary asked, pausing. Snow was beginning to fall again, in soft, downlike flakes, making star patterns on the window.

"Not any more than everyone else," Veronica conceded. "Tomas is the one who'll really get into a lather."

"Veronica, has anyone been around here that we know? Anyone from Rathcormac?" Mary asked, pursuing her own thoughts.

The girl shrugged. "No. Not that I know about. The men would have mentioned it. Why?"

"No reason," Mary said absently. "Give us a kiss, now. I must go. We'll talk about your problem with the men next week."

Mary held onto the girl so long, so desperately, that Veronica clung to her hands when she released her. "Something's the matter, Mary! Here I am bothering you with my troubles, and sure, you don't look yourself at all. What is it? What were you saying about someone from home?"

"Nothing. Nothing. Forget it, darlin'. And don't say anything to the men. It isn't that important."

"We'll be seeing you in time for Mass on Christmas, then?"

"Indeed you will. Rosaleen and I will spend the whole day with you."

The party on Christmas Eve would have been delightful, if she had not such a weight upon her: her heart, which grew heavier as the days went by, had surely turned to lead. Mary was like a walking corpse, in the strange shot-gray taffeta dress with her thick dark hair in a braid around her head. She found it difficult to laugh with Laura at the antics of the children as they opened their presents from each other under the large tree in the parlor. She felt detached, like a pair of eyes watching without really being there at all. Laura gave Rosaleen a beautiful doll with a china face, dressed in the latest fashion in billowy green silk and lace. The first thing the little girl did was turn it upside down to examine its underwear, to the amusement of all three Maddigan boys. The boys restrained their open laughter at such naughtiness by looking away and covering their mouths with their hands, so their mother would not observe their lewdness. When the children were finally settled by the fire, Johnny having presented his book of fairy tales and Rosaleen, her penwipers, Laura bent down and took a large box from under the tree.

"This is for you, Mary," she said, almost timidly. "I hope you like it."

Mary tried to infuse her exclamation with enthusiasm, but what she really felt was dread. The size of the box, with the dressmaker's bow on it, was yet another expression of Laura's friendship and generosity, and it was far too late for Mary to sway from her purpose. She knew she was going to hurt this woman sorely, and her kindness was like a crucifixion: she could hardly bear it.

"Aren't you going to open it?" Laura coaxed her, and Mary's cold fingers fumbled with the satin bow. A fine warm coat was in the box, along with a pair of woolen gloves and a stole, long enough to wrap around her head and neck and then some. Mary tried to speak, but tears came to her eyes.

"I knitted the gray gloves and stole myself," Laura confessed eagerly. "And the coat is gray, because it seems to be your favorite color."

"Yes," Mary managed, "it is."

She had to get out of the room before she made a spectacle of herself in front of all of them. Clasping Laura's hand briefly in thanks, she rose and, squaring her shoulders, made her way through the door before the tears began to flow. Leaning against the closed door, she tried to stop them with her handkerchief. She had just blown her nose and regained some of her composure when she heard a masculine voice.

"Well, would you look at us! I've never seen you so fine. Come here, Mary, let me have a look at you."

Already wearing top hat and overcoat, Maddigan was on his way to the engagement Laura had told her about. Her appearance had distracted him on his way to the front door. She felt nothing, not fear, not even hatred, as he turned her by the shoulders to look at the dress. He did not exist: he was a dead man. Nothing he could say mattered any more. He pulled her under the mistletoe in the hall arch and kissed her cheek when she moved her face aside.

"Ah, Mary," he breathed heavily, reeking of brandy even before going out, "you're a wonder! It's going to be impossible for you to give any of this up. The new year is almost upon us. Merry Christmas, my dear. And God bless you."

Then, he was gone, a blast of cold air greeting his departure. She stood quite still, waiting for the wave of dizziness to pass. She had never fainted in her life, and she was not going to give in to it now. But a shroud of darkness came over her, and though she did not remember falling, she realized she had actually fainted when she opened her eyes again in her own room. Laura and Bridie were both chafing her wrists, their faces filled with concern.

"Oh, Mary, dear," Laura said, when she saw she was conscious, "you've been poorly for several weeks. I'm terribly concerned about you. I'm going to send for my physician."

Mary shook her head slowly on the pillow. "No...no. There's nothing he can do. It's just my nerves. All the excitement, and the fine present.... Please, just let me rest."

Laura and the maid looked at each other, neither knowing

what to do. Finally, Laura rose from the edge of the bed and, following Mary's wishes, motioned the maid along after her.

"It's late, anyway," Laura said, smiling from the doorway. "It must be almost nine. I'll send Rosaleen up."

Her daughter arrived upstairs, her arms laden with presents. Pouting and angry, Rosaleen complained in a whine, "You ruined everything. You weren't any fun at the party, and then you had to go and break it up!"

Mary rose and sat on the edge of the bed, at the point of crying again. "I'm sorry, darlin'. But you're tired, and it was time you came to bed anyway."

"I'm not tired!" the child said, stamping her foot. "I was having a wonderful time. We could have stayed another hour if you—"

The slap Mary lashed out with resounded through the room. They stared at one another in shock, the child with her hand to the side of her face, Mary with hers still stinging from the blow she had delivered. All the anger and fear she had been repressing flared up in her, and her irreverent daughter got the full thrust of it.

"You are never to speak to me like that again! Do you hear me? Rosaleen, you're becoming more impossible every day. You're spoiled rotten! There are going to be some changes in your life, young lady. Starting right now! Get that dress off. It'll be a long time before you wear it again. There'll be no more vanity and willfulness in our family, you can depend on that. Now, get into your nightgown and into bed! I don't want to hear another word from you. I've half a mind not to take you to see the family tomorrow. And unless you're a good girl, I won't."

The child complied quickly to her mother's orders, her lower lip trembling, tears in her pleading eyes. Unmoved, Mary went behind the screen and kicked the taffeta dress off, giving it an extra thrust of her toe for good measure. When she emerged again, Rosaleen was already in bed, with her back turned toward her mother. Mary blew out the candle with all her breath, in a fever of destruction that included the light of the flame, so angry that she knew she would not sleep for a long time, if at all. She had not even checked the baby, but he was quiet and would not need to be fed again until morning.

Rosaleen's sobs shook the bed, but Mary had no compassion for her: she had let her go her willful way too long. It was time for a little discipline. This house was ruining both of them. The child, who had undoubtedly been exhausted from the excitement to begin with, soon cried herself to sleep. Listening to her deep, quiet breathing, Mary felt something inside her melt: she turned over and took her little girl in her arms. The whole thing had not been Rosaleen's fault, though she had been too cheeky for her own good. The fury she had turned on her baby was directed at the wrong person: it was Mr. Maddigan who should have felt the blast.

When all her anger had subsided, the warmth of the child's sweet body against hers finally began to lull Mary to sleep: she felt completely drained. Her eyelids grew heavy, her vision blurred and suddenly, peacefully, she escaped back to Ireland again, the land of youth. She saw the beech tree covered with moss and ivy near the bank of the softly flowing river, and the hawthorn of the hedgerows leading to thatched cottages with wildflowers growing from the roofs. The clothes were drying on the potato plants in the field, and someone was baking pratie bread. She was a small child again, following her nose to her own cottage, where her mother was bent over the hearth. She was safe, so safe. Nothing could ever go wrong in a land like that, with the crop good and her mother's skirts to bury her face in, breathing the earthy, pungent odor of her. . . . Someone knocked on the cottage door, and that was unusual, for it was open to all. But they knocked again. . . .

Mary opened her eyes, with a fleeting regret that her dream was not reality. Rosaleen did not stir. Then she heard it again. Someone was tapping lightly, but urgently, on the door, which she had forgotten to lock. Oh, God, she thought . . . not him. She left the bed quietly in the darkness, groping with her eyes closed to increase her sense of touch, until she found the key and turned it firmly in the lock.

"Mrs. Noonan?" a muted male voice said. "It's Kevin. For God's sake, Mary, open the door!"

Without hesitation, she turned the key again and opened the door wide enough to see him. He was standing in his heavy outdoor clothing, with a lantern in his hand. The house was dark and completely quiet, and he obviously did not want to arouse anyone.

"What is it?" she asked, whispering through the partly opened door. "Kevin, it must be the wee hours of the morning?"

"It is that. You have to help me, Mary. A terrible thing has happened, and I don't know what to do."

She grabbed her shawl and put it over her flannel night-gown before slipping into the hall.

"We're right above Mrs. Maddigan's room, so tell me about it in a whisper."

"It's himself," he said. "You're the only person I could think of. You've a head on your shoulders, and you won't talk like Bridie would. Mary," he raced on in a pressured, monotone whisper, "Mary, he's dead. Now, don't get excited, please. He's at that woman's house, and he's dead as a mackerel and we can't leave him there. She's in hysterics!"

Rather than the excitement he had expected, everything about Mary, including her voice, became very still, almost calculating. "Slow down, Kevin. I won't ask what woman, because it doesn't matter. Are you sure he's dead?"

"Yes, God help us, and in an indecent state, too! She wants him brought home, so no one will know he was there. I can't manage it myself. I can't tell Mrs. Maddigan, and Mrs. Balfe and the maids would talk."

Mary put her hand on his arm to steady him: even the light from the lantern was shaking on the walls. "It's all right, Kevin. Get hold of yourself. Let me get my coat and shoes. I understand."

She returned almost immediately, with the gray wool coat nearly covering her nightgown. Without speaking another word, she and Kevin went quietly down the dark stairs, and within minutes, they were in the hansom.

"It isn't far," Kevin said, still keeping his voice down, though there was no one on the street and all the lights were out in the houses around the Square. "It's right here on Beacon Hill."

The house was within six blocks, and Mary could see a light upstairs, reminding her of her mother saying, "A light in a house late at night bodes no good": everyone else was sleeping peacefully. Kevin helped her out of the carriage, still with no set plan in his mind.

"Sure do you think we can get him upstairs, into his own bed?"

"We'll see, first, if we can move him at all. You lead the way, Kevin. Sure I don't know this house."

She caught fragments of his low voice as they proceeded up the steps and through the door: "Mrs. Paddington . . . widow . . . for six months . . . I couldn't tell a soul . . ." Though the entry hall was dark, Mary could see from the lantern

Kevin carried that it was as magnificent as the Maddigans', and the sweep of stairs they climbed was even more imposing.

"Where are the servants?" she asked just before they reached the second-floor landing.

"She gave them the night off for Christmas Eve. Even her personal maid isn't here. A fine setup for a rendezvous. She's always been discreet. Mostly, they met at another place she has outside of town."

Mary had no opinion of the widow Paddington, even when she saw her pacing the hallway in a light peignoir with her somewhat frizzly red hair flowing down her shoulders. She was obviously beside herself, but not with grief.

"Thank God you're back, Kevin!" the woman exclaimed, rushing toward them. "You have to get him out of here! Did you get someone to help you? I'll pay you well." When she saw Mary, her whole body stiffened. "I thought you were going to get a lad."

"It's all right, ma'am," Kevin said nervously. "Mary's that cautious with her tongue, and she's a strong woman, too. Have you . . . uh . . . did you get something on him?"

The woman covered her face with both hands, shaking her head. "I couldn't go back into that room. I'll never be able to go back in that . . ."

"It's all right, ma'am. We'll take care of everything," Kevin said, shrugging his shoulders at Mary. "You just run along, now, and no one will be the wiser."

Before the words were out, the woman fled down the hall and disappeared through a door. They did not see her again that night: Mary was not to see her again for many years. Out of modesty, Mary let Kevin, who was trembling all over, protesting he had never touched a corpse—"sure, it's the women who do that"—enter the room and dress Mr. Maddigan.

"Be sure you get all his things," she called after him, still keeping her voice down, though there was no one to hear them. "Dress him completely, Kevin, and get his wallet and all. If we're going to make this look right, nothing can be missing."

When she finally entered the brightly lighted bedroom at Kevin's bidding, Mary was overwhelmed by its furnishings, the like of which she had never seen. Dainty, curving chairs touched with gold, more delicate than those in Laura's room, stood against the walls, with one pulled close to a mossy-green velvet chaise longue. The headboard of the canopied bed was the same mossy color, as was the satin bedspread, which was pulled back from the rumpled white satin sheets. The whole scene was illuminated by a lovely gold-and-crystal chandelier. She knew she was avoiding looking at the fully dressed body on the floor, which she had caught out of the corner of her eyes upon entering, but Kevin brought her back to the reality of the situation.

"For the love of God, Mary," he entreated, "stop gawking at the room and give us a hand! It's nearly four in the morning, woman. We've a lot to do, yet. Sure, he's heavy! And he's beginnin' to stiffen up."

They decided on the study, the one place the children were not allowed to enter. Mary supervised laying out the body; or, as the case was, seeing that it lay as naturally as at Mrs. Paddington's. That was not difficult: the problem had been in getting it home at all, rigid as it was. Lividity had occurred on the left side, where he had been lying, and, after they carried him in, supporting him on both sides as though he were merely drunk, there had been little difficulty, except for his weight, in secreting him in his own study. When she had put his shoes on the proper feet, Mary checked his pockets to make sure that his wallet and keys were there. Stepping backward, to the chair he would have thrown his coat on, if he had come in drunk, she looked over their work and was satisfied with the effect.

Once everything was taken care of, however, she began to tremble. Kevin poured a large glass of brandy and, with some difficulty, gave her a sip first, downing the rest himself.

"Holy Mother of God," he exhaled, "that it should come to this! I won't have to drive him to his bad women any more, poor man. It's been a rotten quandary, Mary. Whether to tell it in confession, that is. Sure I was only doing my job, but I felt like a procurer or something. It wasn't so bad in the summer, when I could wait outside in the country; but he wouldn't have me do that in the cold. I had to sit downstairs in the kitchen, downing tea, trying not to imagine what was going on."

He was babbling, a natural reaction to nervousness, Mary reflected. Aside from the shaking, she still felt quite clear and level-headed. That letter was here in the study someplace: she must retrieve it before it fell into the wrong hands.

"Kevin, dear, I'm sure it's been a horrible shock for you," she said, taking the brandy snifter from his hand and guiding him to the door. "We mustn't be talking in here, in case someone's about. You go to your room now, and try to get some sleep. I'll just check everything again, to make sure it's all right; then I'll go along, too."

"I suppose it was his heart," he whispered. "I think it was his heart, don't you, Mary? Or apoplexy, perhaps, something burst in his head. Sure, he wasn't in the physical condition for...that kind of exercise, would you say?"

"Try to forget it," she told him. "I'm sure you're right. I think he overestimated his capabilities. Go along with you now. Everyone will be up early: sure, it's Christmas Day."

As soon as Kevin went out the door, she locked it and quickly, methodically searched the room, starting with the desk: no letter. Her heart began to thud heavily; perhaps he had not written it at all: the whole thing had been an empty threat to torment her with. However, a locked cherrywood cabinet against the wall sharpened her perceptions; of course, he would have some place to keep important papers, even cash. She had tried to ignore the body on the floor; but now she drew in her breath to lean over it, extracting the keys again. Her mind turned over with confusion: there were so many. But the cabinet door indicated a small one; at least that narrowed it down. If her fingers would only remain steady. On her fourth try, after what seemed forever, the cabinet lock turned and she opened it wide. There were piles of assorted papers there: contracts, cargo bills, accounts. On the bottom shelf, she found a metal box, which required yet another key: tears of frustration and fear came to her eyes. But with the key ring at her disposal, it was not hard to open it. It contained mostly money, in large bills, which she riffled through quickly to get to the bottom. And there it was, along with a small pile of letters, all written in the same copperplate hand, which was not his handwriting, tied together with a piece of string.

The bastard *had* written the letter, then: it was addressed to the British Constabulary, Cork, County Cork, Ireland. She did not stop to read it, shoving it into her deep coat pocket along with the bundle of letters: God knows who else he might be holding those over. Then she locked the box and replaced it in the cupboard, turning the key in that small lock, too. She looked around the room once more before hurrying to the door: his coat and hat were thrown over the leather chair; the brandy glass, with still a little at the bottom, was on his desk. Everything was all right. With a shock, she realized his keys

197

were still in her hand. She would have left and probably locked the door from outside! Her nerves alone gave her the needed initiative to return to the body, with its gray, bloated face and glazing eyes. She could not touch it: nothing could make her touch it. She placed the key ring unsteadily on the desk, as though he had done it on coming in and, picking up the brandy snifter, drained it for courage. There was hardly enough to feel the sting of the liquor, so she poured out a little more and drank that, too.

With her inside warm and relaxed from the drink, she went down the small corridor to the kitchen and crept quietly up the back stairs to her room. Rosaleen and the baby were still sleeping soundly. The cold light of early dawn was trying to pass through the falling snow to the window. Kneeling close to the window so she would not have to light a candle, she read Mr. Maddigan's letter quickly and opened one of the others, a love letter signed by a woman named Kate. Then, with a shock of recollection, she went to her dresser and dug deep behind her things for her reticule, from which she carefully extracted the unopened packet, weighing it thoughtfully in her hand. She would destroy it, along with all the letters, as soon as possible; in the meantime, she hid everything in the deep pocket of her coat.

But then a kind of cowardice seized her: she could not bear to be here when the body was found. She wanted to console Laura, but she felt more like a hypocrite than she had during the preceding weeks. She and Rosaleen would leave early, anyway, for Mass with the family. Mass! She sank into a chair and put her hand to her forehead. She could never receive the sacraments again, because she could never confess. She had not murdered, because she did not have to, but she had committed it in her mind and intentions. She could never tell a priest that, or her reason for contemplating it, which was much stronger than saving her virtue.

Now that feeling was coming back, one emotion was paramount: relief. Blessed relief. Mr. Maddigan was dead, and not by her hand: she had never thought she could live with that. Her only remaining anxiety was that the body would be discovered before she and Rosaleen left for church.

Chapter 14

MASS at the Moon Street Church was never very edifying. In Mary's mind, the church was too large; it did not have the intimacy of their gray stone chapel in Rathcormac. The painted glass in the windows could not make up for ivied, mossy walls and the familiar churchyard with its tilted Celtic crosses that housed her ancestors. This church, though not large by city standards, echoed too much, the priest's voice was lost in the rafters; and in the winter it was cold. The high ceiling and wooden nave were warmed only by unwashed bodies, the odor of which even incense and candles could not cover, nor Father McMahon's fine Latin liturgy distract from. The whole Noonan family walked briskly back to the pub and had a hot cup of tea before the children opened their presents. As Mary sat little Philip on the floor with the others, who knelt around the tree admiring the lighted candles, she thought of the two that were missing: Seamus and Michael. And Padraig too, in a way, for he sat at the table with the adults, separating himself by the action from the younger Noonans. He was eleven years old, with the blue eyes and black hair of Brian, but a remote, sulky expression in his face, which made him seem older. Observing him, trying not to think of the Maddigan house in turmoil, Mary realized he would be the next to leave: there was something in his bearing which indicated he was only biding his time, until he was a year older. And poor Doirin just coming out of the last shock, too.

Several times, Mary nearly blurted out that her master had died last night, catching herself just in time. Tomas and Brian, who had attended church that morning, as they did twice a year, to keep from getting excommunicated, as Tomas put it, seemed to be in better spirits than she had seen them in a long time. Business must be prospering, and Doirin, lost in a fog for months, was getting better every time Mary saw her.

As if to give proof of her recovery, Doirin made a sharp observation over her tea cup. "Mary, you didn't take communion this morning. I expect it of Brian. He only takes it at Easter, but I'm surprised at you."

Mary had already prepared her excuse. "Sure, I needed something to sustain me before pushing the pram across town," she said lightly. "I broke my fast with a cup of tea and some bread."

"Come to think of it," Doirin said, frowning, "Brian, did you go to communion on Easter? I can't remember, to be sure."

Tomas stood up suddenly, interrupting her line of thought by opening a bottle and offering whiskey for their tea, with a glance at his brother. "A little bit of heaven for Christmas morning," he said and winked, pouring a shot into Brian's cup and looking at the women. "Sure, won't one of you join us? I know Mary doesn't touch the creature, but how about you, Veronica?"

"Why not?" Veronica said, happy to have her whole family around her. "But just a nip, Tomas. No, no, that's far too much!"

"I'll have some too," Mary said, lifting her cup and getting a frown from Doirin. "Sure, it's cold out there," she explained, at their laughter. "The church itself was enough to freeze your soul."

Rosaleen looked up quickly. "It smelled bad in there," she said. "Those people don't seem to wash."

"My, haven't we an elegant nose all of a sudden," Doirin responded. "You didn't wash very often yourself until very recently."

"That's enough, Rosaleen," Mary said, and the child did not pursue the subject further. Instead, she observed her mother carefully, as though she no longer knew what to expect from her.

"I wanted to invite some friends to dinner," Veronica remarked, "but Doirin said she wasn't up to it. Perhaps next year."

"It's nice just to have family this year," Mary said, sipping the burning whiskey in her teacup. "God help us, we've come quite a long way."

Both Veronica and Doirin crossed themselves solemnly to ward off the wrath of God for their prosperity, and Brian and Tomas chuckled.

Tomas stood up and, extending his hand, that clasped the bottle over the table, let whiskey splash on the cloth. "This is a li...bation!" He laughed. "It keeps the gods happy, so they won't do you in!"

"Tomas!" Mary cried, and the women all jumped up, mopping reeking whiskey from their clothes. "Have you gone completely daft, man?"

"He's drunk already," Doirin complained. "Brian, stop laughing, and do something about him!"

Mary had not looked directly at her brother-in-law all morning: she could hardly face him. Doirin's exclamation prompted her to glance in his direction, and she was surprised at the change in him. He was relaxed, laughing uproariously at Tomas's antics: he looked as he had when he was a young man, except for the white in his hair. For a moment, she wondered if he had been drinking, too: but Brian was not a man who drank himself footless. He was happy, that was all: he was just having a good time. Several emotions clashed in her at the same time. She was relieved that he was happy; she loved him more dearly than ever; and, she felt a vague resentment that he would never know what she had been through on his behalf. Which reminded her of the things in her coat pocket....

Soon the children started to open their packages, with the adults gathering around them by the lighted tree. Mary stoked up the fire in the hearth, separating the coals to let them breathe more flames and, before anyone noticed, adding the packet of arsenic and the bundle of letters to the small conflagration. Though she was afraid someone in the family would notice, no one turned around. Flooded once again with relief, she coaxed the destruction of the past few weeks' horror, thinking it was somehow fitting that she burn everything there, among those she had tried to protect.

For the others, the day was lazy, relaxed. The pub was closed, and there was nothing for the men to do but sit around, conversing intermittently, playing with Rosaleen and Darin.

Liam never seemed to play: it was as though he had forgotten how at nine years old. Soon Padraig went to the room he shared with the other two boys, and stayed there until it was time for dinner. Only the women had work to do, preparing the dinner from Veronica's cookbook, trying to make it properly American, with Doirin looking on, directing their activities.

When they were close together by the black iron stove, Mary whispered to her sister-in-law, "Doesn't she do anything around here?"

Veronica pushed out her lower lip resentfully. "Sure, she's a little better than before. But it's as though she's forgotten how to carry her weight. I feel like her maid most of the time."

"You wanted to tell me something."

Veronica glanced quickly at Doirin, who was sitting at the kitchen table. "Not now. Not here. In my room later."

After dinner, which turned out pretty well, except that the turkey was red at the bones and they had left the sage out of the stuffing, Tomas fell asleep in his chair. Then Brian beckoned to Mary. "Come along, I'll show you the improvements on the kitchen in the restaurant."

Thinking he must have lost his mind altogether, she followed him reluctantly down the stairs to the pub. They had both agreed, on the previous occasion, not to spend any time alone together; but she could not keep her heart from pounding dangerously anyway. She knew he did not want to show her the kitchen, though he took her back there. When he turned to face her, it was not to take her in his arms, however, though his face was serious.

"Sit down, Mary," he said. "There's something I must tell you, and it's going to come as a shock."

"I don't know if I want to hear it," she said proudly.

"But you should. You should know everything about me, Mary. There was something I couldn't tell you until now. Do you remember the day we left Rathcormac, and the way I made you all take such a long, roundabout route to find a boat?"

She nodded, her eyes intent on his face. It was only a confession of murder. But why, so coincidentally... now?

He averted his eyes, spoke quietly and without much expression. "When I went to see Mr. McGee, to get the money Lord Leighton had sent for our emigration—and he did send it, never fear—something went very wrong. McGee was in his office, there in his house...the one we used to go to when we paid the rent. He was sitting at a table with this metal box in front of him, and coins and bills piled up beside it. He tried to hide the money when he saw me, but it was too late: he knew I'd seen it and he looked like a scared rabbit. Mary, I was that desperate. You know how it was: we were all hungry, more than half starved. We'd have been dead in a few days' time. Well, I asked him for the money that was ours, to leave that famished land. He said he didn't know anything about any money for us. I told him we had it through the priest that his lordship was sending it, and he fumbled around saying he knew nothing of it at all, that no money had arrived. And him with a bloody big box of it right at his elbow! I don't know what struck me...I was weak as a cat, hardly had the strength to get there. I told him I would take what he had, thank you. And I did, right before his eyes! I took our fare and a bit more and shoved it in my pocket. He began to call me names I'll not repeat to you, and started to yell for help. His wife wasn't in the house, but he had that workman of his around, I suspected. I don't know if it was fear or anger or both: I won't make any excuses. I had to get us out of there. Anyhow, I picked up that heavy metal box and heaved it at his goddam head, before he could make a racket." He paused, swallowed, raised his eyes and look directly at her. "I didn't mean to kill him, Mary. I didn't think I had the strength to even stop him. The corner of the box must have struck him in the temple to make such a...The side of his head was mashed to a pulp, and he was dead as he hit the floor. I didn't even think, then. I got out of there as quickly as I could. I came home and told you all we were leaving right away. On the way back to the cottage, I decided it was the only thing to do."

Mary held up her hand to stop him: tears had risen in his eyes. "I know about it, Brian. I think I've known all along. Don't think about it any more. It doesn't change the way I feel about you." Then, as an afterthought, "What made you want to tell me about it now?"

He swallowed hard, wiped his eyes and nose with the back of his hand. "You *knew?* But how could you?"

"Little things, lots of little things. You weren't yourself at all, until we were safely settled in Boston...until we'd gotten through Immigration. But enough of that. Why are you telling me now?"

"Because it's all right, you see. Paddy McGuire arrived

here last month, and he came into the pub the other day. Everyone that's left back there respects what I did. Even the priest. When the old man heard what had happened, he came up to McGee's and divided the rest of the money among those who needed it most. Some stayed, thinking things would get better. A few of them emigrated, like us. Things haven't gotten better, Mary: it's hell over there. So Paddy, who knew he couldn't last the winter with the crop failing again, got himself on a boat too. They're forming a society of Irish Catholics, and he came to the pub to enlist Tomas and me."

"Irish Catholics?" She considered. "What's to keep him from spreading your story all over town? He might tell the wrong person."

"It doesn't matter." He smiled. "That's what I'm trying to tell you, my darling. When we're united in a society, no one can do a thing. Besides, as yet, there's no law that could send me back there."

"There's no extra...extradition?"

He laughed. "Where did you get a word like that? No, there's nothing of the kind. And even if such a law were made, they'd have to fight several thousand Irishmen to enforce it."

She felt as if she had just escaped being run over by wild horses. She licked her lips to stop their dryness, but her tongue itself was dry. "Well, then," she breathed, "everything's all right, isn't it?"

He reached out and clasped her hand, raising her fingers to his lips. "Everything's all right. Mary, you're a wonder. You knew about it all along, and you still...Any other woman would have been repelled by me. I feel free, now, but it doesn't change the fact that I've killed a man, even if he was an enemy. That'll follow me to my dying day."

"McGee was as much an enemy as the English," she said, melting at his touch. "You'd feel no guilt if you killed an Englishman with a pike. We must forget all that. I keep telling Rosaleen—we must forget it."

"Your hands are like ice," he said, rising and pulling her to her feet. "We should return to the others. Tomas knows about it but the women don't. I'd like to keep it that way."

She nodded her understanding. Their hands parted, reluctantly, the fingers clinging as long as possible. Then, walking separately, they returned to the upstairs flat, where Mary still had to talk to Veronica.

* * *

"I love him. He's the kindest, dearest man I've ever known. We want to marry. We know the problems we face, especially with the family...never mind the Church. Oh, Mary, I need your help so much! You know what Tomas is, and you're the only one who can handle him at all."

"Veronica, darling, he's a..." Mary took a deep breath. "Besides being a Jew, he's three times your age! Sure, I'm completely overcome."

"He's only forty-one!" Veronica protested with a glow in her cheeks. "Mary, you must have loved Tomas once. You must know what it's like to love someone. I'll not go on like this! We've done nothing wrong," she added quickly. "He's a good man. They don't treat their women the way Irishmen do. Sure, you'd think I was the Holy Virgin herself, he's that respectful. He doesn't want me ever to do a lick of work, either. Can you imagine that? He's going to open a store downtown: he says he'll be rich so I can have a *maid*. I don't care about having a maid, Mary. You know that. I'd work my fingers to the bone for him."

Seated with Veronica on her bed with the door closed against the family, Mary scrutinized her young sister-in-law's face, thinking she had never looked more beautiful. Veronica's eyes looked bluer and brighter, transformed by love: Mary could not bear to think of her unhappy. There were difficulties, to be sure, extreme difficulties in the match. But at least they were the kind that might be overcome. If she took Veronica's side in her attempt to marry Mr. Rabinsky, she would be fighting the whole family, perhaps even Brian, and taking on the Church as well. Never having faced that kind of problem, she had no idea where it might end. But Veronica was right: she knew what it was like to love someone and be denied. At the moment, however, her mind could not grasp another problem: she could hardly cope with what she had to face when she went back to the Maddigans'.

"You aren't planning to tell them about it today, are you?" Mary asked, frowning. "Sure, Tomas is footless with drink, and..."

"No, I don't want to ruin their Christmas," Veronica said. "I just wanted you to know the way things are...to see if you would help me. I feel so alone, Mary. Doirin wouldn't even let him come to dinner. Oh, she caused such an awful fuss! I think she's almost well."

Mary smiled at the comment. It was the first time she had done so all day. "Don't fret, Veronica, darling. Though I may get shot out of my perch altogether, I'll stand behind you. God help us." She crossed herself.

Veronica embraced her impulsively. She was warm and full of life, and Mary felt like a dry stick in her arms. "You won't be sorry! Mary, I swear you'll never be sorry. You've such a fine level head on your shoulders, you'll know how to go about this the right way, I know. I can't even think of how to start."

"You might start by talking to the priest. Not that young idjut Father Donelly. He's green as grass and doesn't know his arse from his elbow when it comes to human emotions."

"Mary!" Veronica exclaimed, withdrawing from her arms in shock and amusement, her blue eyes dancing. "But he's a priest!"

"Go directly to Father McMahon, himself, at the rectory," Mary continued seriously, ignoring the interruption. "He'll probably give you a raking over, to be sure. I don't know exactly what the Church's stand is on such things. I don't even recollect anyone ever trying to marry a Protestant. It seems to me, though, that it would be easier with a Jew. After all, Our Lord was a Jew, wasn't He?"

At the Maddigans', Mary had anticipated wailing and lamentation in the household with Laura in her room, either hysterical or drugged by her doctor. So, the extreme silence in the house when they entered the back door, pulling the pram after them, made Mary's nerves shriek. Was it possible then that no one had discovered the body at all? The walk home had been a silent one, except when they had had to lift the pram over small, frozen drifts at the gutters or choose an alternate way when passage through a particular street was too difficult to negotiate. Rosaleen appeared to respect Mary's silence or, with the second sight she sometimes seemed to possess, she may have expected something to be wrong at the Maddigans' too. Whatever the child's reason, Mary appreciated being left to her own thoughts, which she was only now beginning to bring under control. The sword she had been living under for a month was gone: indeed, from Brian's story, it had never existed at all. She had been saved from desperate, irreparable action by Mr. Maddigan's cooperative death by natural causes: her mind still would not face the possibility that she might have used the powder in the packet and then found out that Brian had been safe all along. The irony was too grim; her damnation would have been too complete. She could not think about it.

Only after they had picked up the baby and stored the pram in the back closet and were passing the kitchen was any sign of life in the house recognizable, and that was sitting so still it could have been overlooked. Mrs. Lynch, the cook, alone at the table, did not stop saying her black rosary beads to greet them; the only part of her moving was her fingers on the beads. Mary decided that the body had been found. She put on as bright and unsuspecting face as she could, hating the necessary hypocrisy.

"Good evening, Mrs. Lynch," she said, entering the kitchen with Rosaleen, holding the baby, at her side. "Sure, you must be that weary after such a holiday. With two of us doing the cooking, our dinner was an absolute disaster. You must give me the recipe for your dress—" She would have gone on babbling, having quickly fallen into her role, but the old woman fixed her with her woeful eyes.

"Ach, you wouldn't be knowing," Mrs. Lynch said, feigning mourning and trying to keep the eagerness out of her voice at the same time. "It's a tragic day, Mary. A tragic day! One that will not be soon forgotten by this family. Sure Christmas will always be the anniversary of his passing, to them."

Mrs. Lynch was going to make her draw it out of her, Mary observed, and played the game according to the immemorial rules. Looking shocked, Mary asked, "Passing? Did you say 'passing,' Mrs. Lynch? My God, what's happened while we've been away?"

The cook leaned forward eagerly, her rosary still linked around her stubby fingers. "It's himself!" she declared. "Mr. Maddigan. Didn't they find him dead as a mackerel in his study just before lunch?"

Lunch! Mary thought: they had taken long enough to go about it. With genuine surprise, she said, "No! Was it a heart attack, then? And no one about to hear him?"

The old woman shook her head. "We'd have gone at once, if he had rung for us. The doctor said it happened sometime during the night, shortly after he came in."

As understanding of the conversation penetrated to Rosaleen, she let out a little cry and nearly dropped Philip. Mary retrieved the baby deftly and put her hand on her daughter's shoulder to comfort her, only to have the child squirm from beneath it, as though she did not want to be touched. Tears streamed, uncontrolled, down the little girl's cheeks. With everything that had been happening, Mary had not considered the effect of the death on Rosaleen. Instead of turning to her mother, the child rushed into Mrs. Lynch's open arms, sobbing against the woman's ample bosom.

"Sure, he had his failings," the cook said ritualistically, "but, then, haven't we all? Even if he liked the creature a bit too much, he was good to the children and he loved his wife sorely. Didn't he give her everything?"

Mary sat down, so she could put Philip, who was getting heavy, on her lap. "And how is she taking it?"

Mrs. Lynch shook her head. "Bravely, indeed, courageously. She informed her sons and made all the arrangements herself. She's alone in there, praying, right now."

Mary pictured the study and knew at once that her mind was fatigued. "In where?" she asked.

"In the parlor. Are you daft? Where else would they lay him out? There'll be no proper wake, though, of course, him being Protestant and all.. Mary, you should go in to her. She's that fond of you. I'll look after the baby. Hand him over. Do you want to go too, Rosaleen?"

The child sniffed and nodded her head. Mary shuddered at the thought of entering the parlor, but she knew it was her duty. She had already thought about that. When she reached for Rosaleen's hand, she was surprised to find it was not there: the child had preceded her down the hall. Rosaleen was acting strangely; but then everything was strange today. She found her daughter waiting outside the parlor doors when she got there, afraid to knock and go inside alone. Mary tapped the mahogany door lightly with her knuckles and, without waiting for a reply, slipped inside, leaving the door ajar for Rosaleen.

Laura was not kneeling in prayer, as the cook had surmised: she was sitting on the red velvet couch, dressed in black with a sheer black scarf over her bright curls. Mary noticed that she was not sitting stiff with grief, either; she was relaxed, with one elbow resting on the uncomfortable wooden arm, her hand braced against her chin, considering the coffin. The only illumination in the room was from the candles flanking the highly polished wooden box, which had the black crepe-draped lid open, so the corpse could be viewed, a privilege Mary did not plan to allow herself. Rosaleen, however, a small figure in a long coat with her shawl still around her head, approached without hesitation, crossed herself and knelt down to pray.

Seeing the child, Laura looked up and held out her hand to Mary, who sank down beside her wordlessly. The scarf did not cover her mistress's face, and Mary could see that her eyes were dry: perhaps she was still in a state of shock. That impression was quickly dispelled when Laura spoke, softly, directly to Mary though her gaze was still on the coffin.

"The older boys are very upset. I can't tell about Johnny," she said, in such a low voice that Mary had to move closer to hear her. "I thought of killing him once, Mary, after I learned about the first woman. I just don't have that kind of strength, though. Instead I pretended everything was all right, in front of the boys, even to him. It was impossible to leave, you know, after making that kind of mistake. I may be foolish, but I'm also proud. I'd never let my family have the gratification of knowing they were right."

"Sure," Mary said quickly, almost whispering as Laura had, "you're rambling, Miss Laura. You've had a terrible shock, and you don't know what you're saying."

Laura turned to look at her with a queer little smile at the edge of her lips. "But I *do* know," she said. "You're the only person I could say it to, Mary. I'm quite all right. I think I may be better than I've been in years."

The little girl rose from her prayers and climbed up on the kneeling rail to kiss the face of the man in the coffin: she could not quite reach it and settled on touching his cheek with the back of her hand instead. The two women on the couch watched her.

"I wouldn't let her do that," Laura said with concern.

"Rosaleen!" Mary said quickly. Without turning, the child climbed backward from the rail, crossed herself again and walked up to Laura, her face full of grief.

"You liked him very much, didn't you?" Laura said, putting out her free hand to take Rosaleen's.

"Yes, ma'am. He was very nice to me."

"Yes. He was always good with children," Laura said graciously. "I'll say that for him."

"Cook said there isn't going to be a proper wake," Rosaleen protested. "Sure, it's not right to send a person off alone. Wouldn't he want his friends and family around, saying fine things about him and drinking all night?"

Laura cut off the laugh that escaped from her throat by pretending it was a fit of coughing. When she got herself under control, she said kindly, "I'm sure he would. But we don't have wakes in our family, Rosaleen. To us, they seem irreverent. Do you understand? We do things differently. Tomorrow, his friends and associates will come to pay their respects. And the next day, we will bury him, with a service both here and at the grave, of course. The minister will be there. It isn't all that cold, you see. Or do you?"

The child seemed undecided, but did not wish to appear impolite. She glanced at the coffin, with all the candles burning, and mused, "It's a fine strong box, ma'am. At least the rats won't eat his fingers and nose." Then, facing the astounded Laura, she asked, "Where's Johnny? I want to tell him how sorry I am."

"I...I think he's in the library," Laura stammered. As soon as Rosaleen was gone, she turned a distressed face to Mary, her eyes uncomprehending.

"Mary, that was a morbid, terrible thing to say! Is the child all right? Does she think of things like that often?"

"I thought she had forgotten," Mary said, almost to herself; and, remembering where she was, replied, "I'm sorry, Miss Laura. She really isn't like that. You know how happy she usually is. I guess all this reminded her of...I'm sorry, it's an unpleasant story."

Laura's hand encouraged her to go on. "Please, it's better to talk about things. I feel better already from what I've said to you."

"You may be right," Mary said and nodded slowly. "Sure it's all been pent up in me, and I can't keep it down. It's even in my dreams." She took a deep breath. "It was in Rathcormac, last year, shortly before we came here. The men were away in Cork, where they went up to pick up a penny or so, or some grain...whatever they could to sustain us. We ran out of food altogether, they were gone so long. There was a riot in the city at the granaries, and Tomas and Brian were thrown into jail. There wasn't a grain in the house...nothing. It was winter and even the fields had been dug up for any root or grass people could find. Our cottages were some distance apart, because of our working our own plots of land. Brian and Doirin, my sister, lived some distance away: she was alone there with her children, and I was alone with mine. My mother and father, the old folk, weren't as far, but I was too weak to even look in on them. My children...there were three of them, then...Seamus died on the ship on the way over. My children slept a lot and so did I. We were skin and bones, and that weak. We weren't really hungry any more," she mused in surprise. "I'd forgotten that...we weren't hungry toward the end. And it was the end we were fast approaching, to be sure. Well—" She stopped suddenly, realizing she would have to revise part of her story to spare Laura's feelings. "Well, an animal came our way. I'd killed a few chickens in the past and I'd seen a hog being butchered. . . . Ah, well . . . I . . . prepared a broth out of the animal, saving the meat for when our stomachs could take it. The broth restored us a little, and some of the meat gave us a little more strength. So I decided to have a go at getting some of the broth and meat to my parents. Rosaleen, God love her, went with me . . . you know how she is, always with me.

"I don't know what I was expecting. If we were near death, the old people would be . . . I wasn't thinking right, I guess. I expected to find them alive."

"Oh, Mary!" Laura said, embracing her. "I had no idea . . ."

"The point of all this is that they weren't alive. They'd been dead for days. And the rats . . . the rats . . ."

"Oh, my dear, don't go on: I understand," Laura said, with a shudder. "And Rosaleen . . . little Rosaleen . . . saw that?"

Mary nodded, her vision blocked by tears and the black taffeta shoulder of Laura's dress, against which she was held closely.

"We buried them," she said, weeping, "in the floor of the cottage, Rosaleen and I. It was all we could do to dig a hole in that hard, cold earth. We barely covered them, when I think of it, now. And we heaped a few stones on top of them." She sat up, her face wet, and Laura wiped it with her crumpled lace handkerchief, handing it to Mary for her nose. "The men came back . . . the next day? . . . I don't know . . . with some grain. Doirin and I had used all the broth and meat by then anyway. We were able to come here, because his lordship, our landlord, sent money to his tenants to emigrate."

"And you've kept all this to yourself, all this time?" Laura said. "That's what famine is. . . . I've ignored it, Mary, it seemed so far away. I was here, frittering away money on useless things to fill my life, while you were actually *starving*." It seemed too much for her to comprehend. She squeezed Mary's hand to express her feeling. "Mary, my good friend . . . my dear, good friend, I hardly know what to say. I want you to stay here with me very much: not just to care for Philip, but as my companion. You and your daughter are to stay here for as long as you want." Her eyes wandered vaguely to the coffin, and she stared at it as though seeing it for the first time. "He might have told me what was going on in the world. He might have given me credit for having some brains...some compassion. Matthew was a very selfish man, insulating me so much against reality. He only did it out of guilt, you know."

Mary felt so relieved from telling her troubles that the top of her skull ached, as though it had been lifted off. She no longer felt any rancor for anyone, even the dead man under the candles. Unconsciously, she responded with a homily that was completely Irish.

"We all have our faults. Sure, none of us is perfect. We only pass this way once...and there's so much to learn." She paused thoughtfully, as though the old words had a new, sudden meaning. "Let's say a little prayer for him, to send him off right. Sure, he was no worse than most of us."

Part II

ROSALEEN

Chapter 15

ROSALEEN'S problems with her mother seemed to have started that Christmas, first with the humiliating slap in the face and then with the carved wooden dog Darin gave her when they were alone. She took the small dog upstairs with her when she left the coffin in the parlor, and put it on the nightstand by the bed. The tears that escaped over Mr. Maddigan's death released a torrent she had been holding back all day, and she sobbed until she was overcome by hiccoughs and felt sicker than she had at the dinner table. Her mother was so abstracted all day that she did not even notice that Rosaleen refrained from eating. Liam said that the adults were all tipsy, anyway: he had seen his father tipping the bottle into their teacups immediately after Mass. Though Rosaleen knew her mother did not ordinarily drink spirits, she hated them all at that moment, and especially her mother.

When she opened the little brown package containing the carving, Darin had told her with awe in his voice, "It's Murphy, Rosie. Sure, he's a blessed saint if ever there was one. If it wasn't for him, none of us would be alive today."

The odor of cooking turkey was heavy in the air when the girl extracted the story from her cousin, bit by bit, as he understood it: he had been trying to figure it out for a long time, and there was no longer any doubt in his mind. At first she would not believe it: it was too terrible, her mother would not do anything like that, even if they were starving. Darin tried to impress on her that Mary was a "blessed saint," too: what she'd done had taken courage. Gradually, the impact of the shock diffused itself: all Rosaleen felt was numb. Then the turkey was served, with the red blood still in its small bones, and the sickness she felt was not from the sight of blood, but from what it recalled so vividly. She must have eaten Murphy. Her dear, kissing, wag-tailed Murphy, whom Darin had given her as a little puppy and she had raised with her own love. She remembered the broth, how hot and rich it had been in her empty stomach; her mind shied away from the meat she had consumed later. Her mother had killed her darling Murphy and fed him to her! She would rather be dead: starving was not so bad, you just went to sleep. She would rather have him still running the fields, chasing rabbits, bounding around happily with his pink tongue hanging from his smiling mouth. But then there would be no one to look after him, there was no denying that: even Darin, for whom she would lay down her own life, would not be here.

At some point during the hiccoughs brought on by crying, she decided that Murphy was, indeed, a saint, because he had saved Darin from dying. Her feeling about her mother was ambiguous, suspended somewhere between hatred and love. She wanted to feel the same about her as she had before, but it was difficult, and not only because of the dog. Her mother was so quiet lately: she did not seem to care about anyone. She was especially strict toward Rosaleen, and without her usual gentle affection. Though she did not acknowledge it to herself, for a few minutes, Rosaleen wished Mary had died, instead of Murphy.

Death was already very much a part of Rosaleen's consciousness, though she did not know it, and no one would have imagined it in her, because she was such a bouncing, joyous child. What her mother would not discuss and had told her to forget had tucked itself deeply in her personality, and her reaction to it was to get as much out of life as possible, every minute, every day. Death was the great enemy of life; consciously, she feared and hated it, and nothing anyone said about an afterlife consoled her. It was physical death she could not cope with and blocked out of her mind: the memory of seeing her brother tipped from under a piece of fraying canvas into the roaring Atlantic; her grandparents half-eaten by rats. At an impressionable age, she had seen death at its ugliest, and she spent the rest of her life rebelling against it, though it seemed that she was simply livelier than others, in the same way she was naturally prettier.

One of the early problems of living to the fullest was that other people did not seem to understand, and certainly did not appreciate, it...especially her mother, who walked around the Maddigan house as though she were walking on eggs, not timid, but fearful of displeasing by the presence of her daughter. Mr. Maddigan had understood, but he was gone. The Maddigan boys did not comprehend it, but found her highly amusing, just as Auntie Laura did. And Darin...well, Darin was so much like her that they might have shared one soul; she could tell him anything, act silly, act naughty: he understood.

The best times in her childhood, the ones she cherished, were when Mary was not around. From the first year in Boston, the summers at the Cape became her special time: the long, lovely summers without much supervision. Even when Darin was unable to go, it was a good time. Her mother stayed in Boston with Philip, and Rosaleen and the Maddigan boys were left to the wide-open, permissive hands of Auntie Laura, to roam the beach, to swim, to boat, to take side trips with Kevin, who was a rascal and full of fun, and to stay up late, snacking and telling stories and playing games. Summers at the house at Idle Cove were one long party, completely suited to Rosaleen's expansive freedom. But they were always interrupted in the fall, when the party-goers were sent to school again, and Rosaleen came back under her mother's discipline.

By 1849, the year the parochial school was finished, Rosaleen had spent a year reading the books in the library, without supervision, picking up facts where she found them, discarding those that bored her. She had also learned to sew much better than her mother, who had never had the knack of handling a dainty needle. The skill had not interested Rosaleen much at first, until Laura offered the child the small remnants from a chest under her bed. They were nothing like the material from what Mary called the "rag bag," dull strips of cotton, gabardine and black wool. Laura's remnants were pieces of satin, pale-blue brocade, yellow taffeta and strips of laces. Within two months, Rosaleen's china-headed doll from Christmas had a whole new wardrobe, in the latest style from Laura's *Ladies' Magazine,* sewn neatly and quickly, under Laura's expert scrutiny, bound and buttonholed, trimmed with lace and cord. And the little girl's enthusiasm did not stop there: soon she was carefully making impractical gifts for her mother, Veronica and Doirin.

Rosaleen loved pretty things and, from the first white party dress, was inordinately fond of clothes, but sewing for herself was limited by the few garments Mary felt were necessary and the material she could afford. Her mother was proud, as only an impoverished peasant can be: she would accept no handouts of old clothing or material from Laura. She would look after her own. So when Rosaleen outgrew the fine lawn dresses Laura had made, and which she had hardly been allowed to wear, she went back into long gray skirts and blouses, which she could now sew better than her mother, though she was allowed choice of neither pattern nor fabric. After working with Laura's splendid remnants and helping make the brightly colored quilt, the child found sewing for herself both tedious and dull.

The Sisters of Notre Dame de Namur came from Philadelphia to staff the new parochial school at St. Mary's in the North End, but their arrival hardly caused a ripple in the Irish community, which could not afford the tuition. It brought keen excitement to the Noonan household, however, where they had been saving for the event, and it caused almost as much dissension as Veronica's continuing struggle to marry Mr. Rabinsky. Rosaleen was eight. There had never been any question about her attending the school, and Liam was anxious to go, too. Eleven-year-old Darin was a problem, though. Schooled in the streets and at the Noonan Pub, he had no intention of being hauled away to a classroom at his age. Padraig flatly refused, and the subject was not pressed: big for his age, Padraig already looked like a man, and his stubbornness was legendary in the family. He had already lingered longer than Michael because of Doirin's illness, though everyone felt he wanted to follow his older brother to sea.

When the dispute over Darin's schooling came under discussion, Rosaleen eagerly made the trip across town with Mary and Philip, who was able to walk part of the way.

"I can read and write!" Darin screamed with his eyes flashing. "Hell, I know my catechism! I can even figure up a tab at the bar and give proper change. I don't need no schooling! I'm too old!"

"You're never too old to learn," Brian argued patiently, running his hand through his white hair. "Sure, Darin, it's the opportunity of your life. If we'd stayed in Ireland, you'd have no chance to go beyond the hedge school gathered by the priest. You should be thankful we've enough money to pay your tuition."

"Save your money," Darin replied sullenly. "I'd rather help out at the pub and earn a bit myself."

"I'd like one of my sons to go to school," Doirin said plaintively. "Sure, the others aren't worth a thing, and never will be! Michael's not been heard of for these two years. He may be dead, for all we know. And Padraig—great, stubborn lump that he is—will never get any further than little Philip, there. He's not a moron, of course, but if you get three words a month out of him, you're doing well. Darin, I want one of my sons educated. I'd like one of my sons to be a priest."

"A priest!" Darin cried in horror, his blue eyes widening. "Jesus Christ, Ma, you don't expect it to be me! Sure, if you want someone to pray for you, ask Liam, who's on his knees in church all the time."

"Liam isn't *my* son," Doirin said, with a hateful glance at Mary, which must have hit its mark, because Mary gave an almost imperceptible gasp. "Damn you, Darin! Do you want your cousins to be smarter than you are?"

"They won't be smarter," Darin responded. "Their heads will be full of book-nonsense, that's all."

"One more word out of you, and I'll cane you!" Doirin screamed, at which point Veronica and Rosaleen withdrew to the little-used parlor. For some reason Rosaleen did not understand, Irish people always seemed to congregate in the kitchen. Veronica sank down in a chair near the fire, shaking her head, and Rosaleen saw how pale she was, with her blue eyes deep and sad, as though the strength were just about drawn out of her. Unsure what to say and not wishing to discuss the problem being aired in the kitchen, Rosaleen knelt down beside her.

"And how's everything going with you, Veronica? Is there any progress at all in your marriage plans?"

Veronica heaved a deep sigh. "When it's even mentioned, there's a row. Father McMahon's more sympathetic than they are," she said, tossing her head in the direction of the storm-filled kitchen. "Brian's taking my side, now, but Tomas and Doirin are insufferable. The priest has finally agreed that if we raise our children Catholic, we can be married in church, but not at the altar, only in front of the rail."

"What's wrong with that?" Rosaleen asked. "If it were me, I'd not be married in church at all."

"Oh, Rosaleen!" Veronica said, widening her eyes, "don't ever talk that way, darlin'. If you aren't married in church, you aren't married at all. You'd be living in sin. Your children wouldn't be legal: they'd be illegitimate."

Rosaleen had never heard the word, but she got its meaning from the context and inflection of Veronica's words. "That isn't fair! Sure, it wouldn't be the fault of the children!" She thought about it for a moment. "They could be baptized, couldn't they?"

"I don't know," Veronica said lifelessly, against the rise and fall of voices in the other room. "Mr. Rabinsky's synagogue feels as strongly about the whole thing as our church. Did you know they don't even accept converts?"

"Well," Rosaleen said, "I don't think I'd really want to be a Jew anyway. People seem to dislike them even more than the Irish, if that's possible. But I think he's such a nice man! I think you should get married and have children and be happy. No one in this family seems to know how to be happy."

Veronica patted her cheek and smiled slightly. "Darlin'," she said softly, "didn't you know they're doing what makes them happy, right now? I think it gets their blood up. I really think they enjoy it."

"I hate it. I've always hated it," Rosaleen said vehemently. "Row and nag. That's all they know how to do. Sometimes I think of joining the nuns, but I wouldn't do that either, I guess. There aren't any pretty dresses there."

Unwittingly, she made Veronica laugh, which brought a smile to her own lips: she liked to see people happy, even at her own expense. "Darin will go to school," she said. "There doesn't have to be a row."

Veronica raised her eyebrows. "Oh? And how's this to be accomplished, young lady?"

"I'll talk him into it," Rosaleen said smugly. "Ma's always saying, 'You get more flies with honey than vinegar.' I wonder why they don't try it?"

Darin did not respond to Rosaleen's sweetness, however; it was so unlike her that it made him suspicious. When one method did not work, she was always perfectly adept at another: she flattered, cajoled, and even got angry. He was as stubborn about going to school as Padraig was about everything else. Finally, without really being aware of it, she resorted to the deadliest Irish method of all, jeering.

"If you want to spend your life running jars of grog to people too drunk to come and get it, it's no skin off my nose. You're as daft as your mother and Padraig."

"I am not!" her cousin flared. "Jesus, Rosaleen, don't ever say I'm like my mother! We all know she's crazy. And I'm *not* as stupid as Padraig."

"You're just as uneducated," Rosaleen fired back at him. "And it looks like you want to stay that way."

"I don't want to be a priest!"

"You don't have to be a priest, Darin." Rosaleen laughed suddenly. "They wouldn't take a devil like you into a seminary anyway. You should just be interested in more things. Do you think your mother would turn into a lump over someone leaving if she had something to think about besides herself and her family? You should learn to *speak* better. Do you know what you said a while ago?"

He looked humiliated. "No. What?"

"'I don't need no schooling'! That's not only bad grammar...it's street talk, like some illiterate mick in the pub! The Maddigan boys would never say anything like that."

"The Maddigan boys, is it?" Darin said sullenly. "Sure, they've had advantages I haven't."

"But you have one, now! Going to school's an advantage that most of the poor hoodlums on the street aren't going to have! Tuition costs money. Your father wants to do what's best for you, Darin. Never mind your mother's crazy ideas."

He sat quite still, with his hands around his knees, on the stairway going down to the pub. She observed his pretty profile, his tousled black hair, his long lashes and pouting lower lip: she loved him so much, he just had to listen to her. She did not want to see him tending bar like his father when he was grown up.

"The Maddigan boys, is it?" he repeated, almost to himself; then his blue eyes turned to glance at her, and he sighed. "All right, Rosaleen, I'll go for a while. I'll see what it's like. But I'll be goddamned if I'll wear one of those stupid little caps!"

"You can put it in your pocket on your way home," she said and smiled before throwing her arms around his neck. "Oh, Darin, I'm so glad!"

He disentangled her arms and pushed her away roughly. "Don't do that! How many times have I told you not to do that? It's stupid...and you're a stupid little girl." He cast his eyes to heaven. "Jesus! What did I ever do to deserve a cousin like you?"

"You saved my life," she said pertly. "You hauled me out of the raging river so I wouldn't drown."

"Your recollection of that heroic act is distorted," he told her. "The River Bride's a lazy old thing and it was about a foot deep where you were."

"I was almost a baby!" she protested. "I know I would have drowned if you hadn't come by."

"Well, you don't owe me noth...anything. I'd have done the same for a hurt duck or a litter of kittens in a bag."

"I love that about you, Darin. You care about every living thing, sort of like St. Francis. He cared about every little bird ... even the wolf ..."

"Get on with you! I'm no saint, to be sure. I couldn't be a saint any more than I could a priest. So don't look at me like that," he said, his own blue eyes imitating the worship in hers. "And if you throw your arms around me again or kiss me," he said with distaste, "I'll shove you down for sure."

She was too old to get tearful over his threats, or for her lips to tremble uncontrollably; besides, she was confident of his affection and did not believe his words. He was just talking boy talk. She knew there was a special relationship between them: the one constant thing in her life.

Laura helped Rosaleen make her school uniform, a long dark-blue serge with hardly any waist which buttoned down the back, adorned only with the embroidered white letters S and M transposed over each other on the left breast. At first Rosaleen was enthusiastic and felt almost like a novice in her black lisle hose and matching shoes; but it did not take long for the novelty to wear off and the drab uniform to depress her. Within a few months, she could not wait to get home to get out of it. Initially, all students were put together under different nuns, in order to sort out their educational levels, because some had been trained to some extent in Ireland and others had no schooling at all, regardless of their age. By Christmas, classes were formed, and Rosaleen was delighted to be put in the higher level, under the same nun, Sister Agnes Marie, as Darin and Liam; though her education already surpassed theirs, the Mother Superior decided not to put her above that level, because of her age. When school adjourned for the holidays, Rosaleen looked forward to its reopening in spite of the uniform: she would be with Darin every day.

As always, her good fortune was either short-lived or balanced by what she considered a personal misfortune. Before the Maddigan boys got home from their school, Mary made a decision that sent Rosaleen into a tantrum of weeping protest.

Approaching quietly from Laura's room with little Philip in her arms, Mary caught Rosaleen staring into the mirror of the chiffonier in the nursery, holding her hair up with both hands in imitation of a new hair style, giving herself sidelong looks from under her black lashes.

"Do you like what you see, then?" Mary asked, putting Philip down to run around and play with his toys. Though her voice was as cheerful as usual, Rosaleen caught the hint of a jeer in it. She dropped her hair and stood at attention, away from the mirror. If there was one thing her mother disliked, it was any hint of vanity. Though she indulged her in other ways, she was quite merciless if she thought anything was damaging her character, and one of the more serious things seemed to be liking the way one looked.

"I was just thinking of tying my hair back," Rosaleen lied without blinking. "The boys will be home tomorrow, and I want them to see how grown up I am. They'll be so proud that I'm attending school."

Mary arched one well-formed eyebrow: she knew Rosaleen far too well on the surface and recognized a hasty lie when she heard it. "Sure, you're a bit young to care what any boy thinks, Rosaleen." She smiled. "In ten years or so, you might start giving it consideration, I suppose. But if you're going to live in a house with so many boys older than you, I'll not have you making an idjut of yourself. Anyway, I'm afraid you'll not be romping and playing games all this holiday season...not with Monica Devlin flat on her back in bed. There'll be too much work to do."

Monica Devlin was one of the maids, middle-aged and very industrious. She had developed a cough the week before, which now had her laid up in her room with camphor and turpentine and other ill-smelling medicines on the table by her bed. Rosaleen's heart sank: she had looked forward to the holidays, to seeing Johnny and his brothers again and enjoying all the fun the season brought. Her face went rigid, and she bit her lip to keep from saying something she might regret.

223

"Am I to look after Monica, then?" she asked. "I'm sure if I hung about her room, I'd get the sickness, too. You wouldn't want me to be sick when you go to visit the family on Christmas Day, would you, Mother?"

Mary scrutinized her for so long that she began to feel hot around her collar. She realized, too late, that what she had said did not sound exactly charitable; and whenever she tried to manipulate her mother, she usually failed anyway. Mary turned away with an exasperated sigh, which seemed to come right from her heart, and Rosaleen felt a moment's guilt for distressing her.

"No," she said wearily, beginning to fold Philip's clothes, "you won't be put in a sickroom...though I think it might do you more good than harm. Monica's work isn't getting done. There's all that silver to polish, and the household linen to iron...never mind the dusting that's been neglected. The dining room and the parlor have acquired an inch of dust already."

Rosaleen was aghast. "You want me to be a *maid?*"

Mary did not look around at her, continuing her tasks. "I don't think a little work will harm you, if that's what you mean. You aren't a fairy princess, you know: you should have some responsibilities. I should think you'd be delighted to give the Maddigans a hand when it's needed, they've been so good to you."

"I won't polish silver!" Rosaleen declared, trembling all over, her blue eyes blazing. "I won't dust the parlor! Auntie Laura wouldn't want that."

"She isn't your aunt," Mary said levelly. "You must get it out of your head that you're a member of the family, Rosaleen. Sometimes Miss Laura doesn't realize what she's doing. I'm careful not to take advantage of her generosity. You must be more mindful of it, too. I'm a servant here, no matter what she chooses to call it, and you're a servant's daughter. So please don't act so high and mighty, young lady. You'll do as you're told."

That was when, to her mother's surprise and distress, the tears and screaming began. Rosaleen did not remember what she had said, later; but she knew she had been hauled bodily and none too gently out of the nursery, where Laura could hear her, into their own room and thrown down on the bed. Still, she continued to sob and beat her fists on the pillow.

"Stop it!" Mary commanded. "Stop it, at once! *Rosaleen,*" she said harshly, grabbing her daughter's long hair and pulling her up from the pillow to face her, "I won't have this! Do you hear me? You're acting like a raging maniac." Then, realizing that Rosaleen had completely lost control of herself and was hysterical, she administered a sound slap across the face to bring her out of it. "I swear to God, you're as daft as Doirin! Who do you think you are, anyway...to carry on so over a bit of work?"

Her mother would never have accepted the answer to that question, had it been given: quite simply, Rosaleen thought she was Rosaleen, and she could not imagine being anything better. She did not mind the work as such: it was the degrading position she was put in, filling in for the maid. Everything in her rebelled against doing anything so menial; her dignity was at stake. And she would also be missing a good time.

The next morning, a few hours before the boys' return from school, both Rosaleen and her dignity were marched down to the dining room and all the household silver laid out before her, several days' work, even if she hurried, which she did not. Within a short time, she found herself fascinated by the beauty of the heavy Georgian patterns and, meticulously, began to clean every trace of tarnish from them. As she polished, she spun a fantasy that all this loveliness was hers. With an apron over her everyday gray peasant dress and her hair unbraided, she saw herself as Cinderella oppressed by a wicked guardian, who would be totally abashed when the butterfly within her emerged from its cocoon. Lost in her imagination, she did not hear the boys arrive and only realized they were there when they burst in upon her.

"What on earth are you doing?" Harry cried with surprise when he saw her in the soiled apron with tarnish smudges on her face.

Johnny expressed the same displeasure with the simple exclamation, "Rosaleen!"

She looked up at them with just the proper amount of abashed dignity and sweetness in her face. "Mother asked me to help," she explained. "One of the maids is ill, and there's just too much for the others to do."

"But..." Johnny said in bewilderment, "this will take forever. I wanted to teach you chess!"

"I'm going to see Mother about this, at once," Harry said, in a new and deeper voice: like Darin's, his voice was beginning to change. "Better yet, I'll have Matthew do it! He's the man of the house, now, and she really listens to him."

Rosaleen shook her head. "There really isn't anyone else to do it, and I can't disobey my mother. She's that grateful to the family for its kindness to us. Maybe I can see you tonight, after I dust the parlor and..."

As she had intended, her martyred voice had an effect on her friends, though rather a different one than she had expected. Harry shed his school jacket and rolled up his shirt sleeves. "Come on, Johnny, get a move on you. If we all pitch in, it'll be done in no time, and Rosaleen will be free for the rest of the holidays."

Johnny, still smaller and paler than his brother, did not obey him at once. His gray eyes looked troubled through his spectacles, and he wavered between doing as his brother told him or what he thought was correct. "We haven't seen Mother yet, Harry. Surely we should go up there first."

"Matthew's with her—her pride and joy," Harry said without rancor. "If we don't show up, they'll come down to us. Besides, I want Mother to see this: I don't approve of Rosaleen doing this sort of thing, in the least."

The decision made for him, Johnny took off his jacket and hung it carefully over the curved back of one of the Hepplewhite chairs. "I was going to help you," he explained shyly to Rosaleen. "I just thought we should see Mother first. But Harry's right. This way, she can see what's happening for herself."

Laura's interview with her oldest son took nearly an hour, by which time a great deal of silver had been polished. Though Johnny said relatively little about school, applying himself fastidiously and nearsightedly to his task, Harry kept up a steady stream of chatter, which had all of them smiling by the time Laura and Matthew, now taller than his mother, appeared in the door.

"What is this?" Laura said. "Why, you dear things, you're helping with Monica's work! And I can see from the smudges on her face who started it all." She walked from one chair to the other, embracing her sons and kissing their cheeks, ending with Rosaleen, whom she hugged from behind. "What a good girl you are! And, imagine, thinking of it all by yourself."

"Mother suggested I do it," Rosaleen said fairly, since Laura would probably hear about it anyway. "She didn't want me caring for Monica in her sickroom."

"Well, I should think not!" Laura said. "You might get ill, too."

"Matthew, come and give us a hand," Harry said, polishing

a teapot fiercely. "If we can get this stuff out of the way, Rosaleen will be free to be with us during the holidays."

Matthew, though smiling, demurred. He was very much like a younger version of his father in appearance, dark-eyed and dashing, very close to being a man. Rosaleen had heard her mother and Laura discussing his entrance into Harvard, and if it could be arranged in a couple of years. Everything in the Maddigan household seemed to suffer from Laura's break with her family to marry beneath her; though Mr. Maddigan was rich and, apparently, powerful in the financial world, the people Laura called the "Brahmins," with a bitter tone in her voice, would never accept his sons.

When Laura withdrew to show Matthew some papers she had received from the lawyer who was handling her end of the business until Matthew was able to do it, Rosaleen said as tactfully as she could, "I don't understand the people here in Boston. Your mother would like to be friends with them, I think, but they're so unfriendly, aren't they?"

Johnny ignored the remark, but Harry smiled widely. "'No Irish Need Apply' to Boston society," he said. "If you didn't come over on the *Mayflower*, or within the next hundred years, you're an outsider. And heaven help you if you marry someone who *is* an outsider! Someone 'beneath you,' as mother did. We may be able to buy and sell them, but their doors are locked to us, because our name is Maddigan. It doesn't bother me."

"It does me," Johnny said quietly and unexpectedly. "I want to go to Harvard."

"There are other good schools," Harry said. "I may have to go away to study medicine, but I'll do it. Of course, Harvard is the best. Though they're murdering each other at the Medical School right now. You heard about Dr. Parkman, didn't you?"

"I think your mother's trying to get you in there," Rosaleen said with a nod: everyone had heard about the doctor's disappearance. Johnny looked up hopefully, but Harry continued burnishing the tea set.

"No chance at all, I'd say. Unless she does something like endow a chair. And that would be a bit pretentious without Father being an alumnus. Without that, and with our name, it's impossible."

"You could always go to Boston College," Rosaleen suggested: it was the only college besides Harvard that she had heard about. Harry's reaction to that was a loud laugh.

"Under the Jesuits!" he chortled. "No, thank you, Rosie. Though I suspect it would be proper training for Matthew, who's going to be a banker."

Rosaleen did not understand. Liam wanted to go there, and he did not want to be a banker. "Why?" she asked. Harry, embarrassed by the implication in what he had said, did not answer. "Why?" she persisted.

"Historically," Johnny said, without interrupting his silver rubbing, "the Jesuits have acquired a great deal of land and money wherever they go."

Rosaleen laughed. "That's daft!" she said with confidence. "Priests take a vow of poverty."

The brothers looked at one another and discontinued the conversation.

"How's old Darin?" Harry asked suddenly. "I hope he can come to the Cape with us next summer. It wasn't the same without him last year."

"He's going to school with me," Rosaleen said enthusiastically. "He's doing pretty well, too, except that he spends too much time on his geography and his grade in mathematics is down a bit. I don't know why he doesn't like math: it's my favorite subject, because it's so easy."

"Easy?" Johnny said. "I don't do well in it at all. I have to study my head off. I prefer the classics."

"The what? We don't have that, I'm sure."

"Latin, Greek, the humanities," he stopped to explain. "It's like discovering whole new cultures, Rosaleen. I brought a mythology book for you."

"Thank you," she said as sincerely as she could, because she did not wish to appear stupid twice, by asking what that was, too.

"Old John's going to be the family scholar," Harry said, too good-natured to actually tease his younger brother. "The classics aren't altogether practical, Rosaleen. Our Johnny's a bookworm."

To her surprise, Johnny appeared more pleased than offended by the appellation, which was one of scorn at her school, though Ireland remained the land of "saints and scholars" in the minds of even the most ignorant Irishman in the North End, having heard it often from the pulpit to boost morale.

"A scholar's a fine thing to be," she defended Johnny. "At one time, scholars came to Ireland from all over the world to learn the Latin and the Greek."

She did not expect quite so much appreciation from Johnny, whose hands stopped moving altogether while he stared at her like a thankful puppy, as though her approval were actually important to him.

"When we finish this," he said with glowing eyes, "I want to teach you chess. You'll like it, Rosaleen: it's very exciting, and a game can go on for hours."

"Who ever heard of a girl playing chess?" Harry asked, without the least understanding of the qualities of Rosaleen's mind. "It takes strategy and patience, aggressiveness and intelligence—all things a girl is better off without."

"Rosaleen isn't like other girls," Johnny defended her. "She's quite intelligent, you know."

"I'm not denying that," Harry said. "She's bright enough. But it's more important for a girl to be pretty and sweet, and I'd rather she kept those qualities, both of which," he said gallantly, "she has in abundance."

Rosaleen was accustomed to compliments. She had heard them as long as she could remember, but usually they were about the way she looked, rather than the sweetness of her personality. She didn't know how to respond to that, so she remained silent. She had never heard boys talking about her as though she were not there, and though she found it gratifying, she felt like an eavesdropper, so she changed the subject.

"Harry, is it true that Professor Webber cut Dr. Parkman up and burned him in the laboratory furnace? Will the janitor really get the three-thousand-dollar reward?"

Mary was nervous and exhausted, almost constantly angry at her daughter for something, usually for not helping more with the work. Sometimes she even felt angry about the time Rosaleen spent in the library reading, though they had both agreed that she should do it. Mary loved Philip, but he was more work than all her own children together had been. Though she had put all her strength into toilet-training him, his poor little brain could not grasp it, and she had to clean up after him several times during the day, washing his clothing out, so he would be clean and perfect if Laura sent for him. When she left him in his crib for a nap to spend the required time with Laura, almost invariably she came back to a frightful mess, because he frequently woke and played in his feces, spreading the filth all over the linen and the wall. It seemed her arms were constantly immersed in dirty water, and she could not get the odor out of the room. And Rosaleen was no help at all. Even more sensitive to the smell than Mary, she gagged and ran from the room when she was needed, though she was almost as fond of the child as her mother.

Many of the tensions Mary felt were centered around Rosaleen, and she was frequently cross with her. She wanted more for her daughter than she had known in life, but not of material things, which the girl fastened on so greedily. Her daughter was more beautiful than she had been, and she did not envy her this. Rosaleen was a Noonan, and it gave Mary pleasure just to look at her, but she recognized the danger of being too beautiful, and the shallowness it might cause. Already, Rosaleen was vain, and Mary could not let her grow up too fond of herself, because real beauty came from within, as it did with Veronica.

She worried a lot about Veronica, too. She knew her young sister-in-law was in pain, and there seemed to be no end in sight for her unfortunate marriage plans. Mary was afraid that the prolonged argument with the Church would make her ill again. When Mary visited the pub, she watched Veronica carefully for any sign of the hectic flush or the cough of her former illness. No matter what the weather, she visited there on her day off, glad for the long walk and the company of Veronica, and Brian, if he showed himself upstairs. She tried to talk to Liam, to love him, but her son avoided her with dark looks that made her feel guilty, just as she felt guilty over her punishments of Rosaleen. Her emotions were in turmoil, and she could not seem to understand them enough to get them under control.

If her life had been set to music, her love for Brian would have run through its jangling cacophony like one sure chord, the only dependable emotion she felt. And dear, gentle Brian was probably as unhappy as she was, perhaps more unhappy than anyone. Though she longed to see him, she would have stayed away if possible, because of the pain in his eyes. When they met, their glances held with a feeling like a benediction. It was difficult to look away, regardless of the fear of discovery. He was a normal man, blighted by the need for love. From what she had felt in his arms that one time, she knew she was a normal woman, but everything stood between them, and the added guilt of loving her sister's husband hurt almost as much as that love. She had considered their situation long and sadly, knowing that even if Doirin and Tomas were removed, there was no hope of their ever being together. The Church was explicit about family relationships: "Thou shalt not marry thy brother's wife" was like an eleventh commandment, just as strong as the law about marrying within the third degree of kindred. Though they did not move toward each other physically, their love itself was regarded as a sin.

The family was more comfortable than it had ever been, materially, but Mary found herself weeping more often: for Philip, over Rosaleen, in anger toward Laura when she interfered between her and her daughter, and, probably most of all, over the fate that kept her from the only man she had ever loved. A fate that tortured both of them. She wanted desperately to talk to someone, but she had to carry the burdens herself. The catharsis of confession was lost to her, unless she told the priest she had once contemplated murder, which she could not bring herself to do. She had no friend, no relative to whom she could confide the problems which were causing her exhaustion, and she worried even about the excessive weeping, which had been prominent in one stage of her sister's breakdown. She did not want that to happen to her. One evening, in desperation, she sought Rosaleen in the room they had once shared together, though Mary stayed with Philip in the nursery now, in an attempt to relieve some of her anxiety. If she could come to terms with her daughter, perhaps she could handle the rest on her own. To her surprise, Rosaleen was lying on her bed weeping too.

"What is it, darlin'?" Mary asked softly, sitting down beside her, the comforter, never the comforted. "Sure, what's bothering you? You can tell me about it."

Her daughter wiped the tears away, sniffed and set her chin at a proud angle. "It's nothing, Mother," she said, with her lower lip trembling. "You wouldn't understand."

"Perhaps, I would. Indeed, I would," Mary said and nodded. "Sure I've been a bit down myself, tonight. You went to visit Veronica, today, didn't you? Did something happen there?"

"Veronica wasn't home. She was at the rectory with Mr. Rabinsky," Rosaleen said. "It's Aunt Doirin, Mother. The things she says. She and Darin had an awful row. I hate her!"

Mary was silent for a moment; then, "She doesn't think before she speaks. You mustn't pay that much attention to her."

"She thinks, all right!" Rosaleen flared, her eyes filling

again. "Everything she says is calculated to hurt. I don't care if she is your sister, she's a dreadful woman! Do you know what she said today? She said Veronica's going to die of consumption anyway, so nothing really matters. She said it's a wonder we haven't all gotten it, because it's that contagious. That's when Darin told her to shut her gob and go to hell. I asked him about consumption later. He said it's tuberculosis, and it is contagious, but his mother had no right to say such awful things." She wiped her eyes with the back of her hand. "Is it true, Mother? Will we get it, too?"

"Not if we take care of ourselves," Mary said, her mind on Doirin. "Sure we haven't gotten it yet, have we? And Veronica's cured. Rosaleen, what made her talk about such things to you children? Why was Veronica at the rectory with Mr. Rabinsky?"

"I forgot to tell you," Rosaleen admitted with a shamed face. "Aunt Doirin upset me....The dispen...dispensa... the thing from the Church came through, I think."

"The dispensation?" Mary cried, her spirits rising. "Veronica and Mr. Rabinsky can get married?"

"Yes. That's what set Aunt Doirin off. She said it didn't matter, because that 'Jew' would have a corpse for a wife anyhow. She said we're all going to die from it. I don't want to die, Mother! I'm more afraid of death than anything."

"Don't talk like a coward." Mary smiled, elated at the news: at least one of her worries was over. "Everyone has to die, Rosaleen, sometime. It's better not to think about it, and to keep your soul in a state of grace. Oh, my! I'm that relieved! Aren't you happy for Veronica, Rosaleen?"

The girl did not reply, though under other circumstances she would have been delighted for her aunt. Once again, through a fluke of mood, of diverted communication, she and Mary had come close for a moment, only to ricochet apart because of their differing concerns. Mary did not know how near she had been to hearing about her daughter's greatest fear. Rosaleen never spoke of it again, because she was reprimanded carelessly as a coward, and she continued to believe that she was alone in her fear of death.

Chapter 16

MORE THAN any bride, Veronica deserved to walk down
the aisle in flowing white with the music playing. Instead,
the wedding was almost surreptitious, with only Mary and
Rosaleen, Brian and Darin in attendance. Veronica was
dressed in drab gray taffeta with a full-flounced skirt and
carried a small bouquet of hothouse violets. Rosaleen helped
her sew the dress hastily in her own room at the Maddigans',
because Doirin could not be told about the wedding until it
was over, or Veronica would not have been able to stay under
the same roof with her. She and her bridegroom were married
on the steps in front of the altar rail, not on the altar as other
people were, and the priest performed the service in a per-
functory manner which would leave the couple little to remember of their wedding ceremony.

Veronica looked as though she were dressed to go on a
trip, which, indeed, she was: across town in a cab to Mr.
Rabinsky's new store, where they would live upstairs. Her
box of things was already in place on the roof of the waiting
horse cab, so that when Brian invited the couple to a little
party he had planned, it was impossible for them to delay.
Veronica kissed him and smiled.

"Thank you, Brian, for everything, darling. We'd love to
come, but we have to be married in an Orthodox ceremony
this afternoon. I wish you could attend that, too, but the
Church won't allow you inside a church of another denomi-

nation. Thank you, Mary, Rosaleen. Dear Rosaleen..." She smiled, hugging the child. "Darin, you devil, I love you! I love you all! But sure, you'll perish in the cold if I don't get going. Goodbye!" she said, mounting the steps of the cab. "Come to see me. Please!"

Mr. Rabinsky, smiling happily, seconded the invitation from his seat above them. "You must come to see us. Our door is always open to you, my dear friends... and relatives," he added, almost timorously, and they were gone.

Mary wept openly in the blustery March wind, and Brian put his arm around her shoulders to comfort her.

"There, it's all right now, isn't it? Sure, they're as happy as any couple I've ever seen. They have each other. Please, Mary, don't cry. I can't bear to see you cry."

"It's from relief," Mary said, half laughing. "I'm so glad they finally got to marry. I was so worried she'd do something foolish, during that long wait. But she's married, and in the Church, too. And her children will be Catholic, if there are any."

He nodded with a faint smile on his lips. "Everything's worked out just fine. Well, what d'ya say, now, we have a party of our own? I hear there's a fine tea shop on Boylston, with cakes and white linen and everything. And we'll take a cab, just like they did."

The children's faces lit up, but Mary was reluctant. "Sure, it's throwing money around, Brian. Anyway, I'm not dressed for it. What you see beneath my fine coat is my black uniform!"

"It looks just splendid. If you hadn't told me, I wouldn't have known. I don't see you often enough... you or Rosaleen," he added quickly. "What d'ya say, kids? Do we have a right to celebrate?"

"Yes!" came in unison from both Rosaleen and Darin, who had his cold hands plunged deep in his pockets.

"Well, all right," Mary agreed. "It is *bitter* cold and we can't be standing around on a street corner."

"We have a right to something," Brian said earnestly; then, more cheerfully, "Darin, my boy, get us a cab. One of the big ones, so we can all ride in comfort."

Rosaleen ran along with Darin to the place with a trough where they knew cabs stopped, and together they rode back to the church. "Isn't this wonderful?" she said to Darin as they jerked along to the clop of the horse's hooves. "Your father's in a queer mood today. I've never seen him happy before. I guess it's having his sister marry. Though that's supposed to make people sad, isn't it?"

"After a wait like that and all the fighting that's been going on? Sure, he's probably glad to have it over with. He isn't usually happy. Can you imagine being married to that witch of a mother I have? I can hardly stick it myself sometimes. If the Church won't allow divorce, at least it should condone murder, in special cases."

Rosaleen laughed. "What an awful thing to say! But I understand what you mean. Have you noticed how well my mother and your father get along? It's a pity they didn't marry, instead of the way it worked out. Except that then you'd be my brother." The conversation brought her father to mind: she did not think of him often. "By the way, how's my father doing? Is he still walking both sides of the road most of the time?"

Darin smiled, with mischief in his eyes. "You're too hard on him, Rosie. He's a very funny man. I don't think I could survive without him around, drunk or sober. He's more fun when he's drunk, of course."

"He has no responsibility."

"No. But then don't you think there may be men who were never meant for responsibility? Well, there they are, then...cabby, pull over here!"

The tea shop was very grand, and Rosaleen was conscious of the cheap, ill-fitting clothing Brian and Darin wore, grateful that she and her mother had decent coats to hide the clothes beneath. But she loved Darin so much she could not really be ashamed of him, and she began to feel defensive, instead, when people turned to stare. Brian ordered tea and cakes from a dignified waiter, who did not bring their order until he had seen to some people who came in after they did. Inside, Rosaleen fumed at the inequality, reducing the waiter to no more than a maid in her eyes, regardless of his stuck-up manners.

She studied the ladies' fashions almost greedily; until now, she had only seen such frocks in the fashion plates of Laura's magazines. The women themselves she both admired and ridiculed, because her mind was astute. Their manners were easy and unaffected, like Laura's; and, like her, they seemed to know nothing about life. The bits of trivial conversation she overheard, about people and parties, were notable only for their shallowness. Yet these were probably the people who scorned the Maddigans. Her gaze wandered to the bright chandeliers, the striped silk fabric on the walls. It was truly an elegant place, and they had no business there. She was almost surprised that the management had not barred their entrance. But at least she knew how to behave correctly, from Auntie Laura's coaching.

The most awkward moment, which came close to humiliating her, came with the cake cart, which was artistically laid out with pretty pastries, each on its individual doily. Though she had spent a lot of time in the kitchen and at Laura's little teas for the children, even Rosaleen had never seen anything like it, and the other members of her family, not knowing what to do, sat gaping, while the waiter stood by with two forks in his hand. Rosaleen quickly grasped that the forks were for serving the pastries, the way cook served vegetables with two spoons, but she knew the names of only two of the pastries.

"Ah," she stammered, "we'll have petit fours and Napoleons, please."

Brian and Mary looked at her gratefully as the waiter put the tiny pastries on their plates, asking who wanted the Napoleons. Darin stared hungrily at the cart. "If you don't mind, sir, I don't want these picky little things," he told the waiter. "I'd rather have that great big chocolate one at your elbow . . . the one all heaped with goo."

The man was there to do their bidding, albeit unwillingly: Darin got the pastry he requested. This encouraged Brian to speak up.

"We're after having a little celebration," he explained diffidently. "We'd each like two, please. Ladies, select your own."

Their plates were heaped with pastries, and a fine hot metal teapot sat on their table with china cups, and they finally relaxed once the waiter left, glancing over his shoulder with disapproval.

"Sure, I think we offended him slightly," Brian remarked in his soft voice. "Is it they don't have enough to go around, do you think?"

Even Rosaleen laughed, raising her napkin daintily to her mouth, because she had already taken a bite of pastry. Mary, who had been tense before, smiled, and Brian, encouraged by his success in making her happy, continued to joke relentlessly.

"Wouldn't Darin be the one to want the one with the mess of 'goo' on it, now?" and "Rosaleen, darlin', you're so dainty,

I can hardly remember you dipping into the only bowl of potatoes in the house with both hands" and "Do you recall when we first went into Dugan's Pub and didn't know what a menu was? It took our fine Mary to decipher that tea-soaked scrap of paper covered with flyspecks and piccalilli so we could eat!"

Though their voices were subdued, the merriment at their table elicited disapproving stares from the people around them, which increased their hilarity almost as much as if it had occurred in church. When a woman with a jet-trimmed bodice raised a lorgnette to look at them, Rosaleen went into a convulsion of laughter and had to hide her whole face in her napkin. She wondered if having fine manners meant having no fun; if that was the case, she would be shocking people all of her life.

When as much pastry as they could eat was gone and the teapot drained, Brian's customary sadness began to return. "I wish Veronica and her husband could have come," he said. "Sure, it's a grim day when a man can't toast his only sister's wedding."

"We'll do it another time," Mary said, and Rosaleen had never before noticed the richness of her mother's voice. "It's been a grand party, Brian, and we thank you for it. I don't know when I've had such a good time. I haven't been this happy in years. Not even at my own wedding, as I recall. Everyone was drunk on poteen and leaning against the cottage wall."

"Everyone but you and me," Brian remembered. "Sure, we nearly danced our feet off that day...just you and me. And then his lordship came riding along with McGee, and gave you a gold sovereign because you were the prettiest bride he'd ever seen!"

"Is that where you got your gold piece, Mother?" Rosaleen inquired. "I remember Pa looking for it all the time, but you had it hidden well in a crack in the chimney."

"You knew where it was?" Mary smiled with surprise.

"Yes. It was so pretty. I remember you said you had to spend it for cereal when—"

"We won't talk about that," Mary said quickly. "Sure, weddings in Ireland were happy occasions, with the fiddling and the dancing."

"We danced the old way, holding hands and waists and fairly flying!" said Brian. "I nearly had a heart attack when his lordship rode up that day, Mary, and us dancing as mad as the pagan Celts!"

Mary laughed aloud, completely relaxed now, and Rosaleen saw how pretty she could be. "With Tomas and the rest of the men at our feet from the drink, the women clapping and Fiddler Murphy fairly forcing the music from his violin! His lordship wasn't a bad man. As landlords go, he wasn't bad."

"I'd like a wedding like that," Rosaleen cried. "Do I have to be married in a church? The wedding today was depressing."

"Indeed you do," her mother said. "If you aren't married in church, you aren't married at all. The dancing and laughter comes afterward. It's a bit too early to worry about that, though." She smiled. "Someday you'll find yourself a good Irish Catholic boy, and there'll be no trouble at all."

Rosaleen was content with the answer. She did not dare look at Darin, for fear he would see her choice in her eyes. On that happy day, she was completely unaware that there could be any shadow over her future.

They parted on the sidewalk outside the tea shop, each family to go its separate way home. As they walked up the hill, Mary began to hum a tune, which Rosaleen had forgotten, and Rosaleen sang the words in Gaelic, her breath coming out in puffs of steam in the cold air. She wished it could always be like this, with her mother humming and her singing as they walked along together. It had been that way once. She wondered what had happened to them.

Darin was expelled from St. Mary's just before Rosaleen's birthday, toward the end of the second year, and Rosaleen rushed to his defense without a second thought. Lifting her chin indignantly, she knocked at the door of the Mother Superior's office herself, an office to which she had never before gained admittance. She had only seen the Mother Superior from afar. An accented voice bade her enter, and she stood directly before the head of the convent community. The nun was sterner and older than she had expected, and her sharp black eyes under the white wimple made Rosaleen hesitate; but she was determined to help Darin, so she had to proceed.

"I'm Rosaleen Noonan," she announced. "My cousin's been expelled, Reverend Mother, and it isn't fair! He didn't even have a warning. You just told him to go. I think it's shocking. Darin's a fine boy and—"

"Did he tell you he wasn't warned?" the tight-faced French nun asked coolly. "Because if he did, he's added lying to his other transgressions."

Rosaleen thought quickly: Darin had not told her anything. Her brother had reported to her what had happened, and he had said nothing about warnings at all. "No, Darin didn't say that," she told the nun. "He doesn't lie! But if he was warned, he didn't tell me that, either."

"Does he tell you everything?"

"I...think so. He usually does. Do you mean he did have warning, then?"

"Twice," the nun said, beginning to write again. "I told him one more time and he was expelled."

"But what did he do, Reverend Mother? I know he curses sometimes, but he doesn't mean anything by it."

The incident during religion class was still burned into her mind. Darin, who sat in the back of the class because of his height, dozed off during Bible History, and his desk tipped over, throwing him on the floor. He had risen quickly, clutching his ribs, exclaiming, "Jesus Christ, I damn near killed myself!"—which made everyone laugh right in the middle of Religion. That would be one point against him, she guessed.

"Your cousin, I believe, is a bit too old for our school," the Mother Superior explained. "It isn't just the cursing, though that's pretty bad. And it isn't *just* his making up soubriquets for his teacher, which the younger children emulate."

Haggy Aggie, Rosaleen thought: the nickname Darin had affixed to Sister Agnes Marie, which everyone had copied, because it fit her so well. "If it isn't those things," Rosaleen demanded, "what is it, then? Darin's a good person. I don't know what he did to deserve this. His mother will be raging."

The nun placed her pen carefully in the groove beside her inkwell and spoke as gently as possible in the face of such unintimidated loyalty. "He's older than the other boys. He's almost thirteen, and his voice is changing. He's told the younger boys things they've no right to know: there have been complaints from their families. And he's told them stories he could only have heard in his father's establishment. In short, my dear, he was corrupting the boys of nine and ten. His mind obviously isn't on his education."

Stories? Rosaleen wondered: he never told any to her, and Darin shared things with her. She would ask him about that, later. "He's very popular with the other boys," she pleaded. "They follow him around all the time. He can't shake them off. What stories do you mean, Reverend Mother? Something about the customers at the pub?"

"More likely something *told* by the customers at the pub," the nun said acidly, "and some of it about priests and nuns. Remarks you have no right to hear."

"Everyone will miss him," Rosaleen said lamely, not fully understanding what had happened.

"They might," Mother Superior said with an air of dismissal. "We won't."

In her frustration and with an unconscious urge to communicate with the woman in her own language, Rosaleen said, *"Merde!"*

She did not know what it meant, but she had heard the governess say it once when she pinched herself on the desk. If her attempt had been to get the nun's full attention, she succeeded. The woman looked up with wide dark eyes, the hint of a smile on the edge of her lips: she had been a country girl before heading a religious community.

"Where did you hear that?" she inquired, and Rosaleen said, "Mamselle Boucher, the governess where my mother works, said it once when she was upset. She taught me French for a year. Did I say something wrong?"

The Mother Superior scrutinized Rosaleen with more interest.

"Dites-le en anglais, s'il vous plaît," she instructed her. *"Comprends-tu?"*

"Oui, je comprends, mais," Rosaleen said, *"je ne sais pas le mot en anglais."*

"Bon. Le mot n'est pas gentil."

"Qu'est-ce que vous voulez dire?" Rosaleen asked timidly. *"Je ne comprends pas tout."*

"Écris-tu en français, aussi?"

"Oui...je l'écris mieux que je le parle."

Mother Superior smiled. *"Intéressant . . . très intéressant . . ."*

"Puis-je aller maintenant, s'il vous plaît?" Rosaleen asked nervously, and was dismissed by a wave of the nun's hand. She felt her staring at her back as she left the room.

When they left for the Cape at the end of June, Rosaleen had no idea that it would be her last summer there with Darin, though he was unusually quiet, conversing mostly

240

with Matthew, his particular friend. He did not run down the dunes or splash in the water as he had done in the past. She knew he was unhappy. She knew he had come there under a cloud, his mother hardly speaking to him. Things were worse than ever at home. Doirin took the expulsion as a personal affront, and even his father, generally supportive in what was at best an unhappy household, seemed hurt and humiliated. His proud gift of education had been flung back into his face. When Darin asked if he could go to the Cape with the Maddigans for the summer, his mother snapped, "Do as you please. You will, anyway."

For a woman who was thrown completely off balance when her sons departed, Aunt Doirin did not try very hard to keep them at her side, Rosaleen thought. No matter what Darin thought of her, her attitude hurt him: she was the only mother he had. And there was no way he could erase his father's disappointment, either. Padraig, so big and clumsy that he had not been allowed to carry ale before, was given Darin's job for the summer, with an uncertain understanding about whose it would be on his return. To Rosaleen, it appeared that Darin had been expelled from home as well as school, and she did everything she could to make him happier. But he seldom smiled; he even seemed to go out of his way to shun her company. She did not attempt to fight the jealousy she experienced when she was excluded from his friendship in favor of Matthew, who had little to do with either his brothers or Rosaleen any more. Since his father's death, Matthew took being head of the family seriously, though he was only fourteen.

Liam's unexpected acceptance of the invitation frequently extended to him proved to be more of a consolation than she could have imagined. Her brother really was not too bad; perhaps he was just growing up. At least he talked more now; in fact, when he was with Johnny, it was difficult to shut him up. The two boys, both self-conscious and interested in their studies, got on famously, and Rosaleen and Harry either had to listen to their discussions, which were increasingly pedantic, or go search for something else to do. But Liam and Rosaleen became friends, too, frequently walking the sand together during the day, and playing chess and lighter games with Harry and Johnny in the evening.

Until now, Liam had clung to Aunt Doirin, an attachment neither Rosaleen nor her mother could understand. He only agreed to come to the Cape after Mary promised to look in on her sister, and Padraig assured him that he would be there, too. Liam seemed to pry himself loose cautiously to have a look at the world, and in the company of his sister and the other boys, it would have been impossible for him not to enjoy himself.

The three boys and Rosaleen were lying on a blanket on the beach one day when she asked them, "What's happened to Darin? He doesn't want to be with us any more. I know he has troubles, but he used to share with us. You're almost the same age as he is, Harry, can you explain it to me?"

Liam and Johnny were, in fact, the same age as Darin, and Harry a year older. Harry's fair complexion flushed slightly, but he was always direct, if frequently amused by her questions, and he attempted to explain. "He's going through a difficult time, Rosie. It mixes one's head up. It isn't just the voice changing, which is pretty embarrassing sometimes. He's changing into a man. It'll happen to you, too," he added mischievously. "By the time you're twelve, you'll start to be a gorgeous, curvy woman!"

"Is that when it happens?" she asked reflectively. "I have three whole years to wait! I'm sick of doing what other people say. When I'm a woman, I'll do exactly what I please."

Harry's laughter bewildered her: without trying, she had said something funny...again. That sort of thing kept happening with Darin and Matthew, too, as though their minds were somewhere she could not follow, and they saw everything from a different frame of reference. She looked to Liam and Johnny for an explanation, but they were sitting rigidly, staring at the sea: if they knew what was going on, they did not show it in their faces. Liam looked uncomfortable beneath his apparent ignorance, and he finally felt it his duty to reprimand her.

"Rosaleen, you mustn't go around asking such questions." His clear, immature voice was high. "You should discuss such things with Mother. And you must remember that when you're a woman, it'll be a very great responsibility. You can *never* do as you please. It's important that you realize that. Women have a very important, almost hallowed, place in society. In my opinion, they carry civilization from one generation to another. Historical continuity is dependent upon them."

She did not understand much of it. Johnny sniffed and blinked a few times before he entered into the discussion.

"Women are important, of course," he said, agreeing with his opponent before he tore him down. "But, Liam, when it comes to history, how many have really been outstanding? You can count them on one hand. And whatever they accomplished wasn't due to excessive morality: Cleopatra, Queen Elizabeth, Catherine the Great . . . and . . . well, I can't even think of five!"

"That isn't what I meant," Liam protested. "When I said 'historical,' I meant the continuity women bring to history as mothers of great men. Actually, though, I think you should add some names to your list. What about Mary, the mother of Jesus, and Joan of Arc?"

"I'm sorry," Johnny apologized, "but I don't believe in that mystical stuff. Oh, I know Joan was a person: they have the trial records to prove it, and she did some remarkable things. But I don't go along with her 'voices.' I realize your religion feels differently about such things, and I respect your views, of course."

Harry and Rosaleen looked at one another. He jumped up and brushed the sand from his hands. "I'll race you through the tide to the tide pools!" he said. "This sort of thing bores me stiff!"

He would have been surprised at how hard Rosaleen was trying to follow the conversation. Though she was usually moving, she was interested in what the boys said; but she did not want to hurt Harry's feelings, and it was fun to help search the tide pools for the little creatures and bits of algae Harry put into jars. So she rose and ran barefoot into the tide. The last words she heard were:

"Speaking of continuity, take Messalina as an example."

"I'd rather talk about Mary. Who's Messalina, anyway? I've never heard of her at my school."

"Prominent women seem to be only saints and sinners."

Rosaleen looked all these names up in the library later that year, but immediate events took her mind off them for the rest of the summer.

After a leisurely tea with Laura, Rosaleen detached herself from the others and went looking for Darin, to whom she had hardly spoken in days. She may have been lonely for his company, but afterward she attributed it entirely to a premonition. She found him and Matthew waiting outside the stable with a box at his feet. Their reaction to seeing her told her that something more than a horseback ride was taking place, and she ran to confront them.

"What are you up to? Darin, what's in that box?" she asked suspiciously. "Where's Kevin?"

"Rosaleen," Matthew interrupted, "you must understand. There's nothing else Darin can do. I only wish I were free to go with him. It'll be a marvelous experience, seeing the world."

Ignoring Matthew, she concentrated all her attention on her cousin. "You're going to sea! Darin, you can't do it! You can't leave me! And what about your mother? How can you do this to her? You know what happened when Michael went away!"

"Rosie," Darin breathed through clenched teeth, "I was hoping this wouldn't happen. You've caught me out, but I want you to keep quiet for a while, until we're safely away from here. As for Michael, I'm going to look for him: our paths will have to cross sometime. And Mother...well, Paddy's still at home, and Father's with her. Will you visit her for me, Rosaleen? I don't want anything bad to happen to her."

"No, I won't! I'll never go near that flat again. If you do this, it'll be on your conscience, because I'm not going to help! If she gets sick again, it'll be your fault."

His eyes were grim, and he had a hangdog expression on his face. "She doesn't give a damn anyway. She won't grieve for me the way she did for Michael. It'll be good riddance to bad rubbish. Don't be so stubborn, Rosie. You know I don't want to leave *you*. You and Aunt Mary are special to me."

After every conceivable stratagem and entreaty failed, she finally revealed herself for what she was: a broken-hearted little girl. "Can I go with you, please?" she sniffed. "I want to see the world, too. No one will know, Darin, if I dress like a boy."

He smiled and gave her a hug. "Darlin', you'd never pass for a boy, and you'd puke at the sight of a whale being rendered and boiled down. Be a good girl, Rosaleen. Do the things you have to do, the things right for you. I've never told you before, but you're very clever. Keep going to school. I'll be back before you know it. A whaler only stays out of port two or three years."

"Three years! Why, you'll be all grown up in three years! Sure," she said, lapsing under stress into her old speech pattern, "what if someone hits me or knocks me down? Liam can't defend me, he's too little and puny."

He laughed and tousled her hair. "That hasn't happened for a long time. You can look after yourself better than anyone I know. You aren't a baby any more, and you really have your wits about you." He released her and she tried to scramble back into his arms. "Is Kevin just about ready, Matt? I want you to get back here before too late. Your mother will worry. She's a nice lady. Please give her my regards."

"You're leaving right *now?*" Rosaleen cried.

"It's best that way. I was hoping I wouldn't see you. I don't want another row with my family, so there's no sense going back to Boston with New Bedford so near. I'll get a ride out to Nantucket somehow."

"Let me ride with you! I just want to see you off."

"No, Rosie. I don't want any more scenes. Just let us go quietly. Don't tell anyone. Matthew will be back tonight."

Kevin appeared with the light buggy, all hitched up and ready to go. He looked frightened when he saw her. "Be a good girl, Rosaleen," he implored from his seat with the reins in his hands. "Sure, I don't want to get into any trouble. Please don't tell Mrs. Maddigan."

Darin stooped to give her a quick kiss on the cheek before leaping into the buggy. Matthew followed with more dignity. She watched them go down the sandy road with sparse trees overhanging it, her heart bursting inside of her. As soon as they were out of sight, she ran screaming to Laura.

"Aunty Laura! Aunty Laura! Darin and Matthew have run away to sea!"

Laura's hysterics lasted until Matthew returned after dark with an explanation; then she remained tearful, because she had lost Darin when he was in her care. Before breakfast the next morning, after a sleepless night, she settled down to the difficult task of writing to Darin's parents. Liam volunteered to carry the letter to Boston, so he could be with Doirin when she heard the news.

"I'll never forgive him," Liam told Rosaleen, when he was packing his things. "You'd think he'd have some consideration for his mother. He knows she's...sensitive."

Rosaleen, still devastated by her loss, exploded, "Sensitive! She's crazy, Liam, the way she does things! She drives people away, and then she goes crackers because they're gone. She doesn't care who she hurts, and she's had it easier than anyone, with everyone else doing her work and looking after her. I've never been able to understand why you like her. And you treat your own mother like dirt."

He grew silent, walked to the window with his hands in his pockets and stared sadly at the ocean. "I'm sorry about that," he said at last. "I know I've been unkind. I misunderstood something a long time ago, Rosaleen. Never mind what it was, it doesn't concern you. Anyhow, I felt sorry for Aunt Doirin, and she seemed to give me more attention than mother. Besides, we were the only ones who liked to go to church every morning. Remember when I came to school with my jaw swollen last semester, and I said I had a toothache? It wasn't a tooth. I caught Father one night when he was sober and asked him about what I'd overheard. He hit me so hard for what I'd thought that I crashed into the wall. He said there wasn't any truth in what I'd thought, and he'd kill me if I ever mentioned it again." He turned to face her, his lower lip drawn in to keep from trembling. "Aunt Doirin was all I had, during that time. Can you understand that? When she went . . . got sick . . . I wanted to help care for her. I still feel I have to. Ever since you went to live at the Maddigans, she's the only mother I've had."

"Pa hit you that hard?" she said, narrowing her eyes. "Ma would have his hide on a wall for that."

"Don't tell her. I deserved it."

Rosaleen studied this brother she had never really understood. "Liam, a lot of that was your fault. Ma and I don't understand you. If she's seemed to ignore you, it's because she can't reach you at all. She thinks you're without affection for anyone."

"It'll be different now," he said, tying a rope around his box of clothing. "You can't imagine how I feel. I want to be close to her again. I've been sinful...she's my mother, after all! We'd better go down to breakfast, so I can catch the train."

The morning post arrived during breakfast, and Laura glanced through it abstractedly while the children ate. She lifted one letter on cheap stationery to look at it more closely and let out a moan.

"Oh, God, it's from Mary!" she said. "I'll never be able to face her again. Here, Liam, you read it."

He perused the lined sheet of paper with his mother's childish handwriting on it, his eyes widening with shock. His hands began to shake. Clearing his throat, he read as slowly as possible,

"Dear Miss Laura,
Please keep the children there until I write you otherwise. There is an illness in Boston, mostly in the North End, and many people are dying from it. It is called the cholera, though I am not sure about the spelling."

Harry looked up from his plate and exclaimed, "Cholera! In Boston? I thought it only occurred in filthy, poor countries. My God, it can be a plague! I'm sorry, Liam. What else does she say?"

"They say the drinking water has been contaminated by the sewage. There are so many people that the privies have overflown and the filth has gotten to the wells. Hundreds of people are sick. I regret to tell you that my husband, Tomas, is one of them, but I do not think he has the serious sickness. As I have told you in the past he does not drink water very often. I am leaving Philip with Bridie at your house, so I can look after him. My sister is not good at such things. She will not even go to church.

"Philip will be safe. Do not worry about him. Your part of town is safe. Bridie has strict instructions not to leave the house until this is over. Philip will not be anywhere near the sickness.

"I am so grateful that the children are safe with you. Tell Rosaleen I am very sorry I made a fuss about her going to the Cape this year. I was wrong. Please give my love to her and Liam. And please assure Darin that his family is all right.

Love,
Mary"

Liam put his hands together as though in prayer, crushing the letter between them. "How does she know Father doesn't have cholera?" he said desperately.

"I don't know," Rosaleen answered, torn between her concern for her mother and her own horror of disease and death. "I know for a fact, he sometimes mixes his whiskey with water."

"Some people say alcohol prevents infections," Harry volunteered. "Most patent medicines contain a lot of it. Cholera! It kills millions of people in places like India every year."

"Harry," his mother cautioned tearfully, "be more careful what you say. I'm sure your father will be all right, Liam. I only wish your mother didn't have to go into that place to nurse him."

Rosaleen's throat swelled with emotion until tears came to her eyes. Darin was gone. Her mother was in danger, and her father might be dying. She might be left all alone in the world with no one to look after her. Maybe everyone in Boston would die: Uncle Brian, Veronica, Aunt Doirin: she would be an orphan on the streets. She began to sob uncontrollably, and Laura rose to embrace her.

"Poor darling," she said. "Now you've frightened her, Harry. She's such a loving child. I've never seen anyone closer than she and her mother are."

When Mary had written the letter from the Maddigans' house, Tomas's symptoms were no more serious than intestinal flu, vomiting and diarrhea, which confined him to his bed in the hot flat above the pub. Brian continued to serve drink downstairs, because the general fear of the water made the men turn more and more to alcohol. Mary sat alone with Tomas, trying to make him comfortable. But it was soon evident that he had the fulminant form of the disease: the watery diarrhea increased, his skin began to wrinkle from dehydration and he became delirious, demanding a 'drink,' and Mary ran downstairs to the bar.

"Brian," she said breathlessly, "I can't give him the bad water. Fill up a pitcher of ale! He's that thirsty, I must give him something."

"Ale? For God's sake, it might kill him, Mary! Sure, give him hot tea, instead. I don't know about this disease, but when one has typhoid, the wrong thing in the stomach can cause perforation."

She tried the tea, but her husband's head rolled on the pillow, his eyes became sunken, and he continued to fail. After Brian closed the pub, he came upstairs to help her, both of them staring helplessly at the sick man.

"God in heaven, he has it for sure," Brian said quietly. "It's the way it's been described to me, Mary. Our cook died today, so we'll have to continue our own cooking up here. Where's Doirin, for God's sake?"

"In her room," Mary said wearily. "You should be there, too. It's my husband, as she told me. You shouldn't be exposed, too."

"He's my brother," he said irritably, rising from the chair beside the bed quickly. Mary heard him hammering on Doirin's door. "Come out of there, woman!" he demanded. "You're needed! Your sister's ready to drop! The least you can do is prepare some decent food for us. You don't have to come near Tomas at all."

"Get your own food," said the sharp voice from within. "I'm praying for the souls of all them that's passing."

"You're a bloody coward, that's what you are! Sure, I'll get the food, all right, but you'll not have a bit of it."

Brian went into the kitchen, and Mary heard the crashing of pots and pans. He was seldom angry, but when he lost his temper, there was no controlling him. She glanced at Tomas, incoherent in the bed: she dared not leave him to calm Brian or make a meal. Besides, she knew he was capable of cooking: that wasn't what had brought on his fury. She herself was too tired to be angry with Doirin any more. Within a short time, he brought two bowls of potatoes back to the bedside, after knocking on Padraig's door to give him some.

"Eat," he said, pushing one gently into her hands. "We're back to the old food, but it was always nutritious. Go on, Mary, eat, please. We must keep our strength up. If Tomas had eaten more and drunk less spirits, he might have been stronger and not become ill. And after you've eaten, I want you to lie down in the parlor and rest for a few hours. I'll take care of him."

Mary consumed half of the potatoes, forcing them down slowly with her spoon. Then she got up and said, "You're right. It won't do for us to get sick, too. But call me in two hours."

Before lying down in the parlor, she went to Doirin's door and rapped softly, so Brian could not hear. "Doirin, I'm leaving a bowl of potatoes outside your door. You must eat something."

"I'll not touch anything you've touched," came the reply. "I'm sure the cook gave the disease to Tomas. You can get it from food, too, they say. I won't eat or drink until you get him out of here."

"I've washed my hands a hundred times today," Mary said. "The food's from your own kitchen. It's all right."

There was no answer: Mary could hear the faint murmur of a voice saying the rosary.

"Doirin, don't you want to know how Padraig is?" There was still no reply, and she did not offer the information that the boy was well, safe in his room, where Mary herself had put him to keep him off the streets. He was a big, strong boy, but children and the young seemed particularly susceptible to the illness: she wished Padraig were at the Cape with the other children. At least that was one worry off her mind.

She woke after midnight, in the middle of a terrible dream. There were no potatoes, people were dying of hunger and fever in the ditches. She was in her cottage, almost too weak to move, and her children were sleeping, because they were dying of starvation: she must do something. She opened her eyes suddenly and realized it had been a nightmare. She was in the Noonan flat, and Brian had not awakened her!

He was trying to force some cold tea between Tomas's dry lips when she entered the bedroom. She was shocked at how much Tomas had failed in the hours she had slept: he did not look like the same man, he was so wasted and dry. The tea poured down the corners of his mouth: he was not swallowing it.

"I can't get him to take it," Brian said, when he realized she was beside him. "He's losing all the liquid from his body. God, what a mess it is!"

"You sleep," she said. "You look ready to drop yourself. I'll clean up here. Brian, are you all right?"

He nodded his white head, but did not look at her. "I'll just—" he began, but suddenly made a dash for the bucket beside the bed and began to retch uncontrollably. Mary went to his side and held him by the shoulders, her heart beating fast with alarm. When he finished, she wet a clean white cloth for him, which he wiped all over his face.

"It's nothing," he said. "It'll be all right, Mary. It's just the stench in here, I'm sure."

"Go lie down in the parlor," she commanded. "I'll open the rest of the windows. Sleep."

Her own stomach was uneasy, with nausea coming on, but she knew it was not the odor of the room. She was inured to that from taking care of Philip. Opening the windows did not give any ventilation in the Boston summer: the heat clung damply. On nights like this, one could hardly stand to sleep under a sheet. She checked Brian to see if he was sleeping and returned to Tomas's bed, to have another try at giving him some tea, before changing the soiled linen. Tomas was dying for lack of liquid, and she could not get him to drink. She was seized by panic at her inability to help him, and her dream came back to her, as though the whole thing were happening all over again. Desperate situations required desperate measures: that is what her dream was telling her. Once again, they were all dying, and she could not just sit here and do nothing about it. After bathing Tomas's body, so he could be comfortable, she washed her hands thoroughly with brown soap in the kitchen and descended the stairs to the bar.

Taking the largest pitcher she could find, she set it on the metal grille beneath the draft ale. When she turned the spigot, nothing happened at first: she had never operated it before. But, after several tries, the ale foamed out into the container, filling it quickly until it overflowed and her hands were covered with foam. Wiping the head off the pitcher with her palm, she rushed upstairs again. If Tomas would not drink tea, perhaps he would take the ale. But before attempting to give it to him, she took a sip herself in the hope of settling her stomach.

Her husband was not completely unresponsive, and the taste of the drink reached him in whatever limbo his mind dwelt. He began to drink greedily until he started to choke, and she had to remove the cup for a few minutes before putting it to his lips again. The expression on his wasted face changed. He opened his blue eyes once and gave her a grateful glance before falling into a heavy, comatose sleep. Relieved that she had gotten some liquid into him, she was equally alarmed that she might have killed him, but she did not have time to think about it, because she heard Brian in the kitchen retching again. She rushed to him with the pitcher and poured him a large glass of ale.

"It settled my stomach a bit," she assured him. "I don't know whether it'll kill or cure, to be sure, but it's a change, at least. I'll have one, too."

Tomas lived until six o'clock the next evening; by then, both Mary and Brian were still suffering only the first symptoms of the illness, but they had not gotten worse. The only thing Padraig and Doirin, still in their rooms, received was ale, of which there was an abundant supply in the bar, and boiled potatoes prepared by Brian and not scorned by his wife after twenty-four hours of fasting. Though they suffered vomiting and diarrhea, Mary noted that neither she nor Brian was wasting away as Tomas had: she was almost certain they would survive. The side effect of her treatment from the fluid they had forced was that they were both tipsy when Tomas's end came. And they ushered him out of the world as he would have wished, with something like a wake.

"Sure you don't think my forcing ale on him killed him, do you?" Mary asked, after they laid the body out. Brian gave the idea some consideration and shook his head.

"It hasn't killed us. We haven't gotten any better, but we're not worse, either. I think poor Tomas was too far gone when you began it with him. At least he died drunk."

"Just as he lived," Mary agreed without rancor, taking a large gulp from her glass. "Did you give Doirin and Paddy some supper?"

"I don't think so. We didn't have any, did we?"

"I don't remember, Brian. I'm a bit fuzzy in the head. Do you think it's the illness?"

He gave a lazy laugh. "No, love, I think it's the cure. Sure he looks peaceful, doesn't he? A fine-looking man was Tomas."

"Yes," Mary agreed. "He lived his life fully and died in his prime."

"Aye. Tomas wouldn't have wanted to be old. It wouldn't have suited him at all. I should open the pub, so everyone can come to the wake. At least I should tell Paddy and Doirin to come."

"Doirin disapproved of something," Mary said, trying to remember what it was. "I don't think she'd appreciate the invitation."

"There's enough brew for everyone. I filled two pitchers an hour or so ago. And," he added slyly, "I've a bottle of fine Irish brew in the cupboard."

Mary shook her head. "No whiskey. It isn't part of my treatment. It might do someone harm. Ah," she exclaimed, seeing Padraig standing in the door, "here's Paddy! How are you doing, love?"

The big boy grinned foolishly. "I feel fine," he said thickly. "I see Uncle Tomas is resting well, now."

"Indeed," his father confirmed, "as well as he ever will. Are you hungry, lad?"

"No. Drinkin' this stuff all day sort of filled me up. Is Ma still confined to her room then?"

"We've not seen her for two days," Mary said; then she frowned. "Brian, do you suppose she's all right? She might be sick in there."

"The drinks have been disappearing from her threshold," he said. "If she's ill, it's the little people themselves have been taking them. She stopped mumblin' her beads several hours ago, though. Should I have a look?"

Padraig came in and sat on the edge of the bed, still unaware of his uncle's demise, and filled his glass from the pitcher on the night table. "Pa, this is fine stuff. You never let me touch it before. I can't imagine why not."

"I've something finer, but Mary's afraid it might perforate us," Brian answered. "Our insides might not be up to it at all." He refilled his glass and raised it toward the figure on the bed. "To our grand Tomas...not the best brother a man ever had...but maybe not the worst, either!"

Padraig and Mary raised their glasses, too; then Padraig looked more closely at his uncle and leaped to his feet. "Jesus Christ, he's dead!"

His exclamation was answered by a new voice from the doorway, speaking as thickly as the rest of them, "Sure, it's not himself you see there. It's only his shell. He's singing with the angels in heaven above, and passing the bottle around."

They all looked up dully as Doirin came across the room with her rosary hanging over her fingers and her glass in her hand. She lurched against the dresser and steadied herself by hanging onto the back of Mary's chair, holding out the glass for a refill. Brian complied carefully, but the ale still ran over the top and drenched the rosary. Mary, not Doirin, was troubled by this; she sprang up and attempted to dry the beads with her wrinkled apron.

"Sure, they've been blessed! It isn't proper to spill brew on them...even at a wake!"

Doirin withdrew the rosary from her administrations and held it above her glass. Her dark eyes were dull and her lips were smiling faintly. "And, now, they're blessed again!" she said, dropping the beads into her glass and mumbling, "Hail Mary, full of grace, the Lord is with thee..."

"I believe to God she's…" Mary whispered in amazement, and Brian chuckled warmly.

"…drunk," he finished. "And I believe to God we should all stay this way forever."

Chapter 17

HER FATHER was long buried when Rosaleen returned to Boston for the school year. The news of his death had come to the Cape in August from her mother. The letter was neatly pressed when Laura received it: she had instructed a maid to run a hot iron over mail from Boston several times, under the prevalent impression that pestilence could be cauterized away by such a precaution. The family at the Cape had followed newspaper accounts of the plague in a virtual panic. Tomas Noonan was the six hundredth fatality of the summer cholera, and another hundred deaths were to follow, most of them concentrated in the poor areas inhabited by the Irish. And, though Harry kept protesting that it was not real cholera, but some other vicious dysentery, the resulting deaths were just as final.

In later years, Rosaleen wondered if anyone had mourned Tomas besides his brother, Brian. She and Liam had such mixed feelings about his death that they were difficult to express. Rosaleen was more relieved that she was not there than stricken over the loss of someone she had avoided for years. And Liam, who had lived with him, was ambivalent, trying to mourn without involving himself in hypocrisy.

"He was funny sometimes," he said the night after they received the news. "If you could stand to be around him when he was drunk. He was fond of you, Rosaleen, but he didn't care for me much. He preferred Darin, because he was more jolly. Of course, he was completely selfish. But he was our father, wasn't he? I think we should say a rosary for him."

Frightening as the newspaper accounts had been, Rosaleen did not really grasp the reality of death in such numbers until she returned to school in the North End in September. The autumn leaves were blazing brightly under the overcast gray sky, but there was black crepe on nearly every door, and almost everyone wore a black band on his upper sleeve like the one she wore. Still, the impact was not personal until she reported to class and found many of her classmates missing forever. Only then did she cry sincerely; and, again, when the nun read off the list of names at the service held for the dead students.

She could not really tell what her mother felt about her father's death. After the first few minutes of her reunion with her children, Mary did not speak of Tomas again. Rosaleen finally concluded that her mother was "forgetting" Tomas, as she had so often counseled Rosaleen to "forget" the famine. Mary was more concerned about Darin's running away, and its effect upon her sister, than her own husband's death. And Liam, who really appeared to be given to good works these days, went out of his way to look after Doirin once again. Perhaps because she had been unkind to her son, Doirin was suffering as much from his loss as she had from that of Michael. That she did not slip completely over the edge again was due completely to Liam's attention and Mary's frequent visits to look after her.

Rosaleen would not go to the flat above the pub, in spite of her mother's entreaties that she do so. Several times the situation developed into a fight between them.

"How can you be so heartless?" Mary cried, her face red with anger. "We're trying to keep your Aunt Doirin from getting sick again. Imagine how she feels, with two sons gone already. Rosaleen, you think only of yourself for sure."

"I'm not needed there, Mother. She has enough people handling her with kid gloves. I'd make a mess of it. She drove Darin away with her meanness, and I hate her for it! If I went there, I'd tell her what I thought of her, and undo everything you and Liam are doing to keep her sane."

There was grief in Rosaleen's heart, but it was not for her father: it was from losing Darin. She waited constantly for a letter from him, but she did not reproach him when nothing came. The distances were so great; mail might be shuttled from ship to ship at various ports. There could be innumerable delays. She was certain Darin would write when he had a chance. She loved him: he had to write. But the weeks and months passed without a letter, and she was left to fantasize about his love for her.

The school year was brightened by only one thing: she was excused from further penmanship classes in order to continue her study of French with the Mother Superior. Though she was flattered by the unusual change of schedule, she tried to bargain at first, in order to get out of Religion class. She knew her catechism by rote and nearly went to sleep from boredom every day. She soon learned that Religion was one class from which no one was excused, however: it was the basis of the parochial school system. The book of Greek myths Johnny had given her fit nicely in her lap during class, though, and it could easily be slipped into the desk when she was called upon and had to rise to recite. She stood up promptly and unrepentantly, giving the correct answer to any question, even when it was asked out of sequence:

"Who is God?"

"God is a Spirit, the Creator of heaven and earth and all things."

"Where is God?"

"God is everywhere."

"If God is everywhere, why can we not see Him?"

"He is a Spirit and cannot be seen with bodily eyes."

"Who is the Pope?"

"The Pope is the Vicar of Christ on earth."

"Can the Pope err?"

"The Pope cannot err when teaching a doctrine of faith or morals."

Rosaleen did not understand the meaning of some of the answers, but it did not bother her. When a statement was being elucidated, she was already deep into her book of myths again, sometimes just staring at the pictures. The Greek gods were more interesting: they had human emotions she could understand. They did not become flesh just once, to preach and die. Whenever they wished, they took human form, usually to seduce young maidens, which Rosaleen took to mean that they hugged and kissed them, with the remarkable result that the girls had babies who, in turn, became heroes. She was particularly fond of the sensuous, swooning engravings of these activities, which she dreamed about for hours, particularly just before she went to sleep. The images in her mind made her feel nice things in her body, and the god or hero usually had Darin's face.

In no way did she reject her own religion, which was so entrenched in her that she feared sin greatly. She truly loved Christ. She always wept on Good Friday and rejoiced on Easter Sunday, when the whole earth seemed to resurrect itself from the gray death of winter. Emotion swelled her throat whenever she heard the Gospel story of Christmas: the couple searching for lodgings, the birth of the baby Jesus who had only the sweet breath of gentle animals warming him. And then, as magnificent as the crescendo of a symphony, the three kings of the Orient coming in splendor to worship the Child, bearing Him royal gifts.

The logical, unromantic part of her mind, which dealt so well with figures, nudged her belief sometimes. For instance, what happened to those fine gifts, since Jesus grew up so poor? Her mind stored up questions to ask Johnny when he came home for spring vacation. Occasionally, they were worded like statements to catch him off-guard, because she liked to show him that she could think, too:

"The Greeks and Christians were alike, you know."

His bewildered gray eyes stared at her through his lenses. "I'm almost afraid to ask. In what way?"

"The stories of Dionysus and Christ. Dionysus brought wine to the people, like Christ changing water to wine at the marriage feast at Cana. And Dionysus's followers fell upon him and ate his flesh, but he was always resurrected again in the spring."

Johnny observed her thoughtfully. He never laughed at her ideas like Harry and Matthew. "You have a peculiar mind," he said at last, "to draw such an unusual analogy. Actually, it's very perceptive of you. I'd never noticed the connection, myself. Since the Greeks preceded Christ by a couple of thousand years, maybe the Christians lifted the whole body-and-blood and resurrection story from them."

Rosaleen was shocked. "No! I know Christ lived and died and everything that happened in the Gospels is true. It's just a coincidence."

"Well, maybe," Johnny said, always respectful of her religion, though he was not a churchgoer himself. "Have you heard anything from Darin?"

"No," she said, with a falling voice. "I'm worried about him, Johnny. We saw those little boats they use to go out after the whales, in New Bedford, remember? What if something's happened to him?"

Johnny allowed himself a smile. "Rosaleen," he said gently, "Darin's too young to be in one of those boats. It takes strong men to do that. He's probably a cabin boy, safe on the ship. The closest he's come to a whale's when they're stripping it and boiling it on deck. You mustn't worry."

"He could have slipped and fallen overboard. We'd never know. Just like we've never heard anything about Michael."

"We *would* know if anything happened to the boys. The family would be notified or it'd be in the newspapers. I read the paper every day. You mustn't worry."

"I haven't looked at a paper since last summer at the Cape. That was so awful. What if I read one now and saw Darin's name there?"

"You're awfully fond of him, aren't you?" he asked hesitantly. "I mean, you seem fonder of him than of your own brother."

"Liam's all right. He's learning Latin, you know: he and two other boys go to the rectory every day after school. But Darin," she said softly, her gaze far away, "he's very special. He saved my life, you know."

"Yes, I know," he said, staring into her pretty face wistfully. Then, suddenly, and with more humor than he usually displayed, "I have a wonderful idea! Why don't you go fall in the Charles River, so I can save your life, too!"

Mary was difficult to be around at that time. Maybe it was Tomas's death that made her worry so much about everyone else in the family. If she was not concerned about Veronica's approaching confinement, which she was convinced her young relative would not survive, she was upset about Doirin and the mess that was always going on at her place. Rosaleen stayed fastidiously away from the pub, but she heard about the troubles there secondhand and pretended to listen, because her mother needed someone to discuss things with.

Regardless of the occasional friction between them, Rosaleen loved her mother, when she thought about it, and felt more than a little sorry for her. Taking care of a severely retarded youngster, no matter how sweet he was, and running back and forth between the Maddigan house and Doirin's was not much of a life; besides, she was a widow now as well, and her hair was turning gray in places, though it was still long and thick and envied by Rosaleen. Usually she put on an interested face and thought about something else when her mother was unloading her problems to her; or she played with little Philip, who was a constant delight to her. When she had compared him to a puppy that would never grow up, the simile had been appropriate. The six-year-old boy was still a grinning, sweet-faced baby who did not even talk, and Rosaleen adored him.

"Anyway," her mother said, "it won't hurt you to visit her once in a while. You find time to see Veronica. Except for Liam, who's gone most of the day, she won't have anyone. She'll be alone, and that's dangerous. You know what happened to her before."

"Who'll be alone?" Rosaleen asked, hugging Philip. She had heard only part of the tirade.

"Doirin, of course! Don't you even listen?"

"Is Uncle Brian going somewhere?" Rosaleen asked in confusion, realizing she had given herself away. Her mother was ominously quiet. Still holding Philip tightly, but now for her own protection, Rosaleen looked at her and, for the first time, saw something like naked pain in her face. Mary controlled her expression quickly and sighed.

"Of course your Uncle Brian will be there, but that isn't enough for Doirin. She'll be missing Padraig as much as she's missed the other boys."

"She doesn't miss Darin," Rosaleen said contemptuously. "She only pretends to so everyone else will do her work. But...is Padraig going to sea?"

"Not to *sea*, Rosaleen. Didn't you hear me at all? He's going to work on the railroads in the West. Do you know what that big clod said to me? He said the only reason he hadn't gone to sea with the others was that he's afraid of water. From the trip from Ireland! But now he's found himself an escape, all right...on dry land. Oh, God," she said, pushing her hair back, "is there no end to it at all? I know Doirin's unpleasant to be with, but think of Uncle Brian. He's been good to you. Please visit her, so she doesn't go crazy again. I can't be everywhere at once, and she won't even speak to Veronica."

"Aunt Doirin's a bitch," Rosaleen said flatly.

"I know, but...Rosaleen! Where did you hear that word?"

Darin had often employed it in describing his mother, but Rosaleen thought it best not to say so: he must be protected at any cost. "Female dogs are called that, aren't they?" she said quickly. "I don't know why, though, because dogs are so nice."

An unwilling smile came to Mary's lips, and she turned away. "Your aunt isn't a dog, darlin'. And female dogs go around mating with any male. The word isn't nice when it's applied to women."

"I thought it meant snapping and snarling a lot, and Aunt Doirin does that," Rosaleen said, setting Philip down on the bed and moving behind the screen to prepare for sleep herself. The room had virtually become her own. Mary slept in the nursery with Philip, because she was afraid he might get up and start roaming at night: the stairs were too close.

Mary banked the fire in the grate while she waited for Rosaleen to emerge in a long flannel nightgown.

"So, how's everything at school, then?" she asked. "Did you give Reverend Mother your tuition?"

"Yes," Rosaleen said, without getting into bed. This was her special time of the evening, when she prayed on her knees for Darin's safety: it was time she had to have alone. "Two dollars a month is dear enough. Especially when some students don't have to pay at all. If their families don't have any money, they get their tuition free."

"Thank God, we can afford it," Mary said. "Brian's giving me Tomas's earnings from the pub. He says we own half of it. And Reverend Mother's giving you the French lessons free. Though I can't for the life of me see what good French is for you."

"With enough education, maybe I could be a governess," Rosaleen said. "Of course, Reverend Mother wants me to be a nun."

Mary was silent for a moment. "And what do you think about that?" she asked carefully, her breath suspended. "Would you like to be . . . a nun?"

"No," Rosaleen said, and her mother began to breathe again. "The only thing I can think of doing is becoming a governess, if I have to work."

"A governess, is it? Like Mamselle Boucher?" Mary considered. "Sometimes they have difficulties with their employers. Mamselle and Mr. Maddigan—" She stopped short, as though she had been thinking aloud.

"What?" Rosaleen asked. "Mamselle and Mr. Maddigan . . . what?"

"Nothing, darlin'. A governess has a peculiar position in a household. You're a good Irish girl and you're too pretty: I want you to be virtuous and chaste."

There was that word again, the one she heard so often at

school and which even the dictionary did not define well enough for her. "Does that mean you don't want me to marry...or that I'm not to hug and kiss anyone?"

"Of course I want you to marry. You'll know all about it when you're older." Mary smoothed her apron, as she often did when she was troubled or thinking seriously. "I want you to be a good girl, Rosaleen," she said softly. "I love you."

The words had not been spoken for so long that Rosaleen did not know how to respond to them. Finally she muttered, "I love you, too, Ma."

Mary started to speak, but thought better of it and took Philip by the hand. "Well, goodnight, then."

After she left, Rosaleen fell on her knees before the nightstand and began her impassioned prayers, speaking in a whisper, almost aloud. Her heart hit her throat when the door opened again suddenly.

"Rosaleen," her mother said.

Without time to get up off her knees, Rosaleen turned with as much dignity as possible. "Yes?"

Her mother stared, forgot what she was going to say. "Rosaleen, you aren't praying to that wooden dog, are you?"

Rosaleen shook her head, though the dog represented something important to her. "I'm praying to Our Lord and the Virgin Mary, Mother. Did you forget something?"

"I...I never mind. I wish you'd get rid of that bloody thing!" Mary said before she disappeared into the hall again.

A letter from Darin finally arrived, written at Christmas five months before and difficult to decipher. In spite of being artistic, he had never written well. If Rosaleen could not restrain winces at his grammar and punctuation, she forgave him everything and pored over the precious letter in her room as though it were the finest literary work imaginable. It was from Darin, and it was the first letter she had ever received addressed to her, alone:

My darling Rosie,

It is Christmas here but you would never know it. the people in Japan are not christians even. they pray to idols of a fat man named budda or they are shinto and wear yellow robes. it is cold here but we will be leaving for the south pacific as soon as we take on supplies. I saw my first whale in the south atlantic about two months after I left you. I cant describe the site of it. it was a sperm...that is a big whale with lots of oil in its head...fine oil. You probably burn it in the lamps at the Maddigan house. it don't seem rite to me to kill a grand fish like that just to lite lamps. but if people used candles I wouldnt have a job.

I do the same things here I did at Pa's pub...I carry things around and take them to the captan and his mate. the captain is a fine fella and he likes me...I like him too. his name is williams. the mate is a son of a bitch and I wont even tell his name...in case he falls overbord some day and you would think it was murdther. he is english of course. I dont even like to here him talk but he has some books in his cabin...and I steal them long enough to rede them and put them back before he knows.

Im sorry you felt so bad when I left. I think about you a lot...my funny pretty Rosie. no matter what hapens you are my little Rosaleen. I will bring home something nice for you. you can rite me in care of this ship...the rover...in valparaiso, chile. we will stop there during the year. I am looking forward to heering from you. please say hello to Johnny and Harry. I am writing Pa and the family.

all my love,
Darin

O, god. Rosie. after I wrote this I just heard about the sickness in Boston last summer. the captain came back with some newspapers. is every one all right? O, god...Im so scared for all of you. please rite as soon as posible if you are alive.

I hope you are alive, darling Rosie.

all my love for ever
Darin

She answered passionately and immediately. There was no time to lose: Darin must know she was alive. She told him about his parents and her mother and her father. She could not lose a second in reassuring him. She wrote until dinnertime, neglecting her homework, and she continued again until ten o'clock, spilling out all her feelings, thanking him for his letter. The next morning, she was tardy at school, because she waited for the post office to open, so she could post the letter at once.

She reread Darin's letter five times during classes, still with the same awful urgency. She realized she had not told him about Padraig's leaving: she must write another letter. No, it was better not to tell him that: he would worry about his mother, perhaps. And with good reason...Doirin had not spoken since Padraig had left. Mary continued to go over to do the cleaning for her, and Veronica, who was expecting a baby at any time, had to look after Doirin during the day, until Liam got back from school. Doirin did not even notice that Veronica was in the house, apparently. No, she could not tell Darin the bad things. He was too worried already.

Then suddenly, during her French lesson, Rosaleen realized that Darin would not receive her letter for many months. She stopped in the middle of an exercise, her blue eyes widening with horror.

"O, my God!" she cried in a tone that brought the Mother Superior to her side at once.

"Rosaleen, what is it? Are you all right?"

Rosaleen began to cry. "It's awful! Reverend Mother, it's awful! Darin's at *sea*. He heard about the cholera in Japan at Christmas. He thinks we all might be dead! And...the letter I wrote him won't get to him for...months and months."

The nun studied her with troubled dark eyes. She put her hand on Rosaleen's chin and turned her face so she could look at her directly.

"You're very fond of Darin, aren't you, Rosaleen?"

"Yes. Oh, yes!"

"You love him like a brother," the nun suggested hopefully.

"No, Reverend Mother...I love him more than anyone. Darin's the most wonderful person on earth."

The nun drew in her breath slowly, and her hand gripped Rosaleen's chin until it almost hurt. "You must remember he's your cousin, my dear. The Roman Catholic Church is very decided on the matter, as you must know. Darin's your *cousin*, Rosaleen—*ton cousin*," she emphasized in her native language.

Rosaleen stared at her without comprehension. "I know that, Reverend Mother. I know he's my cousin. We're so much alike. I guess that's why I'm so fond of him. I love him because he's my cousin, and I'm glad he's in my family."

"*Alike?*" the nun said, stiffening. "My dear girl, from what I saw of Darin, I hope you're nothing alike! I know that you don't curse, and, I'm relatively certain there isn't any other similarity." The frown lines on her forehead deepened, and she softened her tone. "In what way do you think you are alike, Rosaleen?"

Intimidated, Rosaleen shrugged slightly. "I don't know, Reverend Mother. I mean, I can't put it into words. We've always been very close and Darin's looked after me."

Uncomfortable about the way she had handled the discussion and embarrassed by the emphasis she had put on the relationship, the nun abandoned the subject with relief.

"*Très bien, ma petite*," she said kindly. "*Continue l'exercise, s'il te plaît.*"

Veronica made the trip by cab to Doirin's every day, until she was so far along in her pregnancy that her doctor forbade her to leave the house. For the first time, Mary realized that the demands were too much for her: she could not be in three places at once. Though she could take Philip with her anywhere and continue caring for him, she wanted to be with Veronica for her confinement, and she could not do that and administer to Doirin at the same time. She had been fairly lenient with Rosaleen until then, she felt, but this summer her daughter must give her some assistance, even if it meant a tooth-and-claw battle about Rosaleen's not going to the Cape. If she could only remain reasonable during the encounter, Mary felt she could get Rosaleen to comply; but as much as she loved the girl, it was not going to be easy. Rosaleen was selfish and headstrong, two qualities Mary did not admire in the least, and the time had come for her to give a little, before Mary herself became ill.

She waited until early June to approach Rosaleen, hoping to catch her daughter at the right time, just before school was out for the summer and before preparations for the Cape were underway. Rosaleen had been in a happy mood since she'd received her letter from Darin and was slightly more approachable than she had been in the past. She had even planted an occasional affectionate kiss on her mother's cheek before leaving for school, and this little act had filled her mother with warmth. She did not like to deprive the girl of her summer holiday, which she seemed to enjoy so much, but she could see no other way out. Liam was not capable of doing the personal things for Doirin that had to be done, any more than Rosaleen was equipped to cope with childbirth yet or the days of care which followed it. Someone had to take charge of Veronica's baby until the young woman was capable of it herself... if everything went all right during the delivery, which worried Mary a great deal. Though she felt it "indecent" for a man to assist at this time, she was relieved that Saul Rabinsky had insisted upon the doctor's care. Veronica was a small girl without the wide hips needed for an easy delivery. Mary dearly loved Veronica and wanted to help her: she must make Rosaleen understand.

She found her daughter in the library, sitting at the long mahogany table, which was polished high enough to catch her reflection, poring over a large volume with absolute concentration. Before Mary could clear her throat to get her daughter's attention, Rosaleen became aware of her presence and quickly pulled a folded newspaper over the book she was reading before calmly raising her gaze to the doorway.

"Mother," she said quietly, "what are you doing here?"

"I find it a bit difficult to see you alone." Mary smiled. "If you aren't studying, you're praying at night in your room. What are you reading so intently there? The book under the newspaper," she clarified, when Rosaleen looked blank. "It must be that interesting."

Rosaleen became tense as she pulled the volume from beneath the paper, but her voice was even when she answered, "It is. It's a book about whaling, mother. It's just published. It hasn't been very well received, but I like it."

Mary moved to her side and picked up the book. Rosaleen's behavior was so peculiar she wanted to make certain she was reading what she said. The book, called *Moby-Dick*, indeed seemed to be about whales. Hating herself for being suspicious, Mary opened the flyleaf. "It just came out, you say? My goodness, it's marked two dollars! Rosaleen, where did you get it? You don't have that kind of money."

Mary expected her daughter to say that Johnny had sent it, a statement she would not be able to refute. The two of them were as thick as thieves, and when he came home he would back up her story, even if it was not true.

Rosaleen was silent for a moment, as though attempting to fabricate a story; but instead she faced her mother with a reproach.

"Mother, I need a bit of money of my own to spend. Not much...just a little. I could save it up for the things I want."

"That's quite agreeable to me," Mary said, "as long as you work for it. Now, where did you get the money for this book, Rosaleen?"

Her daughter glanced away and swallowed hard. "I used my tuition money to buy it," she said in a barely audible voice.

Mary fought back the fury that galloped through her veins and burned her cheeks. She turned away to take a deep breath and get herself under control, feeling Rosaleen's eyes upon her back. The girl expected a good whacking, and she deserved it; but Mary had promised herself to deal reasonably with her tonight. In a way, her daughter had worked right into her hands, though she had not meant the summer to be a punishment for her. When Mary turned back to her, Rosaleen looked away quickly.

"If your tuition's behind almost a month, it will have to be paid again," Mary said evenly. "You know how hard I work for that money."

"Uncle Brian gives you money from the pub, too," Rosaleen muttered. "We have a share in that. It isn't as if all we had was what we make here, Mother."

"I don't quite understand that 'we,' Rosaleen. Sure, I think the money that's earned belongs to the person who earns it, don't you? And, to be just about it, my dear, you don't raise a hand in this house unless it suits you. Which it seldom does. The money from the pub's being saved for a rainy day, for all of us. Most of it's going right back to pay the loan off, so don't think of that as something to be spent on foolishness. Rosaleen, what you've done with your tuition money is the same as theft. Surely, you knew you'd be found out!"

Rosaleen's blue eyes flared. "I don't care! I had to have this book! And since there was no way to get money of my own, I borrowed the tuition money last month! If I had a kind of allowance, like the Maddigan boys, I wouldn't have had to do it!"

Mary drew in her breath and counted, as patiently as possible: she must control her own temper this time. "As it happens, I do have some work for you. I hadn't thought of reimbursing you for it, but hoped you'd do it out of the good of your heart."

"You do?" Rosaleen asked hopefully, the fire draining out of her. "I'll do it, Mother! I'll do anything to make up for the money I took for this book! Please, what is it?"

Mary pulled out the chair beside her and joined her at the table, sitting sideways to face her. "As you know, Veronica's baby is due soon, and your school will be out by then. Someone has to take care of—"

"The baby!" Rosaleen cried, her eyes shining. "Oh, Mother, I'd love to do it! I—"

"Not so fast there, love. Someone will have to look after *Veronica* and the baby for a while. There's a lot about that you don't understand, and I'll have to do it. In fact, I want to do it. Veronica's a dear, giving girl, and I want to help her." Mary paused, knowing that what she was about to say would not be received so readily. "Working off two whole dollars will take you the rest of the summer, Rosaleen. And for a while at least, it's Doirin who'll be needing the help."

She stared directly into Rosaleen's stricken face, wanting to add that she would look after Doirin later, they could change places when Veronica was up and only needed help with the baby, but she held her tongue. Already she had Rosaleen working for pay, rather than out of the goodness of her heart, and she would not change her stand further.

"What about Philip?" Rosaleen said suddenly, in an attempt at bargaining, but Mary was firm.

"Sure, I can take care of Philip at Veronica's. Or, if you'd prefer, you can take him to Doirin's and look after the both of them."

"I don't know how to take care of Aunt Doirin," Rosaleen said in a hushed, strained voice. "She scares me, and I don't even like her. What about Liam?"

Mary shook her head. "Your Aunt Doirin has bodily functions just like the rest of us. It isn't proper that your brother should help her with them. Veronica or I have been going over there and cleaning the house, after we get her out of bed and ready for the day. Then we give her something to eat and a cup of tea. Brian's bought a fine commode, so we don't have to take her outside to the privy any more."

Wrinkling her nose with distaste, Rosaleen said, "You mean, I have to help her with the toilet? Ma..."

"Yes, just as someone may have to help you someday,"

Mary cut in. "And you have to clean her, and care for her like the invalid she is."

Rosaleen was silent; finally, she answered, "Well, she's Darin's mother, I guess. How long will I have to do it?"

"For the rest of the summer, off and on. You won't be going to the Cape this year," Mary informed her quickly. "And if you've any mind to get the Maddigan boys involved to save you, forget it. One word to anyone here, and I'll tell them about the stolen tuition money."

Rosaleen did not know it got so hot in Boston during the summer: this was the first year she had been there during the sticky, humid three months. Upstairs, over the pub, the heat rose and collected so even the open windows gave no relief. Her job was not really too difficult for a strong young girl, though it had its distasteful side. Disliking Doirin as much as she did, she found it loathsome to look after her personal needs and swore to herself that she would never be in a similar dependent position. She would look after her health so she would never be sick. Apart from taking her aunt to the toilet, she had to admit that the job was not too bad, except for the heat and the fact that she was not at the Cape with the others.

For the most part, Doirin sat in one place all day long, responding to nothing that was said to her, as though she were completely deaf. She ate very little, and that almost had to be forced upon her. Things were almost normal while Uncle Brian was in the flat, before he went down to open the pub at noon. He was a kind, helpful man and, when she looked closely, she could see Darin in his face. But she could also see a settled sadness there. His life with Aunt Doirin had been terrible, whether she was ill or well, and he had lost all his sons because of her. Rosaleen spoke frequently about Darin with him and saw the light come back into his eyes at the mention of his son's name. And, while he was present, Rosaleen was a perfect little nurse, looking after his wife. But once she was alone with the woman, she could not refrain from abusing her verbally, knowing she did not hear anyway. Until now, everyone had coddled their patient, much to Rosaleen's disgust. Now she handled Doirin the way she felt the woman should be handled.

"Drink your tea, Aunt Doirin! Do you want to curl up and die? Open your mouth, stupid! That's better now, down the hatch with the lot of it! Good. Keep it open . . . here come your mashed potatoes. Open. Remember when we didn't have any potatoes at all? You can take a bigger bite than that. Good. Now, here comes another one...."

Surprisingly, in the first two weeks that Rosaleen looked after her, Doirin gained five pounds at least. Her face, which had been thin and almost wizened, filled out enough that even Brian noticed it.

"Rosie, darlin', I don't know what you're doing, but you're good for her," he said with a crooked smile. "I swear to God, you've got her eating! At this rate, she'll be better in no time at all. By the way, is there any news of Veronica?"

"Not yet. Mother's there every day. The baby's a week overdue, and she says that isn't a good sign," Rosaleen said, plumping up a cushion behind her patient on the couch. "Uncle Brian, were any of us a week overdue?"

He looked uncomfortable. "Sure, how am I to know that, dear?" he replied. "I'm just a man. Birthing is a woman's thing. Back home, it was usually all over before we came home from the field, or the pub, if it took place at night."

Rosaleen studied him solemnly. "Is that true? I didn't imagine it that way. I think a man should be there when his baby's born: I can't picture it any other way. I know that Uncle Saul will be there. He's just wonderful to Veronica."

As it happened, the baby was born at night and even Mary did not know about it until the next day. Though very weak, Veronica had come through the birth well. The child, a tiny girl, was in fine condition, except for size, and Mary set about correcting that with frequent feedings—so frequent that Veronica got very little rest during the first week. Rosaleen did not see the baby until Sunday, on her way to the pub, and she fell in love with her at once.

"Oh, look at her," she cooed, as the baby lay in Veronica's arms. "All that curly dark hair! Veronica, she's so pretty! And her eyes are blue."

"Your mother says that'll change," Veronica said and smiled, kissing the little forehead. "She says they're a 'murky' blue, which means they'll probably be dark like Saul's. I hope so." She watched Rosaleen as she stroked the tiny hand. "Is everything all right, Rosaleen? I mean, with your looking after Doirin. I know it isn't easy."

"It's just fine," Rosaleen said. "Of course, I'd rather be at the Cape, but... she's gained weight, you know. Uncle Brian says it's like a miracle. She *eats* for me."

Doirin also took her share of badgering about other things,

though she did not respond at first. Reasoning that bullying her into eating worked, Rosaleen continued the therapy in other areas of her life, too. When Doirin would not raise her arms to get her blouse on in the morning, it was thrust forcefully, like a sack, over her head, blotting out all light and air, until her arms eventually began to struggle upward toward the sleeves.

"You're just lazy, that's what you are!" Rosaleen taunted. "I think you're the laziest woman I've ever known. You've never done your share of work as long as I can remember! That's right," she said, reaching through a sleeve for Doirin's hand and pulling it roughly through. "If it weren't for you, Darin would never have left! You may be quiet, now, but you had a tongue like a viper when you weren't sick. You were the meanest woman in the world. Give me that other hand! I don't blame your sons for running away. I hate you, too. Come on, now...it's potty time, you great baby!"

One morning, Rosaleen got such a shock that she ran into the kitchen to Brian, though, white-faced. He looked up from his tea and rose to his feet at once, "Rosie, what is it?"

"Uncle Brian, she's bleeding! All down her legs. Her skirt's drenched with blood! What's the matter with her? She's hemorrhaging...is she going to die?"

"Rosie, calm down. If it's what I think, it's nothing at all. It just hasn't happened for a long time, since she's been sick. Veronica's up and around, now, isn't she? Run and get your mother, dear, I'll watch Doirin."

When Mary had been with Doirin for a few minutes, she came back to the kitchen. "It's all right," she declared, piling her sister's skirt into Rosaleen's arms and speaking to Brian. "It's what we thought. She must be getting better to have her normal flow. You can go on downstairs to work, Brian."

"What shall I do with this?" Rosaleen cried, half-covered by the soiled skirt in her arms.

"Wash it, please," Mary said, starting back to her sister's room. "She only has one other one, and it'll take ages to get it dry in this humidity. Watch Philip a moment, too. I have to get her dressed again."

Mary washed her hands and put a kettle on the stove for tea, while Philip banged the pans. Rosaleen did not move from where she stood; she was angry, frightened, confused. Her head ached from the heat of the kitchen, and every time Philip crashed one pan against the other, the sound resulted

271

in more pain. Finally, she said, "Ma, why did Doirin bleed like that? It frightened me to death."

Mary, who was laying out the tea cups, stopped and turned to her. "I'm sorry, Rosaleen," she said sincerely. "You poor thing, you don't know. Sure, I had it in my mind to tell you when you were a little older. Come here, darling."

Rosaleen walked into her mother's embrace and pressed her head against the starched white front of her apron. The warm, pungent odor which had consoled her when she was a tiny child was gone. "It's been an awful day," she said and sobbed.

"Of course it has," Mary said in her comfortable lilting voice, which had not changed or lost even a hint of its brogue. "You mustn't be frightened, though. It isn't something one talks about, but when a woman's old enough to have children, she has a monthly flow...from that area. That's all that happened to Doirin this morning, Rosaleen. Since she's been ill she hasn't had it, but now it's started again. You'll have it too, soon, because you're growing up. When a woman's pregnant, she doesn't have the flow."

Rosaleen raised her head to look up at her mother's face. "Does that mean Aunt Doirin's going to have another baby?"

"She is not!" Mary replied forcefully. Then, realizing her own overreaction to the idea, she explained more calmly, and not without a certain gratification, "Sure, she and Brian don't even share the same bed any more."

"What difference does that...?" Rosaleen began, but decided not to press a subject that made her mother so obviously uncomfortable. There had been questions in her mind for some time, and there was really no one with whom to discuss them. She wished Darin were here. But, lacking that, maybe she could talk to Johnny when he came back from the Cape: he was always well informed about everything.

Chapter 18

IN EARLY August, when the heat was at its worst and Rosaleen hardly had the energy to clean the apartment, Doirin rose suddenly and began to pace the living room. Shocked, Rosaleen dropped the broom and dustpan and moved quickly to her aunt's side. It was almost impossible to keep up with the swiftness of the woman's movements and she repulsed Rosaleen with her flaying arms when she tried to contain her, muttering something about the Blessed Virgin and how she knew everything now. Though she was hesitant to leave her in a state of such activity, Rosaleen ran down the stairs for Brian.

"She came to life all of a sudden!" she cried at the bar, and her uncle's blue eyes were uncomprehending. "Aunt Doirin's almost running around the flat!"

They both rushed upstairs to find Doirin in the same condition, active, but apparently unaware of them.

Drawing in his breath, Brian grabbed his wife's arm and entreated her softly, "Doirin, come, sit down, dear. I can see you're feeling much better, but it's too hot for running about."

He was dragged along with her while she made another course of the room. Recognizing her activity as eccentric, he finally threw both arms around her to hold her still. "For Christ's sake, woman! What's the matter with you?"

She became calmer in his arms. Within a few minutes, Rosaleen was able to assist her to the couch, where she sat upright and tense, with her hands fidgeting in her lap. Only Brian's arm about her seemed to keep her in place. He spoke comfortingly with his soothing voice, but Doirin did not appear to hear him at all.

"Uncle Brian," Rosaleen suggested, "I've found she doesn't pay any attention to kindness. She only hears you when you yell at her. Aunt Doirin," she said firmly, "you stupid thing! I know you can hear me well enough. Why are you being so crazy? Only naughty children act crazy to get attention. You're no better than a bad child . . . a stupid, bad woman!"

Visibly shocked, Brian opened his lips to protest, but before he could speak, Doirin repeated clearly, "Stupid and bad. Evil. But the Blessed Virgin will save me. Brian, I want to go to church!"

"Ah, Doirin," he said, "I don't think you're able yet. Sure you've been sick a long time."

"Take her," Rosaleen whispered. "I'll help you, Uncle Brian. Just let me comb her hair a bit."

They walked her the few blocks to St. Mary's, one of them on either side of her, both glancing surreptitiously at her face and trying to appear as normal as possible. She did not mutter or act peculiar, however: their only problem was keeping pace with her. But once she was inside the church, standing at the holy-water font, she began to behave erratically again, by dipping both hands in the font, crossing herself repeatedly and bathing her whole face with the holy water. Rosaleen's startled eyes met Brian's, and in the one second of distraction, Doirin broke free. She ran down the aisle with her skirts and shawl flying and prostrated herself at the foot of the Virgin's statue, extending both hands out to her sides on the floor, as though she were on a cross. They moved forward, genuflecting automatically before the altar, where a ruby lamp proclaimed the Host was present, and knelt nearby on the hard floor, while Doirin muttered her prayers half-aloud to the Virgin. The sun had dimmed in the windows when, by unspoken mutual consent, they rose to take her home. She was perfectly calm and obliging.

Rosaleen went home to Beacon Hill with elation and ran up the back service stairs to the nursery, where her mother was feeding Philip.

"Ma! Ma! Aunt Doirin's well again!" she cried as she burst into the room. As Mary looked up, Philip knocked the spoon out of her hand and spattered meat and gravy over the front of her white apron. She rose quickly, mopping at herself with the towel she always kept nearby at dinnertime.

"Philip! Philip!" she said irritably, but changed her tone at once. "Oh, my poor baby," she cooed at the smiling face of her charge, "I know you didn't mean it." Then, to Rosaleen, "What do you mean, she's well?"

She told her mother about the day's events and added, "She's a little confused and there's a lot of religious talk, but I'm sure Uncle Brian will be able to look after her, now. He closed the pub for the evening, just to make sure she's all right. Isn't it wonderful?"

"Indeed it is, if it's so," Mary considered. "It took much longer, last time, and she came out of it more gradually. It's a pity we don't know more about these things."

"I know she's well," Rosaleen said with conviction. "I talked to her this evening. She didn't know who I was at first, but after I told her, she remembered. And she was so happy, Mother. I've never seen her like that... ever. She was smiling and laughing and talking so fast we could hardly answer her! I just know she's glad to be well again. It's like a miracle! I think she saw the Blessed Virgin this afternoon and Our Lady told her to wake up and come to church. She was talking about the Blessed Virgin when she first stood up. And, after she prayed in church, she was ever so happy. Do you think it's a miracle, Ma?"

Mary wiped the food off Philip's chin without answering. Finally, she said, "I can't imagine Doirin happy. The only time I saw her that way she was drunk. So maybe it is a miracle, Rosie. Though I can't for the life of me understand why Our Lady would intervene for her. I'll try to get over there tomorrow afternoon to see for myself."

To avoid watching the mess Philip made at breakfast, Rosaleen had, for some time, taken toast and tea in the kitchen when Mrs. Lynch was cleaning up the table from the servants' morning meal at six-thirty. Though the kindly cook tried to press oatmeal on her, she found she could not stomach it on hot days, after spending the nights tossing and turning in sheets dampened by her own sweat. Usually they chatted together about school or impersonal subjects, but Rosaleen had not been able to share much with the portly lady since she had started to look after Doirin. She had strict instructions from her mother that no one was to know anything that happened in the Noonan family, especially if it was not good.

275

Apparently Mary herself had told Mrs. Lynch about Veronica's baby, though, because the affable woman poured herself a cup of tea and sat down with Rosaleen to chat.

"And how's your sweet little cousin these days, Rosaleen? Your mother says she's a real beauty and doing quite well, now."

Rosaleen was bursting to talk about the breakthrough with her Aunt Doirin, but instead she said cautiously, "She's lovely. I'm going to see her today."

Mrs. Lynch blinked her round blue eyes. "Today? I thought you were with her every day."

Realizing Mary must have explained her absence that way, Rosaleen rallied quickly, "Yes. Her eyes are becoming a pretty amber color, now, just like her father's."

"And they named her Rachel," Mrs. Lynch considered. "It isn't an Irish name, though, of course, it's from the Bible. What's Veronica's husband's name, by the way?"

Fortunately, before Rosaleen could answer, an insistent pounding on the back door distracted the cook. The woman rose quickly, murmuring, "God in heaven, what's all the racket at this hour? It's too early for deliveries."

Rosaleen put the rest of her toast in her mouth and washed it down quickly so she could disappear before she was submitted to any more inquiries about Saul Rabinsky.

"Mother of God! Who are you? What do you want here?"

"Brian Noonan. I must see my sister-in-law."

"But whatever happened to your—?"

Rosaleen was beside the woman at the door at once. Brian was holding a bloody handkerchief to his cheek, and there were red stains down his open shirtfront. His suspenders dangled around his hips, as though he had left the flat in a hurry.

"I...I'll take care of it," Rosaleen stammered, leading Brian through the door by the hand, with a glance at Mrs. Lynch. "Right up these stairs, Uncle Brian."

When they were out of hearing of the cook, halfway up the back stairs, she asked with horror, "What happened?"

"It's Doirin," he said, breathing heavily as he climbed. "I locked her in her room and ran all the way. Sure, where's your mother, Rosie?"

"At the top of the stairs," she said, still holding his large hand. "Right here, in the nursery."

She was trembling so much she did not consider the shock

Brian's appearance might give her mother when she threw the door open and led him through.

"Brian! Holy Mother, what's happened to you, darlin'?" Mary cried, rushing to his side. "Sure, you're bleeding all over. Come, sit here on the bed."

Rosaleen had never seen her mother's face so white: she thought her impervious to shock, strong enough to handle any situation calmly. Seeing her mother grow pale and start trembling did not reassure the girl. Brian sat down on the neatly made white bed and mopped at his cheek with the drenched handkerchief. Without asking for further explanation, Mary grabbed up a towel and wet it in the basin on Philip's bedside table. When the handkerchief was removed, four deep scratch marks were revealed on Brian's cheek, and Rosaleen pressed her hands over her mouth and stared at them.

"You're bleeding," Mary cried, gently pressing the towel against the lacerations to stop the flow by pressure. He grabbed her other hand in both of his and held it to his lips like a grateful child.

"Christ, Mary, she's like a wild animal," he muttered with tears in his eyes. "I locked her in her room. I didn't know what to do! I've never seen her like this before at all. It came on so sudden . . . and me asleep in Tomas's room. I don't know what made me wake up. It was a knife she had . . . the one from the kitchen . . . poised right over my breast. I grabbed her arms and fought her off, but she got me with a swipe of her nails before I locked her up."

"You left her there alone?" Mary asked with concern.

"Your boy's there," he said, taking the towel from her hand and holding it in place himself. "Liam's in the flat."

A low moan escaped from Rosaleen's throat. "You left Liam alone with her?" she asked hysterically. "You left my brother with that . . . ?"

"She can't get out," Brian said quickly. "Sure, he was wakened by the commotion, poor lad. He said he'd stay until I got Mary."

Mary glanced frantically around the nursery, at the disordered breakfast trays and Philip sitting, his face unwashed from his meal, playing with his toys. "God in heaven," she repeated over and over again as she rushed to the closet for her shawl. "I want you with us, Rosie. We'll need every hand we have. Brian, get yourself in order, pull your braces up.

Sure, it's a wonder you didn't trip on them running across town."

"I took a horse cab. He's waiting outside," he said, sheepishly putting his suspenders over his shoulders. "I'm surprised I got into my pants at all!"

Mary left the nursery for a moment and came back leading a bewildered Bridie. "If you'll just clean him up," she was saying, "change him and see that he's in clean clothes. He won't be any trouble. But I always like to have him clean in case Miss Laura drops into the nursery. I don't know how long I'll be. It's a family emergency."

"I've cared for him before," Bridie said, staring wide-eyed at the bleeding man rising from the bed. "Mrs. Noonan, what...?"

"Never you mind. There was..." Mary began, but lost her train of thought and was unable to fabricate an excuse for Brian's appearance.

Rosaleen, more quick-witted, finished the sentence, "...a robbery at the pub. We're going after the police, Bridie. They beat poor Uncle Brian something terrible."

She caught the grateful expression in Mary's eyes as they left, descending the back stairs.

Liam was sitting in a chair in front of Doirin's bedroom door with his hands folded in his lap and his face averted, as though he were saying a rosary, but there were no beads in his fingers. He looked up calmly when they entered.

"It's all right," he said. "I've been listening. I was afraid she might harm herself, but I can hear her in there."

Somehow, his control spread to Mary and Brian, but when Rosaleen caught the sound of labored, hoarse breathing from inside the room, a chill went down her back and the fine hairs on the back of her neck stood up. Mary motioned her away, and she complied without argument. Whatever was behind that door no longer sounded human; she imagined her aunt waiting there, prepared to strike if anyone turned the lock.

"Ma, don't open the door!" she cried. "Leave her alone! Look how her fingernails cut Uncle Brian's face. She's gone lunatic for sure."

Her mother's hand relaxed on the doorknob, and she turned to Brian with questioning eyes, wavering in her decision.

"She's right, Mary. We can't open the door until we're sure she's somewhat reasonable. She has the strength of two men, so help me God. Maybe if you talk to her, she'll calm down a bit."

Mary leaned her head against the door and said in a clear, firm voice, "Doirin, it's Mary. I've come to talk to you. Can you tell me what's bothering you at all? You were always able to talk to me. If something's troubling you, let's discuss it. We're sisters."

She was answered by the sound of a piece of furniture hurled against the door and deeper, more inhuman breathing. Rosaleen's heart was in her throat. She could hardly keep herself from running down the stairs and out into the safety of the hot August morning, where there were normal people in the street. As Mary put her hand on the doorknob again, Rosaleen heard herself shriek, "No, Ma! She's a raving maniac! Uncle Brian, please don't let her open it!"

Mary turned on her harshly. "It's your aunt in there and no maniac at all! If you're after cringing and crying, you'd better get out of here. I can't be thinking of you, too."

"Mother," Liam said in his new, deeper voice, "I think Rosaleen's right. This is more than any of us can handle. You know how I feel about Aunt Doirin. She isn't herself, believe me. It's like the devil's got into her. Maybe we should get the priest."

"The priest, is it?" Mary flared. "How dare you! And from my own son, too! So, you think my sister's possessed, now, do you? If you're so frightened, I think you should all get out of here!"

She reached for the key in the lock, but Brian's hand closed on her wrist, almost crushing it.

"No, Mary," he said firmly. "You don't know what she was like. Sure, Liam may be right. We've all heard of such things often enough."

That was too much for Rosaleen. Forgetting her fear, she took a deep breath and said, "The Devil be damned! He's something to frighten children. Liam, I'm surprised at you. But you're right about one thing—we need help. We don't understand what's going on here."

"I can get some of the boys from down the block," Brian volunteered. "They're fine, sturdy lads and good friends of mine."

"You'll do nothing of the sort!" Mary cried. "Sure what would people think? Family matters should be kept within the family."

"We need Dr. Townsend," Rosaleen said. "He'd know what to do."

Mary looked at her, with eyes so troubled that she did not seem to focus on her daughter's face. "Dr. Townsend...yes," she said, all of her resolve collapsing. "Does anyone remember his address?"

"I can find it soon enough," Liam said. "Pa, give me some change for a horse cab, please."

"I'll go with you," Rosaleen said. Then, studying Mary and Brian, "You must promise not to do anything until we come back with the doctor."

Brian nodded, and tears brimmed in Mary's eyes. "I'm afraid she'll hurt herself," she said. "Please hurry!"

Dr. Townsend was not in his office and they had to take another cab to Massachusetts General Hospital, where they were stopped at a wooden desk by a woman with her hair covered like a nun, who directed them to a conference room on the second floor. They walked quickly through the clean, dark corridors, nearly breaking into a run when no one was about. When they came to the door the nurse had indicated, Rosaleen did not pause to knock. All of the white-coated men talking together looked at the two young people in surprise, and Liam hung back a little; but Rosaleen rushed forward into their midst.

"Dr. Townsend!" she cried, running up to him. "Aunt Doirin's awfully bad! Please come. She hurt Uncle Brian!"

His rosy face was both alarmed and amused. "Young lady, calm down, please," he said, glancing at his colleagues. "Now, who are you...and who's Aunt Doirin?"

It seemed impossible that he did not know her. "I'm Rosaleen Noonan!" she said. "You looked after Aunt Doirin in the basement five years ago!"

Several of the doctors suppressed smiles, but Dr. Townsend remembered. "Rosaleen! My word, how you've grown! Now, what's this about your aunt? What has she done?"

She told him with her lower lip trembling until she had to stop and bite it from time to time, to keep from dissolving into tears altogether. He listened sympathetically with his hand on her shoulder, and then he turned to one of the other doctors.

"Dr. Jerome, this may interest you...the sort of thing you've observed at your asylum so often. A deep melancholia a few years back, and now she's gone the other way. I think we should take an attendant with us."

The man addressed as Jerome had a keen, intelligent face. Rosaleen was confident he could help her aunt.

The light-haired young physician beside him observed, "I tell you it's just the way the Irish are...either up or down. Always extreme. Insanity's built into them. At the rate the asylums are filling up with them, we'll have to switch things around...let them have the streets and barricade ourselves in the mental institutions!"

A wave of laughter swept over the assembly, and suddenly Rosaleen felt her face burning with embarrassment and anger. She began to speak and could not control what she was saying, as though she were detached from her own tongue.

"Sure, my fine doctor," she said, lapsing into the old speech, "the Irish in Boston have had a trip through hell. I'll bet you've never been hungry...or missed a meal at all! You've never lived in a dark basement so full of rats you're afraid to go to sleep at night. Or had your sons run away at twelve...without any real hope of seeing them again. If the Irish are crazy, it's the famine and lack of work that's made them that way. Doctor," she sobbed, "have you ever eaten *dog?*"

A hush fell over the assembly, and the fair-haired doctor looked away, murmuring, "There goes another one."

Dr. Townsend, with no apology, quietly intervened, leading Rosaleen and Liam down the hall. Dr. Jerome followed. Liam's hand reached out to take Rosaleen's.

"Please forgive them," Dr. Townsend said. "It's difficult for us, who didn't go through it, to really understand the famine and your people. Thank God it's over now."

"It'll never be over," Dr. Jerome said. "As long as they live, it'll affect their lives. You know how short their life expectancy is from what they went through. At the rate they're going, it's fourteen years in this country. No wonder they go mad. The frustrating thing is that we can do so little—"

"Did you bring morphine?" Dr. Townsend asked, and the other man nodded. "Rosaleen, your aunt may have to go away this time. From what you've said, things are different than before. There's a very real danger that she will harm herself or someone else again."

Rosaleen did not speak: she was completely drained. But Liam spoke up intelligently.

"It doesn't matter, sir. She won't know the difference. It's probably for the best."

They stopped at the desk for a moment and were soon joined by a large man in a soiled white coat, whose eyebrows nearly grew together over his nose.

"This is Sam Peckham," Dr. Jerome explained, and Rosaleen studied the man, deeply disturbed at the sight of him. A creeping premonition seized her, and she was sorry she had come.

Dr. Townsend examined the gashes on Brian's face and asked him a few questions.

"Has she ever done anything like this before? No? How long has she been depressed this time? Oh, I'd like you to meet Dr. Jerome, Mr. Noonan. He's a specialist in complaints like your wife's."

Dr. Jerome's intense dark eyes probed Brian. "Mr. Noonan, did anything unusual happen last night to set her off this morning? Anything she might have considered threatening?"

"I don't know what you mean, doctor," Brian replied in bewilderment. "Sure, nothing's ever *threatened* Doirin."

"You must forgive me, but you said she appeared much better last night, after a very long time. It would be very natural for you to . . . make a sexual overture . . . which might have frightened her, made her anxious . . . in short, made her come after you with the kitchen knife."

Brian reacted as though the doctor had struck him in the face. "We don't use words like that around here," he said. "Certainly not in front of women and young people!" His blue eyes glanced at Mary's unperturbed face, and he took a deep breath. "Is this really important, then?"

"Yes. Some of us are beginning to think it is," Dr. Jerome replied. "Especially in cases where religious manifestations occur."

"I don't understand what you're saying," Brian said helplessly, "but there's been nothing like that between me and my wife since we came to this country . . . and even before that . . . before the hunger. Maybe it was religion, if that's what you mean."

"And nothing last night?"

Brian set his chiseled lips tightly. "Nothing."

Dr. Jerome patted his shoulder with understanding. "Well, I think we'd better get her out of there and see for ourselves. Do you have the key?"

"You won't hurt her?" Mary asked, glancing at Sam Peckham.

"We'll be as gentle as possible, Mary," Dr. Townsend assured her. "I'd appreciate it if you and the young people would move back, my dear. Stand over there in the arch to the parlor, please."

The silence was thick and hot and sticky as the key turned in the lock: Rosaleen felt sick. Dr. Jerome motioned Sam to his side and gave the door a push with his foot. What sprang from the room was not human: it was the banshee...a witch. Rosaleen drew farther away. That wild-haired, keening creature could not possibly be her aunt. And, most shocking of all, she was naked, with blood streaming from the deep scratches on her arms and bosom. Rosaleen wanted to turn away like Liam, but she was frozen to the spot and could not even avert her eyes.

Quickly immobilized by Sam Peckham, Doirin continued to struggle, contorting her face and screaming obscenities in a growling voice unlike her own. Rosaleen grasped her mother's hand with her own cold fingers: perhaps Liam had been right, perhaps it was a priest that was needed.

"She's hurt herself," Dr. Townsend said. "Hold onto her, Sam, until we can restrain her arms with a blanket!"

The doctors moved almost as one person, wrapping Doirin in the wool blanket from her own bed while Sam held her tight, his face reddening with anger as Doirin kicked at him. When the blanket was wound around her, Dr. Jerome opened his black bag and raised a phial of liquid to her lips.

"What is that?" Brian cried out.

"Medicine to calm her down," Dr. Jerome said, just as she spat it back into his face. He opened another phial patiently. "We want to dress those facial lacerations."

After a short time, Doirin stopped fighting and her knees buckled beneath her. She began to sink slowly in Sam's arms, crying, "My God, my God, why hast Thou forsaken me!" Her head lolled, her eyes rolled back. "Brian?" she said softly. "Brian?"

The silence was more terrible than her cries had been. Rosaleen felt tears running from her eyes. Doirin's body...her poor, torn body...had been beautiful.

"We'd better get her to the hospital before the drug wears off," Dr. Jerome said, rising. "Mr. Noonan, you did the right thing in getting us. Sam, pick her up and carry her."

"No!" Mary cried clearly, struggling to remove her hand

from Rosaleen's grip. She stepped forward and knelt at her sister's side. "Sure, you said you'd dress the wounds," she reproached the doctors softly. "You'll take her nowhere like this. Rosaleen, get a basin of water! And look for her hairbrush. Brian, get her things together, so she can take them with her. She'll not go out of here without a stitch. There, now, darlin'," she said soothingly, brushing her sister's hair back with her hand, until the basin and brush were on the floor beside her. She wrung out the cloth in the cold water, and washed Doirin's face gently, revealing what the woman's nails had done to it. "You were such a pretty girl. Let me wash your face just one more time, dear. Oh, God in heaven, how did this happen?"

Mary did not hold her tears back as she brushed her sister's graying hair and secured it with her own bone hairpins. When she felt she had done as much as she could, she released the patient to the doctors.

"We all must have some dignity," she said, with her hands idle in the bloody water.

For several hours after the doctors left with Doirin, the family remained at the scene of its latest tragedy. Mary and Brian sat at opposite ends of the couch in the parlor, staring into space without communicating. Liam had gone directly to his room and had not reappeared since. Rosaleen moved about the flat, looking out one window and then another, without really seeing anything outside. Though she was still upset, she had to admit that she was also relieved, and she felt guilty about it. They had endured Doirin's presence far too long, to the detriment of her sons and the overextension of work for the others. It did not occur to her to think it would be better if Doirin had gotten well, as they thought the day before. What was done was over, and Rosaleen seldom reflected on what might have been. Besides, other aspects of the episode had risen in her mind to haunt her, and her restlessness increased. She must talk to someone: she needed comfort.

Obviously it was useless to engage her mother or uncle in conversation: they looked like living corpses themselves. Rosaleen made a decision and walked quietly to Liam's room, which she entered without knocking or announcing her presence.

Her brother stared out the window, over the untidy patch of back yard with its trash bins and uneven wooden fence, strung with scraps of discarded paper, as dismal as the alley view of any tenement. His back was to her, and she approached without his noticing, sharing the view for a few moments before speaking his name. She had meant it to come out sounding soft, but her voice was strangely hoarse and it was like a croak, instead, but it did not even startle him, though he was unaware of her presence. He turned a drawn, tear-stained face to look at her.

"Rosaleen," he said, as though there were some comfort in the name. "I wanted to tell you...you were marvelous today."

She did not understand him, and it showed in her slight frown and questioning eyes. He cleared his throat and mopped at his face with the back of his hand. "At the hospital," he said. "You were really marvelous."

"Oh," she said, her voice falling. "The doctors. I don't know what I said, Liam. I just felt so angry at the way people treat the Irish. It's strange, really. I've never been that proud of being Irish."

"I think you are," he said, "in your heart. You proved it today. I stood there like a lump, and you took on the lot of them." His voice wavered and a sob wrung itself from his chest. "Oh, God, Rosie, I feel like something's gone from my life forever! It's worse than if she were dead."

She recognized how much he was suffering and could not quite comprehend it. "But...you said it was for the best. You told the doctors that."

"I know. We did what we had to do...didn't we? I mean, there wasn't any other way."

"No," she said, taking his hand. "There really wasn't. You saw what she did to herself. She's quite mad, Liam. And she tried to kill Uncle Brian. She'll be better off where she is, now. They know how to take care of her. They can give her some of that medicine to make her sleep when she's so unhappy. It's us I'm worrying about."

"Us? I don't understand."

"You heard Dr. Jerome. He said that we'll only live for fourteen years in this country. We've already been here six."

"I heard him, but I didn't pay any attention. Don't worry about it, Rosie. He was talking about statistics."

"I won't even have time to raise a family," she continued, as though she had not heard him. "I was almost six when we got here. I'll die when I'm twenty!" she cried in terror, her hands going to her mouth.

"No, Rosie!" Liam said, putting his arm around her. "That isn't what he meant at all."

"Do you think we should marry?" she asked. "It would be hard on whoever we did marry, wouldn't it? Oh! It means that you and Darin will die at the same time I do!"

"I'm not afraid to die," he said, almost amused by her reaction, not understanding her fear. "And as for marriage," he said and sighed, "I've seen quite enough of it never to do it myself. I'll never marry," he said softly, as though the realization had not struck him before. "I think I've always known that, without even thinking about it."

"I want to," she said. "And I don't want to die. Not until I'm so old it doesn't matter."

"Rosaleen, look at it this way. Even if what the doctor said is true—and it isn't—the thing to think about is what we are to do with our lives. How we can make them count most?"

"I want a husband and a family of my own. That's all I've ever wanted. It's what I'd be best doing."

"Well, then, I'm sure you shall have them. What Dr. Jerome meant was that some people will live longer than others. The ones who die young will balance off the ones who live to be very old. He said an *average* of fourteen years. You know what an average is."

"Yes." She thought about the mathematical probabilities a few moments and raised her blue eyes pathetically to his face. "But how can we tell which we are?"

The Maddigans returned to Boston two weeks early, before Mary and Rosaleen had had a chance to recover from what had happened to Doirin. Mary was summoned to her employer's room shortly after her arrival. Thinking it was Philip his mother wished to see, Mary groomed him carefully, combing his unruly light-brown hair with water to smooth it back, keeping up a weary-voiced, childish prattle to him while she did so, while her daughter looked on.

"Are you going to tell Aunt Laura about Aunt Doirin?" Rosaleen asked and Mary's hands went still on the boy's head.

"Indeed I'm not!" she said, wishing she could overcome the feeling of pain in her chest, the emotional hurt that would not leave her. "There are some things you don't tell anyone, Rosaleen. No one is to know about poor Doirin. Do you understand me? Sure, it's bad enough we have to live with it, without inflicting our sorrow on anyone else. And it's a matter of family pride, too. We don't want people going around saying someone in our family's crazy."

"But she is," Rosaleen replied reasonably. "All of us know that."

Mary experienced a flash of irritability, but managed to control it. "Just do what I say, without any arguments. I'm not going to mention it to anyone...and neither are you, not even the Maddigan boys, do you hear?"

Her daughter nodded. "The servants all know about Uncle Brian coming here covered with blood."

"Well," Mary said, rising to smooth her own hair before going downstairs, "for once, one of your lies came in handy. A burglary at the pub was a good idea."

"Thank you." Rosaleen twinkled ironically, and Mary could not restrain a slight smile. Her daughter was a devil like all the Noonans and there was no getting around it.

"Go on with you," she said, "and we'll follow. I want you to know . . . indeed, to God, you should know by now . . . . I'll not have you making up stories."

Rosaleen preceded them down the stairs, looking back over her shoulder. "I didn't lie about the tuition money," she defended herself. "And, goodness knows, I certainly worked it off! A long time ago. You told me never to lie unless 'it was a matter of life and death.'"

"You remember that?" Mary frowned, recalling the Immigration office so many years ago; she tried to think of some way to put the incident into perspective. "Life and death is what I meant, then. Sure, we wouldn't have gotten into the country at all if I hadn't mistranslated the Gaelic of that young couple. You tell quite a few...fibs, Rosaleen. And I don't think you're faced with life and death that often."

Rosaleen waited until they were just outside Laura's door to say, "It's a matter of degree, isn't it, Mother? I'm very intense. Almost everything that affects me is a matter of life and death, you see."

A Noonan either melted you down straightaway or wore you down through attrition, Mary thought. She was certain her daughter was still teasing her, so she let the matter drop. Besides, she had other things to think about at the moment: she must appear her usual, calm self to Miss Laura, and it was not going to be easy. She took a deep breath, worked her lips into what she hoped was a smile and opened the door.

Still in her gray traveling clothes, Laura was seated at her desk, looking through a small address book. Her pale face was drawn, and she was chewing her lower lip. When they entered, she glanced up blankly, but the expression changed at once into displeasure. "I didn't mean for you to bring Philip," she snapped, "or Rosaleen either, for that matter." Then, seeing their discomfort, she rose and walked toward them, embracing her child in a billow of skirts. "I'm sorry," she apologized, looking up at Mary. "I'm just a nervous wreck, Mary. It's been the most appalling summer! Rosaleen, dear, will you please take Philip back to the nursery? We'll have a chat later, when I come up to see him. I want to discuss something with your mother."

Without a word, Rosaleen lifted the little boy in her arms and exited the room, just perceptibly slamming the door behind her. Laura did not seem to notice: her thoughts were not even within the room. She marched back to her desk and motioned Mary toward a rose faille armchair across from her, not speaking for a while as she continued her vain search through the address book. Finally, she put it down with a sigh.

"I don't know what to do! I know you can't help me, Mary, but I need someone to listen. And sometimes you come up with the greatest good sense. I'm just fit to be tied!"

"What is it, ma'am?" Mary asked with what she hoped appeared to be "good sense" while, in truth, she was still somewhat shaky over her own problems. "You know I'll do anything I can."

"They grow up so fast!" Laura said, almost reproachfully, and Mary waited for her to circle all the way around her problem, before she finally mentioned it. "I had no idea...I hadn't even yet considered it. This summer was simply awful! There was nothing I could do down there, you know: I was completely helpless. Matthew kept after me the whole time. And when he wasn't after me, he was brooding! The brooding's the worst of all, don't you think? You don't really know what's going on in their minds. The other boys were quite reasonable. Harry isn't nearly so demanding...and, of course, old Johnny keeps his own counsel, though he did chime in once or twice in defense of Matthew....What *am* I going to do?"

Mary saw that Laura was really seriously agitated, though the only sense she could make of it was that the boys were demanding something she could not provide, which seemed unlikely, considering all her wealth. "I think if you calmed down a bit, Miss Laura," she suggested, "we could find a way out of whatever's bothering you. Sure, your mind's dashing around like a bird in a chimney."

Laura's gray eyes settled on Mary's face. "I've been this way for most of the summer. You're right, of course. I don't seem to really focus on a problem. That's why I need you." She was quiet a moment; then: "It's Harvard, Mary. Matthew insists on going to Harvard, and I think Johnny wants it, too."

Mary had been in the Maddigan house long enough, close to Laura, to recognize the difficulty. Though the boys were not Catholic, they were Irish, and their mother had been out of favor since her marriage, years ago, to Mr. Maddigan. It was a situation Laura could not buy her way out of: caste was more important than money in this city. "You were looking through your address book," Mary said thoughtfully. "Was it for the name of some one who might help?"

"Yes," Laura replied, downcast. "And there isn't a single person there, who...it's just the names of shopkeepers and charities, as you know. None of my old friends even speak to me."

"Are any of them in a position to help the boys get into Harvard College?"

Laura shrugged despondently, "I don't know. I'm sure they are, though. My friend Catherine married a man who was very involved with the college; but he's dead now, and I saw in the newspapers that she's remarried. Poor John Paddington was a dear boy," she said reminiscently, "but he died several years before my husband, so she was a rather young widow. She married a Bradshaw about five years ago...not nearly so well off, but a fine old family."

The name echoed through the years in Mary's head. "Paddington?"

"Yes. Kate was an heiress, you know. Beautiful girl...except for her hair, which was that sort of frazzled orangey red...the kind that kinks up. She had a terrible time with it in school! When I think of her, I picture her in front of a mirror, struggling with a comb. I remember once, someone suggested slippery elm, and—"

"Well," Mary interrupted, "you never know about old friends. Did she carry on her first husband's interest in the college?"

"Oh, indeed she did! After his death, she endowed a chair in his honor." Recognizing the familiar signs of bewilderment in Mary, she explained quickly, "She contributed a great deal of money to set up a commemorative post . . . a job for a professor . . . in his name."

Mary considered this. "Does that mean she's still well known at the college, then?"

"Oh, yes! As a matter of fact, now that you mention it, she's probably still active, financially, at least."

"Miss Laura, will you just give into a little whim of mine? Write your friend a letter, explaining how clever your sons are, and telling her how they'd like to go to Harvard College. As I said, you never know about old friends. Kevin and I'll deliver it this very evening. Does she still live at the same place?"

"What place?" Laura asked in surprise. "Surely you don't know her?"

"Of course not," Mary said quickly, cursing herself for the slip of the tongue. "I meant the same place as when you knew her last."

"Yes. She stayed in her house on Beacon Hill after her second marriage. It really isn't far away . . . in blocks, I mean. Socially, it's farther than China. Mary, do you really think I should, after all these years?"

"I do. Don't underestimate old friends."

"Well, it's no time for pride," Laura said. "I'll write it immediately. But you won't need Kevin, Mary. It's only a few blocks away."

Mary did not insist on her peculiarity about taking Kevin: she would do so anyway, to reinforce their presence. She had learned blackmail in this house, as a victim, and she did not want to make this too hard on Kate Paddington. She even rationalized that though the woman had been doing something wrong with Mr. Maddigan, it was Mary's service to her, along with Kevin, on that winter evening so long ago that she would be rewarding. Mary could look at that night dispassionately now. In fact, she realized that all the pain and guilt she had been carrying over Doirin's madness had disappeared in the past few minutes. She had been given an opportunity to repay Laura's many kindnesses, and, faced with this challenge, she had more immediate things on her mind.

As soon as the letter was in her hands, Mary decided to deliver it at once, realizing there would be less chance of the woman's husband being home in the afternoon. Convincing Kevin was not difficult. She did not take him into her confidence, however, because she worried that it might give him further ideas. She knew her countrymen were good at heart and loyal to those they served. But she also knew, too well, that working for the basic necessities of living sometimes made them succumb to temptation. Kevin and Bridie had been saving for several years to marry, because they would have to "live out" when they did so, forfeiting their lodgings in the house and adding the expense of rent. She would not point out a way he might reach his goal sooner, though the evidence of the affair had been destroyed when she burned the letters the night of Mr. Maddigan's death.

"I want you to take me to the Paddington house," she told him, as though the idea of going there again troubled her. His mouth dropped open, and his guileless eyes were filled with inquiry. "I've a letter to deliver from Miss Laura... something to do with Harvard College and the boys. I don't like to go into that house again, Kevin. Will you please come with me? I know it's embarrassing, but I could hardly refuse. We'll just give the lady the letter without saying a word. Perhaps she'll have forgotten us."

"Not damn likely, is it?" he said. "But of course, Mary, I'll come along with you. I don't mind telling you I don't care for the memory of that night either, though."

They rode the few blocks in the buggy and, when they arrived at the house, Kevin joined her to go to the front door, which was opened by an indignant butler, who tried to send them to the servants' entrance.

"My mistress wants me to deliver an important letter directly into Mrs. Pad—Mrs. Bradshaw's hands," Mary told him imperiously, and he let them into the hallway while he went to fetch his mistress. Mary felt Kevin give a shudder beside her as he looked up the stairs.

"It's all right," she reassured him, glancing around. "As a matter of fact, it isn't the same at all. The whole place has been redecorated. Do you see? Just pretend you've never seen it before."

The woman descending the stairs was different, too, Mary noted. Though she did not expect to find her clad in a peignoir with flyaway, loose hair, she did not imagine such cool composure and stately dignity, either. The years had been kind to her. In middle age, her body had filled out amply and her distressing hair was lighter, coiled neatly around her head. The moment of recognition came a few seconds later than Mary anticipated.

"A letter from Laura?" the woman said, almost irritably. "Surely, she knows..." Then, facing Mary and Kevin directly, her body stiffened, her light eyes glancing from one face to the other. "It's all right," she said to the butler, dismissing him. "Would you please step into the study?"

They followed her into a cluttered room filled, apparently, with the treasures of both husbands, and totally unlike the one at the Maddigan house, as though study and library had been combined. The shelves of books were scanty, the empty spaces occupied by porcelain figures and ivory carvings of many elephants. The desk, instead of being solid and heavy and masculine, was no more than a table with a few drawers, shiny black and covered with raised Chinese drawings in gold, which matched a sort of highboy in the room. Mary took all this in at a glance, before Mrs. Bradshaw turned to her, having put the safe distance of the desk between them: the rosy color had gone from her face. Without comment, Mary handed her the letter. She and Kevin stood in stony silence, looking at her while she read it, her eyes appearing slightly glazed.

"But this is...!" she started to exclaim, but reconsidered. She took a deep breath, and her eyes wandered to the window. After several moments, she said, turning back to them, "Tell Mrs. Maddigan...I will do what I can." Then, under Mary's steady, not unsympathetic stare, she amended the statement. "Everything considered . . . their mother's name and their . . . wealth . . . I can see no reason why the young men should not attend the school they desire, especially if they are as clever as she says. Tell Mrs. Maddigan she might consider a donation to the college: they are seldom refused. Something substantial, but not outrageous...her lawyer can help her. I'll take care of the rest of it."

Mary nodded, her neutral gaze still on the woman's face. Then, taking her lead, Kevin turned to leave with her. They were nearly at the door when Mrs. Bradshaw asked, "What's your name?"

"Mary, ma'am."

Considering her with narrowed eyes, Mrs. Bradshaw detected no further threat and bowed her head stiffly. "I saw you on the street once...with your little son," she said with a motion of her hand, dismissing them.

The next fall, both Matthew and Harry were accepted into Harvard, after passing the entrance examinations; two years later, Johnny, who insisted upon being called John, joined them there.

Chapter 19

PHILIP died, during one of his many bouts of pneumonia, in the winter of 1859, when Rosaleen was seventeen; and for several days she and Mary were uncertain about their future. Mary was no longer needed at the Maddigan house, and Rosaleen was earning a small wage working as a seamstress for Madame Hurotte, Laura Maddigan's dressmaker. John had violently opposed her apprenticeship, when she left the Catholic school two years before. But Rosaleen did not understand the commotion: she was quite happy to earn some money of her own, in a place where she could make some pretty dresses for herself. She was flattered that Madame Hurotte was impressed enough with her sewing to engage her. Additional schooling and college for her had never been considered. Her mother's discouraging view of her becoming a governess had long ago put such thoughts out of her mind. At fifteen, all she wanted was some money of her own, while she waited for Darin to return again.

He had come back to Boston twice, for only a few weeks at a time, before going back to sea, and each time their relationship had deepened, come closer to what she wanted it to be. Darin was tall and handsome the last time she saw him, and he could not keep his gaze from hers. Though their only physical contact was a goodbye kiss on the lips when he left again, she clung to the memory and built her whole future on it. He had changed, not just in appearance, but in his mind and outlook. The years at sea had not been idly spent. When she received a letter from him now, and they came often, they were properly capitalized and punctuated, if rather florid in style—as a result of his extensive reading. She loved him completely and could think of no better life than working and waiting for him to come home again. Still, she could not imagine herself living anywhere but in the house in which she had been raised.

Because of her long hours at work, she did not see anyone often, but the house was full again, just as it had been when she and her mother had first come there. Harry and John were living at home while they attended Harvard. Matthew, who had graduated and had a year in Europe with some friends, was learning the family business at the bank and finding that the life did not suit him.

In one of her infrequent encounters with Matthew, one Sunday in the library, Rosaleen listened to him complain.

"It's so damned dull, Rosaleen: you can't imagine. I'd rather do something active...like traveling. Just look at this!" he said, pushing a large account book across the table to her. "It isn't that I'm bad at figures. After all, I did train for this. But it bores the hell out of me. Would you believe that in that long column of neatly written numbers, there's a one-hundred-and-twelve-dollar error? I've been over it six times and I can't find it. I don't know if this is the way I want to spend my life."

"Yes," she said, glancing down the column and putting her finger on the ledger. "It's right here. And here. You must have been looking for it in one place, Matt, or in even numbers. You see, this eight should be a nine, and this..."

He struck himself on the side of the head. "You're right, by God! I'd forgotten," he said, "about your talent with figures. The next time, I'll come to you before I lose my mind. Tell me, how can anyone be so beautiful and so intelligent, too?"

Any mention of her appearance still made her blush. "It isn't intelligence, really," she demurred. "I've never been able to explain it, even to the nuns at school. Numbers are just so easy for me. I don't have to add or subtract or multiply: when I look at them, the answer's just there."

"Well, you're being wasted at the dress shop." He laughed. "If it weren't so wildly improbable, I'd hire you at the bank."

She laughed with him, imagining herself in the severe, wood-paneled offices she had seen only once. "I could sit on a high stool like the other accountants with my skirts hanging to the floor!"

"But, seriously, Rosaleen, I'd like to tell you about some of this. If you helped me out at home, I'd have more time to play!"

She knew that Matt was attracted to her, just as Harry was, though both of them kept their distance. The social chasm between them, which had not existed during childhood, had been reinforced during their college years. They made many friends at Harvard, and though their mother still was not accepted, the young men were invited to parties aside from college functions. Only John was a loner. He made few friends and seemed to like it that way. His time was spent almost entirely in his books, but he had more contact with Rosaleen than the older boys, and he still resented her working as a seamstress.

"If I had my money," John had told her, "I'd get you out of there in a hurry and see that you were properly educated. It's unfair that Liam's going to college and you aren't!"

"Liam's going to be a priest." She smiled. "If I'd become a nun as Reverend Mother wished, I'd be going to school, too! You wouldn't want me to be a nun, would you?"

"No!" he cried, his eyes widening behind his glasses. Then, imitating her good-humored smile, "You wouldn't last a month, anyway. I don't know. " He sighed. "Maybe your mother's right. I must say, I haven't cared for any of the literary type of girls I've met. They're either snooty bluestockings or they're too overpowering for me. I much prefer your company."

"And I enjoy yours," she said sincerely. She always felt comfortable with John; in many ways, he was more like a brother to her than Liam. "Sewing isn't that bad, John," she reassured him. "I handle really beautiful fabrics and know all the latest styles. Madame's even discounted material so I can make myself some dresses. And we speak nothing but French at work, which is very amusing. I've learned more there than I ever did in school. And, in some ways, much more about life."

"What have you learned about life?" he asked, frowning slightly. "I told you all you needed to know years ago."

"You did. You were wonderful, and not the least embarrassed, either. But the girls do talk," she said mischievously. "And not about when the next novena is, either. All French girls talk about is men."

There were three French girls sewing with her, and Rosaleen exaggerated only slightly. Two of them were older than she, and Madame Hurotte kept a close eye on them, because she was answerable to her relatives in Paris, who had sent them. So, while they did not actually act out their fantasies, they discussed them very romantically, and the only thing each of them wanted in life was a man of her own. And, though madame was strict with her young relatives, she was firmer still with Rosaleen, because of Mary, who had spoken to her after hearing that seamstresses had a doubtful reputation. Madame admired Rosaleen's appearance greatly and had asked several times if Mary would let her model her creations. But the girl knew the answer would be a flat no. In fact, that was the cause of the current friction between Rosaleen and her mother, because Rosaleen dearly wanted to wear those marvelous gowns, rather than sit at a sewing machine behind the shop all the time. She could not understand why she should not adorn her special beauty and show it off before others. But all her arguments were met with lectures about vanity, which were quite to the point, though she did not like to admit it. It was apparent that her debut before the matrons of Boston would never take place, so she consoled herself with dreams of Darin's return, as though all adverse things would be wiped out then.

The first dawning that her life could change abruptly, and for the worse, came when Rosaleen awoke one morning to find her mother sitting on the edge of the bed, weeping without restraint. Mary had been up looking after Philip for two nights in the chilly nursery, and Rosaleen's mind cleared quickly when she became aware of her.

"Mother, what is it? You're tired out and freezing cold. Why don't you crawl in with me and get warm for a while?"

Responding automatically, Mary took her shoes off and got between the covers fully dressed. Staring at the ceiling, she said, "He's gone, Rosaleen. Our little Philip's gone...."

Rosaleen gave a small cry and burst into tears. They were in each other's arms at once, sharing companionship in their misery. Philip was the one thing they shared without controversy: they both loved him as though he were their own. He was no longer "little," though they referred to him that way: he was eleven years old. The doctor had warned Mary, from the first, that children like him were usually swept away in infancy or the first few years of life by infection or a heart ailment, but Mary had dedicated herself to raising him to maturity. Only her excellent care had brought him that far. Now it was over: the child she loved was dead.

"I don't want you to go to work today," she said, after their tears had drained into silence. "There will be so much to do. I must tell Miss Laura."

"I'll go with you, Mother. She'll be brokenhearted."

"Will she?" Mary asked in a curiously flat voice. "I wonder. She's been so busy with the other boys' activities that she hasn't had time to kiss the child goodnight for a long time now. The only person who's visited him while he was ill is John. Sure, they all abandoned him long before this night," she said bitterly.

"Don't blame them too much, Mother. They're awfully busy with their studies."

"Damn their studies! Matthew hasn't seen him for over two years. And Harry's a good lad, but when he came last time it was to 'observe' him, because he was learning about such things in medical school. Sure, he's been no more than an embarrassment to them all for a long time."

"You talk almost as though he were *your* child, Ma."

"I feel as though he was," Mary said. "Sure, when I lost my poor tiny son, it was Philip I nursed and cared for. I brought him through so many illnesses, and I tried to give him the love he didn't get from his own family."

"If he'd been allowed downstairs, there would have been more feeling for him," Rosaleen said. "But you can't blame the boys for that. That was Laura's doing, and you went along with it."

"I always thought I'd win her over, eventually. For a while, I did," Mary said, turning to brush Rosaleen's dark hair back. "You haven't called me 'Ma' for a long time," she added softly. "You only do it when there's trouble, do you know that?"

Rosaleen nodded. "Yes. When I'm troubled or excited, I lapse into the brogue. I probably always shall. When are you going to tell Laura?"

"We'll let her have her breakfast first," Mary considered. "And we better have our own, I guess."

"I'm not hungry," Rosaleen said, her mouth still salty from tears, her eyes burning.

"Nor am I. But a good deal may be put upon us this day. We must fortify ourselves for it."

She groped for Rosaleen's handkerchief beneath the pillow, blew her nose and braced herself for the day to come.

"Ma?" Rosaleen asked, the full impact of what had happened settling on her, "What about your job? We won't be able to stay on here, will we?"

"Sure, that's the least of my worries at the moment," Mary said sharply.

The silver tray and coffee service had not been removed from Laura's night table when they came to see her. She was still in bed, propped up against pillows with her gray-blond hair unbrushed, sorting through the morning mail for invitations addressed to her sons, the only pleasure she received from their being able to go out into society without her. She did not ask about Philip's health, as though she had forgotten he was ill again. Instead; she looked up with a smile, holding a cream-colored envelope between two fingers.

"I do believe the Addison girl is taken with Matthew. This is the second invitation in a month! They're a very good family.... Mary, what on earth's the matter with you? Is your family all right?"

Mary nodded. Rosaleen was afraid her mother would say something unforgivable and logical, like "Yes, but yours isn't": she was very conscious of their position in the house at this juncture. But Mary was more charitable.

"I'm sorry to tell you, Miss Laura, it's Philip. We lost him early this morning."

Laura paled. She dropped the letter and her hand fluttered to her throat. Mary poured her a glass of water, and she accepted it without speaking, drinking it in little sips, her gray eyes thoughtful. Rosaleen observed that she was not hypocritical enough to cry; but when she finally spoke, she might have been more discreet.

"You did your best, Mary. God knows what you've been through. Let's see," she stammered, rubbing her forehead with trembling fingers. "We must... consider the funeral. I've never thought about it, though I knew it would come someday. I really don't know how to handle this without attracting attention."

Mary stared at her uncomprehendingly, too upset to follow her train of thought. "Attention?"

"A notice in the papers...that sort of thing," Laura said; then, recognizing Mary's state of mind, she added quickly, "My dear Mary. We all know what a sweet boy he was, but other people didn't know him. They didn't even know *about* him. Do you understand? We must handle all this without any...fuss."

Again, Mary nodded, too grieved to assemble her thoughts. "I don't know what to do," she said, turning to Rosaleen, who was almost as tall as she. "I kept Rosaleen home to help."

Rosaleen's only thought was to get Mary away before her mind cleared; she felt her pleasant life collapsing around her. As long as her mother kept her thoughts to herself, they still had a chance.

"She's terribly upset," Rosaleen explained. "I think I'd better take her back to my room."

Deprived of Mary's help in a crisis, Laura's face became frantic. "Has Matthew left for the bank yet?"

"I'll get him, as soon as I take care of Mother," Rosaleen said, and Laura motioned her closer.

"You understand, don't you, my dear? It's the other boys I'm thinking of," Laura whispered.

Rosaleen left her mother on her own bed, insisting that she rest for a while, and hurried down the stairs to the dining room, where she found all three of the Maddigan boys just finishing their breakfast.

"Matt," she said, her lower lip trembling almost uncontrollably, "your mother needs you. Philip . . . died . . . this morning."

Tossing his napkin on his plate, Matthew rose quickly, but the others remained seated. Harry leaned back with a frown, and John slowly put a piece of toast down and reached for his handkerchief. After his first shock of grief, John asked Rosaleen, "Are you all right?"

"No," she said, with tears in her eyes, "but at least I'm alive. I must go back to Mother."

Mary was not in her room, and she heard faint movements in the nursery. Though Rosaleen had loved Philip, it took all her courage to open the door. Her mother was pouring water into the bedside bowl from the pitcher. She looked up when the door opened.

"Come in, Rosaleen, and close that door. Sure, whatever they decide, we must take care of him before they come to get him. I should have done it this morning, but I was too upset."

Mary had prepared many bodies: in Ireland, it was a sign of loving and caring, to which she was accustomed. But to Rosaleen, with her fear of death, her mother's methodical motions over the thing that lay on Philip's bed were grotesque. She immediately felt ill and light-headed, though she dared not admit it, and she tried to follow her mother's quiet instructions.

"Wash his face well, darling," she said, "and comb his hair. It takes lots of water to slick it down. I'll take care of the rest of the bathing. Sure, rigor mortis has already set in. I really should have done this earlier. We won't be able to dress him unless we tear his clothes down the back."

"Ma, his eyes are open!" Rosaleen cried after gingerly approaching the blue-lipped face with the washcloth.

"Ah," Mary said, staring down into the quaintly oriental face with compassion, "I closed his eyes this morning, but not long enough, I guess. They're only open a slit. I hope it isn't too late."

She moved quickly to her dresser, and Rosaleen stood away from the body while she was gone, looking down at it with both fascination and revulsion. She had never seen Philip when he was not smiling, and he was not smiling now. A feeling of cold terror began to mount to her chest. She wondered if, without a mind, he had possessed a soul. And, if so, where was it now? Something had definitely left him: he was like a slab of cold meat. She thought she could not bear it. Her mother came back and forced pennies down on his eyelids, but the eyes remained stubbornly partly open.

"The man from the funeral parlor can do it later, after the rigor goes away," Mary said. "Sure, look at the streaks the tears made when he died, poor lamb. That always happens, and I've never known if they're tears of gladness at leaving this life, or sorrow over ... Rosaleen, where are you going?"

"I don't feel well, Ma," Rosaleen cried, running from the room with her hand over her mouth. She did not make it to the basin in her room before vomiting her small breakfast all over the hall carpet.

Her heart was pounding wildly, erratically: she could not breathe, and she called out for her mother. She tried not to think of death; it was impossible to face its reality. Mary was at her side quickly, wiping her hands on a towel.

"Sure what's the matter with you? Oh, you've been sick all over the—"

"I'm dying, Ma! I can't breathe ... help me!"

"Come," her mother said, slipping her arm around her. "It's all right, Rosaleen. Just relax and take a few even breaths. There, that's fine. You aren't dying at all. You got emotional and took in too much air: it makes you giddy. You don't have to go back in the nursery. Go rest in your room."

The funeral service, in a Protestant cemetery in the North End, was mercifully short, and Rosaleen was kept on her feet by the strong, cold wind blowing in her face and her mother's hand beneath her elbow. With Matthew's help, Laura had made the arrangements so that her sons' positions were not jeopardized, burying Philip far from their parish church, in a cemetery so full of Irish names that "Maddigan" was not distinguishable among them. If Rosaleen had been thinking clearly, she would have recognized at once what was taking place. And Mary, the only person really overcome with grief at the graveside, was accustomed to no other kind of interment and only knew it was a Protestant cemetery and ritual, which seemed appropriate enough to her. The whole family attended the service: only that was important to Mary.

When they returned to the black carriages, waiting in the snow, Mary asked Laura quietly, "Is it all right if I visit my family while I'm in this section of town? I like to be with them when I feel like this."

"Of course," Laura said, through her black veil. "You and Rosaleen take one of the carriages."

"It's within walking distance," Mary said. "We needn't trouble with that, Miss Laura."

Suddenly, John asked, "May I go with you? I've heard about your family for years, Mrs. Noonan, but I've never met them all."

"There's only my brother-in-law...and you know Liam," Mary said. "Shouldn't you be with your mother?"

"She has Harry and Matt," he said with determination. Rosaleen, who did not like to visit the pub anyway, began to feel alarmed. She did not want John to see it or become aware of the fact that the family lived above it. She did not want him to see the neighborhood itself. He was her friend, and she was afraid she would lose him if he observed her origin. Before she could think of a valid objection, Mary reluctantly invited him to come with them. For the rest of the afternoon, Rosaleen saw everything through John's eyes, with increasing mortification.

The North End was still full of tenements, though there were no longer lean-tos attached to them to provide extra living space, and instead of newspapers over the windows to protect the inhabitants from the cold, a few lace curtains were now visible. But the doors and windows still peeled paint and trash was preserved in the icy streets, littered scraps which might have been insects preserved in amber, for their durability: they never seemed to go away. A considerable part of the Irish population had moved to other surrounding areas when the fabric mills opened. Though employed at last, the people who had been beggars and scalpeens in their own country still had no basic rules of hygiene. Only the pub, it seemed, which bore the Noonan name in large gold letters on the window, had been brightened up with yearly coats of dark-green paint, and its very conspicuousness made Rosaleen wince. She was certain that John would forever consider her no more than a pubkeeper's daughter after this visit. She determined not to defend anything, however: she had too much personal pride for that. John had asked to accompany them without an invitation: he could take the shocks as they came.

He was mildly bewildered when they entered the pub by the business door, and his curiosity grew quietly as they ascended the stairs to the living quarters above. But his reaction to the parlor, which Mary kept scrupulously clean for Brian, set Rosaleen's mind at ease.

"It's charming." He smiled broadly, moving to the fire to warm himself. "It has a real country quality...right here in the middle of the city. I've never been upstairs above a store or a pub before. I had no idea how comfortable such accommodations could be," he said, noting the delicately crocheted doilies on the mantel and all the chairs, his gaze finally resting on a bookshelf. "I can see that Liam lives here by the books on the shelves. I suspect he's at classes today?"

"Yes," Mary said uncomfortably. "I'll brew us a cup of tea. Sure we're all after freezing, though we didn't stand long for the service. I'll tell Brian we're here. I don't know if he saw us come in."

"Uncle Brian's family lived here," Rosaleen said diffidently. "When the boys were home, there was lots of life here. Now, with all but Liam gone, Mother tries to look after them. She always brought Philip with her. He liked it here. And everyone was fond of him."

They sat down beside the fire, and John sighed. "Was your mother displeased about the service? It was not a pretty business, was it? Honestly, Rosaleen, I'm so ashamed of my family. I'm grateful that Philip got to come here, though, that he enjoyed something in his short life. I'm sure the people are as cozy and warm as this room is."

"Mother will be angry for a short time, I think, when she starts to feel anything. But she'll get over it, John. She only has to realize that every family has something to hide."

He turned his head sideways to look at her with a smile. "Even yours?"

She opened her lips to speak, and shut them firmly, nodding. "Even ours, I suppose," she said. Mary had been quite firm about her never mentioning Doirin, and she did not want to do it now. "Ah, here's Uncle Brian!"

Even Brian looked different to her today, as though her perception were heightened by John's presence. He was no longer a white-haired old man, bent slightly at the shoulders, hardly worth paying attention to, except for the fact that he was Darin's father. His blue eyes were merry, his face almost unlined, though there was a shadow of the past on it. He had a soft voice and gentle manners, and held out his hand to John at once. The young man rose to shake it.

"I've heard about you and your brothers these many years," Brian said. "I'm sorry I have to meet you on such a tragic day. We were all that fond of young Philip."

"Thank you, sir. I'm grateful for that," John replied without any formality, as though he were quite at home here already. "And for Mrs. Noonan's fine care of him. His life wouldn't have been much without you all. I'm sure you know he didn't have much at home."

"There are things that are difficult for a family to deal with," Brian said, helping Mary lay out the tea tray. They were like a married couple, Rosaleen thought, and a handsome one at that, except for some slight tension she had never noticed before, which held them apart. "I was just telling Mary that in the kitchen. There, lad, sit down again, and we'll have some tea and cakes. It's a cold gray day to be standing around in a churchyard."

John took to Brian at once, and behind his glasses his gray eyes smiled speculatively as he sipped his tea, glancing from Brian to Rosaleen. "There's the most remarkable family resemblance," he finally said. "You, sir, and Rosaleen and Darin are so alike. It's incredible. My brothers and I aren't alike at all. We don't even resemble our parents much. Well, Matthew favors Father, I guess, though I hardly remember him."

Mary nodded slightly. "And you resemble your mother some," she said. "The same gray eyes and fine features and light hair. Poor Philip didn't look like anyone but himself, did he?"

"Not like the family, Mrs. Noonan," John said carefully. "He did resemble other children like him, though. They all have that same open, sweet smile. Mary," he said suddenly, calling her by her first name for the only time in his life, leaning forward to touch her arm. "Do you know the life expectancy of children like Philip? It was only because of you that he lived as long as he did."

Her dark eyes brimmed with tears. "I know," she said, "and I did my very best. But, sure, it wasn't good enough."

Brian changed the subject so spontaneously and suddenly that they all turned to stare at him.

"Good God! With your news, I almost forgot. I had a letter from Darin yesterday. He's—"

"—coming home!" Rosaleen cried, spilling her tea over into her saucer. "He's coming home! Why didn't he write to me? Oh, Uncle Brian, where's his letter?"

Brian shook his head. "He isn't coming home . . . not for a while yet." He smiled at her enthusiasm. "And the reason he wrote to me was really remarkable. You know how he's been looking for his brother Michael all these years? Well, he—"

"He found Michael?" Mary asked in amazement, wiping her eyes with the back of her hand.

"No. No." Brian chuckled, shaking his head good-naturedly. "If you women will stop jumping on my words before I can speak! He ran into Padraig, instead, in San Francisco. Well, not Paddy himself, really. He saw his name on a pub. Remember the great incoherent hunk old Paddy was? Well apparently he's done all right for himself. Darin's going to stay on with him for a while. He said to give his love to all of you."

Rosaleen, whose heart had expanded at the thought of Darin coming home to her, felt it contract in her chest like a burned cinder. No wonder he had written to his father: he knew the news would not delight her. To think of him in America and three thousand miles away was more difficult than not knowing where he was, or having him halfway across the world. "I suppose he'll be coming home by ship," she said, attempting to hide her disappointment. "It's a long, hard trip overland."

"And expensive." Brian pondered. "Yes, he'll sail home for sure, Rosie. He can always get a job on a ship. There's no telling when we'll see him, but I think it'll be during the summer, somehow." He caught the intent expression on John's face and apologized, "I'm sorry, lad. I shouldn't have brought up family matters at a time like this. But then of course you know Darin."

"Yes," John said. "He went to sea for the first time when he was staying with us. And I've liked to hear him talk about all his experiences since. My God," he said, shaking his head slowly. "We're the same age—and all the things he's done, while I've been muddling my way through school."

"You'll have your trip to Europe this summer, after you graduate," Mary said. "Sure, what you've done will count for more in the long run, John. And what do you mean by 'muddling,' for heaven's sake? Your grades have been better than your brothers' right along. John's a scholar," she told Brian, knowing that he would appreciate the label. "He's a very clever boy."

Though Rosaleen heard their voices, she did not hear their words. She had a lot of planning to do. In a way, it was probably better to hear of Darin's return this way, instead of having him appear suddenly when she was not prepared for it. If he was arriving in the summer, she would need some pretty summer frocks, the best she had ever made. She would talk to madame about obtaining some really nice fabrics, and copy the latest fashions from the magazines from Paris. In this, she was fortunate, she concluded: skirts were getting fuller, layering out with many petticoats. That, along with the lower necklines, made the dresses the prettiest she had ever seen. Her only real problem was to get enough remnants of sheer white batiste and crinoline together to accomplish all those petticoats.

And, of course, there was the added consideration of whether or not her mother still had a job.

When they entered the Maddigan house, Mary moved darkly and silently up the dim staircase, leaving the two young people standing in the hall. The house was quiet. The chandelier above them was unlit and the lower floor was getting dark. Rosaleen knew that cook was preparing dinner, though the odors were too confined to the back of the house to permeate far. Laura was in her room with Harry. Matthew, who had gone to work from the funeral, would be coming in late. The house was so familiar to Rosaleen that it was an entity made up of separate cells like a beehive, and she usually knew what was happening in it. Right now, Laura's room was a question, though, giving off unfavorable vibrations: she was afraid there was trouble there. The silence of such a busy entity at dusk on the day of a funeral was almost uncanny, and she shuddered in her warm coat.

"You're cold," John said with concern. "Come, there should be a fire in the parlor."

"I have some things to do upstairs."

"Warm yourself first. Your fires will have burned out up there. Give your mother a chance to get them started again."

She allowed herself to be persuaded into the parlor, in spite of everything that was on her mind and the things she wanted to think about. They warmed their hands at the crackling fireplace, staring at the familiar porcelain figurines on the mantel without seeing them.

"Is your mother going to stay in the nursery?" John asked suddenly. "It might upset her awfully."

"I don't know. I don't even know what Mother will do here, now. John, do you think we'll be here at all?"

"Who? You and your mother? Good heavens, Rosaleen, how can you ask such a thing? You know how much my mother depends on yours. Do you think she'd actually let her go? I suspect she'll be kept on as a sort of companion, if nothing else. Forget it, my dear, you've nothing to worry about."

"Maybe not. What a terrible day. Though things weren't bad at Uncle Brian's, I guess. Mother's mind wasn't with us all the time, I'm afraid. She's sadder than I've ever seen her."

"Yes. It'll take her a while to get over Philip, though she brightened a little when... Rosaleen, may we talk for a moment? Not about Philip or our mothers. I don't get to talk to you nearly enough. And there's something I've wanted to say for so long. I hope you won't laugh at me."

"Why would I do that?" she asked, glancing at him for the first time since they had come into the parlor. His face was tense, and he could not meet her eyes, but she hardly noticed. She was tired, a little confused: angry with Darin for staying in San Francisco, elated about his eventual return. When John put his hand under her elbow and guided her to the velvet sofa, she complied without question, sitting down beside him.

"As you know, I'll graduate in a few months. I'll be of age in March, you know. Rosaleen, I think you're the most beautiful girl I've ever seen. I love you. I've loved you for as long as I can remember. Will you marry me after graduation and go to Europe with me?"

Rosaleen was speechless. She had never realized his feelings, never in her life considered such a proposal. She wanted to refuse him immediately, because her mind was full of Darin. But she was flattered, and she did not want to hurt John's feelings. "I don't know what to say. I never dreamed..."

"Well, at least, you didn't laugh," he said with relief. "I don't expect you to answer right now, Rosaleen. Wait until graduation, if you want. But let me know by then, please." His words came in a nervous torrent, as though he had lost control of his tongue, a situation Rosaleen recognized only too well, and she felt sorry for him.

"I'm all mixed up right now," she said as kindly as possible. "I didn't expect this, John. I..."

"I'm sorry. I felt I had to tell you, now, before Darin comes home. I know it's Darin: I've always known. But I want you to think about it a lot. He isn't the right man for you, Rosaleen. He's restless and he likes his freedom. Overlooking the fact that he's your cousin—because cousins *do* marry sometimes—I'm afraid he'll ruin your life. And I can't stand by and see that happen. I love you too much." He put his hand over hers, and she could feel it shaking. "If you marry me, you'll have everything I can give you, Rosaleen. Not just material things, which really don't matter much. You'll have all of my love, all the time—for the rest of our lives. I'll be there when you need me. You'll have security and contentment. That may not sound very exciting, but I think contentment is happiness."

"It all sounds very nice," she said helplessly. "But I can't even think right now. I'm tired, John. All mixed up. It was dear of you to say this. I won't forget it. I promise. There are months and months to think of it, aren't there? I'll give you my answer this summer."

"After he comes home." He nodded. "I suppose it has to be that way. I panicked when I heard he was in the country: I've thought about it so long. You're so *beautiful*, Rosaleen, and I'm afraid he'll think so, too."

Chapter 20

HE WAS tall and confident. His small, beaked cap, pushed jauntily to the back of his head, revealed curls so black that they did not catch the sunlight. With his fair skin tanned by wind and weather, he could have been a sailor from the Mediterranean, except for the startling blueness of his eyes beneath strongly arched brows. Instead of timorously approaching the servants' entrance, he sauntered up to the front door of the Maddigan house and lifted the lion-head knocker heavily several times. A young man with vast experience of the world and its manners and customs, he no longer respected the difference between classes, but felt he was the equal of any man alive. Standing in the hallway, hat in hand, he looked without curiosity at the room to which he had never before been admitted.

Rosaleen rushed down the stairs, stopping for a moment to look at him, while she tried to still her leaping heart. Then, lifting her billowing skirts, she called his name and ran breathlessly into his arms.

"Darin! Oh, Darin! I thought you'd never come, or I wouldn't be home when you did! I thought...How lucky you arrived on Sunday!"

He tipped her chin back to study her face, a half-smile on his lips. "I didn't," he confessed. "I just got around to seeing you."

Rosaleen's eyes, so much like his own, snapped open

widely, and she flushed. "How long have you been in town?" she demanded. "It's bad enough you wrote to your father instead of me!"

He pressed her to him and laughed warmly. "I got home yesterday afternoon. Pa told me you worked late, so I waited until this morning to see you. And what a sight you are, Rosie!" Holding her away from him, he let his gaze scan her from face to waist and back again. "My God," he said wonderingly, "you even have your mother's figure! Now, there's a miracle."

She had thought he was admiring the dress she had made so carefully, without realizing that his interest was engaged by her figure. "My mother's...?" she began, in an attempt to feign modesty, but her tongue spoke instead. "I have not! It's my own! Mother's waist is much larger than mine."

"It wasn't always," he mused. "I had a terrible fixation on your mother once. No, it was really on her figure," he clarified. "And, until this moment, I haven't seen its like again."

"Darin, you're terrible!" she cried, her vanity and jealousy fighting; then she laughed. "You haven't changed much! There are those who always thought you were terrible."

"Reverend Mother," he said, his eyes twinkling. "She did me a great favor. And, I believe to God, she was right. If you find me shocking, it's because I don't beat about the bush. I never have, really, except with you. I don't even have time for that, now. You'll have to accept me as I am."

His voice had reached a serious level as he spoke, and with the banter over, they grew silent. Their eyes met and clung, as they had in the past, but this time Rosaleen felt the difference and knew he did, too. The love they had confessed so many times in letters was difficult to speak, but the gaze between them was deep and intense. In another moment, their lips would have met with abandon, but they heard footsteps on the marble floor.

"Darin? Is that you, Darin?" John's voice asked. "Well, I'll be damned! We were expecting you, but not this soon."

While the two young men shook hands, Rosaleen turned away to control the sudden blush that made her face burn. To kiss Darin here would be indiscreet, anyway, she told herself: if John had not interfered, it might have been her mother. She did not want to face her mother yet.

"No," John was saying. "It's been a most peculiar summer, really. Matthew didn't want to leave Boston. Harry's dug in at the laboratory, and, well, I'm supposed to sail for Europe soon. Mother didn't want to go to the Cape alone, so everyone's here for once. Besides, the Cape lost its appeal after Rosaleen started working. Things were boring there without her."

"John was supposed to start his trip right after graduation," Rosaleen said, turning back to them in control again. "He's been dawdling around, reading everything he can about Europe."

"Well, no hurry, is there? As a matter of fact, I'm glad I didn't leave. Here's Darin, who's seen it all! I can get it right from the horse's mouth."

"I can tell you what's not in the books," Darin said, dismissing him with a smile. "It's Aunt Mary I should be talking to now, though. Is she at home?"

"She's with Mother," John said. "I'll get her. Why don't you go into the parlor where you'll be more comfortable? And, oh," he said turning back to them at the foot of the stairs, "Rosaleen and I were having a picnic this afternoon. Would you like to come along?"

Darin shrugged slightly. "That'd be nice," he said. "Thank you." Then, to Rosaleen, as they walked to the parlor, "Sure Johnny's grown into an amiable fellow, hasn't he? The cat had his tongue when I knew him."

"He doesn't like to be called that now," Rosaleen said, opening the heavy red drapes, which had been closed against the sun. "He's *John*. And he doesn't like to be called 'old' John, either. He always hated it."

"I don't remember calling him anything. He was usually off somewhere with a book. Am I wrong, or does he fancy you? Not that I'd blame him in the least."

"Let's not talk about him," Rosaleen said. "I want to hear what you've been up to."

"I told you in my letters, everything I should. And more besides, if you remember. Come here, Rosie."

Their gazes met, and she looked away quickly: her mother would walk in at any moment. Indicating the armchair for him, she sat down on the settee, noting the twinkle of comprehension in his eyes. "You're marvelous," he said softly. "Just as devious as ever. They'll have to know sometime."

She nodded. "Later. Not the first few minutes you're here. I haven't breathed a word, you see. I've kept everything to myself. It was even more precious that way. I prayed for you every night, Darin. Every day you were away wasted a day of my life."

"Indeed?" He smiled, raising his eyebrows. "Are they numbered, then? We have our whole lives before us, Rosie, darling."

Unable to express her dark fears of a short life, she remained silent, staring at her hands in her lap, and Darin apparently misunderstood her attitude.

"Were you and John going on this famous picnic alone, then?" he asked.

She shook her head. "Kevin's taking us. The only time we go anywhere alone is when we go ice-skating. Otherwise, someone always seems to be about, either Kevin or Bridie, or both. Laura and Mother aren't sure we're just good friends, I guess."

He grinned at her appraisal of the situation. "More mischief can happen on the grass than on an icy pond, dear Rosie. Kevin can't be much of a duenna, though. He was quite a heller when I knew him."

"Darin!" she whispered. "You really must watch your tongue. And as for Kevin, he's married and quite settled and respectable, now."

He gave a mock shudder. "Is that what happens? Sure it sounds like a dreadful fate."

She considered him for a moment with narrowed eyes. "You really are the most dreadful person. You don't take anything seriously."

Before he could reply, Mary rushed into the parlor and approached him with open arms. "Darin, darlin'! Sure it's been far too long," she cried, smiling, as he rose to embrace her, too. "Would you look at the height of him? Oh, you're a fine beautiful lad, to be sure! You look like your father, many years ago."

"Aunt Mary!" he said, holding her at arm's length, as he'd done with Rosaleen. "You're looking very fine yourself, lass, and no more uniform. It never suited you. It was too stiff!"

In her new position as Laura's companion, Mary had been asked to abandon her black uniform and starched apron, and she wore neutral, ladylike frocks selected by Laura. Because of the summer heat, she wore a light cotton with a small gray-and-white flower print, with collar and cuffs of sheer white lawn. Rosaleen observed that the gray in Mary's dress matched that in her hair, and though her waist had widened, her bosom was still full and high. Since Darin's earlier remark about her mother's appearance, she had experienced a vague jealousy, which was laid to rest when she saw them together. Her mother looked old, to her eyes, and Darin tall and strong and young.

"You've seen your father, then," Mary asked. "Oh, I'm sure he was happy at the sight of you!"

"Of course. He closed the bar." Darin smiled. "We lifted a few of your own in the parlor."

"Did he talk to you at all about your poor mother?" Mary asked, suddenly serious, casting a pall on the reunion. "I used to go see her as often as possible, Darin, but it was no help at all. I've been only once in the past two years. She just doesn't know me."

Releasing her from his arms, Darin turned toward the mantel and rested one arm there, staring down at the clean-swept, unused hearth. "As a matter of fact, he had the heart not to speak of her," he said. "He behaves like she's dead and gone, and it's the same thing, isn't it? There was no love between any of us when she was sane—if she ever was. There's less between us now," he finished, facing his aunt again and looking her directly in the eyes. "I've no intention of going there, Aunt Mary. I want you to know that straightaway."

Mary hesitated only a moment. "Maybe if she saw you, Darin... Sure, it's a terrible place, and I'd like to have her out of there."

He shook his head. "If she saw me, she'd probably go crazy again. That's how much she cared for me. Michael was the one she wanted. It was his leaving that set her off. Paddy and I discussed it, and neither of us feels any guilt. And, if you'll be so kind, I don't want any laid on me, either."

"We all feel it," Mary replied, bowing her head, "in one way or another, I guess. It isn't easy to have someone in your family...leave like that. I keep thinking, if we'd only done more. But," she said and sighed, squaring her shoulders and abandoning the sad subject, "there seems nothing we can do, now. Have you heard nothing of Michael at all?"

"No, I stopped asking, finally. He could be dead, I suppose. At first I thought we'd hear that, if it were so. But, knowing Michael, there's a good chance he didn't give any home address when he signed on."

"But he was just a boy!" Mary protested. "Surely they'd have asked about his family?"

"With all the orphans on the street at that time?" Darin asked, shaking his head. "It was during the famine, remember. I like to think he settled on one of the Pacific islands, like so many sailors have. I don't believe we'll ever know."

"And Padraig? What's he doing out there in San Francisco?"

Darin laughed suddenly. "He owns a bar. What else do you think he'd be doing, but the only thing he knew? He's quite happy and business is good. It's a very wicked city," he added, smiling in a manner to confirm it.

"Is he married?" Mary asked with concern.

"No," he replied and, when he saw her expression of dejection, "Aunt Mary, you should know that Irishmen never rush into marriage until they're caught. Look at our fine Liam! He'll never be rushed into it at all. A priest, for God's sake."

"There are worse things," Mary said, beginning to bridle. "In the old days, boys married young, when they should. Sure, your father was only a lad of twenty. Back home—"

He walked forward with a smile and hugged her again. "Back home, men needed extra hands for the fields, darlin', and bred so many there wasn't food to put in them when the bad times came. Don't worry about me, Aunt Mary. My time's at hand, as the Good Lord said. Now, where's John and the grand picnic hamper he should have? We're all going on a picnic, Aunt Mary, though I don't know where."

"On the Charles," Rosaleen volunteered, rising quickly. "We go out beyond Cambridge, where it's countryside. I'll get John."

Mary's gaze followed her daughter until she had left the room. "She's vain and flighty and I worry about her," she said.

"Well, love, you don't have to worry today," Darin said, squeezing her around the waist. "You've a built-in chaperon."

She smiled up at him. "So I have. With you along, I can rest my mind. You'll not be needing Kevin at all. Sure, it's good to have you home, darlin'."

The sight of him unsettled Mary more than she revealed: it was like seeing Brian again over thirty years ago, when she sat on the stone fence by the hedgerows waiting for him to come down the path. She could hardly remember being so young, so full of love. She had deliberately put the moments of passion she had felt out of her mind forever. A cruel fate had taken even that from her. She loved Brian in a quiet, settled way, now: if he felt the same way about her, there was no way of knowing. They had never mentioned their feelings again, or given them the least expression, since the day Doirin was taken away.

If Doirin had died instead, perhaps it would be different: though they could never marry, or be lovers, there might at least have been a touch of the hand, a kiss on the cheek between them; perhaps it would have been a living torment, but it would have been preferable to the guilt they felt regarding Doirin. Nothing had been the same since the day her sister was carried away, calling for Brian.

Mary tried to keep busy and active to keep from going over the whole thing like an endless circle in her mind, but the sight of Darin, so tall and young, stirred emotions in her she had believed to be dead. She stayed in the parlor for a long time, deep in thought. The pain of it was not so terrible, now; for that, she felt she should be grateful, but she knew she was not. Even the pain of love was better than no love at all. She let the old pictures rise in her mind, to tempt herself into passionate despair once again, but they did not have the same effect as they once had. The part of her that should be filled with loving a man was barren: guilt had washed all romance from her life.

When she pondered her sister's madness, which she often did, she could not really find what she and Brian had done to contribute to it, unless it was in ways more subtle than she could comprehend. Perhaps, years ago, Doirin realized she did not have her husband's love, and her mental state had plummeted from there. There was no way to know. The one person who could have told them no longer spoke at all.

Mary wanted a better, fuller life for Rosaleen, one such as Veronica, through sheer persistence, had attained. None of it had been easy, of course, with the built-in biases of Bostonians; but Veronica had overcome even that, with her sweetness and devotion. She had helped her husband become a respected merchant, though he would have been more respected if he were a Gentile. Veronica had many friends of both faiths, and her children were the happiest Mary had ever seen. In spite of her frailty, Veronica had borne three, all of them girls, and they were devoted to their parents. They would never show the ingratitude she had heard in this room today.

As she grew older, Mary felt a certain bitterness about most children. Only Philip, in his happy innocence, had been constant. Rosaleen's affection was rarely seen: the girl had her desperate most of the time. The fatal Noonan beauty and charm were on her, but she did not seem to have Veronica's goodness and compassion to go with it. Mary seldom saw Liam. When she did, his kiss on the cheek was abstract and cool, though he professed to love her, had to tell himself he did, anyway, to obey all the commandments. Laura's boys, too, had flown from her like leaves in the autumn: they might as well have gone away like Doirin's. Matthew and Harry were so caught up in their rounds of social activities and work that sometimes their mother did not see them for days, even at dinner. John was a puzzle. Though always at home, since he had finished college, he was usually in the library or his own room. He never visited his mother's suite. But Mary understood something about that. Only John had never forgiven his mother's secretiveness about Philip, living and dead, though there seemed to be more to it than that. Mary, who had been deeply troubled about Philip's lack of attention from his mother, and the way he was hidden away, had come to terms with it. After all, her family was the same way about Doirin; and the Maddigans had a social position to maintain, as well.

Mothers only wanted their children to profit by what they had learned through living, to follow a path with the most contentment at the end. Why did none of them listen? Rosaleen was at a dangerous age, too beautiful to live in a house with three young men of a different social level. She must be watched carefully, or she might find herself ruined: both Mary and Laura agreed on this, though Laura was only worried about her sons getting into some scandalous entanglement. Yes, it was time Rosaleen was married, and as soon as possible. But the girl scoffed at her mother's suggestions of going to church parties and Irish socials in the North End, the only place she would find the proper kind of husband, both Irish and Catholic...and she could have her choice of any of them. Her daughter was at a serious time of her life, and Mary did not know how to handle her.

With a sigh, Mary rose from the deep chair, with her hand on her back, which ached sometimes now. Without thinking, she went to the window and drew the red plush drapes so the sun would not discolor the furniture and stood for a moment with both hands on the drapes.

"My mother was right," she said almost aloud. "It's a thankless job, to be sure."

* * *

"I don't like to dance with my arms all stiff at my sides," Rosaleen said cheerfully, as she spread out the cloth on the lawn near the river and opened the hamper, addressing John and Darin who were assisting. "The jig and the reel aren't for me! I'd rather float around a ballroom in a man's arms, with my skirts swirling around me. I consider *that* dancing! Mother just aggravates me to death with her talk of Irish halls and those murderous pipes!"

"How many ballrooms have you graced, then?" Darin asked, settling himself next to her on the grass.

She looked at him and laughed. "None, silly! You know I wouldn't fit in there. John, how many seamstresses attend the grand Boston parties?"

"Perhaps more should," he said noncommittally. "I don't like that sort of thing myself, but I'm certain you'd be a sensation, Rosaleen. We must arrange it sometime."

"Oh, you don't even dance!" she said, turning again to Darin. "Harry and I dance sometimes at home. Unfortunately, no one in the family's musical, so he has to hum the music."

"You could ask Mother to play," John suggested. "I haven't heard her do it for years."

"That would be a mistake." Rosaleen smiled. "She'd have at least a litter of kittens if she knew we were dancing! Laura's steadfast in keeping her sons away from me when I'm home at all," she told Darin. "I don't know whose virtue she's protecting."

"Yours, of course." John smiled. "It's the female of the species that must be protected. All men are beasts."

They laughed at the remark, especially coming from shy, bookish John. "I always know I'm safe with you, dear," Rosaleen said, tapping his hand.

"Now there's an insult." Darin grinned. "Sure you aren't going to put up with it, John?"

John shrugged. "It doesn't matter. What's spoken in blessed innocence can't be insulting. Rosaleen only thinks she knows me."

"Ah, you've a dark side, then?" Darin teased gently, with a glance at Rosaleen. "But, sure, you've never been far away from this Puritan town."

"They had a dark side, too, I suspect," John said idly, pouring the lemonade. "Don't be condescending, Darin. I probably know more about life than you do, when it comes right down to it. You've traveled a lot, but do you know what

317

you've seen? Are you informed about what's going on in the world?"

Darin rubbed his smooth chin. "I know what I've seen, but we'd probably see things differently. I read the papers, if that's what you mean. Since I left the whaler, I've seen some of it firsthand. A few years back, we put into Constantinople during the Crimean War. I was in India before the mutiny that put it under crown rule. My God, but the English are busy causing trouble all over the world! One day I'm sure they'll have their own."

John was visibly impressed, and Rosaleen was proud of Darin, though the subjects did not interest her much. She would much rather both men lavished all their attention on her: after all, that was why she had taken so much trouble making her dress. So she felt she must join in the conversation, to call attention to herself and demonstrate that she was clever, too.

"They will have," she sparkled, picking up Darin's remark about the British, "if Mother and Uncle Brian have anything to do with it! Did you know they're still putting money into some revolutionary cause? It started as a famine fund, and now they're sending guns!"

The remark did not have the desired effect upon Darin, who narrowed his eyes thoughtfully. "If it ever comes, I want to be there."

"In Ireland?" she asked, horrified. "I'd never go back there! Never! I've tried to forget all about it."

"So have I. But if it came to fighting for what was always ours—I'd go, for that."

"Chicken?" John asked, passing the plate. His diversion was successful: the heroic Celt disappeared as the hungry sailor reached for a drumstick. But Rosaleen remained troubled by Darin's talk of fighting and dying.

"Life's too short to worry about such things," she said moodily, shivering slightly. John rose quickly to put her shawl around her shoulders.

"This is no talk for girls," John observed. "The thought of war's enough to make them shiver on a warm day. Tell me, Darin, what do you plan to do now? Will you be in Boston for a while, or is it back to sea again?"

"The sea's my livelihood, but I'll be around for some time," Darin replied, watching John and Rosaleen together. "Is there nothing stronger than lemonade in that hamper?" he asked, tossing the contents of his glass away. "You didn't happen to bring any beer, John?"

"Sorry, we don't keep it on hand: I didn't think. And there's no place around here to buy it, either."

"Don't worry, it's a fine picnic," Darin said, flushing. "You wanted to hear about some of the places I've visited, John, in preparation for your own trip. When are you leaving?"

"I'll be around for a while," John said, almost echoing the other's words. "I plan to spend a year abroad, mostly in the Mediterranean, after I visit France, of course. But I'm in no particular hurry. It'll still be there when I decide to go."

Rosaleen thought it was a wretched picnic and nearly said so. At another time, she might have enjoyed the thrusts and parries of the two young men, but today she wanted to be alone with Darin, for whom she had waited so long. While they talked about Naples, and Syracuse, Athens and Crete, she tried to think of some way to end the excursion. Suddenly, her face brightened.

"Darin," she interrupted at the first chance, "have you been to see Veronica yet? She has the most adorable family."

He understood the suggestion at once. "I wanted to see her this afternoon. She was always so good to us, wasn't she? Our Aunt Veronica," he said to John, "is a very fine, but delicate, lady. She'll take it amiss, I'm afraid, if I don't see her today."

"Of course," John said, and Rosaleen knew he understood more than he should. "You must meet your family obligations. We can continue our discussion another time."

Darin drove the buggy to the Maddigan house, where they parted with it and John. Rosaleen could feel John staring after them as they walked down the hill toward the Common. The awareness made her feel wretched, but she did not know what else to do. She wanted to reach for Darin's hand: she restrained herself, walking at his side in silence.

"You didn't tell me he was in love with you," Darin said softly, moving his hand to enfold hers. "Is he a rich boy being gallant to have his way, or has he declared himself to you?"

She swallowed hard. She had not wanted to tell him of John's proposal, for fear Darin would think he had less to offer her. Still, John was a good person, and her friend.

"He asked me to marry him. It isn't the way you think."

"Good," he said, his hand tightening on her. "I like the fellow. I wouldn't want to kill him. Rosie, I love you: I didn't know how much until today."

"You know how much I love you."

319

He drew in his breath and let it out slowly. "Yes, I think I do. But love isn't always wise, is it? You'd be missing a fine life by refusing him. He can give you everything."

She stopped walking and looked up into his face, feeling the blue magic of his eyes and not avoiding it. "You're the only one who can give me what I want, Darin. Things don't mean that much to me. I only need you."

During the week, Darin met Rosaleen every night at Madame Hurotte's and walked her home, through the green Common and up the hill, leaving her in the brick-bounded back garden, with his kisses burning on her face. They would have only part of the next Sunday together, because there was a family dinner at Veronica's house, which both of them had to attend. Saturday night, on the way home, they sat together in the Common as usual, and talked.

"Shall we tell the family about our marriage tomorrow, then? Everyone will be together, and we won't have to say it more than once," Darin asked.

The tone of his voice told her he was not looking forward to the announcement any more than she, and she could not understand their mutual reluctance to share their secret.

"I don't think they'll be so delighted," she said. "I've heard remarks about cousins marrying."

"So have I," he said. "My mother said something once about their children being odd."

"That's nonsense!" she said quickly. "John said cousins can marry. And he told me there's every reason to believe that the Egyptian pharaohs married their own *sisters*." She shuddered.

"Did anything bad happen?"

"I don't know," she said lamely. "He said the mistakes could have been thrown in the Nile."

Darin laughed, breaking the tension. "I shouldn't, but I like that fellow. All right. Let'd do it this way, Rosie. We'll get everything arranged—the license and the priest—and then we'll let them know. Their objections won't come to much in the face of all that."

"Yes, that's fine." She nodded eagerly. "Is there any way we can get away from Veronica's tomorrow, to have some time to ourselves? I can't be in the same room with you without it showing in my face."

He thought for a moment. "We'll have to spend a few hours

there. But after dinner, I'll get us away somehow, darling. Leave it to me."

The solution to the problem was simple and natural, aided by Liam's departure at four o'clock, shortly after dinner, to return to his Catholic college out of town. As Liam bent to kiss his mother goodbye, Darin stretched and rose from his chair, and began pacing the room restlessly.

"That was a grand dinner, Aunt Veronica, dear, but with the heat in this room, I think it'll put me to sleep for sure. Wait up, Liam, I'll have a walk with you." Then, turning to Rosaleen, Darin asked, "Rosie, how'd you like to have a look at my ship? There's plenty of light left yet. We could get to East Boston and back by horse tram in a couple of hours. It's grand and cool down by the water, at the wharf."

Her face full of childish delight, she asked Mary, "Oh, Mother, may I? You wouldn't mind, would you, Aunt Veronica? I've never been on one of Darin's ships before."

"Of course not, darlin'." Veronica smiled indulgently as she helped the maid clear the table. "Sure, you've little enough time for outings, working the hours you do. Just run along, the both of you, and have a nice time. You don't mind, Mary?" she asked mildly. "The young people have too much energy to be cooped up too long at family gatherings. They should enjoy themselves while Darin's at home. God knows when we'll see the lad again."

Mary nodded agreement. "Be sure to take your shawl, Rosaleen. It can get chilly by the water in the evening."

Rosaleen heard their burst of laughter as she closed the door behind her, and her mother's amused voice saying, "By all the Apostles, the two of them are Noonan, through and through! You wouldn't think the O'Shea girls had a hand in it at all."

They walked with Liam, whose narrow shoulders hunched in his dark suit of cloth heavy enough to make a saint perspire: he needed only a clerical collar to look completely like a priest, though he was not a seminarian yet, but only teaching at his college. When their paths divided to take separate buses, he held out his hand stiffly to Darin.

"Good to have you back," Liam said tightly, his pale face serious. "I'm sure we'll see each other again before you leave."

"Indeed to God, we will." Darin grinned. "I hope you didn't take anything I said this afternoon amiss, Liam. I'm as good a Catholic as I ever was. It's just the idea of your becoming a priest that set my tongue wagging."

"I considered the source," Liam responded aloofly. "You've never shown any respect for the clergy or the nuns. Rosaleen," he said, turning his attention to her, "get home early enough to keep Mother from worrying."

"Yes, Father," she teased. "And don't be angry, Liam, you know there's no harm in Darin at all."

"Have a nice time and get home early," her brother repeated before running to catch his horse-drawn bus. He was barely out of earshot before Darin laughed.

"Jesus! What a little prig he's become since he got the calling from heaven! Of course, he always was an odd sort of fellow. How can you bear him at all?"

"I don't see much of him," she said without thinking, adding quickly, "I'm very proud of him! He's made his way through the Catholic college on scholarships, and now he's teaching to earn the money to go to a seminary abroad. It's a pity, for Mother's sake, there isn't one in Boston. And, Darin, you were the terrible fellow today, with all those jokes about priests! You can't blame him for being offended. I thought the Devil had got into you, myself."

He took her hand, and they walked along the cobbles to their bus stop. "Being around him made me nervous. It's such an unnatural kind of life. Sure, he made me feel the way one of my shipmates did, when I knew he liked boys."

They walked in silence for a few minutes, enjoying the living warmth that flowed between their hands. "Why shouldn't your shipmate like boys?" Rosaleen asked suddenly. "I think that's nice of him."

"Forget it, darling," he said, realizing, not for the first time, the depth of her innocence. "I shouldn't have said that. You know, Rosaleen, I really haven't lost my religion. In fact, I didn't know how important it was until I went away. In a lonely port, after months at sea, there was always one place I knew I'd feel at home: a Catholic church. I'll wager I spent more time in church when I was away than I did the whole time I was here! And I received the sacraments, too, whenever I could. There were a few hassles in the confessional along the way."

"What about?" she asked directly.

"Well, the priests spoke different languages in all those ports," he said quickly. "Communication was difficult to hilarious."

"Oh." She sighed. "I thought you meant you'd sinned so much!"

322

"Sinned?" he asked, as though the word were unfamiliar. "I only broke the usual commandments, Rosie, dear. You know how I curse. And it's difficult to respect my mother, no matter how hard I try. I didn't commit *adultery* or covet anyone's wife, if that's what you're after. As far as the commandments go, I'm a pretty decent fellow, I guess. And everything that's left over, after the commandments, I don't consider sinning at all. I'm a Catholic *fundamentalist*, you might say." He grinned. "I accept the literal word and nothing that's merely implied."

She was greatly relieved that he was still a good Catholic: it would be a point in his favor when they went to see a priest about getting married.

Chapter 21

WHITE CLOUDS moved against the blue sky like the billowing sails of the clipper they watched on the horizon, beyond the forest of masts in the harbor. Rosaleen had thrown her light shawl over her shoulders, and her hair blew in the salt wind from the sea, touching Darin's face as they stood close together at the wooden railing overlooking the piers. As Darin slipped his arm around her narrow waist, beneath her shawl, its warmth penetrated the light fabric of her fluttering dress, communicating something to her that, until now, she had felt only in daydreams, a melting in the soul, a feeling of warm honey pouring downward from her heart. If she had been with anyone else, she would have found the sensations alarming; but with Darin, she knew it was natural and right, though she tried to steady the quickness of her breath.

"Rosie," he said softly, in the lilting voice to which she was so accustomed, "I do believe we should make our arrangements as soon as possible, darling. There's just so much a man can stand and remain honorable."

Then she realized he was experiencing the same emotions she was fighting back. She knew little of men and their passions. When John had told her about making love and having babies, he had not mentioned these feelings, though he had been delicate and almost poetic. But now she recognized the urgency of desire, its almost frightening compulsion, wondering that no one ever spoke of it, for it was by far the loveliest thing that had ever happened to her.

"Yes," she said quietly. "We'll go to the rectory as soon as possible. I'll go to work late one day...say I'm sick or something. Oh, Darin, I want you to kiss me! I want you to hold me."

"I think we better walk around a bit," he said, withdrawing his hand reluctantly. "I haven't shown you the different ships yet, except for the clipper leaving for Europe. You won't find any whalers here. There aren't many of them about in New Bedford now, either, now that there's petroleum, thank God. Whaling was a bloody business and one I've been glad to be away from for the past few years."

She listened, almost without hearing, as he pointed out the various wooden ships and explained about their riggings. Even his voice had a magical quality which did nothing to subdue the wonderful, half-frightening feelings she was experiencing, without even touching his hand. Instead of banishing the fire within her, though, she found herself nurturing its wonder by studying his face. How beautiful he was, with his perfect features and fine lips, the clear deep-blue eyes, the line of his hair around his ears; how tall and athletic, with his catlike, rolling stride, as though, even now, he were balancing himself on the deck of a ship. She not only loved him, as she always had, she loved him madly, insatiably, could not have enough of him, wanted to throw herself in his strong arms and hold him closer than she ever had, and the feeling was as heady as too much wine, as invigorating as the sea air. Dusk was coming down as he put his arm around her without realizing what his touch did to her.

"Where's your ship?" she asked, after a long silence. "I thought you were going to show it to me."

"I am. I thought we'd just stop at the tavern up ahead," he said, indicating the painted wooden sign extending from the frame building, "and have some refreshment. I'm fair dying of thirst. It may not look it, but it's respectable enough. It caters mostly to passengers; otherwise I wouldn't take you in there."

"I'd like a cup of tea. The breeze is getting chilly."

"They've something better—a fine mulled cider. It's a great treat, Rosie." He smiled, putting his arm beneath her elbow to guide her through the door. The place was not as clean as Uncle Brian's pub, but there were no sailors hanging about, either: the few people sitting at the stark tables did not appear to be passengers, at the moment, but the only seamen were officers.

The cider, served hot in a pewter mug with a cinnamon stick, was delicious, and Rosaleen noticed its hardness the moment it touched her tongue. She drank it slowly so that her mug was still half full when Darin ordered another for himself.

"Why do Irishmen drink so much?" she asked, studying the lovely picture he made across from her. "Everyone just takes it for granted. There are cartoons in the newspaper of 'Paddy,' with a jar in one hand, a cigar in the other, and an unshaven jutting chin...looking like an ape."

"Is it my habits or my appearance you're commenting on?" he said and grinned; then, more seriously, "I think it's a habit developed in the old country, where the mists were cold and life not all that pleasant. Thank God the women don't do it that often, or we'd have no one to keep us respectable at all. Do you disapprove of my drinking, then, Rosie?"

"I approve of everything about you." She smiled lovingly. "I suppose I shouldn't, with the example of my father before me."

"I'd never do that to you," he said, leaning forward to touch her hand. As he did so, his knees inadvertently pressed against hers under the table, and the meeting of their eyes was deep and dangerous. He pulled his legs back quickly.

"If you're finished with your drink, we'd better take a quick look at my ship. It's getting dark out, and I don't want to get you home too late."

Except for the light from the cabins of some of the docked vessels, and an occasional lantern swinging on deck, the harbor was wrapped in the first gray darkness. Rosaleen heard a sailor singing on one of the vessels they passed; aside from that, there was only the sound of the snapping breeze against rolled canvas and the creaking of wood. She began to feel slightly nervous in this dark, unfamiliar place.

"Darin, is it safe here?" she asked, looking around more carefully. "It's so deserted and quiet."

"Safe in the port of Boston?" he laughed. "Oh, darling, you don't know how safe it really is! Oh, there may be a few rough lads about, but they're nothing to worry about at this early hour. If you could see some of the ports I've been in, you'd realize that those in New England are the tamest in the world."

In spite of his reassurance, she moved closer to him. Rosaleen was too fond of life to put herself in peril, especially just a few days before her marriage, the sweet goal she had looked forward to for so long.

"Sure, nothing's going to hurt you," he said softly. "My ship's right here—isn't she a beauty? And I know everyone on board. Here, give me your hand, I'll lead you down the gangway; the tide's out and she's lying low."

Rosaleen did not doubt that it was a most remarkable ship, because Darin told her so: actually, it seemed pretty much like all the others to her, as they toured the deck and bridge and gazed upward in the growing darkness at the tall masts. The cry of a seagull made her jump slightly.

"I'll show you the cabins—the captain's, the mate's, and my little one—the second mate's. Maybe you'll feel less uneasy down there."

"Below deck?" she asked, suddenly claustrophobic with old, half-forgotten memories. "Darin, I don't think I can."

He looked at her in surprise at first, but his perception was sharp and he pulled her to him in an embrace. "No, no, it isn't like that ship was at all! It's really quite homey and pleasant, Rosie. God, do you think I'd bring you here to show you the hold? We only stow cargo there."

Her anxiety lessened by his soothing voice, she accompanied him, still fighting the terrible memories of that other ship. They were startled by a sudden light glaring in their faces and the sharp words of the watch, holding a lantern in front of them.

"Put that down, you bloody idjut!" Darin commanded. When the light was lowered, Rosaleen saw a bearded man in a striped shirt with small brown eyes, glowing like a rat's.

"Ah, it's you, sir." The seaman smiled, revealing several missing teeth. "I'm alone on watch. You startled me: no one's due back until morning. But I see you have a lady with you." His voice was syrupy with implication. "So, I won't be botherin' you again."

"I'm showing my cousin the ship," Darin said firmly, but his tone did not discourage the sailor's widening smile and rakishly raised eyebrows.

"Your cousin, is it?" he said, raising the lantern again. The smile disappeared suddenly from his face. "By God, it is! I beg your pardon, sir."

Rosaleen was relieved to be away from him; as they descended the polished wooden stairs, the striped shirt still glimmered before her eyes. Somewhere in her mind, she saw the shirt picking two small boys up under its arms and knocking their heads together; a dirty, torn striped shirt tossing a bucket of beans and bread into a large metal basin, as though throwing them to pigs. And, finally, she saw many striped shirts standing on a deck behind a small bier covered with a canvas sack, heard her mother murmuring, *"Ashes to ashes, dust to dust..."*

Though Rosaleen was uncertain about the pictures in her mind, they raised terror in her heart. Had such things really happened? She felt light-headed.

"This is the captain's cabin," Darin said, opening a door and taking a lantern off the wall at the foot of the stairs. "Someday I'll have one like it, Rosie. Come in, isn't it fine?"

She nodded, hardly stepping through the door, her vision slightly blurred, the creaking hull rocking beneath her feet. After paying the same homage to the quarters of the mate, she followed Darin to his own insignificant room, which contained a narrow bunk built into the wall, a table, a chair and a shelf of books.

"I feel peculiar," she finally admitted, sinking down on the chair.

"Ah, darling, it was probably the drink and maybe the motion of the ship. I'm sorry. Is it a bad little sailor I'm marrying, then?"

She shook her head emphatically. "I'm not seasick, really."

"I should think not! You and I were the only ones who never got seasick on that terrible voyage twelve years ago."

"Has it been that long?" she asked, pressing her fingers to her temples. "I hardly remember it, yet...there are pictures in my mind, Darin. I don't know if they really happened...not all of them. And, now, suddenly, 'fourteen' comes to mind."

But she remembered what that meant almost immediately, with a flash of fear: the doctors in the hospital the day Doirin was taken away, one of them saying, *"They'll live about fourteen years from the day they arrived in this country."* And it had already been twelve! She was eighteen: she had only two years to live!

Darin was at a complete loss when she burst into tears, a condition he had never dealt with in a grown woman. He went down on his knees before her and embraced her impulsively.

"Darling, darling, please! Is it that old trip you're remembering? I did the same thing when I first set foot on a ship again. It took me weeks to get it out of my mind. I wouldn't have brought you here if I had a brain in my head! I shouldn't have." He began to kiss her tenderly on the cheeks and neck. "Oh, God, will all that always be with us, I wonder?"

Her fears calmed beneath his touch, she began to experience some of the sensations she had felt earlier in the afternoon, and soon she was kissing him passionately, full on the lips, with a rare sort of wildness in her heart. Before he realized what was happening, he was responding, his emotions rushing forward with all the love he felt for her. The hands that had been around her waist moved upward to her breasts, and she responded to his caresses.

"Darin," she whispered, between kisses, "love me. Love me! Oh, darling, make love to me, now."

Their lips parted suddenly, and he drew away from her with wide blue eyes.

"Rosie," he said, breathing heavily, "darling, we're seeing the priest soon. It isn't right. No, I can't, Rosie. As much as I want to, I can't."

"How do we know we'll be here tomorrow?" she murmured. "Oh, Darin, please."

"You're talking daft, my darling," he said. "There's a wildness in you."

"Yes! And it's in you, too. I can feel it, Darin," she cried. "We're so much alike. Are you saying love isn't 'decent'? But that's our parents talking; not us!" She put both hands to the neck of her best dress and, with one motion, pulled it open to the waist; some of its small pearl buttons scattered on the floor. "Look at me, Darin. I'm beautiful; I was made for our loving. I've waited so long!"

He gasped at the sight of her full young breasts, exclaiming softly, "Oh, God. Your skin's like cream, Rosie." Drawing her to him, he kissed what had never been touched, ran his fingers gently over her pale-pink nipples, making her breasts swell with sensations she had not imagined existed, her whole body swooning with surrender like the women the gods had touched in mythology. When he kissed her with his tongue probing her lips, as he had never done before, she felt it an intimation of his body penetrating hers, and she fumbled wildly with his shirt to slip her hands beneath it and feel his naked flesh.

"Oh, God, Rosie, it's good! I've never felt like this before," he said, drawing her down with him to the floor. "I want it to be good for you too—perfect. Let's get out of these clothes, so there'll be nothing between us. Nothing. And no shame in it, either."

"There isn't any shame, there shouldn't be," she whispered, desperately untying her sash, slipping off her full skirt and petticoats, leaving them where they lay beneath her, a cushion against the wooden floor. Completely nude, she felt only the excitement generated by the awed, almost stunned expression in his eyes. While she was undressing, he had discarded his clothing, too, and their bodies met full-length, incredibly smooth and warm, in what was only a prelude to the rest of the hour of lovemaking. When he finally took her, there was one sharp pain, but she was so ecstatic, so completely open to him, that she hardly felt it. All she knew was that he was inside of her, moaning with pleasure, as close as she would ever know him, and that was everything.

As strictly reared as they had been, neither of them had even thought to extinguish the lantern.

Staying out of each other's arms after that night was impossible. Even when he walked her home from work, Darin's arm was tight around her waist, and the kisses in the garden became a torment, because they could not have each other completely. Rosaleen was not surprised when, instead of taking her home, he suggested they stop for a cup of tea at the Noonan flat over the pub: she was grateful he had found a solution. His father always stayed downstairs, waiting bar, until after eleven, and they were alone again, at last. After a few kisses in a close embrace, tea was forgotten, if it had ever really been considered, and they went to Darin's room.

They dared not undress completely, in case they heard Brian's footsteps on the stairs; but their loving was more precious for having been stolen, and they lay together afterward kissing tenderly, caressing each other's face and hair.

"You know we can't go on like this, Rosie," he said at last. "As difficult as it's going to be to face the family, darling, we must get married as soon as we can."

With her face against his neck, beneath the curve of his jaw, Rosaleen was too happy to feel any guilt, but she made a small sound of agreement. Unconsciously, her ears were straining for the sound of Brian's footstep, the possibility of it heightening the moment with a dash of fear: the same sort of fear she felt at the prospect of telling the family they were going to marry.

"I wish we could have this a little longer," she said faintly, "before the explosion. They aren't going to like it at all, Darin."

Darin laughed softly, the sound of it vibrating against her cheek. "You've always been a dreadful little coward, Rosie," he said affectionately. "Sure, you're going to have to straighten your backbone and come to grips with life. You can't avoid unpleasantness forever, darling: only a vacuum has no ripples. At any rate, I'll be here to face this with you."

"As you always have." She smiled with contentment.

"As I hope I always will, sure." He kissed her forehead and let his lips rest there. "We'll do it the way we agreed: everything will be ready for the ceremony before we even tell them. And, so you won't have second thoughts out of fear, we'll take care of it tomorrow."

"Tomorrow?" Rosaleen said, raising her head to peer at his face through the darkness in alarm. "That soon?"

"That soon." He smiled. "Today's Wednesday. Three days for banns, and we could be married this weekend. Don't you want to be married to me, darling?"

"Yes. Oh, yes!" she cried sincerely. "More than anything in the world, Darin! You know how much I love you."

"Grand," he said, rising, pulling her up to sit with him on the edge of the bed. "We'll meet at the church tomorrow morning. Oh, by the way," he said, reaching into his pocket and putting something very small into her palm, closing her fingers over it, "it's one of the buttons from your dress. I found it on the deck of my quarters. Did you get the others sewn on?"

She laughed and kissed him on the cheek. "Of course! I had the rest of the card of them."

"Then I'll keep this one in a special place, darling... to remember," he said.

The spires of the church shone brightly in the sunshine when she hastened to meet him next morning, dressed demurely in her working clothes, a gathered gray cotton skirt and long-sleeved white blouse with a yoke of lace that burst into a small ruff at the neck, banded by black grosgrain ribbon. She saw him from half a block away, sitting pensively on a flat stone in the churchyard, twirling a small bunch of violets, and she nearly ran the remaining distance between them. The sound of her hurried footsteps on the gravel made him look up, and he sprang to his feet to meet her. Entwining hands, they looked into each other's faces. Her eyes were radiant; his were slightly troubled.

"You're the one who looks frightened now," she smiled.

"I didn't sleep a wink last night," he confessed. "Sure, I've never been married before, Rosie. It's a dreadful responsibility, but one I embrace sincerely. Being married to you will be wonderful."

"I want to be your wife," she said, searching his eyes lovingly. "In all the world, you're all I want."

"Well, then," he said, taking a deep breath and glancing toward the church, "this is it, Rosie. Mass isn't over yet; I've been listening to the music. He'll be out soon, sure. D'ya really think we should approach him before he has his breakfast?"

"There are three priests here now." She smiled. "We don't have to wait for the one who's saying Mass! Or are *you* losing your nerve now?"

"Sure, I never had any to lose in this matter," he said, nearly crushing the violets between his hands and becoming suddenly aware of them. "Oh, these are for you!"

He proffered them awkwardly, and she rescued the ragged flowers, taking their bruised petals to her nose.

"They're lovely."

"I wanted to get you red roses: I know they mean love. But the street seller didn't have any, and besides, they'd be so conspicuous."

"These are fine," she said, pinning them at her throat. "Violets mean faithfulness, and that's important, too. Oh!" she cried, puncturing her finger with the corsage pin and putting the wound to her tongue.

"I hope that isn't an omen," he whispered with frightened eyes, and she looked up at him with a laugh.

"Darin, you're *terrified!* And so *Irish*. We left all that behind us, with our lost banshees and fairies! Pricking my finger just meant that I'm nervous, too."

They began to walk toward the rectory, without touching hands. "Rosie?" he asked quietly. "If he asks if we...should we tell him?"

"No; indeed not! It's none of his business."

His eyes smiled slightly. "I think perhaps it is, but, I agree with you. It was too wonderful: something to be kept to ourselves. Even if you didn't..."

She waited, but he did not complete the sentence. "I didn't what, Darin?" she finally had to ask.

He licked his lips nervously. "Nothing...never mind. You'll find out soon enough when we're married."

The heavy oak door of the rectory distracted her from further questions. She waited for him to lift the knocker, and as soon as it struck the wood, her heart began to hammer almost uncontrollably. "I've this terrible feeling," she whispered. "It's like a premonition..."

The rectory housekeeper, a scrawny woman with a neat white collar on her dress and disheveled hair, opened the door and peered at them short-sightedly.

"Yes?"

"We'd like to see a priest," Darin said boldly, adding, "if you please."

"Which priest is it you'd be wanting to see, then? Reverend Father's saying Mass, and Father Aherne's off to the school."

"We'll take anyone that's left, then," Darin said amiably, and they followed her through the door into a chilly little hallway, scented strangely with candles and cabbage. She left them standing there while she went to fetch the priest.

"It'll be Father Donelly, then," Rosaleen said, a note of gloom in her voice. "For some reason, Mother can't bear him, though I've always thought him rather nice-looking, myself."

"D'ya know him well?" Darin followed. "Is he hard-nosed or a liberal sort of man?"

Rosaleen shrugged. "I always avoided him at confession: I don't know. Mother still calls him a 'young idjut,' though he must be at least thirty-five."

She was interrupted by the appearance of the priest himself, tall, heavy-set, with a rather long face and limpid blue eyes. Darin came to attention, sizing the priest up from his fair, thinning hair to his black shoes. Their height was almost equal, and Rosaleen felt very small between them.

"Well, then?" Father Donelly said coolly. "Mrs. Kelly said you asked to see me."

Darin took a deep breath. "We wish to marry," he said firmly, and the priest's expression changed slightly, turning almost to disgust.

"Come in here," he said, opening a door into a small officelike room, dark-paneled, with the sun shining brightly through the lace curtains. Indicating that they should sit down, he took his place behind the desk and opened the drawer to take out some papers. "Very well. Are you both of age?"

They nodded, both speaking their ages at the same time, and Rosaleen felt the muscles over her stomach cramp until she was breathless. She understood why her mother did not like the man: he was a cold fish, indeed. She would have felt more at ease in a doctor's office, being examined for a mortal disease. She wanted to get up and leave, to simply withdraw, taking Darin with her, so they could come back when another priest was at leisure, but she could not do it: such was the control of the Church and its ministers on her life.

"Names?" he asked, with his pen inked and poised over the paper. When neither of them spoke, he looked up at them, repeating, "Names?"

"Darin Noonan," Darin spoke up clearly, on the edge of anger, and Rosaleen said faintly, "Rosaleen Noonan."

There was a cold silence, which made Rosaleen shiver in the lace-shadowed sunlight. The priest put down the pen with deliberation and folded his hands on the desk, his eyes no longer attractive, but a pale, icy blue. "How can that be?" he asked, without looking at them, as though he were in a confessional. "How can you both have the same surname?"

Rosaleen swallowed hard, beginning to feel sick, but Darin said cautiously, "Because we're cousins, Father."

The slap of the priest's hand on the desk was so sharp that it startled them both to their feet. He began to pace the small area between the desk and the window, cradling his chin in one hand, his elbow supported by the other. Then, suddenly, he turned to them. "How close is this relationship? Either you're fourth cousins, with the same name, or you're blithering idiots without any religious training at all!" He narrowed his eyes, as though seeing them for the first time. "But you aren't fourth cousins...you look too much alike. Haven't either of you been to school and received any religious instruction? What, in the name of God, made you come here?"

Rosaleen could not speak, and Darin began, "Father, we know there's some doubt pertaining to the marriage of cousins, but we don't see—"

"You don't *see*...no, you don't see anything at all!" the priest raged, becoming paler, instead of flushing. "I repeat, haven't either of you even learned your basic catechism?"

"Sure, I had some of it in Ireland at the hedge school," Darin said, searching his mind, "and a bit of it, here, but..."

Rosaleen, thoroughly frightened by now, knowing she was

going to hear the worst and wanting to get it over with so they could leave, spoke up for the first time. "I went to St. Mary's, Father. I don't remember anything about cousins."

"'There'll be no marrying 'within the third degree of kindred,'" the priest quoted, narrowing his eyes to see if the words took hold. "Surely you remember that."

She knew the words by rote: the problem was that they had never meant anything to her. It flashed through her mind that as a small child she had thought "kindred" had something to do with kine: pigs. She had never understood the words; and, yes, she had been too busy with the books concealed in her desk to pay any attention to explanations. "The words weren't ever explained," she said. "Father, I swear I didn't know what they meant."

"They mean that cousins can't marry . . . or second cousins. Or even third cousins!" he bellowed. "Anything within that limit is incest! The most ancient and heinous sin of all. You're a credit . . . a real credit . . . to our school: the nuns would be proud of you!"

"Father!" Darin protested angrily. "You've no right to speak to Rosie like that! Sure, she was a fine student, and it isn't her fault, entirely, if she misunderstood something that wasn't properly explained."

"This is outrageous," the priest considered more quietly. "But we must consider its ramifications. Since you want to *marry*, you must believe yourselves in . . . love, or what passes for it, nowadays. You haven't been intimate, have you?" When there was no answer, he said more plainly, "You haven't behaved like animals?"

"Indeed to God, no," Darin said, angered. "We have not behaved like animals!"

"Then my only suggestion is that you never see each other again. I'd report this to your parents, if I knew who they were: apparently, they've been very lax with you. Say," he said suddenly, "you couldn't be related to Liam Noonan, could you?"

"Who's he?" Darin asked quickly.

"I thought not," the priest said, relaxing slightly. "You will not see each other again, alone . . . do you understand me? And I want you both to go to confession and receive absolution, if possible, for this—perhaps *unintentional*—sin. But never forget its seriousness! I also suggest you review the basic tenets of your religion, before you plunge yourselves into hellfire, for sure."

335

Once outside the rectory, Rosaleen was ready to collapse from the war of emotions the priest had unleashed in her. Darin led her, without speaking, to his father's apartment over the pub, where he poured her a small glass of whiskey and a larger one for himself. He had risked Brian's being home, but he had to take her somewhere quiet until both of them recovered from the initial shock of the priest's tirade. To his intense relief, his father had gone out to the Haymarket for produce to supply the restaurant, as he did every Monday morning.

Rosaleen sat on the edge of the couch, taking small sips of the liquor, until she realized that the warmth inside did her good and drank down the rest in one gulp, holding out her glass for more.

Darin shook his head, his eyes serious. "No. It'll make you drunk. You aren't accustomed to it, Rosie."

He pulled up a chair and sat in front of her, waiting for her to speak, but her mind was in such a turmoil that she was dumb for a long time, staring almost frantically into space.

"Rosaleen," he said at last, "we haven't much time before Pa gets back. We have to discuss this, darling." He drew in his breath, as though in pain. "Is it all right, do you suppose, for me to call you that? No matter what he's said, I do love you...so much! The Catholic Church isn't the only church, Rosie. It's just the only one with such a rule. Queen Victoria and Albert are first cousins, did you know that? Look at all the children they have, and none of them odd at all. Would you consider being married in another church?"

"They're Anglican," she said, not quite rousing herself from her stupor. "Would you consider taking to the Church of England, which everyone knows was established so their king could marry all the women he wanted?"

"Well, another church, then."

"There's only one church. You know it as well as I do. Darin, I'm so confused...."

"Yes, I know you are," he said sympathetically, but without reaching out to touch her. "He's a terrible man. The worst one we could have talked to, I think. He had no right!"

"That's just it...he did," she responded quietly. "Now that he's told us ... in fact, as soon as he told us ... I remembered that part of the catechism, Darin."

"But you didn't know what it meant."

"Only because I was inattentive." She sighed. "Oh, Darin," she cried, her eyes filling with tears, "I love you so much! And it's an awful thing we've done."

He sat staring at her in silence, with hurt blue eyes. "I don't think we should discuss it right now," he said at last. "We should both think on it awhile. Sure, you're far too upset to make any sort of decision, at all. I'm going to take you home now, darling. You won't have to pretend you're sick, you really look it. I think we should both think about it for a week, because it's a big decision . . . changing churches . . . and one that won't be approved of by the family. I want you enough to do it—remember that! The question is your own belief and what you'll have to face later if you choose me."

She rose and gathered up her shawl, as though she had heard only part of what he said. She wanted to be home, right now. She wanted to lie down on her bed and let the tears flow without restraint, to try to relieve some of the pain in her heart. She could not face the guilt yet, because she did not feel guilty for loving Darin, but she was hurting very much and she had to be alone.

"I guess that's the best thing," she said in a vague, dreamy way. "I'll go home, now. I have to think." She felt the wilting violets at her throat and tore them from her blouse, throwing them down on the couch.

Chapter 22

MARY did not understand Rosaleen's sudden illness and knew even less how to treat it. One day her daughter had been in fine and blooming health; the next, she came home from work pale and shaking and had locked herself in her room all day, saying in a muffled voice through the door that she felt too sick to eat. As the week wore on, Mary became alarmed at Rosaleen's symptoms, which began to resemble Doirin's more than a little. She lay in her dark room with the blinds drawn, almost too weak to move, pale as wax, speaking little and sleeping a great deal, to avoid being awake. Her mother would have been relieved to feel a temperature on her brow and see a flush on her cheeks, as Veronica had exhibited: consumption was curable, at least. What she sensed was a sickness, if not of the mind, of the soul.

"Would you like to talk to Liam, darling?" she finally asked softly, when she came to pick up a dinner tray that had hardly been touched. Rosaleen shook her head in her tangled hair spread out on the pillow.

"I'll be all right, Mother," she said weakly. "I just need a little time."

"Madame Hurotte's concerned about you. She sent one of the girls around to ask after your health today. Rosaleen, we're all concerned, darling. If there's something weighing heavily on your heart, can't you talk to me? I'm your mother, after all."

Again, there was a shake of head, and Mary rested her hands in her lap with a sigh. "Let me brush your hair, at least. It's a sight."

"Tomorrow," Rosaleen said without expression. "I'd like to sleep now."

She did not rally until the following Sunday, when she suddenly became agitated and wanted to rise and leave the house, saying something about its being "too late," and Mary had to hold her down.

"Sure, you're as weak as a cat from not eating all week. You stay in bed, now: you aren't after going anywhere in this condition. Miss Laura's having her doctor come by tomorrow." Then, with exasperation, "Rosaleen, you're acting like your Aunt Doirin, for God's sake!" And she burst into tears. "I'm sorry, but I'm so worried about you!"

Contrary to her mother's orders, Rosaleen slipped out of bed as soon as Mary left the room and, holding onto the bedposts for support, tried to reach the armoire to get her dress, in spite of the way her head was swimming. She felt herself sinking, as she had once before, and managed to cry out before she fainted. When she awoke, she was in her bed again with Mary and the doctor bending over her, all thoughts of reaching Darin dispelled by the frightening episode.

"There we are," the doctor said. "With us again, are you, young lady?" She stared blankly into his partially familiar face. "She's very anemic," he said to her mother. "She needs a bit of building up, I think. Her lungs are clear, Mrs. Noonan. No need to worry about that. And her heart's strong. I'll leave a tonic for her, and I'll see her next week. As for you," he said, addressing Rosaleen like a child, "you're to eat everything your mother offers you, do you hear? One's body can get into serious trouble by neglecting it so."

"What about her job?" Mary asked him at the door. "What shall I tell them at the dress shop?"

"Tell them she needs rest and a good deal of building up. With the long hours she's been working and the way she's been eating, I'd say she should rest for a few weeks. I'm leaving some drops which should relax her: give her two drops, three times a day."

The laudanum, a standard medication for nervous complaints, made Rosaleen's head dull, and in her already weakened condition she slept almost continually, waking only when Mary brought her tray and gave her more drops. Under the opiate, her dreams were more pleasant: she spent all her time with Darin in green fields and along a half-remembered flowering river bank. Then, abruptly, her dream world was shattered. Mary came into her room one day and threw the drapes open with a loud clatter of the drapery rings. After so much time in the dark, Rosaleen had to shield her eyes with her hand. Mary stood over her angrily.

"Get up! Go out and sit in the garden for some air. This room's gloomy and stuffy, and the doctor's prescription's only making you worse. Sure, I won't have this happen again in our family." She opened the armoire and threw some clothes on the bed. "Get up, Rosaleen! Get dressed and go to the garden!"

Darin had called at the door twice that week, not knowing that Rosaleen was ill, because Mary had not left her long enough to make her usual visit to the flat over the pub. The first time, Mary had said Rosaleen was out: she did not know when she would be back. And today, not wishing to talk about her illness, because it was so much like his mother's, Mary said that Rosaleen was not seeing anyone. She had observed the hurt in the boy's blue eyes; but better that, she thought, than his knowing his cousin was going the way of his mother. The next time he called, she wanted to admit him to talk to a lucid Rosaleen. Sensing that her daughter would be better off without the drops, she had thrown them away before coming into the room to rouse her.

Rosaleen was still weak and confused as her mother helped her into her clothes. She realized she had only been dreaming of Darin and that she must get to him to tell him her decision. There was no one with whom she could trust a message or letter of that nature: she had to get well and carry it herself. She was ready to go anywhere with him, do anything, even change from the one true Church. Without him, she felt that she would surely die. Her illness had been the beginning of her decline to the arms of death, the dark, cold arms that were ever threatening, that must be avoided at any price.

Once the medication was withdrawn, her will to recover was so strong that, by the next day, she was able to go out by herself to the brick garden with its flowering plants, and breathe the sweet, clean air, tipping her face to the sunlight.

She was sitting in the comfort of a flared-back white wicker chair with her shawl thrown loosely around her shoulders and an unread book in her lap, listening to the birds sing, when a gentle voice said, "That's the prettiest sight I've ever seen."

She opened her eyes to find John standing over her in a summer suit, his eyes adoring behind their lenses, the small gray eyes which were so familiar.

"Hello, John." She smiled. "I didn't even hear you approach."

"That's because I was walking on tiptoe," he said, pulling up another garden chair to sit before her. "If you were sleeping, I didn't want to bother you. I've nearly been out of mind, Rosaleen. Mary wouldn't let me see you."

"My eyes were closed," she teased him. "I might have been asleep."

"I thought you were, at first." He smiled. "But I saw your lashes flickering, and realized you were turning your pretty face to the sun like some ancient pagan goddess...simply soaking it up."

"My goodness, you're getting absolutely poetic!" she chided softly. "I'm nothing so grand as that, as you know. I didn't know scholars turned into poets."

"Quite often, really," he said, studying her. "You're pale, Rosaleen. There's all the sun you'd ever need in the Mediterranean, you know."

"But that's very far away."

He grasped her hand between his and took it to his lips. "Not really, my dearest. I've been waiting around in the hope that you'd go with me."

She remained silent, examining with surprise the thrill that his lips on her fingers sent all the way up her arm. She glanced at his worshiping face, and found it impossible not to compare him with Darin, so perfectly beautiful in every way. John was plain: not homely, in the least, but not one of God's favored creatures, either. If he had not been her friend for so long, it would be quite easy to ignore him...even be unkind, before such transparent devotion. Everyone should hide some of his feelings, especially around a person who did not respond to his love. Even with Darin, there was always some little doubt, some tantalizing curiosity about the steadfastness of his love. John was so open, so vulnerable, his pale eyes and sensitive lips showing everything he felt. It was flattering to a girl, of course, but she could not take him seriously, and at the same time she did not want to hurt him, because she knew now what vulnerability could do, the

341

extent of its devastation. She felt that in the presence of so much love, she should love somewhat in return; but all she felt for him was a twisted sort of compassion. She was too young to realize how much of youthful passion was based not as much on character as on physical beauty; and she would never have admitted to herself that she had rejected him, long ago, simply because he was plain and not much taller than she.

"I won't be going anywhere for a while," she said, turning her face back to the sun, completely aware that he was adoring it. "I really think you should start your trip, John," she said as carefully as possible. "It's the end of July already, and you don't want to travel the ocean in the winter. I remember. The storms in the North Atlantic were terrible."

Pictures of the storms drifted through her mind unbidden, along with the striped shirts of sailors, the same things she had recalled when she stepped onto Darin's ship, bringing a cold screaming sensation to her chest which made her heart rate increase frighteningly.

"John," she entreated, reaching for his arm. "Get Ma, please! I don't feel well, at all."

They were at her chair again almost immediately, and Mary observed the terror in her daughter's wild blue eyes.

"It's all right, darling. We'll take you right up to your room. Sure, your bed's all made up fresh and the room's been aired. John, would you help me, please?"

He assisted Rosaleen only as far as the door, which, with murmured thanks, Mary closed in his face. Struggling to hold her daughter upright, Mary tried to pull down the covers. Rosaleen began to feel better when she was on her back, but when Mary made a move to get a cool cloth for her forehead, she clung to her skirt. "Don't leave me, Ma, please! Stay with me. Sit down beside me. Don't go away!"

Mary submitted quietly to the request, brushing her daughter's dark curls back from her pallid forehead. "Sure, I wasn't going to leave you, darlin'. I was just going to—"

"Ma, will you tell me something? It's been bothering me so much. I think it's about the voyage to America."

Her troubled brown eyes widening with something like comprehension, Mary nodded cautiously: the trip was not something she wished to remember, or discuss. "Of course, Rosaleen, if it will help you. Though, God knows, that was a long time ago and there's nothing much to be gained by thinking of it now."

Rosaleen, who had swallowed too much air during her anxiety attack, felt her heart returning slowly to normal, though she could still feel it pounding. "Ma, I keep seeing sailors in striped shirts." Mary nodded and clasped her hand tightly. "And a single bent basin, with a sailor throwing awful food into it from a bucket."

"Yes," Mary said softly, taking the white hand to her cheek and holding it there, "you remember more than I thought you would. Too much for a tiny child."

"And a short canvas bag, a sack, with lots of people standing around...more sailors. And someone saying, 'Ashes to ashes and dust to—'"

Her mother moaned, pressing her lips hard against Rosaleen's hand. "Mother of God! Mother of God!" she cried painfully, tears starting from her eyes, pouring uncontrollably down her cheeks, unable to answer the question Rosaleen was asking, suddenly realizing too much.

"It happened, then?" Rosaleen prompted her. "I wasn't imagining it?"

Mary was silent for a moment, brushing at her tears and sniffing. "Indeed to God, you weren't imagining it...though I thought I'd made you forget. It was poor little Seamus's funeral, such as it was, that you've remembered, Rosaleen, dear. He died of the fever, and they buried him at sea."

"I knew I had a brother Seamus and that he was dead," Rosaleen said wonderingly. "But until I stepped on Darin's ship the other night, I'd forgotten the rest."

"The ship!" Mary exclaimed. "Sure, that's what this is all about. Oh, Rosaleen, I'd never have let you go, if I'd realized it would bring back those old, bad memories." She leaned down to embrace her daughter, rocking her slowly, between tears and laughter. "Oh, God! At least we've got to the bottom of what's wrong with you, darling! I thought..." She shook her head, not wishing to mention her thoughts about Doirin again. "But it was the ship...of course it was! It was what caused your fever. Mother of God, that Darin causes problems! His poor father's fair out of his mind at his leaving again so suddenly."

Her daughter's body stiffened in her arms. "Darin's *gone?* His ship wasn't to sail for another six weeks!"

"Indeed it wasn't!" Mary said angrily. "So what does he do but leave that ship and his good position on it, and sign onto some old tub on its way to the Orient! He's wild and he's that restless. He doesn't care for anyone's feelings. Poor Brian did everything he could to make his stay pleasant, and he left without even a goodbye to anyone...not his dear father, or Veronica or me. Just a note to Brian saying he was sailing that day. Sure, Brian had to find out the rest on his own."

Rosaleen was unable to grasp the fact that Darin was gone. Though her head was clearer than a few days ago, she was confused about time. "What day is it? What's the date?"

"Why, it's the fifth of August, Rosaleen," Mary said. "You've been sick almost three weeks."

Three weeks! *August.* But it couldn't be, she thought: John hadn't contradicted her in the garden when she'd said it was the end of July. But John would not contradict her, out of kindness, knowing she was ill. "Ma, has it really been that long?" she asked in a whisper. "Didn't Darin come to see me at all?"

"Yes, he did," Mary admitted uneasily; then burst out suddenly, "Sure, I didn't want him to know you'd had a break-down! About a week ago, I told him you weren't seeing anyone. I didn't want to remind him of his poor mother."

Rosaleen kept remembering the violets, the way she had discarded them, as though they were nothing, when she tried to reconstruct events as Darin had seen them. He had waited to hear from her, without knowing she was ill; then he had come to the house, not once but twice her mother said, to be put off by lies that made him think Rosaleen did not wish to see him again. She was angry with Mary for not telling the truth; but she could understand it, too. She knew her mother's dread of insanity or anything that resembled it, and recognized that Mary had not wanted to upset Darin speaking of his mother's condition. It was a terrible mixup, but he would return: she knew he loved her as much as she did him. He would be away two years, three at most, and they would be older, better able to handle their decision. If she had been truthful with herself, she would have realized she felt something like relief that facing the family with the news they were leaving the Church could be postponed. The important thing was for her to regain her health and soundness of mind as quickly as possible, for Mary's remarks about Doirin had not escaped her. Rosaleen determined to leave all symptoms of her aunt's disorder behind her forever. Death was one thing; insanity, another. She would not give in to either, no matter how much pain she was feeling. Somehow she must survive, not just for Darin but for herself.

As the days passed, the calendar became her worst enemy. At first, she thought it was just because she had been ill: her whole system seemed disordered. But during the ensuing week, she could not overlook the empty, gnawing sensation in her stomach, or the number of mornings she felt nauseated when she got up. Her young body had built up again quickly on the many forced meals, sunshine and fresh air. Her state of mind, in spite of all that had happened, was as serene as she could will it to be. Therefore, there was only one reason for her new symptoms, and it struck icy fear into her heart.

Somehow, she must avoid discovery, just in case she was wrong, which she hoped almost desperately. All her life, she had planned to have Darin's children; but without hope of marrying him right now, her situation was too awful to think about.

The first thing that came to mind was total expulsion from a horrified and furious family. Even her mother's love would not extend so far, especially if she knew the identity of the baby's father. All her previous pain and confusion were forgotten: she was surprised at how clearly her mind worked. She even pretended she was having her period for Mary's benefit, while she searched day and night for a solution that would save her from shame.

One night, she stood at the head of the stairs, staring down into the darkness below, with the intention of hurling herself down, but she was afraid she would kill herself and abandoned the idea quickly, knowing it might not work anyway.

"Sure, it's a strange thing," Veronica once told her. "Some women miscarry by stepping off a curbing, while others can fall two stories without losing a child."

She did not really want to lose her baby: her heart yearned for it. And though she had her weaknesses of character, perhaps, she knew she could not commit murder. So she lay in her bed, unable to sleep, her mind racing on like the needle of her sewing machine. When the answer came to her, it was so simple that it took the rest of the night to examine all the angles of it before she fell into a deep sleep toward morning. She awoke, refreshed and settled, ready to face the most curious events in her life.

Studying herself in the mirror after breakfast, she concluded she was doing no one a disservice. Her color was back, her eyes, which had faded during her illness, back once again to their clear dark blue, surrounded by long black lashes. She even looked innocent, she decided critically, and that was most important: but she practiced a wide-eyed expression just to make certain. After all, she was not protecting herself: she was thinking of her child's future. And bringing someone else happiness into the bargain. She could not think of Darin now, any more than he had thought of her when he went away before finding out what had happened. When she moved down the front stairs, she did so with her head held high, completely forgetting that she had tried to throw herself down the same stairs the night before.

"I'm beautiful," her mind repeated. "Beautiful, clever and brave, forsaking everything else for my baby."

She found John where she knew he would be, in the garden with his morning coffee and a book, looking rather despondent, until he became aware of her presence and rose clumsily to his feet. "Rosaleen! Oh, my dear, you *have* recovered thoroughly. You're absolutely radiant. I was just sitting here thinking..."

She sat down gracefully, spreading her full skirts around her, letting her white hands caress the smooth fabric. "What were you thinking?" she asked, smiling up at him.

"I was thinking about what you said," he replied, unable to take his eyes off her as he took his seat again. "It is getting late in the summer, and I've wasted two months here. I'm going to leave on my trip as soon as I can make arrangements, Rosaleen."

She held his glance with her smiling eyes. "You've given up on me, haven't you? Just because I've been so sick."

"No! No, my dear. It's only because you're well again that I feel I can leave. I'm not a complete fool, Rosaleen. I know by now that you'll never accompany me. Things don't always work out the way we'd like them to."

This was the kind of opening she was awaiting, but she went dumb for a moment with the realization of what she was about to do, the finality of it. "John," she said breathlessly, "I do want to go with you. I want to be your wife. Really I do."

He could not believe his good fortune. "Are you sure you're quite well?" he asked. "Just the other day, you were a little confused about dates."

"I realized that later," she said and laughed. "My dear John! I'm perfectly well, and if you'll still have me, I'll marry you."

"Have you!" he exclaimed with relief. "Oh, Rosaleen, you don't know.... We'll get married at once!"

"What about your mother? I've never been certain she'd approve."

"Damn my mother!" he said, his face glowing. "We'll be married immediately. We can even be married in your Church, darling. I took instructions early in the summer."

This did surprise her. "You've converted?" she asked in disbelief.

"Converted? God, no! I'm not such a hypocrite. You know how I feel about religious matters. I ... well ... in the interest of understanding Catholicism better, I took instructions. The kind one takes when one's going to marry a Catholic. You know, raising the children in the Church and all that. Rosaleen, I wanted to marry you so much; I think I did it out of hope."

Her quickly calculating brain put one more obstacle out of the way. "I think that was fine of you," she said sincerely. "But where did you take this instruction? At St. Mary's?"

"No. St. Peter's in Cambridge. I was at the college library a lot, and..."

Cambridge! Relief flooded through Rosaleen at the word: she could never go back to St. Mary's and risk meeting that awful priest again. Cambridge. Of course. John spent most of his free time around Harvard, digging into the library for obscure passages in even more obscure works. "We can be married there, then," she said quickly. "I don't want a large wedding, John. I just want to marry you and be out of Boston soon. I want to forget Boston altogether for a while." She realized that by making the arrangements so hastily, there had been nothing of romance in her speech. Looking over at him, almost pleadingly, she asked shyly, "Aren't you going to kiss me?"

When he fell on his knees on the cobbled walk and embraced her, kissing her gently, the same extraordinary thing happened that had happened when he had kissed her hand the other day. She studied his face more intently, and thought: No, it could not be *him.*

"I'm going to tell Mother now," he said, springing up. "I'll be honest with you, Rosaleen: she isn't going to like this one bit. But she has nothing to say about it, you see. I'm over twenty-one, and my fortune's in my own hands. She can go on yearning for her old position in society, but I'll have you. And which one of us will be the happiest?"

The Maddigan house was in quiet upheaval for days following John's announcement. There were considerable goings and comings from Laura's room, with both Matthew and Harry conferring with their mother, and the activity communicated itself to Rosaleen, making her apprehensive. But John assured her repeatedly that everything was going to be all right. Along with worrying about the closeted conferences of the family, she had her own mother to deal with, something she had not taken into consideration: Mary violently opposed the marriage.

"Sure, you must still be out of your mind from your illness?" she exclaimed. "Rosaleen, it isn't suitable at all, don't you see that? You'll be an embarrassment to the whole family. Miss Laura and Matthew aren't pleased with the match at all. Matthew has a place to maintain now—one that was hardly won—and his brother marrying a poor Irish girl, no more than the child of one of their servants, would be a catastrophe for him, for certain."

"I thought Matthew liked me."

"He does! Sure, they all do, you know that, but it's on a different plane altogether that they're seeing this. They don't approve any more than I do! I don't know what you're thinking of, child! If you're marrying for money and what it can give you, it'll only make you unhappy in the end. You'll never be accepted in their circles! And there's your religion to consider, too."

"John's already taken instructions, Ma: our children will be Catholic. And he's Irish...well, half Irish, anyhow. It's almost the way you wanted it: 'a good Irish Catholic boy'! Besides, you're wrong about my marrying for money: it means nothing to me at all. I'm very fond of John, and we've always been close."

"I can't complain about him personally," Mary said. "He's always been a good lad for sure. But there's something else you should be thinking of, too." She let the suggestion hang heavily on the air, before reluctantly explaining it. "Rosaleen, I'm thinking about your children, darlin'. Sure, there's a history of mental problems in both families, isn't there? Marriage should be avoided when that happens: it's liable to occur again."

Rosaleen flushed, partly with her hidden secret, but mostly with anger. "Are you trying to tell me I can't marry the man of my choice because Aunt Doirin's crazy?" she asked. "That just isn't fair, Mother! And I won't have any of it!"

"It isn't just Doirin," Mary said quietly. "It's little Philip, too. Sure how'd you like to have to face the raising of one like him?"

"I won't have to! You're talking absolute nonsense, Mother. Harry told me that doctors believe that such children are born to older mothers most of the time. Aunt Laura was in her forties when she had him! It seems shocking to me that anyone *that* old would be involved in...such activity at all."

Her mother studied her with compassion. "You're very young, Rosaleen. You know nothing of the world. Whatever happens, I want you to know that I opposed it," she said, reaching out to stroke her daughter's smooth cheek. "And whatever happens, I want you to know that I'll be here to help."

That evening, John rushed ecstatically up the stairs to her room, hardly knocking on the door before he entered. Rosaleen, who had been gazing thoughtfully out of the back window over the garden, turned just in time to be embraced and lifted off her feet into the air. "It's settled!" he cried. "I don't know what I said, but they've all agreed to it, Rosaleen! They think you're a lovely girl, you know. In fact, Harry even said he'd have done the same thing himself, if he'd had the courage. Courage! I told him a man didn't need courage...only love."

"Put me down," she said and smiled. "I'm getting dizzy! Tell me all about it. What *did* you say, for goodness' sake?"

"I don't know!" He laughed. "I said so many things. But, there was a rather queer response when I threatened to take my part of the fortune and move to Europe forever. I didn't think they cared for me that much, but they simply wouldn't hear of it. Within twenty minutes, they'd agreed to everything. On their terms, I must say, but..."

Rosaleen, who had learned a little of finance from Matthew, did not want to curb John's jubilation about being cared for too much to let him leave. Quite obviously, his share of the money was tied up in the bank, in bonds and notes, not the cold cash he pictured in his mind: he was a complete innocent about such things. She was sure his withdrawal of funds would work a hardship on the company. In total ignorance, John had said the right thing—made the right threat.

"Of course they care for you, John. Did you ever really doubt it? But what are their terms?"

He laughed. "I pretended to be serious about them. But they're exactly what we wanted to do, anyway! They agreed, with relief, I might say, that we should be married at St. Peter's in Cambridge: they aren't known there. There's to be no publication of the marriage in the newspapers. You don't mind that, do you?"

"No, of course not."

"Then a little duplicity comes in, but it doesn't matter to me, darling, if you don't mind. When we return from Europe next year, it will appear that I've married over there. I don't know how they plan to work that, but..."

"...it'll cover up my humble antecedents," Rosaleen said slowly, feeling slightly hurt. But she was in no position to haggle over details. When she returned next year, it would be with a child, and she would never accept a lesser position in the household than she deserved. "Yes," she said and nodded, "that's best. Matthew, particularly, has worked very hard to come up in the world. I wouldn't dream of being an embarrassment to him."

"Mother wants to see you, darling," John said, kissing her gently. "I want you to go in there with your beautiful chin up high. Let them know from the beginning that you're their equal...and better. For you really are, you know."

The interview with Laura went very well, Rosaleen thought: the woman was genuinely fond of her, and Rosaleen had grown up in her house. Though she kept her dainty gold-trimmed desk between them and looked like an aging, be-curled porcelain figurine, Laura seemed to have her wits about her more than ever before.

"My dear Rosaleen!" She smiled faintly. "Please sit down. I must say, you've caused quite a stir in the family. We had no idea things had progressed so far between you and John. Has he discussed everything with you?"

Rosaleen tilted her head so that her deep-blue eyes looked down on the woman, without any attempt at the arrogance of which she was perfectly capable. "He has. And I agree that under the circumstances, it's the best thing to do. You've been like a family to me, Aunt Laura: I wouldn't do anything to distress you."

"You know that your mother doesn't approve. She thinks our life won't suit you. That you'll feel uncomfortable and out of place."

"Mother's concerned with things like station," Rosaleen replied calmly and with as much poise as she could muster. "I'm not. Mother wouldn't fit into another way of life. She's still a peasant—good, hardworking, honest—and *she* would be miserable under other circumstances. However, Mother and I are not the same. Our background and experience is even different, isn't it? I've lived in this house so long. I'm more familiar with its ways than any place, Aunt Laura. Because of your kindness, I've come a long way, and I hope to learn even more in Europe."

Laura studied her like a wary bird, though her hands, which were usually active and fluttering, lay with a peculiar stillness on the desk. "Your manners are good, and you do have taste. I've seen to that," she said crisply. "But if you think you'll ever 'pass' in society, you're wrong, Rosaleen. Fortunately, John's the youngest son, with no aspirations higher than the top shelf of his bookcase. Matthew's quite another matter, my dear. He's courting, and hopes to win, a very wellborn young lady. By the time you come back, they may be married and living in this house. The presence of all of you here together is unconscionable: a solution will have to be worked out before your return. You must understand from the outset that your background will be kept to ourselves. It will be shared with *no one*. I have to think of the older boys."

Rosaleen felt the sting of the words, but the expression in Laura's eyes belied them: the woman was doing the best she could to keep up appearances, and setting things straight at the beginning, so Rosaleen would not be upset later.

"I understand, Aunt Laura. You know I wouldn't do anything to hurt them. I'm fond of your sons. There is one small thing I'd like to request, though." Laura leaned back with a troubled look in her eyes. "Oh, it won't be too difficult! John thinks you agreed to his wishes because you loved him too much to see him go away forever. It made him very happy. I'd like him always to continue in that belief, Aunt Laura. If anything comes up to dash his illusion, there's no telling what I might do. I won't see him hurt." Her eyes were cold and her expression unrelenting as she watched to see that Laura understood.

When they made their vows on a late August morning in Cambridge, with only the immediate family present, Rosaleen was very conscious of what she was doing to John, and added an unspoken vow of her own: "...and I'll always be faithful to him." Though Darin still lived in her heart, she would not encourage thoughts of him or long for what should have been. She would be true to this good friend, who was saving her life, though he was ignorant of the fact. And she would make him as happy as possible. She would defend him against his uncaring family, with whom he had always rated only slightly higher than poor Philip, because of his introverted ways. She knew the standard she was setting was high, and that she had been weak and willful in the past, but her decision at the altar rail was as firm as her hand in his. As Mrs. John Maddigan, she would be a different person: the epitome of what a wife should be. And if there was a little spite in her decision, it only added excitement to her future life. First, she honestly wanted to please John; but underlying the wish was an irrepresible urge to show them all.

The wedding was hastily put together, and Rosaleen dressed at the church, instead of at home. She wore the simple white chiffon gown she had made to wed Darin. There was so little pomp accompanying the affair that she realized the occasion bore the mood of Philip's secret funeral, but she did not let John notice it, too.

Mary and Veronica were the only ones from her family in the church; and it amused her that they were the only people there who knew how to follow the Mass. The Maddigans were the ones who were out of place. They finally gave up trying to stand and kneel at the right times and sat despondently in their pew. The nicest thing about it, in Rosaleen's mind, was that she would be spared their presence in any gathering later. Their luggage had already been sent to the ship, and she and John were to go to the ship right after the ceremony.

"Take good care of yourself, darling," her mother entreated on the church steps, holding her tearfully for a moment. "Sure, it's dreadful that you're going so far...among Frenchmen and Italians and Greeks and God knows what-all!"

"They won't bite her," John reassured Mary, beaming. "Of course, they might like to kidnap her: I'll have to be careful about that. Have you ever seen anything so *beautiful?*"

"I haven't," Harry said, appearing beside them, "and I intend to be the first to kiss the bride." He was not really cheerful, but his manner was less reserved than that of Matthew and Laura, and his eyes had been watching the couple thoughtfully. He embraced Rosaleen and kissed her for so long that she nearly lost her breath. "My God," he said, with an attempt at a smile, "John's the only one in this family with an ounce of good sense."

Rosaleen found herself shaking Laura's gloved hand, instead of embracing her as she had done in the past, their eyes meeting levelly, not as rivals, but as future combatants. Matthew's sendoff was cool. Slipping an envelope into her hand, he said evenly, "I think you'll find something to do with this in Paris. I wish I were going there again, too."

"Good luck to you," Rosaleen replied, forgiving the sudden distance. "I hope you're soon as happy as we are, Matt."

He smiled ironically. "To be happy, I should have taken another course years ago. But thank you, things may work out."

She kissed Veronica and accepted a little envelope from her, too. "Not enough for a Paris gown," her aunt smiled merrily, whispering in her ear. "But perhaps you can pick up a little something for your new home."

"Thank you." Rosaleen smiled, hugging her, more grateful for her thought than for Matthew's. "I'll get something that will always remind me of you and Saul."

Veronica's deep-blue eyes went serious. "Sure, child, it isn't the frills and reels that make a happy marriage. Remember my wedding? What a dreary, wonderful day that was! And what a beautiful marriage it's been!"

Then, suddenly, it was time to go, and John was still deep in conversation with Mary. "I promise you, I'll guard her with my life, Mother. May I call you that? For that's what you are to me, now. I've had two wishes granted on the same morning!"

Rosaleen's hands felt cold when, alone with her new husband in the carriage, he took them in his to kiss them. He was still unrepressed in his joy, and while it did not communicate itself to her entirely, she was pleased to see him so happy.

"I love you," he said, kissing her often and exuberantly; then, with a swift change of mood, becoming thoughtful and gentle, "Rosaleen, your hands are like ice. You're frightened, aren't you? I want you to know that I've thought about it a lot, and we don't have to hurry into married life. I want you very much, darling, but your feelings come first. We have a very large cabin on this new ship of Matt's, which I haven't yet seen. We can sleep apart until you feel—".

"No!" she said quickly; then, realizing her enthusiasm

might not seem maidenly, she lowered her eyes and whispered, "I want to be your wife, as soon as possible, John."

His breath was very warm on her face when he kissed her again. "I love you more than I'll ever be able to say."

She had tried not to think about this part of getting married to him; she had pushed it to the back of her mind, though she recognized the urgency of it, if her child was going to appear to be his. And now, this very night, it was upon her: there was no ignoring it any longer, and she felt ice in the pit of her stomach.

She leaned her head back wishing that somehow she could suspend consciousness for awhile, dreading the thought of the inexperienced, hot caresses of the man at her side.

Chapter 23

THE STATEROOM surpassed anything Rosaleen might have imagined, if she had thought about it beforehand at all: she could not grasp that people traveled so sumptuously on shipboard. The best cabins she had seen were the ones Darin had shown her on his merchant ship. This room was decorated like a beautiful boudoir, with satin furniture and a large bed covered in gold velvet; even the windows were draped. It might have been a suite in one of the best hotels. Their luggage, John's two trunks and her small one, was waiting for them when they entered, along with baskets of fruit and several beautifully wrapped boxes. She stood dumbfounded, staring around her, much to John's amusement.

"Well, what do you think of it? Aren't you going to open your gifts? Mother would be terribly disappointed if you just stood and stared at them," he teased.

"I don't know what to say." She smiled weakly. "Sure, I've never seen such a room in my life! It's far grander than your mother's, even."

He threw his head back and laughed. "Darling Rosaleen! I know you're quite overwhelmed, because you've lapsed into the brogue, my dearest...just as you've always done when you're excited!"

"I'm sorry," she murmured, her dimple showing slightly: she was too comfortable with him to be embarrassed. Already she felt the rocking of the ship beneath her, though, and it made her ask suddenly, "John, what's belowdeck?"

"What a curious question," he said. "Why do you want to know, my dear?"

"You said it was a passenger vessel. Does that mean there are people down there, too? Is there a steerage?"

"No," he answered, shaking his head, not understanding but trying. "There's ballast and merchandise going from here to France, Rosaleen. These ships don't carry passengers in steerage. Whatever made you think such a thing?"

She shook her head without replying: she must put the old thoughts completely out of her head. The discussion with her mother had helped a great deal, and she was no longer plagued by phantoms. "Did your mother send all the presents?" she asked, suddenly curious at such a large gesture from a disapproving Laura.

"We'll look at the cards and see."

The fruit and one box was from her mother, and she tore the tissue off with childish anticipation, drawing a white cotton nightgown, trimmed with blue ribbons, from the box. "Oh!" she said. "It's beautiful! God love her, it cost her a lot."

John studied it with a frown, muttering, "Good God! But it's the thought that counts," he added quickly. "She certainly wants to see that you're covered from your toes to your ears, doesn't she?"

Laura had sent lingerie of pure silk, embroidered and trimmed with lace: camisoles, petticoats, even drawers, and Rosaleen concealed them quickly. There was a red velvet robe for John, which made him stare in bewilderment. "Handsome, but not very practical," he commented. "I packed my friendly old flannel one. But this will do on a grand occasion..." He started to say "like this," but thought better of it, not wishing to frighten his bride any more than she was.

Rosaleen had to put the box from Madame Hurotte's, wrapped with its distinctive ribbon, on the bed to open it, thinking it, too, was from Laura until she found the small card inside. "It's from madame!" she cried in surprise. "How did she know? No one was supposed to."

"I suppose Mother bought the silk things from her and inadvertently told her all in one of her flutters," John said. "Ah, now that's more like it! Leave it to the French!"

The peignoir of lustrous pale-blue slipper satin spread itself over the bed, releasing a matching nightgown of sheer georgette and lace. Tucked into the corner of the box were a pair of dainty blue satin slippers, which Rosaleen lifted, drawing in her breath. "I never thought I'd have anything so lovely! It's made for a princess. Oh, John, just look!"

He put his arms around her from behind. "Wait until we get to Paris, darling, and you'll see how a real princess dresses. I know you love fine things, and you should have them. You shall, Mrs. Maddigan. After three years of making lovely things for the wretched hags of Boston, whom not even the best clothing can save, you've come into your own. Your mother always says, 'The world's unevenly divided.'" He laughed. "My division would have the most beautiful women wearing the most beautiful garments! And, you, Rosaleen, will be a perfect marvel."

"You're daft," she said, still not comprehending the good fortune in her hands. "Something like this is incredibly *dear*. I have three fine dresses in my trunk, and you can only wear one at a time. They'll do me fine until they wear out."

His chuckle was affectionate in her ear. "We'll see, dearest. Oh, it's going to be fun showing you the world, Rosaleen!"

The sea was smooth and the weather good when it was time to retire that night. They had had an almost sumptuous dinner, at which Rosaleen deliberately drank two glasses of champagne to calm her nerves. When she chose what to wear to bed, however, she still selected the modest white nightgown her mother had given her. Propped up with pillows, she lay waiting for John, trying to adapt a frame of mind that would get her through the coming ordeal, though she expected it to be blessedly short. He came to her side of the bed dressed in his new robe, carrying two more glasses of champagne, and sat down to offer her one, which she accepted with a shaking hand.

"I rather thought you'd wear that one," he said, touching his glass to hers with a tiny clink. "Rosaleen, I know you're nervous, and it's natural, considering your upbringing. But I want you to be as happy as I am. I'd prepared all the things I wanted to say tonight: it was sort of a lecture, and too pedantic for the occasion. We know each other very well: we trust each other, darling. I'll be very considerate; I love you so much. But I want you to enjoy marriage the way you should, not as this damned restrained society of ours dictates. So just relax, my dear, and trust me." He paused to sip his drink, without looking at her. "The first thing I want you to do is to get out of that idiotic sack! And the next," he said, smiling and moving to his side of the bed and removing his glasses, "is to drink your wine and pretend you're a pagan. Throw away the Puritan chastity-belt mentality and be an ancient Greek!"

"You're daft!" she smiled, but the drink helped her shed some of her inhibition—and the nightgown. He slipped between the sheets as naked as she, and the inexplicable tingle she had felt before from his kisses extended down her whole body as she felt the smooth warmth of his body against hers. "You're . . . absolutely . . . daft," she repeated, as she surrendered to his kisses, surprised at the new loveliness of him.

Without the distortion of his glasses, his eyes were large, worshipful, half-ironic, gray; and combined with his other features, unnotable by themselves, they produced a handsomeness that was remarkable. At first she tried to resist the sensations his searching lips evoked in her, arguing with herself that it was not decent: she loved Darin. She did not know whether it was her mind or her body, or both, that finally surrendered, realizing that the feelings his lips and hands created were for the man, himself. He had a quality she did not understand; something that Darin, with all her love for him, lacked...an unconscious facet of soul or personality that aroused her with a touch, made her abandon herself completely, in a way she had never dreamed. Her body shuddered beneath his in almost an agony of surrender, which blacked out everything else, even her own identity. He stayed with her as long as he could, and his hand was still entwined in her long hair when he lay back on his side of the bed, their sides still touching.

She lay silent in the darkness, feeling as though all the layers of her being had been stripped away: she had never been truly naked until now. She had not known there was so much pleasure in the world, but she was slightly disturbed that she did not understand. Finally, because she could say anything to John, she whispered, "What...happened?"

He turned to kiss her gently. "Only what should always happen, Rosaleen. But I didn't dare hope it would this first time. Are you all right?"

She nodded in the darkness. "Yes! I didn't know it would be like this."

"Well, now you know, and I'm so glad."

"How did you know?" she asked, and he was silent a moment.

"That's an answer I believe you deserve. Rosaleen, I'm a

very sexu…passionate man. I began to realize it years ago, when I was still in prep school," he explained.

"Prep school! You were just a boy."

"Yes, twelve to be exact. Since then, I've made it my business to explore what goes on in the world. First, through books—those 'dull' classics aren't as lifeless as people imagine. And there are other works, if you know how to find them. And I completed my education…almost anywhere I could, darling. Passion is elemental, but it can also be highly refined. Again, one has to know where to look. I was always terrified that somehow the family would find out, but even my brothers didn't know. There'd have been a terrible scene if any scandal had erupted. Mother, particularly, would have had the vapors. But I just don't understand the guilt over such things. Especially when men are so two-faced about it. I've run into some very prestigious citizens in my quest."

"In Boston?" she asked, interested and almost disbelieving, and he laughed softly.

"Even in Boston. And New Bedford, when we were at the Cape, and even in the little town where our school was located. I hope you aren't displeased with me."

She shook her head. "Just amazed," she said. "I thought I knew everything you ever did."

"Yes," he said, kissing her on the lips. "So did everyone. Sometimes it's fortunate to be the 'stranger' in the household: no one pays that much attention to you. As long as you aren't shocked, it doesn't matter. I've always had my own ideas about such things, which I'll probably discuss with you at length sometime, poor darling. You see, Rosaleen, I don't condone or believe in either guilt or 'sin' when it comes to sexuality."

She put her arms around him and drew his head down to rest on her breasts, smoothing his hair. That's all very well, she thought, but I wonder how you'd feel if you knew about me? And she made another oath in her heart never to let him know, certain it would plunge him into despair; and always to be faithful to this really remarkable man who was her husband.

The Paris of Napoleon III and his beautiful Spanish empress, Eugénie, was a city devoted to fashion and the arts. To Rosaleen, who spoke the language fluently and had heard stories of it in Madame Hurotte's shop, it was a little bit like coming home. Their hotel suite was regal, and the first day of their arrival, John took her shopping to make her choices and be measured for a couturier wardrobe. She felt out of place in her ruffled skirts when all the other ladies were wearing frames beneath theirs, to hold them out still further. The age of the new *crinoline*, which was not crinoline at all, but a light cage worn under petticoats increasing the diameter of the hemline to four feet all around, had arrived, though still violently rejected in both England and America. When Rosaleen had said her three dresses were quite suitable, she had been ignoring fashion, as did the rest of her countrywomen in Boston; but once in Paris she realized how badly out of style they really were. And her desire to wear the frilly hoopskirts was motivated by something else, too: in a few months, the fortunate hoopskirt would conceal her pregnancy. Though she could have revealed it at any time, she still had not mentioned it to John. She did not want to spoil his grand holiday by concern over her and was determined not to tell him until she could no longer hide it.

The nausea, which she had discovered could be held in check on the ship by eating soda crackers, was already abating, and she had never felt better in her life. When John took her to the dressmaker's shop, it was like putting a child down in a candy store. He watched in amusement as she evaluated the fabrics and patterns, talking rapidly in French to the designer, who was captivated at once by her knowledge and vivacity, and produced one frock that needed only a few hours' alteration for her to wear while the rest were being made. She left with her hands gingerly touching the sides of the unfamiliar maroon taffeta skirt, held out stiffly by a Tavernier hoop, in a matching Eugénie hat perched forward on her shining black hair with a sweep of ostrich feathers at one side. Once she became familiar with the swaying hoop, she felt very elegant, but John did not like the fashion.

"I can't get close enough to you," he complained, though he was exceedingly proud of her when he took her to the museums and the finest places to dine.

Rosaleen's interest in art was stirred at first, not so much by the paintings she saw, but by the single word "invaluable" which she heard attached to them.

"Someone must have bought them at one time," she said. "Only who could have that much money, John?"

"The Renaissance paintings you saw today weren't actually *bought* originally, darling. They were commissioned.

The artists probably never had enough to live on. It's their quality and age that makes them so admired now."

"But what about all the artists we see on the streets? They're selling their paintings, aren't they? Some of them are quite good, too."

"Yes. Some of them will probably be valuable someday—if one has the eye for that sort of thing. It's safer to buy in the galleries, where someone with knowledge has already appraised them for future worth. Art can be a very good investment, I guess, though that isn't why I enjoy it."

"As valuable as real estate?" she pressed him seriously.

"Good God, I don't know! Perhaps more valuable, if you were able to purchase something very good. Rosaleen, what are you up to? Do you want to buy a painting, darling? Because if you do, you only have to say so."

"The envelope Matt gave me," she said. "I told you it contains an enormous amount of money: a thousand dollars. He told me to spend it in Paris, but you wouldn't let me buy my own dresses. I was thinking of buying a house with it when we got back."

"A *house?* For that amount? Oh, my dear, when we buy our house, we'll have it built ourselves, and *I'll* give it to you."

"Would it be foolish, then, to buy paintings with the money, John? Is it all right if I use it that way?"

"You can use it any way you like, you know that. We'll contact a good gallery first thing in the morning."

She purchased a few paintings and had them crated to send home; but the experience stirred something inside her, a recklessness almost akin to that of a gambler, and she grew restless after her money was spent. All she had left was the fifty dollars Veronica had given her for something for her home, and though one part of her mind told her she was being frivolous, she decided to buy another painting. Knowing she could not go to the better galleries to purchase anything at that price, she thought perhaps she might search out something on the street. She did not confide her intention to John when he left her to spend a day in the National Library. Without considering that "ladies" did not walk the streets of Paris, especially on the Left Bank where she had observed the artists, Rosaleen set off on foot with a small map in her hand. Accustomed to walking anywhere she wanted in Boston, she felt no hesitation about doing so in Paris. During her walk, several coaches stopped to offer her transportation; she declined, but was much impressed by the kindness and chivalry of Parisian men.

Later, when she showed John the small painting she had acquired, she was surprised by his reaction.

"You walked to the Left Bank and mingled with the people there! Rosaleen, you must be out of your mind! Don't you ever do anything like that again. Do you understand?" Then, noting the chagrin in her eyes, he put his arms around her. "It isn't safe for a woman to roam the streets alone, darling."

"People were very kind," she said, still hurt by his angry words. "Several of them offered to give me a ride."

"Men?"

She nodded. "They're very gallant here, John. The nobs in Boston wouldn't give you a lift if you were limping."

"You didn't...?"

"No. It was a lovely day, and I wanted to explore things on foot. What do you think of my painting?"

"Huh? Oh, the picture. Yes . . . it's . . . different. Rather peculiar, really, but I like it, I think," he said, his mind dazed with what might have happened to her. "Rosaleen, darling, come, sit down. We must have a little talk."

There were times in the ensuing months when Rosaleen wished she were a man, so she could go about as she pleased while John visited his various libraries; but knowing it would upset him if she went against her word, she contented herself with reading books about art and sightseeing with the various couples they met in the best hotels.

As the weather cooled into autumn, she and John traveled south into Italy, staying in Florence for a month while she indulged herself in the museums, with more appreciation than she had experienced at first, in Paris, because of her reading.

After they toured Rome, he unexpectedly announced, "We're off to Naples and Capri, darling, while the weather holds. My friend Edward Dove has rented a villa there, and I promised him we'd visit. I know you'll enjoy him and his wife. And we must see the Blue Grotto, he says. I'm very interested in the area myself: the island's supposed to be beautiful . . . and Tiberius's palace was there."

Four months pregnant, and beginning to feel it on the long coach rides, Rosaleen thought perhaps they too should lease a permanent place somewhere. But she did not express the wish to John, who was enjoying every moment on European soil, being thoroughly drenched in its history. By the time they reached Sorrento and took a boat out to the island, Rosaleen was exhausted, but within a few hours, she was glad she had raised no objection to the trip. Edward and Pamela Dove were completely delightful, their rented villa something out of a dream. Without the usual letters of introduction for a grand tour, she and John had met no one from Boston, until now, and it was a relief to reminisce about home and chatter about their experiences in Europe with someone who would understand.

Edward Dove was a serious young man and an historian, and had been at Harvard with John. The two young women escaped their ponderous conversations to chat and show each other their wardrobes and talk about clothes. Pamela was not giddy like Laura, though she came from the same place in society; she was gentle, spontaneous and intelligent, if not in a bookish way, at least about many of the things Rosaleen wanted to know. A bride herself since spring, she and Edward had been in Europe longer than the Maddigans. and Pamela had much to tell Rosaleen about things their husbands would not have noticed: family life in France and Switzerland and Italy, and all the people she had met and stayed with by invitation; the customs and scandals in different countries; even where bargains could be obtained and the way to haggle for them. Within a short time, the two women were like sisters, and not once did Pamela even think to ask about Rosaleen's pedigree or family, which led Rosaleen to believe that she was accepted as someone in the same station of life, an illusion she did nothing to contradict.

Capri was such a lovely place, with its blue skies and chestnuts and laurels, that Rosaleen decided it was the right time to tell John of her condition: they could settle and stay there until the baby was born.

But when she and Pamela joined their husbands for supper on the patio one evening, they heard the men discussing moving on.

"In another month, the wind and rain will be coming in from the Tyrrhenian, John. I have it on the authority of my gardener! It's been a marvelous summer, but I won't be unhappy to move on."

"To Greece!" John said with an exultant laugh. "I can hardly wait to get there, Edward. There's been so much to do and see...and read! But I've been holding myself back from rushing there at once. Ah, Rosaleen!" he said, looking up and taking her hand. "We've had such good fortune, darling. The Doves are migrating to Greece, too. We can travel together."

"And we can go on to Egypt, when it gets too cold there," Edward put in. "I'm sure Egypt's always pleasantly warm."

In Rosaleen's mind, France and Italy were civilization: she was not so sure about their future destinations, especially with regard to her confinement. She had not yet had time to be frightened by it, but the first small shock of panic quickened her heartbeat. What was she to do? If she went along with the present plans, she might be in some ungodly wilderness when her baby was born, and die of infection, or have him in the lobby of a Cairo hotel. On the other hand, John was so keen on Greece. She lifted her hoop skirt in back and sat down in the chair a servant held for her.

"It sounds very exciting." She smiled, touching the stem of her wineglass. "Where shall we be in the spring?"

"In the spring?" John laughed. "I haven't thought that far ahead. Let's see," he said, looking upward with dreamy eyes, "we really don't want to spend too much time in Egypt, do we? There's nothing much there for the ladies . . . and it is not a particularly healthy place to stay. If we come back to Greece in late February, we can spend more time there. I suspect we'll be back in Italy by spring, dear."

Rosaleen sighed faintly and lifted her glass. "We'll be here in April, then. I think it's the loveliest place on earth!"

Though Rosaleen did not know it, she carried her baby the way her mother did, low in the pelvis, without showing, so she carried out her deception for the sake of her husband's trip until January, in Cairo. She would have kept her secret longer if she had not confided it to Pamela in a moment of concern. The men had planned a trip to Giza to see the pyramids, and Rosaleen was afraid to make it, not knowing what conditions they might encounter: she had to talk to someone about it, without spoiling the trip. But instead of merely staying at the hotel with her as Rosaleen had planned, Pamela, greatly incensed over what she considered Rosaleen's "sacrifice" for so long, marched right down to the men's lounge and told John. He immediately rushed up the stairs to their room and flew through the door.

"Rosaleen!" he cried with disbelief. "Is what Pamela told us true? Why on earth didn't you . . . ?" He sat down beside her on the bed and studied her face. "Darling, how far along are you? I swear, I had no idea."

"I'm fine." She grinned up at him. "Really, I am! I shouldn't have said anything to Pam. I wanted to tell you myself. I've wanted to for months, but there didn't seem to be a proper time."

"She called us selfish pigs," he said, shaken. "And she's right...she really is. How long has it been?"

"From the first," she said, feeling completely honest about it, because she had been with him so long. "It happened on the boat, I guess. But, really, there's nothing to worry about, John. I feel very well. I just didn't think I should take a coach ride out into the desert."

"A coach ride?" he said, and she saw a glint of humor in his eyes. "It was going to be a *camel* ride, darling. I rather think you did the right thing."

Their eyes met, and they both started laughing.

"Oh, darling," he said, holding her in his arms, "I'm so happy! You don't know.... Oh, Rosaleen, you little idiot! We'll have to leave this place: it's very unsanitary. We'll go back home at once."

"No," she said, kissing him, her steady blue eyes reassuring. "We'll go back to Greece for the winter: I know you love it there. The baby's due in April, John. I'd like to be someplace civilized by then, in Italy or France."

"Are you sure you don't want to be with your mother, Rosaleen? I think perhaps we should go back, where we know you'll get proper care."

She shook her head like a stubborn child. "Really, John, women have babies in the most improbable places...even in Egypt and Greece. Of course, we don't know the mortality rate, though, do we? I just want to be with you, and somewhere a little more...advanced."

"You'll have the very best, darling. From now on, I'll look after you every minute."

"No. That would be terrible for both of us. You'll continue your research, while I prepare for the baby." She was silently thoughtful for a moment. "Of course, you can pamper me when you're at home. I'm going to need you very much."

Jason Brendan Rory Maddigan was born in a lying-in hospital in Rome on March 25, 1860, and baptized six weeks later. He was extraordinarily beautiful, the living image of his real father, perfect in every way: and Rosaleen nearly fainted with relief at that news, though she had to inspect him for herself to be certain. She had tried not to think of it before he was born, but during the two months in Greece when it was too chilly to get out much, her mind kept examining the fact that her baby was the offspring of cousins, and cousins twice over, at that. She was terrified that he might be grossly deformed, or worse: mentally deficient like Philip. She could not communicate her fear: she had to live alone with it, and it festered inside. But now her relief was so great that even the pangs of childbirth were forgotten.

She had tried to be brave during her confinement, but any pain alarmed her and she ended up carrying on in an extraordinary fashion, crying out for "Mary," without knowing if she called upon Our Lady or her mother. She was certain her death was imminent, in this strange black-and-white hospital with its crucifixes and ghostly white nuns. Actually, the pain was forgotten almost at once. Within two days, she was up and around, hovering over her son's bassinet, worshiping, but feeling slightly guilty at what she saw. John was delighted that the child looked so much like his mother; anything else would never have entered his mind. His protection and devotion had been unwavering: she knew she meant everything to him. She was determined to have another child as soon as possible, one that would be his own.

John was still doing research for a book he intended to write, and he spent his days in the Vatican archives, just as he had in the library in Athens. When they had been abroad for a year, they made the decision to stay on, to avoid a winter crossing, and the reaction from Boston had been surprising. After receiving one of Rosaleen's long, dutiful letters, Mary wrote back that they were "all that disappointed" over their thoughtlessness in "prancing around Europe yet another year." Neither she nor John understood the drift of the letter, and they heard nothing directly from Laura, because of John's stubbornness about writing to his mother. Rosaleen had to explain every time she wrote to Mary that he was just too busy with his studies to write home.

The time they had together was precious, especially when they took Rory out in his pram on Sunday, strolling in the sun through the Borghese Gardens not far from their rented house.

One Sunday afternoon, when they were passing through a section of town where there seemed to be a greater abundance of ragamuffins on the street than usual, and John had given out all the change in his pocket, he said, "Good God, I think this country's made up mostly of children, and cats! There are more cats in Rome than I've ever seen. I was about to say there weren't any dogs," he added, as they passed a littered cobble alley, "but there's a whole family of them right here!"

A shaggy yellow bitch with two puppies was panting by a doorway under the affectionate eyes of her master, an old man in tattered clothing, leaning on a stick. They bid him *buon giorno* with a smile, and he acknowledged the greeting by taking off his hat to Rosaleen, his eyes following them as they continued on. Suddenly, Rosaleen froze like a statue, her knuckles white on the handle of the pram, and John looked at her with alarm. Without explanation, she handed him the pram and ran back to the alley with flying skirts. Frowning, John turned the unwieldy vehicle and followed her. He stopped in surprise when he found her kneeling on the foul pavement of the alley with her skirts spread around her like a flower. She was cuddling a scruffy yellow puppy to her cheek, and she looked up at John with radiant eyes.

"Can I have him?" she asked, dodging the licks at her face. "Oh, John, please! I *must* have him."

"But darling, you wouldn't want to leave the little fellow when we go home."

"I'd never leave him behind...never! He can accompany us in the cabin on the ship," she said rapidly, extending her hand to stroke the puppy's mother.

"Attenzione!" the old man cried as the bitch showed her fangs, and John warned her at the same time,

"Be careful, Rosaleen! She's a surly one. Look, you could have any dog you want when we get back—not a mutt like this, but one with breeding."

His wife looked up with pleading eyes. "It has to be this one," she said. "Oh, John, I haven't asked for anything else."

This was true, almost to the point of annoying him. She admired many things, and her taste was unerringly good; but when he offered to buy something, she would draw herself up and, sounding like her mother, would say, "No, I won't hear of it! It's too dear. You mustn't waste your money on everything I like, John."

What she liked was French furniture in muted rose and beige; a particularly fine bolt of lace in Florence; small marble statuary of the most excellent design; several paintings, both in France and Italy, at an auction in Rome; and a *pietra dura* table, low and round, made of black marble inlaid with colored stone flowers, leaves and birds. When he thought about it now, all she had required during the whole trip was the wardrobe he had insisted upon in Paris, and a fine cotton layette for the baby. How could he refuse her anything...even if it was a flea-infested puppy of undecided breeding?

"Of course you can have him," he relented. "Though, of everything we've seen, why you should insist upon an ugly little mutt like that I can't understand."

"He's beautiful," she defended her prize, standing up with the puppy against her white throat. "Give the man something generous for him, please. Come on, Murphy, I want you to meet Rory! That's it, little one...into the pram. You're a member of the family now, and don't you forget it. Oh, what pretty babies...."

"Rosaleen," John said, putting his wallet back into his pocket, "please don't put him in with the baby until he's had a damn good bath! I swear to God," he said and laughed, "I'll never understand you! You even named him on the spot."

One person, it flashed through her mind, would have understood instantly; but those were dangerous thoughts, and she pushed them out of her mind, as she had been doing all year.

Chapter 24

THE MADDIGAN household had been upturned for days, the new servants cleaning and recleaning, shifting furniture, polishing the silver in preparation for John and Rosaleen's return from Europe. They had been away almost two years, and Mary thought that Laura was even more excited than she was. Rosaleen's letters, which Mary had shared with Laura, were complete, lengthy, and arrived almost every two weeks, more often during the past winter. Because of them, Mary had felt closer to her daughter in her absence than she sometimes did when she was home. Though she did not share the enthusiasm for foreign places and the queer people Rosaleen seemed to enjoy, Mary read and reread every word about her little grandson, Rory, and could hardly wait to hold him in her arms.

The house had been a gloomy sort of place since the young couple left: she had not dreamed it could be so empty. And though she had new and important duties, not really as housekeeper, because she was connected with the family, now, but taking care of everything the former housekeeper had managed in the past, she spent most of her time with Laura, trying to keep her spirits up. First, Harry had taken rooms of his own when he went into practice as a physician: his gaiety was missed. Then, something peculiar happened to Matthew, which changed his whole way of life. Though they did not speak of it in so many words, Mary knew that there had been a rejection in his suit for the hand of the estimable Miss Addison, since no wedding materialized, though she did not have the courage to press for details. Matthew grew bitter, reclusive: he worked at the bank, which he did not seem to enjoy, and spent his time at home, either in the den or his room, remaining silent at the dinner table or expressing himself only in monosyllables when addressed. He looked particularly pained when his mother communicated news of the happy couple in Europe, and once even threw down his napkin and left the table to avoid hearing about the singular beauty of Capri.

It was the awareness of Matthew's disappointment, along with the birth of Rory, that changed Laura's mind about John's marriage.

After several adoring letters from Rosaleen, describing everything the beautiful baby did, Laura said thoughtfully, "It would be so nice if they could live here with us, Mary. It would bring the house to life again. There's nothing like a child for doing that."

"I doubt they have such plans, Miss Laura," Mary said proudly. "They were given the clear impression when they left that they'd be living elsewhere. And why shouldn't they want that? It's that difficult for a young couple to adjust to the ways of their family, after being apart so long. Two women under one roof is like having two cocks in the barnyard. It never works out."

"I don't know why you say that. I'm almost inconspicuous in my own house, you know that. I keep my peace and the house runs itself."

Laura did not miss the unabashed scorn in Mary's eyes, though a smile came with it, and she pouted like the pretty girl she must once have been. "Well, I recognize that the servants keep things running," Laura admitted.

"You were after hiding this marriage from everyone," Mary reminded her calmly. "Sure, you aren't going to embrace my daughter to your bosom openly, now, are you? What would people think?"

Laura did not bat an eye. "It can be got around somehow," she said, as though she had already considered it. "They've been away so long, people will think John married abroad: that's all they need know. Of course, there's the matter of the servants."

Though she distrusted what she was hearing, Mary could do no more than put in a word for her old friends. "Sure, they've been with you forever, Miss Laura. It would be ungrateful to turn them out now. It'd be like evicting loyal tenants on a farm back home. I know you too well to believe you'd be so unsympathetic, for it's a kind heart you have."

"We're doing very well without a housekeeper, since the last one left," Laura said. "I wouldn't turn them out in the street, Mary," she defended herself quickly. "No. I'd send Kevin and Bridie along to Harry: he has no help at all. And Mrs. Lynch is getting along in years... she must be close to seventy. I don't like to be uncharitable, but her meals reflect it. Haven't you noticed?"

Mary admitted to herself that it was impossible not to notice, and the poor old thing talking away to herself at the kitchen table when she was not throwing that slop together: perhaps it was that which made Matthew so bilious at table. "What happens to old servants," Mary inquired sadly, "when they've worn themselves out like cart horses and can no longer earn their keep?"

"They're retired with a life pension," Laura said, "and, in cook's case, someone to look after her."

Mary's silence gave consent. "And the younger lasses? Sure, none of them are ready for a pension?"

Obviously, that was a more difficult problem, but Laura's wits were agile when she was pressed. "For some time, I've been thinking of staffing the house at the Cape. A watchman living there alone makes it get musty. Do you think the girls would adapt to the Cape? It gets very cold there in winter."

"Since you're determined to get rid of the lot of them," Mary said with a sigh, "I'm sure they'd take to that better than living in some cellar or going onto the streets like some I've heard of."

"Mary!" Laura said, shocked, but she was too curious to contain herself. "Is that really true? Right here in Boston?"

"Indeed it is. Good Irish girls, too. Though I'm sure they weren't the first to pound the pavement here. Liam says..."

"Yes? What does he say?"

"Sure, it isn't fit for our ears, but he's that indignant. Why is it, I wonder, that religious men know more about the evil going on around us than others do?"

"It's part of their job, I suppose," Laura replied, admonished out of her inquisitiveness. "He'll be leaving for Europe soon."

"He and Rosaleen will cross each other on the ocean," Mary said and nodded, not really sad to see him go: a budding priest in the family was a nuisance. He would be more likable when the Jesuits in France got through with him, and he was more charitable toward the world. The Catholic college in Worcester had only been a stopgap: there was no seminary yet in Boston. Liam had taught for two years to earn the money to go abroad for the priesthood and, with his education, had chosen the Society of Jesus. Though she knew she would not see him for years, Mary felt more relief than sorrow. She felt a constant reproach in his eyes for having left Doirin where she was, but there was no alternative: Mary could not have her raging at Brian with a knife again.

Gradually, the servants were replaced, and Laura was proud of her broad-mindedness, though Mary worried at the results. She had never gotten used to blacks: they frightened her a little, and when she found out that most of them were slaves escaped from somewhere south, she confronted Laura with hot brown eyes.

"I don't understand it at all! Faith, they frighten the breath out of me! They're every bit as lackadaisical as the Irish servants, but I'm sure there's murder in their eyes when I reproach them. Where did they escape from, anyway?"

Laura smiled indulgently. "Mary, my dear, please sit down and I'll explain to you. It didn't occur to me that you were unaware of... Don't you read the newspapers? Don't you know what's going on?"

"Only the Irish ones," Mary replied obstinately, "and I've only time to read the obituaries there."

"How gloomy!" Laura said, biting her lip to keep from laughing. "My darling Mary! These people were brought to this country as slaves to work in the fields in the South. No, please, don't look like that! It wasn't just Americans who did it. Most were brought by the British before the Revolution, though, not to our credit, the Southerners have continued the practice."

"The British made slaves of them too?" Mary asked, slightly mollified. "They made them work in the fields for them too?"

"Too? I don't know what you mean. But let me assure you it's coming to an end! That's what all the fuss is about. The North simply won't tolerate such a condition, and our new President, Mr. Lincoln, is very much against it; he says the country can't 'endure half slave and half free.' These poor people I've hired have *escaped* to freedom, Mary, at the risk of their lives! And," she said smugly, "most of them were house servants to some very prominent people down there. They know what they're doing, you must admit that."

"I've never seen a black man with white hair answering a door anywhere before," Mary grumbled. "And if poor old Mrs. Lynch made a mess of meals...well! Aren't you just a bit tired of chicken and—"

Laura held up her hand. "Something must be done about that, I admit! I was thinking of writing to John and Rosaleen: maybe they could bring back a French cook."

Though she was equally suspicious of that idea, Mary began to feel sympathy for the servants, who had suffered under the British as much as her own people. She could never quite let down her defenses to mingle with them in the kitchen, because they were so different, but they seemed jolly enough among themselves and had no malice in them that she could detect. She ceased to lock her door at night and tried to be friendly, because they had been abused and fled here for safety: but she was too Irish to accept them entirely, and they were aware of her condescension.

She wondered what Rosaleen would say when she arrived home to a houseful of black Africans. But she had a word or two to say to that young lady, too, with all the bloody big boxes that had been arriving at the house for almost two years: the girl would make a pauper of her husband! John's room, which they had wanted to clear for their arrival, was heaped to the ceiling with crates labeled in foreign languages, and they had to fix up Harry's old room for the couple. It was obvious that Rosaleen had gone completely daft and bought up most of Europe.

But the baby would have a place, Mary smiled: Rory would stay in the nursery with her. She had, after all, come here to care for children.

The coach arrived earlier than expected, laden with trunks and boxes, and so many people descended from it that Mary and Laura stood on the steps with their mouths open. It took a moment for them to revive enough to embrace the travelers. Even John kissed his mother, making it obvious that all old wounds were healed and he was starting afresh with her. Rosaleen held Mary for so long that she was assured of her daughter's enduring love, though she could not really get that close to her.

"What in the world do you have beneath that skirt?" she

asked, backing up to look at her in her fine French clothes. "Sure, that isn't a petticoat at all...it feels like metal!"

Rosaleen laughed enchantingly. "It *is*, Mother. I'll show it to you later. Right now, I want you and Aunt Laura to meet your new cook. Monsieur Giraud," she hailed the fat man with a mustache, who was standing by almost at attention and moved forward quickly. "Aunt Laura, this is Monsieur Giraud, your new cook. Monsieur, Mrs. Maddigan. And—"

"But it's a *man!*" Mary exclaimed, before Rosaleen was faced with introducing her mother. "And who are these women?" she asked, appalled, staring into two shy faces. "Rosaleen, you've dragged the half of the continent home, for sure!"

John intervened quickly. "Mother, Mary, this is Thérèse, whom I've employed as Rosaleen's maid. Come here, Carmela, *cara*...Rory's nurse, Carmela. She's been with him from the first, in Rome."

If the foundations of the house had shuddered, dropping stones on her, Mary would not have been more astounded: she hated the Italian woman immediately, but that did not stop her from lunging for the baby in her arms and quickly moving into the hallway with him, followed closely by Laura.

"Oh, the little lamb!" Laura exclaimed, grabbing at Rory in his long dress and shawl. "He's the image of his mother! He's going to be as beautiful as she. Mary, please let me hold him."

But Mary was not about to relinquish custody of her grandson, who had already melted her heart with his clear blue Noonan eyes. She had waited too long for his arrival to share him with anyone, even his other grandmother, who was pulling almost frantically at his clothes. John came through the door with Murphy prancing on a leash and laughed aloud when he saw the two women.

"If you keep it up, I'll have to make a Solomon-like decision," he said. "Mary, please let Mother have him for a moment, before he goes back to Carmela. He needs a nap."

Laura gently took the child from Mary's arms, glancing at her son with gratitude; but what she saw distracted her from Rory.

"Good heavens, what's that?" she cried, catching sight of the large yellow dog. "John, we've never had a dog in this house!"

"He'll only be here until we get our own place," John said,

wondering if he had offended Mary, because of the expression on her face, a mixture of disbelief and shock. "Mary, dear, there'll be plenty of time with the child later."

"Where did Rosaleen find him?" she asked, through tight lips. "Did you go to Ireland, then, after all?"

"No, only as far as England. Rosaleen didn't want..." He checked himself. "Oh, the dog. She found him in Rome, and his name's—"

"—Murphy," Mary said with resignation, as her daughter and the new servants stepped through the door, and Carmela came forward to relieve Laura of the baby, who laughed up at her. "I swear to God, this isn't the day I thought it would be."

"The dog's all right," Laura put in quickly, her fingers still entangled in Rory's knitted shawl. "John, about your house..."

"I've never seen such a three-ring circus," Rosaleen said and laughed, taking her husband's arm. "Oh, my, it's good to see familiar faces! Is it possible to get a cup of tea, Mother? And may we go to John's room to take off our wraps?"

"John's room!" Mary said sharply. "It's Harry's room we've fixed up for you. Sure a fly would break his neck trying to get into John's room!"

When they finally sat down to tea, Rosaleen was out of her hoopskirt and dressed in one of the simple day dresses she had taken with her. That seemed to make her more approachable, though John was ill at ease in his mother's sitting room. They listened to all the news at home: the implication of Matthew's disappointment, and concern over his low spirits; Harry's success in his practice, now that he had come to his senses and given up research; and the day-to-day matters that concerned the two older women. As they talked, Rosaleen sensed an urgency beneath the banalities, noticed the way their eyes met frequently in some understanding and moved quickly away, as though the time were not yet right for something.

"Everyone's all right, aren't they?" she finally asked uncomfortably, and Mary assured them that everyone in the family was fine.

"Darin's back. Did I write you that? He returned last fall and married a few months later. A fine girl named Peggy Hanrihan. But I know I must have written that to you."

"We've been traveling," Rosaleen said, with as much control as she could gather, because her heart turned over at the mention of his name. And though she knew she should not resent his marriage, it pained her deeply. "Your letter probably hasn't caught up with us yet. How's Uncle Brian, Mother? You never mentioned him."

"I've never seen him happier," Mary said, with the first open smile since they'd gotten home. "He has his son and Peg to look after him and help him now. Sure, what he's needed most was a bit of companionship in his life."

"We all need that," Laura interrupted inconspicuously, apparently seeing an opening for the mysterious silent communication between herself and Mary. "I must say it's been lonely in this house without you two, and you stayed away so long! It's given me a lot of time to think. I hope you weren't too upset by my attitude about your marriage."

John remained silent, studying her face carefully; but Rosaleen, too relieved to be home for caution, smiled. "We've been far too busy and happy to even think about it, Aunt Laura. So don't you think about it, either. After all, you *were* doing what you believed right, with Matthew's planning to marry and bring a wife into the family. We've forgotten all about it: you forget it, too."

Her words gave Laura the courage she needed, though perhaps she did not say things as she had rehearsed them for so long. "The point is, my dear, Matthew didn't marry, and the ways things are going, I doubt he ever will. For some time now I've recognized my mistake...my mistaken way of thinking when you married. What I'm trying to say is...oh, dear! Would you young people consider living here?"

Rosaleen was speechless, not at the opportunity, but at seeing their plans dashed. She and John had decided upon a small, manageable house in the country, where he could work on his book and she could care for Rory, and the other children they planned. She gave John a quick, startled glance, unable to reply, and saw that he was smiling faintly, having figured out his mother's motive some moments earlier.

"That's very kind of you, Mother," he said amicably enough, "but the fact is that we have other plans. We don't want to live in Boston at all. But we'll be close enough to see you often enough. You were probably wondering about all the crates I sent home: well, those were for our house...Rosaleen's house. And we have brought our own servants."

"Crates?" Rosaleen asked, bewildered. "What crates, John? We didn't buy anything big enough to ship back ahead of us."

He patted her hand affectionately and smiled. "You didn't, darling: you were too damn tight. But I think you'll find just about everything you admired, right up there in my room: from the inlaid marble table to the French furniture. If I did my job right, I didn't miss anything."

"It was *you*, then?" Mary burst out in surprise. "Sure, I was going to rake Rosaleen over the coals for certain, thinking she'd gone mad with your money."

"Don't worry about that, Mary," he said gently. "Your daughter's as thrifty as you are. If she hadn't felt so out of place in Paris, I'd have had to twist her arm to replenish her wardrobe."

"But..." Rosaleen said, completely overcome. "Oh, John, you shouldn't have! That *pietra dura* table was too hundred thousand lire! And the Louis XV chairs were each—"

"The first thing she did, Mary," he explained lightly, "was learn the complete monetary conversion for each country. I've never seen anyone do it so fast! Then she limited her purchases to no more than a few dollars each. She has some kind of abacus in that pretty head of hers, which works with remarkable swiftness."

Rosaleen was shocked at his profligacy. "My dear John, I just can't believe it. You need someone to manage your money!"

His pride in his expenditure was unabashed. "Tomorrow we'll have some of the crates opened, sweetheart, and we'll see if you're as morally upright then. We'll have to see if anything was damaged in shipping, anyway."

"Damaged!" Rosaleen cried, her blue eyes terrified. "Sure if anyone damaged a piece of it, I'll have his heart on a skewer!"

The difficulty they found themselves in with Laura over where they should live was settled temporarily by their mutual agreement to stay in the Maddigan house until they could either find one of their own or arrange to have their dream house built. Both of them preferred the elegant half-timbered beauty of the houses and small manors they had seen in Normandy, though an architect who could undertake such a problem would have to be found, because that sort of house was completely in conflict with the logical Colonial clapboards of New England, straight and bare as the soul of the place, decorated only by their charming black shutters.

In the meantime, there were many distractions from even

looking for land. John, anxious to get to work on his book, holed up in the library, grateful for his proximity to the one at Harvard; and Rosaleen, who had thought all she would be doing was caring for Rory, came home to a large stack of letters from people she had met abroad. A prolific letter writer, she was hardly finished with the first ones before the invitations began to pour in, from New York, Philadelphia, and even Boston. She was soon as thick as ever with her good friend Pamela Dove, and when she asked Laura if she could invite her to tea, she was surprised by her mother-in-law's awed reaction.

"Dove? Not the girl who married young Edward? But my dear, that's Pamela Bradshaw! She's from one of the very best families. And the Doves aren't badly placed, either. She's your *friend?* Of course you can invite her. But Rosaleen, I must warn you that she may not come. I mean, her older relatives might prevail on her to snub you, here. Associations abroad can be rather loose, I understand, but once people are back in Boston...well, I think you know the problem we've had about my marriage."

Pamela did come, though, and invited Rosaleen and John to dinner at her house in return. Laura, too old to be envious, was quick to appreciate the opportunities opened by Rosaleen's beauty, charm and intelligence.

The young woman was accepted by their own age group for her ready wit and interest in people, which she revealed by being an excellent listener; Rosaleen still wanted to learn and had an open warmth about her very few tried to resist. And though her beauty startled some and fascinated others, it was soon overcome by her very natural charm, so that envy was avoided. The young women trusted her: she was obviously completely devoted to her husband and did not know how to flirt with their men. Even the older, stodgier members of Pamela's circle could find no fault with the chicly dressed and well-traveled young woman who had sprung up so suddenly among them: when she was with them, she seemed to enjoy the company of older people, listening to their reminiscences about Europe with interest, conversing with them in both French and Italian, enthusiastic about her own interest in art and, more important, revealing herself as a simple, devoted young mother who, though she doted on her baby son, was respectful enough of their age to ask them serious questions about childrearing.

By the time that first evening at the Doves was over,

Rosaleen had made many more friends, both young and old, and the steady stream of invitations that came to the Maddigan house put Laura into an emotional state which was a combination of elation and fear.

"Didn't they ask about your family?" she inquired closely, wringing her lace handkerchief in her lap. "Surely they wanted to know who you were?"

"Some of the older people made veiled inquiries," Rosaleen replied happily, glancing through her invitations. "I managed to put them off rather obliquely, by referring to a tragedy I didn't feel up to discussing. So we spoke mostly of Europe, and the places they had been."

"Rosaleen, my dear," Laura said, pointing to the invitations in the young woman's lap, "it's within your power to completely restore the family's position in society or destroy it altogether, I think. We must consider how to handle any situation which may occur."

Rosaleen shrugged. "I'm not worried, Aunt Laura. I can't possibly accept all these invitations. John would be quite worn out attending so many functions. Besides, it just isn't important. The first time was fun...like Cinderella's ball. But aside from Pamela and a few others I met, I'm content to stay home. I'd like to study music and—"

"But it *is* important," Laura said, "to my family and yours. You must start thinking about Rory's future, my dear."

At the mention of Rory, Rosaleen looked up at her thoughtfully. "You're saying that what I do now will affect Rory later?"

"Yes. You don't want your children to have the lonely childhood my sons suffered, do you? They should grow up in the position they deserve."

Rosaleen tapped several of the invitations on her knee, staring out the window onto Louisburg Square. "I want my children to be happy, Aunt Laura. I want them to have a place in the scheme of things."

"Then, for goodness' sake, accept. One thing's bothered me very much since you've been back, especially when you say it before the servants. From now on, you're to call your mother 'Mary,' except in private, of course. I've already discussed it with her, and she agrees."

"I don't like it," Rosaleen said later to Mary, in her upstairs room. "I want as much for my children as she does, but it

379

can't come between us, Mother. I know you'd agree to almost anything to keep things running smoothly here, but..."

"The fact is, I'm an embarrassment here. I should leave altogether, Rosaleen. I'm sure Veronica would make a place for me, and I have some money saved and some coming in every month from our part of the pub."

"No! I won't have it, at all. You belong here: besides, everything would fall to pieces without you, Mother. I was wondering why she sacked the servants: now I know. It was so they wouldn't be around, knowing our relationship."

"The new ones are black, you know," Mary said, and Rosaleen smiled.

"I know...I couldn't help noticing," she said, watching Mary look up quickly, humor flicker in her dark eyes and laughter come to her lips.

"Sure, you're a dreadful girl!" she said. "I don't know what society wants with you at all. But, Rosaleen," she added, more seriously, "it's true what she says about Rory's future. I don't want to see him in limbo like her boys. He wouldn't be fish nor fowl nor good red meat, as they say. I want the very best for that darling child. So if you have to call me Mary in front of people, sure it's no sin and no harm to me. There is one thing, though..."

For a moment, it was as though Rosaleen were a child again, anticipating her mother's thoughts before she spoke them.

"I can't send Carmela all the way back to Italy," she considered, "but there's no reason in the world you shouldn't share the care of him, Mother. That's what you really want, isn't it?"

A beatific glow spread over Mary's face. "Yes! That was what I was hoping for when you came back. And after a few weeks of watching the goings-on about that poor baby, I really think it's essential that he has one firm hand in his little life, Rosaleen. And I can see it isn't going to be yours or his father's, or Laura's . . . or that plump little Italian's . . . who kisses him all over and sings to him all day!"

"All you want to do is give him a firm hand and spank him when he's naughty?" Rosaleen grinned, and her mother lowered her eyes. "You're such a stern, harsh woman and not loving and maternal at all? Is that it?"

Mary shook her head with a defeated smile. "Sure, if everyone else is going to spoil him, why can't I have my part in it? He's so lovely, Rosaleen! He's a Noonan, through and through, and not like a Maddigan at all!"

The words had a sobering effect on Rosaleen. "Mother, I want you to help me: you'll be good for him. But there's one restriction; and I must be firm about it. Rory's to stay in his own neighborhood and here in the house. You'll not be trailing him across town to the pub, as you did with Philip. I won't have him near that place. Do you understand?"

Mary did not understand, of course: she dearly wanted to show the baby off to Brian. But she agreed to the rule, thinking it was part of Rosaleen's intense reaction to her own childhood. The girl had never liked the pub, and she probably thought it would be a bad influence on the little boy as he grew older.

"All right," she said, crestfallen. "I would like our family to see him, though, Rosaleen. He's as much a part of them as the Maddigans."

"I'm sure they will," Rosaleen said softly. "Please don't worry about it. There's something else I've wanted to discuss with you."

"Indeed?" Mary said rigidly.

"It's Aunt Doirin." Rosaleen sighed, the very thought of the woman upsetting her. "I met a physician from New York, when I was in Florence. He specialized in such things. He gave me the name of an excellent small facility that handles people in her condition. It isn't far from Boston. I think we could manage to get her out of that awful asylum and move her there, Ma. We'd have to be discreet—even John doesn't know about her—but..."

She had never seen such happiness on her mother's face: Mary was inarticulate with joy. She moved forward quickly and embraced Rosaleen as though she would never let her go. With tears streaming down her face, Mary gasped, "Sure, Brian and I could look after everything, darling. We'll do it this very weekend."

"It's very expensive," Rosaleen warned her, "but don't tell Uncle Brian that. I don't want his family to know. John's given me an outrageous allowance, and I'll take care of it."

"We'll pay our share," Mary said quickly. "I told you things are better now."

"You'll pay a minimum amount, Ma, just to keep Brian happy. You really couldn't handle it otherwise."

"Oh, Rosaleen, I didn't think you cared for poor Doirin at all! I didn't think anyone cared but me... and Brian, of course.

You've made me so proud, my darling. Sure, it's a fine woman you've grown into."

"A rich one, at least," Rosaleen said, patting at Mary's tears with her lace handkerchief. "I'm not a noble person, Ma. I'm sorry. But I've thought about Doirin a lot, since I was sick two years ago and had just a taste of the pain she must feel. Maybe my motive's purely selfish...hoping that if it ever comes on me again, someone will do the same for me." She brought herself out of such gloomy thoughts, taking a deep breath. "I *do* want to see you happy, Ma. I really do! I'm not at all proud of the deception that's going on in this house. And if it weren't for Rory, sure, I'd lapse into the brogue whenever I wanted to!"

Chapter 25

NO ONE confronted Matthew about his behavior, which was upsetting the whole family; Laura and Mary tiptoed around the subject, keeping their voices lowered to a whisper when he was in his study, afraid of making things worse if they mentioned anything to him. The young man had a broken heart, and only time would heal it; in the interval, he was to be given every consideration. That was the way such matters were handled by two aging women, who knew very little about men: they faded into the wallpaper to let him work his problem out, hoping that things would turn out well in the long run. But not Rosaleen. She had hardly settled under the roof again, before she marched right up to the door of the study and rapped on it, not at all gently.

When Matt opened the door, scowling, she did not ask to be admitted: she pushed past him into the room, while he stared after her with disbelief.

"Same old room!" she said, her skirts swirling as she turned on the balls of her feet to examine it. "The one your father died in, as I recall. Do you have something like that in mind for yourself, Matt? Close the door."

He did so reluctantly, a frown mark already permanently set between his dark eyes. Taking his place behind the desk, he remained silent until, after a few moments of no speech at all, for Rosaleen did not help him, he finally said, "Frankly, I don't much care whether I live or die."

Such words were worse than blasphemy to Rosaleen's ears: everything about her was a confirmation of life. Death was the Great Enemy, to be avoided in every possible way. "Is it a broken heart you have, now?" she asked with bitter Irish sarcasm, which thinly masked the outrage she felt. "Sure, it's a poor man who goes down for the count at the first refusal in his life." Then, more gently, for she understood loss, "Did she really mean that much to you, Matt?"

He sighed deeply. "It isn't a broken heart, Rosaleen. It's a broken life!"

"Was it the old thing?" she asked. "The problem of class among the Brahmins? I thought you had overcome that."

"No. The thing with Ada was just another man. It was a disappointment, but I haven't even thought of it for a long time. It's my *life*, Rosaleen: I hate my way of life. A man should be able to choose, not be *destined* to uphold the family business, just because he's the eldest son. With all my heart, I hate *banking:* it's dull, meticulous and completely meaningless to me. I could hardly bear to hear your letters when you were abroad: I wanted to be there so much."

Rosaleen sat down in the red plush chair and studied him, his face pale in the slanting light from the heavily draped window, his wide mouth, so like his father's, tight with frustration. "But surely you could take a trip," she suggested. "You don't have to remain at the bank all the time. What happened to the man who looked after things for your mother after your father died? Isn't there someone like him who could take over, so you could get away for a while?"

He shook his head and stared at his hands, clenched together on the desk before him. "That man, who's mercifully dead, now, left things tangled up in a Gordian knot... while another upright member of the board extorted all he could. Things were a mess when I took over. I've only now got them completely straightened out. The whole damn load's right on my shoulders. I wish I had a brother who could help shoulder it, but what do I have? A dedicated physician and, God help me, a scholar!" He laughed harshly. "You're the only one with the brains to do it, and you're a *woman.*"

She assessed the problem silently, her eyes wandering over the paneled walls. "No one would have to know that, would they?" she finally said in a small, tentative voice, and he looked up with another weary frown.

"What do you mean?"

"It's probably quite daft," she demurred, "but it would give you a chance to get away for a while."

"Come out with it, Rosaleen. I can't second-guess you, love. I never could."

"Well, could you teach John and me what we'd have to know, so he could take over while you were away? He wouldn't like it," she said, anticipating Matt's objections, "but it's his responsibility, too, isn't it? And, actually, he wouldn't have to do anything but take what I prepare to the meetings and such."

"It's quite mad, as you say," he replied, but then the expression on his face lightened slowly. "Do you really think you could do it?"

She shrugged prettily. "I don't know. But you've always said I was good with figures—"

"Good?" He laughed suddenly. "You're fantastic. But you must realize that John can't string more than a few numbers together, and even that would bore him senseless."

"He isn't that bad," she said in defense of her husband. "He had all the preliminary math that you did, and he's very intelligent. Mathematics does bore him, though. On the other hand, he likes to spend the money well enough, and it wouldn't hurt him to be bored long enough for you to have a rest!"

"There are other things, though, Rosaleen," he said thoughtfully. "You see, I'd like to get out of it altogether. Besides, there's no way I can nip in and out of Europe before the war starts."

"What war?" she asked, alarmed.

"Surely you know that the Southern states have seceded?"

"Of course, but John says they're just being naughty children to have their own way." She laughed. "A war between the North and South is impossible! Why, we're still one country. Well, at least we're all Americans. I can't imagine Americans actually shooting each other."

"Let's hope you're right, my dear. As a banker, I have to plan the other way, though. You know, Rosaleen," he said dreamily, "I wish I *had* gone off to sea with your cousin that summer at the Cape. That's what I really wanted to do."

The memory disturbed her sweetly, but she fought the emotion back. "And look at him now," she said scornfully, "tending bar in his father's pub! He has nothing. Not even an interesting life."

"But think of what he's *had!* Complete freedom. I've never

had that in my life. The goddam bank's been tied to me like a ball and chain ever since Father died."

"We can't change the past," she said sincerely. "But Matt, we can do something about the future. I'm going to talk to John right now. The sooner you start training us, the sooner you can relax. 'Go to sea' for a while, if you like." She smiled, as she rose. "Your mother's going to raise Cain, of course, but she can't prevail against all three of us."

Actually, Laura had no inkling of what was taking place in the library when she retired after dinner every evening, with a glow of relief that Matthew was coming around, at last. And Mary, who usually knew everything that was going on, only suspected something, without pursuing it. Her mind and heart full of her grandson, she was too occupied to worry about what Rosaleen might be up to now.

Mary and Laura tiptoed into the nursery to see the sleeping baby, under the watchful dark eyes of Carmela, for whom they had both developed a mild abhorrence, because she was closer to Rory than they, and the child loved and depended on her.

"Sure, everything's perfect, now," Mary said softly, when they were once again in Laura's room. "It just goes to show that if you wait long enough and weather the storms, there's peace and contentment waiting for you. I'm forty-six years old, and I've never been happier in my life. Sure, I wouldn't be young again for anything. Would you, Miss Laura?"

Laura winced as she sat down to take off her shoes. "I wouldn't mind being forty-six again," she said. "I have ten years on you, Mary, and my bones are beginning to tell me about it. But you're right, my dear. Everything is pleasant now. As for being really young again, I don't know—I really don't. I wouldn't make the same mistakes twice, though. Everything would be very different; there would never be a Matthew Maddigan in my life. I've gone over all that in my mind for years, but there was no undoing what I'd done."

"We tend to do that as we get older, I think," Mary said from experience. "But sure, you just think in circles when you remember. If you hadn't married Mr. Maddigan, and I had avoided Tomas, as I should have, neither of us would have that gorgeous child upstairs to love. Family's the important thing. And now, even young Matthew's looking happier."

At that very moment, Matthew was in the library, shouting at his brother in a rage.

"Goddammit, John, apply yourself! Your eyes keep sliding to your own work on the end of the table, and you don't listen to a thing I'm saying! You've been doing it for two weeks! Can't you get it through your head that this is more important than something that didn't even happen twenty-five hundred years ago?"

"Sorry," John said, with a helpless glance at Rosaleen. "I know it's really important; honestly, I do. It's just that it's so damn dull. My mind doesn't function like yours and Rosaleen's, Matt."

Rosaleen got up and removed John's carefully laid-out notes to the window seat, and returned to him with a smile, extending her hand. "Out of sight, out of mind?" she asked softly. "John, you don't have to learn all of it: Matt will only be away a short while. But you simply must understand the basics of what we're discussing, because it will be you who'll be presenting things as head of the bank and president of the board."

He murmured something amiable and clung to her hand as she took her place beside him again.

"John," Matthew said, attempting patience, "you know as well as I do there's going to be a war...or do you? Do you really believe the Southern states are just being 'naughty children' or was that for Rosaleen's benefit? I assure you she won't collapse at the thought: we've already discussed it."

John nodded. "It was for her benefit," he admitted; then, suddenly, there was a transformation in his whole manner. He straightened his shoulders, and his eyes became intense behind his glasses. "I hate the thought of war, but if it's the only way to stop slavery in this country, it can't come soon enough. I'm in agreement with President Lincoln about that subject, at least. We can't endure as human beings, as long as there are slaves among us."

Matthew raised his eyebrows. "Good God! We've a red-hot abolitionist among us—and I thought he was living in ancient Greece! Have you any conception of the financial implications to the North, if such a war occurs?"

"Well, it would be mobilized, of course," John said. "It does seem absolutely rotten to capitalize on that. I suspect you're leading to weapons and such things?"

"Wrong. I'm talking about mills closing, because there

387

isn't any cotton, and about saving our investment there, before it happens."

"Saving your investment?" Rosaleen asked, appalled. "Pulling your money out? Matt, thousands of people work in the mills: it would be unemployment and fam...hunger for them!"

"They'll go on the dole. There's nothing we can do about it, Rosaleen: it's going to happen anyway. You must learn that our interests must be protected first, because the solvency of the Northern banks is what will win a war in the long run."

"There isn't that much dole," she said, "and you don't know what unemployment is! It seems to me there's a perfectly logical solution to keeping the mills running, Matt."

"Indeed?" He smiled. "You're very good at figures, my dear, but...well, let's hear your great economic proposal, anyway."

"Find another source of cotton," she said simply. "The finest cotton in the world comes from Egypt, and you have ships. Not the right kind, of course, but you could trade them for merchantmen. No one would be taking luxury ships abroad in the middle of a war, I'm sure."

Her suggestion was met with silence; she thought she must have made a fool of herself, that perhaps her idea was completely implausible. In the future, she would remain quiet about anything she did not understand, learn the basics of bank management and leave the big decisions to those who knew about such things. She nearly fell out of her chair when Matt jumped up.

"Goddammit!" He started to pace the library, and she was at the point of apology when he swung around to face them. "Out of the mouths of babes! It's...feasible. Yes, Rosaleen, it's altogether feasible. Of course, we won't be able to get as large a supply unless we went farther afield. And if we did it immediately, we'd corner the market for Eastern cotton before England had the same idea. They're much more industrialized than we are. Jesus, God! It's a brilliant suggestion."

Rosaleen was shaken by his words; she experienced something gratifying and completely new to her, without knowing what it was: a taste of power. "If it'll do England out of anything, I hope you'll carry it through," she said, basking in the warm glow of the new feeling. Then she had another thought, splintered through with fear. "But what if there isn't a war?

And pray God there isn't, Matt. Your ships would be gone and you'd have all that cotton piled on the docks and..."

He put his hand up to check the flow of words. "Rosaleen, don't ever go back on a good idea when you've had one. Whatever happens, we'd suffer no loss; and if things work out the way I'm almost certain they will, we'll have considerable gain. You must learn how to *speculate*."

She did not know what the word meant, but did not want to spoil the moment by telling him so. "May I borrow some of your books about banks and stocks and things like that?" she asked, and he was in the act of piling several forbidding tan leather volumes in front of her when another thought struck like lightning. "Matt! Those damned Southerners will keep selling their cotton to *England!* England might go in with them. Sure they were all English once anyway, weren't they? What can we do?"

Matthew and John both started laughing, though for different reasons. Her husband, still holding her hand, kissed it quickly.

"Goddam the king and up with the Irish! Darling, it's a good thing Mother didn't hear all that."

"Rosaleen," Matt said and smiled, "for the time being, at least, we can leave the governmental decisions to the President, and the military, if it comes to that. I may be wrong, but I think their answer would be one thing: blockade."

She could not resist asking the meaning of that word; and, when he explained it to her, she leaned back in her chair with a sigh. "Lovely!"

"I don't know what you have here, John," Matt said. "She's either the loveliest monster in the world, or she's a daft genius! However, I think we're ready to get down to business in a small way. Tomorrow you'll both accompany me to the bank, and I'll acquaint you with the physical part of it, which only a few people know. Then, gradually, over the next few months, you'll take over, John. In name only, I suspect. And God help both of you!"

Rosaleen was pregnant again, happy about it, but almost too busy to experience morning sickness. Between her work for the bank at home and her continuing social life, which she tried to limit to one function a week, she barely had time enough for Rory and her husband, and she tried to make it of the best quality she could. After reviewing John's day at the bank thoroughly right after dinner in the den every evening, they went to their rooms, which were furnished with the furniture John had so extravagantly purchased in Europe. They had a bedroom and by combining John's and Harry's rooms, a sitting room and a dressing room as well.

"It won't be for long, dear," she told him gently, after Matt had been gone a month. "Perhaps through the summer. Then you can get back to your own work, and we can start thinking of our house again."

"I think about my work most of the time while I'm at the bank," he said wearily. "If it weren't for your making all the decisions, I think I'd go insane, darling. I'm like a small boy dreaming out the window most of the day. But I've had some really fine ideas about my book. The best that can be said of all this is that it's given me more time to consider it before committing anything to paper."

"I know," she said sympathetically, kissing him. "But it's better for us to be inconvenienced for a while, than that Matt have a breakdown. He was very depressed."

John nodded, holding her hand against his cheek. "If anything happened to Matt, I'd be stuck with it permanently. Actually, Rosaleen, I'm really rather proud to be able to fill in. I feel as though I'm carrying my own weight, and I've never felt that way before. Of course, you're doing the difficult part. I'm just showing up every day and presenting your work. I appreciate it, darling, I really do. It won't be too much for you, though...with the new baby coming?"

"I traveled all the way to Egypt and back to Rome carrying the first one." She smiled. "This time I'm almost sedentary!" Then, to lighten his spirits, "Remember the camel ride you'd planned?"

They laughed together over the sentimental recollection, and when John announced Rosaleen's condition to their friends the Doves one evening, all he had to say was, "Rosaleen won't be riding camels for a while."

"I won't be, either!" Pamela cried happily, and the two young women withdrew together to discuss their babies and childrearing, while the men had a marvelous evening with their own scholarly interests. When they were with friends, the bank was totally forgotten. So Rosaleen was able to rationalize her love of dinners and parties as relaxing for John, though it was she, and not her husband, who was taking a firm place in the circles of their many friends.

Matthew had hardly arrived in France in April when Fort Sumter was fired on, and the war he had anticipated began.

While the President was calling up 75,000 Union troops, Rosaleen was writing a swift message to her brother-in-law, telling him to remain where he was for the summer, assuring him that everything was under control at the bank. The figures she sent him were so conclusive that Matt decided to finish his vacation.

As far as Rosaleen was concerned, the war meant only keeping the situation at the bank steady; she worked long hours and made some far-reaching decisions during this period. In the whole household, only John read the papers with interest and trepidation, though the news of major battles, especially the first encounter at Bull Run, which the Union lost in July, filtered down even to the black servants. At peace with their grandchild, Mary and Laura could not have been further from what was happening in the world, a little to the annoyance of Rosaleen, who was struggling hard with other banks and industry to convert the shoe factories into retooling to make boots and military gear and trying to carry through her cotton deal, now that the blockade of Southern ports was actually in effect.

"You're behaving as though you have blindfolds on," she said with asperity to the two older women at tea in Laura's suite one afternoon.

Laura and her mother sat on the white silk sofa with Rory between them, an arrangement which had become customary with them when they were both in the same room with the tiny boy. "Aunt Laura, please don't give him tea biscuits! He's only eighteen months old! Mother, you didn't give us anything solid until—"

"Sure, it's all right." Mary smiled. "It was soaked well in cream. You began to have your praties at about his age, mashed up with milk, and you thrived on them, all of you."

"Potatoes are nourishing," Rosaleen said. "Cookies with icing in between will only make him fat. I don't want him to be a little roly-poly. He's too lovely. Anyway, as I was saying, I don't see how you can ignore the war the way you do. Even the servants know what's happening more than you do! Everyone thought it would only last a short time, but so far the Union Army's getting beaten! It may last a whole year."

"Sure, darling, we've already had our troubles," Mary said. "As long as they don't march right through Boston, we aren't letting ourselves be concerned. If it had to happen at all, it's just fortunate it came now, instead of twenty years from now, when Rory might have to go."

"Amen," Laura said, kissing the child. "And all our sons are safe, too. Everyone knows that only poor boys go to war."

Laura's illusions about that were dispelled, and total hysterics occurred, when Harry came by a few months later to announce that doctors were needed in the Union Army and that he had volunteered to go.

After giving his mother a light sedative, Harry came downstairs, where Rosaleen and Mary were sitting with stricken faces.

Mary flew at him at once. "Sure, you'd no right to do this to your mother!" she cried. "She doesn't need such shocks at her age at all. You weren't even called up, Harry. You had to go and volunteer! I swear to God, I've never heard anything so daft in my life. You had a nice practice: your mother's so proud of you..."

He held up his hand to check her excited words. "There, there, Mary. If you keep it up, I'll give you a sleeping draft too. Mother has you to look after her, so I know she'll be fine. There's nothing physically wrong with her, except, maybe, lack of exercise, which is a breeding ground for hysteria. I don't have to justify myself to anyone, so I won't remind you of all the Irish lads who've left their families every few years to fight the British, will I?"

"Left and got themselves shot or hanged!" Mary spat back at him. "Sure, there was many a mother at home who spent most of her time in church from losing sons that way. And you're not going to fight. You don't *have* to go. The selfishness of children is criminal! Sure they're a worry from the cradle to the grave."

He gave a deep sigh and looked to Rosaleen for help, but she only shook her head.

"Without mother's embroidery, I feel the same way, Harry. This is totally unnecessary, and an awful waste. With all your work and education."

"Rosaleen," he said patiently, "I don't think you've been properly Americanized, even now. And I'm not really going out of any great patriotic concern myself, I guess. Conditions are deplorable down there, with more injured coming in every day. Never mind that they're short of medications or that they're doing amputations under whiskey, both as anesthetic and antiseptic, or that there just aren't enough doctors there! I have to do what I consider my duty, as a physician and a man."

"Amputations?" Rosaleen said, frowning.

Harry's nerves were drawn so taut by the afternoon's emotions that he cried, "Yes, goddammit! Shells blow arms and legs and heads off! Do you think they're *playing* at war? They're using real ammunition—bullets and powder! Men are being killed like flies! And the ones who aren't killed outright are dying of infection. I'm sorry," he said, his voice falling. "I shouldn't talk like that to you."

But his brutal words had reached Rosaleen, penetrated her total ignorance of the horror of war, touched her with his compassion. She walked into his arms and held him tight, tears running from her eyes.

"Harry," she said. "Dear Harry. Oh, God. Take care of yourself. *Please!*"

Her mother was not mollified. Without another word, Mary walked out of the parlor to look after Laura. Passing the black butler with a silver tray of mail on the stairs, with hardly a pause in her stride, she shot him an angry look from her flashing dark eyes.

"You!" she said accusingly, making him back up against the stair railing to let her pass, wondering what he had done now.

With decision following decision at the bank, it was no longer feasible for Rosaleen to stay home; judgments had to be made on the spot, not in the evening at home. And John, who was more liberal in his thinking than most men, was the first to point it out.

"This war isn't just going to go away," he said one Sunday in the garden, shortly after Carmela had taken Rory upstairs for his nap. "This arrangement at the bank isn't going to work out, darling. The summer's nearly over and Matt will be home soon. In the meantime, would it be too hard on you to accompany me to the meetings? I just can't think about financial things fast enough, Rosaleen. I feel a perfect idiot. If you were beside me, I could confer quickly with you. You'd only have to be there for the meetings, which we'd know about beforehand."

Rosaleen, looking lovely in a softly ruffled, low-cut blue dress, which intensified the color of her eyes, fell silent for a moment. "Wouldn't the board resent a woman's being there?"

"Probably. But to hell with them! There are advantages to being their employer, though I usually don't exercise them. You have a better brain than the lot of them. I don't see why

393

it should be wasted, just because of your sex. Of course," he added, "you *are* pregnant, and it might be too much for you."

"Don't be ridiculous, John. It would be easier to be there on the spot than to sort things out at night. The baby has nothing to do with it. I've never felt better in my life; or, perhaps I should say, since I was carrying Rory. You know that pregnancy agrees with me: it makes me feel just grand! However, there are a few things I'll have to do first. Can you hold them off until Wednesday?"

The next day, with a sheaf of papers in her drawstring purse, she descended on Madame Hurotte's shop, setting it into total commotion with her demands.

"Madame, I need a complete new wardrobe," she said, putting the papers into her old employer's hands. "Here are some designs I worked out, last night...in the order in which I'll need the dresses. The first, as you can see, will have Eugénie riding-jacket tops, curved down into the skirts. I must have one of these by tomorrow evening."

"Tomorrow evening!" madame cried. "But you know our schedule here."

Rosaleen gave her an ironic smile. "Because I know it, I know you can do it," she said. "I'll pay the girls extra. All of these tailored frocks are to be in subdued colors, though I don't object to attractive textures. I'll select the materials now. I'm going into business, madame," she explained, "and I want to look as unfeminine as possible."

The young woman who entered the boardroom on her husband's arm to sit beside him at the head of the long, highly polished table on Wednesday was totally unprepossessing in her plain skirt and jacket. Her hair was coiled severely into a knot on her neck; her hat, with its narrow brim, concealed most of it. In the course of the meeting, John Maddigan, whom the members had come to respect—though very differently than his brother—conferred several times with his wife, making a clear decision quickly on every occasion. And, though Mrs. Maddigan's presence was never explained, the board members, ruthless businessmen all, recognized at once who was making the decisions, and that she was not to be flattered or catered to in any way. Even a request to light a cigar in her presence was met with a cold, sharp look from the blue eyes.

"Business as usual, gentlemen. Mrs. Maddigan's quite familiar with the odor of tobacco," John would answer.

And, as the weeks passed, with Rosaleen wearing her conservative tailored garments which neutralized her sex, she began to experience the peculiar exultation she had felt in some of the sessions with Matt: the sensation he called "power." These men were not dull-minded, though their thinking was not as creative as hers...and they respected her. Not for her pretty face and frocks, not for the Noonan charm, but for her mind as a businessman.

She found herself becoming two people, though she recognized that one had always been latent within her. The men at the bank, who did not move in her social circles, might not have recognized her at one of the many parties she attended. Though in the months since the war had begun ostentation had been subdued, and many of the functions were in aid of the army or to purchase medical supplies, Rosaleen's particular "style" had not been affected, because it had always been simple and unadorned, merely a setting for the sparkling gem that was herself. If the other ladies looked somewhat drab and ordinary, because they were hesitant to wear their diamonds during a national crisis and had new gowns devoid of ruffles and ornamentation, Rosaleen still appeared the same, in her old Paris gowns without hoopskirts, and without jewels because she had none of her own.

She was still the one people were drawn to, her vitality and charm undiminished, her youthful beauty full and vibrant. Though she did not understand her particular attraction, she enjoyed it to the fullest, often wondering what these people would think if they saw her business self.

Chapter 26

WHEN MATTHEW returned home in early August, without notifying anyone he was coming, his presence was a relief to everyone but Rosaleen. His mother hung on his arm, airing her complaints about Harry's abandonment, and John rushed forward with a smile to shake his hand heartily, telling him how well he looked and how good it was to have him back. Rosaleen dutifully kissed him on the cheek, though she was uneasy about having her eventful, gratifying business career cut short, with no warning at all. Until she saw Matthew again, relaxed and tanned, so obviously ready to take over his duties once more, she had not realized how much her work at the bank meant to her, nor fully recognized the curious pleasure being in control brought to her life.

Through all the greetings and conversation the next day, Rosaleen observed that Matt was inattentive. There was a certain aloofness in his friendliness, as though his thoughts were not quite with the family, and he gave no indication of hurrying back to work, even postponing a survey of the transactions of the past four months' business. She did not have time to dwell on his peculiar attitude, however, because of a disturbing development in her own family.

She was in the nursery helping Carmela get Rory ready for bed, when her mother slipped quietly into the room and stood by the door, instead of entering into the bathing and dressing of her grandson, which usually meant so much to her. Only after Rory was kissed by both his mother and his nurse and tucked away comfortably and Rosaleen had reluctantly started to leave the room did Mary speak up.

"Come to my room for a moment," Mary whispered, the muscles of her face sagging with what appeared to be fatigue. "I must talk to you."

Once inside the room that had been hers for so many years, and which had been cheerfully redecorated to accommodate Mary in her new position as companion and unrecognized housekeeper, Rosaleen's suspicion that something was amiss was confirmed.

Mary informed her, "Rosaleen, I hate to tell you this. Sure, everything's going so well for you, right now, and the Noonans seem far from your mind, but..."

Her first thought was of Darin, and she was surprised at the emotional jolt her apprehension gave her. "Is everyone all right?" she asked carefully, and she braced herself for bad news.

"It's Doirin, darling," Mary said quietly. "I told you what a case she was when we went to move her to the new convalescent home. A wraith of herself, altogether, and with those horrible bedsores."

"Yes." Rosaleen nodded. "But you said the care in the new hospital was excellent, Ma."

"Indeed, it was," Mary agreed gratefully, "but it's her lungs now, Rosaleen. The doctor says she won't last the week."

"Consumption?" Rosaleen whispered, thinking of Veronica. "But why didn't they tell you before?"

"Not consumption, dear, pneumonia. She lies there in one place all the time. And though they've been turning her, and even trying to make her walk a bit, she's just too weak. She's dying, Rosaleen, and there's nothing anyone can do."

"Fourteen years" went through Rosaleen's mind, the time set by the doctor that day Doirin was institutionalized: her aunt was dying right on schedule. And what about the rest of them? For the first time since her marriage, Rosaleen was concerned about her own health. She wondered if she should confess to John that she might not live to see her children raised. Her long silence puzzled Mary, who knew she had never been that attached to Doirin.

"What is it, Rosaleen? I didn't mean to upset you, in your condition. I just thought you should know. I'll be going there every day, but I'm not asking you to come, darling. And, of

course, there'll be arrangements to be made when it happens."
There was a catch in her voice. "Brian and Darin will take
care of that, sure. I was wondering, though, if you'd like to
attend. You haven't seen anyone since you came back, and
you and Darin were so close. I know how the Maddigans feel,
but sure I can't understand your not seeing him."

Rosaleen's heart raced, and her hand went to her chest.
"No, Mother, I won't be able to attend. I'll send flowers, but
I just can't go. You know how much I hate funerals."

Mary nodded mournfully. "I thought perhaps you'd overcome all that. Your morbid fear of death is something I never
could understand. Sure, it'll come to all of us, and if your
faith's strong enough, it's nothing to fear at all. Ah, you aren't
going to Mass as often as you used to. That's a mortal sin,
you know."

Rosaleen turned and put her hand on the doorknob, wishing to flee. "It isn't easy," she muttered. "I make visits to
church, sometimes, but you must realize it'd be as compro-
mising to Laura if her daughter-in-law were known to be a
Catholic as it would be if the other secret was out. I'm sorry
about Doirin, Mother. Sorry for you. And when John and I
have our own house, which should be soon now that Matt's
home, I promise you I can do anything I want...including
going to Mass."

The funeral was held a few days later, but Rosaleen was
at a meeting with John at the time. Both of them had begun
to wonder when Matt was going to take over again, so they
could announce his return. As they drove home in the carriage, Rosaleen took her hat off and ran her fingers through
her tightly combed hair.

"I want to get out of that house, John," she said. "We
should be alone with our children. I'd like to get away from
Boston altogether."

"I've noticed you've been a bit down the past few days,"
he said, putting his arm around her. "Is anything wrong?
You haven't had words with Mother, have you?"

She shook her head. "I hardly see her, except at dinner.
Sometimes my mother annoys me, though. You wouldn't believe the fights she and Carmela have in the nursery. And
neither one tries understanding the other. Has Matt said
anything at all to you about going back to work?"

"He's a strange one," John admitted. "He seems much
happier since his trip, but it's almost as though he were still
on vacation. Rosaleen, I want very much to get back to my

own work. This whole thing has made me quite miserable, but I hate to prod him. I guess we'll just have to wait a bit. And, darling, as soon as he says he's taking over again, we'll have our own house, I promise you."

She leaned her head against his shoulder. "I don't know what I'd do without you," she said. "You're such a dear man, I want you to be happy, doing your own work. And, John, if anything happens to me, you must marry again: promise me. I don't want my babies raised by two foolish old women."

"Don't ever talk like that!" he cried, raising her face and looking into it with alarm. "I couldn't survive a day without you, Rosaleen." Then, with a sympathetic smile, "You're exhausted, darling. I want you to stay home and rest. Too much has been put upon your narrow young shoulders."

Rosaleen slept late the next morning, and played with Rory in the garden after lunch. When Carmela took him away for his nap, she remained in the garden, trimming away dead roses and trying to imagine the baby that she would have soon, but her thoughts would not come into focus to plan the future. She was oppressed by what had been in her mind since her conversation with her mother: who will be next? She would have been better off at the bank, where her intellect was challenged and she was unable to consider the fate of the Noonans. More than Doirin's death was depressing her, though she was not completely aware of it: since Matt's return, she had been living in limbo, expecting him to take back his position any day. She was unable to function under such circumstances. Putting down the garden shears, she drifted into the house like a ghost, wondering how to employ her time for the rest of the day.

She was making her way toward the study to do some work when her steps were arrested by the front door bursting open, with a spate of male voices and laughter, and the appearance of Matt and another man in the hallway. Even before her eyes registered who it was, her heart gave a rush. The way the tall figure stood in the subdued light, with legs slightly apart as though on a rolling ship, paralyzed her for the crucial moment in which she might have slipped into the study.

"Rosaleen!" Matt cried, moving toward her. "See who I've found ... and this time I'm not going to let him get away!" He took her by the arm, nearly dragging her to the hall, and she could smell the alcohol on his breath. They must have met in a bar somewhere, her mind said, anger beginning to rise. It was abominable of Matt to bring him home: she could not handle it. "You're in the presence of the two newest recruits in the Union Army!"

The blue eyes that looked into hers were quite sober: they could look away no more than hers. It had been so long since she had seen him, and nothing had changed. Her knees were like water, and her chest heaved with feeling. Thoughts could be suppressed: his presence could not.

"Darin," she said with only partial control and a nod of her head, in an attempt to break their gaze, to behave as normally as possible. "It's... been a long time."

"Yes."

"Forgive me," she said, averting her eyes with difficulty, feeling the color drain from her face. "I... it's a surprise to see you. I'm ... ah ... sorry about your mother. I would have attended the funeral. . . ."

He waved his hand in negation and let it fall heavily at his side. "I didn't go either."

How stupid of her! Of course he would not have gone; and she had stayed away out of fear of seeing him. But here he was, right in her house! The rush of love she experienced was so strong that she wanted to flee up the stairs, lock herself in her room: hers and John's. And she realized for the first time that it was not sexual love: it was more powerful, going back over so many years.

"You're looking fine, Rosie," he said. She tried not to look at him again.

"I'm well, thank you," she managed; then, suddenly, Matt's words reached her mind. "The Union Army! What in God's name are you talking about?" she cried, turning on her brother-in-law, who stood by smiling, oblivious to everything passing between the cousins.

"I met Darin at the recruiting office," he said, swaying slightly. "I went down to get my orders. I signed up the other day. And who do I find signing up too! My old friend here," he said, throwing his arm around Darin and thumping his shoulder. "I must admit," he said with a silly smile, "that we celebrated a bit before coming home."

She would have been furious if Darin were drunk, too; but, he was not, though he probably held his liquor better than Matt. He was not entirely resigned to the shoulder-thumping camaraderie and moved away from it, supporting his companion with his other arm. "You're walking both sides of the road, man. You'd better get some coffee in you before you speak to your mother," Darin said.

"You're out of your minds, both of you!" Rosaleen cried, "Matt, your mother won't be able to stand this! And Darin"— her eyes met his briefly again—"you...you have a wife."

"I feel sick," Matt said, looking pale, and before Darin could assist him, he ran toward the kitchen.

Disgusted, Rosaleen made no move to help him, calling after him, "You damn well should!" Then, in a more normal tone, to Darin, "I know you aren't responsible for this, but..." She looked up into his amused but still unhappy eyes. "It's no laughing matter," she continued helplessly. "My God, do you want to get yourself killed?"

"Not if I can help it. Our motives are different, Matt's and mine, Rosie. Though part of them is similar. Something's happening that we feel we should be a part of, you see, and neither of us is fond of his job. Sure, Matt's always been full of adventure and couldn't do anything about it. Now, he's found a way out."

With the full realization of the catastrophe setting in, Rosaleen began to feel desperate. "If you had to join, why didn't you go into the navy? It's safer. Darin, why have you been working at your father's pub when you loved the sea so much? I don't understand any of it."

"Neither do I...now," he said, with nothing but sadness in his eyes, looking away from her. "You were married, and I guess I felt I should be married, too, Rosie. Peg made me promise not to go back to sea...so, I'm escaping by land. I like to keep promises, whenever I can."

"You're running away," she said softly.

"Again. Yes." He straightened his shoulders and drew in his breath. "You made a fine marriage, Rosie. John's a good man." Then, reluctantly, after a pause, "Are you happy?"

She nodded almost imperceptibly. "Yes. I was until today. Is there any way you and Matt can get out of this?"

"Sure, we don't want to, darlin'. We both went in there with clear heads and our eyes open. I came with him today to see you once more before I left. I'm sorry if it's upset you, Rosie. To tell the truth, it's upset me, too."

They were standing five feet apart, but she felt her spirit leave her to meet his in an embrace somewhere in between; in another moment, her body might have followed, but Matt came staggering back, wiping his face with a wet cloth.

"I'm better now," he announced roughly. "A cup of hot

.offee was just the thing. Rosaleen, I apologize. Please forgive me. I had no right barging in before you in that condition."

His presence had a sobering effect on all of them. Darin slapped his seaman's cap against his leg and moved to the door. "I must be off. I've some explaining to do at home myself," he said. "If I don't see you again, Matt...you being an officer and all...the best of luck to you. And," he added, with a long look, "God bless you, Rosaleen."

"God bless you," she cried softly, running toward the door in time to watch his tall figure descending the stairs to the street. She leaned against the doorframe, her legs unable to bear her weight, trembling all over. "God bless you, my darling," she whispered to herself, her gaze following him until he was lost in a blur of tears.

"Matt planned it from the beginning," she said bitterly to John, after the day's upheaval. "He planned it from Europe! He never intended to come back to the bank. You know where that puts us, don't you? We'll be right here until the end of the war."

"Do you mind terribly, Rosaleen?" he asked. "It does appear that the responsibility for the bank, and Mother, has been thrust upon us, for a while, at least. It wasn't what I planned; not at all what I'd planned."

"I don't mind for myself, John. I've been happy, really. I like working at the bank. But you've sacrificed enough already. I simply won't allow any further delay in the work that means so much to you. Let me take over the duties you hate so much, while you write your book."

"I can't do that," he demurred, clasping her hand tightly in appreciation of her thoughtfulness. "I'm worried about you, darling: you do too much! I want you to stay at home until after the baby comes. It isn't that long, now, you know. Only four months. After that, perhaps we can discuss it again."

The delay in taking charge of things was difficult for Rosaleen. The war, and their contribution to it, was very personal now: she wanted to guide the investments at the bank in the hope of ending it sooner. And though she did so with her work at home for John, she felt she needed total independence in her decisions. He was a gentle, kindly man who, though he supported the cause in theory, lacked the ruthlessness to carry through on some of her suggestions. Frustrated in her business dealings, strangely restless after seeing Darin again, she did the only thing left to her: she ventured into society more, not as the dazzling social beauty of a few months previously, but as an organizer of committees and functions to help the army in every possible way. And her image among the elite of the city, instead of being diminished, was strengthened by her total, unwearying support of the Union and her splendid loyalty to her brothers-in-law. The younger women were caught up in her enthusiasm; the older ones shook their heads apprehensively, but with admiration for this unusually brave young woman, so active and dedicated in spite of her approaching confinement.

She had just returned from an operatic performance to raise funds for the Medical Corps when her son John Michael was born in the Maddigan home, with only her mother's aid, in December 1861.

"You aren't going to stay home with your own baby?" Mary cried, when Rosaleen told her she was going back to the bank. "Sure, do you want me to get a wet nurse, like Laura got for poor Philip? I just don't understand you, girl."

Sitting at her vanity with Thérèse briskly brushing her long hair, Rosaleen laughed into the mirror at the reflection of her mother's disapproving face. "I'll be gone only four hours a day," she said. "He doesn't have to nurse more often than that, does he? It was certainly enough for Rory."

"And that's another thing," Mary was reminded. "That child's behaving badly. I've never seen a little one so jealous of a baby, Rosaleen. Even that dim-witted Carmela's aware of it. She made motions the other day indicating she wouldn't leave Rory alone in the nursery with poor little Michael."

"She's not dim-witted, mother," Rosaleen said patiently. "She speaks her own language as well as you speak yours. And she's awfully good with children."

"When people come to this country, at least they should learn the language," Mary said. "*Good* with children? Sure she spoils them to death! No child can endure that much fondling and kissing. Until a child's three years old, he's an uncontrollable little animal, and he needs a good cuff for his own good, now and then."

"I haven't seen you doing it. As a matter of fact, when you and Laura have him, all you do is 'fondle and kiss' and stuff him with sweets. I know I'm no better. But Rory's a very appealing little boy. And don't let me catch anyone cuffing him, either."

"He bit me!" Mary cried, until now reluctant to admit it.

"When I said he had to leave my room to go to bed last night, he *bit* me. Sure, I won't be savaged by any brat alive. I guess I'll have to take your punishment, Rosaleen. Your boy's been cuffed."

Rosaleen turned from the mirror to face her mother, her blue eyes clouded. After dismissing Thérèse in French, because she was another emigrant who did not try to learn the language, Rosaleen confessed.

"He bit me, too, and I bit him back, Mother. I ended by crying later. I don't know how anyone so adorable could develop such a beastly habit. You're right: he must be taken in hand. Perhaps if we treat him like a person, instead of a plaything, he'll respond like one. But that will mean everyone—including Laura."

Mary shook her head slowly. "We can't go that far. Sure he's all Laura has, Rosaleen, with the other boys away. She and John have never been close, though it's as much the fault of one as the other, you know that. Sure, she'd be completely out of her mind with worry right now, if it weren't for Rory."

Rosaleen ran her hand through her loose hair with a sigh. "He isn't a ball to be bounced around to make adults happy," she said. "But I know, Mother. How would you like to take Rory out? In the mornings, when the baby's getting so much attention? Laura has you going out to check the casualty lists every morning anyway, doesn't she?"

"Yes," Mary said, almost holding her breath. "But I thought you didn't want him dragged about town the way you were."

"It didn't do me any harm, I guess, or Philip, either. In fact, it was fun to go with you all the time. Would you like to take him with you in the morning? I know he's a handful."

"Of course!" Mary smiled. "Sure, he has too much energy to be cooped up here. It'll help him wear a bit of it off. Does that mean I can take him to see Brian, too?"

"Yes," Rosaleen said, turning back to the mirror: now that Darin was away, it was safe to take the child there. Her initial caution had been to keep him away from Darin, for fear some instinctual urge would draw them together, or reveal to Darin that the child was his.

"I didn't tell you, because you don't like to talk about those at the pub," Mary said. "When I was there the other day, Peg told me she's in the family way herself, and Brian will have a grandchild next year."

404

"How can that be? Her husband's been away since August."

"How, indeed. Well you may ask, you who keep your secret until you're five months gone! The sad thing about it is that Darin doesn't even know. If anything happens to him, he'll never know."

"Nothing's going to happen to him!" Rosaleen flared, and struggled again for composure. "Mother, if she needs anything..."

"She doesn't. They're well off enough there. Except perhaps a husband, to be there at her side."

"What's she like?" Rosaleen asked before she could stop herself.

"Sure, she's a fine girl, Rosaleen. A good Irish girl from County Kerry. God help her, I think she made a bad marriage, though. Darin's that restless, he couldn't settle down for even one whole year."

"He didn't mistreat her, though?"

"Indeed not. He's more like Brian than your father....I mean..."

"I know what you mean: I was there, Mother....Peg," she said, looking at her own face in the mirror, "is she pretty?"

"Pretty is as pretty does," Mary said, observing her daughter regarding her perfect face. "Yes, I guess you could call her that, though her coloring's a bit low. She has a fine head of golden hair, with just a touch of red. And a beautiful skin with only a few freckles. It's unusual for a redhead to escape the freckles altogether, but she only has a few."

"Green eyes?"

"How did you know?" Mary asked in surprise. "Yes, rather light. As I told you, her coloring's low. She's a bit on the plumpish side, but a fine figure of a girl."

The picture of Darin's wife was now complete in Rosaleen's mind. She hated her completely, but she felt sorry for her, too. Before her mother could say anything more, she said lightly, "If you take Rory out this morning, bundle him up well. It's very cold out. Please give my love to Uncle Brian when you see him."

Everyone in the family read the newspapers now, including Mary, who quickly became the real authority on the battles, though she had no idea where the place names were, the only important thing in her mind being whether the Union won or lost. Letters from Matt and Harry came through sporadically, from small towns in the South, which Rosaleen had to look up on a map. Most of their correspondence was to their mother. So, they said very little about their hardships or experiences, which soothed Laura, who imagined them out of danger. A more descriptive letter from Harry arrived at the bank for John, and when Rosaleen brought it home to him, she insisted on reading it, to find out what was really happening, but John withheld it from her, his gray eyes thoughtful and sad.

"I don't want you to read it, darling," he told her. "Your mind should be free of picturing such things. War is terrible . . . dehumanizing . . . though sometimes it brings out the best in men, too. The losses on both sides are staggering, as you know; but, there's no need for you to have it described so graphically."

She slipped out of bed that night and went barefoot down to the library, taking the letter out of the desk where she had watched him secrete it. She was concerned about Harry and Matt; but she was in a panic about Darin, from whom no one had heard since he had left. When he was at sea, she could imagine his activities: now they were incomprehensible. Lighting a lamp, she sat down by the fireplace with her feet under her to protect them from the cold. The letter described a nightmare of dismembered limbs and stinking bodies, piled up like cordwood. But she read it to the end in spite of her horror, driven to know the worst, intent upon the truth. Harry told about the cases he treated, and often lost. He still complained about lack of medications and bandages and spoke woefully of the extreme youth of many of the dead. One statement stayed in her mind for the rest of the war:

The thing that troubles me the most, John, is the dead who cannot be identified. Men . . . or what is left of men . . . so completely blown apart and disfigured that even the army coroner cannot piece enough of them together to say, This is John Smith, or Bill Jones; his family must be notified. I think of their wives, mothers back home in New York or Illinois or Massachusetts, who will never know, except by their perpetual absence, what has happened to them, while they lie in some unmarked grave or in a mass burial at the site of a battle little known to anyone, part of a green Virginia field and Mother Earth . . . anonymous.

She was sorry she had read the letter. The casualty lists were more real now. And not seeing a name on the lists no longer reassured her: between the lines, she saw ghostly, invisible names that would never be printed.

Chapter 27

AT ROSALEEN'S insistence, John stepped down from his position at the bank in January, with the announcement that Mrs. Maddigan was replacing him; and when Rosaleen arrived the next day, carrying Matt's battered leather valise, three board members resigned.

Calling the meeting to order, she remarked, "We are fewer today; but in the end it will make us more. It's fortunate that the ones who left were the ones who were so old-fashioned they were bordering on senility. You who've remained are more youthful. Your active brains will more than cover the loss."

The most youthful man there was forty-eight: the acknowledgment was a success. They already knew, from John's conferences with her, who was making the decisions: they liked the way she thought. And if, in spite of her tailored clothing and the attempt to subdue her appearance, several of the men fell in love with her, it helped matters more than it hindered them. She was so businesslike, so cool, with only an occasional flash of humor and charm showing through, that there was not a man in her employ who would dare make any advance to her. Within a few months, they had done a considerable amount of reorganizing and profits were higher than they had ever been.

She had watched them work for almost a year: she knew the way each man thought and approached problems. Without undue ceremony, she appointed the first vice-president: Frank Connell, an astute and aggressive Irishman, who was married and an Episcopalian, but whose main interest in life was not money in the hand, to be spent, but money on paper and the grand game of power. He was an expert in stocks and real estate. She gave him a handsome raise, and had him do the daily work that Matt had done, so she could appear only a few hours a day and at meetings, doing her research and planning at home. He was the only person to whom she ever revealed her background, and even he was not actually certain afterward he believed it.

"As long as I trust you, you've a fine, grand future before you, Frank. Right now, I trust you altogether. But I've eyes in my head and long ears, too: one slip, dear man, and you'll wish you'd never left Monaghan."

Somehow, it came out sounding like an Irish curse to him: he admired her, but he feared her, too. And she never made a better choice in business in her life. With him, in later years, she surreptitiously began to buy up and improve real estate.

John Michael, whom everyone called Michael, because Mary had started it, had his second birthday two and a half months after the "bloodiest single day of war," the battle of Antietam. Lincoln's subsequent issuance of the Emancipation Proclamation finally boldly announced that the war was not just for the preservation of the Union, but for freeing the slaves.

When Mary read the proclamation in the paper in September, she was surprised. "Sure, I thought the whole thing was over them," she said. "What's all this talk about 'preserving the Union' then? Mother of God, you'd think the President was an Irishman, going about things cart before the horse! But then politicians and Irishmen have a lot in common: they all know how to cod and dissimulate. Emancipation, indeed! And two years into the war."

Antietam was not a decisive battle; though it kept Lee out of the North, neither side won it. Its main interest for Mary at the time had been its horrendous statistics: twelve-thousand Union soldiers killed, wounded or missing, the Confederate losses even higher. When the lists came out, everyone but Rosaleen, who looked at them with different eyes, was reassured and life resumed as normal. The whole thing, including the proclamation, was forgotten on the day of Michael's party, which Pamela and her son, Edward Dove III, attended, along with the children of some of Rosaleen's other friends.

The cake decorated by Monsieur Giraud drew exclamations from the adults and older children, though Michael's gray eyes were fastened only on the two candles glowing on top. There were gifts not only for him, but for all the children, though Rosaleen had ceased giving something equal to Rory every time she bought something for his brother. The older boy was still untamed, but Mary's process of civilizing him seemed to be taking: she had convinced him he was a big boy, and should no longer be jealous of his brother.

Amid the squeals and shrieks of the children's games, Rosaleen and Pamela tried to keep some order. As usual, John and Edward stood near the fire lost in scholarly conversation, ignoring everything, including the other guests. After the gifts were opened, Laura motioned to Mary to be accompanied to her room; and Mary left reluctantly, smiling back over her shoulder.

Completely absorbed in keeping seven children from committing mayhem or getting burned on the firescreen, Rosaleen was startled by her mother's hand on her arm: she thought she was out of the room.

"Mother, what is it?" she asked, holding the squirming Michael at her knee.

"The newspaper—I picked it up this morning and didn't look at it, with the party and all." Mary's lips trembled. "It's Matt, Rosaleen. At Antietam, three months ago! Miss Laura saw it. I've sent Cornelius for the doctor."

If she had stayed at home like other women, as her mother often entreated, Rosaleen would never have survived the next two years of the war. With mostly small children and uncommunicative old women for company, her mind would have dwelled entirely on Darin's fate, which sent her into a panic when she thought about it too long. Almost from the moment she heard of Matt's long-unreported death, she realized the pattern of her life was set for better or for worse: she and John would never have their house, and the future of the bank was entirely in her hands. There was Laura to care for now, too: always frail, the news of her son's death had left her almost an invalid. Laura's only happiness was rocking her grandchildren, while she talked quietly with Mary, in her room which had almost become a cell, and which she did not leave even for meals.

As a compensation for John, who began to grow bitter over his helplessness in making his promises to her come true, Rosaleen consulted with Frank Connell, then told her husband about a surprise she planned.

"It would be nice if we had a sort of retreat, in the country, dear. We don't have enough time alone any more, and soon there'll be another baby to complicate things even more here. It wouldn't be too expensive to build a little house just like we wanted, perhaps just beyond the outskirts of Cambridge, John. Of course, you'd have to plan it."

He looked up from his desk with the first boyish expression she had noted in some time. His gaze wandered to the library window for a few moments, and she could almost hear him thinking; but when he turned to her with a smile, the leap his mind had taken surprised her. "No one will know about it but us," he said, rising. "We'll have our own hideaway, darling! We can go there on weekends, whenever we want. It doesn't have to be a large house, just for the two of us. We could even sell the place at the Cape, since no one goes there any more."

"I'd like to keep it for the children." She smiled. "It's such a grand place for children...remember?"

"Yes," he said, drawing her into his arms. "It was the only place I could be with you for months at a time. I'll see that our little house is built, darling, just the way we wanted it! I'll go out tomorrow and buy the land. And then there'll be workmen to consider, and..."

"That will take a good deal of time from your book," she said, kissing his happy face. "There's someone I can put you into touch with who'll be a great help, I think."

Their daughter, Cliona, was born before Rosaleen was allowed to see the house. John supervised its building with the same attention he usually poured into his own work, getting stacks of books on France from the Harvard library for their lithographs, and consulting almost daily with Frank Connell.

"It isn't going to be inexpensive, Mrs. Maddigan, with all the things he wants," Frank had told her. "It's a beautiful spot, and we got it for a song, because it's so far out, but the house is going to be a bit peculiar."

"It's all right, Frank. John's enjoying it, and after Matt's death...well, he needs some joy in his life. The house may be 'peculiar' to you, but I almost think I'll recognize it!"

Her mother objected to her baby daughter's name and, rocking the tiny child in her arms beside Rosaleen's bed, told her about it without restraint. "Sure, it isn't a Christian name at all, Rosaleen. Just because you were daft about the fairies when you were a child is no reason to name her after the Fairy Queen. It's not only unchristian, it's indiscreet. Cliona's an Irish name if ever I heard one, and you're supposed to be hiding your background."

"Look at her," Rosaleen said and smiled. "She's a fairy princess if ever I saw one, Mother! Those beautiful tiny features and blond hair. We'll give her a saint's name, too, at baptism, the way we did with Rory. No one in Boston, except the Irish, would recognize the name as such. And"—she shrugged—"what if they do? My husband's Irish, isn't he?"

"An Orangeman," Mary said, never forgetting the distinction, "but a good man, for all that...the best. What's he about, anyway? He's been running around as though he'd a fire beneath him lately, instead of staying in there with all those books. There's a look of total inspiration on his face."

But Rosaleen kept John's secret. "He has a great idea about his book, I suspect." She smiled calmly. "He's just running from one library to another, I guess. You know how he is."

"I've never seen a man get so excited over words," Mary agreed. "What's this grand book about, anyway?"

"The Greek gods and their relationship to other religions. It'll be a very scholarly work: I doubt I'll understand a word of it, but I'll try."

"Greek gods. Fairy princesses! I'd think the whole household altogether heathen if you hadn't been attending Mass every morning, darling. Since you go to St. Mary's, so you won't be seen, you really should drop in on Brian and Peg and baby Sean when you're down there. I can't understand the way you've grown away from the family. Aren't they good enough for you any more?"

"It isn't that," Rosaleen said, lowering her eyelids to hide the expression in her eyes. "Mother, you of all people know how busy I am. As soon as Mass is over, I'm off to the bank. When I'm finished there, it's home as quickly as possible to be with the children. And the evenings are for John, when he isn't working."

Mary put the small bundle into her arms. "It's time she was fed. She's so *small*, Rosaleen, and she never asks for anything. You must nurse her more often during the day to put some weight on the poor babby. You aren't going back to work very soon, are you? She needs you."

"I'll not go back until she's just fine, Mother."

"It seems to me the whole family could get together sometime. At Veronica's, perhaps. You haven't even seen little Sean... or met his mother, for that matter. And Brian always asks after you."

"We'll see," Rosaleen said, lifting her bedjacket to put the baby to her breast. That was not something she wished to discuss at the moment, but since the subject had arisen naturally, she asked, "How old is Sean, now? About two? Does he favor his mother or his father?"

"He's a Noonan, Rosaleen. He and Rory are enough alike to be brothers, though I swear to God no one has the energy of that Rory! I wish you could see them together, and Brian hovering over them—all with the same blue eyes."

The remark about Rory and Sean made Rosaleen hold her frail baby tightly; it would not do to get upset when Cliona was nursing: a mother's feelings could give a baby colic. Trying to breathe naturally, she asked quietly, "And still no news at all of Darin?"

Mary clenched her lips and shook her head. "After all this time, I don't think there will be."

"Mother!"

"I'm sorry, but saying it won't necessarily make it so. If Darin could write, I'm sure he would have. And what about Harry not writing his mother, either? Sure they wouldn't shoot a doctor, would they?"

"Of course not," Rosaleen said without conviction. Hearing someone else express what she had felt for so long tore at her heart. "It'll all be over soon. General Sherman's finally beating hell out of them. The boys will come home, just wait and see. They *have* to."

Spring was abundant with new life in the country around their little Norman house, which John had built near a pond surrounded by willows. They had spent many happy weekends there since the house was built, and that April, Rosaleen was setting out the garden she had planned so long, though it was doubtful the children would be able to enjoy it, unless she could convince her husband to allow them to come. To John, this place apart was important, not only so they could be together one weekend out of the month, but because he had become completely infatuated with it as a place to do his

413

work, setting one wood-paneled room aside as his study. His book was nearly completed, and he was beginning to relax.

"When things are back to normal, let's go to Europe again," he suggested, standing over Rosaleen, whose hands were deep in the rich earth, putting in her bare-root rose bushes and the annuals she hoped to see every year in the future. Already daffodils and alyssum were blooming near the entrance; and the tulips she had planted in the fall made a handsome bed of red along the walk. She had not dreamed that growing things could be so satisfying: after a weekend here, she returned to Boston completely renewed.

"I'd like to stay here," she said, looking up from under the wide brim of her straw gardening hat. "I think I'd like to stay right here, forever... and bring the children, too."

"You're different here." He smiled. "More relaxed. Perhaps that's what made me think of Europe. Seeing you under that hat, smiling at me with your dimple showing." He crouched down beside her. "I'm singularly blessed, my darling. No man ever had a more perfect wife, even when she has mud on her cheek. Remember when you knelt down in that alley in Rome when we got Murphy? My God, there are four dogs at the house! Everything you touch seems to multiply, Rosaleen. When you said you wanted to get a female for him, I didn't think you meant to keep all the puppies!"

"He was lonely. He wasn't living a normal life," she explained. "And who could part with puppies like that? Besides, each of the children has a puppy of his own. Cliona's too young, yet, but there's one marked for her."

"That makes one left over. You see, I *can* calculate! You know, the place is rather a zoo, though. It's difficult to get much done there with all the comings and goings and rompings around. I love every moment of it... the place was never so lively! But being here alone with you makes me selfish. I really think we should go back to Europe for a summer."

Rosaleen removed the dirt from her hands with a washing motion and sat back on her heels. "Sometime. John, about that extra pup... it'll have a little owner before long. That's why I can't think of Europe right now."

"Good God!" he said, dumbfounded and delighted. "Well, as I said, everything seems to multiply! Come here, darling, and give me a kiss. I love you, Rosaleen, more than I can say in words. You're the best thing that ever happened in my life."

That weekend they stayed an extra night, and when they

returned to the Maddigan house on Monday, Mary greeted them at the door waving a newspaper in the air, unable to control her joy.

"It's over!" she cried. "It's over! They're signing the surrender today . . . at Appa . . . Appa . . . mat . . . oh, some Indian kind of place! Sure, we'll find out about our boys, now, won't we, Rosaleen?"

"I'm sure we will." Rosaleen smiled, not feeling at all optimistic. "Things will sort themselves out. We'll hear something."

"Something *good*," Mary corrected her, catching the inflection in her voice. "Now that this terrible war's over, nothing bad can ever happen again."

President Lincoln was shot at Ford's Theatre one week later, and the whole North mourned as a train draped in black took his body home to Illinois.

A party at Veronica's for the whole family was the last thing Rosaleen wanted to attend, and she did not think Darin would like it, either. From what she had heard, he still had not recovered from his stay in the prison camp and his long trip back from Georgia. And a party with all the children, including her new baby, Mary Rose, seemed out of the question; but she did not know how to get out of it.

"Darling, it'll be nice," John told her in their room the day it was announced. "God knows, Darin's had a difficult time of it. The accounts I've read about Andersonville are unbelievable. He hasn't seen any of the family for four long years, Rosaleen. I'm sure it'll cheer him up to have everyone there welcoming him back. I really don't understand your objections."

"He's lost a leg," she said tightly. "He'll be sensitive about that. The man's probably exhausted: it'll be too much for him."

"Are you thinking of him or yourself, Rosaleen? You can't know what he's thinking, darling. You just don't know how to handle his infirmity, do you?"

"No," she admitted. "I can't think of him like that. He wouldn't want people to see him like that."

"He's coming to the party: that should say something. I think it's only decent for us to attend. Besides, I'd like to see him again: I always liked him, you know."

"I'm nursing," she said. "Mary Rose is colicky, anyway. I can't endure..."

He gave an exasperated sigh. "All right. Leave the children at home. It's just for a few hours. Mary won't like it, she's anxious to show them off. Rosaleen, just this once, I'm going to have to put my foot down. It would be insulting for you not to be there."

"His little boy, Sean, will be there," she considered, thinking: and his wife, too. She could not do it. "And Veronica's children."

"Who are quite humanly grown up by now," he said, studying her face through his glasses, with his hands shoved into his pockets. "I haven't said anything, because I felt it was none of my business. But I think you've treated your family rather badly since we married. Perhaps you're just going by Mother's guidelines, Rosaleen, but we shouldn't exclude the Noonans completely. I think you've been rather unkind."

"I've been busy!" she flared, starting to pace the room. "You know what my schedule's been, John. The bank, the house, the children...four babies in six years. I don't know what you expect of me!"

"You have time for your friends...why not your family? I liked your Uncle Brian a lot when I met him, and Veronica, too. Is there some reason you're not telling me?"

The question was dangerous: it brought Rosaleen up short. It would be better to attend the function than have John start wondering, especially since he knew how much she'd once cared for Darin.

She wanted to see Darin very much: she had prayed every day for his safe return. But she wanted to see him alone, to talk to him and reassure herself about his mental condition after such an ordeal. She did not want a crowd around. And she would now have to do something about Rory's going to the pub, which would mean trouble with her mother. She was confused, in emotional upheaval: no wonder her poor baby girl was so cranky.

"All right," she agreed finally, seeing no way out. "But the children will stay at home with Carmela. That should eliminate some of the confusion. Rory would make sure all the attention was on him the whole time. They'd see how spoiled he is."

John laughed fondly. "They already know. Besides, he's not a bad boy, darling. He's a charmer. He got that from you full-force. In fact, he's very much like you."

"Like me!" she said. "I must say, that doesn't give me any consolation. What do you mean, like me?"

416

"He twists everyone around his little finger, with the pure charm of him. He looks exactly like you, except for the dimple. I wonder why he didn't inherit that?"

"My dimple was an accident!" she said.

"An accident?" He laughed. "What do you mean? An accident of nature, certainly, and a remarkably lovely one."

"John, I'm sorry," she apologized, running her hands through her hair at the temples. "You must think I'm daft. I *have* felt upset. Please, just go tell Mother we'll be there...without the children."

Before leaving for Veronica's, Rosaleen made her customary afternoon visit to Laura, and found her rocking Rory on her lap, with Mary sitting nearby. When Rory saw his mother, he struggled free of his aging grandmother and rushed to her, throwing his arms around her peacock-blue taffeta skirt.

"We were invited to the party, too! I like parties, Mother. I want to go!" he cried.

"Not this time." Rosaleen smiled, crouching to hug him. "Your cousin's been away a long time: he isn't well, darling. It'll be a gloomy party, Rory, with lots of grown-up conversation."

"Mm, you smell good," he said, nestling his head against her neck. "I bet you'll be the prettiest lady there. Did cousin Darin really get his leg cut off? How can he walk with just one leg?"

She looked helplessly at Mary, who shrugged indulgently, and said, "The doctors made him a new one, darling, out of wood. He walks quite well with it." Then, to Rosaleen, "Sure, it's only natural for a child his age to want to know everything, and something like this is very interesting to them."

"You shouldn't have said anything at all," Rosaleen whispered, rising to greet her mother-in-law. "You're looking well today, Aunt Laura. So Rory's to be your companion this afternoon? I hope he brought some toys."

Laura's faded face and washed-out gray eyes showed little emotion. Her gray hair was still carefully done up in youthful back curls, though the black frock she wore was an old one. She had ordered nothing since Matt's death, wearing only the black dresses from her closet: the one she had on today had a perceptibly greenish cast from age. Rosaleen made a mental note to supply her with new ones.

"Maybe Darin will know about Harry," Laura said, in a

tremulous, faraway voice. "They were both in the war. Darin should know where he is."

"I'll ask him, dear," Rosaleen said, bending to kiss the top of her head. "But you know John's doing everything—"

"John!" the old woman said with unusual vehemence. "He couldn't tie his shoes without you! I don't know what any of us would have done without you, Rosaleen." Laura's eyes filled and she fumbled for Rosaleen's hand. "I couldn't take care of the bank, you know. I was never good at figures."

"It's all right," Rosaleen said, having been through the conversation before. "Everything's just fine, Aunt Laura. You should be very proud of John: his book's being published, you know."

"What book? I didn't know about a book. Why doesn't anyone tell me anything?"

Rosaleen studied her with concern, glancing quickly at her mother, who indicated by a motion of her head that they should leave. They got Rory settled with his toys and said their goodbyes to Laura, assuring her they would only be gone a short time. But when they started for the door, she suddenly whined, "Mary, are you going, too? I don't want to be left alone."

Rory ran to her side and began to slowly rock her chair. "It's all right, Grandmother. I'm looking after you today, remember?" he said in his best grown-up voice, adding slyly, "As soon as they're gone, we'll play a card game. You beat me last time, but I'll get my pennies back!"

"I beat you last time," Laura's voice said faintly. "I'm sure I can do it again."

Outside in the hall, Rosaleen turned to her mother with alarm. "She's getting worse. She's been forgetful before, but..."

"The doctor says it's little strokes. I can almost tell when it happens. She gets confused for a while, but she's all right again soon. It happened last evening again. There's nothing that can be done about it. The best medicine for her is young Rory." Mary smiled. "He lets her win at cards, you know."

Rosaleen was touched: no matter how she fought it, she loved the boy better than her other children. Sometimes she was too hard on him because of that.

"Do I look all right?" Mary asked, straightening the bodice of her gray satin dress, lifting a hand to her dark hair. "This is such a special occasion, I want to look nice."

"You look lovely, Mother," Rosaleen replied, putting her

arm around her mother's waist to walk down the stairs. wish you'd wear a bit of color . . . but then you never have."

"Sure, it's too late to change my ways, now. Is it a red Kerry petticoat you'd be putting on me or one of your blues? You wear too much blue, I think, though I know it brings out the color of your eyes."

"Will Rory be all right with her?" Rosaleen asked the question really on her mind. "I mean, if she got really ill?"

"Don't worry about him so much. The lad has his instructions, and he has as level a head as ever you did. If his grandmother acts the least bit strange, he's to run to Cornelius, who'll get the doctor. You know, Rosaleen, I've been thinking. If we find out that Harry's dead, we shouldn't tell her at all. It'd be the end of her, for sure."

"Well, there you are!" John exclaimed from the entrance hall, looking up at them on the stairs. "And don't you both look marvelous! Mary, darling, you're absolutely regal. How on earth do you keep such a splendid figure?"

"Devil take you," Mary said, flushing with pleasure. "Sure, you shouldn't talk about such things, John: it isn't decent! You just do it to embarrass me."

Laughing, he escorted them both out to the carriage.

They had no sooner taken off their wraps and entered Veronica's tidy, overdecorated parlor after embraces from their hostess and her husband in the hallway than Rosaleen regretted coming. A feeling of panic seized her as she took her place on the red velvet settee, scanning the familiar bric-a-brac and ferns. Nothing had changed since the last family reunion: the night she and Darin went to his ship. Mistaking her expression for apprehension about seeing her cousin, Veronica sat down beside her.

"We all feel the same way," she reassured her with a nervous smile. "We'll just have to carry it off the best we can. Sure I haven't seen Darin yet, but maybe the affliction's slight enough to ignore. The thing we must show him is our love and warmth."

Rosaleen put her own hand over her aunt's. "I love you," she said sincerely. "The few times I've seen you at our house with Mother, I've wanted to explain, Veronica. If you all think me dreadful, you've every right."

"Not a bit of it!" Veronica said softly. "Sure your mother explained everything to us when you were married, darling. Saints above, don't you think we understood, after all we'd

419

been through together? It's important for your children that you make a better sort of life, if they're to make their way in the world. I've read articles about you in the newspaper...whenever you attend a charity or any function at all." She lowered her voice and said mischievously, "You may think your mother disapproves, but did you know she saves all those clippings? Honestly! She has them in a shoebox in her room." She giggled.

Time had not changed Veronica, Rosaleen thought with a smile. In her late thirties now, only the Noonan trait of early gray hair had touched her: her face was almost as youthful as ever, though somewhat thinner. "When are they coming?" Rosaleen asked, glancing at the door to the hall.

"Sure, they were supposed to be here at the same time as you," her aunt said, rising. "Something must have held them up. Excuse me, Rosaleen. I want to see to the refreshments. If cook made the punch too soon, it'll be all flat when they get here."

Her vanishing form was instantly replaced by that of Saul Rabinsky, still slight, but bald on top. His familiar wide, pleasant grin made Rosaleen respond in turn. "Uncle Saul! Where are your girls? I hope just because I didn't bring my tribe..."

"You didn't know? Mary kept it to herself? That I can't imagine," he said, taking the place Veronica had just vacated. "They're in a convent school! Ah, you heard me right, my dear. Our nice, half-Jewish daughters are at a school with the nuns in New York. We want the best education for them"—he shrugged—"so we have to send them away. Veronica says St. Mary's is full of 'hard cases' and 'riff-raff.' Rosaleen, do you ever get the feeling that everyone's pretending to be something they aren't?"

"Dear Saul!" she said compassionately. "You must miss them terribly."

"I do," he said. "There were never three sweeter children. But," he said and sighed, "I still have my Veronica, and that's enough."

A cool wind coming in from the hall made Rosaleen straighten her shoulders, though a shiver went through her. "I think they're here. Where have John and Mother got to?"

"It's all right, I'll greet them. Poor Darin," he said with a mournful face. "Would you ever have imagined it?"

John drifted in from the dining room with a glass of wine

in each hand. "Here, darling, maybe this will warm you. It's a beastly day."

Rosaleen drank the wine in one gulp, listening to the muffled voices in the hall. She heard Brian's soft accent, and that of a woman and a child, but no other; perhaps she had been right in the first place: Darin had not come. But when Saul ushered the group into the parlor, his tall form stood above the others, and her chest tightened. She had not thought about his physical appearance, though her mother had told her he had lost weight in prison. Only her heart recognized the man across the room, and it went into instant alarm for his welfare. His thin face was older than his father's, the blue eyes flat and sunken into dark sockets. He limped badly. And his shoulders, those great magnificent shoulders, were bowed, with no flesh on them at all. As Saul brought the family forward, she put her wineglass aside unconsciously.

"Little Rosaleen!" Brian cried, his blue eyes merry, stooping over to kiss her with sheer delight. "Sure, it's been too long, darling, but aren't you a beautiful sight altogether? Now, you haven't met Peg here...or little Sean, either. Ah, John! Good to see you again, man!"

Darin stood away from his family during the introductions, and Rosaleen had to concentrate on the woman and little boy, though she wanted to look at him, greet him. Peg almost curtsied, as though she were a servant, but there was no reaction in her pale-green eyes and worn face when she said, "It's a pleasure, I'm sure."

She was plain, terribly plain, though perhaps she had not always been so. Four years of not knowing if her husband was alive or dead had left its mark, and Rosaleen felt sympathy for her, wondering if she knew she had been deserted in the first place. Her son clung to her skirts like a shy little mouse, which almost destroyed any resemblance to Rory. He did not appear to be a happy child.

"Hello, Sean," Rosaleen said, leaning forward, trying to coax him to her, but he hid behind his mother, with only his dark curls and one blue eye peering out with curiosity.

"Come on, lad," Brian said, attempting to show him off. "Sure, this is your friend Rory's ma. Don't you want to meet her?"

Sean shook his head, staying where he was. "Mary's Rory's ma," he protested quietly, and Brian threw his head back with laughter.

"Wait until I tell her that, sure!"

The moment could be avoided no longer. Trembling inside, Rosaleen looked up and said, "Hello, Darin."

He nodded slightly, avoiding her eyes, and held his hand out to John. They clasped hands tightly, neither man speaking, until John finally said, "It's good to have you back, Darin. You don't know how much everyone worried...though it's nothing to what you've been through."

The awkwardness was interrupted by the appearance of both Veronica and Mary in the room. All the women were drawn together by Sean as though by a magnet; and whether intentionally or not, Saul led John and Brian into the dining room for a drink, leaving Rosaleen to talk with Darin. She did not know where to begin, but her nervousness was gone now in his presence, and she looked up to meet his eyes directly, surprised to see the same affection there, though their blue was washed out from pain and the conditions he had somehow endured.

When he spoke for the first time, his voice was soft. "I only came today because I knew you'd be here."

And, with some self-consciousness, he stiffly walked the few feet to the settee, sinking down on it with a sigh, which nearly broke Rosaleen's heart. Without even thinking, she reached out and took his hand.

"How did it happen?" she blurted out. "Was it a shell?"

He turned to look at her, and she saw a glimmer of the old wild amusement in his eyes.

"No. A minor infection." He smiled. "Jesus Christ, Rosie, do you realize you're the only person who's even *mentioned* it? I've been stumping around for three days, with them averting their eyes. And what does Rosie say in greeting, after four years? 'Was it a shell blew your leg off, Darin?'" He laughed quietly. "You don't know what a blessed relief that is."

"Then maybe I'd better add that you look terrible," she said, close to tears. "You must take care of yourself, darling, and get some flesh back on your bones, before something serious happens."

He laughed softly again. "Leaving the lower part of my leg in Georgia isn't serious enough for you, eh? I'm glad you called me 'darling,'" he said, wringing her hand. "Actually, I'm fine, Rosie: I look grand, believe me. You should have seen me three months ago."

"I've read about that place. It was inhuman. I don't know how you survived it."

"I had something to think about that got me through it. Though I don't know how long I'd have lasted if the war hadn't ended."

"Was it as bad as they say?"

He was silent a moment, studying her hand in his. "Do you remember the famine, Rosie?"

"No...yes. I try not to."

"Well, darling, that was a picnic compared to Andersonville. Not many of us lasted as long as a year there."

"A year?" she said, bewildered. "You were only there a year? Darin!" she cried, sitting up straight. "What about the rest of the time? There wasn't a single letter from you!"

"I know," he said without inflection. "And I'm sorry about it, now. There wasn't anyone I could write to, Rosie. I wanted to write to Pa, but she was there. I wanted to write to you; God, how I wanted to write you! But you were married, with a child and another on the way, the last time I saw you. You knew I was running away. I figured I'd just keep on running, with nothing to come back to, or get killed outright, like so many of the others. I didn't know about Sean. I didn't know about him, Rosie, or I'd have... You believe me, don't you? I've never lied to you."

"Of course I do. I always knew you weren't aware of Peg's condition, Darin." She paused thoughtfully. "And now what? I want you to know I'm in a position to assist in anything you want to do."

"Ah, yes!" he breathed with a smile. "A lady banker. Pa told me. God, that it should come to this! I don't need anything, Rosie. Nothing I can have. There's the boy to raise and educate properly. I don't want him to turn out like me. Business has never been better at the pub: I should be able to save a tidy sum." He shrugged his bony shoulders. "I just don't care."

"Get away from that place," she implored. "When you're better, of course. Do something you really love...really want to do! It's the only thing that holds people together, Darin. Go back to sea."

"With one leg, love?"

"Well," she reasoned, "Captain Ahab only had one leg! Sure you have an advantage, Darin. You've more than a peg down there."

His laughter was cut short be a fit of coughing, and he reached for his handkerchief to cover his mouth. "Rosie, Captain Ahab was a bit mixed up inside, wasn't he? I'm not up to chasing white whales, or windmills, either, dear. I've never had any objection to the normal, everyday evil of this world. No. I love that boy, and I want to be with him. And the only way I can do that is by settling down and working with Pa. Don't look so stricken, darling. Sure, I'm more fortunate than some who haven't even a job to come home to. For the first time in my life, I feel all level-like. Nothing matters very much any more except Sean. Present company excepted."

His resignation was almost more difficult to take than his physical condition; but Rosaleen realized he was still ill and probably not thinking clearly yet, so she did not press him.

"And what about you, Rosie? All we've discussed is my problems."

"What about me?" she asked.

"I sense you like your work, odd as it is. And I hear you've four children now, which doesn't really surprise me. What I can't understand is how you missed a year. It would be downright agonizing for any man who didn't keep you pregnant all the time."

"Darin!"

He smiled his slow, sad smile again. "Sure, what are your children's names? I know one's Rory. I hear of little else from Aunt Mary."

"Uh, yes. And there's John Michael. Mother's got everyone calling him Michael," she said rapidly, with renewed nervousness. "My older daughter, Cliona, is blond like Michael. And my baby is so much like Mother...dark eyes, dark hair...that we named her for her: Mary Rose, actually, because John wanted Rosaleen. She's different from the others: I don't know why...that is, I'm not really sure. The others were so *good,* and she's so independent...a little cranky."

"Like Mary," he said, and they both smiled. "You're uneasy speaking to me about your children. You shouldn't be, Rosie. God knows, I'm glad you're happy. The die was cast a long time ago for us: I've accepted it, though I'll always love you." Their eyes met in the same way they always had: it was an effort to wrench her gaze away.

"There are things that need saying between us," she nearly whispered.

"Can we meet somewhere, then?"

"No!" she cried softly, her blue eyes widening with alarm. "Darin, it's *that* I have to say, my love. Nothing's changed with us. It never will. I've always known that. But when I married John, I made a vow—not just in church, but to myself.

I'll never hurt him. Ever. He's the best and truest man alive. I'll do anything in my power for you, and don't hesitate a moment to ask. But our only meetings will be like this one, with everyone around and safe. And we can't speak of us like this again."

His fingers moved uneasily beneath her hand. "You make a dreadful vow," he said tonelessly. "But you're right, of course, Rosie. We've made our separate lives, and we must live them as best we can."

The clapping of Veronica's hands jolted through their brief intimacy, and their hands fell apart as though they had been surprised kissing.

"Come along now!" she cried clearly. "We can all visit later. There's a fine feast on the table, and all you can drink too. And," she sparkled happily, "you'll not find a single pratie there! We'll never risk depending on one thing again."

Rosaleen fought back the impulse to assist Darin to his feet. But he would accept no help from anyone. With her heart breaking, she put on a brave smile and looked down into his face, blowing him an affectionate kiss before taking John's arm to go into the dining room.

"Well," John said with concern, "you had a long chat, but you look cheerful enough. How does he seem?"

"He's a Noonan, my dear," she said, patting his hand. "He'll be just fine. He isn't bitter and he won't accept help. He'll survive. We have an inborn compulsion to hold onto life."

Part III

MARY ROSE

Chapter 28

SHE LOVED her father dearly: her greatest pleasure was looking after him and assisting him with his work. He was gentle and intelligent, and he treated her as though he had a particular affection for her, too. The two years in the convent school in France were the worst of Mary Rose's life; she would have run away back to Boston if she had had the money, and if her sister, Cliona, had not been there to hold her back. The summers at the Cape were bad enough; but two whole years out of his presence were almost enough to make her despair. Strangely enough, it had been Cliona who had fallen ill and brought them home, instead of herself. And now that things were back to normal, she told herself she would never leave him again.

The days of Mama dragging him off to Europe were over; he seemed to prefer the peace of his study, instead. Mary Rose had never understood her mother's restlessness. But then she sympathized with very little about her mother, in spite of what others said. That she was a great beauty no one could contradict: her picture was in the papers constantly. Mrs. John Maddigan, banker, philanthropist, collector and, incidentally, wife of the noted scholar. Fortunately the newspapers said nothing about her being a mother. But then even her brothers and sister would not agree with her on that: they all dutifully adored her. Mary Rose had tried to discuss it with Cliona just the other night, in the large front room they shared, which had an adjoining dressing room just like their parents'. It had been redecorated again while they were away, so they hardly recognized it or felt at home here. Mama was a fanatic about decorating, though she seldom took the people who had to live with her ideas into her confidence first. The room, which had once been her Grandmother Maddigan's, she was told, though she did not remember the woman at all, she was so young when Laura died, was decorated in what Mama considered appropriate for young ladies of their station: virginal white, with lots of eyelet embroidery and blue satin ribbons.

"Why blue, Cliona? Isn't it supposed to be pink for baby girls?" Mary Rose hated blue.

Her sister was sitting on the white carpet with one of the dogs, her long blond hair bent over its shining yellow coat, petting abstractedly. "Mama loves blue, you know that," she said. "I think the room's very nice, Mary Rose. You know she only does these things to please us. It was meant as a surprise."

"Shock's a better word," Mary Rose said, sitting down at the vanity to observe her own face. "I liked our striped wallpaper with the roses. The roses beside my bed had faces, and I was familiar with every one of them: some of them smiled, some frowned, one stuck out its pistil tongue. I miss my familiar flowers."

"What?" Cliona inquired shyly. "I'm sorry, I didn't..."

An intimate conversation with Cliona was out of the question, unless you sat directly on her left side. She was deaf from scarlet fever at seven and terribly self-conscious about it. The one flaw in what otherwise seemed like complete perfection to Mary Rose made her compassionate toward Cliona, and saved the lovely creature from the not infrequent swells of envy she engendered without really knowing it. Cliona was, indeed, like a queen of the fairies, drifting untouched at the outskirts of life, with innocent gray eyes and that peculiar abstraction which was so attractive to people, who did not know it was due to her deafness.

Looking at her own face in the mirror, Mary Rose experienced the usual discontent with it. She was the dark-eyed freak in the family, and her hair was not even black like her mother's, but dark-brown and so fine that tiny wisps showed in an aura around her head, no matter what she put on it to hold it down. Her Grandma Noonan told her she was the only O'Shea in the whole family, and Mary seemed proud of the fact that she was like her. Though Mary Rose recognized that her features were good, she could not help comparing her strong bone structure with Cliona's delicate face and her mother's beautiful one.

Raising her voice so she would be heard, she remarked,

"Why is Rory the only one who looks like Mama? I think it's such a waste."

"You're too hard on yourself," her sister said. "You have a wonderful face. But, Mary Rose, it won't be nice long if you keep frowning like that. Pretty is as..."

"...pretty does!" Mary Rose laughed at their grandmother's frequent saying, when she caught them before a mirror. Cliona laughed softly, too. They were both very fond of Mary, despite her old country ways.

"You look like her," Cliona said, rising and brushing off her petticoat.

"Don't do that," Mary Rose said evenly. "You'll have dog hair all over that ghastly white rug!"

"What? I'm sor—"

"Never mind," she said louder, throwing her hairbrush down. Her sister was almost as untidy as Mama, and she could not understand it, because Cliona was otherwise so sweet. "Cliona, do you think she'll go to France with Rory again in the summer?"

"I don't know, I'm sure. Has he got himself into a scrape again?"

"Probably. We haven't been back long enough to hear. At least he can't get kicked out of another college." She grinned wickedly. "There aren't any left, and he's twenty-one. What in the world will he do with his life?"

They both loved their older brother very much, though their reactions to his escapades differed. Mary Rose was amused by them; Cliona was constantly upset.

"He worries me so much," Cliona said. "I pray for him all the time. His education's all in bits and pieces, you know. He hasn't a degree."

"His education's fractured," Mary Rose smiled. "He's fortunate someone hasn't done the same to his skull. It's extraordinary, really... He has more friends than anyone in the family, from every school he ever went to. And, if he hasn't changed his haunts, from the people in the North End, too."

"Not that awful pub!" her sister exclaimed with distaste. "I could hardly bear it when Grandma took us there that time. It smelled of liquor and tobacco smoke."

Mary Rose made a wide rainbowlike gesture. "And had 'Noonan' painted across it in gold letters two feet high!" She laughed. "How that must upset Mama! No wonder she never goes there or mentions it. She'd have Grandma's scalp if she knew she took us there. Grandma as much as said so. She swore us to silence...remember?"

"She shouldn't have done it. We were so little," Cliona said; then she giggled. "Wasn't it a shock to see so many people looking like Rory? Even that old man, Brian. And that boy...what was his name?"

"Sean, I think. That's Irish for John, you know. The shock was in seeing so many who looked like Mama," she added sullenly.

"Don't be hateful, please," Cliona implored. "I don't know why you have it in for Mama so. She's always been wonderful to us, and Father loves her so."

Though Mary Rose was only sixteen, she was not entirely insensitive, and her motives were clear enough to her. She could not help loving her mother; if she had no one else, she would have adored her. The twist that turned everything against Rosaleen was the very fact that "Father loved her so." She had never been able to do anything about the fact that her mother came first with him.

In spite of the fact that the woman was so independent and appeared to lead her own life, without any particular concern for him.

"Don't fret about it," she told her sister, and Cliona was just about to say "What?" again when there was a knock on their door.

"Come in!" Mary Rose called.

Mary entered quietly, closing the door carefully behind her, and had to brace herself as the two girls rushed into her arms.

"There, now!" she cried, flushing with pleasure, nearly hitting Cliona with the hammer she held in her hand. "Sure, it's like a nest of little doves in here. Though the dear, sweet birds never coo 'Come in!' at the top of their lungs. I came to help you put your crucifix up, Cliona, darlin'. Where do you want it, over your bed as before?"

"Yes," Cliona said and smiled, holding her grandmother around the waist. "We've hardly had time to talk to you since we came home, Grandma."

"Are you feeling better, now?" Mary asked, looking down into Cliona's face. "Sure, you're still a bit peaky, I think."

"I'm so much better! I liked the convent, really, but the nuns kept it so cold. I suppose they don't feel it themselves, in their habits."

"I complained to them," Mary Rose said. "I told them someone would get sick, and you did! Grandma, they only kept it cold because they're so tight with money. And with Papa paying what he was, too! I hated it there—every minute of it. I couldn't even get my tongue around the language. I've never been good at French."

"Sure, you're not like your mother at all," Mary said, putting a nail in her mouth while she lined up the crucifix on the wall.

"So I've been told," Mary Rose almost whispered. "Grandma! What happened while we've been away? Not what Papa wrote in his letters. What really happened? What's Rory been up to? Is he in or out of favor this month?"

Mary slammed the hammer against the nail, nearly crucifying Christ for the second time. "Revolution, I think. Sure, it's difficult to keep up with him."

"Tell us about it," Mary Rose said, dragging her grandmother by the arm to the pale-blue sofa. "It was excruciating not knowing what he was doing. He came to see us last spring, you know. Every girl in school fell in love with him! We were terribly popular afterward."

"He didn't stay long, I hope," Mary said shortly, and Mary Rose laughed at the implication, which went right over her sister's blond head.

"Only a day. I suspect it was too quiet for him. Besides, the nuns made him uncomfortable . . . eyes like hawks, that sort of thing. I don't think they believed he was our brother, we're all so unlike. What did you mean when you said 'revolution'?"

"He's in thick with that lot at the pub again. They're always plotting treason . . . not against this country, you understand: they're after the English. Your brother, who, with remarkable insight on your mother's part, has only an allowance until he's thirty, has been spending everything on guns. You remember the fine gold cufflinks your mother brought him from Italy last time? *Gone*. And a few old volumes from the library, too."

"Oh, dear!" Cliona said faintly. "Has Mama caught him out?"

Mary's dark eyes sparkled. "What do you think? What is it she says of herself: she's eyes in her head and long ears, too? Sure, you can bet your bottom dollar she caught him out!"

"What did she do?" Mary Rose asked evenly, anger beginning to rise in her chest. Why couldn't that woman keep out of things? Rory was no fool. He had often spoken to her about getting the British out of Ireland: what he was doing was patriotic. He did not like the British any more than Grandma did.

Mary's senses were atuned to nuances and inflections: she was well aware of Mary Rose's jealousy of her mother, and her fierce loyalty to her brother. "You must understand, child," she explained calmly, "it isn't the *cause* your mother's against: I don't believe she thinks about it at all. It was the *guns*. Rosaleen hates weapons. Sure, during the war, she'd have nothing to do with the making of them, though she could have made a lot of money then. Guns killed your Uncle Matt. And it was a shell hit the hospital tent your Uncle Harry was in. And your cousin Darin lost a leg in the war."

"We know all about that," Mary Rose said impatiently. "Tell us what she did about Rory."

Mary sighed and settled back in the sofa. "Well, she was all ready to go out that evening...all dressed up in her blue satin with the sapphires your father gave her. She must have spies, I swear. There was a call on the telephone...I always knew mischief would come from that unnatural machine. She flew out of here without even a wrap on: the rest of it I have from Brian. You can imagine the surprise of all those loafers and guzzlers and plotters in the bar when that lady came trouncing in with her skirts flying! Brian said she was so angry that her eyes were as bright as the sapphires on her neck, sure. You know, from being around men in business so much, your mother's developed a...somewhat peculiar vocabulary, though, of course, you haven't heard it. And I can't repeat what she said to them...just that it was something to the effect that if they wanted to fight a war, they should get off their...bar stools...and do it, instead of sneaking guns to poor peasants who'd hang for possessing them. Then she turned on her own cousin, who was behind the bar with his pa, and read him the riot act...something about encouraging her son to wickedness and contributing to the dismemberment of the whole human race."

"Oh!" Cliona exclaimed. "Grandma, that wasn't very kind. I mean, he does have a wooden leg from the war."

Mary patted her hand. "Never a bit of it, darling! Those two have known each other forever. Apparently, Darin infuriated her more by doubling over with laughter, and she hurled an ale mug at him. Fortunately, that missed. Then she grabs your brother and marches him out of that place forever."

"Was that the end of it?" Mary Rose inquired cautiously.

"You might say so," Mary said. "Except for him paying her back for the gold cufflinks and the books."

"What?" Mary Rose cried. "On his allowance, it'll take him months."

"Not as long as that," Mary said. "She has him supplementing his income. She put him to work."

Knowing her brother, Mary Rose had misgivings. "Not in the bank?"

"Good Lord, no! That'd be like giving a bear a honey jar, for sure!" Mary laughed. "No. Rory's working on the docks."

Both of the girls looked blank.

"What docks?" Cliona asked. "Hasn't that something to do with courtrooms? What is he doing?"

"The docks, my darlings, are where the merchant ships come in. Someone has to unload them and carry the cargo to the warehouses. Your brother's doing exactly what Brian did when we first came to this country. Of course, the poor, dear man ruptured himself doing it."

"That," Mary Rose said, "is hateful!"

"Poor Rory." Cliona sighed. "Maybe if we gave him our allowance."

"Sure, do you want to be sent to Australia instead of France?" Mary asked. "I must admit, that was my first reaction, too. But Rory's a wild one. He's been spoiled to death. I'm as much to blame as anyone. It's time someone took him in hand, though it's a late date to be starting."

"Mary Rose," Cliona said with a frown, "wasn't Rory coming from Ireland when he visited us last spring?"

The nursery had long since been turned into a dingy sort of attic with dustcover-draped rectangles stacked against the walls, and Rosaleen was as particular about the temperature as if her children still resided there. Standing in the late-afternoon light with the shades drawn, she surveyed the catastrophe, realizing that the whole thing had gotten out of hand. After she had adorned every wall and hallway in the house with paintings, until there was no space left downstairs, the paintings she had purchased during the last few years had to be stored up here, some of them not even uncrated.

She raised the window shades, which usually protected her treasures, and pulled several of the canvases out to look at them in the light, her expert eye assessing their worth. Boston, she decided, was not yet ready for the Impressionists; though she loved the misty quality of the Seurat in her hands, almost as much as the first painting she had purchased on her own that day on her honeymoon. She kept that on the

435

wall of her own suite, not because the early Manet was now so valuable, but out of pure love of it. It had been her wedding gift from dear Veronica, who was gone so long now that her face was almost as misty as the colors on the canvas before her. Who would have dreamed that she was so ill at that last family gathering? She should have realized, as Mary did, that Veronica and Saul would never have sent their girls away for anything but their own protection from the consumption that was killing her. She shivered slightly at the thought: death still bothered her, though, thank God, everything had been fine for the past ten years.

But she had sent her girls away to school, too, Rosaleen reflected, much to Mary Rose's dismay. Her reasoning had seemed logical at the time, though there was a strong emotional element in her decision, too. She wanted to give them everything she had not had as a girl: the convent school in France had seemed just the thing. She would have gloried in it at their age; instead, she was working ten hours a day over a sewing machine. Of course, there was also what she termed to herself "Mary Rose's problem." The girl was too attached to John, and he loved her too much to discourage it. The school had, in that sense, been a desperate attempt to wean the girl, so she would not end up an old maid, fetching her father's papers and slippers. And already it was starting all over again, with Mary Rose in the library, hanging on her father's every word. There was no harm in that, by itself: he was a well-informed, fascinating speaker. It was the hostility toward herself that was difficult to bear. Her daughter had made a rival of her, and it was an extremely uncomfortable situation. Rosaleen found herself behaving differently to John in Mary Rose's presence, so the girl would not observe the deep affection between them, the laughter and solid friendship, and turn it against her mother.

Rosaleen pulled another painting out, whisking the dust away from her face. This one was already framed in heavy gilt, a passionate, romantic Delacroix. She giggled a little and bit her lip: it was so old-fashioned, though probably worth a fortune to someone. Indeed, it had cost her a good deal at auction, but she had no idea why she had bought it; perhaps the bidding had gotten so high, she could not resist. She dumped it against the other larger canvases, with its painted side against the wall. She had to make a decision: they would not survive another year up here, regardless of how much she protected them. Seeing a spot on her finger, she looked at it closely under the window with her heart beginning to pound; but what she had mistaken for a fleck of paint was only a smut from the covers, and she sighed with relief, nearly stumbling over Rory's easel as she turned away.

Unwittingly, she had invaded Rory's corner of the attic; usually she avoided it, having been warned away... and also to keep her skirts clean. What a mess that boy created! The paint-smudged, oily rags alone were enough to start a conflagration. He must have been up here recently: the linseed oil on one rag was still damp. Curious, ignoring warnings, she lifted the cover off the canvas on the easel and stood back to appraise his latest attempt. That was what he hated, though Rosaleen could not understand why. If he was going to paint at all, someone should look at his work, even if, as in this case, it was only half finished. He was meticulously attempting to copy her Renoir nude, which she discerned propped against a shipping box behind the easel. Suppressing a smile at her son's choice of a model, she had to admit that the copy was *good*. He had always liked to draw: that talent had been evident since childhood. And after accompanying her to galleries and museums abroad, he had added oils to his experiments early. She was proud of him, but she had done nothing to encourage him. With his energy and propensity for trouble, the company of artists had not seemed very safe. But, seeing what he had accomplished on his own, she wondered....

The sound of his step coming heavily up the stairs made her replace the cover quickly and whirl around to her study of her own paintings once again. She quickly picked one up to look at it as the door opened.

"Jesus Christ, who left the shades up?" And, seeing her standing there, his blue eyes widened and his face went as blank as an angel's. "Mother! I'm sorry. I thought...I didn't know you were here."

"Obviously," she said, turning away to keep from smiling. "I'm glad you're conscious of the care of these paintings, though your dedication to them is rather crudely expressed." She slid a look at him and caught him grinning. "How did it go at the docks today?" she said, stacking one frame against the wall and pulling out another.

"God, it's cold out! I'd kiss you, but I'm sweaty and dirty. Actually, it isn't that bad. I wouldn't want to make my living there, but doing heavy work is quite nice. I use so much energy that I come home...shall we say, *serene?*"

"That's a change. Maybe we should keep you there longer.

Your serenity might give us all some rest." She wondered briefly if he was attempting to trick her, but dismissed the idea at once. Rory was many things, but all of them were out in the open: he did not deliberately deceive. If he did, he would not have been caught so often.

"Well, I'd like that," he said, digging into his pockets, "but there are so many other things to do. I was able to quit today, because I have your payment...in full."

She stared at the wad of bills in his hand, trying to maintain her composure. "But you've only been there two weeks," she said at last.

"And fine weeks they were, Mother darling." He smiled, putting on his best Noonan Pub accent. "But I regret to say that, due to my sudden wealth, I'll be seeking other employment."

He looked and sounded so much like Darin that she was filled with a sudden rush of love. But that had happened too much in the past; at this stage of his life, it was crucial to be firm. All right, she thought quickly, how did he do it? The docks: that was the clue. What might stevedores do to amuse themselves between jobs? A picture came to her mind of a little boy with a deck of cards, letting his grandmother win. "Rory, you've been gambling!"

"Oh, my God," he said weakly with a twinkle in his eyes, "it isn't spies, after all...it's the sixth sense for sure! Mother, what am I going to do with you?"

"The question is, what am I going to do with you?" she said, fighting the impulse to run and hug him. "I might try tears."

"No, don't do that! You've never been unfair. It's always been a pleasant sort of war."

"Perhaps for you. Rory, you don't realize how much worry you cause!" she cried with exasperation.

He put up his hand. "None of that, either! The banshee was left shrilling in Ireland."

She went silent. She had found in the past that he could not endure that. Quietly, deliberately, she put down the painting in her hand, and raised another for inspection. An unknown artist, she thought, to put her son out of her mind: but unknown for how long? If you keep a painting long enough...

The painting dropped as she was engulfed in a big, sweaty hug. "Rory, for the love of God! You scared the life out of me! Let go!" But he picked her up and swung her in a circle in the center of the attic, until they both dissolved into laughter at the helplessness of her struggles. "You big oaf, put me down! I have a proposal for you. It's important."

"I didn't like the last one. It proposed me to hard labor."

"I'm *serious*," she said, frowning, and he set her gently on her feet. "I ignored your warning and I looked at your work. It's *good* . . . not original, of course . . . but you might make more of it than as an art forger. Have you ever considered studying art? I nearly said 'seriously,' but you aren't serious about anything."

"As a matter of fact, I have," he replied uneasily. "I love to paint. But I didn't think you'd ever consider it."

"I probably wouldn't have earlier. But you're twenty-one, and you've shown no direction. If I invest a few years in you, will you invest a few in me?"

"I don't understand," he replied, completely serious.

"We hope, but we don't know if you can make it as an artist. You'll be closer if you learn technique."

"But it takes more than talent," he finished for her. "It takes that special spark. I know. I've thought about it."

She wanted to reassure him, tell him he was wonderful; but she was not sure, and she did not want him to be let down.

"You go to Paris to study," she said, wondering if she could bear the separation. "And *you* decide if you have it, Rory. Be honest with yourself, because otherwise this could really lead to disaster. You've seen them—the ones who don't have it—standing on the streets trying to sell a painting to buy more paint, or absinthe."

"Yes. The burned-out boozers," he reflected. "And if I decide against myself? What's the alternative? What do I owe you?"

"The same amount of time in a gallery we'll open," she told him, fearing his reaction.

"A gallery," he considered, walking toward the window. "That isn't a bad idea." He turned suddenly, his entire face animated and smiling. "It's a deal! I love you, Mother!"

They all knew about the Noonans, though they had no particular place in their lives and were hardly worth mentioning. The girls would not have known about them at all if it were not for their grandma, who could not resist her occasional stories. Rosaleen would have been surprised at how much Mary Rose knew, against the unspoken pact in the household, which had not died with Laura. Everything Rosaleen did was for the benefit of her children, including hoarding priceless paintings in the attic. True, she derived her own satisfaction from that...it allayed some restless yearning in her; but, essentially, she was always acquiring security against the future. She had learned too young that the world was an unstable place: she did not entirely trust her own good fortune. More like Mary in that respect than she realized, she was a frequent toucher of wood and often threw spilled salt over her shoulder, feeling somewhere deep in her that when things were best and brightest, the sky might fall in.

Rosaleen would not have appreciated her mother's confidences to the girls, which was a regression on Mary's part. Rosaleen worked hard, both at the bank and in her social life, to hold the sky above them on her narrow shoulders: to preserve what she had thus far gained for them.

Mary Rose, with her own turn of mind, saw the whole thing differently. Her mother was a snob: she cut the Noonans. She did nothing to help them get out of that pub, where they actually *lived*. Her mother was restless, frivolous, extravagant: a judgment she had picked up, in part, from Mary. And, most despicable of all, her mother was cold to her father: she did not understand his needs in the least. Now the woman was packing Rory off to Europe, just as she had Cliona and herself, so she would have more freedom to go out into society.

Mary Rose had been home only three months when Rory left, taking most of the excitement in the house with him. Cliona consoled herself by reading, preferring romantic, moody novels in which the lovers died before consummating their union: Mrs. Radcliffe and the Brontës were on her shelf, along with the Douay Bible, her old catechism, and several religious books presented to her by her uncle, Father Liam. Liam visited often and spent more time with Cliona than with his mother, who somehow did not have the proper kind of pride in him an Irish mother should. Mary Rose was more fortunate in her activities, she felt: she spent as much time as possible with her father.

She perceived John as a great scholar, terribly misunderstood; after all, each of his three books had been met with an outcry from the clergy. She doubted that her mother had even read them; but *she* had, several times and carefully. The workings of his mind were fascinating. Gradually, in sifting through the myths, with all the proper Greek quotations, he revealed Christianity for what it was: a plagiarism. The taking of the body and blood of Christ at Communion was stolen from the story of Dionysus, whose body was rent and consumed by his followers, though he was resurrected again every spring. Hera, the mother goddess, had been transmuted into the Blessed Virgin. Of course, it was no wonder her father was persecuted by the clergy, which she had always suspected to be narrow-minded. Mary Rose herself believed every word her father wrote and, at the age of fifteen, proclaimed defiantly to her mother, "I'm not going to Mass any more. I don't believe in God: I'm an atheist!"

"Oh?" her mother said, with that superior, ironic look of hers. "What happened between you and God, darling? Have you had some sort of fall-out? Did you pray for something for Christmas that you didn't get?"

"No. I'm an atheist, because father's one."

"Nonsense, sweetheart! Your father isn't an atheist: he has all those gods and goddesses."

What could Mary Rose say to something like that? She was not even able to create a scene with the woman, and she thought it was because her mother did not care enough.

But her father cared. He listened to her and conversed with her like another adult. Now, at sixteen, she was proud to be his assistant, carefully copying out manuscript in her neat, rounded handwriting, because it was too much of a strain on his eyes. She spent quiet, happy hours with him, and brought him tea when his energy seemed low. He paused often to take off his glasses and rub his eyes. His fine gray eyes were bloodshot more often than she had ever observed before, though his smile was frequent, gentle and kind. Voluntarily, she started to read to him from his research books, if there were no Greek or Latin quotations in them, while he sat back in his chair with his eyes closed, nodding and listening to her.

Her life was as perfect as it would ever be, one tranquil day running into another. It pleased her to keep the library, where he always worked, tidy for him, with his books and papers in their proper places, his pens at hand always wiped clean, beside his inkstand.

She was totally outraged when, once a month, her mother dragged him off somewhere, as she always had, for the weekend. Only then was the house empty, and Mary Rose completely bereft.

The garden at the cottage was blooming early this year, and Rosaleen felt her usual satisfaction with it. Things had not gone well at the bank that week: Britain was at war again, this time against Egypt; and Germany, Austria and

Italy were forming a rather disturbing Triple Alliance. The market was shaky: no one knew what might happen. But everything faded away at the mere sight of her roses.

"Oh, John," she breathed, "this place was the best idea you ever had! I'm glad now we kept it secret. Two days a month is just about right to get away and be together, without distractions."

"Darling," he said, slipping his arms around her waist and cupping her breasts in his hands, "it's the best time of all. Always has been."

"Not outside!" She laughed, slapping at his hands.

"There's no one watching. Or do you object terribly to the scrutiny of the birds and the bees? Which gives me a perfectly delightful idea."

"Later." She smiled. "Living with a libertine has taught me not to exclude morning, afternoon and/or evening. But I do want to take a look at my garden first to make sure that boy from the farm's been watering everything."

"It's a long walk: I wouldn't blame him if he didn't. Maybe we should come more often. Or get someone from Cambridge to do the job. The city's getting closer than the farm." He looked around him and took a deep breath. "It won't be long before our cottage is on Something-or-other Square in North Cambridge. I'll hate that. I love it here. You're right, darling, we absolutely *need* to get away."

"You've seemed tense," she said, inspecting a budding bush for aphids. "Are your eyes bothering you?"

"A little," he admitted, plunging his hands deep into his pockets, "but not half as much as our daughter. The poor girl! She has so much love in her. And she's so beautiful."

"But she doesn't know it. I can't understand it," Rosaleen said. "I was always aware of my looks... maybe because people remarked on it all the time. Do you think we haven't given her enough self-confidence? I've always told the children they were beautiful, because they are. Of course, Mother doesn't hold with that. Do you think she may have discouraged Mary Rose?"

"I don't know. Maybe because they're all lovely... with the possible exception of Michael... she doesn't believe what we've told her. You know what she reminds me of?"

"Mother? I'll go along with that."

"No. I didn't know your mother when she was young... well, I did, but I was too young to appreciate her. Mary Rose reminds me of a Spanish gypsy: the same large, flashing eyes and dark hair. Only I wish to God she'd flamenco off with someone her own age and leave me to my own devices."

"John, dear, that isn't kind! The poor girl adores you. She should have friends, though."

"Rosaleen, my library's like a classroom! When I reach for one of my notes, it's all stacked up with my manuscript. She's deplorably neat. If I stop for a breather, or just to rest my eyes a minute, she's forcing tea down my throat. I really don't want to hurt her feelings, so I drink the damned stuff. But the human body can hold only so much liquid, and that causes interruptions, later. As well as an upset stomach from so much tannic acid."

Rosaleen laughed. "Maybe you should tell her. In a way, she's just playing mother: she needs someone to look after. Eddie Dove was always very fond of her, but he hasn't been around since the girls came back. It's a pity he isn't more like his father. Eddie's inordinately fond of sports. I suppose," she said thoughtfully, her voice trailing off, "it's time we started placing the girls in a position to get husbands. But when that happens, hardly any of the children will be at home."

"You miss Rory," he said, taking her hand. "So do I. The house is like a tomb without him. The element of suspense is gone."

"He's thoroughly exasperating," she reflected fondly. "If Paris doesn't settle him down, maybe it will wear him out."

"He'll be all right." John smiled. "But, in the meantime," he asked plaintively, "can't you do something to bring another male into Mary Rose's life? Why don't you give a party? Maybe some poor scholar will show up."

"All right," she said, kissing him on the cheek, "you know I'd do anything for you. A party it is! I'll have all my friends contribute their sons from Harvard. I suppose I should invite their daughters, too."

"No!" he protested jokingly. "Give our girls a chance. Eliminate the competition, so I can settle down and work. Sometimes, I just give up and have her read to me."

Chapter 29

THE PARTY, and those that grew from it, did not distract Mary Rose much. She found that she loved to dance, but the young men struck her as either callow or insensitive, though she was popular with them. As her confidence grew, she noticed that Cliona was becoming increasingly shy; her sister had turned down the last two invitations, preferring to stay home and read. One Friday evening in late autumn, Mary Rose, who was admiring her dress for the following evening, a striking light-rose silk with a postilion skirt, draped upward in the front and falling into a small train in back, decided to try to penetrate her sister's timidity.

"Do you think the neckline's too low, Cliona? There's certainly no one to whom I wish to show off my body. Should I wear a shawl over my shoulders, do you think? I wish you were going with me tomorrow night: I don't like to go alone."

"What?" Cliona asked, looking up from her book. "I'm sorry, Mary Rose. Did you say something about staying home?"

She walked to the sofa and carefully sat down on her sister's left side. "I said I don't like to go to the party alone, dear. I wish you'd come along."

"I'm sorry," Cliona apologized, "but all that bores me very much. I'm not as fond of dancing as you are."

"You could just sit and talk. All the boys like you. You wouldn't lack companionship."

Cliona closed her book with quiet decision and gazed directly at her sister. "They've been polite," she said quietly, "most of them. But, because of my deafness, they treat me as though I'm stupid, or a little fey. It's bad enough to be so fair, without that complication. And since I don't care about them anyway, it's much more pleasant to stay home. I haven't your life and vibrance, Mary Rose." She smiled sweetly. "You're growing up to be so beautiful."

"Do you really think so?" Mary Rose asked, flushing with pleasure, distracted from her intention of understanding her sister better. "You know, I really don't think of myself as plain any more. There's a certain way that boys look at you and, well, you know you're attractive. The trouble is, I feel the same about them as you do. There's just something missing, isn't there?"

"I hadn't considered it that way," Cliona said thoughtfully, "but now that you mention it... Do you think it's because none of them are Catholic?"

Mary Rose laughed. "What's that got to do with it? Papa isn't Catholic, either. It isn't as though we were going to marry any of them."

"Isn't it? In the long run, that's what it comes down to, I think. If I ever marry, I want to marry a Catholic man. There would be no understanding between us otherwise."

"Uncle Liam's really gotten to you, hasn't he? I don't have any such reservations at all. I just don't think the right person will ever come along, from what I've seen. I want to show Papa my new dress," she said, rising. "He keeps telling me I should wear more color. You know, I'm glad we were only children when bustles were in style. I don't know how Mother sat down in them. He'll be able to give me an opinion of the neckline, too."

"He's gone," Cliona said, returning to her book.

"Gone? They weren't supposed to leave until tomorrow morning."

"They left right after dinner. I wonder where they go every month," Cliona said, without real curiosity. "They've done it as long as I can remember."

Mary Rose looked at her dress with displeasure: all the joy had gone out of having it. She had intended to surprise her father with the color. "Well, maybe Grandma can tell me about the neckline. Do you know where she is?"

"She had a telephone call just before I came upstairs. I think she went to her room."

"That's unusual. She's never had a call before that I can remember," Mary Rose said, picking the dress up in her arms and leaving the room. She wanted someone to admire her choice of colors.

She knocked lightly on the door of her grandmother's room, but there was no reply. Putting her ear against the door, she thought she heard a sound within; but no one answered when she tapped again, more insistently.

"Grandma? Are you all right?" she asked, and, still getting no reply, quietly pushed the door open. She was stunned by what she saw.

Dressed completely in black, Mary was sitting in the chair next to her bed with her rosary beads over her fingers, her face expressionless and pale. She did not seem to notice anyone had entered the room.

"Didn't you hear me?" Mary Rose asked cautiously as she approached her. "Grandma, what on earth's the matter? You look dreadful, dear. Are you sick?"

Throwing the rose dress on the white counterpane, she knelt down before Mary, whose dull dark eyes finally came to rest on her face. Though her face did not change, she reached out her hand, and when Mary Rose grasped it, it was icy cold.

"I can't reach Rosaleen," Mary said, as though her lips were numb. "Not that she would be much good in a situation like this, but... Darlin', Brian died this afternoon, and I'm feeling too weak to go to the wake."

"Brian?" Mary Rose asked, finally remembering that he was the man Mary spoke of so often, a Noonan relative. "I'm sorry, Grandma. You were good friends, weren't you? But wasn't he awfully old?"

"Seventy-three. Sure, it's a good many years, indeed, but I always thought I'd go before he did. It's such a shock, Mary Rose. I haven't been able to weep at all, and I can hardly stand up on my own two legs to walk. Rosaleen should be here."

The ember of hostility in Mary Rose, never completely cool, was easily fanned to flame. "It's awful of her!" she cried. "Doesn't she even leave a telephone number when they go away? I always thought you knew where they were."

Mary shook her head slowly. "If I could just get on my feet, sure, I could go in the small carriage. I *have* to be there, love!"

"And you *shall* be there," Mary Rose said firmly. "Cliona and I will help you, Grandma. Where is it we're going?"

"To the flat above the pub. Where else would a wake be held?" Mary said, with a little more life in her eyes. "Would you girls really do that for me? You know what a wake is, don't you? If you're like your mother, I wouldn't blame you if..."

Now fully aware of what she had let herself in for, Mary Rose could not back down. "Of course I know what a wake is," she said. "You've mentioned them many times. And,"—with less determination, facing the specter of that awful, smelly pub—"I'm nothing like my mother! I know she doesn't go to funerals: I think she's silly. You just rest here a moment, and I'll get Cliona."

If I can, she thought, as she hurried back along the hall. Her sister had an even greater aversion to the pub than she did, and neither of them would know how to act around her mother's shanty Irish family and their friends.

The two girls assisted Mary up the stairs to the Noonan flat, and Mary Rose heard the sounds of fiddling, laughter and an ungodly wailing up above them. She gave a quick glance over her grandmother's back to Cliona, who, with lips set, seemed to be bearing up, probably because she could hear only half the din up there. It was really a terrible place, in an awful part of town; and though Mary Rose knew she was not in an actual den of iniquity, she had her misgivings, which were reinforced by the odor of whiskey and tobacco smoke wafting from the open door on the landing. The flat was packed with seamy people, mostly middle-aged men or older, though some women were keening beside the plain wooden coffin, set up on carpenter's horses under the windows at the far end of the parlor area. And she noticed as they passed, more women were in the kitchen, actually *preparing food* for the crowd. The violin was played by a bone-thin little man in threadbare clothes, the music more like dance tunes than mourning for the dead. Though her grandmother had told them about wakes, they were hardly prepared for this. Mary Rose's only reassurance, in the midst of such strangeness, was that the people in the room parted respectfully when they saw Mary, leaving an open pathway straight to the coffin for her.

Though neither girl had ever attended a funeral before, because their mother did not think it good for them, walking toward the body was the least of Mary Rose's worries, as they passed between the rows of smelly men. She wanted to be objective about them, rationalizing that poor people probably did not have the facilities to wash often; but they were such an unknown quantity to her that her heart rate picked up with fear. If nothing could happen to her here, with her grandmother and her family, why was she so frightened? She knew Cliona was experiencing the same emotions: her gray eyes had widened enormously under her dark bonnet.

When they reached the coffin, Mary said a few words in Gaelic, which dismissed the wailing women. Fearing she might faint, Mary Rose held her arm more firmly, but her grandmother shook herself free from the girl's support and leaned over the still body of the white-haired man, whose face appeared almost young, the wrinkles of age smoothed out by the hand of death.

"Oh, Brian, darlin'," her grandmother said, almost to herself. "Sure, you look like a boy again, my love. Mother of God, that it should come to this for you and me."

And, before Mary Rose could check her, Mary put her lips firmly on those of the corpse, with her gnarled hand stroking his face. It was not Mary but Cliona whose legs gave way then; and as Mary Rose turned to support her sister, she found herself staring into a face very much like Rory's. The young man had reached Cliona first, and, half-carrying her with Mary Rose attempting assistance, he led them to the safety of a bedroom, which appeared to be the only unoccupied room in the flat.

"She'll be fine now," he said, letting Cliona's body sink down on the clean white counterpane. "Mother has some smelling salts. I'll get them."

Mary Rose sat on the edge of the bed, loosening Cliona's bodice and chafing her wrists, while her eyes scrutinized the room. It was very tidy, with books she would not have expected to find there, stacked neatly on the shelves and lying on the desk and crisp lace curtains on the windows. Cliona gasped and half-opened her eyes before the young man came through the door with the bottle of salts in his hand, but he sat beside Mary Rose and put them under her sister's nose anyway.

"Wakes can be a shock to those who aren't accustomed to them," he said softly, his voice lilting slightly, but with no other trace of accent. "It's really a curious custom. We thought

Father Liam was bringing Aunt Mary. If I'd known, I'd have come for her myself."

The young man's voice and face affected Mary Rose strangely: they were both so sensitive, so gentle. The heart that had been tripping along in fear a short time ago began to do the same thing now, swelling into her throat as it only did during the "Hallelujah Chorus" of the *Messiah*. Until now, she had never been struck dumb in her life. She was grateful that Cliona raised her head at that moment, saving her from conversation.

"There, now," he said and smiled slightly, raising her sister's shoulders until she was in a sitting position. Still blurry from her faint, Cliona's eyes fastened on his face with all their innocence and beauty, and her breath caught sharply.

"You aren't Rory," she whispered, "but you look like him."

"No, I'm not Rory." He laughed gently. "But I think I know who you are, now. Please forgive me, but, dressed in black like that, I thought you were a couple of maids who'd come to help Aunt Mary. You must be Cliona and Mary Rose." He looked from Cliona to Mary Rose and nodded, still smiling. "Yes, you're Mary Rose! You look so much like Aunt Mary."

"You," Mary Rose said, almost in a whisper, "are Sean."

He held out his hand to grasp hers, and the touch nearly paralyzed her. "It's been a long time," he said, his blue eyes holding her gaze, so she could not look away. "You were only little girls the last time I saw you. But you've both grown into perfect beauties."

"What happened to me?" Cliona asked with both hands on her cheeks. "I feel so..."

He pulled his eyes away from Mary Rose's. "You fainted a little, Cliona. Overcome by that three-ring circus out there."

"I've never fainted," she protested softly, not taking her eyes off his face. "I remember, now. It wasn't the people. Grandma *kissed* that man in the coffin right on the lips!"

"I must say, it startled me, too." He smiled shyly. "The 'man in the coffin' is my grandfather."

"Oh, I'm terribly sorry," she said quickly. "It's Brian, of course. I wasn't thinking. Where are we?" Cliona asked, looking around the room.

"My room," he replied. "It was the only place I could bring you. I locked it against the flood of people this afternoon. I've a paper to write, and I didn't want everything scattered."

"You're a student?" Mary Rose asked awkwardly.

"Yes, at Boston College," he said, the full attention of his

449

blue eyes on her face again. "As you know, Father Liam teaches there."

"Are they going to make a priest out of you, too?" she surprised herself by saying. His soft laughter made her feel gauche and terribly young, but she loved the sound of it.

"They don't do that. There's no pressure from the priests there. It's a choice a person has to make for himself, you know...or he wouldn't be a good priest, would he?"

"And have you made that decision?" she asked carefully, but his reply was interrupted by the door opening and a tall man coming into the room. Mary Rose recognized him at once: she remembered him. He had not changed that much with the passing years. His body was tight and strong, his handsome face had the same wicked smile on it she remembered. His rolling walk did not betray his wooden leg.

"I just came to see if the girls are all right," Darin said. "Apparently, everything's in order. Your grandma was worried about them. Sure, I'm that sorry for the terrible mix-up: Liam's just now arrived." He studied their faces, as though looking for something there.

He smelled of alcohol, but he was not drunk, Mary Rose noted. And though the smile came quite naturally to his face, his blue eyes looked sad and bruised.

"I'm sorry about your father, Cousin Darin," she said sympathetically, imagining how it must feel to lose one's father. "We came with Grandma, because there was no one else to bring her, and she was feeling poorly."

"What about your mother? Does she know you came tonight?"

"She wasn't home," Cliona volunteered. "She'd have probably made other arrangements, if she had been, but..."

"She wouldn't have come herself," he said without malice; indeed, he seemed to understand. "I didn't expect her. We all know about Rosaleen and funerals. Is she keeping well, then?"

"Yes," Cliona said and nodded. And Mary Rose, remembering the story about her mother's tirade when she came here to drag Rory out of the pub, said, "I'd like to apologize for Mother. I understand she was very rude to you when she came after Rory. She shouldn't have said the things she did."

A faint gleam came into his eyes, a crooked smile to his lips. "Don't ever apologize for Rosie," he said softly. "She wasn't rude, child, she was glorious! I've never seen her so angry...though I was completely innocent. Sure, I'd never

450

encourage the boy to guns. How is your brother, anyway? Do you hear from him often?"

"Not really," Mary Rose replied. "He only writes to Mother and Father. He seems to be enjoying his studies in Paris, though."

"I'll bet he is!" the tall man smiled. "Of all the queer decisions I ever heard of, that was the queerest of all. Taking everything into consideration. He's a fine lad, though. I'm uncommonly fond of the rascal. Now, are you young people going to stay closeted in here with the vapors or are you going to join the crowd? I know you don't entirely approve of all this, Sean, but it's what your grandfather knew and deserves. He was a fine sweet man; and his friends are here to honor him."

After Mary Rose danced with Sean, the crowd no longer seemed threatening to her; in fact, it might not have been there, for all she noticed. Her attention was completely on her partner, with the fiddle music swelling around them.

"This seems almost pagan," she whispered, when they stood clapping on the sidelines, and he smiled his gentle, but half-ironic smile.

"What do you mean...*seems?* The whole thing probably goes back to the heathen Celts, when a harp was used and they danced with abandon around a bonfire!"

"I really don't know anything about them." She laughed. "Grandma claims they were all saints, scholars or poets. Which are you, Sean?"

"A little of the latter two, maybe," he said cheerfully. "She didn't tell you everything. Caesar said they dyed their hair blond, wore golden neck torcs and nothing else into battle."

"How interesting!" she sparkled up at him, and his blue eyes widened with amusement. She flushed. "I mean, how interesting that you've read Caesar!"

"My subject's Latin."

"Really? My father..."

"I know." He grinned. "I've read him. I shouldn't have: his books are on the banned list. He must be quite a fellow."

The fiddle stopped long enough for the fiddler to refuel. They found a spot against the wall to sip some punch, and Mary Rose surveyed the room.

"Where's your mother?" she asked.

"Cooking," he replied. "No, there she is over there with your sister and Aunt Mary."

The woman he indicated was plain, her expression not very pleasant. Mary Rose was surprised that she was blond. "She looks unhappy," she said with sympathy. "She must have cared for your grandfather a lot."

Sean took a deep sip of his punch, well laced with illegal potato liquor, the old-country poteen. "She always looks that way. She's a very religious woman," he said, without rancor.

Mary Rose tried to imagine that woman and Darin married: it made no sense at all. "I like your father. He's a very handsome man, isn't he? You're rather like him."

"Not at all." He smiled. "I gave up trying to be like him a long time ago. I love him dearly, but he's a bit of a rascal, like your brother. Every time I did anything like him, Mother spanked my pants off."

"But rascals are so much fun!" she cried. "They keep things lively."

"Yes. But they can also do that," he said, indicating his mother with his glass, "to those around them. I prefer a quieter, more ordered life."

"You didn't answer my question," she said, her tongue becoming freer from the punch. "Do you mean to be a priest?"

"Good God, no!" He laughed. "Whatever gave you such a strange idea?"

"I don't know: Boston College, and Uncle Liam. Oh, Sean, I'm so glad!"

When the music began again, she felt slightly dizzy and put the glass aside. "Sean, dear, would you mind dancing with Cliona? The poor girl's been sitting there with Grandma and Father Liam all this time. She isn't having any fun at all."

As he spun Cliona out onto the floor, Mary Rose took her place beside Mary and her uncle. She did not particularly care for Father Liam: he was strict and prudish. But she tried to make conversation with him for a few minutes, before leaning close to her grandmother's ear. "Grandma, may we come to the funeral tomorrow, too?"

When Rosaleen returned from the cottage on Monday morning, she was shocked to hear of Brian's death, but not in the least cross with the girls for going to the wake and funeral with Mary.

"It was very sweet of you," she told them, when she went to their room immediately upon her arrival and learned what had transpired in her absence. "How's Mother taking it?"

"She hasn't left her room since she came back from the funeral Saturday," Cliona said. "We've been taking trays to her, Mama, but she isn't eating much."

"She's living on tea," Mary Rose put in with less hostility than usual. "You can't imagine how upset she was, Mama. When she kissed the dead man, Cliona fainted away and had to be revived."

Rosaleen drew in her breath. "You fainted?"

"Yes. But I was all right later, Mama," Cliona reassured her. "Everything was very strange, but really not the least unpleasant."

"I think it's a marvelous way to send off the dead," Mary Rose said with real conviction. "With music and dancing and laughter, instead of too much grief. Of course, there were those wailing women."

"What women?" Rosaleen asked.

"The ones that wept and cried over the coffin. Surely, you've been to wakes?"

"Of course," Rosaleen said, not wishing to admit that she had not, but remembering what she had heard of the custom. "The women are hired, sometimes."

"That's what Sean said," Mary Rose cried, her interest rising. "I didn't believe him! Mama, what do you know about Cousin Darin's wife?"

The impact of the name was still the same: Rosaleen stiffened imperceptibly. "Very little. I've only met her once, shortly after the war. Why do you ask?"

"I was just wondering. They seem so ill-suited to me. He's such a beautiful, charming man, and she...well, she's a bit of a stick, you know. Do you suppose his losing his leg did that to her? Of course, Sean says..."

"Sean seems to have been very talkative." Rosaleen smiled. "Is he like his father?"

"Not at all," Cliona defended him. "He looks like him, of course, but he has none of his wickedness about him. He's intelligent and very gentle."

"Wickedness?" Rosaleen asked, frowning. "What on earth gave you that impression?"

"It isn't an impression. Uncle Liam told me. He said Cousin Darin's a very wayward man...that he's always been wild. He said it's what he wants to prevent in Rory, because they're a lot alike."

"You pay too much attention to my brother," Rosaleen said, trying to keep her voice even. "Liam's views have always been a bit distorted, in my opinion, and I don't know what he was talking about. I must go to Mother now, my darlings. I feel dreadful that I was away when this happened."

"If you'd left a telephone number," Mary Rose said, "we could have reached you in time. You really shouldn't go off without letting anyone know where you are. What if something happened to Grandma? She's getting old, too."

"You're right, darling. It won't happen again," Rosaleen said as she closed the door. She stood outside in the hall a moment, trying to compose herself. Her mother seldom spoke of the Noonans since the episode with Rory, not wishing to bring down Rosaleen's wrath on her head, and it was extremely disturbing to come home and have her daughters chatting so openly about them. Another death: poor Brian! Not all her sympathetic magic could keep that from happening, and it was as frightening to her as ever. But there was no time to think of her own feelings right now: her mother needed her.

The drapes were pulled in Mary's room, and she sat in the darkness, just as the girls had found her. Before Rosaleen spoke to her, she went to the window and let in the light.

"It's stuffy in here, Ma," she said. "The room needs airing." She raised a window slightly, allowing some cold air to enter, before sitting down on the bed beside her mother's chair. An untouched breakfast tray was at the old woman's elbow, and she really did look poorly. Her face was tearless, hopeless, putting a fear into Rosaleen she had never experienced before. Her mother had given up: she was going to die, too! And Rosaleen did not know what to do or say to bring her back. Helplessly, she reached for the teapot on the tray.

"The tea's still warm," she said, pouring a cup and adding sugar and cream. "I know you don't drink it this way, but the girls say this is all you've had. It won't do for you to get ill. Please drink it."

Mary obeyed like a child, taking a few sips and then waving the cup aside. "You weren't here," she reproached her daughter. "I needed you, and you weren't here."

"It'll never happen again. Do you want to talk about it, Ma? I know Brian was your oldest friend, the last link with the old country, really. It must be hard on you."

"Friend?" Mary said, her dark eyes flashing up at Rosaleen. *"Friend?* You must know he was far more than that."

Realizing her words had somehow struck fire in her mother like a flint, Rosaleen began to feel better: there was life in her yet. "Well, he was Doirin's husband, and you go back a long way," she said, still without sympathy: this time, on purpose. If she could make her mother angry enough, the battle was half won. "Of course, if I remember right, Doirin was never much of a wife or mother even before she went mad. I recall feeling a little sorry for Uncle Brian at times."

The attack was on Doirin, something her mother would never condone; but to Rosaleen's amazement, Mary's large, haunted dark eyes blazed.

"Sure, she was good for nothing! The life she gave that man! And when she was finally sent away, it was too late," she said.

Rosaleen waited patiently, but the statement was doomed to incompletion. "Too late for what, Ma?"

Finally, the tears came, in a rush, a flow, streaming down the wrinkled cheeks. "Too late for *us!* Sure, he was the only man I ever loved! I adored him altogether. I've worshiped him since I was fifteen! I only married Tomas because he looked like Brian."

As the old woman sobbed, her shoulders shaking, Rosaleen sat perfectly still, unable to take in what she had just heard. Her mother and Brian? It was impossible. But she knew in her heart it was only too probable, because she had given her love to a Noonan man, too. The situation was like a tangled web in her mind, with no beginning and no ending, and she found it difficult to breathe. With a rush of pity, she put her arms around Mary and tried to soothe her.

"There, darling, I understand. I just didn't know, that's all. He was a lovely man."

After several minutes, the sobs grew less and Mary reached for a handkerchief. "There was nothing wicked in it," she said, her chest still heaving. "He was my sister's husband, and there was never any harm in it. Well, maybe once, sure, but it was only a kiss. And we paid for it the rest of our lives. Doirin..."

"Did she know?"

Mary shook her head miserably. "I don't think so. But sure, his affection was divided from her, and she must have sensed that. All these years, I've felt that Brian and I were the cause of her madness. Didn't she go after him with a knife? Wasn't it his name she was calling when they carried her away?"

"Ma, no! Don't dwell on things like that. She never once attacked you, did she? If that had been the problem, she'd have gone for you, too, and more murderously, I think. She was all tied up and religious inside. She went after him for some other reason altogether."

"That may be so." Mary sighed deeply. "We could never have had each other without sinning, anyway. He was my sister's husband. Sure, it was never meant to be. If it had, I'd have been the oldest one when it came time for him to marry."

And Darin and I wouldn't have been cousins, Rosaleen thought; though they had not been as restrained as their parents. She realized she was not sorry for what she had done. How could a couple live forever on just a single kiss?

"Sure, if I had the whole thing to do over again, things would be different. What are the flames of hell compared to what we endured in life? But I shouldn't be saying such things to you, darling. You're a fine wife and mother: you're twice blessed. I feel better for saying it, though, and for getting the tears out, too."

Rosaleen kissed her on the cheek, leaving her lips there for a while. "I'm glad, Ma. Don't ever worry about saying it to me. I understand some things better, now."

"Don't be after telling your upright brother about all this," Mary warned in a firm voice. "He'd flay me alive, if he knew. He was a rather horrid child, you know, but that was probably part of it, too. He saw and heard some things he couldn't understand. I think it made him draw away from life altogether. If he'd turned out a saint, I wouldn't have any regrets, but sure he's a pompous son of a bitch. Meaning no disrespect to myself. He's working on your Cliona, and on Darin's Sean, too. Watch out for him, Rosaleen. He'll be whisking your lovely daughter off to a convent, if you don't guard her. Our fine Father Liam's opposed to the flesh."

Rosaleen remembered Liam, as a boy, standing by the window saying he would never marry, after all he had seen. "I know," she said, and added with a twinkle, "Sure, that's his loss, isn't it, Ma?"

"Rosaleen!" Mary cried, with life in her eyes. "By all the saints, you're the one! You're as shocking as Darin, and that's no mistake. But," she said and smiled sadly, "I don't know what my life would have been without the Noonans."

Sean had never called, as she had asked him to on the day of the funeral. It was almost Christmas, and Mary Rose's restlessness was apparent even to her sister. Their life together had been peculiar since the wake, neither of them speaking much, except about unimportant, everyday things. The confidences they had shared had ceased abruptly. Mary Rose, no longer hanging over her father in the library, was the one who was reading, now, in an attempt to teach herself Latin. Cliona, the bookworm, worked on embroidery or dreamed out of the window when they were together in their room.

"Stop pacing," Cliona said suddenly. "You're like a caged tiger, Mary Rose. Why don't you take a walk or something?"

"The snow's too deep." Mary Rose sighed. "I think I'll ask Papa to teach me Latin."

"You've had some Latin: you didn't like it, remember? You've always said you were bad at languages."

"Living languages," Mary Rose corrected her with some asperity. "This one's dead. You don't have to be so careful of the pronunciation."

Cliona smiled. "Remember how you got into trouble at school in France? How did it go . . . what you put on the blackboard?"

She laughed at the memory. "I didn't make it up. I saw it on Rory's textbook, once:

"'Latin is a language
As dead as it can be . . .
It killed the Romans long ago,
And now it's killing me.'

"But I've changed, Cliona. I'm really interested in it now. I want to read Caesar's *Gallic Wars* in the original. He talks about the Celts, and Vercingetorix, the Gaul . . ."

"And," Cliona said in a soft, sad voice, "Latin's Sean's study at college. Mary Rose, please be careful. He's a lovely boy, but he's our cousin."

"Our *second* cousin. Cliona, how much do you tell Father Liam in your talks with him?"

Cliona blushed. "Our talks aren't like that. He isn't my confessor. I don't tell him anything."

"Good! I've been afraid to say anything to you, but I'm so terribly fond of Sean! I think I'll go mad if I don't see him again."

"Mary Rose!" Cliona whispered, her eyes pained and her face paling. "It's impossible. I like him, too, but . . ."

"But there *is* a way to see him that's perfectly respectable!" Mary Rose said triumphantly, ignoring her sister's warnings.

"Instead of going to Mass in Cambridge, we can go to the North End this Sunday. What Mass do you think he attends?"

"Eight o'clock?" Cliona asked, her fearful eyes full of adventure. "Yes, I think early Mass, since he attends Boston College. They'd expect them to take the Sacraments, wouldn't they?"

"Mmm. But Sean isn't ordinary or that religious, I think. I think he probably sleeps in and goes at nine!"

"What if Mama finds out? She'll wonder why we're going to St. Mary's."

"She doesn't need to know. We usually go earlier than she and Grandma anyway. We'll leave at the usual time and walk, instead of taking the carriage. It should take us just about that long to get down there."

The next Sunday, as Sean knelt in church, he had no feeling of being watched, though two pews behind him his pretty cousins' eyes did not leave him. Mary Rose, who thought Cliona had come along just for a lark, watched him with his dark head bowed, so full of love she could hardly contain it, seeing only him in the entire, crowded church, trying to think of some way to bring them together again. She did not notice her sister's gray eyes worshiping in the same direction, as though there were an aura around the kneeling young man whose hair caught the colors streaming through the stained-glass window.

Chapter 30

JOHN made a bargain with Mary Rose: he would instruct her in Latin an hour a day, if she would continue to leave him to his own work the rest of the time. Though it was put more diplomatically, Mary Rose grasped its essence, and agreed at once with passionate exclamations about her interest in the language, her absolute need to read Caesar in his own words. The request did not strike John as odd, but admirable, because of his own devotion to the classics. Even Rosaleen was more optimistic about her daughter, though both girls had ceased attending any parties or social functions. There was time enough for that, since they were both obviously immature for their age, without the least interest in boys. In a way, it was a blessed relief, because Rosaleen had found herself imagining the things that might happen to them, from her own experience.

"There's time enough for all that later," she told John with a sigh. "We were trying to rush them, and some things won't be rushed, my dear. Let them enjoy their books and dreams a little longer: it's a happy time of their lives, and wonderfully innocent."

"You aren't going out as much yourself," he observed. "I want you to enjoy yourself, darling. It can't be exhilarating married to a recluse like me. If you're too busy at the bank, you must learn to delegate authority."

"It isn't that," she confessed quite seriously. "You wouldn't have noticed, because you seldom go with me, and the only friend you see is Edward Dove. But it's been happening gradually, John, since the end of the war. That was probably the only time I could have broken into the 'right' social circles, with everyone so patriotic. Since then, they've regrouped, and the Brahmins have really become Brahmins. Everything is based on family with them, now more than before. Many of my old friends have made themselves quite inaccessible: they've built a wall. Actually, it isn't altogether a bad thing. The 'old families' weren't always the most interesting or brightest, and it doesn't matter that much to me, now that your mother's gone. I did a lot to please that woman, and I guess I succeeded for a while, long enough to keep her happy, by imagining her family had its proper place again."

"This regrouping of the casts is something quite new to me," he said with a frown. "Has anyone cut you?"

"No," she said, "not outright. I still have my own friends, and I'm happy with them. But they're composed of literary people and even an occasional artist. It's ever so much fun, and I like it. But what I'm trying to tell you is that the children won't be in society as your mother knew it. Their name and religion are against it. The girls can't hope to marry into any of the 'good' families."

"But that's fine." He smiled. "They're inbred and a little moronic anyway. You know, Rosaleen, I don't care who they marry, as long as they have a marriage like ours. I just want them happy, that's all."

Though neither parent knew it, the girls were miserable, suffering all the pangs of first love, dismayed at their inability to see their adored one as often as they wished. Sometimes, if they were fortunate, they saw Sean on Sunday at St. Mary's; when they did not, the whole week was ruined for them. That suited Cliona's romantic, tragic nature: she wept quietly at night and read more poetry than Father Liam would have recommended to someone of her turn of mind. Having selected an impossible love object, she wanted nothing more than to dream of him, seeing Sean and herself as star-crossed lovers with no possible future. At least, that is how it seemed to her, before she began to feel jealousy for her sister.

Always practical, Mary Rose was more overt in her pursuit of Sean. It was she who had suggested going to St. Mary's in the first place; and she did not give up when he did not appear sometimes. For four months, the coldest ones of winter, she insisted on continuing their quest, knowing full well that *sometime* he had to become aware of their presence. While her sister flew like a white moth around a dangerous dream, Mary Rose knew what she wanted and meant to have it at any cost. She was determined because she was madly in love. If Cliona dreamed of laying down her life for Sean, Mary Rose wanted, quite directly in her own mind, to share her life with him.

One Sunday, in early spring, with the green buds just showing on the trees, she felt particularly optimistic. Indeed, if he did not see them today, she would put herself right into his path: worshiping from afar was not quite satisfactory any more. To her delight, he was at Mass: her heart nearly stopped when she saw him, and she was filled with irresolution again. The meeting might be awkward. She had decided that he had not visited for the very reason Cliona had pointed out in the first place: he was a good Catholic, and she was his second cousin. Unlike her mother at the same age, there was no mistake in Mary Rose's mind about the consequences of such a union. She had learned her catechism well, and it had been explained to her. She would die if he turned and fled at the sight of her. She knew quite well that he had been attracted on the evening of the wake, and again at the funeral. He had not taken his eyes off of her. She did not want to frighten him with her presence, for fear he might do something extraordinary, like flee all the way into the priesthood. If she were to make a move, it must be casual at first.

"Mary Rose, what are you doing?" Cliona whispered as they stood outside the church. "If we stay here, he'll see us. What would he think? I can't stand it. I'm leaving!"

Her chance to escape was thwarted by the people pouring out the door; and, almost immediately, they heard a familiar, lilting voice exclaiming, "Mary Rose! Cliona! What in the world are you doing here? It's so good to see you!"

When she looked up into his face, Mary Rose's composure deserted her completely, banished by the delight in his remarkable blue eyes.

"I'm glad to see you, too!" she said in a rush, while Cliona remained stricken dumb at her side. "It's been such a long time!"

"It has, too long." He smiled. "We must go somewhere to talk. Come on, there's a coffee shop down the street. I usually stop there on the way home, to have a moment of peace before all that studying." He stepped between them with a hand on each of their elbows, steering them away from the crowd and through the churchyard. "Forgive the route," he said and smiled, "but it's much quicker this way. Though it's almost spring, it's still cold. No one's afraid of ghosts, I hope?"

"Of course not." Mary Rose laughed. "I don't believe in them for a minute!"

"That's heresy," he said. "You can't be Irish and not believe in ghosts, and a lot of other mad superstitions, too. I saw one once."

"You?" Mary Rose started, finding herself perfectly ready to accept anything he said.

Cliona picked her way along the path through the dead leaves as though she were floating. All this was too much for her: her beloved's hand on her arm, strong and firm, and a graveyard, too. All of her most Brontë-esque fantasies had come true. She could not have spoken if addressed directly; she was so full of the sweet melancholy of knowing she could never have him, while something in her yearned for him in a very real way, which did not fit into the proper mood of the books she had read. She was grateful that Mary Rose was able to keep the conversation going without her, especially since he was on her right side as they walked, and she could not hear him very well.

"Yes," he said, ushering the girls into the nearly empty coffee shop and holding their chairs until they were seated at a round table with a checkered cloth. "I think the ghost was my father's fault, really. One night he was telling stories about the sea, complete with ghost ships and spectral crews and God knows what-all. Let me assure you, he can tell a fearful story when he has a mind to, on a dark night in the wintertime! Anyway, when everyone was asleep, I thought I heard something on the stairs. I got up and opened the door, and..." He held them both captive with his untroubled blue eyes, until Mary Rose begged, "What did you see?"

"I don't think I'll tell you." He shrugged. "You don't believe in such things and would surely call me a liar."

"Sean!" she cried, her dark eyes laughing, and he laughed with her.

"All right, then. You won't believe me, but it's true. There was a small person on the stairs shaking a fist at me. I was frightened half to death. I slammed the door and ran back to my bed and hid under the covers, afraid to peek out."

"How old were you?" Mary Rose asked, fascinated.

"Seven or eight. But I saw it."

"You were dreaming! Some of Grandma's stories did the same to me. Mother made her stop telling them."

He shook his head seriously. "I thought that myself, and bit my lip hard to make sure I was awake. My mother frightened me worse by her explanation the next morning. She said it must have been the ghost of my grandmother I saw, and her quite mad in her lifetime! A ghost is one thing, you know, but a *mad ghost*. It makes my flesh crawl even now." He laughed, rubbing his arms.

"Did you ever see it again?" Cliona asked quietly with no trace of disbelief in her fine gray eyes.

"I never went out on the landing again after dark," he told her. "I try to avoid it, even now."

"Was your grandmother really mad?" Mary Rose asked. "She was our grandmother's sister, and she's never mentioned it."

"Apparently," he said, fastening his attention back on her face. He had hardly stopped staring at her since they had entered the shop, not even to look at the waiter when he gave their order for three coffees. "A lot of us are, really. There's no shame in it. Every year, more and more are taken away. I haven't an explanation, though I've thought about it a lot. Even when we're at our best, there's a touch of lunacy in us. You must have noticed."

"In the Noonans?" Mary Rose asked, considering it thoughtfully. "No, not really."

"No, in the *Irish*," he said with a gentle smile.

"Now you *are* joking." She laughed. "You're really *too* bad! I don't want to hear about the crazy Irish. I want to know about Grandma's sister, Doirin."

"Oh, that," he said, his voice falling. "I really don't know much about it, only what Mother told me that morning. When my father found out what she'd said, there were some very definite words spoken, and it wasn't mentioned again."

"I'll find out," she said like a conspirator. "If Grandma won't tell me, I bet Mother will. She's very straightforward."

"Where are they today?" he asked, handing their coffee around. "Sugar? I should think you'd attend Mass with your family, instead of coming down here."

Cliona poured several spoonfuls of sugar into her coffee and began what amounted to perpetual stirring while she stared into his face, certain not to be caught at it, because he had hardly looked at her directly at all.

"Our whole family doesn't go to church together," Mary

Rose explained nervously. "Only our mother's Catholic, you know. Father's a pagan."

He choked on his coffee, and continued laughing after he had put a handkerchief to his mouth, his eyes bright with amusement.

"But he is!" She smiled. "He's a bona fide pagan. My mother will tell you."

"She doesn't have to," he said, between laughs, "I've read his books! I think we're in the same family situation, Mary Rose. My mother's a Catholic in the extreme, and father's a pagan, too. It makes strange bedfellows...I mean," he said quickly, flushing slightly, "it makes a peculiar match. What about your own convictions, coming from such a household? Are they sort of half and half?"

Her smile died and she grew silent, not knowing how to answer; then, "And what are yours?"

"Well," he said, more seriously, "the Church is something we grow up with, isn't it? I'm not the sort of person who doesn't ask questions, though. It's difficult to accept everything on faith. Father Liam's given me some dressing-downs for my curiosity, believe me."

"I guess I'm the same way," she said.

Cliona became uneasy and abandoned her stirring spoon to pull her coat off the back of the chair. "Mary Rose," she said quietly, "we really must go home. We've stayed longer than usual. We'll be missed."

As he walked them to the door, close behind Mary Rose, Sean asked softly, "Did I say something wrong?"

She shook her head. "She's right. We must go. Sean, it's been lovely! May we have coffee again next week?"

Cliona would not return to the North End, and Mary Rose continued to go alone, meeting Sean for Mass and talking in the coffee shop, until the weather became warm and they could take long walks together. For months, they walked side by side without touching; but by autumn, their hands linked and the time together was richer than ever.

One morning by the Charles River, with the blazing gold and yellow leaves falling on them where they sat, Sean said, "You know quite well what's happening, don't you?"

"Yes," she said, tracing the veins of a maple leaf with her finger. "I've always known, Sean. I didn't come to the church by accident. Why didn't you come to see me at our house?"

"I couldn't. You weren't out of my mind for a single hour

all those months, but I couldn't come to see you. I thought it better never to see you again. But I'm glad I did, Mary Rose, you don't know how glad."

"I think I do." She smiled as he kissed her hand. "We have a problem. I think we should face it directly, Sean. My background's different; maybe I've spent too much time with my father. I don't think my faith's as strong as yours. I love you, but I don't want to deprive you of something important to you. It just wouldn't work."

Her words were stopped by her first kiss, and she clung to him returning it, letting her lips wander to his cheek and eyes. She could not let him go: she would not...unless he wanted the Church more than her.

"I love you, darling," he said softly. "That's all I know...all I want. To hell with the 'third degree of kindred.' Will you marry me, cousin?"

"Of course I will. I decided that months ago." She smiled.

"And that," he said moodily, "is just the beginning of our problem."

"Yes. Whenever I've tried to think about it, my mind veers away. Your family...my family. Cliona's very upset already. She'll hardly speak to me. The amazing thing is that she hasn't said anything to Father Liam."

"Oh God," he moaned, "that would be a brouhaha! We won't be able to marry in the Church. He'll have apoplexy."

"My father will stand by me," she said with conviction. "I think he's the only one who will. I won't be disowned entirely, but..."

"I'm sure of my father, too: he has no great love for the Church. But Mother..." He became thoughtful. "People don't really die from things like that, do they? In any case, it isn't something we must face at once. I've still two years of college to complete, darling. I won't be able to support a wife until then. Maybe we can pave the way gently, so none of them will be hurt too much."

"Yes," she agreed, searching his eyes, melting inwardly with the love she saw there. "It will be all right. It has to be! I must make sure that Cliona keeps her mouth shut, though."

"In the meantime," he said and smiled, "we can start skipping Mass on Sunday, so we'll have more time together."

Father Liam came to dinner every Sunday, even when John and Rosaleen were away: Mary Rose could not remember it ever being otherwise, and it had never upset her until now. He had a way of dominating the dinner conversation, usually trying to provoke a discussion, which would really be an argument, with her father. But, with little interest in any philosophy that took root after 399 B.C., John remained safe within the confines of his own discipline. He had learned long ago never to argue with a Jesuit. The interplay between them provided Rosaleen with some hidden amusement, though it bored Mary and the girls into eating faster than usual.

For the first time, Mary Rose began to size her uncle up, watching closely for his strengths and weaknesses. He would be her greatest opponent, this frail middle-aged man with thinning blond hair, whose black clothing draped his sticklike limbs loosely. Though she knew his mind was well developed, the rest of him impressed her as a mere husk of a man, dry and unfulfilled. She knew he was quite humorless, a grave defect in anyone. He was also given to arrogance, as though he alone had the ear of God, and only through him might lesser mortals be saved. Before, her dislike of him had been calm and unimpassioned: it was more active now. Especially, because she feared him.

No matter how fast she ate, ignoring her mother's raised eyebrow, Mary Rose did not manage to get away before, his attempts with John failing, he turned his attention to the "children."

"And what are you doing, Mary Rose?" he asked, with a smile. "I know your sister's devoting a good deal of her time to the Altar and Rosary society and her sodality, but I've heard very little of your activities during the past months. I can only hope they're as noble."

Touching a linen napkin to her lips while she swallowed the morsel of roast beef in her mouth, Mary Rose cleared her throat and said quickly, "Papa's teaching me Latin. I've been studying a great deal."

His face beamed like a grinning skull. "Latin, is it? A fine study, indeed. But to what purpose? Young ladies really don't need it, unless it's to follow the Mass more carefully."

"Not Ecclesiastical Latin, Uncle Liam. Classical."

His expression was less indulgent. "Ah, you intend to assist your father with his studies? But, John, I thought you were working almost entirely with Greek?"

John, who had eaten lightly, as he did more and more lately, took a small sip of wine. "I don't see that it matters," he said with irritation. "Latin's as noble a study as Greek, and Mary Rose prefers it. We're into the *Gallic Wars* already: she's really applied herself."

"Caesar's *Commentaries* can't make amusing reading for a young lady," the priest insisted. "And you know the danger of Latin as well as I. Petronius and Catullus can be found on any library shelf."

"Most of the Romans kept the golden mean," John said. *"'Integer vitae scelerisque purus'*—there's more nobility than sin in Latin."

"What about *'Carpe diem, quam minimum credula postero'*? Hardly the thing for young minds, I think."

"I could almost get that from my Italian," Rosaleen said, suddenly absorbed. "What was it, Liam?"

He shook his head, with a supercilious smile. "Never mind."

John looked at Mary Rose questioningly, but she shook her head as a confession of ignorance. "It's Horace, out of context." He smiled at his wife. "It means, 'Seize the day, put no trust in the morrow!'"

Rosaleen looked confused. "What's wrong with that? I've always thought that way. The book I've just read exalts the idea!"

Liam's lips grew thin. "What, might I ask, are you reading?"

Ignoring John's eye signals, she smiled sweetly at her brother and replied, "Edward FitzGerald's translation of the *Rubaiyat*. There's a new edition. My dear Liam, I think we should cheat death any way we can, for as long as we can." Suddenly, she raised her glass of red wine with bravado, quoting,

> "'Come, fill the cup, and in
> The fire of Spring your Winter-garment of
> Repentance fling; the Bird of Time has
> But a little way to flutter . . . and the Bird is
> On the Wing . . .'

"It's my Credo!" Rosaleen laughed, delicately sipping the wine.

"Rosaleen, how *can* you!" Liam flared. "And with your daughters at the table! What you call your *Credo*, so sacrilegiously, could be your damnation. John, how can you tolerate this? Don't you pay any attention to what your wife reads?"

"What a tempest in a teapot," Mary said, rising. "Sure all this foolishness is enough to give a person indigestion, Liam!

467

In fact, I usually have an attack when you've been to dinner. You don't sound like a proper priest at all. You're beginning to sound like some kind of fire-and-brimstone Puritan. Sure I thought Rosaleen's poetry was pretty, and it was written by an Irishman with an old name, too. And it has more sense in it than you'll ever know, in your sequestered, celibate state. Now, if you'll all excuse me, I'm going to my room to say a rosary for committing the sin of Anger."

"Mother!" the priest cried in shock at her back as she marched out of the room. "My goodness!" he said, placing his napkin beside his plate. "I haven't seen her like that in years!"

"Darling," Rosaleen cajoled him, putting her hand on his arm. "You weren't always so stuffy. It must be age that's stiffening your mind as well as your joints. You know we're all very fond of you, but sometimes you are a real pain in the—"

No accident made John spill his wine with the quick exclamation, "Good heavens, what an oaf I am! Cliona, darling, will you call the maid? The linen will be stained forever."

"More wine?" Rosaleen asked her brother with a sweet smile. "It's a very good vintage."

"Thank you," he said, proffering his glass, still unnerved by his mother's tirade, but determined to ignore it. "It was a fine dinner, Rosaleen. It always is. Though the cuisine was definitely better when you had the French cook."

It was not an uncommon complaint from him: he had adored Monsieur Giraud's cooking, watched him leave with genuine sadness years ago, after Rosaleen sacked him in favor of plainer, more nourishing food for her young children. The present cook, Mrs. Walker, was of the old New England breed with both her recipes and her accent: difficult to converse with, but masterful with roasts and chops and fish and her homemade relishes, of which corn was the great favorite. Rosaleen did not wish to go into the matter again with her brother, who had spent so much time in France and longed for rich sauces. Besides, the thought of Mrs. Walker diverted her attention.

"Mary Rose," she said suddenly. "What have you been doing to cook? She complained to me about it. She says she wants 'kitchen to m'self,' with no one hanging over her."

Hardly recovered from the episode between her Uncle Liam and her grandmother, Mary Rose still held her napkin to her lips to hide the laughter, which had now disintegrated to only a controllable smile.

"I don't bother her, Mother," she defended herself. "I've just been watching how she does things. I'm learning to cook."

Her mother looked at her with exasperation. "Whatever for?" she asked innocently. "You really must be more careful, or she'll walk out on us."

Later, in Mary's room, Rosaleen and her mother laughed about the incident with Liam.

"It reminded me of the night I got my dimple," she said. "Whatever started that? I don't remember."

"God knows," Mary said, smiling and shaking her head. "The Time Bird's fluttered too far for memory.... Oh, but sure, I do recall, now! Young Darin was after defending you from your father over something, and that plank of wood on boxes gave way."

Rosaleen grew quiet. After several minutes in the past, she said quietly, "You're right, Mother. The Bird of Time has flown some, since then."

John was not well that winter. The least activity tired him, and his eyes were bothering him more than ever. Mary Rose finally concluded her lessons with him, feeling it was too much strain for him to devote his time to teaching her: she was well enough equipped to continue on her own. Her father needed rest, and during the long weeks between Sundays, when she could not see Sean, she lingered over him like an angel of mercy. But she was mature enough now to recognize that too much of her ministrations definitely bothered him. Her only fear was that he was hiding his condition from her vivacious mother. When Rosaleen packed their trunks with the intention of taking him to Italy in the spring, Mary Rose was so horrified she did the unthinkable: she burst into the study when her mother was working.

"I must talk to you!" Mary Rose said, closing the door and leaning against it as her mother looked up from her desk in surprise. Taking off the glasses she had been wearing with a single quick movement, as though to hide them, Rosaleen nodded.

"What is it?" she asked in a brisk businesslike voice Mary Rose had never heard before. Was this the way she was when she was away from home? Mary Rose was quite intimidated by this unfamiliar person, but she held her ground.

"It's Father," she said. "You simply can't haul him off to Europe this year. You probably haven't noticed, but he hasn't been well, Mother. I'm sure he wouldn't reveal it in front of you, but he tires easily. And his eyes..."

Her mother put down her pen and closed the ledger on the desk, biting her lip thoughtfully. When she addressed her daughter again, it was in a more familiar tone.

"You always make me the villain, dear. The fact is, I'm quite aware of his condition. I've made several appointments with the doctor, which he hasn't kept. So I finally went with him. The doctor could find nothing wrong with him except exhaustion. It was he who advised that we take this trip, and your father is delighted over it. It's been several years since we've been abroad together, and he's looking forward to it, Mary Rose."

"What about his eyes?" Mary Rose asked stubbornly.

"They've been examined," her mother said, looking away. "It's a progressive condition, darling." The deep-blue eyes looked back at her daughter, and there were small frown lines between them. "You aren't a child any more. I'll be quite open with you, but don't let it go beyond this room, please. Your father's forty-four years old. If his eyesight continues to deteriorate at the rate it is, he'll lose it before he's fifty. I don't mean to shock you or worry you, my dear, but that's the prognosis."

"He'll be blind?" Mary Rose said with a sinking heart. "Really *blind?*"

"We don't know that for sure. I said only if it continues this way. We're hoping and praying that it won't happen." Her mother was silent for a moment; then, "Would you like to go with us, Mary Rose? You've never been to Italy, and we're going to stop to see Rory in Paris."

Mary Rose straightened her back against the hard panel of the door, her mind nearly paralyzed by the suggestion. They would be gone several months: she could not leave Sean that long. She wanted to be with her father, but she could not leave Boston.

She shook her head almost imperceptibly. "No, it's your trip," she said, feeling that she was surrendering her father forever. "I hate France, and I've no desire to go to Italy, Mother. I...I'm sorry: I misunderstood."

Her mother's eyes were compassionate and her words soft. "There are things you never understood, darling, because you were a little girl. You're very grown-up for nineteen, Mary Rose: I'm proud of you. That's why I've confided these things to you. You see, your father feels...he wants very much to visit Italy again. We were so happy there once, and the climate will be good for him. It's a lovely, lazy country with a wide blue sky and enough sun to revive anyone. He isn't going to work at all: he'll rest and see the sights again. Please don't worry about him. He really wants this trip. He's conscious of his failing sight."

"You'll take good care of him, won't you?"

"What do you think?" Her mother smiled at her.

Mary Rose nodded, suddenly understanding and feeling free. "I know you will."

They had not been to the Cape for several years, and as much as Mary wanted to go that summer, they all stayed in Boston because Mary Rose refused to leave. Though her grandmother was accustomed to the heat by now, she liked the cool, barren shore better, especially because she was in total charge of the house when they were there, with only one servant to help: she found pure delight in sweeping, scrubbing and cooking on her vacation. Mary Rose felt guilty about her decision, and she told them to go without her, because she would be fine alone with the servants. And Michael would be there, too, training at the bank, before his graduation. Such complete freedom was not to be hers, though: Mary was not about to leave a young girl of Mary Rose's age to her own devices for three months.

"It's rather selfish of you," Cliona reproached her one morning at breakfast, the sun shining on her bright hair through the window behind her. "I don't mind, but poor Grandma was looking forward to it, Mary Rose. I know quite well it isn't your Latin studies and access to a library that influenced your decision."

"What do you know?" Mary Rose asked, trying to sound her out. "I *do* need the library, you know."

"The fact you've been going to St. Mary's for over a year tells me something," her sister said, averting her eyes. "I hope you know what you're doing, and that you'll know when to stop. Having Sean for a friend is one thing, but ..."

"There's no reason I should stop, dear," Mary Rose said so honestly that her statement was misunderstood.

"You are just friends, then?" Cliona asked, brightening visibly. "I've been so worried. It's a long time to be seeing a young man. I was afraid..." Then, looking directly into her sister's dark eyes with her luminous gray ones, she smiled faintly and asked, "How is he?"

"He'll be graduating next year. He's well, and he asks about you often." That was an exaggeration, but she wanted to please her sister: kind and innocent as she was, Cliona was dangerous to her, because she alone knew about her meetings with Sean. She had suspected for some time that Cliona was in love with Sean, too, despite her devotion to her religion, which just made her shy off like a moth too near a flame. Cliona's hectic church activities were only a way of running away from her attraction to Sean, though she probably did not realize it.

"I'm...I was very fond of him," she confided suddenly, a blush tinging her clear cheeks. "I saw at once that he was more interested in having you for a friend, though. I'm glad it's only that, Mary Rose. He's very attractive, gentle and nice. But there's no getting around the fact that he's our cousin, is there? In a way, he's closer than a second cousin, even. I figured it out. Our grandmothers were married to brothers."

"Yes." Mary Rose nodded, studying her sister's face. Cliona leaned closer, pushing her plate aside and resting her elbows on the table.

"Did you ever find out anything about his grandmother?" she asked.

Mary Rose shook her head. "I tried to bring it up with Grandma, but she was as close as a clam. I don't think Papa even knows about it: he acted like he'd never heard of Doirin. I was afraid to ask Mama. It's never been easy for me to talk to her. I think that's changing, though. She'd probably tell me about it, but she's in Italy."

"It's a little worrisome to have insanity in the family," Cliona said. "It's hereditary, isn't it?"

"That's what they say: I don't really know. I don't feel insane. Do you?"

Her sister did not laugh, as she expected. "Not really. But I think there's something wrong with me. I dream too much, Mary Rose. Daydreams. And," she said and frowned slightly, "the dreams are so much better than reality. They're enough, you know? I have no desire to make them come true. It would be impossible, anyway."

Chapter 31

MARY ROSE missed a trip to Italy and sweltered in town all summer without seeing Sean any more than usual. He was helping at his father's pub: Sunday was the only day he had free. She hated the thought of his working there, more out of frustration than snobbery, for Mary Rose was not a snob. And, though even her mother had noticed a new maturity in her, no one sensed the caldron of passions boiling within her or the impetuosity that was brewing. A few stolen kisses in some secluded spot were no longer enough for her, and, without real religion to steady her, the only thing that kept her from embroiling herself in a tempestuous affair was Sean's steady character and willpower.

"Don't you think it's hard on me, too?" he asked miserably, as they lay on the grassy bank of the river. "God knows, I've had my little escapades, but I love you too much to make you one of them. I want you for my own wife, the one woman who's both friend and lover, always. I don't want the wretched sort of life my father's lived. I love him, but I refuse to be like him in that respect. I'll make love to you after we're married, and not before, darling. The consequences could be disastrous: I want you always to be safe and happy."

"Happy?" she said, her dark eyes flashing. "If this is happiness, I'd hate to know what misery is!" Then, more calmly, because he turned his eyes from her to study the river, "You're right, of course. You're a gentleman, Sean: you're honor-

able. I don't know why I had to fall in love with such an honorable man." She sighed, and he looked back at her with a laugh.

"You're quite mad, you know," he said, brushing her hair back from her cheek. "You want to plunge head-first into life without knowing the slightest thing about it."

She considered that for a moment; indeed, she was ignorant about the relations between men and women, knowing only the bare facts and that it was not proper to indulge oneself until marriage. Only men seemed to have that option. "What did you mean about 'having your escapades'?" she asked, seeking more enlightenment. "Who did you have them with?"

He groaned and closed his eyes at the mistake of mentioning it; then, fixing her candidly with his blue eyes, he said truthfully, "Tarts. There are always tarts around for boys to seek out. It doesn't make a man feel better about himself afterward. I haven't done it since I met you."

"I know something of that sort of thing," she considered. "Rory got expelled from prep school over something like that."

Sean's eyes twinkled and his lips twisted into a smile. "Rory's a lunatic," he said affectionately. "No different than anyone else, but less discreet about it. The only truly honest man I know, with the exception of my father."

"You mentioned Darin before," she rushed in quickly. "He's a married man. Does he really have love affairs, Sean? Does he talk to you about it?"

"No, he doesn't talk to me about it, darling. He *is* discreet, and that would be unsuitable, wouldn't it? It's been going on for years, as long as I can remember. In a way," he said, his voice falling, "I can't blame him. I love my mother, but I wouldn't want to be married to her. She cares for only two things: the Church and her son, in that order, I think."

"She can't know about your father's infidelity," Mary Rose said, interested. "It would probably hurt her very much."

"It may sound shocking, but I've come to think she's a party to it," he said quietly. "Not directly, but I don't think she's left him any options. Irish women are marvelous mothers, but they often neglect their husbands. If my father had married someone else, he would have settled down to a normal life, perhaps."

"If he didn't tell you about it, how do you know?" she asked with curiosity, not so much about Darin as the subject they were discussing openly for the first time.

Sean sighed and lay back on the grass with his hands under his head, staring into the blue sky.

"From things that were said and implied around the pub when I was growing up. Some of the affairs lasted long enough for me to learn the women's names. They weren't *bad* women; they weren't tarts. Just lonely and attractive. One of them was a widow. Of course, they were virtually banished from the Irish community, by the mutual consent of the other women. Mary Rose, it's always the woman who suffers in that sort of arrangement: the man gets off scot-free. The double standard isn't fair, perhaps, but it exists completely. That's what I was trying to say a few minutes ago," he said, articulating his words softly. "I don't want you to be hurt. I love you so much."

The tone of his voice, the sight of his beautiful profile, made Mary Rose lean down impulsively to kiss him, holding her lips against his tantalizingly, until he finally reached up and pushed her face away, staring into it with excitement.

"I'm glad you're the way you are, my darling," he said, shaking his head slightly in wonder. "God, it's like drinking strong wine! The day we're married will be the happiest I've ever known."

When John and Rosaleen returned from Italy in the fall, Mary Rose knew what she had to do: her father would help her, she was almost certain. She would give him a few days to settle in, before approaching him with the subject of her marriage. Papa would understand and not hold the kinship against the match, and he could influence her mother. It was maddening that Sean had to search so hard for work, with his ability: a job should be waiting for him immediately after graduation. If he would not accept financial assistance from her father, surely he could have no objection to his using his influence. Papa loved her and wanted her to be happy: he could do anything.

She was very much relieved at how well he looked, with his face deeply tanned by the Italian sun and more spring in his walk than he had shown for some time. Though he was not supposed to spend any time working when he was away, he returned with a whole valise of notes and books and the spark in his eyes to get something done. She had to talk to him before he closeted himself in the library again and got cross when interrupted. But her mother's return to the bank and his closing the library door happened the same morning, filling her with panic. She flew into the library without knocking, causing him to look up with alarm.

"Is something wrong, dear?" John asked, half rising from his desk.

"Papa, I must talk to you, now. I don't want to interrupt your work later. I have something so important to tell you."

John relaxed and smiled, extending his arm to her. "You do just that, then. I've heard very little about your summer, except that you read the *Aeneid* and practiced your piano. I'm very proud of you, Mary Rose, but your summer sounded too serene, dear. Weren't there any parties at all? Was everyone else away?"

"I'm anything but serene, Papa," she said, sinking into a leather armchair near his desk and fastening her glowing dark eyes on his face. "What I'm going to tell you must be in confidence for a while, as you shall see. I know I've been a nuisance in the past, and I hope I'm not going to be a worse one, now."

He waved the idea aside with a smile, studying her from behind his thick lenses. "There's something different about you," he mused. "An enhancement of color, a tender glow. If I didn't know you must have been studying so diligently while we were away, I'd say you were, perhaps, in love?"

"Does it show that much?" she cried in horror, putting her hands to her burning cheeks. "Oh, yes, I am! It's terrible, but it's so wonderful, too. I didn't think I'd ever feel this way about anyone."

John leaned forward and took her hands from her face to kiss them and hold them in his own. "I've always been convinced of it," he said. "I suspect that's what you want to talk about, of course. Who is this very fortunate young man?"

"Maybe neither of us are fortunate, Papa. Except in each other." She took a deep, nervous breath. "It's Sean Noonan, Papa, and we love each other so much!"

The complete stillness of his hands did not betray anything but calm, though he averted his face so that she could not see his expression. "Darin's son," he said at last, as though considering all the ramifications of the alliance. "Extraordinary. I haven't seen him since he was a little boy. How on earth did you two get together?"

"The night Cliona and I took Grandma to his grandfather's wake," she said, feeling her tongue trip ahead of itself while cold perspiration ran down her sides in rivulets. "We've been seeing each other for a long time, meeting at church and taking walks. Only since we decided to marry, we haven't been going to church any more, because the Church wouldn't let us marry. There's a rule about cousins."

He stared at some far-off point over her shoulder. "I know. I took instructions long before your mother and I were married. You're both willing to be married outside the church, then?"

"Yes. Only Mother and Grandma, and his mother, will simply die! Both of us think our fathers will stand behind us. Will you, Papa?"

His hands clenched over hers, and he looked directly at her again with his gentle gray eyes. "Your palms are sweating," he said, "and your fingers are cold, dear. Did you have any doubt in the world that I would take your part?" He shook his head with a tight little smile. "It almost seems it was meant to be."

"You mean you will?" she said with a rush of gratitude.

"Of course I will. I owe a great deal to that rule, but I think it's time it was broken. Sean's in college, I understand. When will he finish?"

"Next summer, Papa. And he's having a difficult time finding a teaching position. He absolutely will not marry me until he can support me. I told him it was silly, but he's adamant about it. He's very clever, probably the best Latinist in the area, even better than those at Harvard, I'm sure. But he's young and he's new, and..."

"He won't have an advanced degree. A Latinist, is it?" He smiled ironically. "And all the time I thought your sudden interest was out of inherited scholarship."

"I'm sorry, Papa," she said sincerely, her face a mask of misery. "I wasn't tricking you. And after you gave me the lessons, I really became interested in it."

He laughed and kissed her hands again. "What better reason for scholarship than love?" he asked. "Now, as I see it, the only thing that's really keeping you apart is finding a job for your young man when he graduates? The rest can be handled later. It *is* going to cause quite a stir, though perhaps not exactly where you expect it. Do you think Sean would consider tutoring while he got a higher degree? It won't pay much, but..."

"We don't need much! Oh, yes, I'm sure he would! Do you know anyone who...?"

"Yes, possibly," he considered. "It might even work into an instructorship at Harvard. You wouldn't have much to live on for a while, though, if he persists in his real nobility."

"It doesn't matter, Papa. We only need each other."

"You're every bit as practical as I am, darling." He sighed. "We don't need money, because we've always had it. But I suspect people do need it, for little things like food and lodgings. Don't worry about it at all, sweet. I'll go to Cambridge this week and work something out. You can plan on becoming a bride next June. Of course, it will not be a formal ceremony, with you marching into church over the bodies of all your Catholic relatives, but..."

Mary Rose kissed him exuberantly, knocking his glasses sideways. "Thank you, Papa. Thank you! Cliona's so wrong! Who says the course of true love has to be difficult? I'll tell Sean on Sunday, when I see him. It's too special for the telephone."

On Thursday, John remarked at dinner that he was going over to Harvard to see some of his friends in the Classics Department the next day, without so much as glancing at Mary Rose, whose heart began to pound over the proximity of her mother and her grandma at the table. She was more alarmed at her mother's reaction to such a simple statement, though.

"Oh, John, do you really have to? It's a good distance even in the carriage, and a long walk across the Yard. Surely it isn't that important."

"I'm feeling wonderful," he told her with a warm smile, adding teasingly, "I'll bundle up against the fall winds, little mother, and I'll lean upon my walking stick!"

Mary Rose could see that her mother was not amused; but at least she did not press her objection, which was totally unreasonable anyway. Instead, she turned her attention to Michael, who was preparing for his last term at Harvard.

"Mr. Connell was extremely pleased with you during the summer, dear. He said you're very quick, very astute. You'll make a fine banker. What I wanted to ask you, before your last year in school, is, Michael, are you sure that's what you want? I mean, sure without the slightest reservation or wish to please me? It's very important to me to know that. I don't want any of my children going into a profession thinking it was chosen by birth, and they have no choice in the matter. That's what happened to your Uncle Matt, and you know how that turned out, don't you?"

Michael, who looked very much like John, except his serious blue eyes were without glasses, grinned at her in a way that reminded Mary Rose of Rory.

"I shan't run off to war or do myself in because of it," he assured her. "You know damn well I like it as much as you do, Mother! I love it: it's a constant challenge. I watched them in the board meetings every week and it's more fun than a tennis match. So, no, Mother, I don't want to change my studies this year: I'll charge right ahead with what I'm doing. Conscience clear, now?"

"Yes," she said and laughed.

"Oh, and about that traditional trip abroad," he said, putting his napkin aside. "I think I'll pass on that, if you and Father don't mind. I've been there so often, there's really no sense in doing it again right now. I'd rather plunge right into my work."

"Young idiot," John murmured, smiling at his son and looking at Rosaleen. "How can they all be so different? That's two of them who've refused trips to Europe this year. I don't understand it."

Michael studied his father with affection. "I didn't say I'm never going back, Father, just not at this time. I'll go on my honeymoon. How's that?"

"The best time," John said, "the very best. Anyone in mind?"

"No! Good God, I'm only twenty-one! I think thirty's a good age to marry. Of course, to a much younger girl. By then, you know enough to raise her as you want her to be."

"I wouldn't know." John smiled. "I was twenty-one. And I went all over Europe, and to Greece and Egypt, with my bride of eighteen. I wouldn't change that for anything. Rosaleen, can I tell them about the camel ride?"

"No," she said.

"What camel ride?" Cliona asked with interest. "Mother, you never told us you'd been on a camel!"

"I wasn't." Rosaleen smiled. "It's an old, very private, joke of your father's, which we won't go into now. Did I tell you how well Rory looked?"

The whole family laughed at her transparent strategy of changing the subject, without realizing it was the thought of the camel ride that made her think of Rory. Only John understood and, as he always did, fell right into line with her conversation.

"I went to Paris in fear and trembling," John said with laughter in his eyes, "certain that Rory's effect on Paris would be visible! You know—the Latin Quarter destroyed, the steeple of Notre Dame tilted at a rakish angle? You can imagine my surprise at what we found."

Michael looked slightly bored: he had had quite enough of stories about Rory. Rosaleen, aware of the rivalry that had always existed between her sons, at least on Michael's part, felt uneasy as John continued, unaware.

"No crates of guns in his garret. No booze beneath the bed. The flaming-haired model I'd been so looking forward to meeting, a figment of my imagination. And no Rory, either. He was at class at the Sorbonne."

"I still don't understand how they accepted him," Michael said stiffly. "You'd think they would have written for transcripts and character references."

"Oh, I don't think they're worried by things like that so much," John said. "They're only interested in minds...have been since the thirteenth century. It *was* a surprise to see your brother actually applying himself, though."

"You make it sound more like a disappointment," Michael drawled with a faint smile.

"I must admit, an element of excitement seemed to go out of my life," John agreed with his ready smile. "Actually," he said, more seriously, "I think what he's doing is commendable. He'll have his degree within two years."

"Well," Mary Rose said brightly, "I've always thought that if the bits and pieces of his education were all put together, he'd have a degree by now. Papa, what explanation did he give for abandoning his art studies without telling you?"

"After only a short time among real artists, he decided he didn't have the 'spark'. That's what he told your mother, at least. Whether that was before or after he met his student friends, I'm not sure."

"He's interested in politics?" Michael considered. "The friends aren't anarchists, are they?"

"No," Rosaleen said. "We took the whole lot of them to dinner. They were delightful. Some were in law with Rory; some, philosophy. And I think there was a medical student among them. Their hair needed trimming, they were a little threadbare and quite ravenous. I think, for once, Rory's fallen in with friends with conscience."

"He likes people." John smiled. "And, you must agree, he's always avoided halfway measures. I think he's becoming interested in politics, not just causes. The best way to help society is from the top, instead of on a missionary level. If his views are a little socialistic right now, it's only because he's young."

"They are anarchists, then?" Michael said in the ironic tone Rosaleen loathed. "I fancy he'll return to Boston and start heaving bombs at the bank."

They all knew better than to say anything derogatory about Rory in Mary's presence; and Michael had left himself wide open to one of her infrequent tirades.

"Shame to you for being mean-minded and bad-mouthed!" Mary cried. "Rory wouldn't harm a bee if it bit him. Bombs, indeed! If it's after being a politician he is, sure, he'll do more good for his people than you in that bank! They haven't been able to help themselves much, thanks to that lot of Protestants who came here from England not all that long ago!"

Michael was unintimidated by Mary. Leaning back in his chair, he said languidly, "Just what we need, another Irish politician."

As they prepared for bed that night, John did something that was not customary for him: he sat near the vanity to watch Rosaleen brush her hair. She looked at him with a quick smile.

"You're tired, my dear, and this can't be very interesting for you, especially as I intend to put a cream on my face."

"Don't," he said and smiled, "not tonight. You know, the only thing that bothers me about losing my sight is that I won't be able to see you, Rosaleen. I want to impress you in my mind forever, darling."

She put her brush down and looked at him with concern. "Are your eyes bothering you again?"

"No more than usual, though my head aches a little. After consulting with the physician in Paris, we know what's going to happen...probably sooner than we thought, though. It's

481

curious how a choked-up vessel can bring on blindness, isn't it? I'm resigned to it," he said quickly. "But I keep wondering what it will be for you."

"I'll be your eyes," she said warmly. "I can read to you...except in Greek and Latin. And I'm sure Mary Rose would be only too happy to accommodate you in the latter. And," she said, trying to keep her voice light, "you'll always remember me as I am now. Forty-one isn't young, but you'll never think of me as old. I suspect there are women enough who wouldn't mind that."

"You haven't changed, you know." He smiled at her. "You're more beautiful than when we married. The structure of your face is finer. And, after four children, your body's lovelier than ever."

"My waist isn't quite as small!" She laughed. "But I guess I'd look peculiar at my age, with a waist like a wasp. At least I haven't put on weight...well, only a few pounds. I haven't kept as slim as you."

"You're *curvier*," he said wistfully, and they both laughed. "Is that a word? Your breasts are fuller, and your hips."

"Please!" She smiled. "Spare me. Don't document me from head to toe. I suppose I'm fortunate, but only because I have such a mother. Have you noticed her figure, even at her age? Shanty Irish heredity *counts!*"

"You're too much of a woman for me," he said, suddenly serious. "This last six months can't have been good for you."

"You said you wouldn't mention it again. We've been over it before. What I said before still holds, my dear. There's more between us than just making love. As your constitution improves, that will come back, too," she said, reaching for his hand. "Nothing's really changed between us. Now, what's all this nonsense about going to Harvard to see old friends tomorrow? Can't they come here? I didn't want to make an issue of it at the table. But you know as well as I that you haven't had a jaunt that far all summer."

He shrugged slightly. "It has to do with Mary Rose. I can't discuss it yet."

"A tutor? That would be an excellent idea, John, if she really wants to continue with this Latin business."

He laughed, but he could not share the joke when she gave him an inquiring look.

"Oh, she's determined to continue," he said. "You can't imagine her determination."

"A peculiar girl," Rosaleen considered. "She's looking absolutely stunning. Really happy for the first time I can remember. But Latin! You'd think she'd be interested in young men, by now. And Cliona! She looks more ethereal all the time, as if she'll just float away on a sunbeam. I'm going to have a doctor look at her. Though, God knows, she's active enough with her church affairs. I hope she hasn't fallen in love with a priest."

"A *priest!*" He laughed. "What an outrageous thing to say!"

"It happens." She sighed, automatically touching behind her ears with perfume, though she would do nothing in bed but sleep. "If there's an attractive enough priest in a parish, girls her age flock to confession and committees. Oh, there's usually nothing to it. It's not like in Italy." She laughed at the recollection. "I was never so shocked in my life."

"The village priest with the buxom housekeeper." He smiled. "And the 'orphans' in his house."

"That was bad enough! But that sloe-eyed guide we had who shrugged and said, 'He's a man, isn't he?' Such easy acceptance, and in the country of the Pope's residence!"

"It's the first time I've seen you shocked in years," he said affectionately. "You looked like a little girl again. You know, my darling, you're usually a rather worldly woman. I suppose it comes with spending so much time abroad."

"Hardly!" she defended herself with wide eyes. "One does run into all sorts of peculiar people, quite willing to discuss everything about themselves, but it hasn't touched me personally. I haven't become hard, have I, John?"

"Not in the least, darling. You're perfect: I love you just the way you are." He gave a deep sigh, partly of satisfaction, mostly of weariness. "I'm going to retire now. I've a busy day ahead."

"Wait for me. I really think it's silly not to just telephone for a tutor," she said, turning off the gaslight and crawling into her side of the satin-draped bed, as he took off his glasses and put them on the night table and joined her. "Oh, you're just stubborn!"

Because he no longer came to her side of the bed, she snuggled up close beside him, laying her head lightly on his shoulder.

"Rosaleen," he said, stroking her hair in the darkness, "you've been the single best thing in my life. I can't imagine what it would have been without you. Thank you. You are my beloved, my everything. You've made me completely happy, no matter how I got you."

She could tell by his even breathing that he had fallen asleep, but she did not move from his shoulder for some time. She was wondering, over and over, what he meant. *No matter how I got you.* The words made her feel cold inside. Surely they could not mean what they seemed to mean. And, if they did, why had he waited all these years to tell her that he knew? And, if he had, what had suggested it to him now?

She moved to her own side of the bed, but it took her over an hour to fall asleep, staring at the shadowy pattern of sculptured leaves on the ceiling and the patterns the curtains made on the walls from the gaslit streetlights outside. Finally, weary and unable to unravel the mystery, which she imagined she was making too much of in the first place, she closed her eyes and slept.

Rosaleen grew chilly toward morning, as she always did when the banked fireplaces stopped giving off heat, and she put her arms under the covers for warmth, turning on her side to snuggle up to John's back with one arm around him. She slept fitfully for a while, having a troubled dream about Rory, in which she was unable to distinguish him from Darin in her husband's presence, and as she woke, she realized something was not quite right. The arm she had thrown around John was colder than before and his body curiously still beneath it. Half sitting up to pull the covers around him for warmth, she felt a vague uneasiness.

"John? John, dear, are you all right?"

There was no answer from the man who was usually such a light sleeper that on hearing his name he would turn to embrace her in his arms for another hour's sleep. Her open hand moved along his chest, feeling no respiration, and upward to his neck, which felt cold and stiff. Her heart racing uncontrollably, she got out of bed and ran to his side, uncovering his face in the early light. He might have been sleeping peacefully, except for a small stream of dark spittle that had flowed from the corner of his open lips, staining the embroidered white pillow cover.

"John!" she cried frantically, shaking him. *"John!* Oh ...nooooo!"

Her screams quickly woke the household. Only vaguely aware of the presence of people in the room, she continued to scream hysterically, her mind paralyzed with loss and the ever-present horror of death.

"Rosaleen, darling," a woman's voice said, and there were arms around her, while people, like spirits, drifted by.

"Mother," a sobbing girl's voice said, but she could not respond, because she really was not there. And finally, there was a man's voice, with more authority.

"Mother. Mother, for God's sake! Help me get her to your room, Grandma."

"Call a doctor, Michael. She's had a terrible shock."

Sobs competed with the screams she did not realize were coming from her own throat. Her mind was blank, her body wreathed in pain and terror like cold fire burning through her chest and bowels. She was jolted back to reality only by a firm slap on the face, and found herself looking at her mother in her room.

"What am I doing here?" she asked, looking around with unfocused eyes. "How did I get here? What is it?"

"Sit down, Rosaleen," Mary said, leading her to an armchair. "Sure, you need a cup of hot tea, darling, and the maid's just brought it."

A delicate china cup was forced into her hands, and she focused all her attention on it, knowing there was something she must not remember. With trembling hands, she tried to get the cup to her lips, but Mary had to assist her, though her hands were shaking, too. The hot stream of liquid did nothing to warm the ice in her chest. The saucer clattered to the hearth, shattering like her own nerves, and the deep, heart-wrenching sobs began again, though she did not know why she was crying.

At one point, the doctor appeared and gave her a glass of water into which he had poured a powder, gently forcing her to drink. After that, she remembered nothing, until she awoke again at night.

"I don't believe you," Rosaleen said numbly when they told her John was dead. Michael frowned and glanced at his grandmother.

Mary sat down on the edge of the bed and took Rosaleen's hand in hers. "Sure, darling, you know it's true. It won't change things by denying them. Poor John died during the night, without any pain, in his sleep. You were the one who discovered it, Rosaleen," she entreated, "everyone's that upset, not just you. But there are arrangements to be made. You have to face reality."

"What arrangements?" she asked from her pillow, but the gears of her mind almost slipped into place for a moment.

"Funeral arrangements, Mother," Michael said. "We're thinking of having it tomorrow. We know you don't like to attend funerals, so..."

"We thought you'd want to make the arrangements," Mary said in a voice firmer than her grandson's, "even if you don't attend."

"I need Rory," Rosaleen said, looking around helplessly. "Where's Rory?"

"I cabled him this morning, dear," Michael told her. "I knew you'd want him. But it'll be a month or more until he can get back. I know this is hard on you," he said, brushing her black hair away from her face. "But, please, for us, don't simply go to pieces. *We* need *you*. Mary Rose and Cliona are in an awful state. You've always been the one person who held everything together: the one with strength. Please, for the girls' sake."

"It's all right," Mary said, putting her hand on his arm. "Go to them, Michael. Sure, the poor lambs shouldn't be alone right now. I'll stay with your mother. Everything will be all right."

After he left, Mary turned on Rosaleen. "We've been through this before, years ago! I don't know what happened then, but you nearly had a total breakdown. I'll have no one else in my family drifting off into unreality again, do you hear me? Life's real: it isn't always pleasant, sure, but it's real and we must face up to it. *This morning, you woke up and found John dead beside you.* He was your husband, and he loved you dearly, but he's *dead*. Don't flinch at the word, Rosaleen. Look at me. That's better. It'll be best for everyone to have the funeral over and done with. We should do it tomorrow. Those are facts. Now, if you want to close your mind on the world like Doirin, that will be it. I'll have no more to do with you. And you'll be dead yourself within a year. I know you don't want to go to the funeral. We all know you avoid them."

"But," Rosaleen said quietly, "I do want to go, Mother. John was so dear to me. He was the best friend I ever had."

Tears came to her mother's eyes and she swallowed hard as she bent down to kiss her cheek. "I'm sorry, darling," she said brokenly. "I didn't want to be heartless, but I couldn't let you go on like that. It's a cruel loss for all of us. He was such a dear man."

Rosaleen put her arms around her mother and held her close. The screaming and sobbing had left her throat and chest sore, and her eyes were painfully dry now.

"He was the best man in the world," she said. "I don't know what I'll do without him."

Chapter 32

A WEEK after the funeral, the house was still quiet, and it felt cold in spite of fires on every grate. Mary Rose wore a shawl around her shoulders to come downstairs to use the telephone in the study, without looking around to see if anyone was observing her. She knew Cliona was at Saturday confession with her grandmother, and though her mother was out of bed now, she had been told Rosaleen was in the library going through John's papers. She had to call Sean at the pub, to tell him there was little hope of meeting him because the family would be going to a memorial Mass together in Cambridge. She hoped his mother would not answer, as she once had, because she had questioned him incessantly about what the girl on the telephone was to him. If he was seeing someone, wasn't she fit to introduce to his parents? Weary from grief, Mary Rose decided that if Peg answered, she would simply hang up the phone without speaking to her. Her throat and eyes ached from tears and she felt worn out. Only her love for Sean kept her from descending into a depression like her mother's.

After the hysterics before the funeral, more had followed; her mother woke from her sleep every night, screaming: her grandmother had to stay in the same room with her, though she would not share a bed with anyone, and a cot had to be moved into the room for Mary. Rosaleen's rising to sort out Father's manuscript, in the hope of publishing it posthumously, was the first sign of life her mother had shown. Mary Rose was completely shaken by the depth of her mother's affection for her father. She would not have believed Rosaleen cared about him that much.

As she crossed the deserted hallway, Mary Rose was startled by a sharp, persuasive knock on the door, and, since Cornelius was nowhere about, she answered it. She let out an involuntary gasp when she saw who was standing there. If it had been Sean himself she would scarcely have been more surprised. She had hardly recovered her manners before he asked gently, his intensely blue eyes fastened on her face, "Are you all right, child?"

She nodded and opened the door for him to enter. "I was just surprised to see you, Cousin Darin. It's been rather a long time."

He nodded seriously, his perfect lips set tightly. "Sure, it's a pity that only death brings us together. Your grandmother tells me your mother's poorly."

His words faded and his eyes widened at the sight of the yellow dog, as though he had never seen a dog before, and he asked, "Good Lord, what breed might that be?"

"Mostly golden Lab," she said in surprise. "We've always had them. The first was a mongrel Mother picked up in Rome. This is one of his descendants."

"None of them were called Murphy, were they?"

"Well, yes." She smiled, searching his face. "One of them always is, even if it's a bitch. This is Murphy III."

He nodded, dismissing the subject. "I'd like to see your mother, Mary Rose."

Mary Rose hesitated. Her mother might not want callers. "She's in the library. I'll tell her you're here."

He raised his hand like a benediction to stop her. "She'll want to see me," he said with such conviction that she could only believe him. "I remember where it is. I used to play here as a child."

Shrugging, she motioned him to go ahead and, when he was gone, she closed the study door behind her, intent on her own mission, wondering if Darin really would, as Sean hoped, put all his influence behind them when they announced their wish to marry. She had been so surprised by his presence she had hardly muttered more than a few words to him. After she made her telephone call, she must do something to make amends.

Sitting at John's desk near the light of the window, with

her back to the door, Rosaleen did not hear Darin enter. Though her determination had been to reconstruct the book, page by page, it had worn out over half an hour ago, and she had bowed her head into her white hands, leaning on her elbows with her eyes closed. The days in bed had left her weak, and she found it difficult to eat much. All the joy had gone out of her life, her heart was leaden. It had been a chore just to get dressed, and her hair was wound in a loose, untidy knot on her neck. She did not want to go back to her mother's room and lie down again; but she felt too debilitated to stay up much longer. Closing her eyes against the feeble sun from the window did not help. Every time she closed her eyes, the sights of that horrible morning were impressed as clearly as a picture on her eyelids. If she could just get rid of that picture...

"Rosie," a soft voice said from the doorway behind her, making her raise her head, though she thought it was not real. "Your mother said you were having a difficult time. I've come to help, if I can."

She turned in her chair with a rustle of black taffeta and raised the white oval of her face to look at him with tragic, intensely blue eyes. It was really Darin: tall, more beautiful than ever, and with hardly any gray in his thick black hair. Her lower lip began to tremble uncontrollably and her eyes blurred with tears like a child's. And, like a child, she rushed to him with open arms to bury her head against his breast.

"Oh, darling, darling," he comforted her, holding her tightly against him with one hand around her head and his lips against her dark hair. "Rosaleen, you've suffered a terrible loss, and had a bad shock with it, dear. Things will be better after a time, but weep all you have to, now. That's what I'm here for. I've always been there to comfort you, Rosie, remember?"

She nodded, sobbing against his coat front as though she were five again and someone had soiled her sock doll. "You saved my life more than once," she whispered brokenly, and heard the gentle laughter in his chest.

"No, *only* once," he corrected her. "Oh, God, Rosie! You, of all people, didn't deserve this! I know what it's done to you: I can see it."

"He said . . ." she wept, ". . . he said . . ."

"There, there, now. What was it he said, darling?"

"He said . . . I was the best thing in . . . his life. No matter how he got me, he said . . . it was the last thing he said to me, Darin..."

"Well, sure, it was a curious thing to say," Darin agreed, puzzled, "but it was a grand thing, too, Rosie. He loved you very much."

"What did he mean? What did he mean?" she demanded weakly. "I can't understand."

"When a man's very ill, and knows it, there's no explaining what's on his mind. It sounds to me like poor John knew he hadn't long, love, and he wanted to say it all, even if it didn't make sense."

"He didn't know he was going to die! We thought he was going blind: we were prepared for that. The doctor in Paris said there was pressure on the optic nerve, and it'd make him blind. He told him not to exert himself unnecessarily. We talked about it before we went to bed. And I woke up, and..." She began to weep again. "They did a postmortem," she said with a shudder. "He had a brain hemorrhage. They called it an 'intracerebral hemorrhage,' Darin. Instead of making him blind, a blood vessel ruptured in his head. Mother said the same thing happened to his father. Oh, Darin, if I could only get that last sight of him out of my mind."

He drew in his breath. "I know. I know," he consoled her, staring over her head with pained blue eyes. "He wouldn't have wanted it this way: he had no control over it. Rosie, he wouldn't want you to remember him like that. He'd want you to wipe it out of..."

The door creaked behind him and he turned his head. Mary Rose entered with a silver tea tray, her dark eyes fixed on them. Darin indicated with a quick motion of his head that she put it down and leave. The tormented expression on his face explained why she should do so, and Mary Rose gave an understanding nod and left.

"Who was that?" Rosaleen asked in confusion, raising her head miserably, feeling his lips brush along her cheek as she did so.

"Sure, it was a little *pookah* bringing you some tea." He smiled slightly. "And I think that's one of the things you need. Come along, darling. We'll just sit right here by the table and get something hot inside of us."

She complied without hesitation, but once seated she mopped her face with her handkerchief and said, "I really can't. I'm sorry. Nothing stays down."

"This will," he said, pouring the hot liquid with a flourish and reaching into his pocket for a flask. "I'm putting a dot of something sweeter than sugar into it, and more nourishing, too, for the soul. Now, drink up and see if that doesn't put the flush of life back into you."

He raised the cup to her lips himself, and their eyes met as she drank. "It goes down like hymns, doesn't it?" He smiled. "God, girl, your hands are like ice!" He began to chafe them. "I've had enough of this, now: I won't allow you to go dying, too. That'd put me under for sure, and I mean to be around for a while yet. Here," he said, diluting tea and whiskey in more unequal measures in the cup, "down the hatch, now!"

"I'll get drunk," she complained, the hot glow of the spirits going from her chest to her brain. "Aren't you drinking, too?"

"I don't, much, any more," he said, handing her the flask. "I brought this for you. A few years ago, I began to need the stuff to get through the day; then, more to get through the night. Then I remembered that old bastard Tomas, and all the pain he caused. You might say it had a sobering effect on me."

"You're talking about," she said, her tongue not quite under control, "my father."

His blue eyes were amused. "Indeed I am, darling. But that was a long time ago. We go back a long way, don't we?"

"As long as I can remember," she said, nodding. "It's good to see you, Darin! You're looking fine."

"And maybe your vision's getting a trifle distorted." He smiled, taking her hand. "That stuff's Irish and powerful, my dear. Save some for later, before you go to bed."

"I'm sleeping in Mother's room," she explained a little thickly. "She's sleeping in ours...mine."

He was silent a moment, looking into her face. "You'll be able to go back there," he said at last. "You know, Rosie, you've never been more beautiful: time seems to have slowed down for you. There's a lot to look forward to, yet. Remember that, my dear."

"I feel a little better," she confessed. "Your magic potion seems to have worked, but it's made me a little tiddly, Darin. Did I tell you I'm glad to see you? You've always been there when I needed you, and I've never done anything for you."

"I hope to God I always will be, Rosie," he said seriously. "Just knowing you're around and happy's all I need." He laughed shortly and lightened his voice. "As you say, we go back almost to Genesis. It's only fitting we should come together in a crisis. And, though I'm sure there won't be many more, I'm almost selfish enough to look forward to them." He took a deep breath and studied her with level, deep-blue eyes full of affection. "You must go back to work as soon as you can, darling. You're a worker, you always have been. It'll help take your mind off things. Will Rory be coming home?"

"Yes. He insisted. He was doing so well in Paris: he seemed to have really settled down. He was terribly fond of John. They got on so well always, and they had a marvelous time the last time we were together."

Darin patted her hand encouragingly to divert her line of thought, before she was in tears again. "He's a grand boy. You should be proud of him. I'm glad he's returning to look after you." He paused a moment and, rising to his feet with a grin, said, "Things should soon be lively enough with him around."

By the time Rory returned, his mother was back at the bank in her widow's weeds. Cliona, more accepting of her father's death than the others, had resumed her church work, too. Though his presence was a comfort to all, it was Mary Rose who really clung to Rory. In a single night, her whole life had been turned upside down: she grieved alike for her father and her lost future, behaving like a small, frantic animal caught in a trap, with no way out. During all the greetings and commiserations of his homecoming, her wild dark eyes appealed to him for help, but they did not really have a chance to talk until several days later, when it was he who approached her first, by knocking lightly on her door. Her usual cry to come in was subdued, and he opened the door onto a scene of feverish activity. Her whole wardrobe was laid out around the room. She was busily brushing the dresses and wraps which were not laid neatly on the bed for mending.

"Are you taking a trip?" he asked, in surprise.

"No, not now. But soon, I hope. I just wanted to see what I have, so I could figure out how long it will last if I don't have anything more."

"I beg your pardon?" He grinned, cocking his head in puzzlement. "It appears you have a good deal, enough to last a lifetime."

"It may have to," she said wretchedly. "Oh, Rory, everything's gone wrong! *They*'d say it was wrong from the beginning, but Papa was going to give us a chance! He was going to help the very next day. It's like a sign, isn't it? The one person I could depend on . . . and, maybe, a punishment, too."

She was very close to tears again.

Totally confused, Rory reached out and took her in his arms. "Will you stop with that damn whisk broom? I'm going to sneeze, but maybe that would clear my head. What on earth are you nattering about? I couldn't attach a single pronoun to anything. Come on, little sister! I've known something besides Father's death was bothering you ever since I came home. Let's sit down and talk about it."

"All right. Be careful or you'll slide off that damn blue satin couch," she said, joining him there carefully. "The first time I tried to sit down on it, I landed on the floor."

"I rather like it," he said, running his hand sensually across the smooth surface. "The one I had in Saint-Germain had springs that poked you in the . . . very rude springs. Now, what's all this about?"

"I want to get married, Rory, and there isn't any hope!" she said, close to tears again.

"So that's it! A man. Well, I should have known. What's the problem, Mary Rose? Doesn't Mother approve of him?"

"She doesn't know about him. I know she won't approve, though." Rory appraised her quietly for a moment, recognizing how much she had grown up.

"You haven't got yourself involved with some fortune hunter, have you?" he asked. "Things like that don't work out very well, for a woman. Men don't like women controlling their money, Mary Rose."

"He isn't a fortune hunter!" she cried. "It would almost be easier if he were. Sean won't take a copper penny from anyone: he's as proud as sin!"

"Sean?" he said. "An Irishman, eh? There shouldn't be any problem there."

"Sean Noonan," she clarified, looking up in a few seconds because of the silence beside her. Rory looked as though he had been hit in the middle by a cannon ball.

"*Je-sus* Christ!" he said. "Our Sean? That fine, quiet boy? That scholar? That . . ."

"'Cousin' is the word you're looking for."

"I see the problem," he said, leaning back on the sofa and nearly slipping off. "My God, Mary Rose. Look, I want you to know, I'm not against it. He's a fine fellow, a good friend: I couldn't think of anyone better for you. It's just the religious thing. The family, both families . . ."

"That's what I've been trying to tell you. I told Papa, and he was wonderful about it. He was going to help us. He was going to get Sean a job as a tutor, until he earns a more advanced degree. It's almost November, and he graduates in June. There just aren't any teaching posts open."

"I wish I could help," Rory said sincerely. "I'm still *persona non grata* at Harvard. Though Mother's trying to get that changed so I can read law. My character's changed for the worse: I've settled down enough to handle law, now. If you can just be patient for a little while."

"A little while," she said, exasperated. "Rory, it's been two years already! Two years of taking walks, sitting in coffee shops, holding hands!" Her dark eyes flashed, and she stood up with a sigh of deep frustration with her hands on her hips and tapped her foot. Her brother's blue eyes followed her with sudden understanding.

"You really aren't my little sister any more," he said softly. "You're a woman."

"Yes," she said, lifting her chin defiantly. "And if you dare to lecture me about the pitfalls of..."

"I won't. I know I don't have to, Mary Rose: I know Sean Noonan. I admire him, because we're nothing alike at all. It's strange," he said, frowning thoughtfully, "I know you both so well. He's been like a brother to me, more than Michael ever has. I can almost *feel* the whole situation. It must be costing him, too. A lot more than you know." He rose and put his hands on her shoulders. "If I had any sense, I wouldn't get involved, but I've never been noted for good sense. It's a good thing you told me, Mary Rose. It gives us a little mobility, another person to help. And I *will* help you, in any way I can."

The tears she had been holding back made her eyes shine. "Nothing outrageous," she cautioned him.

"Little sister, the whole thing's outrageous. You've really outdone me this time," he said, kissing her on the forehead.

If Rosaleen appeared to be functioning to her family, it was by nearly exhausting her willpower. The woman who held a relevant and logical conversation at the dinner table, bolstering the spirits of her sons and daughters, quickly went to the room she occupied and nearly fell apart. Even Mary did not know the extent of her daughter's reactivated terror of death. Struggling with it, without understanding its sources, Rosaleen was completely alone. Afraid to go to sleep at night out of fear that she might not wake, she sat up late reading every book that came to hand in an attempt to banish the devils in her mind. She felt something was in cold pursuit of her, which only the warm body of Murphy III, curled up beside her, could keep away. If anyone in the family knew Rosaleen was actually sleeping with the furry yellow bitch, instead of just keeping the dog in Mary's room for company, they most certainly would have looked askance. When sleep finally overcame her, she patted the covers for the dog to join her and cowered in the canine warmth and kisses to her face until both drifted off into unconsciousness.

It was not really a pleasant surprise to find oneself alive in the morning: it meant another day to get through, treading carefully, lest her secret fear be revealed. The first sign of it was usually in the coach on the way to work: nothing specific, but something hidden in her mind, seemed to trigger it. First, the coldness in the ribs, which seemed frozen like the masts of a ship at this time of year, dripping icicles: that was only a warning. If she caught it in time, diverted her mind, breathed naturally, sometimes it ended there or went away. The danger, she had found, was giving in to the fear when it caught her unexpectedly; because then the icy ribs shattered into uncontrollable panic, which triggered her heartbeat until she was sure she was dying, and her hyperventilation increased the threat.

No matter how often she told herself she had experienced a good life, seen much and enjoyed great happiness, that she was ready to give in to whatever overtook her, the will to live was so strong that she found no peace in surrender. She was still young enough: she was beautiful, for yet a while. She loved. And therein was the crux of everything: the wellspring of her being. Only in the memory of Darin's comforting arms about her was there imagined peace. By using all the arguments, old and new, about their situation, she managed to keep from rushing to him for solace. They were cousins: it was forbidden, as she had found to her distress so many years ago. He was married, and though it did not appear a happy marriage, she would take no man from his wife. Though she was willing to destroy her immortal soul, she had no right to take his along with it. She had made a vow, taken an oath unspoken at the altar, never to be untrue to John. But it was easy to rationalize that now: her dear John was dead, forever. And she and Darin were alive.

During the week before Christmas, Rosaleen had to excuse

herself from meetings twice because of the ice shattering in her chest. Both times she was assisted white and trembling to her office by Frank Connell. She knew that Frank, now a widower of sixty, had loved her for years, without his saying a word. As he stood over her, administering inadequately to her needs with a glass of water, a damp handkerchief on her forehead, the apprehension that he would make a pronouncement of his affection prolonged the attack. She was interested in no man but Darin. She was filled with guilt that she had never once called her husband "darling," or said in so many words simply "I love you," when he was so warm with her. Sometimes she wondered if the source of her attacks was this guilty sin of omission.

"You came back too soon," Frank said, rubbing his hand through his full head of white hair in consternation. "Everyone needs a period of mourning, Mrs. Maddigan: one must adjust to loss. If you'll recall, when my Sheila went, I took several months off. I just couldn't function. You think you're some kind of Amazon, and you really are an amazing woman, I've always known that. But for all that, you've a woman's heart and you need someone to look after you."

Maybe she should quickly marry Frank, she thought. He was handsome, kind. But, no, he was too old, even if she had cared for him in that way: he might die beside her in bed one night. This was just one of the bizarre flights her fancy took lately. She would rather sleep with the dog than give herself to someone she did not care about. She rose unsteadily from the leather chair in her office and put the damp handkerchief aside.

"I think I will take this week off. It's almost Christmas and I haven't even bought presents. In fact, the holiday doesn't mean anything to me at all."

It would give her something to occupy her mind, she thought. But she had made only half her purchases when her vision blurred, she became light-headed and the ice began to accumulate in her chest. That night, she announced at the dinner table that she felt they should not celebrate the holidays this year, out of respect for Father. The girls nodded agreement.

Michael said, "I've been invited out anyway. I find this house singularly oppressive since Father died."

"That's just it," Rory said with his usual energy. "God knows how much we loved him, but we can't go on like this! Everyone looks like dead leaves ready to fall from the vine.

Christmas has always been the best time for all of us! Mother, you know Father would want it to be that way again."

"I think it's amazing," Michael said, "the way people attribute what *they* want to do to the dead. Excuse me. I have to make some calls."

"What an ironic little bastard he is!" Rory said, his eyes following him to the door.

"Don't call him that," Rosaleen said quietly. "Don't call anyone that."

"I'm sorry," he said, abashed. "I didn't mean to speak like that before you and the girls. Please, just listen to me! Let's have a party, a really nice one...invite other people in. Part of it is that we're getting on each other's nerves. It needn't be a lot of work. I'll hire a caterer to take care of food and drinks. The girls can put up the holly and evergreen the way they always do, and we can have a tree! The whole thing will be for our *guests*—for their pleasure. It'll get our minds off ourselves."

"Who would you invite?" Rosaleen asked.

"I have friends, lots of them. But we'll keep it small. And the girls must know someone they'd like to invite. How about Pamela and Edward Dove? You've always liked them, Mother."

"They're away," she said sadly. "He's taken a post in England for a year."

"Oh. Well, I'll tell you what! I'll provide some guests. We'll have them in on Christmas Eve, and take it upon ourselves to make them as happy as possible!"

"Oh, really, Rory," Mary Rose began, but Cliona liked the idea.

"I think that would be lovely." She smiled. "Mother?"

Rosaleen was thinking that if she drank enough wine, she might get through it. If it would only warm the inside of her chest the way Darin's flask and soft words had. Besides, she would refuse Rory nothing.

"All right," she said and smiled. "Anything's better than this."

"One stipulation," he said, raising his forefinger. "Do you remember how we used to wait for St. Patrick's Day during Lent, so we could break our resolution for one day? If we gave up candy, we'd have our fill, on that one day?"

"You never gave up candy." Mary Rose smiled. "As I recall, it was olives and pickles one year, and you don't care for either."

He grinned. "That isn't the point. On Christmas Eve,

everyone comes out of mourning, for just one evening. I'm so tired of all this black: it's depressing."

"Oh, I really couldn't do that," Rosaleen said quickly. "A full year and longer is—"

"Sure that wouldn't do," Mary broke in. "Really, Rory, you don't understand, love. Though I don't think there'd be any harm in the girls wearing something pretty, do you, Rosaleen?"

"I think they should," she agreed, smiling at her daughters. "They'll have new dresses for the occasion, if we can get them made that quickly."

Rory gulped down his coffee, half standing. "I've things to do, ladies! Invitations and merriment to extend. As for you, instead of sitting by the fire mooning over your goddam embroidery, get cracking! In spite of the caterer, you've a lot to do! It's only a week away, you know." And he left the dining room whistling "Deck the Halls with Boughs of Holly."

"Sure, he isn't unfeeling," Mary said. "He cares too much. He's trying to cheer us up."

"Well, he succeeded with me!" Mary Rose said, getting up from her chair. "Come along, Cliona. We'll need greens and holly and mistletoe."

"*Mistletoe!*" her sister exclaimed, shocked. "My goodness, Mary Rose, we have no idea who Rory may drag in off the street!"

On the afternoon before the party, Mary carried most of Rosaleen's black dresses from her closet to the room she was still occupying. Her daughter had not gone into her room since John's death, and it appeared she had taken over Mary's room permanently. Raising one gown after another, Mary tried to get some spark from Rosaleen, but her daughter only shrugged.

"Any of them will do, Mother. They're all made of fine fabric and are pretty much alike. I can't see dressing up for strangers. The best I can be is proper, tonight."

"Well," Mary said, with a hint of a wink, "they may not be strangers, you know."

Rosaleen looked up languidly from her chair. "How do you know who's coming?"

"Sure, you have your ways, and I have mine," Mary said. "I have it on impeccable authority that not all the guests will be *strangers*."

"Impeccable, eh?" Rosaleen teased bravely, trying to fight

back the coldness in her chest again. "Good Lord, Mother, who do we know that Rory knows?"

"Well, I think we're after knowing the Noonans for quite a while." Mary smiled. Rosaleen stiffened in her chair.

"The *Noonans!* All of them?"

"Sure there aren't that many now, are there? Darin and Peg and Sean."

Rosaleen's lips felt numb. "Whatever possessed Rory?"

"They're great friends of his, and it's high time they were invited to this house, I think. I've never really understood it, in spite of Laura. Sure, she's been gone these many years, and you're still giving them the snub. You and Darin were that close."

"I haven't snubbed them, Mother, not really," Rosaleen considered, fingering one of the gowns on the bed and holding it up. "After meeting what's-her-name I didn't think she'd be comfortable here, that's all."

"Her name's Peg, as I just mentioned," Mary said, but Rosaleen had ceased to listen. None of these dresses would do: they were black crepe sacks, regardless of quality. "You may think she isn't fancy enough for you," her mother continued, "but you're wrong. Peg's developed some style since you saw her last. Good Lord, that was a long time ago!"

"Style?" Rosaleen asked. "I can't imagine it. What kind of style?"

"Well, they don't have to scrimp and save as they once did. Sure, Peg has some very nice dresses, which she usually wears to church. And not a gray hair in her head, either; but, of course, you can't tell with that reddish-blond kind of hair, but I've never seen one. Now, you..."

"I know. You found a few when you were brushing my hair," Rosaleen said.

"I shouldn't have pulled them, sure. For every one you pull, five more appear."

"That's reassuring," Rosaleen said, lifting another dress.

"You and Darin seem to have missed the Noonan curse of early white hair, though," Mary said quickly. "That's because you're part O'Shea. Black Irish, they were, you know."

"A hint of the Spaniard there," Rosaleen said to provoke her mother. "They landed on the southern coast, Mother."

As anticipated, Mary flared, "Sure, what good Irish girl would have anything to do with a Latin man? If the history books say that, it's a lie!"

"Mother, there's one dress you didn't bring."

When they emerged together from Rosaleen's room, Mary was frowning darkly. She had been surprised when her daughter entered her own bedroom, for the first time since John's death; now, she was only displeased at the dress Rosaleen took out of the closet and put on. The black silk gown was not decent, cut almost to the middle of her creamy breasts, held up by tiny straps far out on her shoulders: she could not possibly have a stitch on beneath it.

"Sure, you might as well wear flaming red, as such a *little* black," Mary said disapprovingly. "I didn't bring that dress because I didn't know it was a dress at all. I thought it was a nightgown."

"It's beautiful, isn't it?" Rosaleen smiled as they descended the festooned stairs. "I bought it in Paris when we visited Rory."

The butler was just letting their first guest into the hallway; it was a slight young man with dark hair and animated eyes, dressed appropriately for the occasion. Rosaleen went forward with her hand extended easily to greet him. "Rory isn't here, yet. I'm his mother, Mr. . . . ?"

The dark eyes moved from her face right down the plunging neckline, and he gave a flustered smile. "Henri Gautereau, madame. I preceded Rory from Paris, where we studied law together. But you can't be Rory's mother, *certainement.*"

"Vous êtes très gentil." She smiled. "I'd like you to meet my mother, Mrs. Noonan."

Mary did not take kindly to having her hand kissed by a foreign gentleman, even the same age as her grandson, and raised her eyebrows over his head with a look of horror which made Rosaleen smile, since they had so recently been discussing Latin men. The cold feeling was still there: death was right on her heels, but perhaps a glass of wine would banish it. Rosaleen took Monsieur Gautereau into the parlor, where the girls were putting the finishing touches on the tree. The doors had been opened between dining room and parlor, revealing a sumptuous buffet and champagne on ice in silver buckets, and she was pleasantly surprised.

"How nice to have someone else do all the planning," she said to Mary. "I've never seen things look so lovely."

"Those doors should be left open all the time," Mary said glumly. "Sure, I hate this parlor, even with the girls' piano here. It's a dark, inside room, and no matter what you do to it—"

"There's a coffin on a dais," Rosaleen agreed.

"You, too?" Mary asked in surprise. "But you were just a little thing then."

"Why do you think I've redecorated it so often? Mr. Maddigan will always be here." She shivered. "Even John felt that way about it.... The young folk seem to be practicing their French. At least, Cliona is. I'd like a glass of wine."

"I'll go out and wait for the Noonans," Mary said. "I want them to feel at home."

Rosaleen thought for a moment that Darin would not come; he would send his wife and son, instead. A pall of gloom settled over her as she sipped her glass of red wine. The whole thing was absurd: she did not know what she was doing. But if he did come, she wanted to see him with his wife: everything would depend on that. The thought was still in her head when Mary ushered them in, and her heart leaped: her eyes met his at once, and he was smiling over the women's heads at her. It took an effort to acknowledge his family.

"It's been a long time," Rosaleen said to Peg with the faintest smile, because she did not want to be hypocritical. "My goodness, look at Sean! The last time I saw him, he was hiding behind your skirt."

"Yes, he's grown some since then," Peg said proudly, with more composure than Rosaleen remembered. She was almost a handsome woman, as her mother had said, but her style was limited to a stiff black dress with a yoke of black lace covered with jet beads, buttoned up beneath her chin, making her look more matronly than her years. Her pale-green eyes had changed very little, and their smile of pride did not include her husband, whom she totally ignored.

"Sean, you'll want to join the young people." Rosaleen smiled. "Do you remember Mary Rose and Cliona?"

His face was so much like Rory's that she could hardly believe the gentle smile. "Yes, thank you, Cousin Rosaleen."

One of the servants immediately came forward with tall crystal glasses of champagne on a silver tray. Mary and Darin accepted one, but Peg shook her head, declining.

"And what have you there?" Darin smiled, struggling to keep his eyes above Rosaleen's neck. "No champagne, Rosie?"

"No, just dago red," she said. "We sent a whole case back from Italy."

"Chianti?"

She shook her head and laughed, her chest warming inside. "No, I told you. Practically homemade, a family affair, table wine. Uh, Peg, can I get you something else to drink?"

"I don't indulge," Peg said righteously. "Sure, it's the Devil's brew, and the Irish are addicted to it. I'm on the Temperance Committee at church."

Wondering how she rationalized the pub, Rosaleen dipped some rose-colored punch from the Revere bowl decorated with holly; she knew it was unspiked, because Rory had not arrived yet. "It's mostly lemonade," she reassured her. "There's no alcohol in it." Her gaze caught the garnet earrings set in gold that Peg was wearing; they were rather nice. A gift of love, perhaps, from her husband or her son? The thought of Darin's giving them to her upset her, and she was relieved to hear them discussing Saul Rabinsky.

"I haven't seen him since after the fire in '72, when his shop was burned with the rest of the downtown area," Rosaleen contributed. "He got a loan to start over again and paid it off very quickly. He was very sweet, actually."

"One of his sons-in-law is running the store now," Darin said. "Saul's pretty old and feeble. He lives with one of his daughters and her family. I drop by sometimes. And he speaks of nothing but his grandchildren."

"They all married good Irishmen," Peg said disapprovingly. "That family always struck me as peculiar. Those girls are half-Jewish."

"The Bible's more than half," Darin said coldly. "Rosie, may I have some of that Italian wine you're drinking? Champagne makes my chest feel numb."

Sensing discord, Mary took Peg by the arm. "Sure we haven't had a good talk for some time, Peg. Let's go over on the sofa and catch up."

Suddenly alone with Darin, Rosaleen lost her composure. "I wonder what's keeping Rory. This party was his idea, after all, and he should be here to host it. There's a young Frenchman over there no one knows, and . . ."

"My, you do run on, don't you?" He smiled. "You're looking marvelous, but you're as nervous as hell, Rosie. Your hands are shaking, and you'll spill wine on that remarkable dress, for sure."

"Oh, Darin, I'm so frightened!" she gasped, and he scrutinized her face.

"I can see that, but frightened of what?"

"I think I'm going as mad as your mother," she said, glanc-

503

ing around to make sure they were not heard. "Strange things are happening to me. I think the most incredible thoughts. My chest is always cold inside: I can hardly breathe."

"Well, I think all Irish are a little mad," he said reassuringly. "I experienced a little of that in the prison camp, but I was always afraid of death."

Darin, not she, had said it out loud: it was no longer something she had to hide. She bit her lip and looked at him with frantic eyes.

"That's what it is," she confessed. "I feel it's breathing down my neck all the time: I can't seem to get away from it. My thinking is wild. Like putting on this dress tonight. I don't know why I did it!"

"I'm glad you did." He smiled, catching her wording and intonation, recognizing the pitch of her anxiety. "We'll have a talk, Rosie, sometime during this shebang, if we can slip away. Ah, here's Rory now! And God in heaven, look what's with him! The boy has taste."

The splendid brown-eyed blonde with diamonds at her throat must have been thirty, but she had a love-stricken glow on her face and glances only for her escort, until she saw Darin and got confused, looking from Rory to the older man and back again.

"Mother, I'd like you to meet Julia Harrington." Rory grinned, "Julia, dear, my mother, Mrs. Maddigan."

"Charmed," Julia said, extending her hand with natural poise, quickly diverting her gaze up to Darin. "And this must be your father," she said, her bold, confident eyes not leaving his face, her smile a challenge. "I was so surprised when I entered the room and saw you. I don't know which I prefer, the younger or the more mature Mr. Maddigan."

Rosaleen almost fainted; the only thing that saved her was a fiery jealousy that melted all the frost inside. She was unable to speak up and correct the misunderstanding, so Rory quickly did it for her.

"No, my dear. This is Darin Noonan, my mother's cousin! Everyone remarks on the resemblance, and there's another one over there," he said, indicating Sean, deep in conversation with Mary Rose, "but he's really too young and innocent for you."

"What a stunning girl!" she exclaimed at the sight of Mary Rose in her cranberry velvet gown. "She reminds me of... I know... one of those vibrant *gitanas* in Spain!"

"My sister," he said with pride, looking again at his

mother, who had an unpredictable expression on her face, one he had never observed before. "I see Henri has Cliona in tow. I've never seen her so animated, Mother. There are roses in her cheeks, and her eyes are like stars."

"I'm sorry," Rosaleen said, covering her annoyance: she had encountered many such cosmopolitan women abroad, and she did not approve of one on her son's arm, in her own home, especially exhibiting such an attraction to Darin. "I'm afraid I didn't catch your name, Miss..."

"Mrs. Mrs. Harrington," the beautiful woman said with poise, her eyes amused, recognizing at once another woman who preferred the company of men and Rosaleen's determination to protect her son.

"You're so young to be a widow," Rosaleen commiserated to obtain her marital status.

"She isn't," Rory said without any qualms, "except to the foreign service. Mr. Harrington's ambassador to some ungodly place not fit for human habitation."

"Where's that?" Rosaleen asked with curiosity.

"London." Darin turned aside to hide his laughter, and Rory was encouraged to further excess. "You told me yourself that England isn't fit for human beings, Mother. Julia decided that, too. So she stayed behind with me."

"Get your guest a drink," Rosaleen said stiffly. "We should be eating shortly."

When the couple left, Darin whispered into her ear, "Rosie, every young man should have an older woman at least once. It contributes to his education."

"Yes, I know," she snapped, "but older women should have better sense than to lead young men astray."

He gaped for a moment, then laughed aloud at her tilted logic. "I hope you don't reason that way at the bank," he said. "Show the lad a little charity. He'll never find a woman like you, so let him do the best he can."

"Stop codding me," she retorted. "I can see what you're about."

For the first time in months, she did not feel cold. Her blood was flowing warmly through her veins, but she did not consider the change an advantage. She was alive with anger, which grew in proportion to the proximity of Julia, who had returned with Rory at her side.

"Rory, this is your party," Rosaleen said, with blue fire in her eyes. "Please see that your guests are served." Then,

"Dammit! Now, where have Sean and Mary Rose got off to? I don't think we're going to dine tonight."

Instantly alert, Rory looked around the room. "They're gone?"

Without waiting for an answer, he shoved Julia toward Darin and whispered, "You keep your paws off this time!"

Darin laughed. As Rory rushed from the room, Rosaleen, who had overheard, scrutinized Darin in a new light as he began to entertain the pretty woman. Unable to bear it any longer, she left to gather the guests at the buffet.

In the darkness of a small pantry, just behind the dining-room door and down a short hall to the kitchen, Mary Rose and Sean were locked in a fervent embrace, both of them full of warm relief that, thanks to Rory, they could spend this holiday evening together. Staying at the party with so many people had finally become too much for them. Every time their eyes met they struck a spark like a flint against metal. Finally succumbing to their emotions, they had slipped out the door, and Mary Rose had led him to a place where she felt secure from intrusion.

"You look so beautiful in red," Sean breathed, pulling her into his arms. "I've hardly been able to keep from putting my arms around you all evening. God, darling, it's wonderful to be here with you."

Mary Rose kissed him as ardently as her innocence allowed, tempting Sean to show her how to really kiss, but, as always, his head controlled his impulse. Things were frustrating and dangerous enough as they were. Her closeness in the darkness and the light scent of her cologne conspired against him in the small space. When he held her close, he could feel the small throb in her neck against his own and the quick beat of her heart beneath her red velvet gown. He kissed her softly on the forehead, but soon found himself searching for her lips again.

A sudden burst of light from the door opening left them both blinking and their hearts pounding.

"Oh...there you are!" Rory grinned in the doorway. "I've been searching the house for you—starting with the bedrooms."

"Rory, you scared the hell out of us!" Sean said, almost angry. Mary Rose, attempting to keep her composure despite her disarray, scolded her brother softly.

"I thought you were the one who trusted Sean implicitly."

"I do...I did," Rory said, "but when you disappeared, I could only think of what I'd do. Sorry. Stay where you are!" He smiled, raising his hand to check their exit. "You're not really missed yet, and everyone's going to eat." His eyes scanned the three-foot-square floor upon which they were standing. "No one could go horizontal here. So, stay!"

"Rory!" Mary Rose cried, but he closed the door, leaving them in darkness again, and Sean could hardly stop laughing long enough to continue kissing her.

While Rosaleen attended to the men's plates, Cliona tried to take care of the ladies'. Rory returned from the kitchen hall and began to serve himself, with a faint smile on his face, working his way along the table closer to Julia, and Rosaleen shot him a warning glance. Beside her, Cliona was trying to answer the questions of a gastronomically indecisive Peg.

"What's that one, then? The thing with the ruffle of stuff around it?"

"Roast beef." Cliona smiled sweetly. "The 'ruffle' is mashed potato. I'm sure you'll like some of that, Mrs. Noonan."

Rosaleen regained her glass of red wine and watched. She had not had a chance until now to really observe Darin's wife. She might have been rather attractive once, but she had the small Irish features that so often get lost in fat. Only her hair, wound in a thick braid around her head, still retained some of its Titian glow: one had to look closely to observe that it was mixed with gray, because it blended so inconspicuously. Rosaleen could only resent lighter hair shades that so easily disguised that sign of aging. She did not trust herself tonight. Her emotions swung like a pendulum, between human charity and envy. She felt competitive and aggressive, qualities of her character she had always been able to leave at work. She wanted to be her calm, charming self, but she felt mean inside, cruel and tormented. She was at odds with two of the women in the room; but realizing it did not change the condition. She continued to look for the worst in them.

"Sure, I don't eat vegetables," Peg told Cliona. "They give me the most frightful gas! Is that orange thing that's all shiny on top a vegetable?"

"I don't know," Cliona said indecisively. "Mother, are candied yams vegetables?"

Rosaleen shrugged in reply, fastening her sharp eyes on the sparkling Julia again.

"I think this will be fine," Peg said, lifting her plate, her pale-green eyes searching the table. "I wish I hadn't worn such a tight corset now. Would there be a bit of horseradish for the beef?"

"I don't see any," Cliona apologized. "I'll run to the pantry for some. I won't be a moment."

When Rory saw Cliona open the door to the kitchen hallway, he tried to call out and nearly choked on the food in his mouth.

"What's up?" Darin smiled, narrowing his eyes, and Rory looked at him helplessly.

"Never mind. I've a feeling you'll know soon enough."

There was no furor that night, however, though Cliona did not return to the party, and Mary Rose and Sean came back very subdued. After everyone had coffee or liqueur, Mary suggested music, and Mary Rose quietly submitted to the request to play "Adeste Fidelis" for them.

Everyone but Julia sang, forming a nice chorus, with Rory's abandoned baritone and Sean's Irish tenor giving body to the women's sopranos.

"What happened to Darin?" Julia asked suddenly in a clear voice. "He was here a minute ago."

"Yes, where is he?" Rory said, looking around. "I need him to help my unfulsome baritone."

Leaning against the piano, Mary smiled. "Your mother wanted him to see the paintings. She's that fond of art," she explained proudly to Peg. "Sure she stored a whole lot of them a year ago and the nursery's filling up again! There are paintings on every wall of the house."

Peg nodded without concern, caught up in the Christmas singing, and Rory whispered wickedly in Julia's ear, in an exaggerated, lustful tone, careful that his breath tickled her white neck.

"Would you like to come up and see my paintings? They're short on talent, but three-dimensional in perspective."

She slid a smiling glance at him. "Whatever happened to etchings?"

Chapter 33

"Whew! That's quite a climb!" Darin said breathlessly at the top of the stairs, and Rosaleen smiled as she opened the nursery door.

"I guess I'm accustomed to it. This was the nursery."

In the orange light from the fireplace the room, empty except for the new paintings stacked against the wall, was as bare as an attic, and Darin surveyed it with surprise as Rosaleen turned up the gaslight.

"You keep it warm enough," he said. "There are some people who don't have it so warm."

"Don't burden me with guilt," she snapped. "I contribute generously to the welfare of those people. And a stubborn, bumble-headed lot they are, too! If the damn fools would let their children attend the public schools..."

He was silent a moment; then, "Rosie, what's the use of having these paintings, if you don't look at them at all?"

"I do. Sometimes. They're an investment, Darin. Protection against the future."

An enlightened smile flickered across his face. "Are you saying it isn't safe to put savings in your bank, then? The way you were talking downstairs, I didn't think you had any future."

"For the children, then." She sighed, moving to the fire to warm her hands. She shrugged her bare white shoulders. "I don't know. I told you I'm a little crazy still."

He joined her by the fire to lean on the mantel so he could see her face. "I guess our problem's that we don't believe in any afterlife, Rosie. I know that's what bothered me in the camp. It was closing my eyes to nothing but darkness that put the cold fear into me."

She looked up at him with disbelief. "Are you telling me I don't believe in heaven? I go to Mass every Sunday."

"Yes," he said and smiled, "but *do* you think there's something after? Honestly?"

"I haven't dared to think about it. This life's fine for me. I don't want to exchange it for anything."

"And you want to live it to the fullest," he said. "Isn't that what I'm telling you? We aren't so different."

She stared at the flames in silence. "What did Rory mean when he told you to 'keep your paws off' of Julia?"

"Ah, well, that's a story too long for the telling, I think. Let's just say your son came out of it as pure as the driven snow."

The veiled admission left her angry, vindictive. "Your wife's a terrible woman," she said. "She's bigoted and coarse."

"Is she? That doesn't sound at all like you, Rosie. Some people don't age well, like some whiskey. She's a tolerable mother, and that's all I've needed from her."

"All?"

"All... meaning everything. At least, since I got back from the war."

"Then it's true. You *have* been whoring! What Rory meant was that you'd taken a woman from him."

He laughed with surprise. "I've never had to lower myself to whoring, darling. Look, it's obvious where this conversation's going, so shall we come right out with it? While you were living in apparent marital harmony, I had some fallow times. Rosie, there are some sweet, compassionate women who aren't what you'd call whores. I've never cursed myself for being a man. In fact, I've only blamed myself for leaping into such an unsuitable match when I came back and found you'd married and were living abroad."

Her eyes widened, her lips parted. "You...?"

"I wanted to hurt you back, and poor Peg was the pawn. But it was a flaming disaster from the beginning. A man can't make love to a wife who's muttering her beads at the same time. So, you see, I didn't hurt anyone but myself. But there have been times..."

"Yes?"

An expression of disgust crossed his face, and he kicked a coal back into the fire. "Sometimes there's been as much hatred as love in me, I think. Though in some mad way, it was all part of loving. Sometimes during the bad periods, you understand, when I was fed up with playing games, gratifying myself but without love—well, then I'd weave a fantasy, and a terrible one it was, too. You'd be begging me to come back, Rosie, and I'd turn away from you with something like pleasure. Of course it was mad jealousy I was feeling. You had a good marriage, and I . . . well, I'd botched it, hadn't I? I might surfeit my body, but my soul was starved." He gave a short laugh. "And would you believe I was the envy of other men?"

She shivered slightly, holding her arms. "I didn't know," she said. "Though if you wanted to hurt me when you married, you did, Darin. I was too young to realize you couldn't live out your life as a monk. I tried to put you completely out of my mind, then . . . not too successfully. There hasn't been a day of my life I didn't think of you, in some way. Sometimes I had to fight to keep you out of my mind. Now, when I worry about death, I think of you. We won't live forever."

"Death, again, is it?" He frowned. "Rosie, what have we to do with death? In our separate ways, we've renounced it, over and over again. We're too full of life for it."

"We're getting older. I'm not the same girl you seduced that night on your ship—"

His head jerked up from his contemplation of the grate; he looked at her in blue-eyed amazement and began to laugh. "I'm sorry," he said, shaking his head and biting his lip for control. "It's just that the peculiar tilt of women's minds will never cease to amaze me. Rosie, there were two people there that night, remember? I wasn't the one who tore my clothes off. In fact, I believe I tried to calm you down. But it was more than a man could bear. It's funny, because I thought of it earlier this evening, feeling that something was happening all over again. That dress . . . good God, I haven't been able to look beneath your chin all night out of fear of disgracing myself! There's only one thing wrong with you, darling. You need a man's arms about you, to love and comfort you."

"Only one man's arms," she said hesitantly, meeting his eyes, fearful she had said too much, afraid he might turn on her.

"Yes," he said, pulling her into them and burying his face

511

against her fragrant hair. "Just as I've needed only one woman. Oh, Rosie, was it all so wrong? Things haven't really changed."

"I don't care," she cried impulsively, raising her lips to be kissed. "Oh, my love...my love. What does it matter? Why were we so afraid? I don't think it was of hell. And if there isn't a heaven, there can't be..."

He stifled her speculations with his lips, holding her close. Neither of them anticipated that their kisses would change so quickly, causing a rush of desire so urgent that he muttered, "Jesus! I wasn't expecting this."

"Across the hall..." she said, clinging to his side as they moved toward the door. "My old room."

The dark room, which now belonged to her maid, was warm enough, though the fire had died down, eliminating most of the light. Pressing her tightly against him, Darin fumbled with the key, finally locking it against intrusion with a loud click. Rosaleen felt herself sinking onto the faint white rectangle of the bed under his weight, her mind blank to everything except that it was Darin, at last, and she wanted him more than life. She did not know if he discarded all of his clothing in the darkness, but her hands stroked his bare shoulders and torso, went behind his neck, drawing his face to hers. She felt the black silk slip away from her breasts and his gentle hands and lips upon them, making her moan even before his hands slipped up her thighs.

"Oh, darling, darling," she cried softly at his touch, and he whispered her name as he pushed into her body with abandon, crying, "Oh, Rosie, I love you so!"

His words precipitated something that had never happened on such short contact before: her body and mind, stimulated together, made her lose herself in a cataclysmic upheaval of her hips, with her head thrashing on the pillow as she cried out with a pleasure almost too much to bear. Her violent surrender took him along with her, and they soon lay still, together, quiet except for the irregular, heavy beat of his heart on hers. After a few minutes, he raised his head from her neck and kissed her half-open lips softly.

"My God, darling, I hardly touched you," Darin breathed.

"It was your fault," she said in a small, awed voice. "You shouldn't say things like that. Darling, you took me with your words."

He laughed softly. "Well there's a miracle." He rubbed his

smooth cheek against hers. "God, I poured myself into you before I knew what was happening. *I love you so much.*"

The sound of steps on the landing made him raise his head and look toward the door. Across the hall, the nursery door opened and a few hollow footfalls resounded in the room; then the door was shut with a creak, and the feet descended the stairs.

"They're looking for us," she said. "I don't think I can go down."

"Me, either," he said, releasing her and lying for a moment on his back. "But we must, you know. Our children are down there, and it'd look peculiar if we vanished altogether."

She pulled the black silk over her breasts and lowered her skirt, while he dressed beside her. "I'm going to need some light," she said, "to straighten myself out. My hair..."

A match lit in the darkness and she heard the soft hiss of the gas jet. When he adjusted the flame, he was smiling slightly. "I keep thinking I'm going to wake up," he said, stroking her shoulder. "Is there any way I can help with the repair? After all, it was I, who put you into such disarray."

"Not unless you're a hairdresser." She smiled at his image in the mirror, as she tucked one black tress beneath another and adjusted hairpins. Her legs were weak: she wondered if she could make it down the stairs. "Is that all right?" she asked uncertainly. "I don't look as if I've been through a hurricane, do I?"

"No," he said, kissing her neck. "You look the same as when you came up here."

"I don't feel the same," she said, leaning her head against his chest and closing her eyes. "I don't feel the same at all!"

They reentered the parlor and separated immediately. Darin walked over to join the women, who were having coffee, and Rosaleen hesitated, not wishing to talk to anyone. She finally retrieved her unfinished glass of red wine and stood against the wall beside a tall plant, where she could watch without being observed. She marveled a little that Darin looked so completely normal. His face was more relaxed and his eyes had a soft glow which only she would notice.

Sudden laughter from the area of the piano drew her gaze

to Rory and Sean, talking together with their finished cups on the polished cherry surface. Her heart swelled at the sight of *their* son...though she could never tell Darin. How curious the whole scheme of things was, she thought with the glass to her lips. Rory's life had sprung from just such a meeting of their bodies. Why had God made things that way, instead of some other? The thought was not new to her: it had recurred frequently, during her adult life, but never so strongly as now, after being loved by Darin and looking at the son of their youth in the same room with him.

"Sure, what on earth are you doing?" Mary's voice said at her side. "Rosaleen, your lips are slack with drink already. You look like you can hardly stand up!" She took the wine-glass from her hand and set it down on a table. "This is no condition to be in at a Christmas party! You'll disgrace the children. I swear to God, you look like you've been struck by lightning!"

After everyone had gone and the gas jets downstairs were turned off, Mary Rose reluctantly followed her mother up the stairs. The two women paused for a moment for a quick good-night kiss, and then Rosaleen entered her own suite of rooms for the first time in months. Mary Rose stood in front of the door to her own room a moment, before she quietly turned the knob. The room was dark, but her hope that Cliona was asleep was banished by the figure sitting at the window, her fine blond hair haloed by the moonlight on the snow. Knowing her sister had not heard her enter, she approached her from the left side, so she would not startle her. But Cliona still seemed unaware of her presence, her pale face lifted toward the clear winter sky with tears running down her cheeks.

"Cliona?" Mary Rose said, kneeling beside her. "Don't cry, please! You know how much I love you."

"Then why did you lie to me?" her sister asked in a small voice. "You said you and Sean were just friends."

"I know, and I'm sorry. I had to," Mary Rose said miserably. "We've been trying to keep this whole thing quiet, until we can think of something to do. We're so much in love, Cliona! But I'd give anything if you hadn't found out that way."

"Well, I did, and I don't think I can bear it," her sister said, raising her handkerchief to her face. "How could you let things get so out of hand, Mary Rose? I would never have had the nerve!"

Mary Rose took a deep breath: she had to tell her now; there was no other way. But she recognized the danger and hesitated a moment before saying, "You were going to be the first to know. We're going to be married, dear. It won't be the way we'd prefer it...in the Church. But we are going to marry, as soon as possible." Taking her sister's renewed weeping to be over religion, she tried to placate her. "I know how you feel about the Church, Cliona. But I've never felt just the same way, and neither has Sean. We know we'll be just as married in another church, a Protestant one. And I was hoping, when I did tell you, we'd still be friends."

There was such a long silence that Mary Rose, remembering her sister's friendlier association with Father Liam, got a cold sensation in her stomach. Finally, Cliona wiped her eyes.

"I always knew you'd be the first to marry. I thought I'd be there near you—a happy aunt to your children. But I just can't."

"Why not? We're still sisters. We always will be. Does the Church mean that much more to you than I do?"

Cliona's head shook slowly. "No, I'll always love you, Mary Rose. It's a different emotion, having nothing to do with religion. But I couldn't stand to see you married to...I just couldn't stand it."

"You'll feel differently when it happens. Papa knew, Cliona. He was going to help us. But now it'll be a while." She sighed. "You won't say anything to anyone, will you? It's going to be difficult enough."

"No," Cliona said sadly, "I won't say anything. I couldn't. Oh, dear, I wish I were as lively and courageous as you are. I wish..."

"What?" Mary Rose encouraged her, but she just shook her head in the winter moonlight.

They met once a week at the hidden cottage: Rosaleen had given Darin a key. She had not thought that the resurrection of their love would so totally control her life, but she ascended with it to a heady joy that did not leave her even when they were apart. In the middle of a board meeting, she would find herself recalling everything he had done and said at their last visit to the cottage...that strange little house that had known only love. She dwelt on every word he spoke, as though it came from the mouth of an oracle. He was more well read than she had imagined, and his opinions were sound. When she pictured his face, recalled his strong arms, she melted like warm honey inside, sinking in fantasy beneath the heavy table to the Persian rug.

Her inattention to decisions could not have gone unnoticed, though no one was brave enough to confront her. Frank Connell, still solicitous of her recent widowhood, was able to cover for her. She kept her eyes averted to hide their shine, a pose that was easily interpreted as mourning, especially since her movements were so precise. Frank continually reassured her that it would pass, that she would need at least eighteen months to be herself again. *But I am myself,* she wanted to reply, *completely myself—the way I was meant to be!*

Instead, she held silence and nodded her agreement.

She had always thought John a perfect lover, because of his experience and indefinable, but certainly sexual, magnetism. But she had been an impulsive, green girl with Darin, surrendering her virginity with her mind fastened on the surprises about her own body, though so full of love it was enough to have him within her in mortal closeness, with no other expectations. She realized now how conscious Darin had been of her innocent sensibility that first night: he had not wished to shock her by his own experience. How could poor, dear John, despite all his intellectual hedonism, have learned in Boston what Darin had traveled the world to discover? Darin had always been curious, inventive, she thought with a smile, imagining the almost Herculean task he had set himself: to find out what women were all about. And, having done so, he had rejected only what did not suit his own idealistic code of aesthetics. Sometimes, as they lay together in the gentle relaxation following love, he talked to her about it, in a soft, almost dreamy voice.

"It's almost a religion in India, Rosie. Some of the temples have their own prostitutes."

"I thought you said you'd never gone whoring," she said without rancor.

"There should be another term for it there...they're almost like priests."

She laughed. "That must have been interesting, indeed, if a little chilly."

He turned on his side to look at her, with laughter in his own eyes. "If you aren't following me at all, it's because I'm expressing this so poorly. There's a prayer there, Rosie... *'Om, mani padme, Om!'* It says, 'O Jewel within the lotus, Amen.'

516

The jewel's perfection; God, I guess, but not as we think of Him. I've always felt that prayer had another significance, though, after spending some time there," he said, stroking her long hair. "A woman's like a flower, Rosie...not in any poetic way, but..." His hand caressed her body, coming to rest between her white thighs. *"Here.* And what's within her brings life...she opens up like a flower. And that dew drop in the flower, that jewel...is life itself. When I'm loving you, it's as though I were trying to reach its source...the source of everything. Oh, damn!" He sighed, embarrassed. "Words are poor things, indeed."

"No. I think I understand," she said, her chest swelling with love for him. They were both devoid of passion, their senses sated, and he took his hand away, throwing his arm loosely around her waist.

"That word *Om,*" he said, "is interesting and peculiar, you know. It's a Tantric one, that begins and ends texts—like our 'Amen' and the Bible's 'Selah!' But it means 'everything'—creation, preservation and destruction. It's chanted in...God Almighty!" he exclaimed softly, interrupting himself.

"What?" she asked.

"I'm a terrible idjut, for sure, Rosie," he said, emphasizing the Irish pronunciation. "Darling, the way I'm loving you, without taking any precautions at all, I'll make you pregnant. Jesus!" He lay back on his pillow staring at the ceiling with a frown. "There's nothing I would have loved more once, Rosie, but it's a little late in life to be going completely soft in the head."

"Don't worry about it." She smiled, wondering how to say it. "We were abroad a lot, Darin. I asked some of my French friends why they didn't have more than one or two children. They told me, and I didn't have any more."

"Well, *vive la France,* and all that," he said with relief; then he turned his head suddenly to observe her with surprise. "Contraception and the Church, Rosie? An incompatible mix: a paradox, you little sinner! You know very well you should grind little souls out for Rome like plaster saints, whether you can feed their living bodies at all. The mark of salvation's twelve to fourteen snotty-nosed kids without socks, though sex really isn't 'very nice,' you know." He laughed suddenly.

Another time, several months later, Darin somehow got on the subject of Irish women, with one of his always direct, sometimes shocking observations.

"Rosie, you're the only Irish woman I know who lies down naked on the bed with your thighs open, darling. I swear, the rest of them are a crime against manhood, even at their best." He laughed quietly. "I think Irish men would really like to believe there are such things as women, but they're never quite sure. The way the creatures with long hair undress for bed's enough to leave them wondering. First, they put a great bloody tent of a nightgown over their clothes to disrobe, throwing things on the floor...a blouse here, a stocking there, skirt, corset, until her whole wardrobe's at her feet. Then the process reverses itself in the morning, when they dress again, with not a bit of flesh to be seen. Not fully certain it's a woman under the nightgown in bed, the poor confused lads have to grope around a bit beneath the tent—if it's allowed, because she has a mind to mothering—until they find what might be the right place and have it off, as quickly as possible, totally unnerved by the wretched silence in the room. Or the mumbling of beads. Not knowing whether they've mated with the covers or what might be a woman, they have to sit around and wait to see if there's another mouth to feed. All in all," he considered, "I guess their aim's pretty good, but it's a wretched process altogether."

Rosaleen laughed. "Mother still undresses that way. She has ever since she discovered there *were* such things as nightgowns, and she didn't have to sleep in her clothes any longer."

"Is it a wonder, I'm asking you, that Tomas drank himself foolish? Irish men aren't perfect, either," he admitted. "Without the brew to keep them somewhat even, most of them would probably commit suicide. Why are we all so up and down, I wonder? There's usually no reason for the depths, which are miserable, and during the ups we're as crazy as kites in the wind."

"It's almost as though your mother was an exaggeration of all of us. I'm sorry, I shouldn't have said..."

"You can say anything you please," he said, kissing her. "That particular idea struck me a long time ago. It frightened hell out of me, Rosie. I think that's why I was so harsh on her."

A melancholy silence fell over them, each remembering the same things.

"You know," she said suddenly, "I don't think Mother was as cold as you think. From what she's said, Father drank before she married him, but...Darin, this will surprise

518

you...it did me. Mother loved your father as much as I love you."

"You're daft," he said in disbelief, rising on one elbow to look into her face. She shook her head.

"She told me after he died. And he was in love with her, too."

"I can't believe it!" he exclaimed, blowing out his breath. "God in heaven, it's like the whole family's mad!" He shook his head, smiling slightly. "I can't imagine them..."

"No, they didn't," she said.

"Well, they should have, poor souls. Rosie," he said and frowned, "do you recollect Fiddler Murphy and the stories he told during the winter months, back home?"

"I remember him, and bits and pieces of the stories." She smiled. "All the heroes and battles, shape-shifting...I tried to turn myself into an otter once."

"An otter? Why?" He laughed.

"They seemed to have so much fun on the riverbank. The River Bride," she said thoughtfully, "where I nearly drowned."

"Do you remember the story of Sweeny and the saint?"

She nodded. "Not from Fiddler Murphy, though. Mother repeated a lot of them to me."

"'Clenched forever in your profane hand,
It will bring despair throughout the land,
The proud will be humbled, all love will go awry.'"

he quoted. "I think we should look for old Sweeny with his wild harp in the churchyard yew."

Though their lovemaking was uncontained, sensuality completely satisfied, they did not spend all their time in bed on their special Wednesdays together. Darin put the house in order, repairing all the problems that had appeared over the years. And he took as naturally as Rosaleen had to gardening. While John had never had any desire to soil his hands with earth, Darin liked the digging, grubbing, planting as much as she did, and he was happy and relaxed when they went in to clean up for tea after an afternoon in the garden.

"Is it in the blood, do you think?" he asked one day in the early spring, out of breath from preparing the flower beds. "I've never grown anything in my life before, but I can remember Pa doing it, dawn to dusk in the spring . . . and my grandfather, too, coming home as dirty as I am now. It was a peaceful life altogether. It's too bad we missed it."

Darin went mad with roses, bringing bushels of bushes along with a small apple tree the next week, bent on planting the flowers against the house in an area she had always reserved for perennials. Rosaleen did not stop him, though he was ready to argue his point.

"The sun's just right there. Picture them in bloom, darling, a solid mass of roses of every color covering the front of the house. One of them's a trailer. It'll grow right over the porch, bearing small pink roses in such a mass we'll have to brace them up!"

"I didn't know you were so fond of roses, darling." She smiled at him, and he grinned back.

"You're named for them, aren't you? Of course I'm fond of them. Actually, you're named after a song, though. A song that doesn't mean what it says."

"'My Dark Rosaleen'?" she asked. "It sounds like a pretty straightforward love song to me."

"Well, it isn't," he said, rolling up his sleeves to get to work. "It's a 'code song,' Rosie, that kept the English in the dark about our patriotism. Rosaleen isn't a woman: she's Ireland, my dear . . . sung about like a mistress her lover would lay down his life for. Can you imagine the joy it gave that subversive lot to sing it right in front of the English?" He laughed; then, more seriously, "There's trouble there again after last year's land evictions."

Rosaleen did not like talk of war, and, watching him knock his knee into place so he could crouch down to plant, reinforced her sentiments. "There'll always be trouble there," she said. "When they get the British out—if ever—they'll fight among themselves. They're still a bunch of crazy Celts: they can't change. They dance shouting merrily off to war and sing sad songs later."

He glanced up at her, his eyes very blue under the blue sky. "Is that a personal comment, perhaps?"

"I suppose it is. At least, partly," she said. He knew how she felt about his leg, the compassion that had torn her the first time she saw him without it, though he had pulled the counterpane over his lower legs when he came naked into bed. To prove that it did not repulse her, for nothing about him could, she had kissed and caressed his body, stroking the inside of his thigh until her hand reached the knee, where there was nothing else beyond. Then, she deliberately kissed the stump and rubbed the scar: she could see the rush of love and relief in his face, though he drew her back up into his arms.

"I love you," he said, holding her head against his neck. "And I'm sorry, if only because of you."

"Does it still hurt?"

"Sometimes, mostly from that damned prosthesis; though I suppose I should be glad enough to have it." She had never seen that: he always carefully hid it under the bed. "At first, there were the usual 'phantom pains.' It felt like the leg was there and injured, though it was not. That went away quickly enough."

"Was it really from an infection?" she asked, looking up into his face.

"Yes." He smiled. "Such are the glories of war. Sure, I had a boot that rubbed...as simple as that. The heel became badly infected in the prison camp...well, I might as well give it a name, Rosie: gangrene. I've never been sure whether they really wanted to save my life: they let so many others die. At the time, I thought they were just torturing me."

She put her hand on his cheek with compassion deep in her eyes. "Torturing? It was so painful?"

He let out his breath in a short, angry laugh. "Without even whiskey for an anesthetic! Those damned Rebel bastards! I'm sorry, Rosie. It'll never go away: the memories, the agony, the screams I didn't even know were my own. I haven't really been the same since. You might live through something like that, but it takes its toll on your constitution."

"You seem healthy enough to me."

"Yeah," he said shortly, kissing her forehead. "I do try to take care of myself. Especially now, when I have so much to...when I have everything, darling."

"All right," she said and laughed, "now I'm deluged with roses! What are you going to do with the apple tree?"

"It goes in front of the house." He grinned, lifting the small white-blossoming plant. "It's that sweet, isn't it? To tell the truth, I bought it because of the blossoms, darling, but it *will* grow up and have apples sometime." With the tiny tree in his hand, he opened his arms and swept her into his embrace. "'Stay me with flagons, comfort me with apples'...but I'll *never* be 'sick of love'! Rosie, this is the best time, ever. Sure, until now, I didn't know what happiness was. It's you, Rosaleen. All you, forever."

"To me, it's you, Darin." She smiled, holding him tightly. "I love you more than I've ever dreamed possible. Whatever the cost, it's worth it!"

"Cost?" he asked, looking at her closely; then he shook his head with a smile. "Sure you're talking like a bloody banker, woman. Now, are you going to help me plant this tree?"

Chapter 34

RORY was restless that summer. Too full of energy to sit around worrying about his readmission into Harvard, he began to frequent his old haunts again. They were on both ends of the social spectrum, for he mixed equally well with the coffee-house intellectuals and the working men at the Noonan Pub, and was as likely to be invited to a wake as a society party. People liked him, and that he should like people in return was as natural to him as breathing: he had never known anything else. His confidence in himself was secure, and he lacked the wasteful defenses of men who cared less for themselves. He approached no man with a negative point of view, though he was not completely naive. He recognized a rogue when he met one, and there were several among his acquaintances on both social levels. He appeared to cultivate them without discretion, but he knew it was better to have them in his corner than center ring. Besides, most of them were interesting fellows.

Even if he had not kept up with what was happening in the world, the news would have trickled to him in his several hangouts. The coffee houses were buzzing with the details of the trial of President Garfield's assassin and with the recent announcement that a German named Koch had finally isolated the tuberculosis bacillus. Rory had been entertaining his parents in France when the President was shot, and it seemed to him that he was the only Maddigan affected by the news. After an initial "Good Lord!" his father had accepted the tragedy philosophically. John lived so much in the past that, to him, it was just one in a long line of politically motivated murders in the past three thousand years.

And if Rory had not been so shocked, his mother's reaction would have amused him. The first thing she thought of was the stock market, sending off several frantic cables to the bank. Rosaleen's concern with world affairs related strictly to finance, and always before Rory had found her obsession slightly humorous. But he was devastated by the news, unable to accept that such a thing could happen "in this day and age." Lincoln's assassination was just history to him: he had been far too young to remember it.

At the pub, where he dropped in on Wednesday to help Sean behind the bar, there was renewed grumbling about the British and talk about arming the Irish again. Since the recent tenant evictions in Ireland, terrorism was again rampant in the countryside there.

Paddy Maloney with a stub of cigar in his mouth, muttered into his beer, "Sure the least we can do is send money to the cause. I already know a ship that's running arms."

"They need a leader more than guns," Rory told him. "If they hadn't turned on Parnell, he might have argued the whole matter in Parliament. Nothing's ever been won by terrorism, Paddy, except more graves in the villages for the rebels. Without a man with a silver tongue to argue their cause, they might as well wait until the British are bloody well sick of them."

"They aren't terrorists, sure!" Paddy exclaimed. "They're patriots, lad. What else could they do about Parnell, who was sinning with a married woman?"

Listening to the conversation while he drew a pint of draft, Sean looked at Rory with a grin.

"My God, you *have* changed," he said amiably. "No cufflinks left to sell?"

Rory smiled slightly and, glancing at the door, raised his eyebrows in mock horror as the men on their way home from work trooped into the pub in a body. "Good God, what a thirsty lot they are! You know, Sean, if those bastards took their drinking money home, there'd be a little less hardship in this section of town."

Sean regarded the men with compassion. "Not for them, maybe. It's a hard life, Rory. Though I must admit I've often thought we're contributing to the Celtic disease." Then he smiled and added softly, "My father says they have to fortify themselves to face the wives at home."

"You should mind what Darin says," Rory replied, lining up the glasses for filling. "I'd hate to see my sister drive you to drink."

But there was no more time to talk. They were too busy filling glasses and joshing with the clientele. Only after closing, when Sean locked the door and Rory was cleaning up behind the bar, did they resume their conversation over their customary pint to end the day.

Sean slid on one of the stools across from his cousin and said, "Your sister will never drive me to drink. Not being able to marry her might, though. When are you going to find a girl to settle down with, Rory? You won't do it playing around with a married woman older than yourself, you know. Or is the lovely Julia still in the picture?"

Rory smiled. "Very much. I'm going to her place from here, tonight. I'm not steady enough to marry yet, Sean. The most I can hope for right now is that I don't disgrace myself again and ruin all my plans."

Sean observed him with curiosity, and their closeness was so friendly, he could ask, "Are you in love with her?"

"I'm always in love with them." Rory grinned. "The trouble is it doesn't seem to last long. I'm in love with all of them! You know, Sean, it's a strange thing. Neither of us is anything like his father. Mine was faithful to Mother until the day he died, and Darin . . . well, you aren't a bit like him, are you? Do you suppose it's reaction? Maybe sons are deliberately unlike their fathers, for some reason or other."

"I'm sure it's true of me," Sean admitted, smiling faintly. "Very consciously true. I love my father, but I don't want to be like him in that respect. Maybe I couldn't be like him, anyway. He's a bit larger than life, you know: I'm a more peaceful man. You're more like him than I am."

"And you're a better man than I am." Rory laughed. "Has there been any breakthrough for you and Mary Rose?"

"You'd know if there had been," Sean said, shaking his head. "I only hope she'll wait for me. This isn't fair to her. She could have anyone she chose. I've never met anyone so contradictory, but life certainly isn't dull with her. She appears to have gotten over her love affair with your father, now. I only wish she liked your mother more."

Rory stared in disbelief. "I thought I was the only one who saw that. She was straight out jealous of Mother, you know.

Now that he's gone, perhaps things will change. Then I'll only have Cliona and her passion for Christ to worry about."

"How's Michael?"

Rory shrugged and took a sip from his glass. "All right, I guess. He's a difficult one to figure out. The only time I see him is at the table, where he usually manages some unpleasantness. He's as ambitious as hell, I think, and Mother's holding him back. He wants the whole thing; the bank, I mean. Just between us, Mother must have some doubts or she wouldn't be so hard on him. He's always liked to bait me, of course. Right now, he's delighting in the fact that he graduated from Harvard ahead of me." He smiled without resentment. "Who cares about the order of succession? I know what I want to do. I just hope I get back into Harvard in the fall and don't have to return to Paris to complete my education."

Sean frowned with concern. "I thought you loved Paris, Rory."

"I did, but it isn't home. And only a damned Harvard degree will do me any good here. There are so many things that need changing, Sean, and I think I'm the person to do it." He grinned. "I'm in a unique position. In Boston, I'm neither fish nor fowl nor good red meat—neither a Brahmin nor an Irish working man—but I can get along with both. I'm in just the right place to initiate changes. That same position is something else that troubles Michael, I think. He's aiming for the top, and he'll never really get there: he's Irish. He'll just get far enough to have a long, hard fall. It's sad."

"I think he's jealous of you," Sean said. "You carry everything off so easily. You always have, if not exactly wisely."

"No, it wasn't wise," Rory agreed. "No one can see that better than I can, now. There's a streak of the outrageous in me that I have to fight all the time."

"I wish I'd had a brother." Sean smiled wistfully. "It isn't easy being an only child. I feel so damned committed, you know. There's no one else to share the load of my parents. I love them both, in different ways. I feel I can't just abandon Mother. If I had a brother, this whole thing with Mary Rose would be much easier. When we marry, there'd be someone to look after Mother, because I'm certain she'll never speak to me again."

Rory pushed his glass aside, and his blue eyes looked intently into Sean's face. "For what it's worth, you have one, Sean. There's no one I'd rather have for a brother; I'm not really content with the one I have. People should be able to *choose* their relatives. If I had a choice, I'd pick you. There's no man I admire more." He smiled suddenly, slightly embarrassed by the confession. "Of course, I won't be able to console your mother when you marry. But, by God, I'll do everything in my power to help toward that end! Then at least you'll be my brother-in-law."

"I'm already your cousin." Sean smiled. "It'll be a confusing relationship, won't it? Second cousin and brother-in-law."

"Couldn't you get a dispensation? I mean, you're almost there, aren't you? What's one degree, one way or another? What does it matter to them?"

"There's no dispensation for rules like that," Sean said, shaking his head slowly; then he looked at Rory with amusement. "You and your sister really are pagans. I think John Maddigan had quite an effect on your thinking."

Rory smiled, taking off his bar apron to leave. "He was quite a man; I miss him terribly. I wish you'd known him better, Sean."

Though he dallied with the ambassador's wife at night, Rory often spent his days wandering around the poorer areas, the North End and Fort Point, trying to assess the problems there. The slums were no longer just Irish: in the past ten years, there had been an influx from Europe, mainly Italian. No one recognized that Rory was out of place there. If they noticed him at all, it was because of his unusually handsome Irish face or his fluent Italian. He did not feel hypocritical wearing his student clothes from Paris, adapting readily to whatever put others at ease. Whole days went by without more incident than an Irish rebel speaker in a park, or someone more level-headed urging the listeners to demand their rights in the city.

Housing was inadequate; waste disposal at a minimum. And, typical of big-city overcrowding, the crime rate was rising, a matter carefully pointed out by the newspapers. Suspecting the statistics, Rory was not averse to visiting the police stations in the area, which were manned almost entirely by Irishmen. He found that the most common complaint was drunk and disorderly conduct, the number of occurrences making up two-thirds of the crimes, inflating the total incidents, the rest made up of petty theft and the southern Italian quick-tempered use of sharp objects, a minimal figure. The newspaper statistics were inaccurate, manipulated, though their cartoons were right in depicting drunken, brawling Irishmen.

He sat in pubs, inconspicuously trying to learn the minds of these people who, except for a twist of fate, might have been his own. He wandered into churches and dispensaries alike, and he was angered by what he observed. The churches took more money than they gave in charity, the priests explaining logically that they looked after souls, not bodies, and their parishes needed support. Rory found an exception to this who was like a fresh, clean breeze. Father Muldough, a frail old man with a small parish in Fort Point, doled out so much to every taker that sometimes he lacked dinner for himself. He and Rory became close friends. At least once a week, Rory came to the rectory with groceries and dined with him, the two men talking late into the night.

The day there was an incident started out like any other, though Rory was to remember it for the rest of his life. He had not planned to go to the North End that day; indeed, the night before, he had decided to take on the admissions office of Harvard himself, confront the administration directly and in person, to end his long suspense. But he slept later than usual, and his grandmother, who still doted on him, prepared his breakfast and brought it to his room. Knowing his aspirations and how much time he spent exploring her old neighborhood, she began to talk about her arrival in Boston as she tidied his room.

"If you want to know why our people are the way they are now," she said, "you should know how far they've come, sure, darlin'. We arrived here in the winter, Rory: the winter of 1847, the worst famine year. Sure, it was that cold! We'd never known anything like the cold here, and us without clothes, dressed in rags and shoeless. We discovered at Immigration that poor, dear Veronica had the consumption on top of everything else. Sure, we were more fortunate than some in the place we found. Is your coffee hot enough? The cellar was warm in the winter; we were warm as bugs in a rug, because the furnace was there. At least we had some heat, and anything was better than the famine, though once we'd been accustomed to neat, sweet cottages in the country, with the fresh air and sunshine."

"You lived in a cellar?" Rory said, his eyes following her

as she dusted his bureau top with her apron "Grandma, I didn't know that before."

"Sure, the house is still there, though I've not entered it for all these many years. There are dirty curtains in the windows now, where once there were newspapers and rags to keep out the cold. It's near the dispensary, on the same street as St. Mary's. Those were hard times, Rory, though now they look good, with all of us together." She smiled and sank down in a chair near his bed. "Brian put up blankets as dividers to give the adults some privacy, for we all slept on the floor. He made pallets out of straw and sacks. Sure, they weren't that bad at all. You'd be surprised, love, how little you can get by with if you have to."

Rory looked troubled. "Somehow, I can't picture Mother sleeping on a gunny sack in a basement. She's never mentioned it."

"That's because she's never forgotten," Mary said. "She was that frightened, the poor little thing! The rats and the darkness made her cling closer than ever to her cousin. Sure, the sun rose and set on Darin in that one's eyes! How is he, by the way?"

"Fine. He seems very well and happy," Rory said. "He's given himself a day off during the week, and it's done him worlds of good."

After she left, Rory dressed in his student clothes and went out, not really conscious of his destination, even when he caught the horse bus to the North End. But when he found himself standing across the street from the house itself, staring at the dirty cellar windows on either side of the steps, he realized he had been driven compulsively to go there. A slatternly-looking young woman with a baby under her shawl entered, leading a small girl by the hand, and Rory felt a lump in his throat. He turned away to walk slowly down the street, his gaze on the cobbles. He almost wished his grandmother had not given him the address; but, in another way, he was grateful for it, though he had almost been moved to tears. For the first time, he realized why his mother was so driven by money: she did not want any of them to be poor again. He had grown up rich and insulated, with no real understanding of the poverty in this area; now, quite suddenly, he seemed to understand, and his direction was even more clear to him.

"Don't go runnin' off, now! Sure you're a bit taken with yourself, aren't you? Do you think you're too good for us, then? It's just one little kiss we're after askin', Miss High-and-Mighty!"

The ugliness of the man's tone of voice drew Rory from his reverie, and he glanced across the street, where three unkempt young men had formed a barrier in front of an auburn-haired girl, blocking her way outside the charity infirmary. Her manner was composed, even a bit haughty, and she effectively shook off a hand that was placed on her wrist. Rory decided the young men meant her no real harm. They were unemployed and idle, simply trying to break the monotony of their day. But he could not stand by and watch a young woman being accosted, especially as it seemed completely unwelcome to her. He crossed the street with long strides, without even looking at the girl.

"Is it something important you have to say to my sister?" he asked with a brogue almost normal to him from time spent at the Noonan Pub. "If not, I'll be taking her along home, where there's work to be done, sure."

The three hoodlums considered his height, the breadth of his shoulders, and looked at one another. Deciding not to confront him, they slunk away slowly, staring back over their shoulders. The rescue accomplished, Rory had every intention of going on his way as soon as the men were out of sight.

"You didn't have to do that," she said in a clear, cool voice. "I'm perfectly capable of taking care of myself."

Her accent surprised him: it was as American as his own. He glanced down at her face, and everything around him seemed to dissolve. Something seemed to break in his chest, and he had to catch his breath. He saw nothing but the pale oval of that face with its long, intelligent gray eyes, under her heavy auburn hair. He was vaguely conscious that she was wearing blue or gray, or something of both colors, but all of his attention was on her face. He stared openly and had a difficult time recovering himself to speak.

"You shouldn't have to take care of yourself," he heard himself saying awkwardly, forgetting both his Irish accent and his customary smoothness. "I don't think they'd have done you any harm, but there is some crime in this area. What are you doing here?"

"I believe that's my own concern," she said, completely dismissing him to walk across the street to the bus stop.

He found himself following her, unable to let her go. Her

rich copper-toned hair was clasped in back by a barrette, instead of a maidenly bow, falling in loose curls down her back. She wore a gray skirt of good material and cut, and a long-sleeved blouse sprigged with a pattern of tiny blue and maroon flowers with a piece of blue grosgrain ribbon tied just beneath the white collar. Slightly tall for a girl, she seemed even taller because of the stately, graceful way she held herself, her willowy figure filled out beautifully in the right places. As they crossed the street, he found his eyes returning to her exceptionally neat, small waist.

No one had ever rebuffed him before; even honorable girls paused to flirt awhile. This girl treated him as though he did not exist and made him feel that way. When they were side by side at the bus stop, he could think of nothing to say.

"I didn't mean to interfere," he found himself apologizing. "It's just that I spend a lot of time here, and I know what goes on. Miss...?"

She did not give her name, reaching into her gray pouch bag to find change for the bus. "I'm quite all right," she said coolly, without glancing at him. "The bus will be along in a moment. Don't let me keep you from 'spending your time here.'"

"I take the same bus," he said in a rush, not knowing which one stopped at that corner.

"How interesting, since several pass here." She held up her hand to attract a passing hansom, determined to elude him at any cost, even that of taking a cab. Hearing the horse's hooves clip-clopping to the curbing over the cobbles, he grew desperate.

"Please! Let me introduce myself," he said to her retreating back, and she turned a gray, half-amused glance to him as she got into the cab.

"That's unnecessary," she said. "I know who you are, Rory Maddigan."

She vanished into the dark interior of the cab and a moment later, she was gone.

He was to spend the rest of the summer looking for her: he could not let her get away. She was what he wanted; everything he wanted. Only a few weeks before, he had told Sean that he loved all women, with no intention of loving just one. Love at first sight did not surprise him: he had fallen in love that way so many times. But this was different. Not only did he feel as though he had been struck clear through by lightning, in a way he had never experienced, he felt that it was not really love at first sight. Aside from the girl's knowing his name, there was something vaguely familiar about her; but as much as he tried, he could not place her. And he could not find her, either.

He started by taking every bus that stopped at that now hallowed corner: the routes divided, taking off in three separate directions, and even by staying on them to the end of their routes, he had no idea where she lived. The pale oval face and gray eyes never left his mind, disturbing even his sleep. He knew he had seen that color hair before, but where it was, and on whom, eluded him. After the first wild dashing about of his mind, he decided to approach the search more rationally.

She had been just outside the charity dispensary when he'd first seen her. The solution was obvious: he must inquire there. Amid the coughing and sniffling patients in the anteroom and the clatter of bottles and odor of medicines at the counter, the rotund but dour nurse was unable, or unwilling, to answer his inquiries. She finally sent him off, telling him she had no time for his kind of nonsense. Deciding that the bustling dispensary was not the place to confront her, Rory returned when it closed for the day and waylaid the nurse as she left, turning on all his charm to invite her for coffee.

She was too tired for any interest in men, and threatened to call a policeman, adding, "Nurses aren't what people think, you know. They just can't accept new ideas!"

Rory had never thought about them one way or another; but, by his actions, he stood accused and realized there was no chance of getting the girl's identification from her.

His life became a nightmare of thinking he recognized her in any redhead he saw on the street, his heart lurching wildly, only to fall again in disappointment. Though he had always been open enough in discussing his current infatuations, he could not bring himself to mention her, even to Sean. The girl was a mystery, a dream, who had vanished like smoke into the teaming city. Rosaleen was the first to notice that something was bothering him.

"You look a little tired, dear," she said one morning at the breakfast table, with the whole family there. "Perhaps you shouldn't get up so early, or shouldn't go to bed so late. Why *are* you getting up so early?"

"I have things to do," he said noncommittally, trying to avoid his brother's hostile scrutiny. "Actually, this whole business of getting back into college is getting on my nerves."

"You should have thought about that a long time ago," Michael said. "You'll probably be the oldest man at Harvard if you do get accepted."

"That doesn't matter," Rosaleen put in quickly. "There were people of all ages at the Sorbonne, and Rory's only twenty-three." She waited until they were alone before she broached the subject again. "Really, Rory," she said before she left for work, "are you all right? They did say they'd give us their decision soon."

He attempted a smile. "I'm fine, Mother. Do you have change for a dollar?"

"Again?" she asked, raising her eyebrows. "I gave you change just the other day. What are you doing with so much chicken feed? You haven't found slot machines in town, have you? Or are you just putting it into player pianos in the bars?"

"I'm riding a lot of buses," he explained wearily. "I'm really taking a look at the whole city. I didn't realize it was so large and complex."

"Yes," she said, studying him, "it really has grown. But that's a curious pastime for a young man. Is that what you do all day long?"

He shrugged. "I help Sean out on Wednesday, when Darin isn't there."

"Oh?" she said, drawing in her breath a little. "That's very nice of you. A job's just what you need. But I have the strangest feeling you aren't telling me everything, Rory."

During the following weeks, he did not ask her for change again. His mother was too perceptive, and he could not share his dream with anyone. It was too personal, too precious; besides, he felt a little foolish at having lost the only girl he ever wanted.

Cliona's behavior was peculiar, and Mary Rose was upset: her whole life seemed to be coming to pieces, unraveling like a piece of frayed rope. Even Sean was acting odd: she could not seem to get through to him. And the heat of summer in the city seemed to intensify everything, contributing to their first violent quarrel, which started over his working at the pub again.

"What else can I do?" he asked her, beneath the revolving fans in the ceiling of their favorite coffee house. "It's a chance to make a little money, and I was born and raised there. If a job does turn up, we'll need money, you know." He looked at her with despair. "No, you don't know, do you? I couldn't take the one job that's been offered, out in the Western Territory, if I wanted to. You're accustomed to so much more, you couldn't stand it."

"I could," she said with flashing eyes. "I'd do anything to be with you, darling. I've learned to cook and sew a little."

"Could you wash the laundry in an iron tub? That school's rural, you know. I don't know what the hell they want with a Latin teacher anyway, though they made it clear that would be only one of my subjects. I have to wait for something better, more suitable for you, Mary Rose. Aside from hardships you can't imagine, it might be dangerous. General Custer was killed near there just a few years ago."

"Stop treating me like a china doll," she said. "Even if you don't say it, you're always reproaching me for being born with money. I can't help it! I'm trying to overcome it. Whether you take that job or not doesn't matter, Sean. Just stop belittling me."

"When you stop belittling me," he said with hurt blue eyes. "There's nothing wrong with working at the pub for the summer. You haven't objected to it before."

"Because it was only temporary, while you were in school," she said. "You're out of college now, Sean: I guess I'm afraid it'll become permanent. I just hate to think of you behind that bar!"

"Be careful, Mary Rose. My father and my grandfather..."

"Oh, stop it!" she flared. "Your father had a chance at some education and threw it away! Grandma told me all about it. How you with a bachelor's degree can waste your time working there is beyond me."

"That's enough!" he said, trying to keep his voice even, his blue eyes angry. "You know damned well that my father isn't well; I've told you all about it. For the first time in his life, he's taking a day off during the week, and he deserves it. You may be ungrateful for everything you've had, but that man *gave* me my education, *insisted* on it when mother was ready to settle for less. Aside from what I earn at the pub, I owe him something. And if it's another summer out of my life, helping him out, at least it's something."

534

"If Papa hadn't died, we'd be married by now, Sean." She sighed. "Now it looks like we'll be waiting forever."

"Not forever," he said, closing his eyes for a moment in thought. He remained silent a long time. When he finally spoke, his voice was tentative but sincere. "Do you want to break it off? I've been thinking for some time that this isn't fair to you, Mary Rose. Maybe it's all wrong, anyway. Not just the business about the Church, but you and me. Our backgrounds are so different, we're bound to clash. It happened just now, and we were both right. And we were both wrong, too. This whole thing could become an Hegelian tragedy, darling. Sometimes, it's almost too much for me."

Her heart clamored in alarm, but she lifted her chin bravely. "Is that what you want?" she asked, but the thought of losing him made her lips tremble and tears start in her eyes. She reached for her handkerchief. "I love you so much, Sean. I'll wait forever if I have to. Please don't ever say anything like that again!"

His hand closed over hers on the table, and he looked directly into her eyes. "No, I won't: I couldn't bear losing you. But I can live with your impatience: I'm impatient, too. You must recognize where I've come from, Mary Rose: I don't think like you. And you must realize that I love my father as much as you did yours."

When she returned home that afternoon, shaken by the encounter, she heard raised voices in the parlor, one of them her mother's, using language she had heard only on the street. She wanted to crawl away to her room to nurse her wounds, but she heard Cliona weeping pitifully between the shouts. She had never heard voices raised in anger in the house before; and if it concerned her sister, she must stand up for her. Putting her own problems from her mind with a deep breath, Mary Rose squared her shoulders and walked into the parlor, where she stopped in surprise at the bizarre tableau that met her.

Her mother and her grandmother, both dressed in black, stood in the middle of the green-and-gold room.

Father Liam, bending over Cliona, who sat weeping on the sofa, addressed the furious women coldly over his shoulder. "That will be enough, now! You've no right to persecute the girl. She's of age, you know, and can make her own decisions."

"Yes, she's of age," Rosaleen cried, white-faced, "she's a

woman, Liam! And she deserves all the joy a woman can have, goddammit! Things you know *nothing* about in your little Gothic cell. Get out of here! Get out of our lives altogether! I've had all I can take of you! Get out of here, before Rory comes home and completely undoes you! I swear to God, if I had the strength, I'd do it for him!"

Mary moved quietly around the confrontation to approach Mary Rose near the door: Mary had been weeping. "Mary Rose, child," she said, with a tremor in her voice, "Cliona wants to take the veil. She's after wanting to enter a cloistered convent, where we'd never see her anymore."

"What?" Mary Rose cried, with a rush of greater understanding than the other two women possessed, but as opposed to the decision as they. "I can't believe she'd...let *me* talk to her!"

Rosaleen turned away in angry tears when she saw her younger daughter approach her sister and kneel beside the sofa.

"Cliona, what's got into you?" Mary Rose asked, touching the long blond hair tied back with a black velvet bow. "You don't have to do this, you know," she said, lowering her voice and speaking directly into her left ear. "Cliona, if it's because of me...oh, God, you'll break my heart! Please, please, forget all about this," she entreated, weeping. "Don't make me choose!"

Cliona raised her tragic gray eyes, puffy from crying, and threw her arms around her sister, patting her shoulders to comfort her. "It has nothing to do with you," she said softly. "It's the way I want to spend my life, Mary Rose. I just can't make them understand. They've both been at it, first Grandma and then Mother. I thought Grandma would stand by me!" she said, weeping. "You can't believe how Mother's been abusing Father Liam."

"Did he talk you into this?"

Cliona shook her head, a sweet smile on her lips. "It isn't the sort of thing one's talked into, dear. I made my own decision. I've known for some time, there was something better than...this kind of world, for me. Oh, goodness! You should have heard the shocking things Mother said to extol the virtues of love and marriage and having babies."

Mary Rose felt as though her heart would break. She knew Cliona's calling was right for her, but she hated it, because it would take her away.

"All right," she said finally. "I think I understand, dear."

Disentangling herself from her sister's arms, she stood up with as much quiet dignity as possible. "Father Liam, it'll be all right. But I really think you'd better leave before my brother comes in. We've had enough trouble for one day. Maybe, if you leave us alone, we can approach this more reasonably."

Chapter 35

DURING the long train ride to upper New York State, Mary Rose and Cliona sat across from their mother and grandmother, remaining as silent as they. Cliona's cause had not been won without argument and another three weeks' preparation, after Rosaleen capitulated in total exhaustion. Even then, she tried to talk her daughter out of a Carmelite convent, which was cloistered, and into entering a more active and socially concerned order; not really because Cliona would be doing something for mankind, as Rosaleen argued, but so they could see her again. That failing, Rosaleen had given in to Cliona's wishes one Wednesday evening when she came home. It was almost as though she had sought advice on the subject, Mary Rose thought; and whoever she talked to had convinced her in spite of herself, using the words "live and let live," which her mother had used for the first time, almost as though she were quoting them.

"I can't live your life for you, Cliona," she said dejectedly. "God knows, what you want is something I couldn't endure. But I can't get inside your skin, any more than you can mine, my dear. I *am* convinced this is what you think will make you happy. If it doesn't, for God's sake and your own, don't be ashamed to leave and come home. You always have a home, remember that. In the meantime, all I can do, I guess, is live and let live."

Still, the situation was not a happy one, and Mary Rose

could not wait to see Cliona settled in the convent and get home, away from the whole thing. For her grandmother and herself, the trip would only last a few days. Her mother had invited them to accompany her to New York City, where she had some bank business she had decided to attend to. But Mary was not interested in "strange" places, and Mary Rose, though she might have enjoyed it, was anxious to get back to Sean. Even the enticement of dining at fabulous restaurants and going to the theater had not made her waver.

To justify herself and stay above suspicion, Mary Rose argued, "I don't like Grandma making the long trip back home alone. The only train she's ever been on has just been to the Cape. Traveling by herself, so late in life, might throw her into confusion."

Of the four of them, Mary was probably the least confused. She had capitulated to Cliona's calling before Rosaleen. Having lost a son to the priesthood, she had been through the whole thing before. And as bitter as she was about Liam, she reasoned that, if a mother is going to lose a child to the Church, it was probably better to lose one to a cloister, where she would not be hanging around your neck all the time. She thought she knew Rosaleen from the ground up; she could not picture her having an insipid tea party with a lot of nuns, even if one of them were her daughter.

All of them were surprised and relieved at how well Rosaleen behaved when they arrived at the convent, a lovely, sprawling close behind high gray stone walls on the bank of the Hudson. As they inspected the buildings, saw the clean little cell in which Cliona would be housed, and had the inevitable tea with the Mother Superior, the only one permitted to talk, Rosaleen was exceptionally impressive in her black widow's weeds. She asked only pertinent, motherly questions which revealed her concern. The only request she made, with some of her business tone, was that the Mother Superior telephone at once if Cliona became ill.

Mary Rose watched the nuns, some of them no older than herself, serving at table keeping silence. Walking the grounds in silence. Praying silently in the chapel, beating their breasts with an inaudible "Mea culpa, mea maxima culpa." She fought back an urge to scream aloud. Though she tried, she was too much in love to comprehend such a life. She wept along with her mother and Mary when they finally said goodbye. Only Cliona did not seem sad.

Embracing them, her face radiant, she said, "God bless

you always." She lingered longer with Mary Rose, with her white hands on her sister's arms. "I know things will work out for your happiness," she assured her, "but it may not be the way you think. I'll pray for you, and for what's right."

Though Mary Rose was not imaginative, the negative tone of the words lingered in her ears, making her heart heavy. She lagged silently behind the other two women, as they walked along the path to the convent gate.

Taking a deep, clean breath of grassy air, Mary said, "Sure, it smells like home. It isn't such a bad life, Rosaleen. When I look back, knowing what I do now, it doesn't seem a bad one to follow at all. No cares or worries; no men or children. The very innocence of it's enough to lighten the heart, sure. The calm, the silence. I think I might have enjoyed it myself."

In spite of the pain she was feeling, Rosaleen laughed. "I can imagine you taking the vow of chastity," she said. "But Mother, the one of silence would defeat you altogether."

Rosaleen slept heavily on the hot summer afternoon, a dew of perspiration on her face from the humidity, the sheet pulled only halfway over her nakedness, her black hair spread on the pillow. She did not hear Darin get up and dress, walk quietly outside. After not seeing him for three Wednesdays, she had rushed into his arms, full of misery and cares, still bruised by the loss of Cliona, her head pulsing from the days spent at the stock exchange in the muggy heat of New York. Only he had the magic in his voice to calm her, the patience to hear her out, putting things into his peculiar perspective, which made him more important to her than anyone else. Then, after he had soothed her completely, he made gentle love to her and watched as she fell into a relaxed slumber.

The soft shower of cool droplets on her bare body was something her drowsy mind could not comprehend: she moved in her sleep a little, as though bothered by the buzzing of a fly. The sensation continued, and she tried to brush it away with her hands, until she woke enough to be slightly startled by its peculiarity. She opened her eyes to find Darin standing beside the bed, bare-chested and smiling, showering her with the roses from his garden, still damp from watering, a brimming basket of them in one hand.

"Darin!" she cried, half rising, with blossoms falling away. "What on earth are you doing?"

He laughed.

"Flinging roses riotously," he cried. "Sharing beauty with you. Oh, darling, you're a vision! You should see yourself!"

"You're absolutely mad!" She smiled, looking up at him with melting eyes, the outside world far away again, where it belonged. "Your beautiful roses," she said softly. "You must have picked them all."

Discarding the basket, he sat down beside her with his face full of love. "I only plucked the blossoms, with never a thorn to hurt you, Rosie. The beauties of life shouldn't be hoarded. They should be surrendered joyfully while they're still in bloom."

By fall, when Rory went back to Harvard, Sean was nearly ready to give up. The money he had saved over two summers, working at the pub, was not enough to marry on, and he could not bring Mary Rose home to live with his family, as he might have another girl he could marry in the Church. The anticipated reaction from his mother alone was enough to discourage him. No matter what stand his father took, his mother would surely disown him. Before they married, they had to have a place of their own, and money enough to live until he could establish himself. As the couple walked by the river under the falling leaves, Rory seemed to be the only hope they had, but even his intervention would take time.

"Rory's reestablished his friendship with the head of the Classics Department," Mary Rose told him. "They were rather close before he was expelled. Papa and Mama spent their honeymoon with Dr. Dove and his wife: they've always been family friends. But Rory says he can't just come out with it at once, asking for a tutorial for you."

"It isn't a tutorial, Mary Rose," he said dejectedly, "it's a paying tutor's job."

"Well, whatever," she said, her own mood rather heavy. "Oh, Sean, I just hate it! You should be going for your advanced degree there, along with Rory. If only Papa hadn't died when he did!"

"I loathe having to have anyone intercede for me. I could go to Harvard on my academic standing alone. This is supposed to be a democracy, but unless your father went there... Look how easy it was for your mother to get Rory back in."

"Not all that easy, from what she's said. If it hadn't been for Rory's good record at the Sorbonne, I don't think they'd have considered it. But you have a better record than he has, Sean!"

"And I'm an Irish Catholic nobody in their eyes, without a dream of crossing the barrier," he said bitterly. "Father O'Reilly at Boston College said he'd try to send a few hard cases my way."

"Well, that's something." She smiled, pressing his arm.

"Not enough to start a family on. Even if I have five students a term, going to their houses every day, it'll still be next to nothing."

"Try to look on the bright side," she said. "We know Rory will help! My goodness, before, I was the one filled with gloom and impatience! I don't feel quite so hopeless, now."

He smiled and stopped walking long enough to kiss her. "You're right," he said. "I'm chafing at the bit, Mary Rose. I want you...want to marry you so much! Jesus, I should have studied something practical. I didn't want to be a *priest,* but that's about all Latin's good for."

"No! My father was anything but a priest," she said, laughing, "and he could have taught at Harvard any time he wanted! Your only misfortune is that there aren't any lay instructors at Boston College. I'm sure they'd have snapped you up in a minute, if there were."

"That's true enough," he said, smiling. "Thank you for standing by me all this time. You must think I'm a stubborn idiot."

"Yes." She laughed, hugging him. "Especially since I'm coming into my own fortune on my birthday in November, and we wouldn't have a care in the world if..."

"I'll never touch that goddam money," he said decisively. "We can leave it in the bank to bear its many litters." He smiled. "And when you're an old lady, you can be rich."

"The only wealth I want is that of being your wife, Sean," she said, embracing him. "Why the Devil don't opportunities present themselves when you're young enough to enjoy them? It's like . . . well . . . old women finally getting beautiful clothes, when they're too far gone to do them justice!"

"That doesn't sound like you," he said and frowned.

"It isn't, as a matter of fact," she admitted, smiling. "It's something I heard Papa say. He was a bit of a 'live for the day' man, you know. I certainly hope he crowded a lot into the years he had."

"Married to your mother?" Sean smiled in surprise. "I'd say he had just about everything. She's one of the most beautiful, charming, lively women I've ever..."

"Sean," she said, straightening her shoulders, her whole

542

body stiffening. "I'd appreciate it if you didn't go into paeans over Mama! I've heard them all my life...it makes me sick! Besides, you shouldn't talk that way about your future mother-in-law," she added, trying to make a joke of it. "Mothers-in-law are supposed to be anathema, aren't they?"

The blanket of snow over the countryside accented by small stands of dark evergreens with white sparkling on their limbs made the clear day look like the picture on a Christmas card, and, walking along the Mill Road, Rosaleen threw the hood of her fur cape back to appreciate the brisk bite of the air on her face. Like some sort of urban fungus, Cambridge had spread to within a mile of the cottage. The only advantage to that was that she could now take the horse bus to the end of the line and walk, instead of worrying about the horses all day when she had brought her little two-seated carriage.

Her small, black figure, carrying a wicker hamper, was the only moving thing under the blue sky and amid the shining drifts. She walked quickly, as she always did when she knew Darin was waiting for her at the cottage. Christmas would be upon them again soon, and she tried to think of what to give him on the first anniversary of their year together. Her mind turned from golden objects to a better memento, which he would really appreciate: a book of poetry was a gift of love. The problem of which poet was not settled before she reached the gateway. The walk seemed to get shorter all the time.

With a good deal of shoving, she managed to free the gate from the drift that had covered the path. Darin had not yet arrived, because the snow was pure and untouched. She lifted her skirt gingerly over her fur-trimmed boots and managed to tiptoe through the snow to the porch, without getting too much snow into her boots. Unlocking the door, she shivered at the cold that had accumulated in the house since last week. She kicked off her boots and slipped into a pair of shoes by the fireplace and began to lay a fire. My God, how I love this house, she thought, setting a match to the paper and kindling. It was truly a haven from outside problems, some of which still walked through her mind like ghosts. She wondered if she would ever get her children settled to her satisfaction. With Cliona away, she should not have included her, but not a day went by without Rosaleen waiting for a telephone call from her daughter, telling her she was going to come home. And Michael...what a constant provocation he was, working with her now at the bank. Though she loved all of her children, she was able to see them objectively. Michael had the instincts of a shark, with a brain to match: all of his schooling was a waste. When she discussed him with her mother, Mary had said he reminded her, in some ways, of Mr. Maddigan, though he did not look like him at all. There was the same coldness there, she said: a lack of humanity. Her mother had instincts about people, Rosaleen reflected: they were usually right. She would no more surrender the running of the bank to that young man than she would give Rory's money to him prematurely.

Rory was really serious about his studies, she thought as she went into the kitchen to light the wood stove and get a kettle boiling. But, after an examination, he still went out on the town, returning home in high spirits, if not gloriously drunk. She felt guilty for loving him so much; perhaps she *had* deprived Michael of affection in the process. But just the thought of Rory made her smile. His liveliness and charm were so much like Darin's: so was his temper. She remembered the three of them trying to hold him back when he heard about Cliona's decision, her mother on one arm, herself on the other, and Mary Rose almost tackling him around the waist. Undoubtedly they had saved Liam's life that day, not by their restraint, but by Mary Rose's reasoning. Now there was a very reasonable girl! She was almost as practical as Mary, and she looked more like her every year. The only problem Rosaleen had with Mary Rose was in making a future for her: Rosaleen had not even an inkling of where the girl was going in life. Several years ago, she had stopped going to parties, where she might have met a young man. Since John's death, all her activities seemed to center around the house. Her persistence had battered down the cook's New England reserve, and she had learned to cook quite well, if plainly. She had even asked Rosaleen to teach her to sew, and for a while Rosaleen thought the activity brought them a little closer. But when she had caught her polishing the silver in the dining room, she put her foot down, suddenly blasted by the memory of nearly being a maid in the house. Mary Rose did not understand her mother's outburst and returned once again to her sullen under-eyelid glances and the refusal to speak if not spoken to first. God, Rosaleen thought, filling the copper kettle at the kitchen pump, thankful it had not frozen. One could almost do without the cares and problems children brought...but could one do without all that love, so freely given?

She was just starting up the stairs beneath the raftered ceiling to lay a fire in the bedroom when she heard the grind of the gate and the sound of Darin's footsteps on the porch. Everything else went out of her mind. She ran back to the parlor just in time to greet him with open arms.

"I knew you were here," he said and smiled quickly, stamping his feet. "I saw the little marks of your boots in the snow. I'd have fallen down to kiss them, but this is so much better."

The first kiss of the week was always warm and gentle, with only a hint of the passion that would follow later in the day.

"Oh, it's so good!" she breathed. "A week's too long, darling. I wish we could go away somewhere together, to a nice, warm place. Alone."

"Well, that might be arranged." He smiled. "I might even know just the place. You've never traveled the Caribbean, have you? There are islands there..."

"Your hands are freezing!" she cried with concern. "I'll have tea in a few minutes, and we can talk about it then. In the meantime, warm yourself by the fire."

He walked to the fire with a laugh. "I left my gloves here last week! Look, darling, while I still have my coat on—and here are my trusty gloves, just where I thought I'd find them—I think I'll have a go at the walk. So you won't have to tiptoe through the snow again. And the rose bushes are laden to breaking, too, with the little red hips still hanging there, bright, in the cold."

"I brought some good things for sandwiches," she said, "and a bottle of our favorite Italian wine."

He raised his dark eyebrows over his affectionate eyes. "Well, since it's the only kind of cooking you know, I'll be happy to join you."

"Oh!" she cried, laughing. "That's it! You'll have nothing at all. And," she added, imitating her mother's brogue "git on with you, now!"

As she assembled sandwiches of fresh-baked bread from the Maddigan kitchen, spreading the dark French mustard Darin liked so well, she heard the shovel scraping the walk and tremendous thumps against the house, as he unburdened his precious rose trees. When the kettle whistled, she took down the Sèvres tea set she had always kept there, washed out the pot with boiling water to warm it, and set out two cups. Darin liked his tea the Irish way, "strong enough to trot a mouse"; so she sprinkled the Darjeeling liberally and poured the scalding water over it, setting it aside to brew.

When the front door opened again, everything was ready, and she lifted the tray and carried it into the parlor with a smile. Darin drew off his coat and boots without looking at her and walked to the sofa, where he sat down almost carefully.

"I must be getting old," he said breathlessly, with an attempt at lightness. "I don't remember that walk being so long before."

She set the tray down and looked at him with a frown. "Darling, your face is gray. You didn't have to do that, for goodness' sake! You hear of people falling over from heart attacks all the time from shoveling snow."

He shook his head and smiled. "It isn't that. If it were, I'd have clutched my chest and stiffened out on the walk: *ker-plop!* Everyone knows the pain and symptoms of the great attack. I'm fine, Rosie. This has happened before."

"Would you like a cup of tea? You're shivering."

"And sweating, too." He laughed, taking slow, even breaths. "That snow's dangerous stuff: you get malaria from it."

"Malaria?" She laughed. "You *are* mad! I have it on the best authority—an Italian guide—that you get malaria from visiting the Colosseum at midnight. It's very romantic, but the mists and vapors of the latitude get you." Though her voice was light, she was truly concerned: he did not look at all well. "Darin, let me call a doctor. There's no sense in taking chances."

He changed his position on the sofa to make himself more comfortable. "I don't need a doctor. I told you, it's happened before. Now, how about that tea?"

She poured a cup and handed it to him, with it rattling slightly in the saucer from the trembling of her hand. "Oh, for God's sake, Rosie!" He laughed faintly. "You know, you're just the person to have for a nurse. The patient gives a gasp or a cough and Rosie goes completely out of her head, running around the room crying, 'He's dying! He's dying! Help!'" There was amusement in his eyes. "I remember once when I wished you were there, though . . . in fact, I *saw* you there . . . but not as a nurse, thank God. I had this crazy fever in the camp, some months after the leg. I guess it wasn't a killing fever, for sure, or I wouldn't be here at all. But it put me completely out of my head, and my throat was that sore. I looked up at the ceiling, and what do I see? My darling little Rosaleen, still a wee girl, shouting, 'Darin! Darin! Those micks in the yard are after me again!' I felt obliged to crack their heads, so I..." A sharp intake of breath checked his words, and he put the cup down with shaking hands. She was at his side at once.

"Darin, what is it? You said it had happened before. You look perfectly..."

He did not answer for a moment. He did not even seem to see her, his gaze turned inward as though assessing what was taking place in him. Then, "My son's dealt with it before, Rosie. Call him. I wouldn't have come today if I'd known. Rosie, please call my son!"

Afraid to leave him, she obeyed his command, rushing to the telephone on the kitchen wall, looking over her shoulder as she cranked it to give the number. From her position, she could only see the back of his head and his wide shoulders over the back of the sofa: she could not determine if he was moving. She spoke her hurried, almost hysterical message into the telephone, ignoring all questions on the other end.

"Don't ask questions! For God's sake, bring a doctor, as soon as you can! Yes," she repeated the directions again, and left the hand piece dangling in her haste to get back to Darin. As she circled the sofa to look at him, she was stopped by the amused, searching expression in his eyes.

"Rosie, I told you to call my son. Why did you call Rory?"

She gaped stupidly, her mind in total confusion, unable to articulate an answer, and he smiled slightly.

"It's so, then? Do you think I never wondered...just a little? Just to look at him? But he looked like you, too, so what was I to think? Men aren't much good at dates, you know."

"I'm sorry!" she said, looking miserable. "I vowed to myself I'd take the knowledge to my grave."

"You and your peculiar vows. Rosie, you never could get away with anything—even a sin of omission. You always gave yourself away." He laughed shortly and paused to breathe more evenly. "But why did you never tell me? Did you think I was a threat to the boy?"

She knelt beside the sofa and took his hand, with her eyes averted. "There were so many reasons at the time."

He nodded, putting his hand over hers, and said softly, "I know. There was John. And all your crazy vows. No, they

547

weren't really crazy. Rosie, look at me." He lifted her chin, and the meeting of their gazes was more poignant than before: she could not look away.

"I'm glad you know, but..."

"I won't tell him. I know it would turn his world upside down. I've always loved that boy, Rosie."

"Please lie down," she entreated, terrified by his loss of color. "You'll be more comfortable that way. It'll take them a while to get here."

"I don't want to lie down," he said stubbornly. "And, if I know Rory, it won't take him that long. Not after the message you gave him. He probably thinks you're ill, and he'll harness flying horses!"

When Rory finally did arrive, he found them in the same position, Darin trying to stay upright on the sofa and his mother at Darin's knees, staring into his face. Just from the look of the man, Rory assessed the situation quickly and motioned the doctor through the door. Darin turned his head to look at him.

"I told her you'd be here soon. You're a man of action, Rory."

"Darin," Rory said and frowned, accompanying the doctor to his side, "for God's sake, what's the matter?"

"It's nothing new." Darin shrugged; then he flailed his arms to fight off the stethoscope. "Get that bloody thing away from me! I don't need a diagnosis. I just want to get home!" He gave Rory an intense look, shifting his eyes to Rosaleen; the two men understood each other, and Rory helped Darin to his feet, supporting most of his weight, to get him to the door. The baffled physician picked up his bag and followed. There was a blast of cold air when the door opened again, and Darin pressed Rosaleen's hand.

"Stay inside, Rosie. You'll catch cold. It's all right!" he reassured her, bending to kiss her forehead. "It's all right...."

"I'm coming with you!" she cried, reaching for her cape.

But Rory said, "No, Mother. There isn't room. I brought your little two-seater. We'll barely fit as it is. I'll send a cab back for you."

Rory draped Darin's coat over his shoulders to protect him from the cold, and the three men left her standing alone with her fur cape in her hands.

When she got home, Rosaleen paced the floor of the study waiting for some word from Rory, but the telephone did not ring. After several hours, Mary slipped into the room, sensing something was wrong.

"It's cold in here, Rosaleen. You've let the fire die. Sure, come along into the parlor and have some tea. If you're expecting an important call, we can hear the telephone from there. Is something wrong at the bank?" she asked, putting her arm around her daughter's waist and leading her to the warmth of the parlor. When Rosaleen did not answer, she said, "Well, I know nothing of such things. Here, drink this."

Rosaleen took the cup and saucer from her hands, saying, "I can't understand why he hasn't called."

"Well, whoever it is will call when he has something to say. I don't like the look of you at all. Drink your tea," she recommended: it had become the panacea for everything from labor pains to grief. "Mary Rose is going to join us. She's been that upset since Cliona left, poor girl! I found her sitting up there in her room, staring out the window, ever so low."

Rosaleen sat silently with the teacup poised in her hands, as still as a statue.

Mary Rose came in and took her place at the fire with the two women, a frown creasing her clear forehead. "It's such a quiet afternoon," she observed, pouring herself some tea. "The telephone hasn't rung at all, has it?"

"No, indeed." Mary smiled. "Are you after waiting for a call, then, too? That wretched machine's put nothing but tension in our lives. Sure, we were better off without it. When someone had something to say, he just showed up unexpectedly. There was none of this heavy waiting."

Mary Rose smiled at her grandmother's quaintness and glanced at her mother, who usually shared her amusement. She was shocked by her face. Rosaleen appeared to have aged ten years just since breakfast. Her inattention was complete: she did not seem to know they were there. Raising her eyebrows, Mary Rose looked quizzically at her grandmother, but Mary only shrugged, so the two of them tried to make small talk to cover the silence.

Though Rosaleen seemed almost deaf and dumb, her mind was overactive, trying to imagine what was taking place in the flat over the pub. They had Darin in bed now, surely; and Sean . . . or Peg . . . must have prevailed upon him to be treated by the doctor. But why didn't Rory call her? He wasn't that irresponsible. She had nearly called several times herself, but she was certain Peg would answer, and she did not know what she would say. Once she nearly threw on her cape to go there, but some instinct checked her: somehow, she knew Darin did not want that. She had recognized that wish in the cottage, when he wanted to get away as quickly as possible: he did not want her to see him ill. Then, suddenly, as though the light in the room was intensified, she saw his face clearly...not as she had seen it last, gray and stricken, but as he had stood over her bed, laughing and bare-shouldered, hurling roses; and something snapped imperceptibly inside of her, as though something had disentangled itself from her heart strings, peacefully and quietly, but leaving her with an immense feeling of loss.

She rose and put her cup down. "I'm going to my room," she said, almost in a whisper. "When Rory comes in, please tell him I'm there."

She was sitting in the tapestry armchair by the fire, looking very small in her black dress, when Rory finally knocked softly and entered. His lips were pale and clenched, his blue eyes wet with tears, when he looked down at her.

"Mother, Darin's gone. He passed away about half an hour ago. He knew he was dying, dear. He said he didn't want that to happen to you again. I didn't know about it, but Sean told me his heart's been bad ever since the war. He'd seen doctors, but there was nothing they could do. It was from a fever in the camp. They said the valves of his heart were ruined by it."

Rory put his hand to the back of his head, rubbing the dark hair so much like Darin's, and began to pace the carpet. "This has been the strangest day of my life. There's so much I can't comprehend." And, in order to put off talking about the past hour, he pulled up a footstool and sat before her, looking up into her white face. "That house...that funny little French house...I didn't even know it was there."

"We've always had it," she answered tonelessly. "John and I went there once a month to get away."

"Is that where you went?" He smiled incredulously with hurt eyes. "We always wondered. And Darin? What was he doing way out there...sick?"

"He was my oldest and best friend. There was privacy there to talk."

"I've known he was fond of you. He asked about you so often. He said you'd grown up together, and been through a lot." She nodded silently. "What I didn't know until this afternoon was how much he cared for me. And...I cared for him," he said, gulping, tears glistening in his eyes. Unable to bear his grief along with her own, Rosaleen leaned forward and took him in her arms, kissing his hair, letting him weep, as she was quietly doing. "It was so *strange*. If Sean weren't the man he is, he might have resented it. But right at...the end...Darin took each of us by the hand: we were sitting on opposite sides of the bed. He held our hands against his chest, and he said, 'My grand boys!' Just as though I were his own son! We didn't even know he was gone, Mother. He just closed his eyes and smiled." He gave a deep sigh. "After tonight, I'll never fear death again. It's so easy to die."

Silence fell between them for several minutes; then he said, "I loved him. I didn't know it was that when we were laughing and fooling around together, but I loved him, Mother."

The tears fell off her dark lashes into his hair, and she drew away to wipe her face with her handkerchief. "So did I. I always have. I'm glad you were there."

Regaining some of his composure, Rory went on, "Darin said he's always tried to be there when you needed him...but now I'd have to do it. But"—he smiled slightly—"'not with any unnatural fascination and dependence.' Those were his words. He said something odd, because I've never thought of you that way. He said, 'Rosie isn't as strong as Mary. She needs looking after.' I hope that doesn't offend you."

"Perhaps he knew me better than you, darling." She smiled faintly. "The poor lad had the task of looking after me since I was three, and it was no fault of his own, either. I hung onto his shirttail like a flea on a dog, as he once put it."

"You're really upset," he said. "You probably want to be alone." He rose from the stool and pushed it aside. "Oh, he sent you something. Maybe you'll know what it means. And a book," he added, reaching into his inside pocket and extracting a small leather volume that had seen better days. "I didn't know you liked German poetry. He sent you a translation of Goethe."

Placing the book in her lap, he deposited something very small in her limp hand and kissed her. "Try to rest, Mother. You look like you need it."

She was still for some time after he left, thinking about what he had told her. Then, feeling the tiny object in her palm, she leaned forward to look at it in the light. For a moment, it made no sense at all. A little pearl? A chip of iridescent stone? She turned it between her fingers and saw the back of it: a *button*. One of the tiny pearl buttons they had searched for on the floor of his quarters on the ship. And he had kept it all these years: the one button she could not find when she sewed them on again. In the vacuum of the past, she heard him saying in Veronica's parlor after the war, "Oh, I had something to get me through it." Completely shaken, she stroked the worn leather cover of *Faust* and opened it with curiosity to a dog-eared page with an inked-in bracket, reading Faust's challenge to Mephistopheles:

> "When, thus, I hail the moment flying,
> 'Ah, still delay, thou art so fair!'
> Then, bind me in thy bonds undying,
> My final ruin then declare.
> Then, let the death-knell sound the token,
> Then, art thou from thy service free.
> The clock may stop, the hands be broken,
> And time be finished unto me..."

She frowned slightly and read it again, trying to understand its message. Was Darin exalting having found the perfect moment...or telling her he had given his soul to the Devil for it? But she knew he did not believe in the Devil....

Chapter 36

NEARLY a month after Darin's death, Mary and her daughter were sitting by the fire in the parlor, each lost in her own thoughts. The financial journal Rosaleen had been attempting to read lay idle in her lap, and she sat with unfocused eyes staring at the flames in the grate. And though Mary continued to knit one of her interminable afghans—her hands did it automatically; she did not even have to count stitches—her mind was far away, as it was more and more often lately, back in Ireland, remembering the happy times there. Between the constantly recurring image of Brian coming up the path as she sat on the gray stone wall, a girl of fifteen, watching him, there were long periods of recollection of the way things had been before the hunger.

Sometimes, in the old, yellowed white dress she had worn for her wedding, she was dancing with Brian that day before the cottage, with Fiddler Murphy playing the strings off his fiddle and everyone happy. Tomas, the bridegroom, had got quickly drunk on poteen and was sitting against the cottage wall on a bench with his cronies, while Doirin and Brian's mother dispensed the festive food—a grand pudding and chicken along with the potatoes—to the other tenants, their neighbors and friends. She had thought at first that it was out of pity Brian asked her to dance, for every girl should dance at her wedding. But it was not long before she knew better, as he looked seriously into her eyes. They had danced in the old way, with closeness and abandon, and she was happy . . . oh, so happy! . . . looking into his eyes with the touch of his hands on hers, knowing without words that he loved her, too. And the music so loud that none of them heard the sound of horses until it was too late to change the tune and fall into a stilted reel at the approach of the landlord, Lord Leighton, and his Northern flunky, McGee. When they finally became aware of them and the music squeaked to a stop, Lord Leighton smiled and motioned Fiddler Murphy to continue playing.

"Please, don't stop on my account," he said from the saddle of his horse. "I've never seen such a joyous occasion, or a lovelier bride and groom, dancing without knowing anyone else is around. All brides should wear wild flowers in their hair, McGee. But none of them would look as splendid as this one. What is your name, my dear?"

"Mary, m'lord." She had curtsied with her heart in her throat in his presence, for there had been stories of Right of the Lord bandied about, though no one knew if they were true, at least not on this estate. "Mary Noonan."

"Well, Mary Noonan," he said and smiled, reaching into his waistcoat pocket and hurling a gold sovereign at her feet, "here's a wedding present for you! Every bride in the world should have so much love in her eyes." And, reining his horse to one side, with McGee following his lead, he galloped up the road back toward his hall. It had been the talk of the village for weeks: how Mary Noonan came into a small fortune on her bridal day. And not one among them noticing that she had not been dancing "with love in her eyes" with her groom at all.

"Rosaleen," Mary said suddenly, without missing a stitch with the needles in her hands, "sure, how much is a gold sovereign worth today?"

Rosaleen looked at her mother from her armchair. "About 123.28 grains of gold," she said. "Equal to one pound sterling, currently nearly three dollars."

Mary sighed, "Three dollars. And I thought it was such a fortune."

Remembering the stories of the gold coin from when she was a little child, Rosaleen asked, "Whatever happened to it, Mother?"

"Sure, it brought no good for a long time," Mary reflected sadly. "You wouldn't believe the times Tomas tried to beat it out of me to spend at a pub. But I kept it safely hidden for a rainy day...or for your wedding." She smiled ironically. "It finally went for grain to get us all through two months of the famine, when Brian and Tomas were away."

"I don't remember him beating you." Rosaleen frowned.

"He'd stopped by the time you were old enough to see it. Brian mopped up the cobbles with him one night in the village, and told him if it ever happened again, he'd kill him for sure."

"You miss Brian, don't you?" Rosaleen said with sympathy.

"Sure, I miss them all." Mary sighed heavily and shook her head. "I still can't believe that Darin's...It makes you feel really old, Rosaleen, when something like that happens." She was silent for a while, but finally said what had been bothering her for weeks. "You might have come to that funeral. He was your friend as well as your cousin. I thought you'd overcome that awful fear of yours after you went to John's funeral."

"I'm not afraid any more," Rosaleen said. "I didn't go because he wouldn't have wanted me to see him like that."

"The nerve of that Sean!" Mary exclaimed, as she had been doing for weeks. "Not 'allowing' a wake, sure! *Allowing!* Darin had so many friends the churchyard would hardly hold them, and no wake to send him off properly. I don't know what the young folk are coming to." When Rosaleen did not answer, she repeated, "'A three-ring circus,' he called it! He said he wanted his father to go in peace."

"The old customs will change," Rosaleen said sadly. "I think Sean was right."

Not eager to fight with her daughter, Mary changed the subject. "How long are you going to continue wearing mourning for John? Sure, it was a year three months ago. You should be out of it by now."

"How long are you going to continue wearing black?" Rosaleen retorted.

"That's different. I'm an old woman," her mother said; then, nodding her head with secret knowledge, she added, "But I know why you're still wearing it."

"Why?" Rosaleen asked, her head turning sharply to look at her.

"You've such a fine skin, black becomes you," Mary said. "Only beautiful women with good skin look well in black. You always were vain."

Rosaleen knew better than to pursue the subject with her

mother. She could not explain her reason for remaining in mourning, so she changed the subject quickly. "You went to the pub yesterday, Mother. How is Peg taking it?"

"Surprisingly well, everything considered. She's a pious woman, and it must sustain her. She did say something that troubled me sorely, though. They're considering selling the pub." She shook her head slowly. "Sure, it's after being there for over thirty-five years."

"They won't realize much on it, with the Italian immigrants that are drifting in," Rosaleen considered. "Within a few years, the whole section will be Italian. No place for an Irish pub. Did she say why they were selling?"

"Something about Sean continuing his education and that there'll be no one to run it. He's finished college, hasn't he? Why in the world does he want more education, then? I know Rory's still going to classes, but Sean went right through: he should be working. Unless he's one of those perpetual students Rory speaks of."

"In his field, he'll need a doctorate," Rosaleen said. "You don't peddle Latin on a street corner or sell it from a cart, Mother. I think it's a good idea." And what Darin would have wanted, she thought to herself. Sean had meant so much to him: he wanted him to have it all.

"He's a good boy," Mary considered. "From the look of him, you can tell he's always been good."

Rosaleen smiled faintly. "You'd think that to look at any of them," she said. "Such angelic faces."

"What do you mean by that?" Mary bristled. "Some boys are virtuous, even if your son isn't among them! You can't judge all of them by Rory...God love him. I knew he'd come to no good from the beginning, with that Carmela kissing him all over, even in places that weren't decent. Our Rory's had so much from women, he just keeps looking for more of the same. By the way, what happened to that married jade he was spending time with? Is she still in the picture?"

"No, she went to join her husband in England," Rosaleen said. Seeing Mary's eyes narrow with curiosity, she added, "I've never had spies, Mother. The trick of it's in reading people, listening to what they say...and don't say. And, sometimes, the newspapers help. They tipped me to the little gun scheme, along with a phone call from Darin."

"From *Darin?*" Mary exclaimed. "But wasn't it himself you were abusing that night in the bar?"

"I had to. So Rory wouldn't suspect." Rosaleen smiled.

"But you hurled a mug at him!"

"I got carried away," Rosaleen reflected. "But you'll recall it missed. I know Julia's out of Rory's life just from the way he's been behaving: he's home studying every night. And," she added, "I've always read the sailings in the paper. I know she left last summer, and he wasn't at all distressed."

Mary breathed a sigh of relief, "You might have told me. And me worrying about his future! Something like that could come out later, after he's made something of himself, you know. A political scandal...even blackmail."

Rosaleen's blue eyes widened. "*Blackmail!* Mother, how do you, with your sheltered life, get hold of such notions? I wouldn't have suspected you knew the word."

Her mother continued knitting in silence. Realizing the conversation had terminated rather abruptly, Rosaleen let herself drift back into her own, more personal thoughts, where she could be alone with Darin. After that first night of overwhelming grief, she realized that she was not abandoned, that he would never die as long as she kept him in her mind. And, after learning the history of his heart condition, she was only grateful that they could spend the last year of his life together. The room was silent except for the click of Mary's knitting needles and the crackle of the fire. So quiet that, when the door burst open suddenly, both she and Mary turned toward it with startled expressions on their faces.

Mary Rose paused on the threshold a moment, and then strode toward them belligerently, still in her outside wrap, the color high in her face, with her magnificent dark eyes flashing.

On the way home from the coffee shop, Mary Rose realized that any prepared speech was out of the question: she just had to get it over with as quickly as possible and then avoid the hysterical scene that would follow. No weeping on the sofa like Cliona for her! As she walked along the icy streets, her step increased along with the memories she evoked of her mother's past injustices, real and imagined: hers was not a situation that could be faced with compassion for the other person. She knew her mother was not the monster she was making her out to be, but her natural jealousy of the woman made the knowledge irrelevant. To protect herself, she had to be on the offensive: her mother was the enemy. She would strike and flee quickly, send for her things later if necessary, but get out of the house before all hell broke loose.

Seeing her grandmother in the parlor with her mother made her pause a second: she did not want to hurt her, too. But the time to say everything was *now,* so she dismissed her scruples and marched right up to the two older women in black, sitting by the fire.

"I've something to tell you, and you aren't going to like it," she said, almost wincing at the bad beginning. "Sean Noonan and I are going to be married! We've been seeing each other for years." The two women did not stir; they simply looked into each other's eyes. "You don't have to make a decision: it's already made! Sean's with his mother right now, telling her, too. And don't shout at me that he's my cousin! We *know* that, and we don't consider it an impediment. We'll be married in a Protestant church, with Rory as witness. Or at City Hall. It doesn't matter. I'm sorry..." No, that wouldn't do. "I don't care about the Church's views on the subject. Neither of us does! The only reason we haven't just eloped before now is that Sean didn't have a job. Well, Rory's changed that...though not the way we'd thought. I don't know how he did it, but he's gotten Sean into Harvard for his doctorate."

She paused, out of breath, surprised by their silence. She must have put them into shock. Her mother said nothing, but she could see that her blue eyes were calculating something, and the expression struck fear into her heart.

"It can be done," her grandmother said in an unruffled voice.

"What can be done?" Mary Rose countered.

"Sometimes Irish boys can be gotten into Harvard, sure."

"Oh, he'll have the money to pay his tuition. They're selling that awful pub! He won't take one cent of the damned Maddigan money. Even my own." Then, in desperation, she made her final thrust. "Papa knew. He was going to help us. He knew everything."

"Well," Rosaleen said calmly, "now we know, too. Mary Rose, dear, please sit down."

"No. You aren't going to get around me! There's only one thing I need to know." She paused heavily: it was almost like asking a favor, but she had to know. "Is it true that Sean's grandmother was insane? We want children, and..."

Again, the inscrutable meeting of their eyes: they might use it as a weapon. But her grandmother turned to her calmly and said, so honestly that she could not doubt her, "Doirin insane? My own sister, sure? She might have been a little bit highstrung," she demurred, "and once . . . yes, once I remember she had what might be considered a breakdown. But . . . insane! The very idea, child! Where did you hear such a thing?"

Rosaleen's blue eyes widened as though she had been pinched, but she controlled the reaction quickly.

"You haven't given us a chance to congratulate you, darling. He's a lovely young man. But what's all this talk of City Hall? I think she should have a grand wedding, don't you, Mother? Let's see, I think Trinity was your father's church. It's been a long time."

Her grandmother rose to embrace her. "Sure, it's wonderful, darling! And you must have a really proper wedding. Neither your mother nor poor Veronica had that. It's strange, I was just thinking this last hour about my own wedding back in Ireland. Do you suppose it was a premonition, then? Rosaleen, I really was . . . that's what made me ask about the sovereign."

"A beautiful white gown!" Rosaleen said with eyes shining. "I'll make it myself! Alençon . . . no, no . . . it must be chantilly lace. Yes, with a veil rather like a mantilla, because of your dark beauty, darling. Only not supported by a comb, I think, but by your hair pulled up to the crown of your head . . ."

For the first few minutes, Mary Rose stood numbly before them; finally, she sank down in a chair.

"I thought . . . Mother, I *really* thought you'd disown me," she breathed, staring in disbelief.

"Darling," Rosaleen said, rising to embrace her from behind, "whatever made you think such a thing? My own daughter! My own beautiful daughter," she murmured, kissing her hair. "I'm just so *happy* for you. Why didn't you tell us sooner?"

"It was the cousin thing," Mary Rose said, still not completely believing what had happened. Then, with a frown, "Mother, you do know about cousins and the Church, don't you?"

"Oh, yes," Rosaleen breathed into her hair, "I know."

Relaxing for what felt like the first time in years, Mary Rose turned to kiss her Mother on the cheek. "Do you really want to plan my wedding? I guess that's a silly question." She laughed lightly. "You already have! Oh, Mama."

"We'll plan it together," her mother said, straightening herself and walking to the fireplace, to turn and face her.

"I know I've been inconsiderate in the past, when you were younger, dear. I thought you would want what I'd have wanted. Oh," she said, arching one black eyebrow, "I heard the jokes about the slippery pale-blue sofa!"

They laughed together. After talking for a few minutes, Mary Rose looked at the mantel clock and cried, "I have to meet Sean back at the coffee house! I have a feeling he didn't make out as well with *his* mother."

With her hand on her chin, Rosaleen surveyed the parlor after her daughter left.

"Mother, we'll have to redecorate the whole thing for the reception. This green and gold appals me! Federal, maybe? Neoclassic? I don't know. White, though . . . with simple lines. And perhaps a mural of spring on one whole wall." She held out her palm as though she already saw it. "A pale background with blossoms . . . almost Japanese . . . maybe with a lovely little bird or two . . ."

"Sure, Rory could do it, if he has the time," Mary suggested. "Or were you thinking of wallpaper?"

"Yes, I was," Rosaleen said: then she smiled and bit her lower lip. "I'd like Rory to do it, if he can control himself so it doesn't come out like a Pompeiian fresco." Suddenly she narrowed her eyes and turned to Mary with a frown. "Mother, what was all that about 'a slight nervous breakdown'? Doirin was a raving maniac."

"Sure, I didn't want to trouble the poor girl," Mary defended herself. "I thought your children would come out queer, if you'll remember, and they're all right. And so is Sean."

They were silent a moment. Rosaleen had a more important example of genetic soundness, but she could not speak of it.

"Peg's going to be that cross," Mary said in another marvel of understatement, and Rosaleen nodded uncertainly.

"She has every right to be, I guess."

"Sure, Peg's a devout Catholic, and Sean's her only son," Mary pursued.

"You're not against it, are you?" Rosaleen asked, and Mary shook her head.

"I wouldn't want to see what happened to me take place all over again, sure," she said.

"I wouldn't, either. I have to make a call, Mother."

Rosaleen locked the door to the study before placing her

560

telephone call, stamping her foot nervously while she waited. "Frank?" she asked. "I hate to bother you, but something's come up. Do you know the Noonan Pub in the North End?"

After a brief moment of silence, he said, "I've heard of it, Mrs. Maddigan. It's a hotbed of Irish Nationalist plots."

"I'm not political," she said. "It's going up for sale, and I want to buy it. In my mother's name, this time. I'll pay twenty-five thousand dollars for it, and not a cent more...or less."

"You're out of your bloody mind! I'm sorry, Mrs. Maddigan. I didn't mean that. I've never questioned your transactions before, but I must tell you it isn't worth a third of that! Not even as a land investment. Never mind the fact that Italians are trickling in."

"Does St. Mary's Church own a lot of land in that area?"

"You know it does."

"Is St. Mary's selling out?"

"No, of course not! The Catholic Church will keep its holdings until hell freezes over. But that's no argument, Mrs. Maddigan: none of us will be around as long as the church. That land can only depreciate in value. I've gone along with most of your schemes, buying up real estate in the names of your family, but this is altogether mad!"

"You're right," she admitted suddenly. "It should be in the name of my oldest son, instead of my mother."

"All right," he said, giving up.

"No one's to know you represent me."

"I know. I know. The same old thing. How much of Boston and Cambridge do you own by now?"

"My dear Frank," she said, smiling, "if you don't know that, you'll have your walking papers tomorrow. Good night, old friend."

She hung up the phone and began to pace the small room, so full of energy she did not know what to do next. Mary Rose and Sean! Oh, Darin, darling, she thought. I wish you were here. Your son and my daughter. We'll have grandchildren together! She went to a cabinet and poured herself a glass of Calvados, breathing in the odor of apples in the brandy. There would be the wedding, the invitations...decorating the parlor for the reception. But it was nearly Christmas. Well, why not! Christmas would be a grand time for a wedding! Only would it be possible to do all that before then?

The telephone rang with a strident, insistent tone that made her jump. Who would be calling now? If it was Frank again with his faintheartedness about the pub, she would really land into him! As the instrument continued its incessant blare, she almost agreed with her mother's opinion of it. Walking over to it, glass in hand, she put the earpiece close to her head; but before she could say anything, a very Irish woman's voice asked, "Is this Rosaleen Maddigan?"

"Yes," she said, puzzled.

"Well, this is Peg Noonan. I know everything you've done."

Startled, Rosaleen said carefully, "Do you?"

"I know all about you, you frightful jade. Sure, you're as bad as your cousin, I'm certain. And him sleeping with every woman in town! I could tell what you were the night we came to your son's party. The dress you had on was enough to shock a person to the grave . . . with your . . . bosom all exposed. And then not expelling that married woman Rory brought from your house straightaway! And . . ."

Rosaleen relaxed, letting out a long breath: she didn't know about Darin and herself, then. Taking courage in that knowledge, she said, "Really, Peg, I don't know what I've done to warrant all this abuse."

"You've taken away my only son! Sure, don't give a single thought to a poor widow woman, with but one son to comfort her old age! Not the likes of you! You're just as selfish as Darin!"

"Peg! Sean's not marrying me. He's marrying Mary Rose."

"And you've agreed to it! Encouraged them in their sin! Oh, I've heard, all right. You've taken my dear boy from the arms of the Church, to live in incest with your slut of a daughter. You've..."

Rosaleen screamed into the phone, "If you've said anything like that to my daughter I'll have the tongue right out of your mouth! I'd hoped to arrange something bordering on the humane for you, knowing you'd be upset. But after hearing what a wretched blatherskite you are, you can go to flaming hell for all I care! If the youngsters wish to marry it's their decision, isn't it? And a better one than really 'living in sin,' in my opinion. Though neither of them would do that, as you bloody well know! There are no obstacles you can cast in their path, Peg. So, if you want to see Sean again, you should reconsider your opinion."

There was dead silence on the other end of the line.

"Peg? Are you still there?"

She heard a loud sound of sniffling. "Sure, I'd see Sean dead and laid out rather than leaving the Church. I don't need him... or your charity, either, Lady Bountiful! He was leaving home to go to Harvard College, anyway, because there won't be home here any more, thanks be to God! There never was a proper home . . . your cousin saw to that . . . and myself never knowing where he was!"

"Keep Darin out of it," Rosaleen said evenly.

"Sure, he *is* out of it, isn't he? And me with only a bit of insurance money and this wicked pub on my hands! Well, I don't need anyone, anyway. I've got myself a job! Father Donelly needs someone to keep house at the rectory, and he's given the place to *me!* So I don't care any more about any of you damned Noonans."

Rosaleen had an uncontrollable urge to laugh: Peg and Father Donelly... now that was a pair!

"Well, Peg," she said more lightly, "if you ever wish to reconsider . . . so you can see your son . . . and any grandchildren . . . all you have to do is say so. And keep a civil tongue in your head."

"You *are* just like Darin!" she said maliciously. "You even talk alike."

Peg hung up with a loud click, and Rosaleen listened to the blessed emptiness on the line for a moment, before cranking the telephone again.

"Frank? What have you found out about the pub?"

"Nothing. It's only *been* fifteen minutes!" he complained. "I've tried to call, but the line's been busy."

"If a man dies intestate, to whom does his property go?"

"His oldest son, if he has one. Otherwise, to his wife... usually its handled by a lawyer. Women are terrible when it comes to business matters."

"Thanks," she said. Frank, thinking she had misunderstood, began frantically to try to justify his last statement when she hung up.

She knew Sean would take care of his mother financially, even if Peg had nothing more to do with him: the deal for the pub could go through as she had instructed. Everything was in order for tonight. She poured a small sip more of Calvados in the snifter and raised it toward the ceiling.

"My God, Darin, how did you put up with it?" She sighed, taking a drink and letting the hot alcohol warm her chest. "Do you think I should wear black at the wedding? You always hated it so. Maybe Mother's right about ostentatious mourning after all. I know what I'll do!" she said with an inspired, conspiratorial smile, imagining his face if she could say it to him. "I'll mourn you in black underthings, my darling: no one will *ever* see them, anyway."

Instead of poinsettias, red roses decorated the stark Protestant altar on that Saturday morning before Christmas week, though the bride carried only white ones against her delicate white lace dress; the only color was in her cheeks and dark, glowing eyes. In the time allowed during Sean's and Rory's holiday break from college, when the wedding was to take place, Rosaleen had almost accomplished a miracle singlehanded. Trinity was full of old friends, the music was just right, the gown she'd made for Mary Rose was the loveliest she had ever seen, though pinned in places at the last minute for just the proper fit. When Rosaleen was not sewing, she was on the telephone to nearly every greenhouse in New England or dashing about with the guest list in her hand. Instead of sleeping at night, she addressed invitations, having carefully inquired the names of those Sean wished to invite. Right up until the last minute, she was supervising every detail, adjusting her daughter's veil, asking Rory, tall and handsome in his morning suit with striped trousers, if he had the ring.

"Right here!" He grinned at her, lifting up his little finger with the gold band securely upon it. "I won't do anything stupid, Mother: I won't lose their ring!"

When she finally walked down the aisle to take her place beside Mary and Michael in the pew reserved for the bride's family, Rosaleen's color was high, almost matching her red velvet dress. The only thing that still bothered her was that no one was sitting in the pew reserved for the family of the groom.

"I thought she might give in at the last minute," she whispered to her mother, looking straight ahead at the altar. "This is terrible for Sean."

"Sure, you wouldn't know it to look at him," Mary said with a smile. "Rosaleen, he reminds me so much of Brian, standing there at the altar. There's the same gentleness and kindness about him. And he looks ever so happy, darlin'."

Rosaleen could not dispute that: the poor young man had waited a long time for his moment. He showed no sign of nervousness at all, but only quiet anticipation as he waited for the bridal march. If there were tears in the church that day when it started and Mary Rose walked regally and slowly down the aisle, they were not shed by her mother and grandmother. They both showed nothing but delight. Only after the vows were exchanged did Mary raise her handkerchief to her face; but then it was to disguise her laughter. Rory had the ring, all right: for a while, he appeared to have it for good. And his sheepish crooked grin at the minister as he struggled to get it off his little finger was more than Mary could stand.

"God love him," she said, stifling her laughter with the handkerchief, while Rosaleen fought to maintain a straight face.

After all the preparation, the Protestant ceremony seemed brief, though it was beautiful. The bride and groom were congratulated on the church steps, while Rosaleen exchanged greetings with old friends, some of whom she had not seen for a long time. When Mary Rose threw her bouquet, she deliberately aimed it at her brother, Rory, as a joke; but it fell instead against the bosom of a startled auburn-haired girl who not only had not put out her hands to receive it, but was apparently upset to have done so.

Sean and Mary Rose ascended into the gaily decorated carriage under a shower of rice that fell like snow, and the guests' carriages followed to pick them up, the procession rattling along the snowy streets until they reached Louisburg Square, which they encircled entirely to attend the reception.

The freshly decorated white-and-gilt parlor was elegant in its simplicity, with the dining-room doors flung wide to a buffet and champagne surrounding the towering, delicate cake. Rosaleen gave a small sigh of contentment: it had all been worth the effort. Every piece of silver in the house shone on the white lace tablecloth, and the black servants were smiling as much as the guests, as they carried trays of slim-stemmed glasses among the gathering. And the wall...Rory's wall...had come out far more lovely than she had imagined.

He had closeted himself in the room, allowing no one to enter while he prepared the surface and experimented with his paints, first using oils but turping the whole thing out because he did not like the effect. He grabbed his meals hastily, hardly speaking at the table, his blue eyes contemplative. When he finally found the medium he chose to use, he ran up the stairs and burst in on Rosaleen at her sewing machine.

"I have it!" he cried with a smile. "The only thing that doesn't shine, or go to powder, is fresco, Mother! I'm going to call someone to plaster over the whole mess...and use that!"

"Oh, my God," Rosaleen said, sinking her face into the

billowing lace of the bridal gown. "It'll never dry in time! It's only a week until the wedding."

"The damn stuff dries so fast, you can only paint a small section at a time," he said. "It'll be perfect. And I won't have to paint in the background, if the plaster's the right shade."

"But you've never worked with fresco before," she argued as he turned to leave.

"Neither had Michelangelo when he started the Sistine!"

His complete confidence unnerved her. But he had painted the wall admirably, just as she had wanted it: the narrow, twisted branches of a tree covered with delicate blossoms against a background of pale ecru, with several dashing birds of Persian blue. The bluebirds were shaped like swallows, but that did not matter: everything else was right.

She stood greeting friends, some of them from the bank, but more from her contacts in society. None of the Brahmins were there: none had been invited. She was practical enough to recognize her limits and never tried to overshoot them. When Rosaleen saw her old friend Pamela, she rushed to her side.

"Pam! I'm so glad you could come!"

The two women embraced, smiling. Pamela had not changed much over the years; if anything, her beauty was even more misty than before. Her coloring and her auburn hair had faded some, but her face was as sweet as it had been when they were both on honeymoon.

"Oh, Rosaleen, you must be so proud," she said and smiled. "Such a beautiful wedding. And your daughter! It hasn't been that long, but I wouldn't have known her."

"It's been too long," Rosaleen said sincerely. "Are your children here? I wouldn't recognize them, either, I'm sure."

"Eddie's in New York, but my daughter's here...school holidays, you know. Have you ever wondered, Rosaleen, where they came from?"

Rosaleen laughed. "What do you mean?"

"Our children. Mine might as well have come from the moon, they're so different from Edward and me. I think young Eddie must be the most boring man alive, with his interest in sports and things. He'll still be punting rivers when he's fifty! And Vickie...well! I've never known such an independent young lady. She insisted on attending college upstate, instead of a good finishing school. Said she'd had all the music and frippery she'd ever need. Now all she talks about is chemistry and biology...There she is over there!" she said, indicating an extremely attractive young woman in blue velvet with thick auburn hair and slate-blue eyes.

"She's very lovely," Rosaleen said, truthfully. "Isn't she the girl who caught Mary Rose's bouquet?"

Pamela sighed. "Yes, she was furious! She says she has no intention of marrying. Rosaleen, she wants to be a *doctor*," Pamela whispered. "Of course, if it had been a nurse we could have really put our foot down: everyone knows that isn't a decent profession. We just don't know what to do with her."

Rosaleen observed the girl more closely. "It isn't going to be easy for her," she said. "Breaking into a man's world never is. Even if you do it from the top as I did. I'd like to know Victoria better, Pam."

Her friend smiled. "You know, Rosaleen, after all these years I still forget that you're running a bank. It hasn't worked out badly for you. You had your husband *and* a family."

"And a great deal of help," Rosaleen said, still watching Vickie as Rory approached her in his relaxed, confident manner. "I hope she's as intelligent as she is beautiful."

"She *is*," Pamela said without pride. "It's dreadful...all those sums and calculations! They're enough to frighten any man off. I think she's what the English used to call a blue stocking. I wonder why they called them that?"

"I can't imagine." Rosaleen smiled. "The children are about to cut the cake, Pam. Come along with me."

After the initial cutting, Mary stayed at the table with the servants to dispense the white cake to most of the guests, the fruit or "groom's cake" to the young ladies who wished to sleep with it under their pillows for good luck in finding a groom of their own. After a single forkful of hers, Mary Rose gave her mother a pleading look, and Rosaleen came to her side.

"We want to get out of here," Mary Rose said *sotto voce,* still smiling at the guests. "Is there any way you can arrange it, Mama?"

Rosaleen laughed and bit her lip. "I know your patience has been sorely tried, my dear, but you should have a look at the presents first. The servants have displayed them: it won't take long."

As the company moved toward the long tables to look at the gifts, Rosaleen slipped into the dining room and took a tiny box from the mahogany cabinet. She studied it in her hands for a moment, feeling both happy and sad; then she approached Mary Rose and Sean and motioned them aside.

"This is my gift." She smiled, putting it into Sean's hands. "Mary Rose opened everything else, so you open this, my dear. And you must promise to accept it."

She saw a flicker of suspicion in his blue eyes and smiled her reassurance. "It isn't anything as vulgar as money. I know your feelings about such things. It's a very sentimental gift, Sean, for both of you."

He struggled with the little ribbon, finally abandoning the attempt to untie it: it was too small for his fingers. By pulling the ribbon over one corner of the box, he finally freed it and opened it. His dark eyebrows raised in puzzlement and he looked to Mary Rose for help.

"A key, Mama?" she asked. "Is this some kind of treasure hunt? Because if it is, we just haven't the time to..."

"No," Rosaleen said seriously. "There's an address in there, too. I know you've rented a flat near the river, but this key's to a very special, funny little cottage, that now belongs to you. It's never known anything but love, so I've carefully selected the new owners."

"A house?" Sean winced. "Rosaleen, you know..."

"It isn't much of a house," Rosaleen deprecated it. "It still needs repairs. Mary Rose, it was where your father and I went once a month all those years."

"Oh!" Mary Rose cried with delight, embracing her. "Oh, Sean, really."

Before he could refuse, Rosaleen said rather sternly, "There *is* a condition to its ownership." They both looked at her with cautious curiosity, and she smiled at them. "It's covered with snow, now. I've sent a servant out to light the fires, and your things are already there. But in the spring, there'll be more flowers than you've ever seen. Your father planted the roses," she said softly, not looking directly at either one of them, "and the apple tree in the front yard. It's a small thing, now, but it'll soon be covered with white blossoms. And someday you'll be able to hang a swing from it. All I ask, my darlings, is that you care for the flowers and the tree."

Sean gave her a gentle hug. "You're a conniving woman, Rosaleen." He smiled. "If I refused, after all that, Mary Rose would never speak to me again."

Insinuating her arms between them, Mary Rose kissed her mother. "You don't know how much this means to me,

Mama," she said. "I didn't know Papa liked roses so much. They're just like my name!"

"My father adored them," Sean said.

"This might be a good time to slip away unnoticed," Rosaleen put in. "Everyone's distracted by the wedding gifts. Now, everything's taken care of: you can take my carriage, and there's food and wine for a week."

She wanted to explain that the cottage was nearly as close to Harvard as the flat on the river, but they vanished through the door to the kitchen before she could finish. She heard their feet running up the back staircase to go upstairs and change their clothes.

"They managed that nicely," Pamela said, coming into the dining room, "with a little help, I think. Oh, Rosaleen, you aren't going to cry now, are you?"

Rosaleen shook her head and wiped her eyes. "Of course not. I haven't lost a daughter...I've gained a very special son."

"That's what Edward thinks, too." Pam smiled.

"Edward? He knows Sean?"

"Of course. Rory brought him around, and you know we can't refuse Rory anything."

That rascal! Rosaleen thought, shaking her head: so, that's how Sean was admitted to Harvard! She looked around for him, but did not see him. "Pamela," she said, "I don't wish to alarm you, but Victoria and Rory are gone."

"I know. I saw them leave. My gracious, how you fuss!" Her friend laughed. "Rosaleen, I don't have to worry about my daughter...you'd better worry about your son. I told you, for such a tiny thing, she's a terror! Rory may have come up against more than he can handle. It may be quite a shock to him that every woman doesn't swoon at his feet."

"But they're together," Rosaleen said. "It must mean she likes him."

"She probably does: she gets on well with men...until she begins to spout her confounded mathematical equations at them, or explains the life cycle of fruit flies, and why some of them have funny wings."

"Fruit flies? What are they?"

Pamela shrugged. "And what they have to do with medicine I'll never understand. And, oh, yes, I forgot to explain. She's very big on the underprivileged. That's what the doctoring's for! She'll bore him to death in an hour."

"I'm not so sure." Rosaleen smiled, wondering if Rory had

at last met his match. "Oh, Pam, the guests are beginning to leave."

"Let me help you. Remember the birthday parties we had for the children, when I only had Eddie?" She smiled. "My goodness! Your mother was there helping then too. What a wonderful woman she is. You're so fortunate to have her still."

"Yes." Rosaleen smiled. "I'm very, very fortunate."

The sadness set in only after everyone was gone, and the empty parlor resounded to nothing but the footfalls of servants cleaning up. The room was a shambles, with strewn wrapping paper and ribbons all along the gift table, the dainty three-tiered cake down to part of the first level, and plates, silver, glasses everywhere. Rosaleen liked to give parties, but she hated the destruction of her carefully planned work. She drifted across the room to the dining-room table and ate a few crumbs of cake, righting a champagne glass that had fallen on its side.

"Sure, it was fine," Mary said, as she stacked the dirty plates. "It was the wedding none of us ever really had, darlin'. You did yourself proud."

"Mother, what are you doing?" Rosaleen asked. "You aren't one of the servants. Let them clean up."

"But I like to do it." Mary smiled. "I'm so full of energy from it all, I could clean the house from top to bottom and run a mile after."

"I wish I felt like that," Rosaleen said; then, suddenly, "Do you really feel like running? Would a nice long walk do as well?"

"Since when have you taken one?" her mother asked.

"Maybe not recently enough. Come on, get your coat and boots! Let's walk to the pub the way we used to."

"The pub, is it?" Mary said, sadness showing in her eyes. "There's nothing there, Rosaleen. It was cleared out weeks ago."

"I know. But, Mother, we really must find someone to run it again." Mary's dark eyes raised sharply to hers. "You must know some of Darin's good friends. Perhaps we could call on one of them."

"You didn't ever!" Mary cried, beginning to smile. Rosaleen's blue eyes were full of humor, and her mother was convinced. "You wicked schemer! Rosaleen, I don't know where you got your larceny, but I admire it. Well, what are you waiting for? Let's get our coats."

They walked together along the icy cobbles under a sky that threatened snow, Rosaleen slowing her pace to that of her mother, in a fur cape as black as her mother's coat. They did not speak for a while, but the silence between them was close.

Finally, Mary said, "I suppose you'll be after running off to Europe again this summer, now that Michael's settled in at the bank?"

"I don't know. I'll have to keep an eye on that one for some time. I haven't really thought about it," Rosaleen replied. "Actually, now that the wedding's over, my life hasn't any real direction."

Mary considered that for a while, picking her way carefully around the ice, fearful of a fall that might break a hip: the end of so many elderly women.

"But there's still Rory to think about," she said suddenly. "When he finishes law and starts campaigning, he's going to need help."

"That's why I bought the pub. Well, it was one of the reasons. It'll give him roots in the old neighborhood."

Mary laughed. "Sure, I was just thinking, with all the Italians coming in, Rory will be the only politician who can thump his fist against his palm and proclaim, 'I'm your man! An American and Irish-Italian!'—seeing he was born in Italy and all."

Rosaleen laughed at the image, but did not fall into the proper mood of what Mary was suggesting. "The man for the pub," she said, "who will it be?"

"There's only one, sure. Darin's old friend Jimmy Desmond. He was one of the bartenders there, and Darin's good friend. A young man in his thirties with a wife and four children...a bit of a dreamer, but what's wrong with that? I suspect he's come on hard times since the pub was closed."

"They won't last longer than today," Rosaleen assured her. "I suppose Peg sold the furniture?"

"No, she left everything there. Couldn't wait to get out to take care of that gowger, Father Donelly."

"You never could stand him," Rosaleen said with curiosity, remembering her own terrible encounter with the man. "Why not, Mother?"

"I'd rather not say," Mary said crossly. Then, picking up where she'd left off a few minutes before, "You know, if Rory's going to help the people down there, he's going to need help, Rosaleen. If you aren't going abroad this summer, it would be that nice to return to the old house at the Cape."

"There aren't any servants there. Besides, what has one thing to do with the other?"

"Well, I was just thinking...you know how much I like to do the housework there...and it's so lovely and cool. And you like to read."

"You're wandering a little, dear. If you want to go to the Cape, we will."

"Good!" Mary smiled. "Sure, it's the perfect place to learn about politics, Rosaleen. And not a soul about to listen in on our plotting and sedition. I think Rory should aim himself high, don't you?"

Rosaleen laughed and put her arm around her mother's waist. "We could be a very upright, honest Tammany Hall, just the two of us," she said. "Watch out for that curbing," she said, taking Mary by the hand to assist her, as her mother had so often done for her as a child. "No, we'll let him start at the bottom...the streetcorner, handshaking level. He needs the discipline."

And, besides, it would take more time, she thought. Her mother's suggestion had pointed out that Rory's career would occupy a great deal of her future, shown her a light at the end of the tunnel.

Still smiling, Rosaleen whispered in her heart, "Thank you, Darin, darling, for looking after me."

ABOUT THE AUTHOR

Ms. La Tourrette was born in Denver, Colorado, but lived in San Francisco, New York and Prescott, Arizona before age six. After her father's death, the family returned to Denver, where she attended Cathedral Parochial School and was raised in the home of her mother's Irish family. She started writing at the age of twelve and has been doing it ever since. With her mother and sister, she moved to California in her late teens, where she attended San Jose High School and, later, San Jose State University, where she majored in English and anthropology.

After her marriage, she lived in Alaska for five years, and two of her three sons were born there. The family then lived in Ireland for a year, where the boys attended the Convent of St. Joseph at Chapelizid, Dublin. After completing preliminary nursing training at St. Margaret's Hospital, Epping, Essex, England, Ms. La Tourrette returned with her family to Boston for twelve years, working as a medical secretary at Massachusetts Institute of Technology, while continuing to write.

She now resides in Santa Clara, California, and has published eight books, two of them in hardcover. She has traveled extensively abroad, and is now working on another novel.

Get Your
Coventry Romances
Home Subscription NOW

And Get These
4 Best-Selling Novels
FREE:

LACEY
by Claudette Williams

THE ROMANTIC WIDOW
by Mollie Chappell

HELENE
by Leonora Blythe

THE HEARTBREAK TRIANGLE
by Nora Hampton